CITY OF
DRAGONS

RISE OF THE SHADOWFIRE

JAIMAL YOGIS & VIVIAN TRUONG

graphix

AN IMPRINT OF

📖 SCHOLASTIC

FOR MY HIGH SCHOOL TEACHER, ALEC HODGINS,
WHO HELPED ME THINK AND DREAM BIGGER. —J.Y.

FOR MY GORGEOUS NIECE, ELLA, WHO I KNOW WILL
GROW TO BE AS FIERCE AS A DRAGON. —V. T.

Library of Congress Control Number: 2022949488

ISBN 978-1-338-66046-3 (hardcover)
ISBN 978-1-338-66045-6 (paperback)

10 9 8 7 6 5 4 3 2 1   23 24 25 26 27

Printed in China   62
First edition, October 2023

Edited by: Emily Nguyen
Creative Director: Phil Falco
Publisher: David Saylor

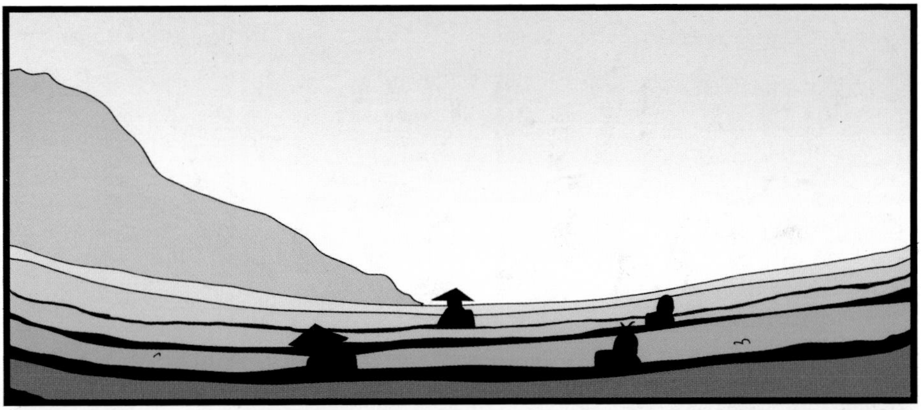

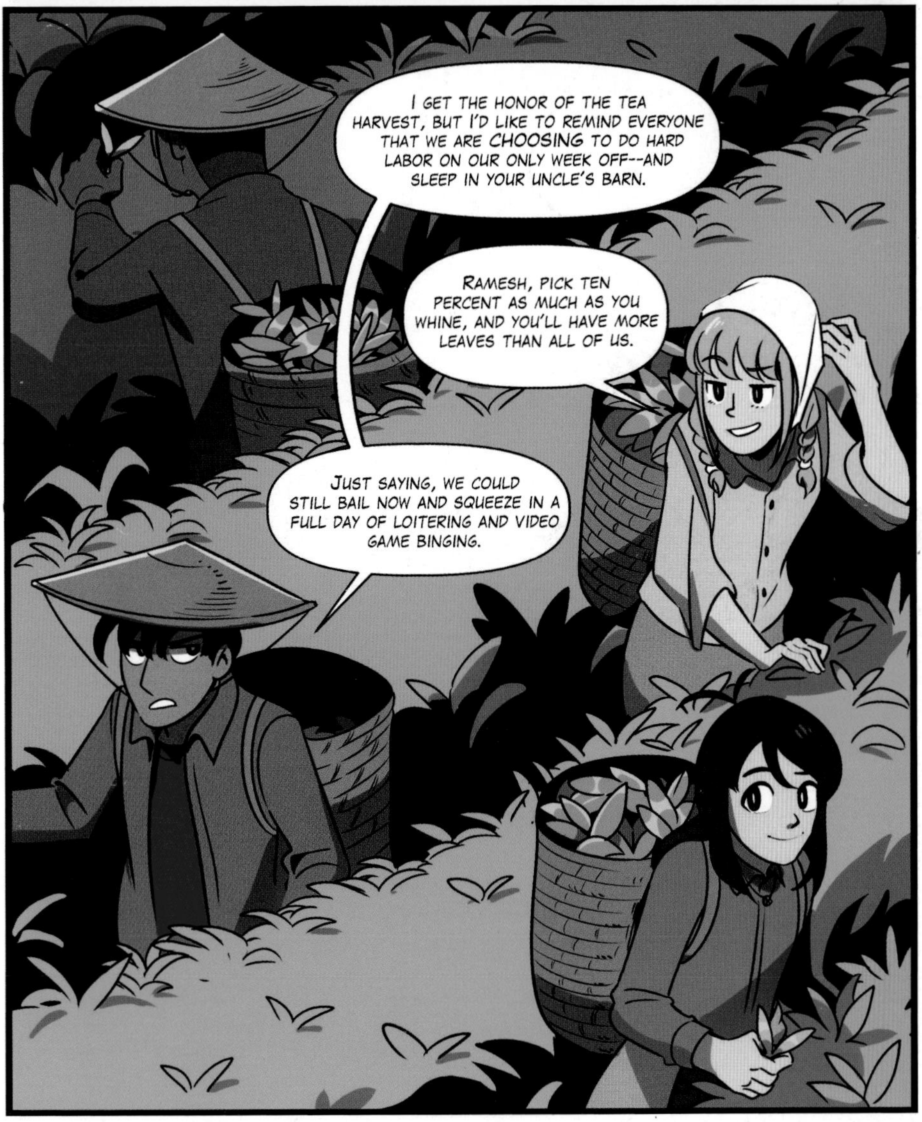
I GET THE HONOR OF THE TEA HARVEST, BUT I'D LIKE TO REMIND EVERYONE THAT WE ARE CHOOSING TO DO HARD LABOR ON OUR ONLY WEEK OFF--AND SLEEP IN YOUR UNCLE'S BARN.
RAMESH, PICK TEN PERCENT AS MUCH AS YOU WHINE, AND YOU'LL HAVE MORE LEAVES THAN ALL OF US.
JUST SAYING, WE COULD STILL BAIL NOW AND SQUEEZE IN A FULL DAY OF LOITERING AND VIDEO GAME BINGING.

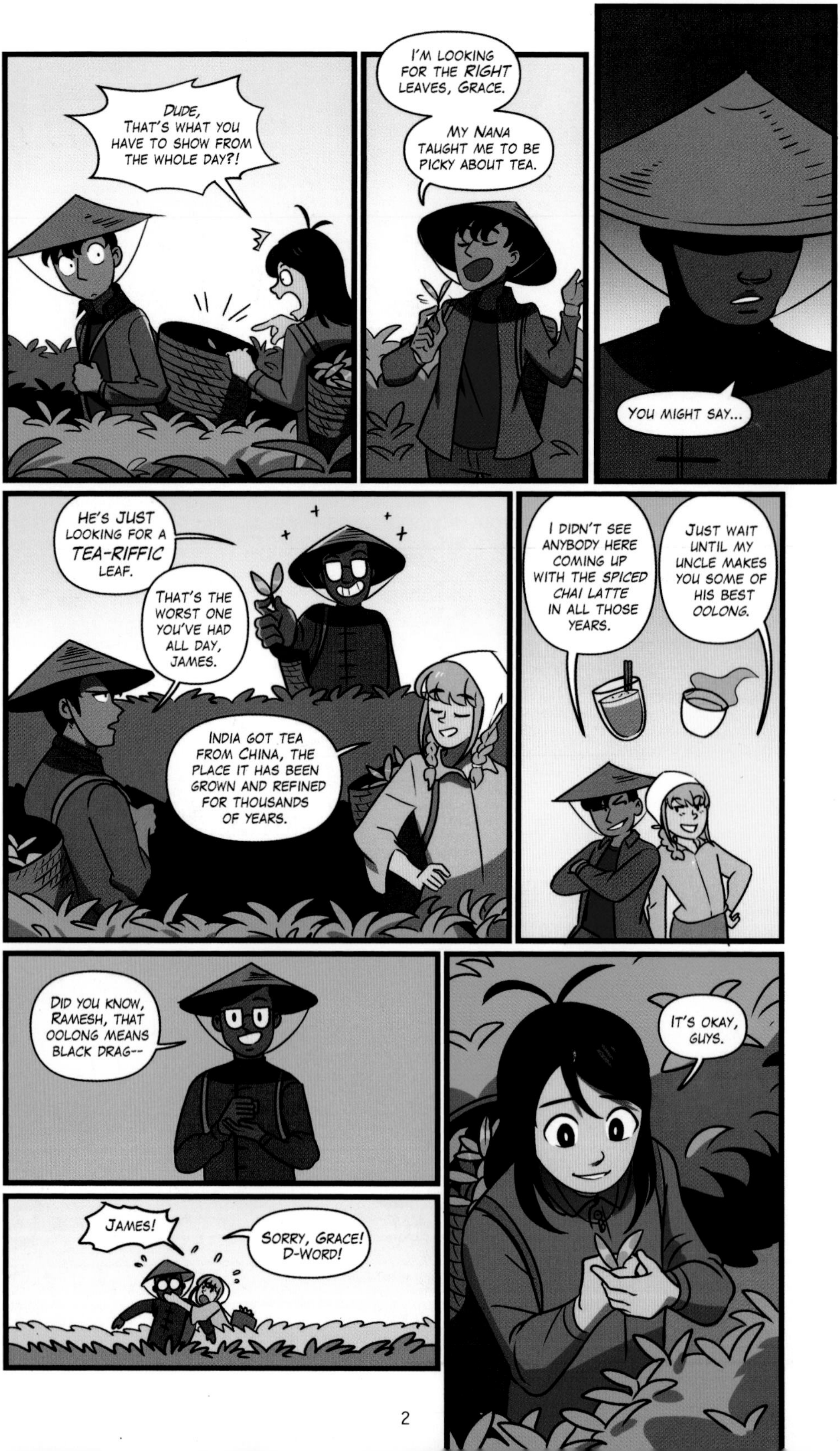
DUDE, THAT'S WHAT YOU HAVE TO SHOW FROM THE WHOLE DAY?!
I'M LOOKING FOR THE RIGHT LEAVES, GRACE.
MY NANA TAUGHT ME TO BE PICKY ABOUT TEA.
YOU MIGHT SAY...
HE'S JUST LOOKING FOR A TEA-RIFFIC LEAF.
THAT'S THE WORST ONE YOU'VE HAD ALL DAY, JAMES.
INDIA GOT TEA FROM CHINA, THE PLACE IT HAS BEEN GROWN AND REFINED FOR THOUSANDS OF YEARS.
I DIDN'T SEE ANYBODY HERE COMING UP WITH THE SPICED CHAI LATTE IN ALL THOSE YEARS.
JUST WAIT UNTIL MY UNCLE MAKES YOU SOME OF HIS BEST OOLONG.
DID YOU KNOW, RAMESH, THAT OOLONG MEANS BLACK DRAG--
JAMES!
SORRY, GRACE! D-WORD!
IT'S OKAY, GUYS.

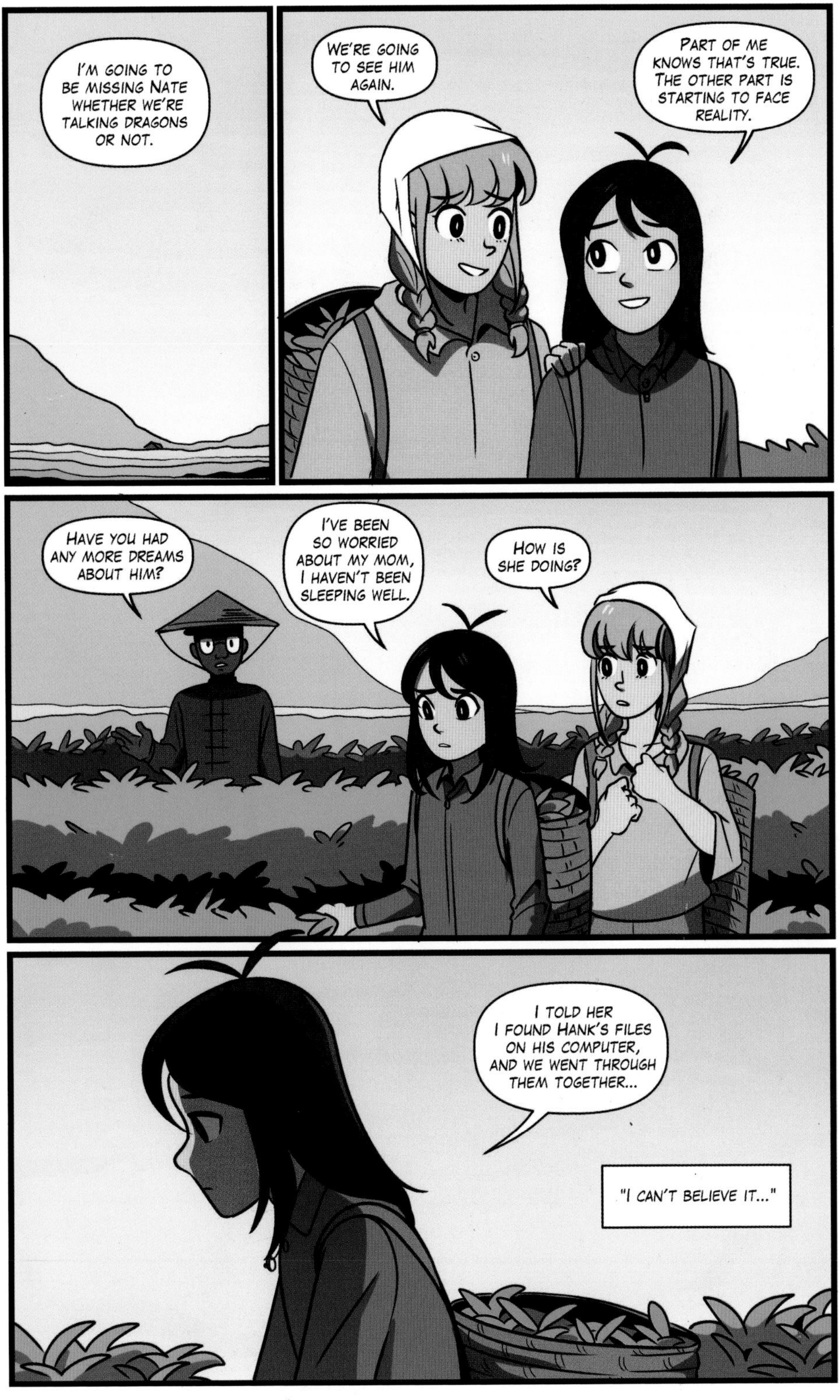
I'M GOING TO BE MISSING NATE WHETHER WE'RE TALKING DRAGONS OR NOT.
WE'RE GOING TO SEE HIM AGAIN.
PART OF ME KNOWS THAT'S TRUE. THE OTHER PART IS STARTING TO FACE REALITY.
HAVE YOU HAD ANY MORE DREAMS ABOUT HIM?
I'VE BEEN SO WORRIED ABOUT MY MOM, I HAVEN'T BEEN SLEEPING WELL.
HOW IS SHE DOING?
I TOLD HER I FOUND HANK'S FILES ON HIS COMPUTER, AND WE WENT THROUGH THEM TOGETHER...
"I CAN'T BELIEVE IT..."

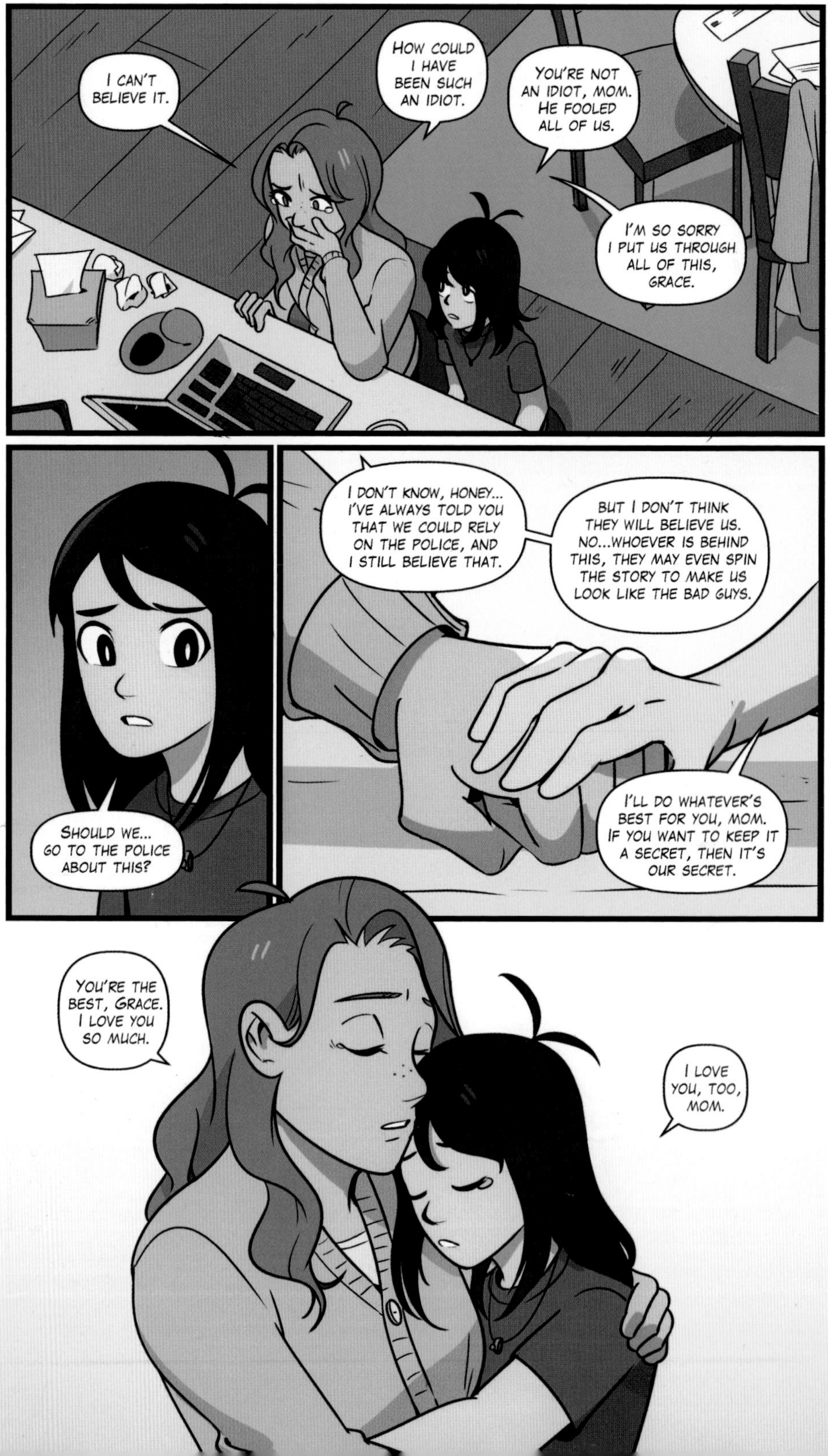
I CAN'T BELIEVE IT.
HOW COULD I HAVE BEEN SUCH AN IDIOT.
YOU'RE NOT AN IDIOT, MOM. HE FOOLED ALL OF US.
I'M SO SORRY I PUT US THROUGH ALL OF THIS, GRACE.
SHOULD WE... GO TO THE POLICE ABOUT THIS?
I DON'T KNOW, HONEY... I'VE ALWAYS TOLD YOU THAT WE COULD RELY ON THE POLICE, AND I STILL BELIEVE THAT.
BUT I DON'T THINK THEY WILL BELIEVE US. NO...WHOEVER IS BEHIND THIS, THEY MAY EVEN SPIN THE STORY TO MAKE US LOOK LIKE THE BAD GUYS.
I'LL DO WHATEVER'S BEST FOR YOU, MOM. IF YOU WANT TO KEEP IT A SECRET, THEN IT'S OUR SECRET.
YOU'RE THE BEST, GRACE. I LOVE YOU SO MUCH.
I LOVE YOU, TOO, MOM.

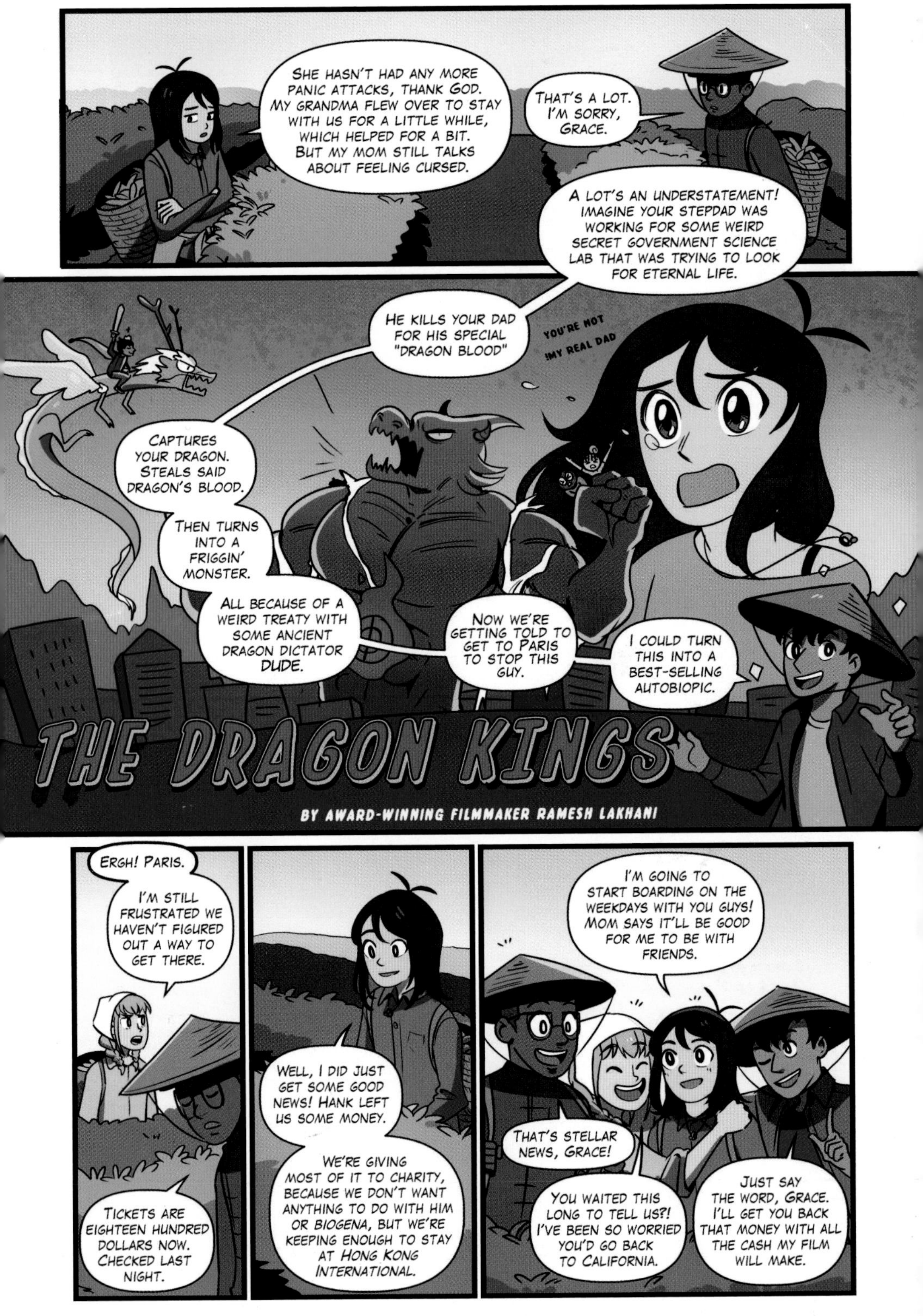

SHE HASN'T HAD ANY MORE PANIC ATTACKS, THANK GOD. MY GRANDMA FLEW OVER TO STAY WITH US FOR A LITTLE WHILE, WHICH HELPED FOR A BIT. BUT MY MOM STILL TALKS ABOUT FEELING CURSED.
THAT'S A LOT. I'M SORRY, GRACE.
A LOT'S AN UNDERSTATEMENT! IMAGINE YOUR STEPDAD WAS WORKING FOR SOME WEIRD SECRET GOVERNMENT SCIENCE LAB THAT WAS TRYING TO LOOK FOR ETERNAL LIFE.
HE KILLS YOUR DAD FOR HIS SPECIAL "DRAGON BLOOD"
YOU'RE NOT
!MY REAL DAD
CAPTURES YOUR DRAGON. STEALS SAID DRAGON'S BLOOD.
THEN TURNS INTO A FRIGGIN' MONSTER.
ALL BECAUSE OF A WEIRD TREATY WITH SOME ANCIENT DRAGON DICTATOR DUDE.
NOW WE'RE GETTING TOLD TO GET TO PARIS TO STOP THIS GUY.
I COULD TURN THIS INTO A BEST-SELLING AUTOBIOPIC.
THE DRAGON KINGS
BY AWARD-WINNING FILMMAKER RAMESH LAKHANI
ERGH! PARIS.
I'M STILL FRUSTRATED WE HAVEN'T FIGURED OUT A WAY TO GET THERE.
TICKETS ARE EIGHTEEN HUNDRED DOLLARS NOW. CHECKED LAST NIGHT.
WELL, I DID JUST GET SOME GOOD NEWS! HANK LEFT US SOME MONEY.
WE'RE GIVING MOST OF IT TO CHARITY, BECAUSE WE DON'T WANT ANYTHING TO DO WITH HIM OR BIOGENA, BUT WE'RE KEEPING ENOUGH TO STAY AT HONG KONG INTERNATIONAL.
I'M GOING TO START BOARDING ON THE WEEKDAYS WITH YOU GUYS! MOM SAYS IT'LL BE GOOD FOR ME TO BE WITH FRIENDS.
THAT'S STELLAR NEWS, GRACE!
YOU WAITED THIS LONG TO TELL US?! I'VE BEEN SO WORRIED YOU'D GO BACK TO CALIFORNIA.
JUST SAY THE WORD, GRACE. I'LL GET YOU BACK THAT MONEY WITH ALL THE CASH MY FILM WILL MAKE.

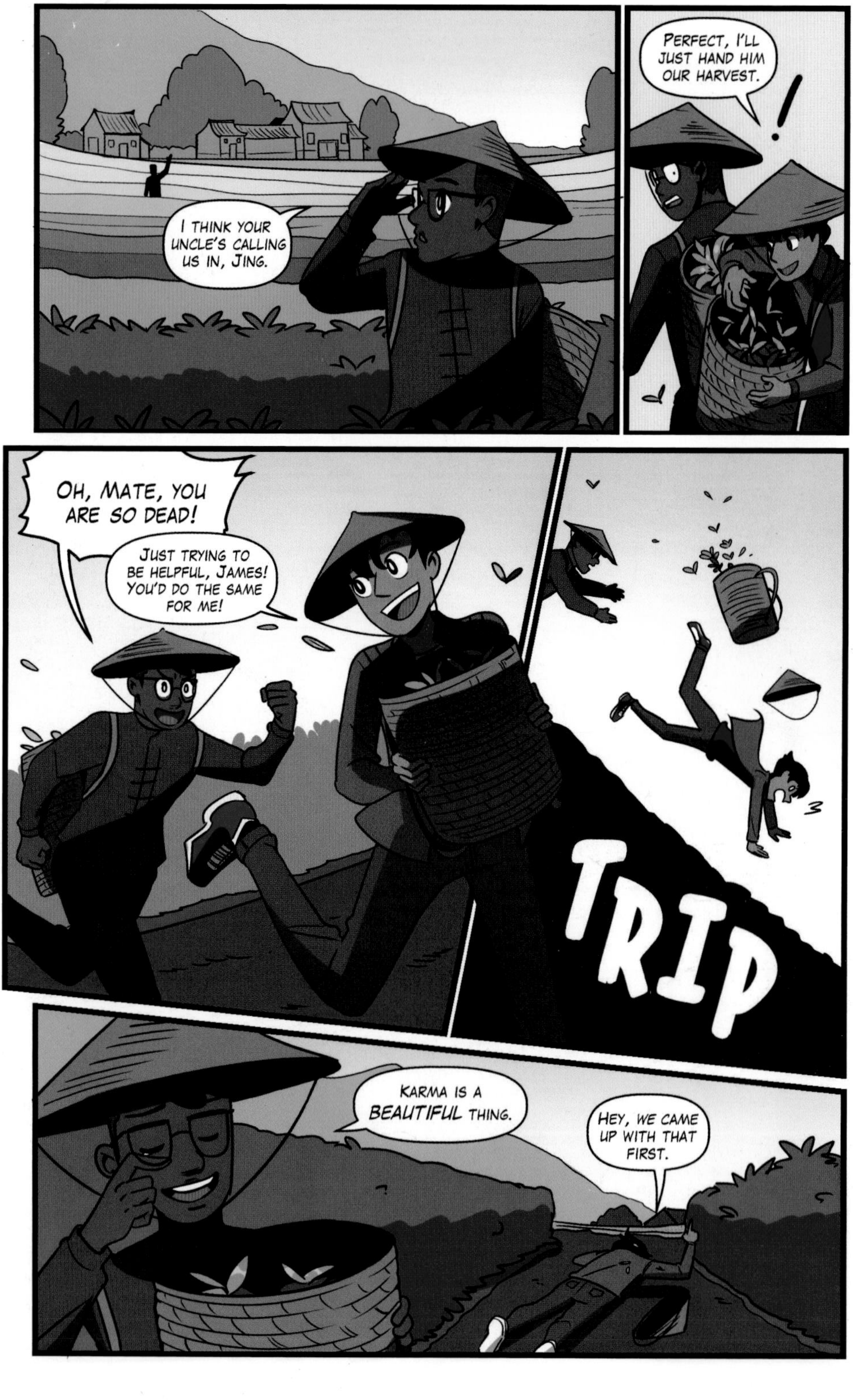
I THINK YOUR UNCLE'S CALLING US IN, JING.
PERFECT, I'LL JUST HAND HIM OUR HARVEST.
!
OH, MATE, YOU ARE SO DEAD!
JUST TRYING TO BE HELPFUL, JAMES! YOU'D DO THE SAME FOR ME!
TRIP
KARMA IS A BEAUTIFUL THING.
HEY, WE CAME UP WITH THAT FIRST.

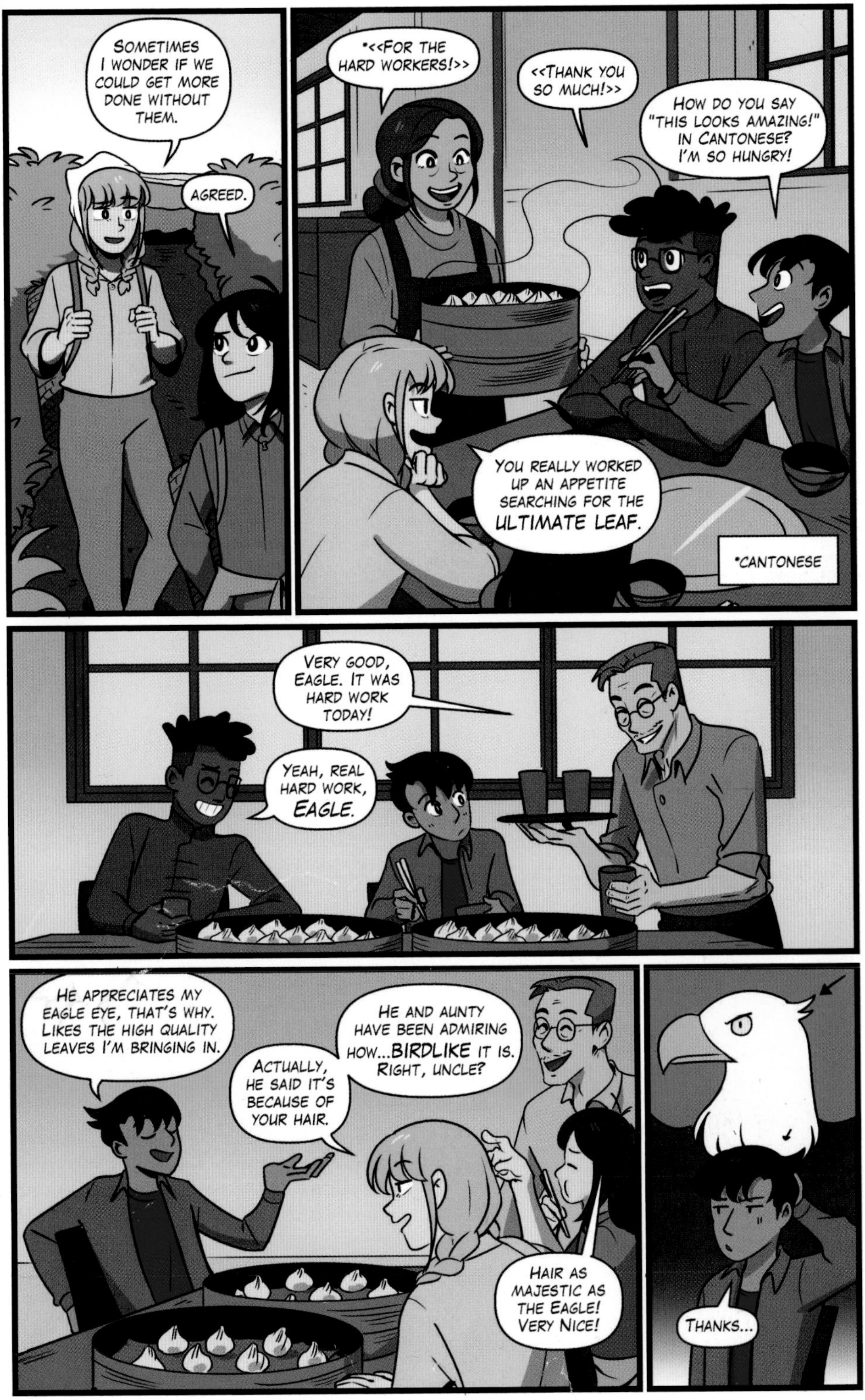
SOMETIMES I WONDER IF WE COULD GET MORE DONE WITHOUT THEM.
AGREED.
*<<FOR THE HARD WORKERS!>>
<<THANK YOU SO MUCH!>>
HOW DO YOU SAY "THIS LOOKS AMAZING!" IN CANTONESE? I'M SO HUNGRY!
YOU REALLY WORKED UP AN APPETITE SEARCHING FOR THE ULTIMATE LEAF.
*CANTONESE
VERY GOOD, EAGLE. IT WAS HARD WORK TODAY!
YEAH, REAL HARD WORK, EAGLE.
HE APPRECIATES MY EAGLE EYE, THAT'S WHY. LIKES THE HIGH QUALITY LEAVES I'M BRINGING IN.
ACTUALLY, HE SAID IT'S BECAUSE OF YOUR HAIR.
HE AND AUNTY HAVE BEEN ADMIRING HOW...BIRDLIKE IT IS. RIGHT, UNCLE?
HAIR AS MAJESTIC AS THE EAGLE! VERY NICE!
THANKS...

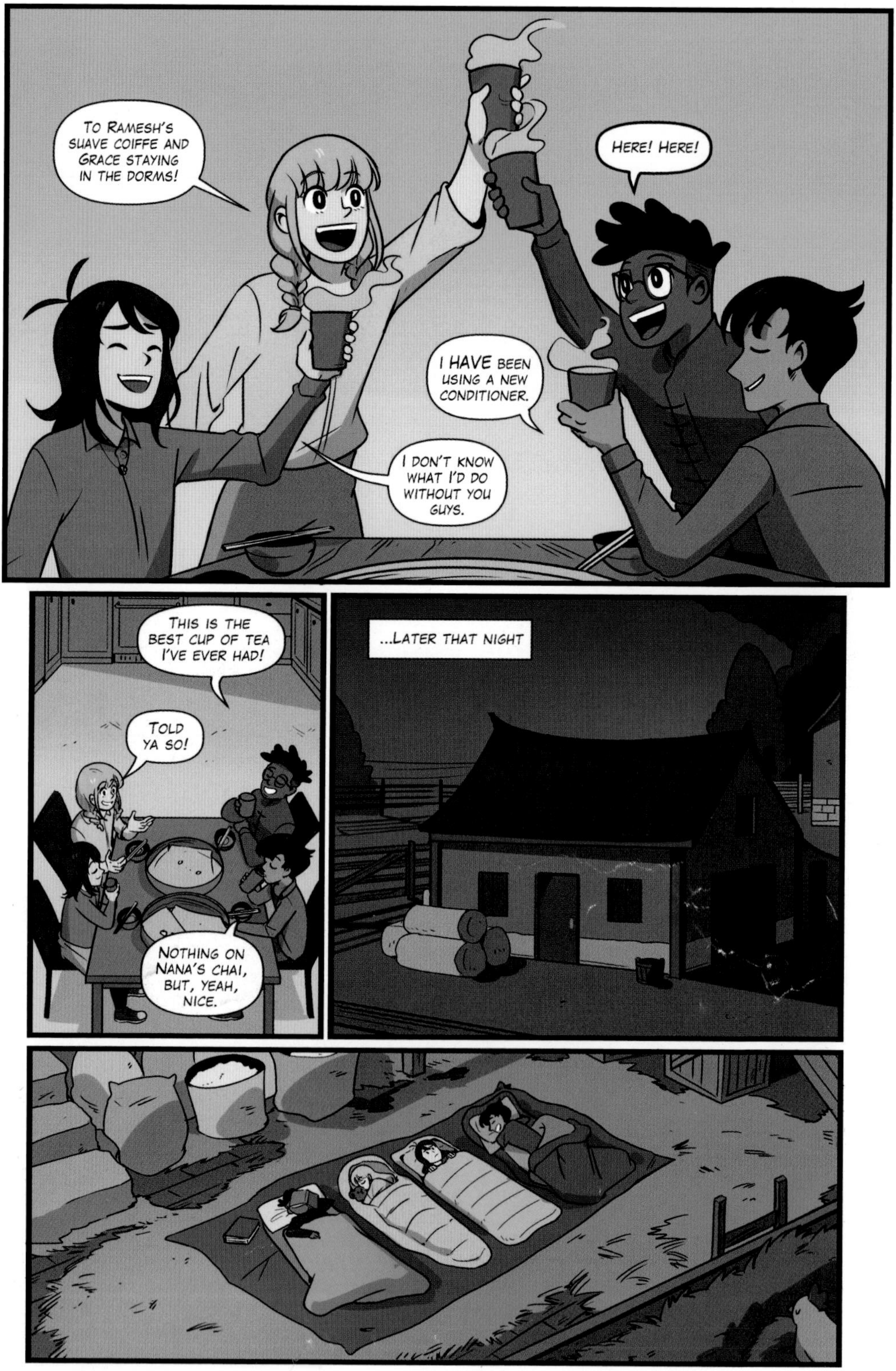
To Ramesh's suave coiffe and Grace staying in the dorms!
Here! Here!
I HAVE been using a new conditioner.
I don't know what I'd do without you guys.
This is the best cup of tea I've ever had!
Told ya so!
Nothing on Nana's chai, but, yeah, nice.
...Later that night

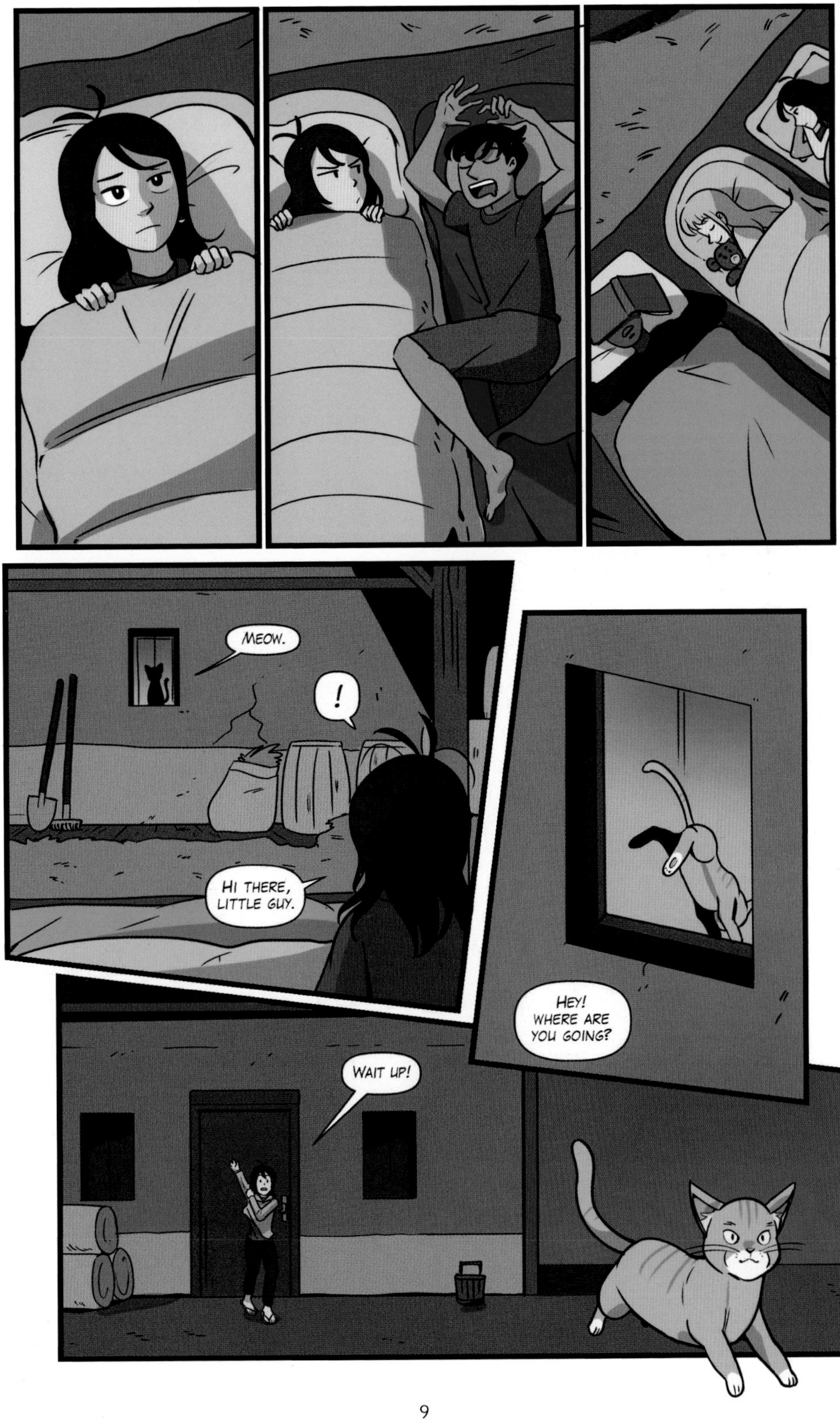

MEOW.
!
HI THERE, LITTLE GUY.
HEY! WHERE ARE YOU GOING?
WAIT UP!

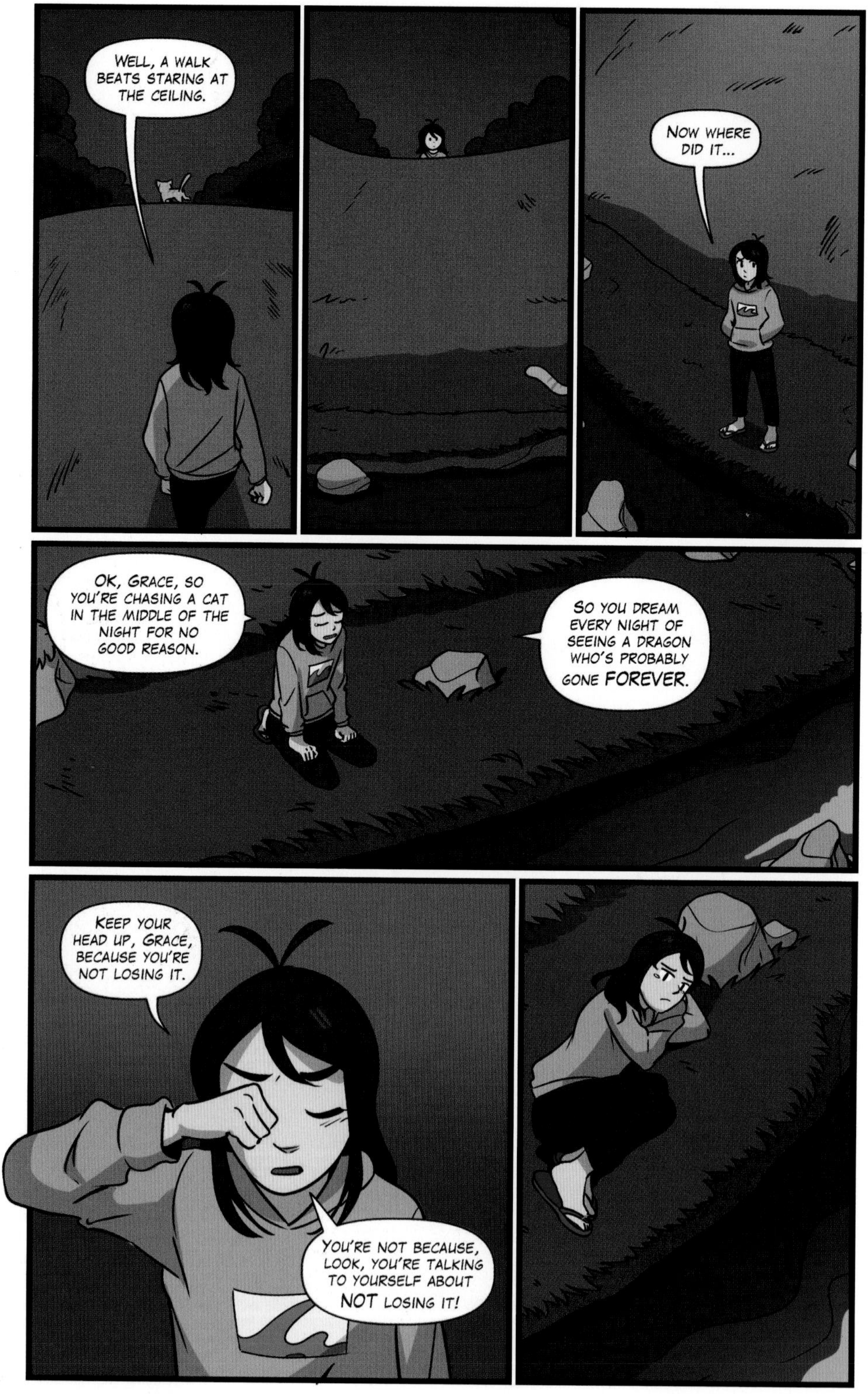
WELL, A WALK BEATS STARING AT THE CEILING.
NOW WHERE DID IT...
OK, GRACE, SO YOU'RE CHASING A CAT IN THE MIDDLE OF THE NIGHT FOR NO GOOD REASON.
SO YOU DREAM EVERY NIGHT OF SEEING A DRAGON WHO'S PROBABLY GONE FOREVER.
KEEP YOUR HEAD UP, GRACE, BECAUSE YOU'RE NOT LOSING IT.
YOU'RE NOT BECAUSE, LOOK, YOU'RE TALKING TO YOURSELF ABOUT NOT LOSING IT!

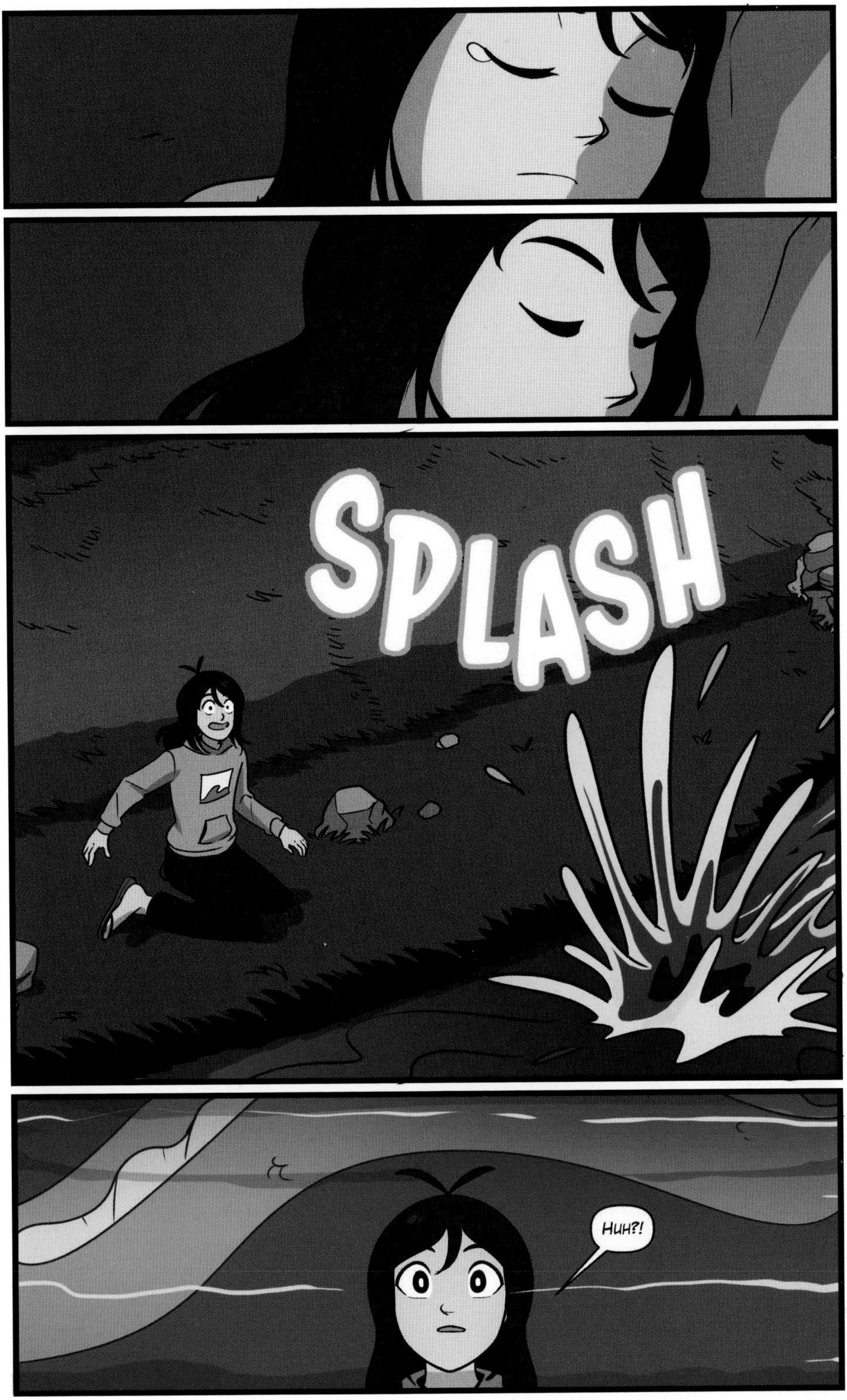
SPLASH
HUH?!

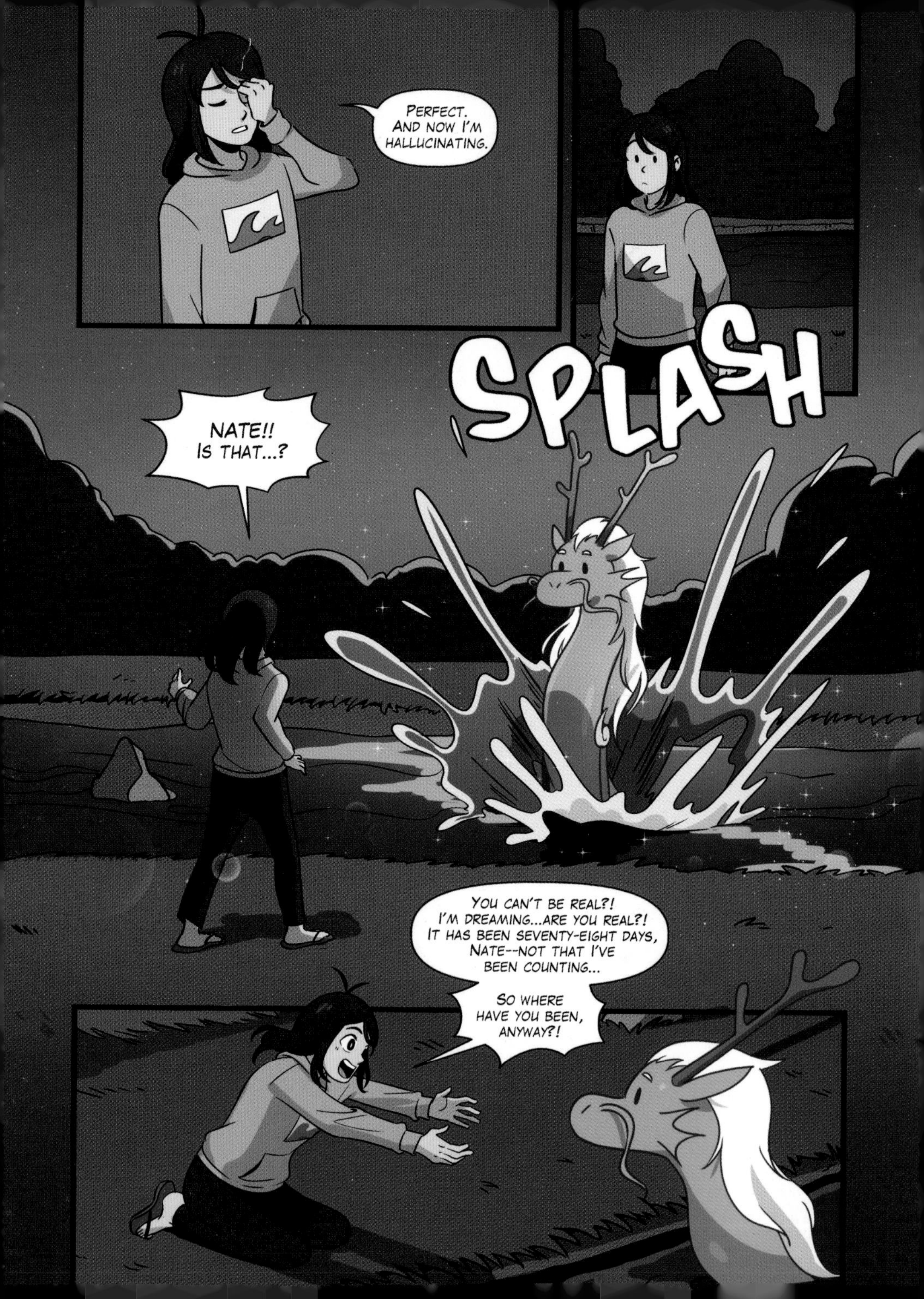
PERFECT. AND NOW I'M HALLUCINATING.
SPLASH
NATE!! IS THAT...?
YOU CAN'T BE REAL?! I'M DREAMING...ARE YOU REAL?! IT HAS BEEN SEVENTY-EIGHT DAYS, NATE--NOT THAT I'VE BEEN COUNTING...
SO WHERE HAVE YOU BEEN, ANYWAY?!

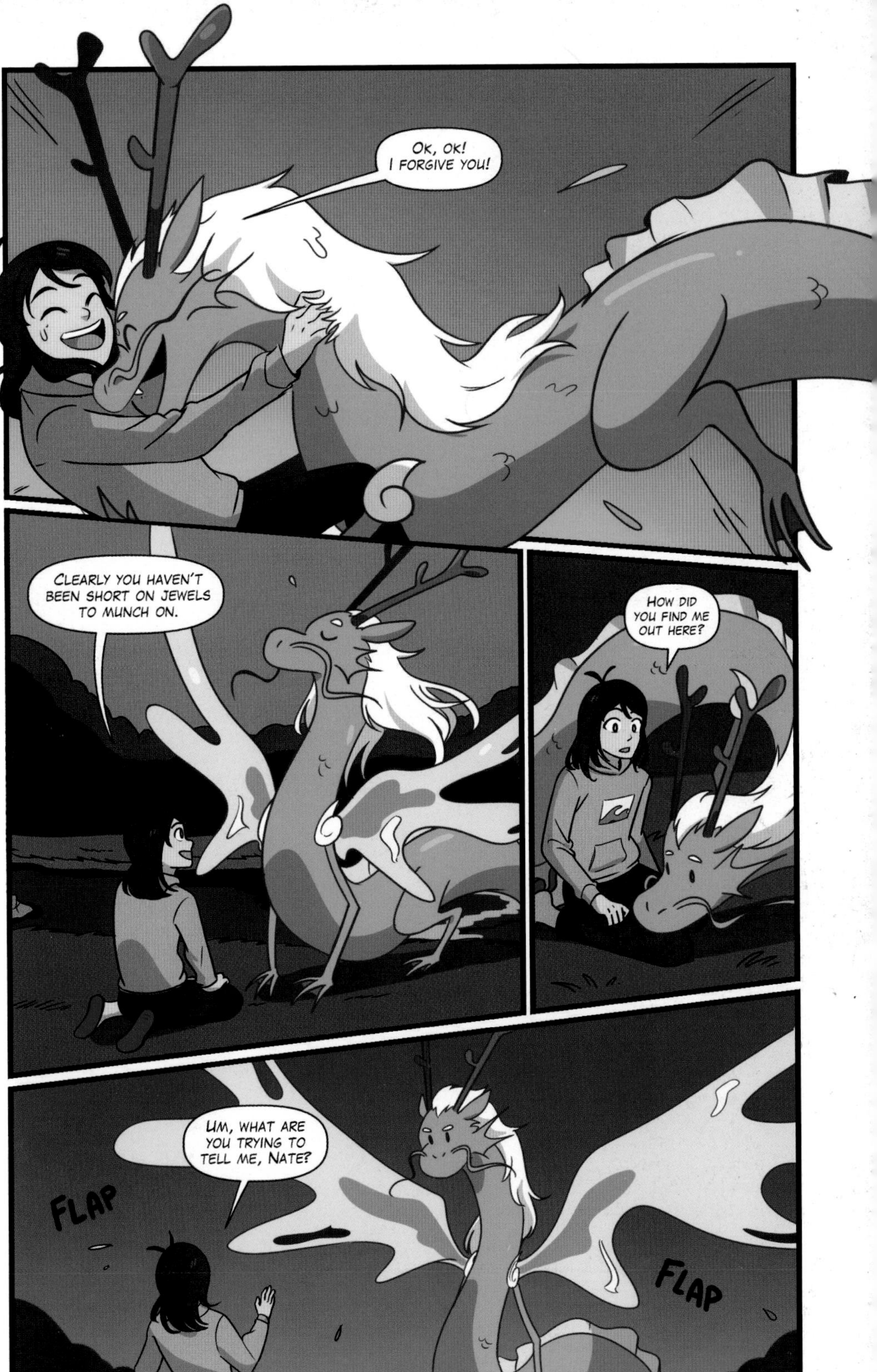

OK, OK!
I FORGIVE YOU!
CLEARLY YOU HAVEN'T BEEN SHORT ON JEWELS TO MUNCH ON.
HOW DID YOU FIND ME OUT HERE?
UM, WHAT ARE YOU TRYING TO TELL ME, NATE?
FLAP
FLAP

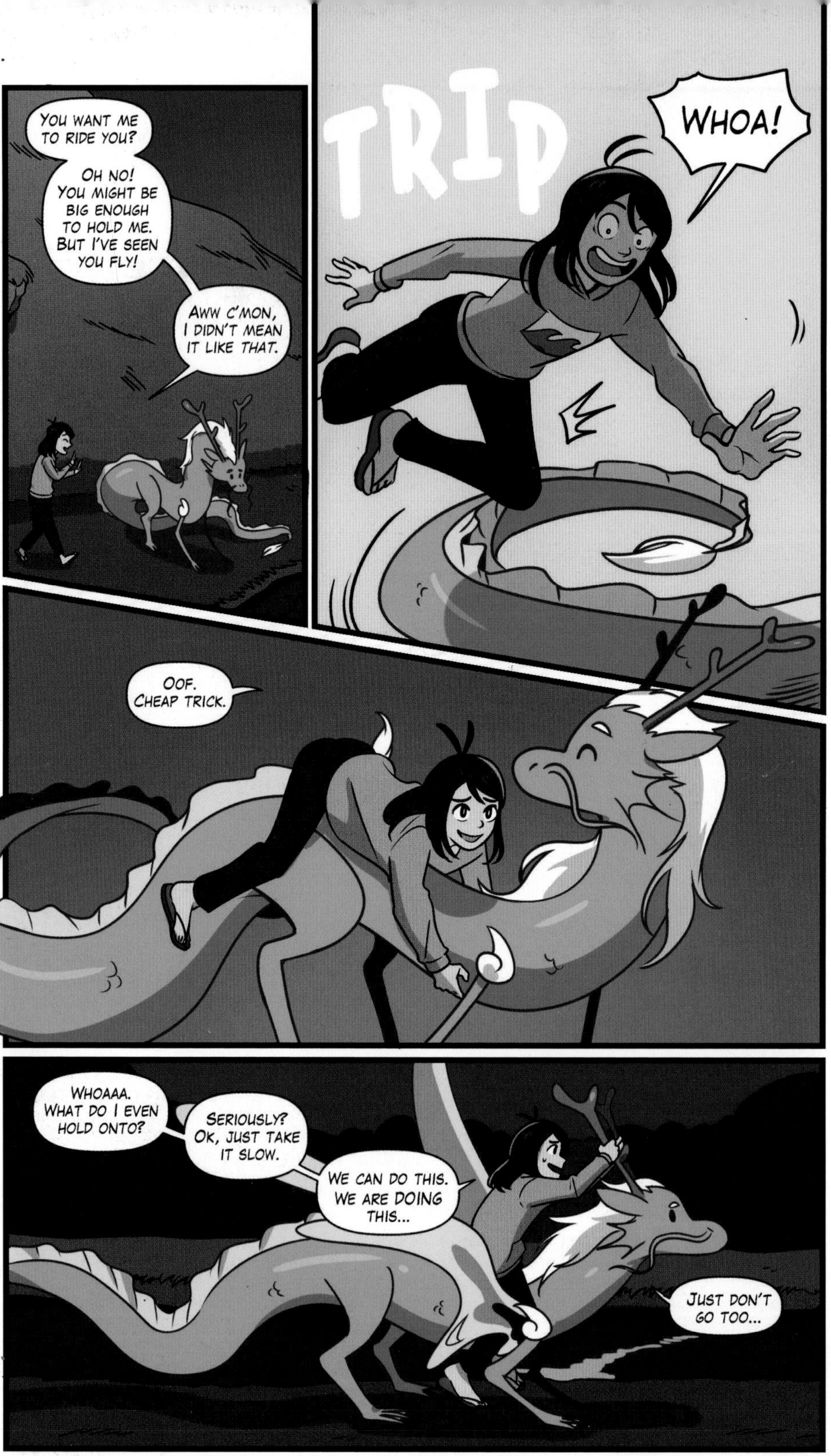

YOU WANT ME TO RIDE YOU?
OH NO! YOU MIGHT BE BIG ENOUGH TO HOLD ME. BUT I'VE SEEN YOU FLY!
AWW C'MON, I DIDN'T MEAN IT LIKE THAT.
TRIP
WHOA!
OOF. CHEAP TRICK.
WHOAAA. WHAT DO I EVEN HOLD ONTO?
SERIOUSLY? OK, JUST TAKE IT SLOW.
WE CAN DO THIS. WE ARE DOING THIS...
JUST DON'T GO TOO...

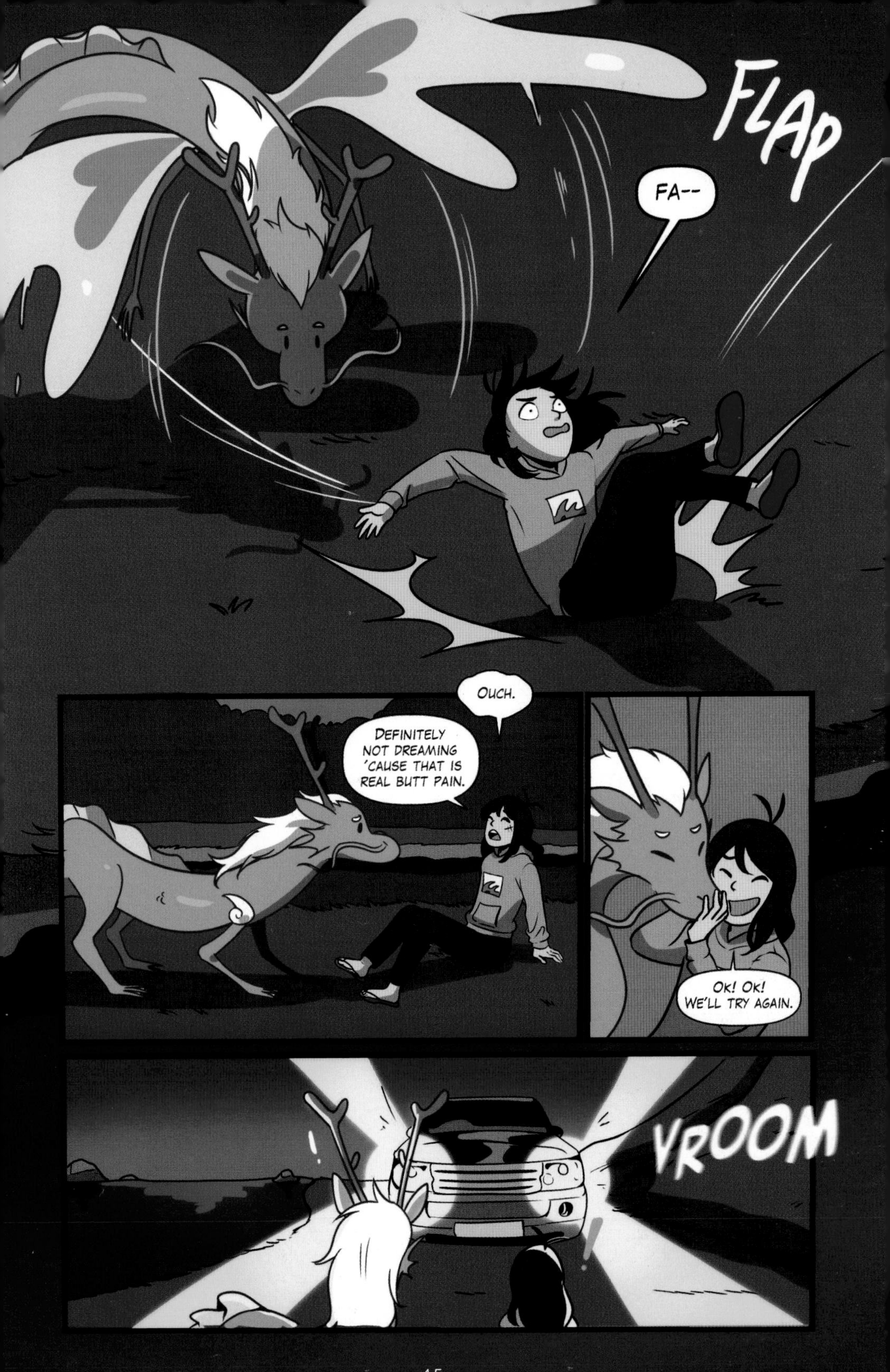
FLAP
FA--
OUCH.
DEFINITELY NOT DREAMING 'CAUSE THAT IS REAL BUTT PAIN.
OK! OK! WE'LL TRY AGAIN.
VROOM

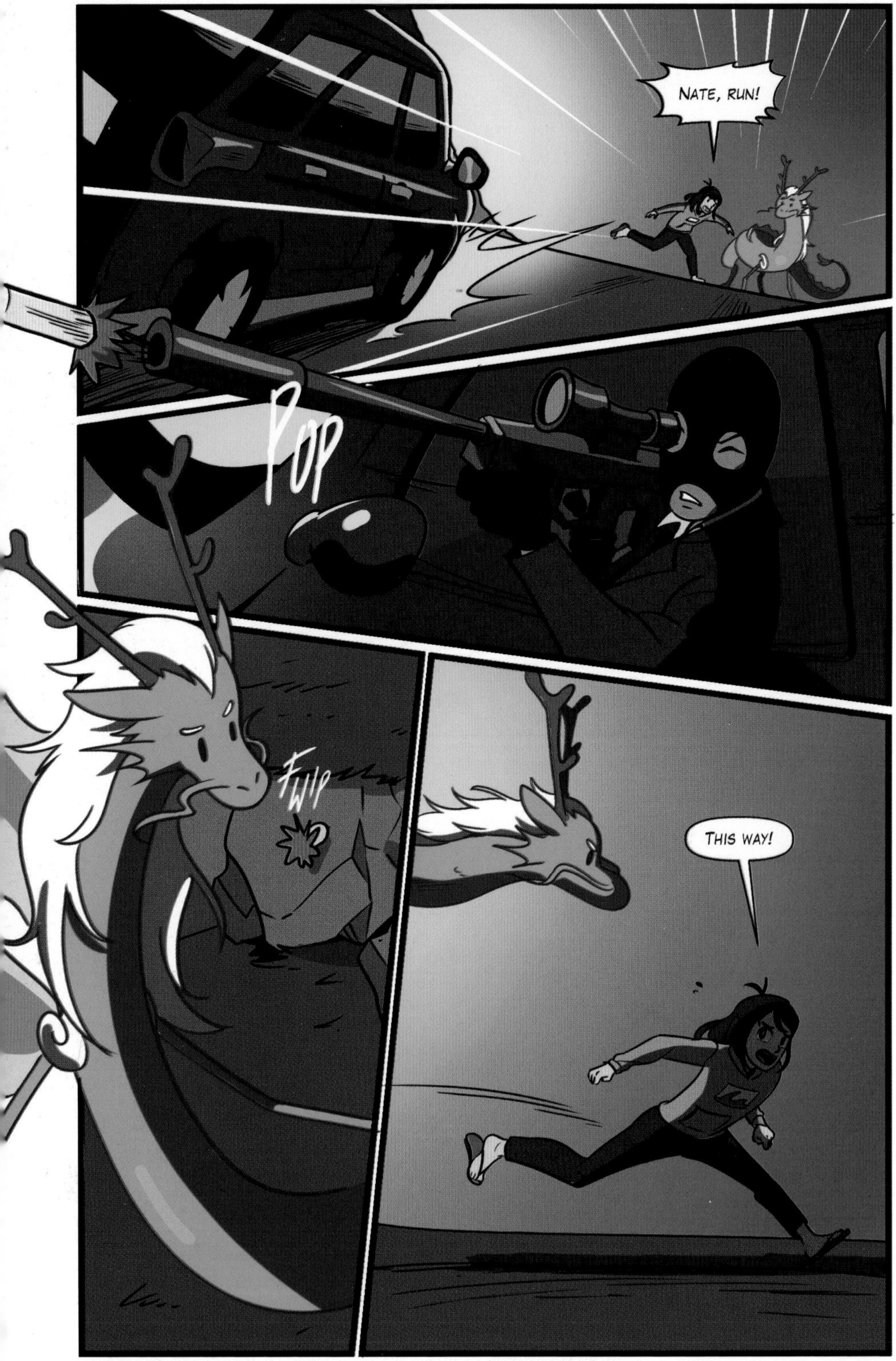
NATE, RUN!
POP
FWIP
THIS WAY!

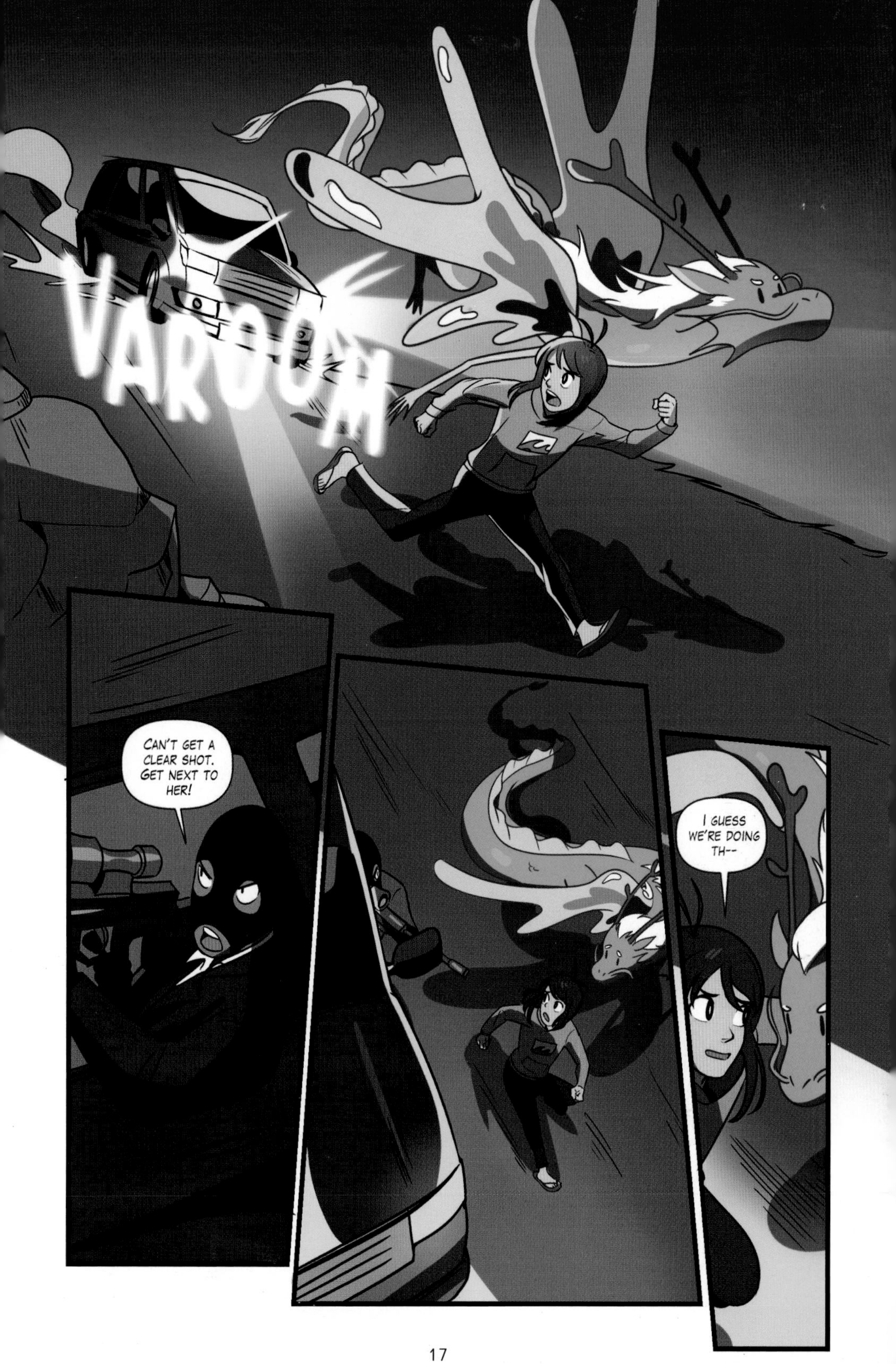
VAROOM
CAN'T GET A CLEAR SHOT. GET NEXT TO HER!
I GUESS WE'RE DOING TH--

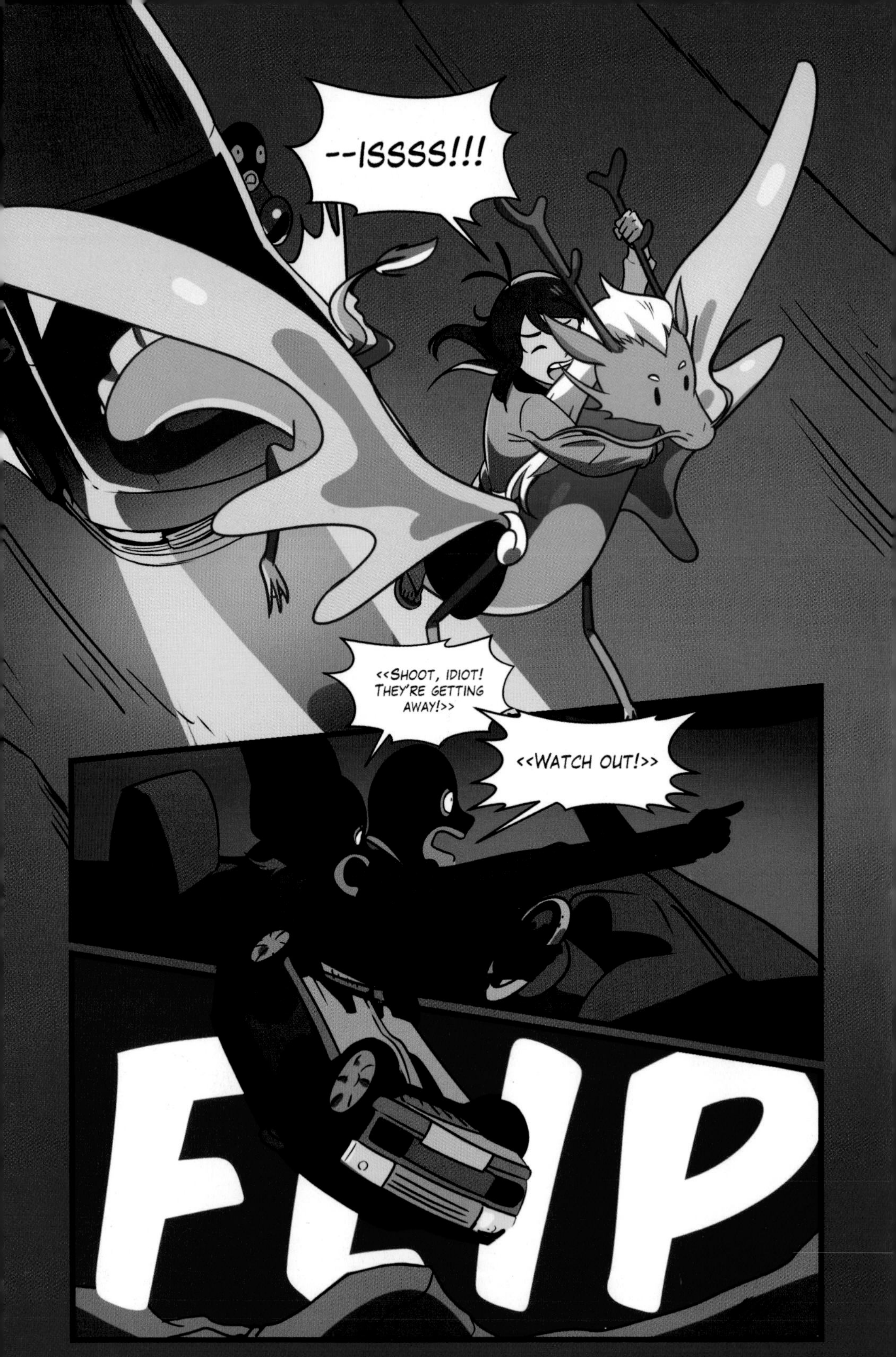
--ISSSS!!!
<<SHOOT, IDIOT! THEY'RE GETTING AWAY!>>
<<WATCH OUT!>>
FLIP

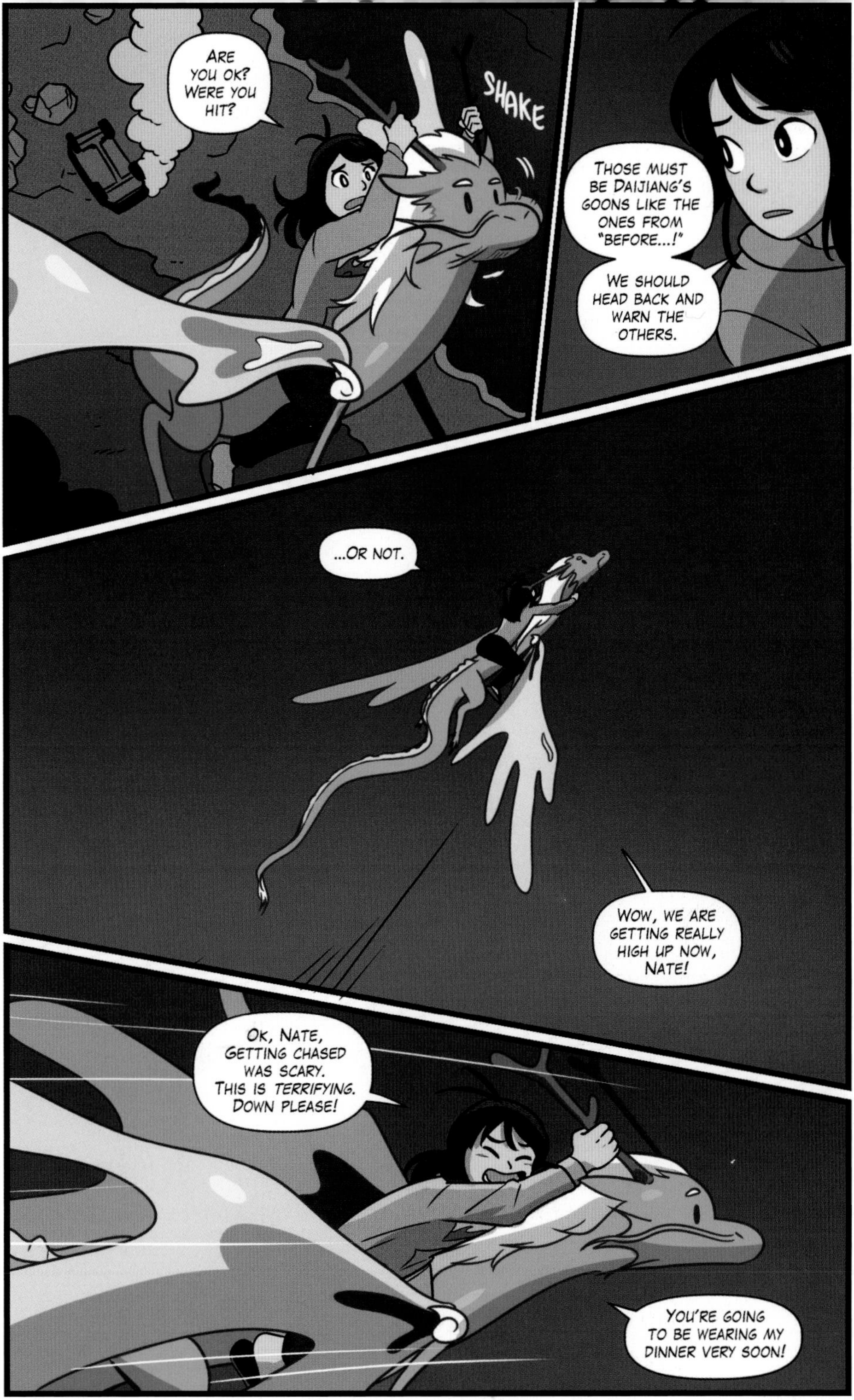
ARE YOU OK? WERE YOU HIT?
SHAKE
THOSE MUST BE DAIJIANG'S GOONS LIKE THE ONES FROM "BEFORE...!"
WE SHOULD HEAD BACK AND WARN THE OTHERS.
...OR NOT.
WOW, WE ARE GETTING REALLY HIGH UP NOW, NATE!
OK, NATE, GETTING CHASED WAS SCARY. THIS IS TERRIFYING. DOWN PLEASE!
YOU'RE GOING TO BE WEARING MY DINNER VERY SOON!

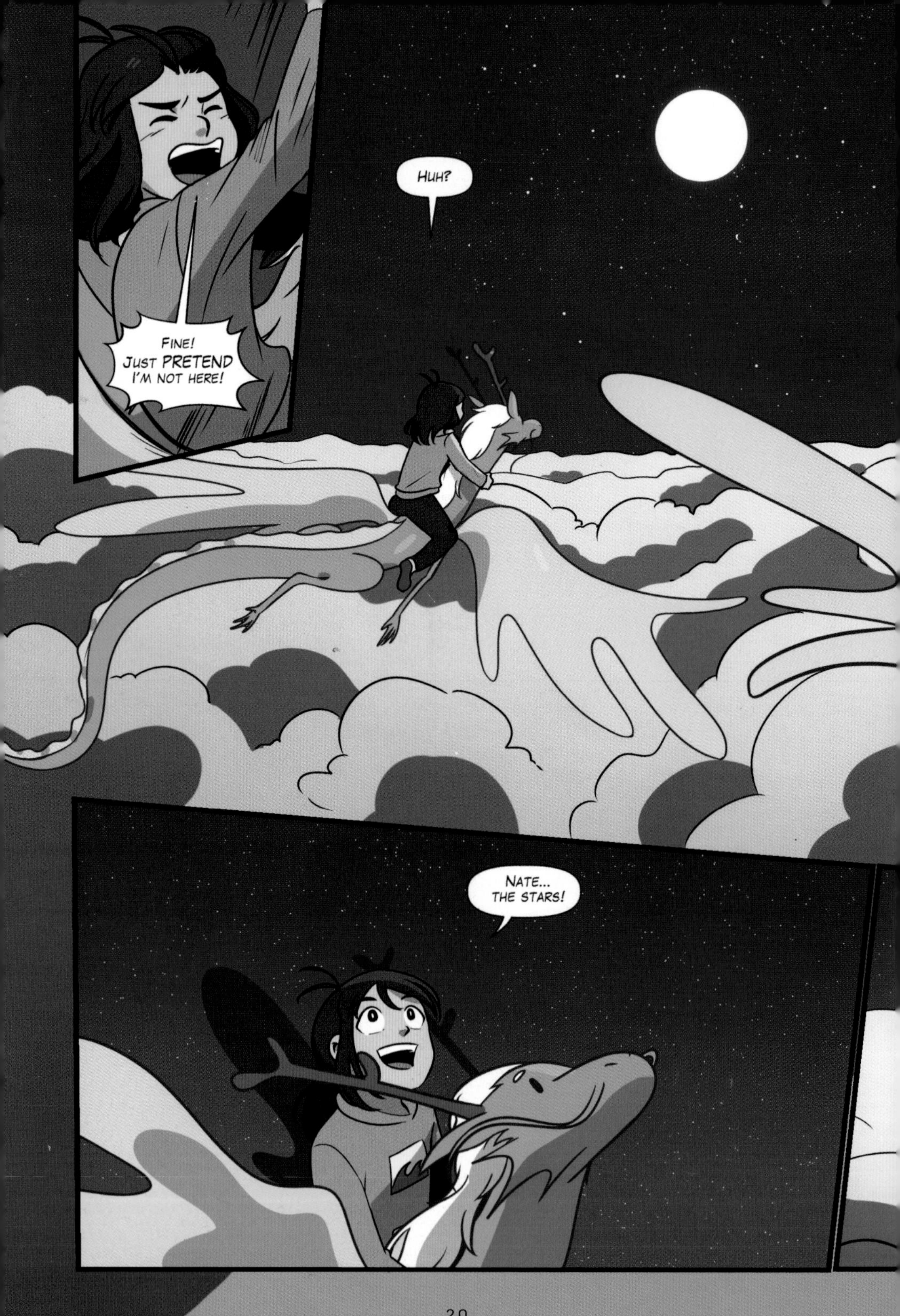
FINE! JUST PRETEND I'M NOT HERE!
HUH?
NATE... THE STARS!

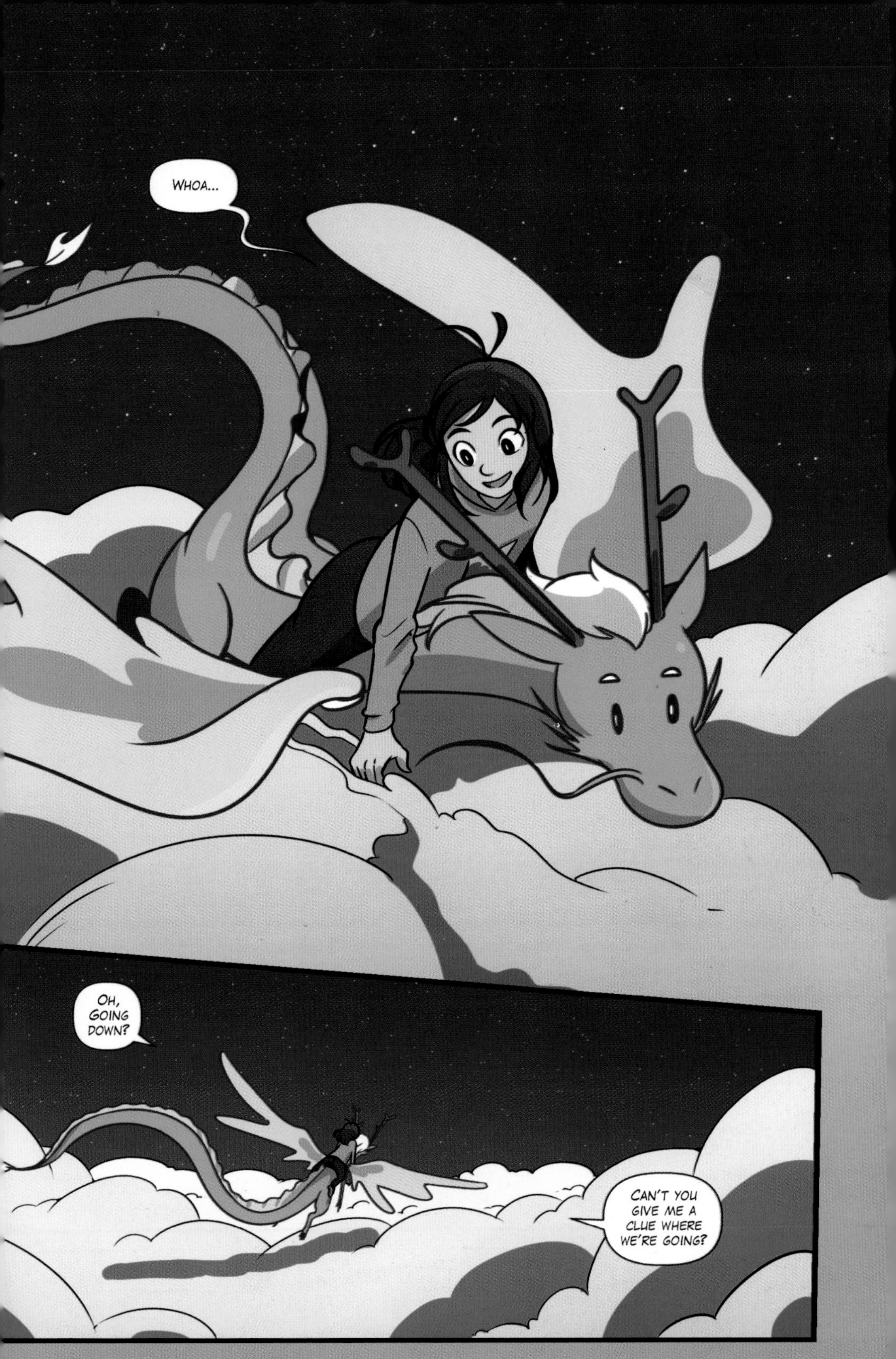
WHOA...
OH, GOING DOWN?
CAN'T YOU GIVE ME A CLUE WHERE WE'RE GOING?

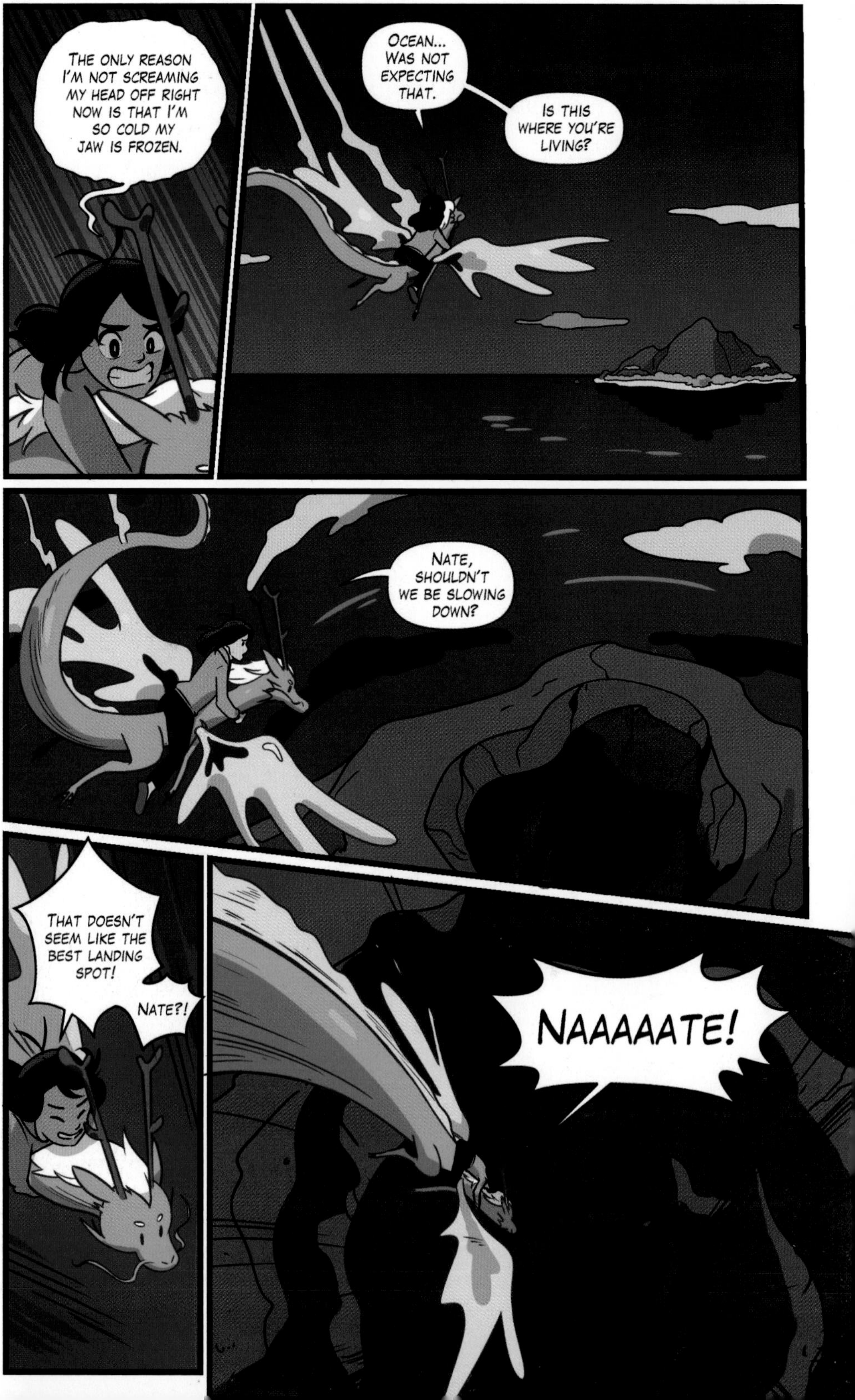
THE ONLY REASON I'M NOT SCREAMING MY HEAD OFF RIGHT NOW IS THAT I'M SO COLD MY JAW IS FROZEN.
OCEAN... WAS NOT EXPECTING THAT.
IS THIS WHERE YOU'RE LIVING?
NATE, SHOULDN'T WE BE SLOWING DOWN?
THAT DOESN'T SEEM LIKE THE BEST LANDING SPOT!
NATE?!
NAAAAATE!

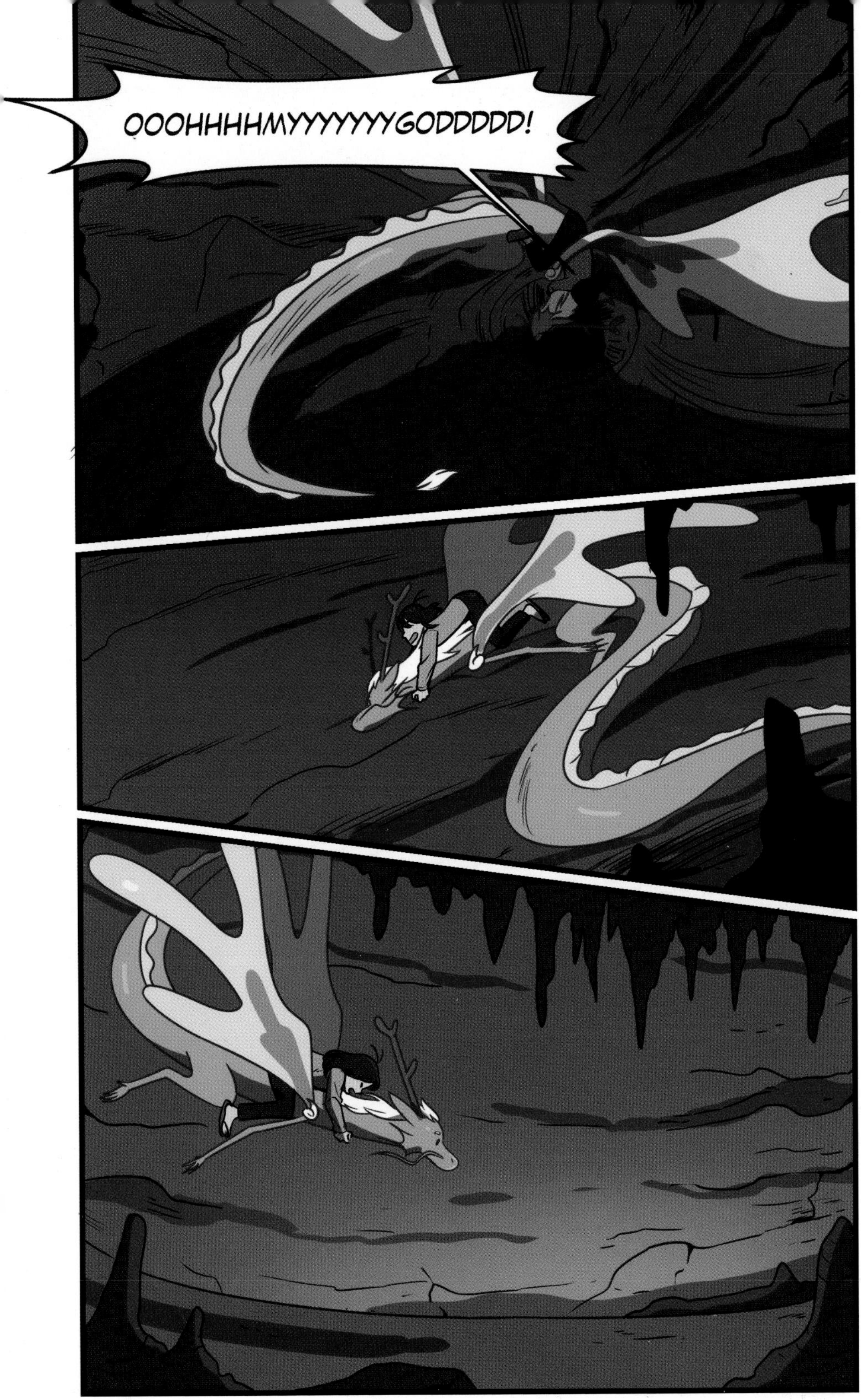
OOOHHHHMYYYYYYYGODDDDD!

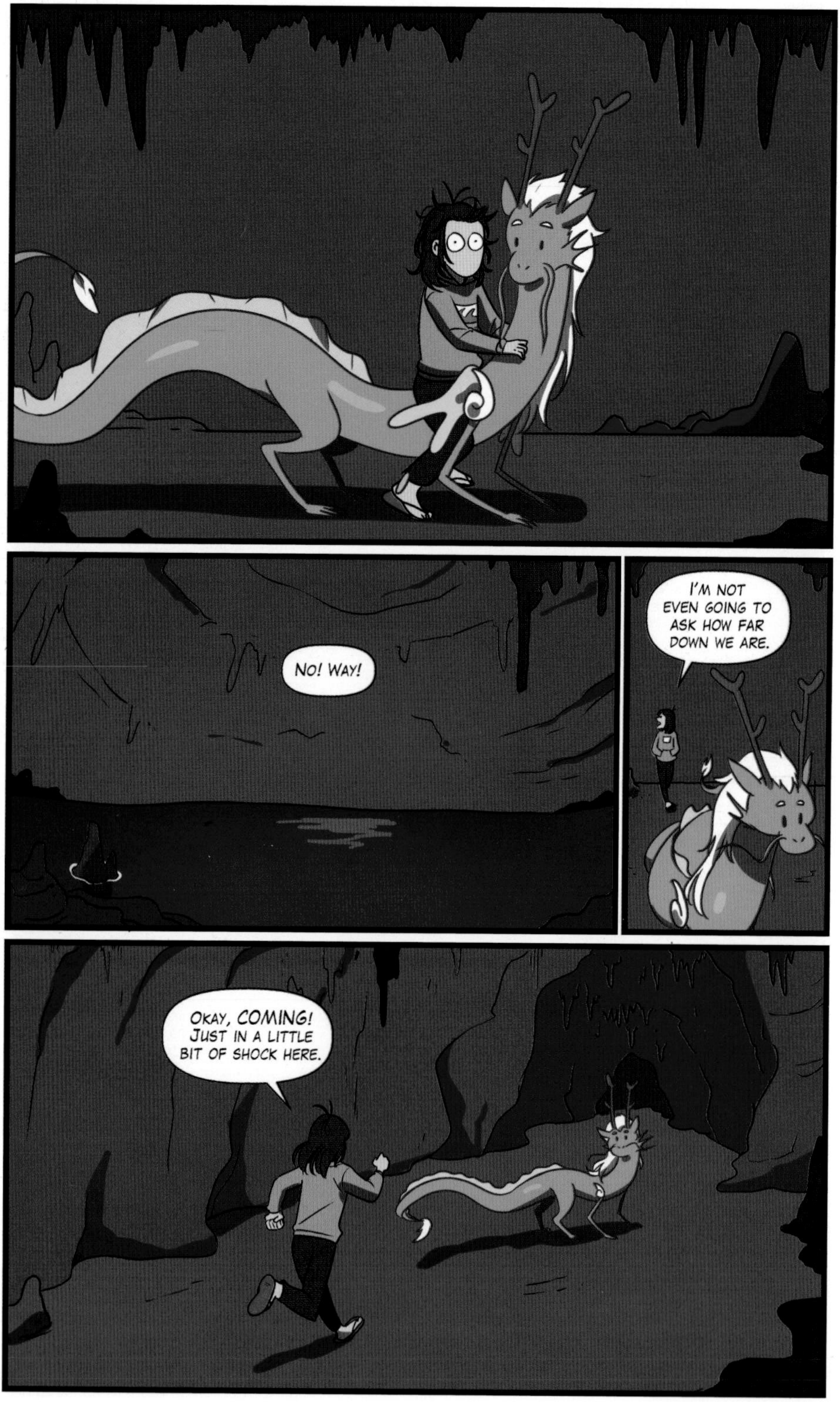
NO! WAY!
I'M NOT EVEN GOING TO ASK HOW FAR DOWN WE ARE.
OKAY, COMING! JUST IN A LITTLE BIT OF SHOCK HERE.

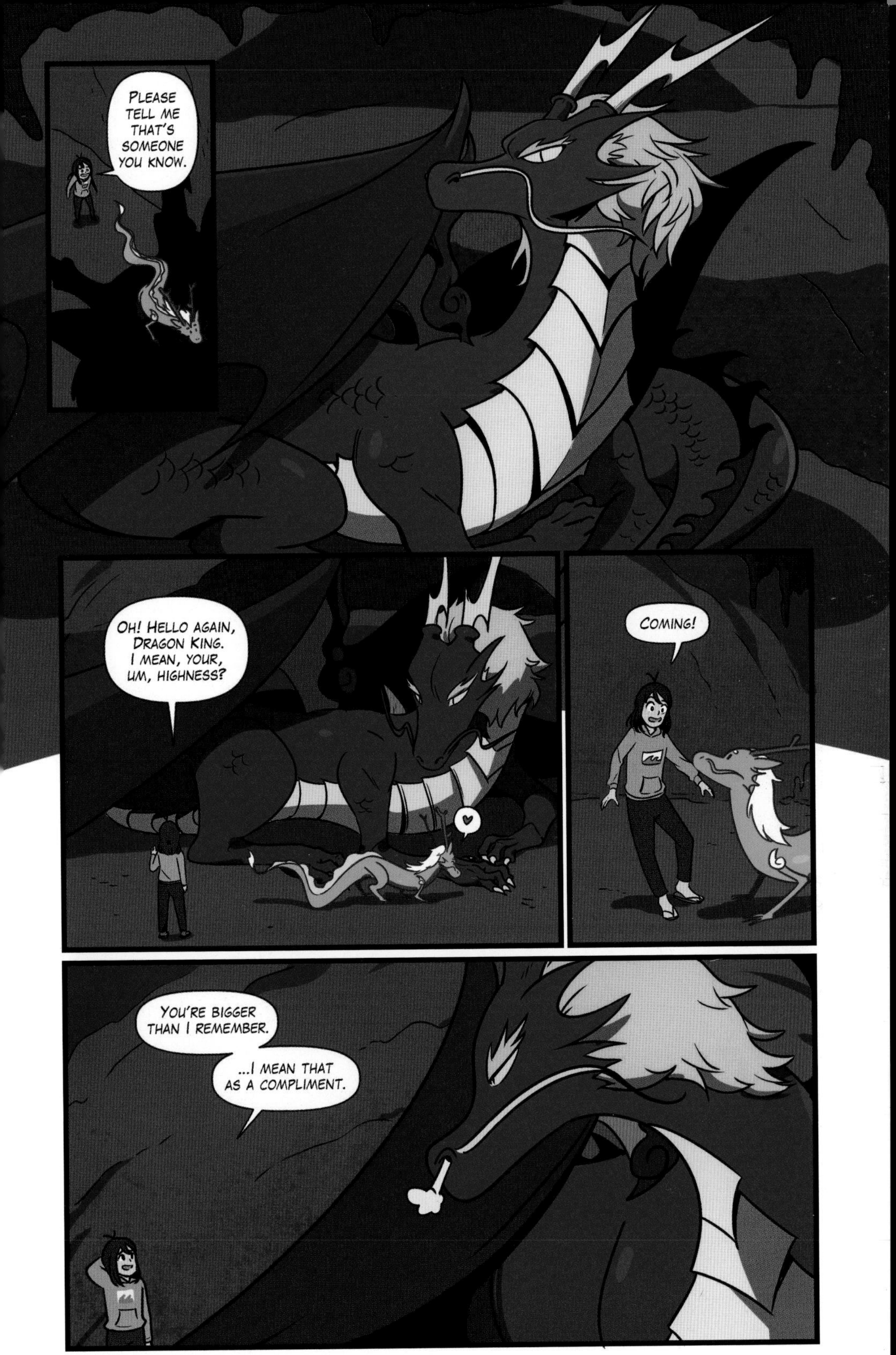
PLEASE TELL ME THAT'S SOMEONE YOU KNOW.
OH! HELLO AGAIN, DRAGON KING. I MEAN, YOUR, UM, HIGHNESS?
COMING!
YOU'RE BIGGER THAN I REMEMBER.
...I MEAN THAT AS A COMPLIMENT.

WHAT'VE YOU GOT THERE?

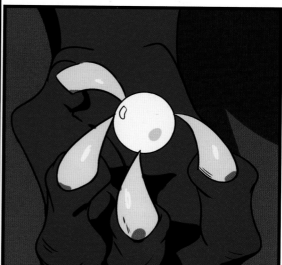

WHOA...

WHERE IS THIS? WHAT ARE WE SEEING?

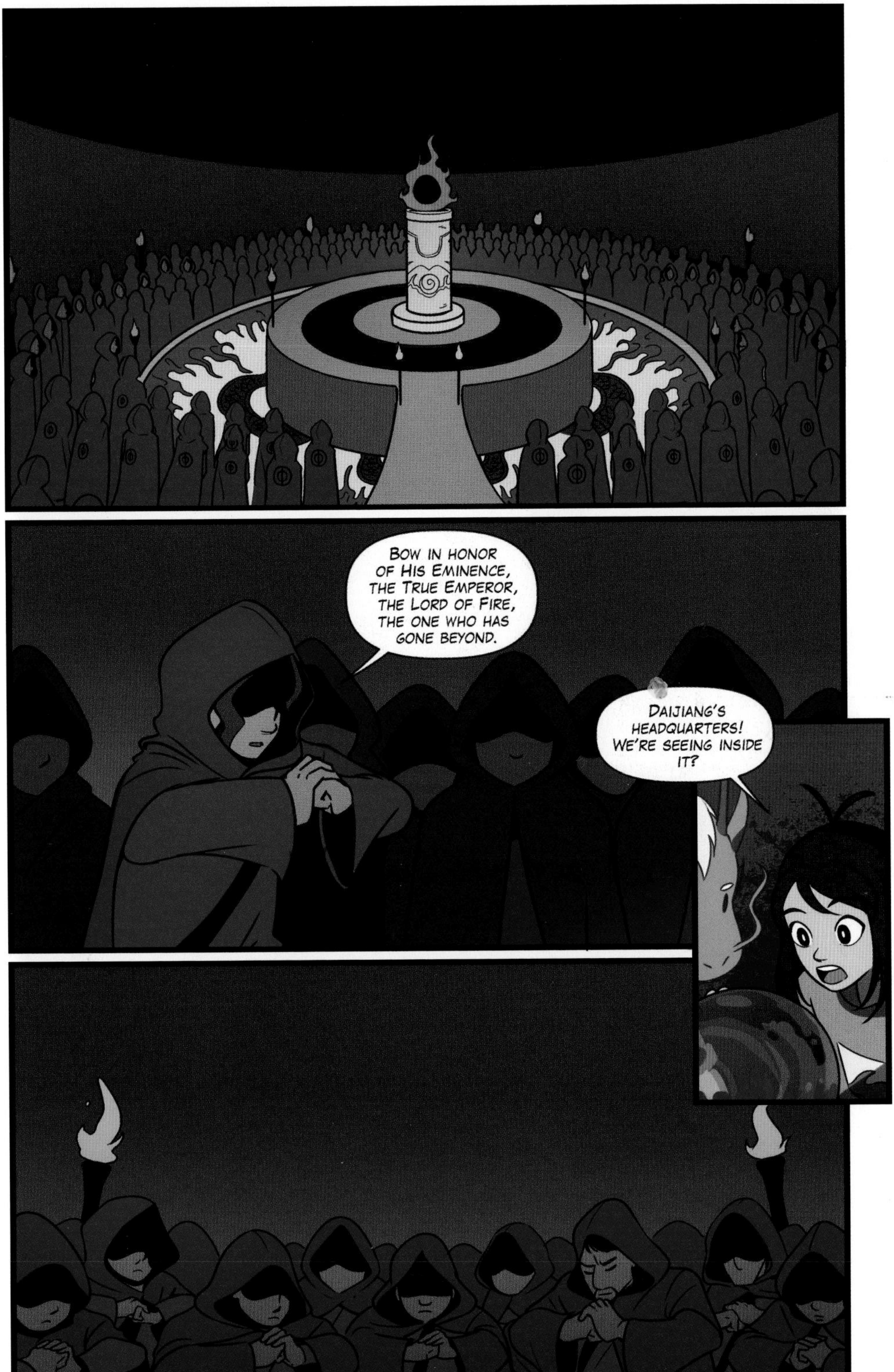
Bow in honor of His Eminence, the True Emperor, the Lord of Fire, the one who has gone beyond.
Daijiang's headquarters! We're seeing inside it?

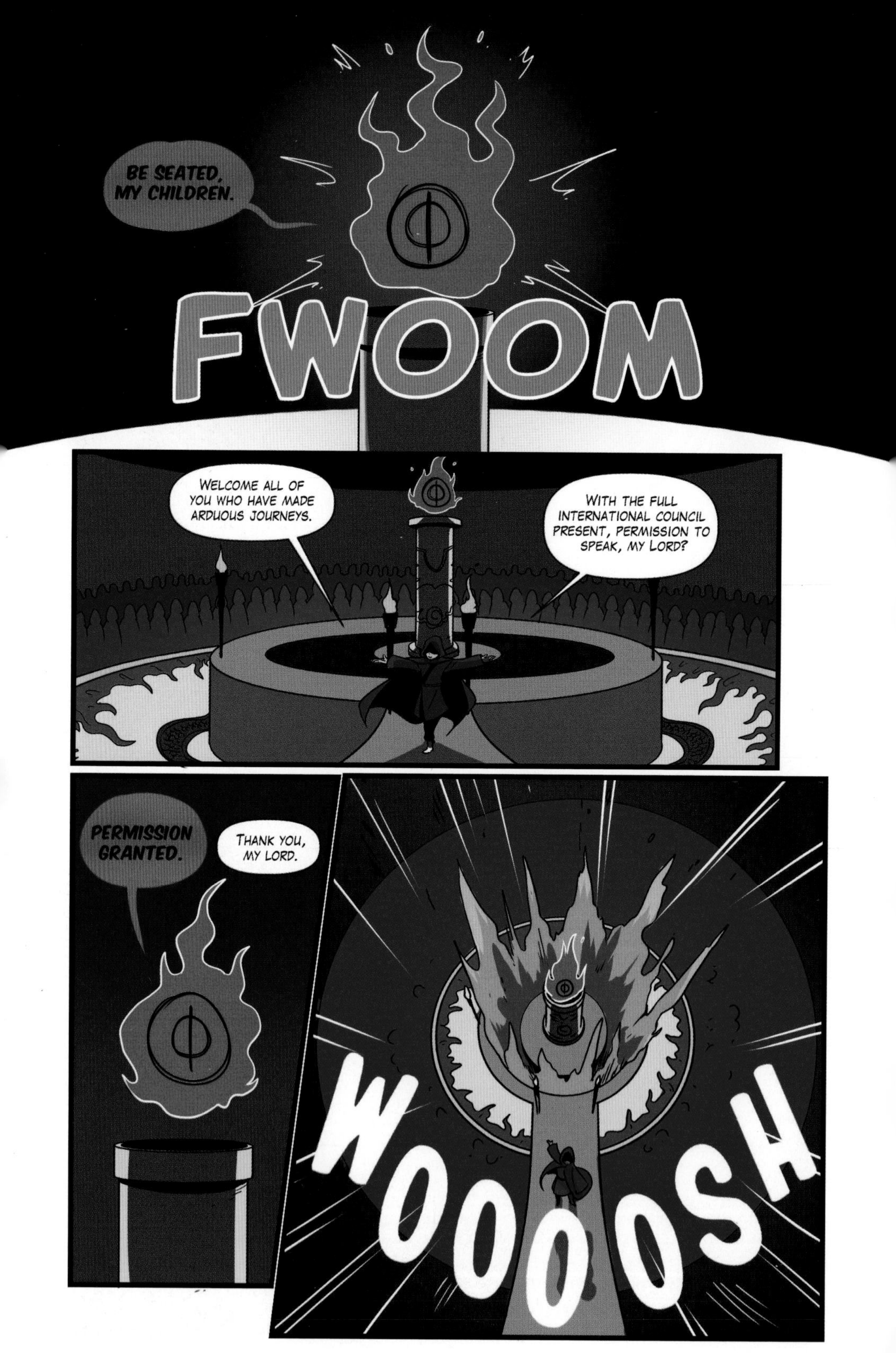

BE SEATED, MY CHILDREN.
FWOOM
WELCOME ALL OF YOU WHO HAVE MADE ARDUOUS JOURNEYS.
WITH THE FULL INTERNATIONAL COUNCIL PRESENT, PERMISSION TO SPEAK, MY LORD?
PERMISSION GRANTED.
THANK YOU, MY LORD.
WOOOOSH

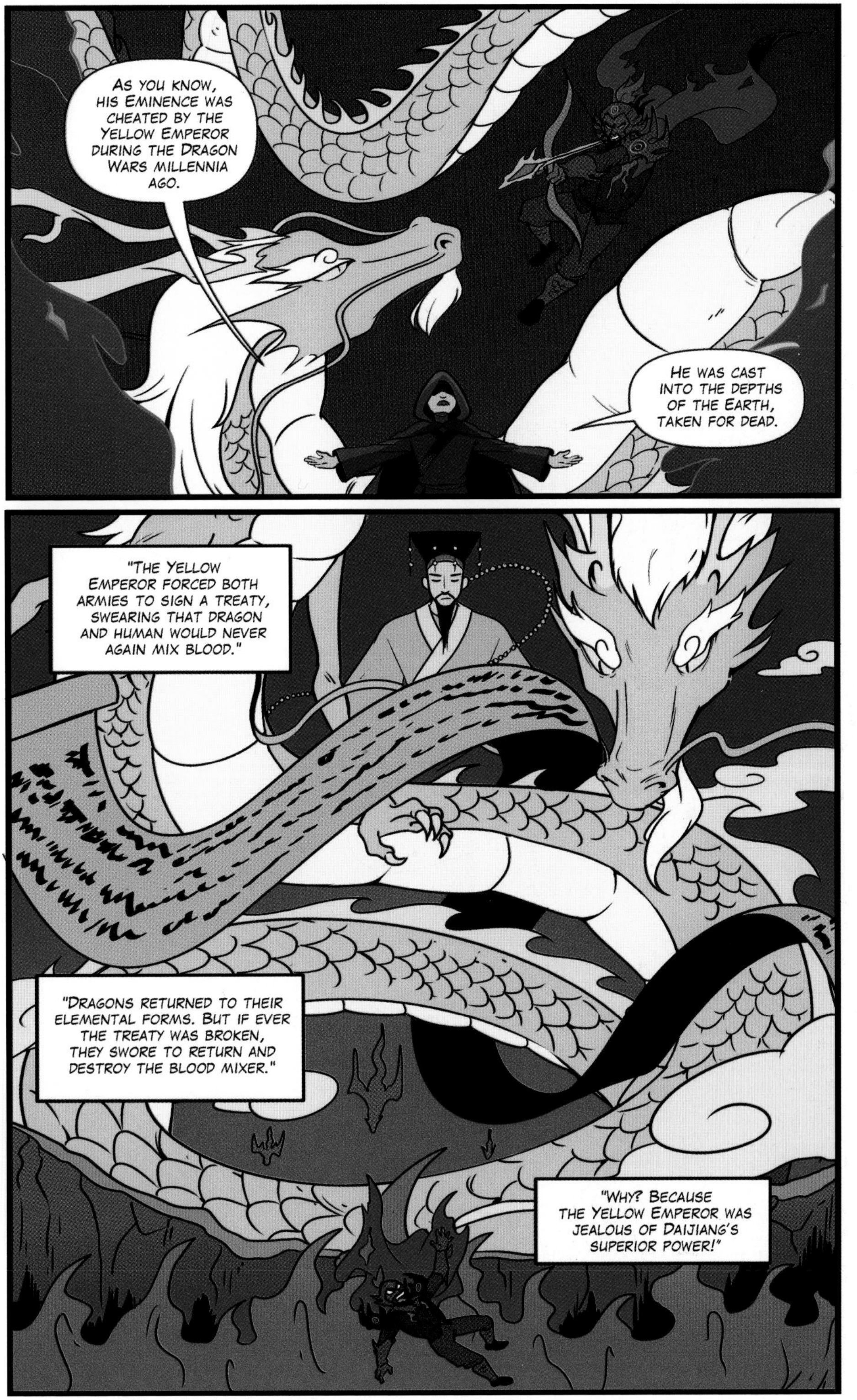
As you know, his Eminence was cheated by the Yellow Emperor during the Dragon Wars millennia ago.
He was cast into the depths of the Earth, taken for dead.
"The Yellow Emperor forced both armies to sign a treaty, swearing that dragon and human would never again mix blood."
"Dragons returned to their elemental forms. But if ever the treaty was broken, they swore to return and destroy the blood mixer."
"Why? Because the Yellow Emperor was jealous of Daijiang's superior power!"

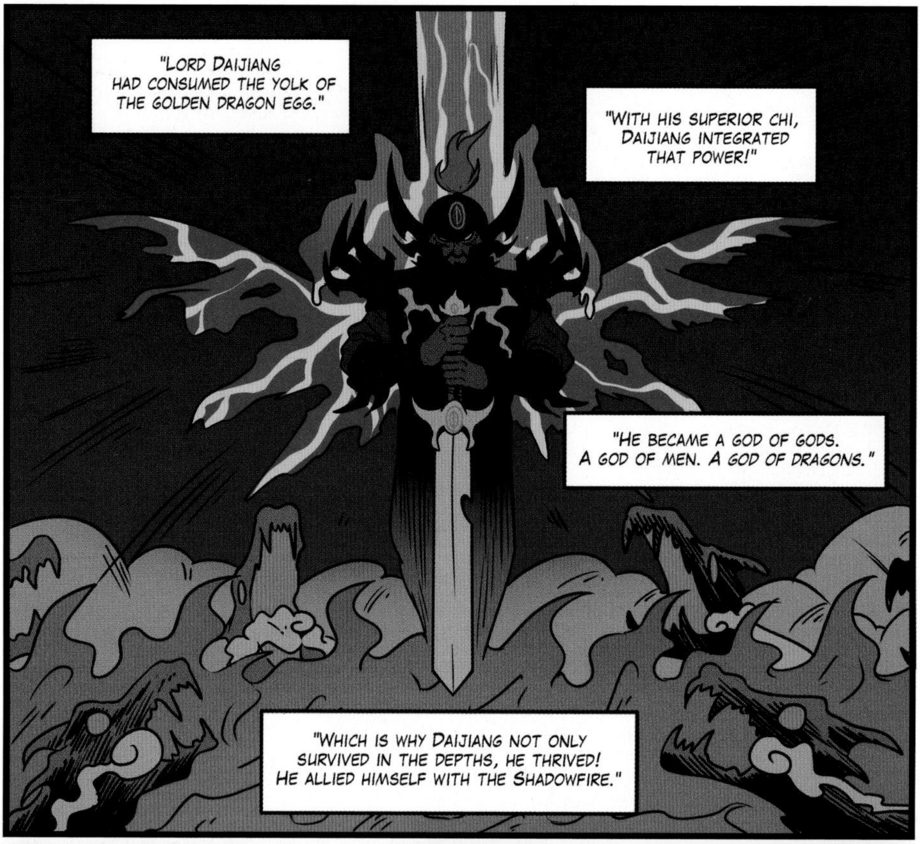
"LORD DAIJIANG HAD CONSUMED THE YOLK OF THE GOLDEN DRAGON EGG."
"WITH HIS SUPERIOR CHI, DAIJIANG INTEGRATED THAT POWER!"
"HE BECAME A GOD OF GODS. A GOD OF MEN. A GOD OF DRAGONS."
"WHICH IS WHY DAIJIANG NOT ONLY SURVIVED IN THE DEPTHS, HE THRIVED! HE ALLIED HIMSELF WITH THE SHADOWFIRE."

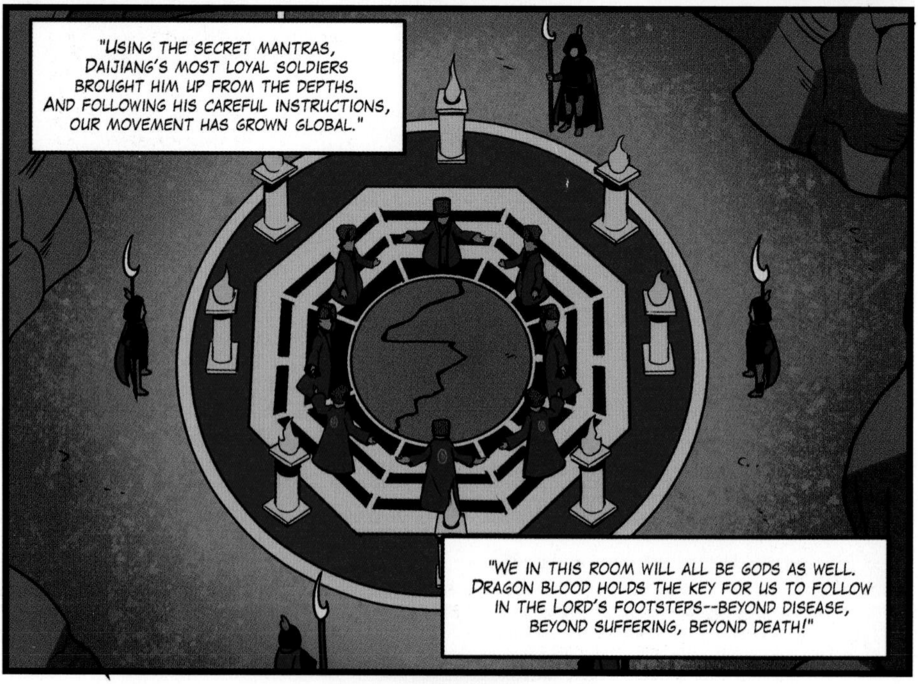
"USING THE SECRET MANTRAS, DAIJIANG'S MOST LOYAL SOLDIERS BROUGHT HIM UP FROM THE DEPTHS. AND FOLLOWING HIS CAREFUL INSTRUCTIONS, OUR MOVEMENT HAS GROWN GLOBAL."
"WE IN THIS ROOM WILL ALL BE GODS AS WELL. DRAGON BLOOD HOLDS THE KEY FOR US TO FOLLOW IN THE LORD'S FOOTSTEPS--BEYOND DISEASE, BEYOND SUFFERING, BEYOND DEATH!"

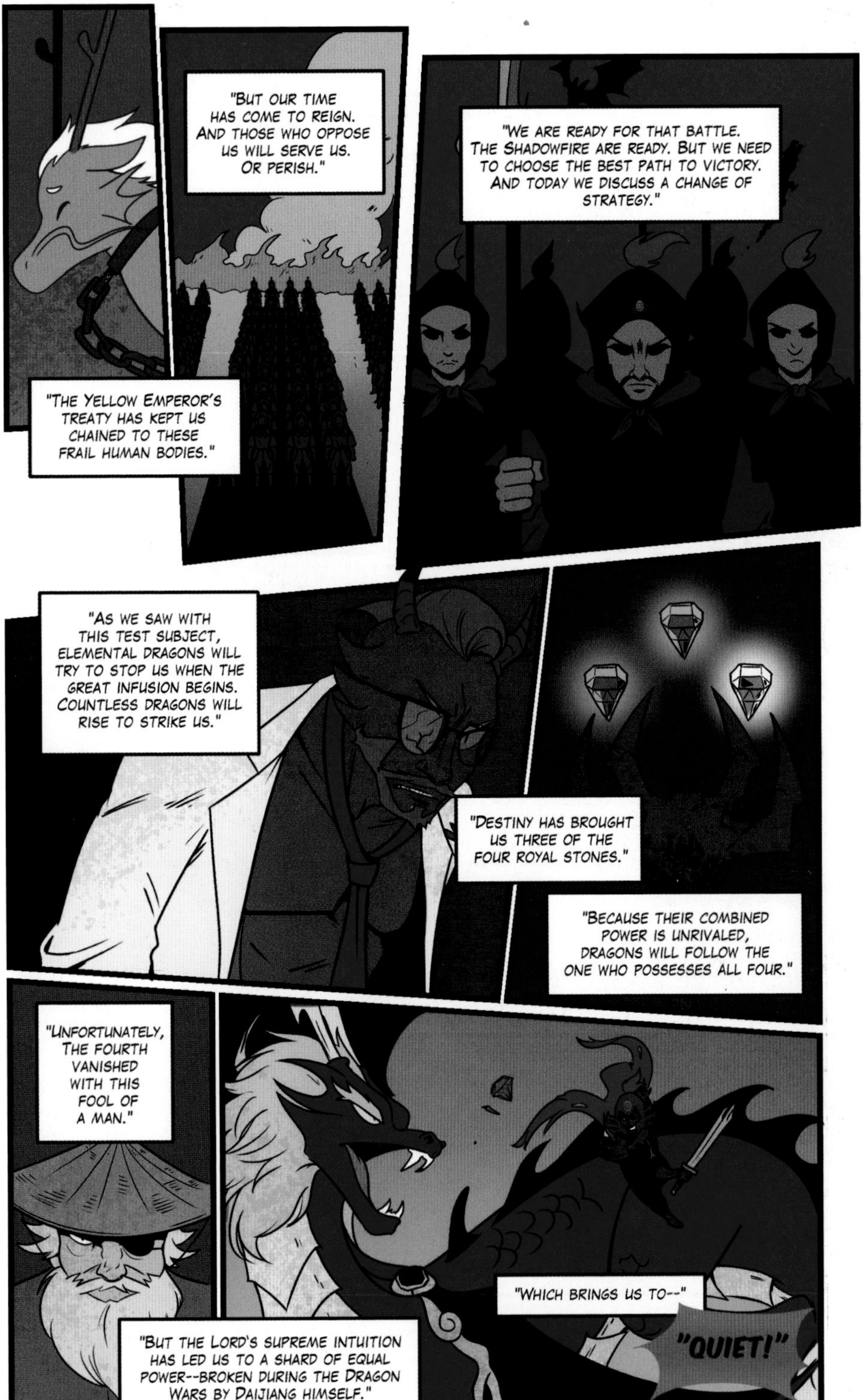
"The Yellow Emperor's treaty has kept us chained to these frail human bodies."
"But our time has come to reign. And those who oppose us will serve us. Or perish."
"We are ready for that battle. The Shadowfire are ready. But we need to choose the best path to victory. And today we discuss a change of strategy."
"As we saw with this test subject, elemental dragons will try to stop us when the great infusion begins. Countless dragons will rise to strike us."
"Destiny has brought us three of the four royal stones."
"Because their combined power is unrivaled, dragons will follow the one who possesses all four."
"Unfortunately, the fourth vanished with this fool of a man."
"But the Lord's supreme intuition has led us to a shard of equal power--broken during the Dragon Wars by Daijiang himself."
"Which brings us to--"
"QUIET!"

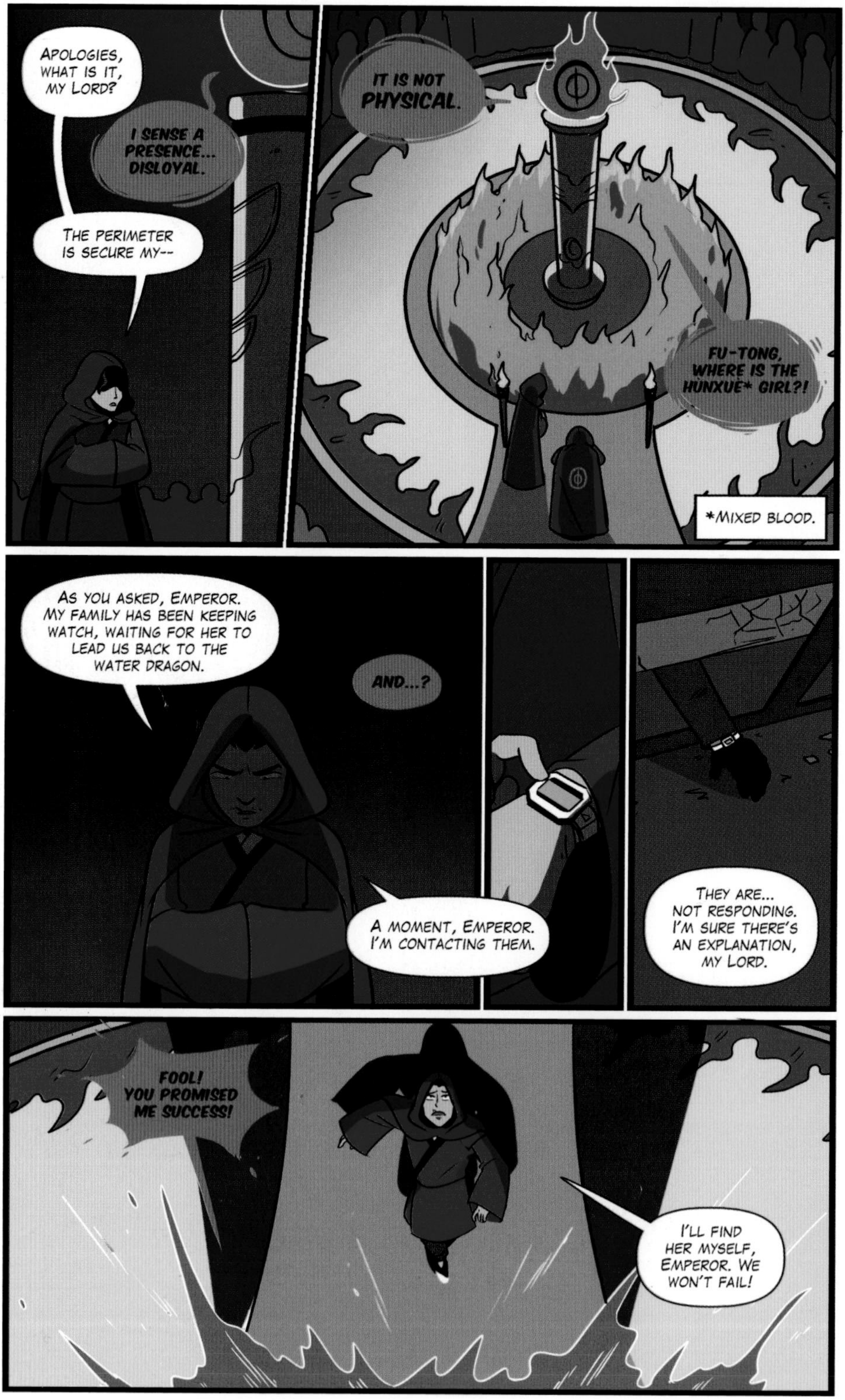
APOLOGIES, WHAT IS IT, MY LORD?
I SENSE A PRESENCE... DISLOYAL.
THE PERIMETER IS SECURE MY--
IT IS NOT PHYSICAL.
FU-TONG, WHERE IS THE HÙNXUÈ* GIRL?!
*MIXED BLOOD.
AS YOU ASKED, EMPEROR. MY FAMILY HAS BEEN KEEPING WATCH, WAITING FOR HER TO LEAD US BACK TO THE WATER DRAGON.
AND...?
A MOMENT, EMPEROR. I'M CONTACTING THEM.
THEY ARE... NOT RESPONDING. I'M SURE THERE'S AN EXPLANATION, MY LORD.
FOOL! YOU PROMISED ME SUCCESS!
I'LL FIND HER MYSELF, EMPEROR. WE WON'T FAIL!

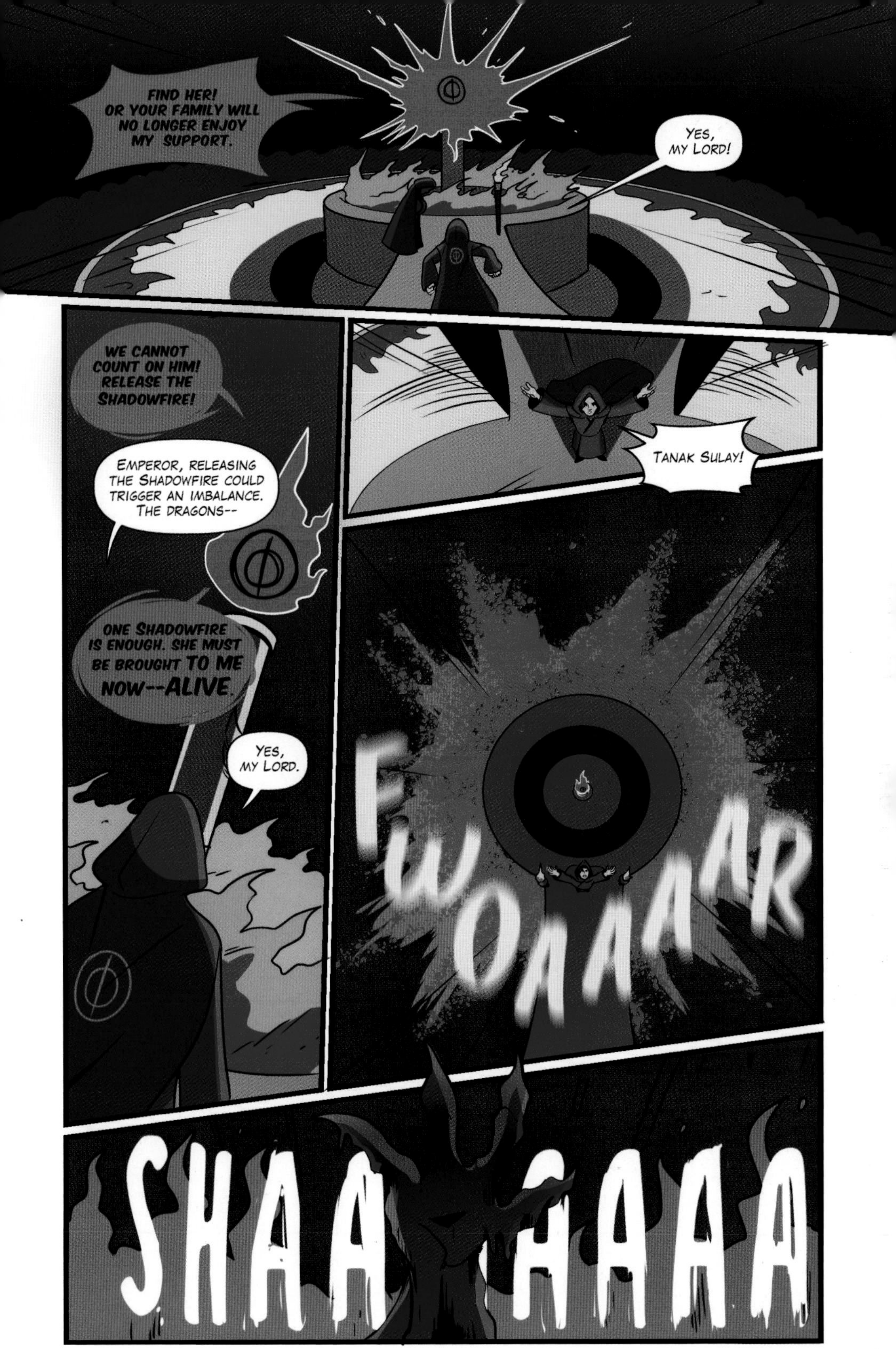
FIND HER! OR YOUR FAMILY WILL NO LONGER ENJOY MY SUPPORT.
YES, MY LORD!
WE CANNOT COUNT ON HIM! RELEASE THE SHADOWFIRE!
EMPEROR, RELEASING THE SHADOWFIRE COULD TRIGGER AN IMBALANCE. THE DRAGONS--
ONE SHADOWFIRE IS ENOUGH. SHE MUST BE BROUGHT TO ME NOW--ALIVE.
YES, MY LORD.
TANAK SULAY!
FWOAAAAR
SHAAHAAAA

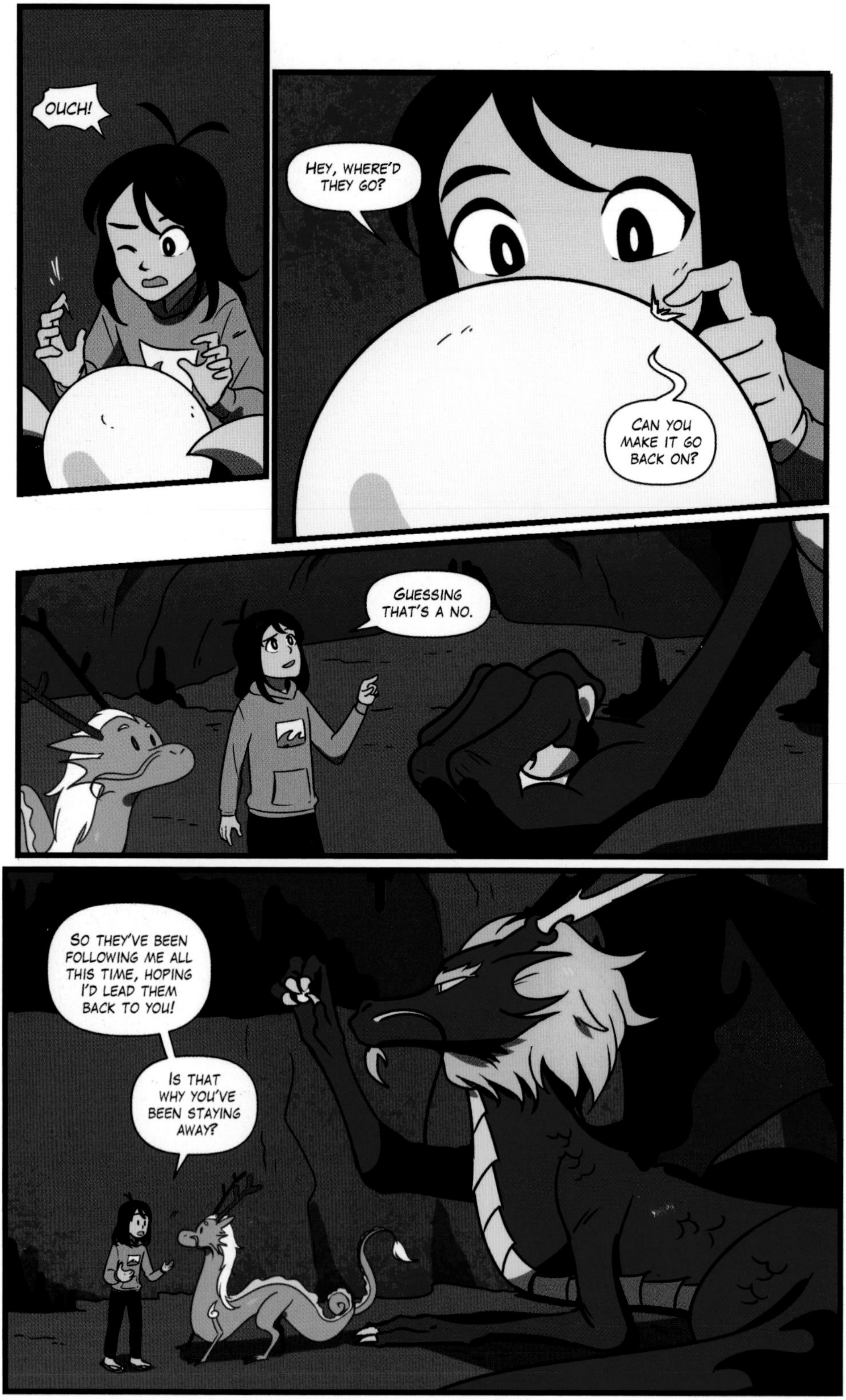
OUCH!
HEY, WHERE'D THEY GO?
CAN YOU MAKE IT GO BACK ON?
GUESSING THAT'S A NO.
SO THEY'VE BEEN FOLLOWING ME ALL THIS TIME, HOPING I'D LEAD THEM BACK TO YOU!
IS THAT WHY YOU'VE BEEN STAYING AWAY?

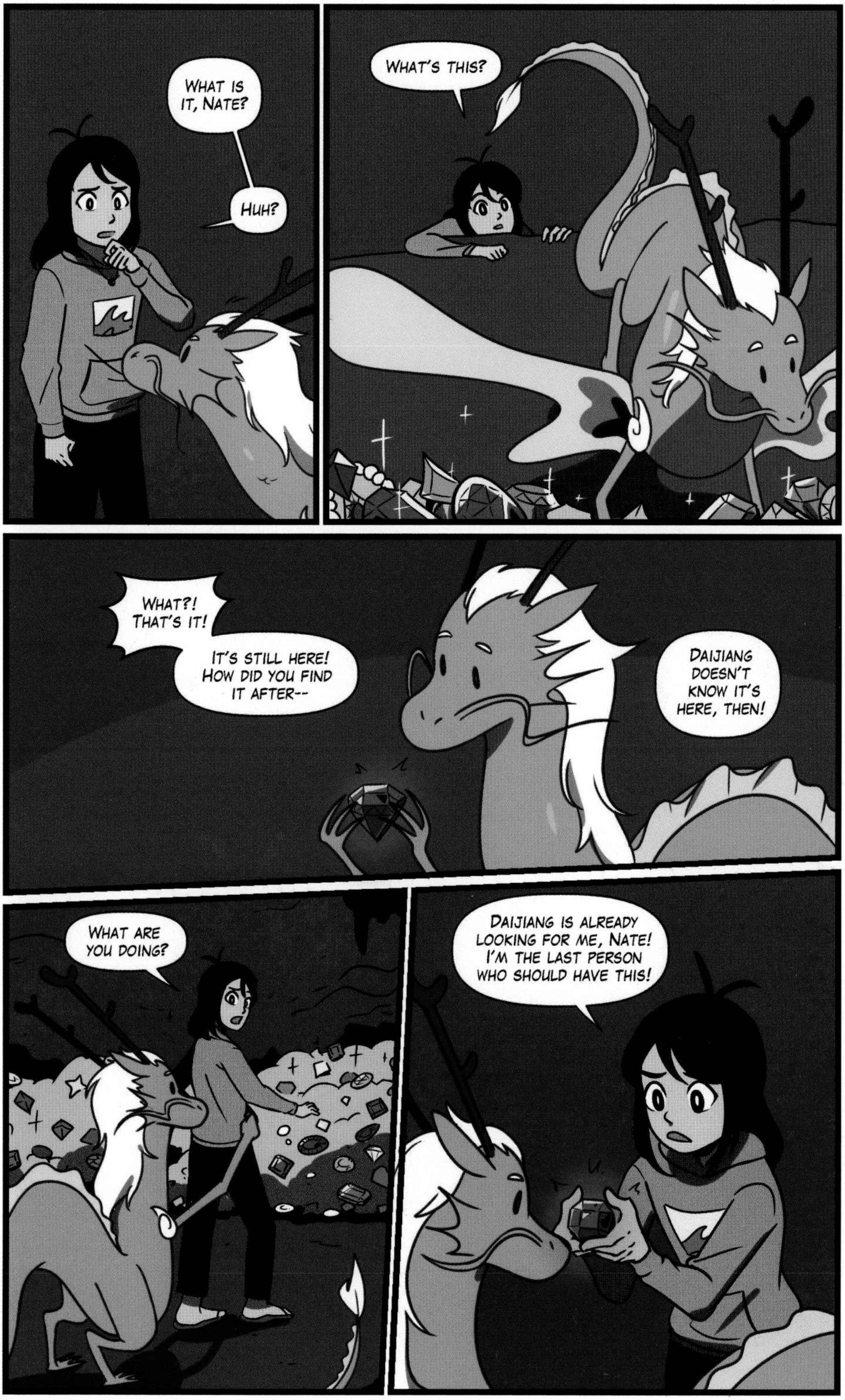
WHAT IS IT, NATE?
HUH?
WHAT'S THIS?
WHAT?! THAT'S IT!
IT'S STILL HERE! HOW DID YOU FIND IT AFTER--
DAIJIANG DOESN'T KNOW IT'S HERE, THEN!
WHAT ARE YOU DOING?
DAIJIANG IS ALREADY LOOKING FOR ME, NATE! I'M THE LAST PERSON WHO SHOULD HAVE THIS!

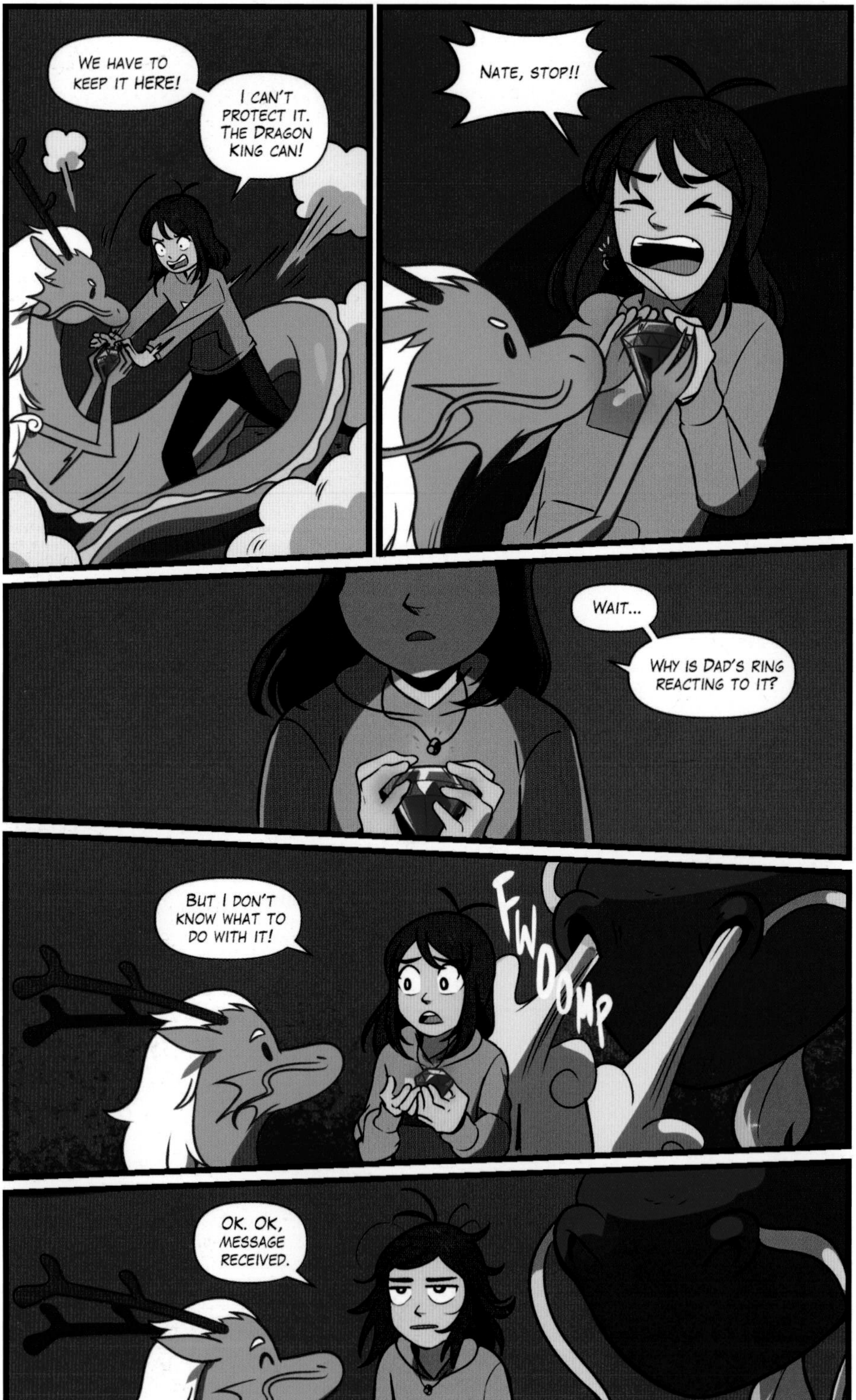

WE HAVE TO KEEP IT HERE!
I CAN'T PROTECT IT. THE DRAGON KING CAN!
NATE, STOP!!
WAIT...
WHY IS DAD'S RING REACTING TO IT?
BUT I DON'T KNOW WHAT TO DO WITH IT!
FWOOMP
OK. OK, MESSAGE RECEIVED.

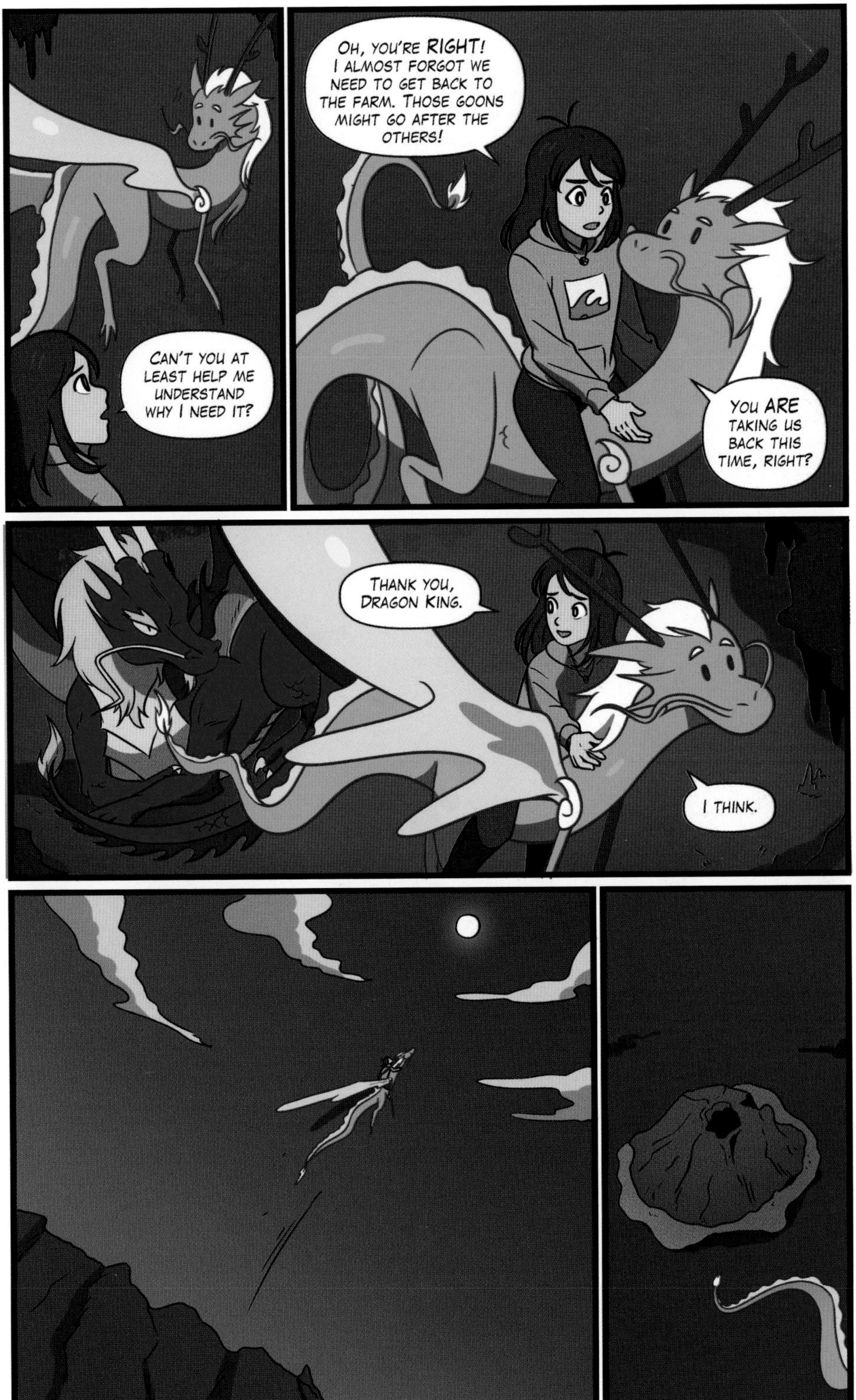
CAN'T YOU AT LEAST HELP ME UNDERSTAND WHY I NEED IT?
OH, YOU'RE RIGHT! I ALMOST FORGOT WE NEED TO GET BACK TO THE FARM. THOSE GOONS MIGHT GO AFTER THE OTHERS!
YOU ARE TAKING US BACK THIS TIME, RIGHT?
THANK YOU, DRAGON KING.
I THINK.

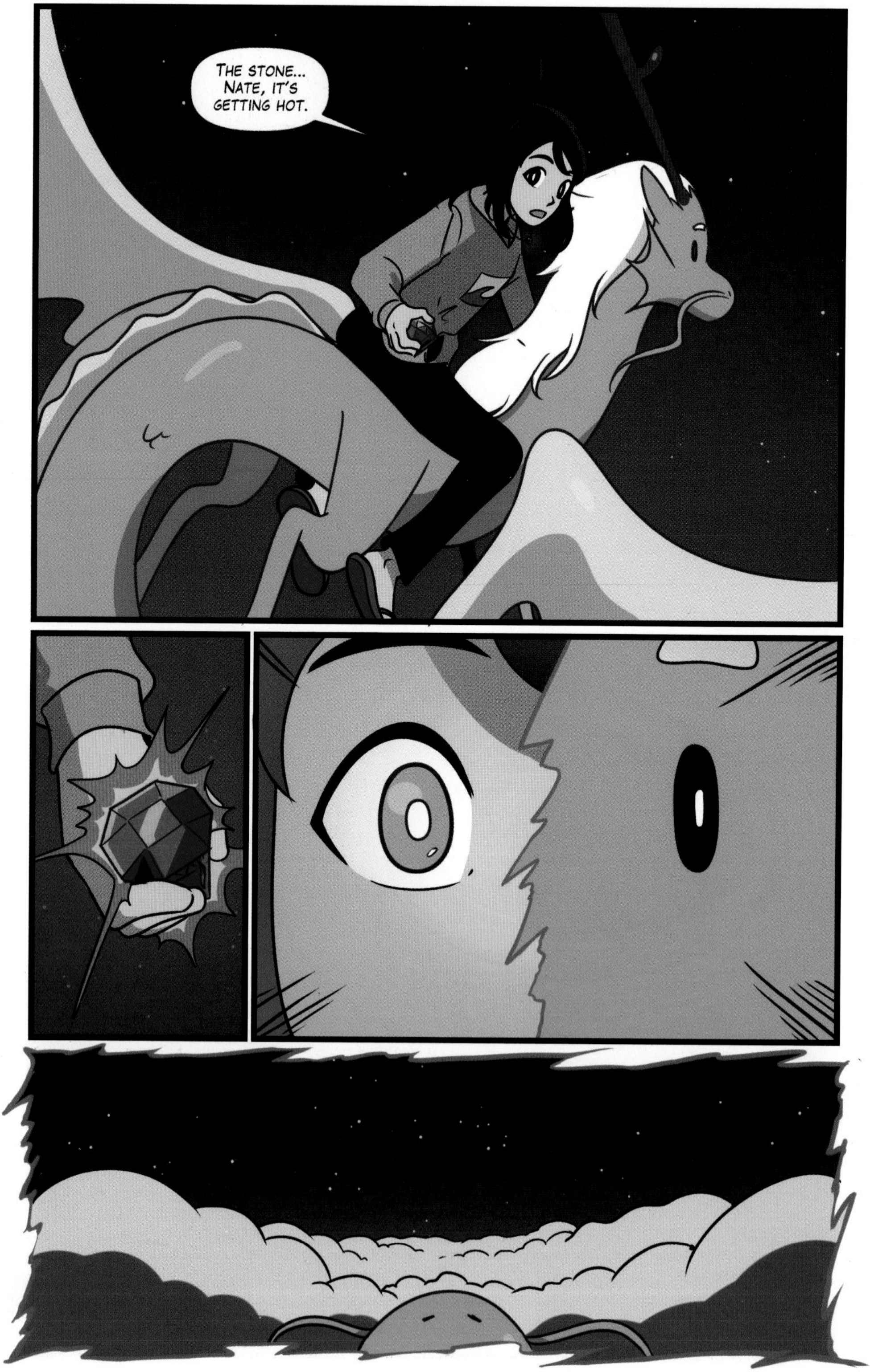
THE STONE... NATE, IT'S GETTING HOT.

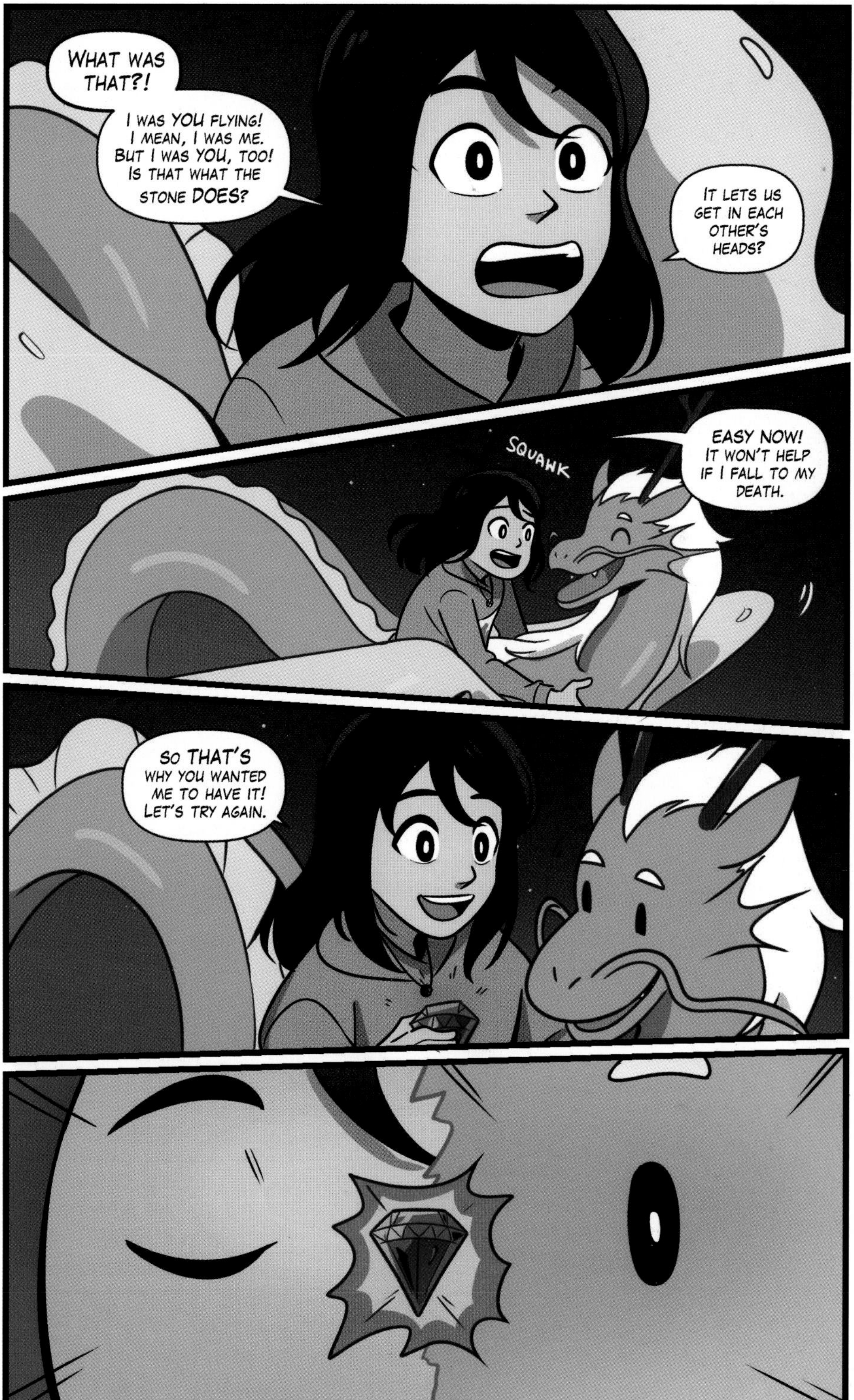
WHAT WAS THAT?!
I WAS YOU FLYING! I MEAN, I WAS ME. BUT I WAS YOU, TOO! IS THAT WHAT THE STONE DOES?
IT LETS US GET IN EACH OTHER'S HEADS?
SQUAWK
EASY NOW! IT WON'T HELP IF I FALL TO MY DEATH.
SO THAT'S WHY YOU WANTED ME TO HAVE IT! LET'S TRY AGAIN.

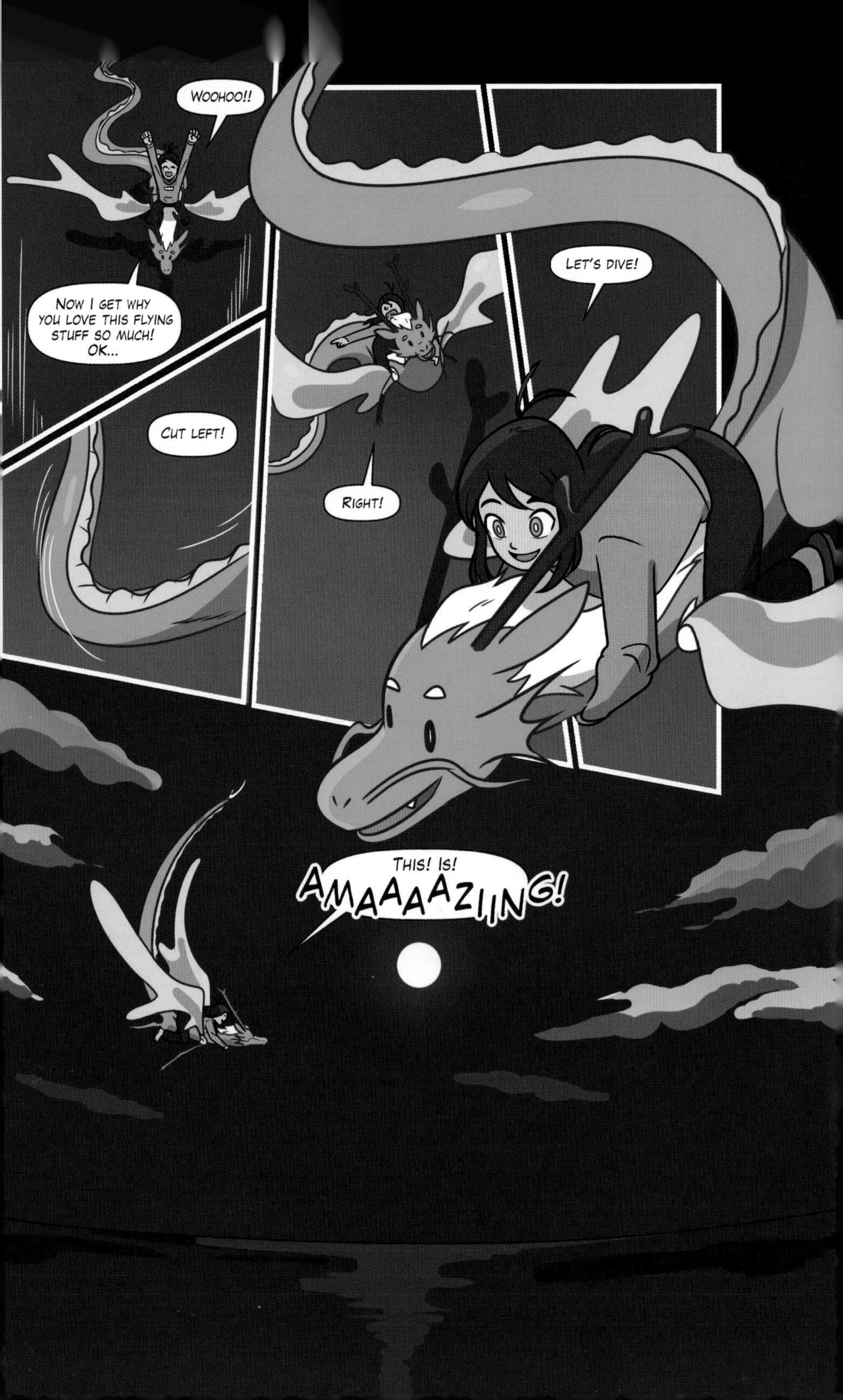
WOOHOO!!
NOW I GET WHY YOU LOVE THIS FLYING STUFF SO MUCH! OK...
CUT LEFT!
RIGHT!
LET'S DIVE!
THIS! IS! AMAAAAZIING!

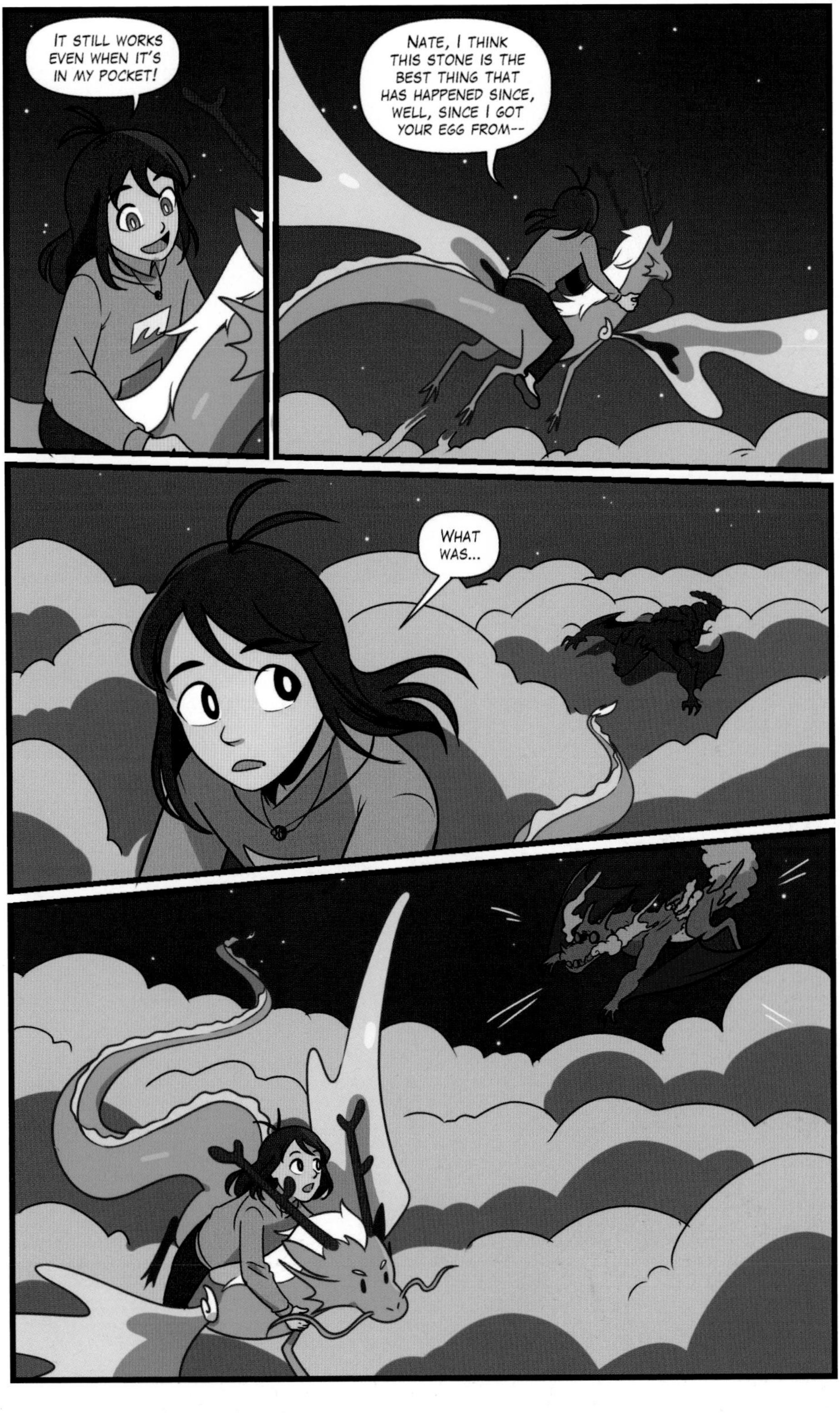
IT STILL WORKS EVEN WHEN IT'S IN MY POCKET!
NATE, I THINK THIS STONE IS THE BEST THING THAT HAS HAPPENED SINCE, WELL, SINCE I GOT YOUR EGG FROM--
WHAT WAS...

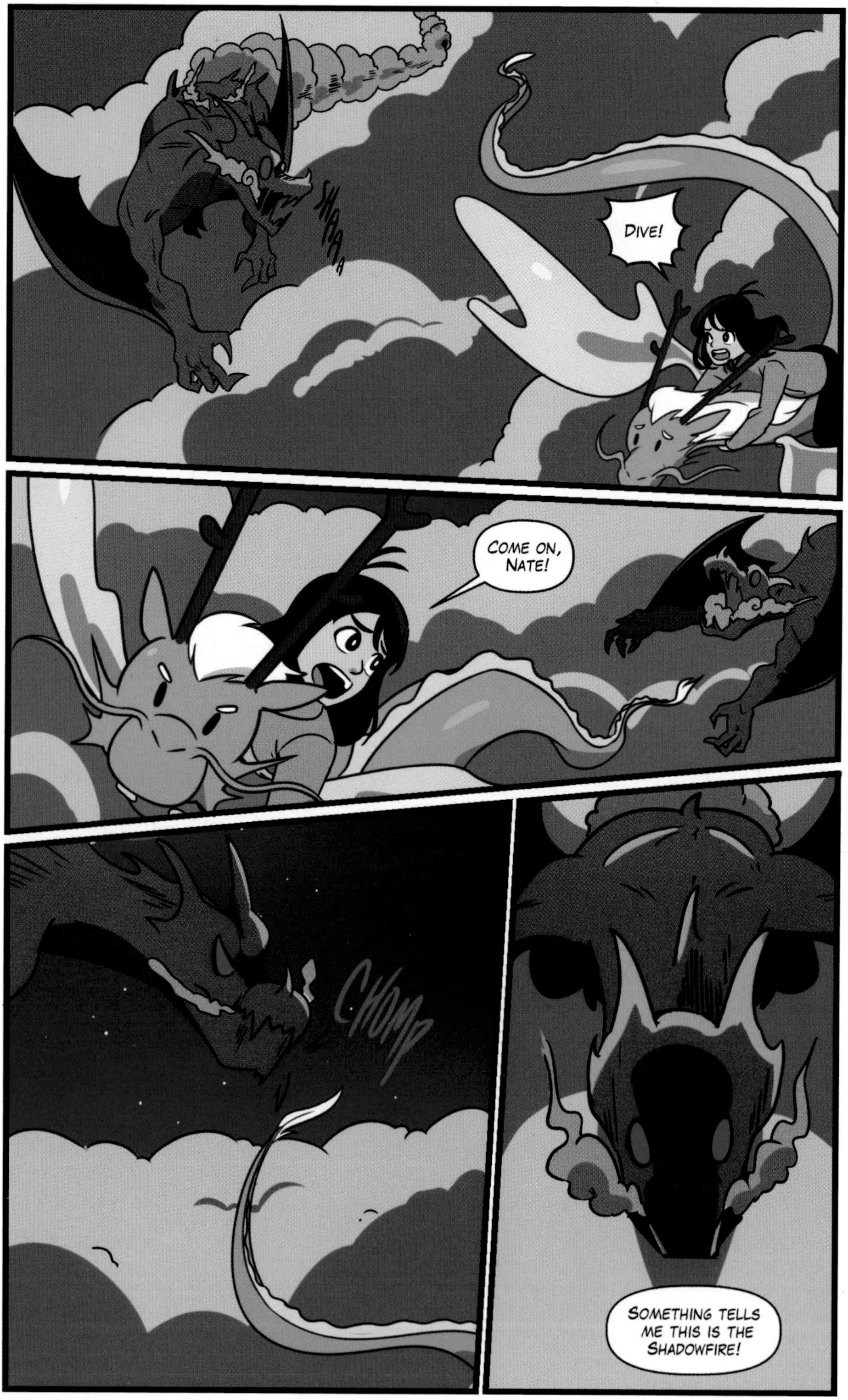
SHAAA
DIVE!
COME ON, NATE!
CHOMP
SOMETHING TELLS ME THIS IS THE SHADOWFIRE!

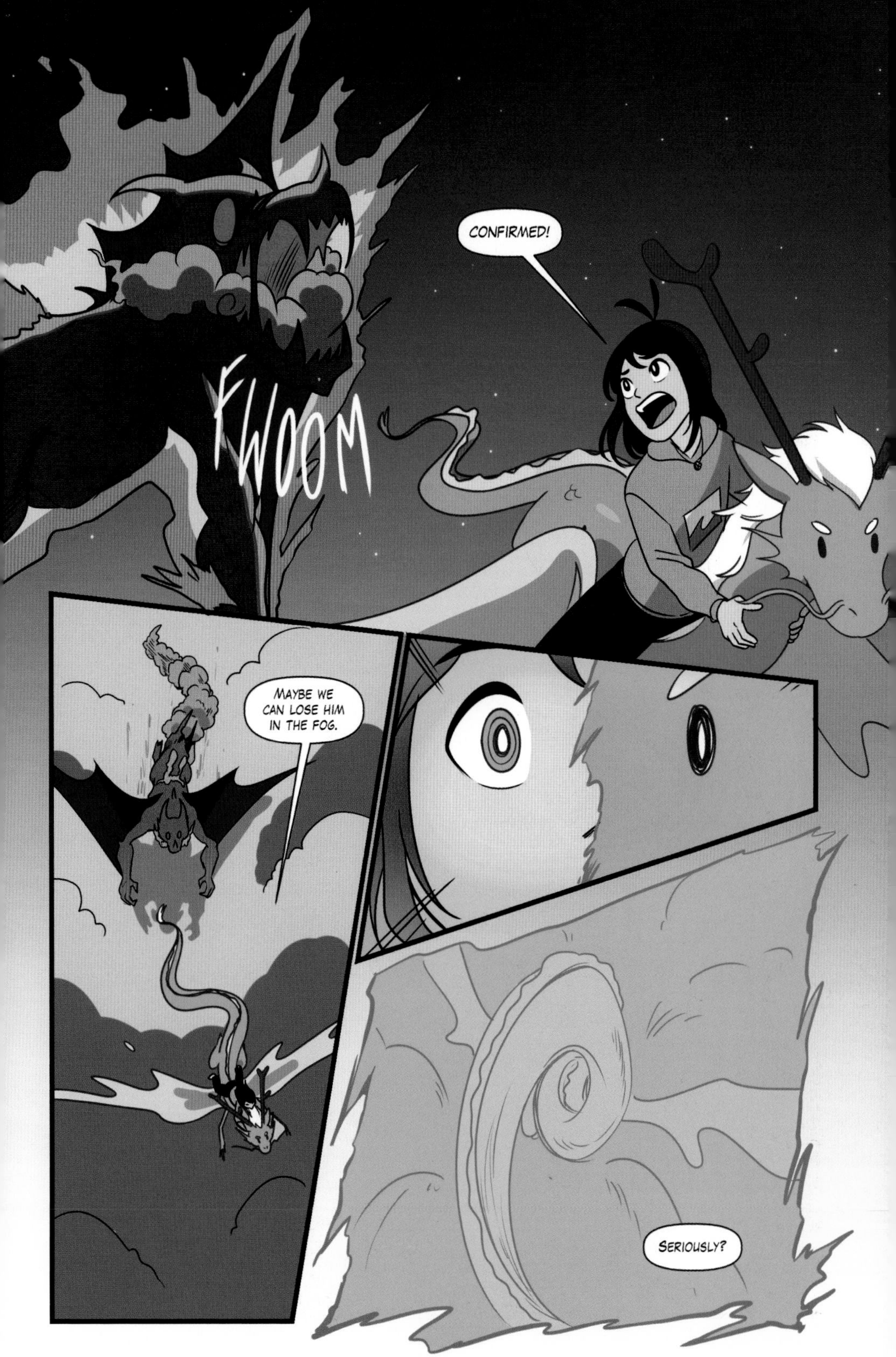
CONFIRMED!
FWOOM
MAYBE WE CAN LOSE HIM IN THE FOG.
SERIOUSLY?

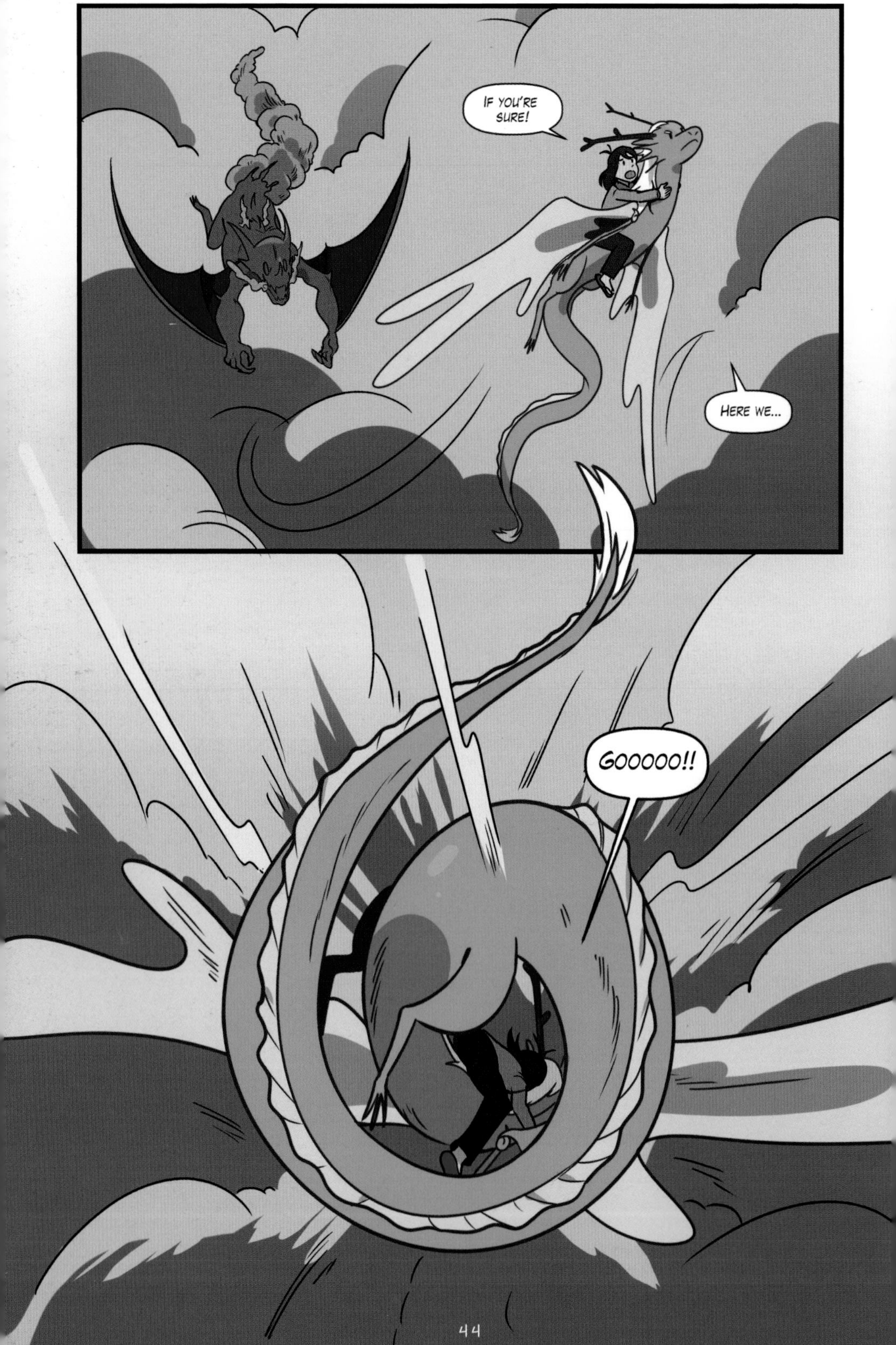
IF YOU'RE SURE!
HERE WE...
GOOOOO!!

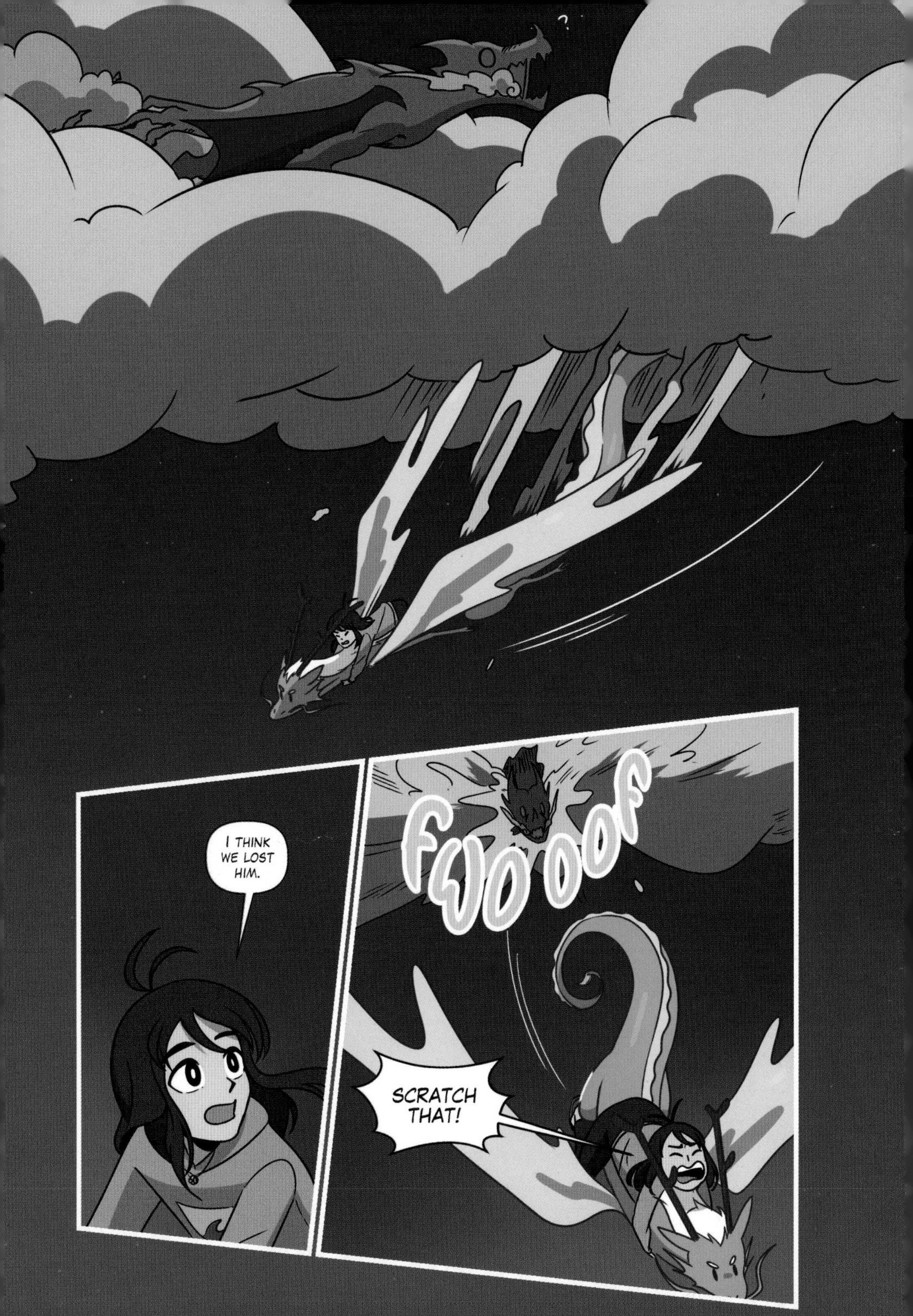
?
I THINK WE LOST HIM.
FWOOOF
SCRATCH THAT!

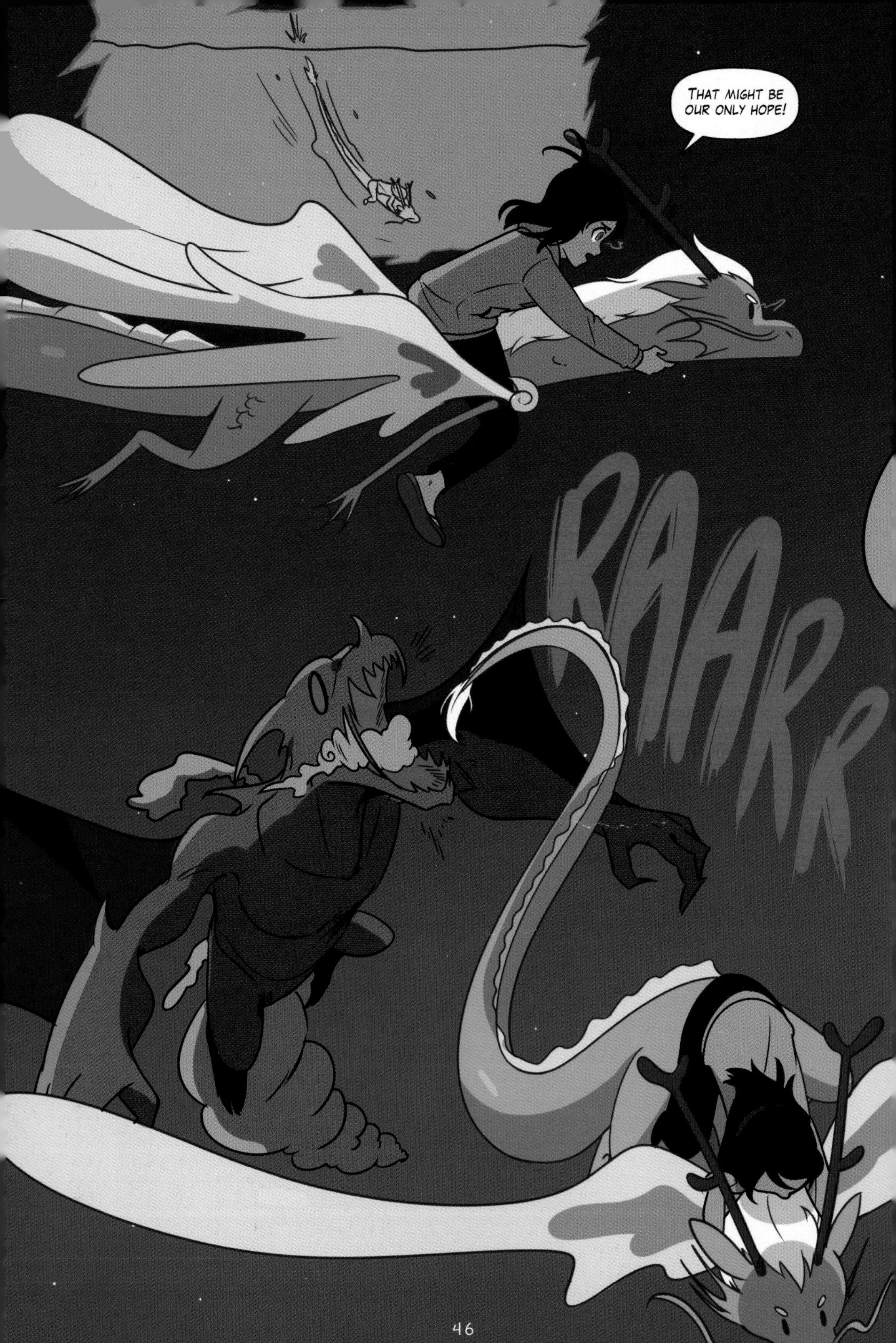
THAT MIGHT BE
OUR ONLY HOPE!
RAARR

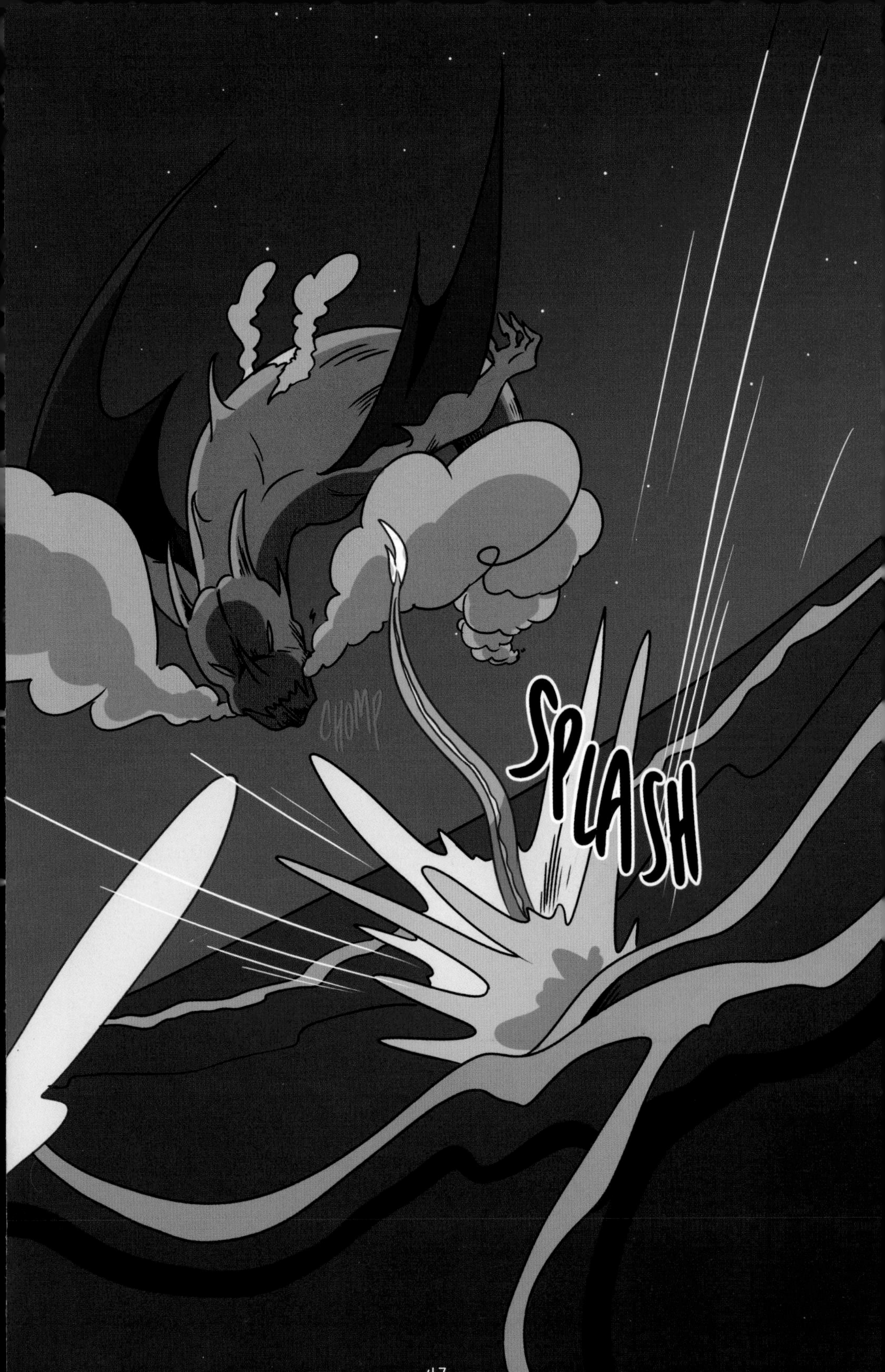
CHOMP
SPLASH

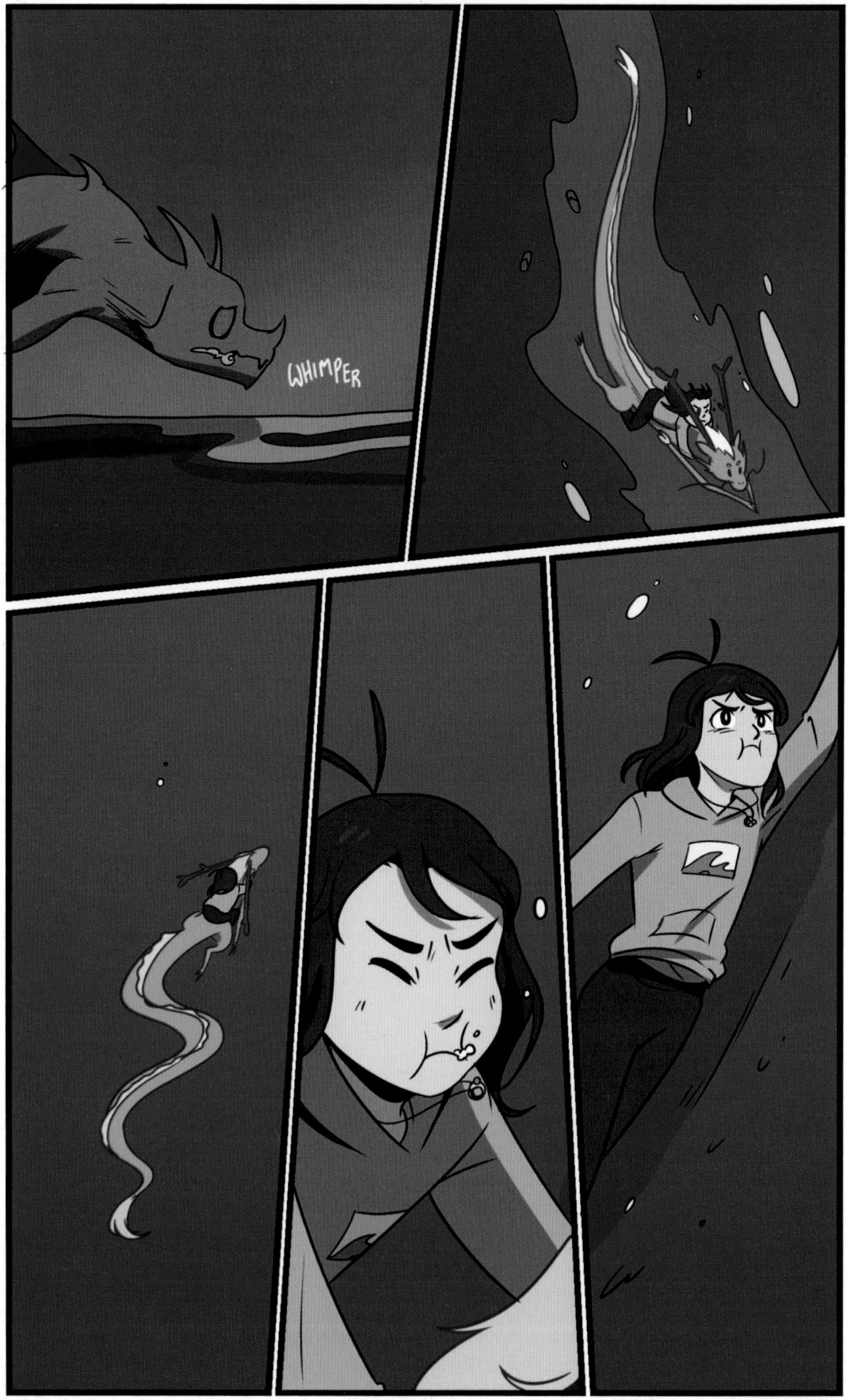
WHIMPER

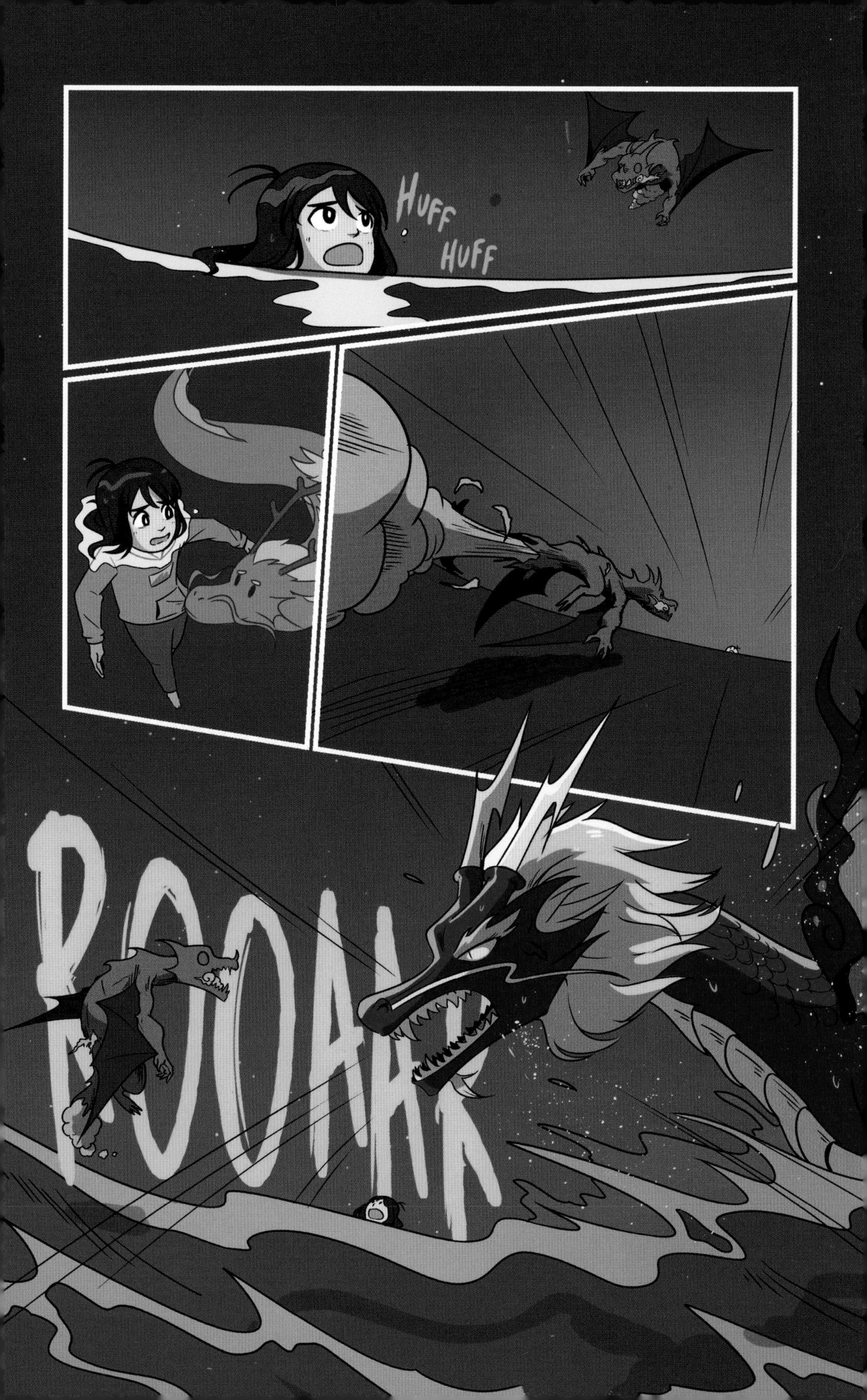
HUFF
HUFF
ROOAR

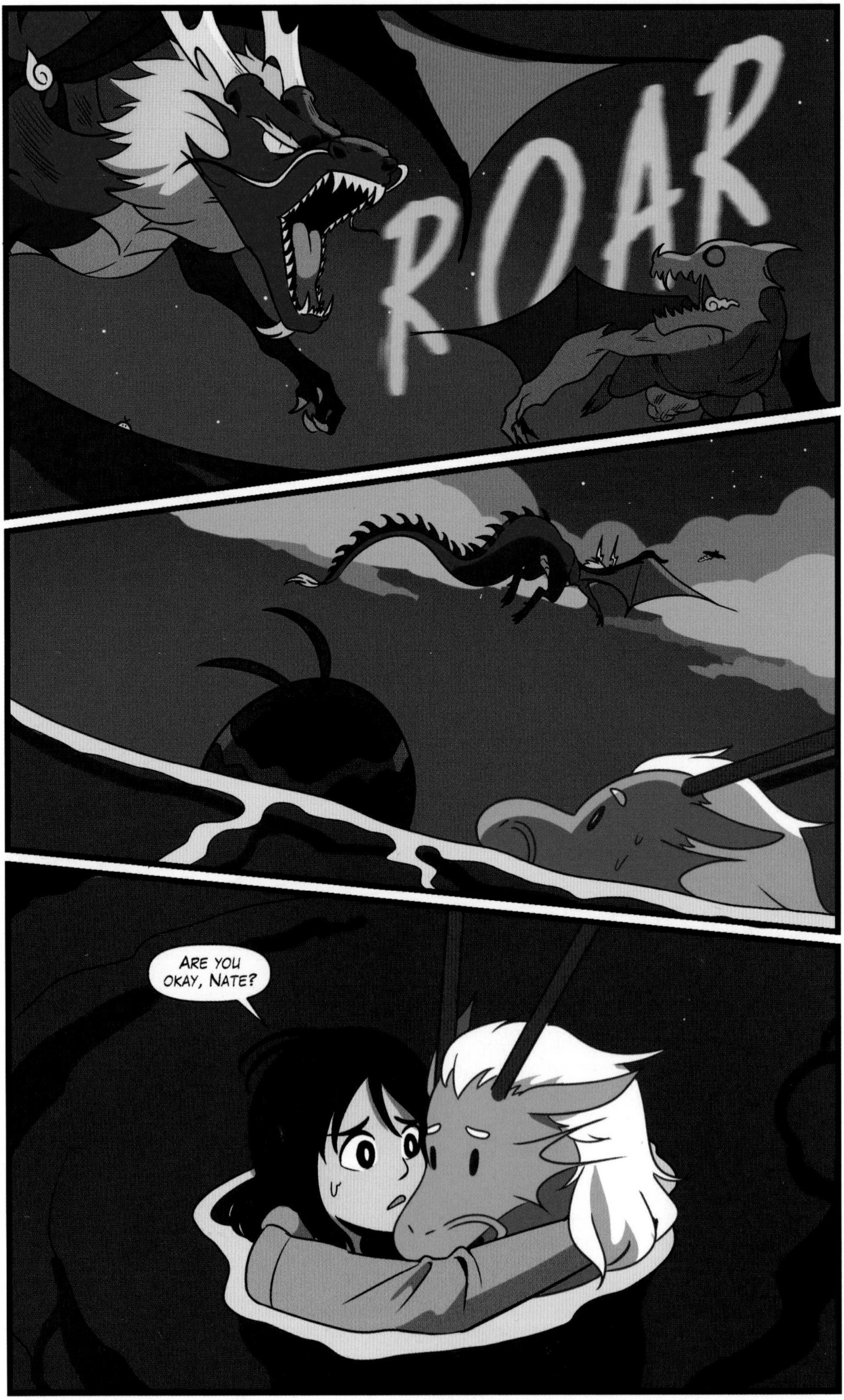
ROAR
ARE YOU OKAY, NATE?

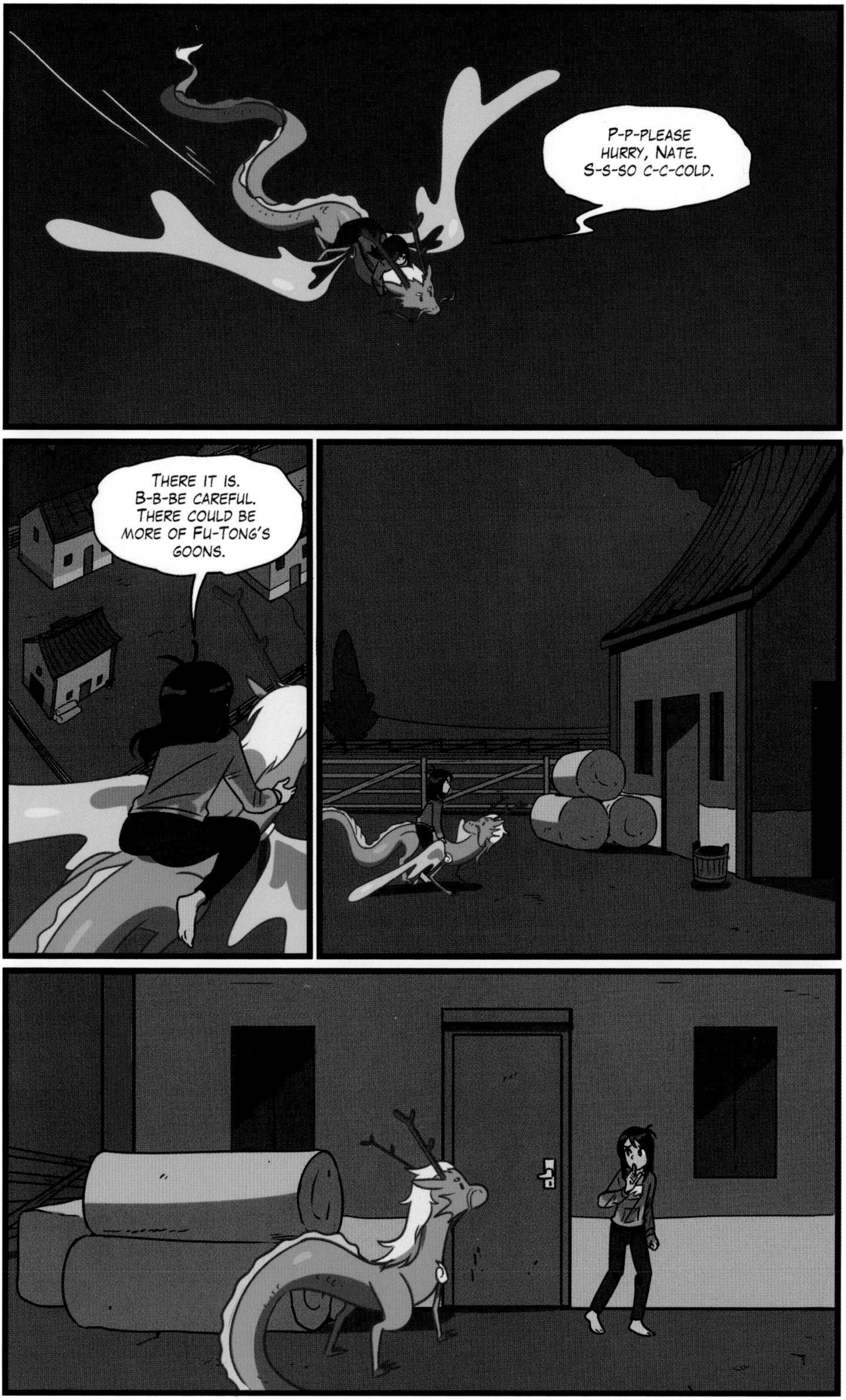
P-P-PLEASE HURRY, NATE. S-S-SO C-C-COLD.
THERE IT IS. B-B-BE CAREFUL. THERE COULD BE MORE OF FU-TONG'S GOONS.

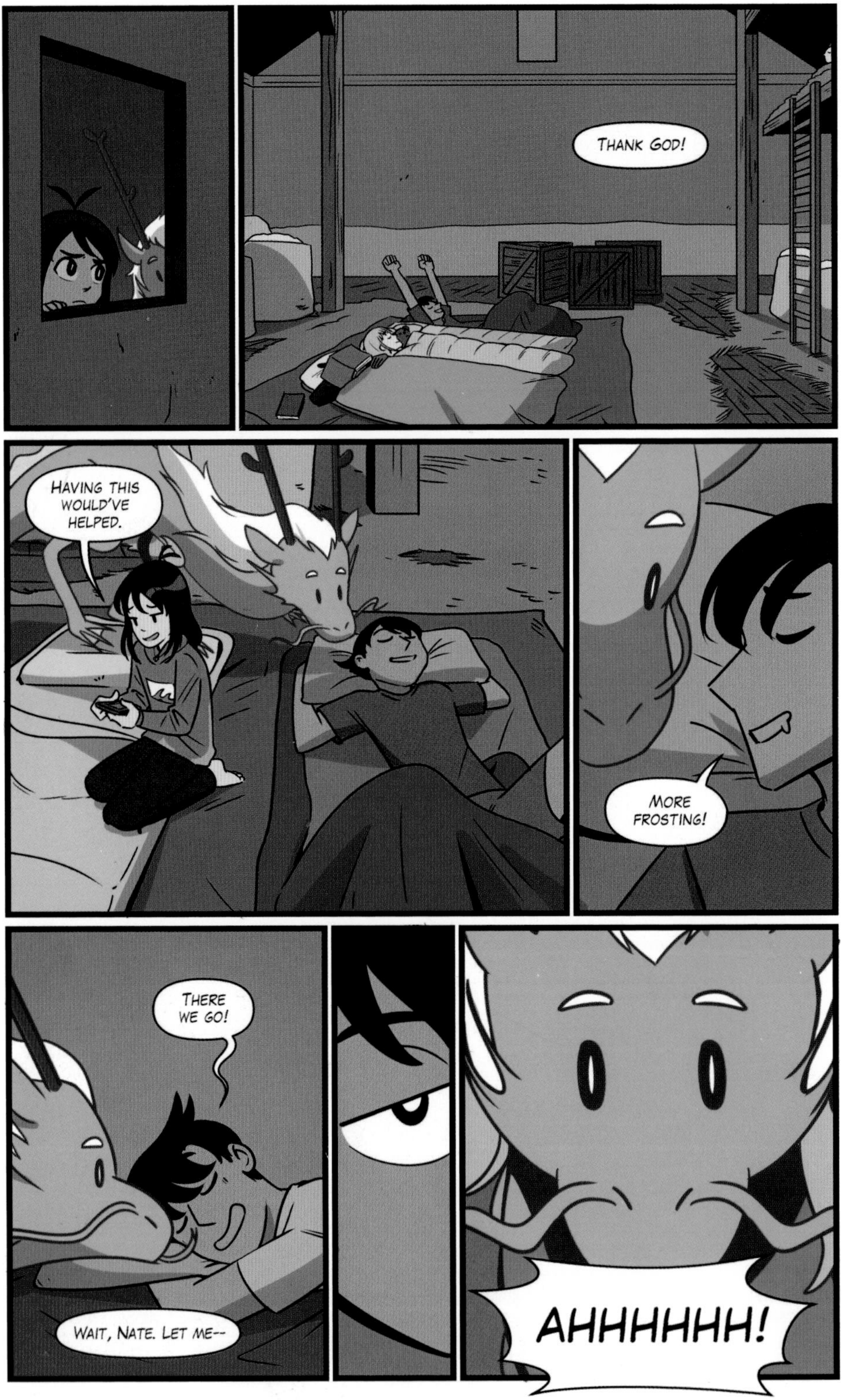
THANK GOD!
HAVING THIS WOULD'VE HELPED.
MORE FROSTING!
THERE WE GO!
WAIT, NATE. LET ME--
AHHHHHH!

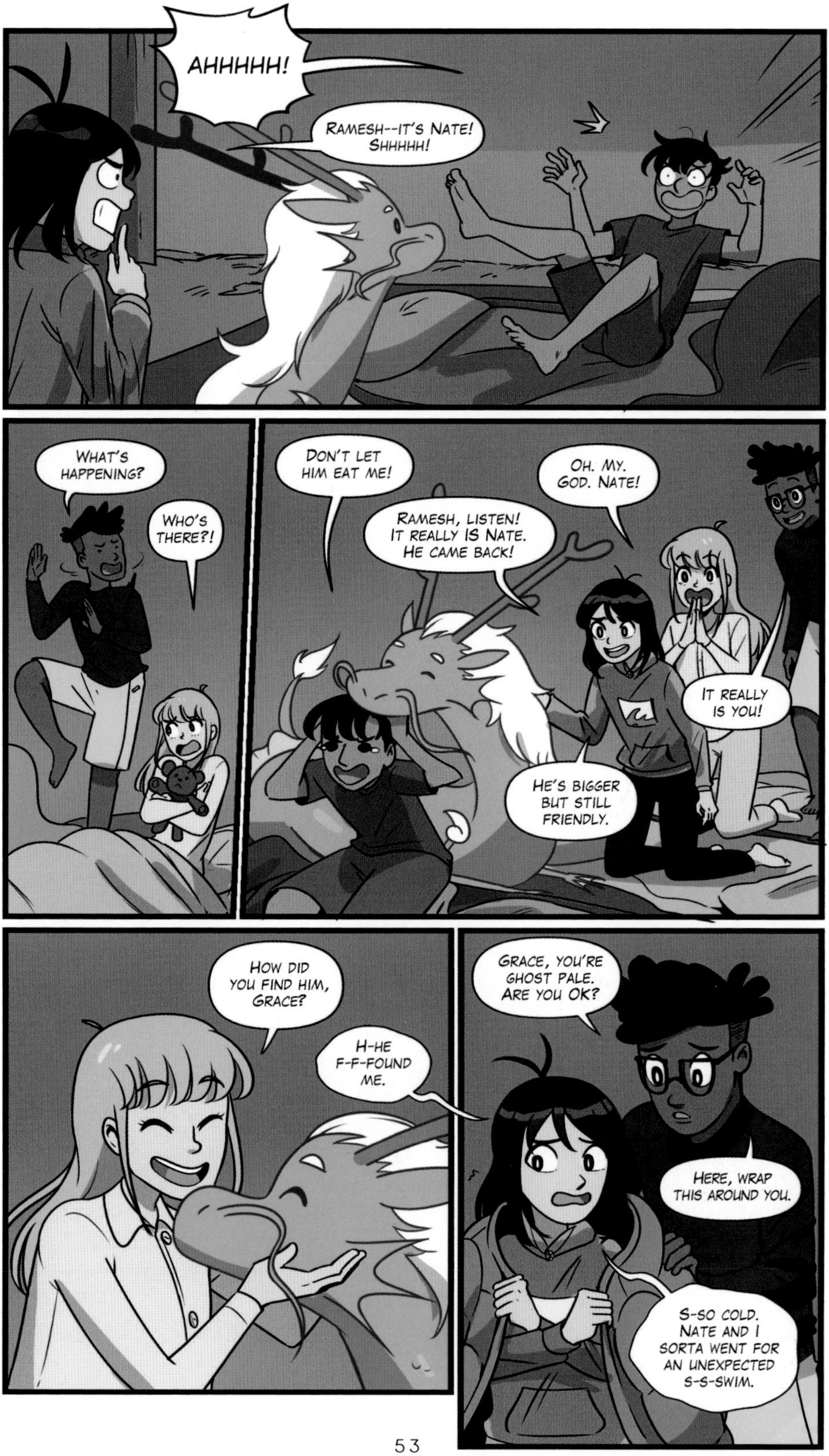
AHHHHH!
RAMESH--IT'S NATE! SHHHHH!
WHAT'S HAPPENING?
WHO'S THERE?!
DON'T LET HIM EAT ME!
RAMESH, LISTEN! IT REALLY IS NATE. HE CAME BACK!
OH. MY. GOD. NATE!
IT REALLY IS YOU!
HE'S BIGGER BUT STILL FRIENDLY.
HOW DID YOU FIND HIM, GRACE?
H-HE F-F-FOUND ME.
GRACE, YOU'RE GHOST PALE. ARE YOU OK?
HERE, WRAP THIS AROUND YOU.
S-SO COLD. NATE AND I SORTA WENT FOR AN UNEXPECTED S-S-SWIM.

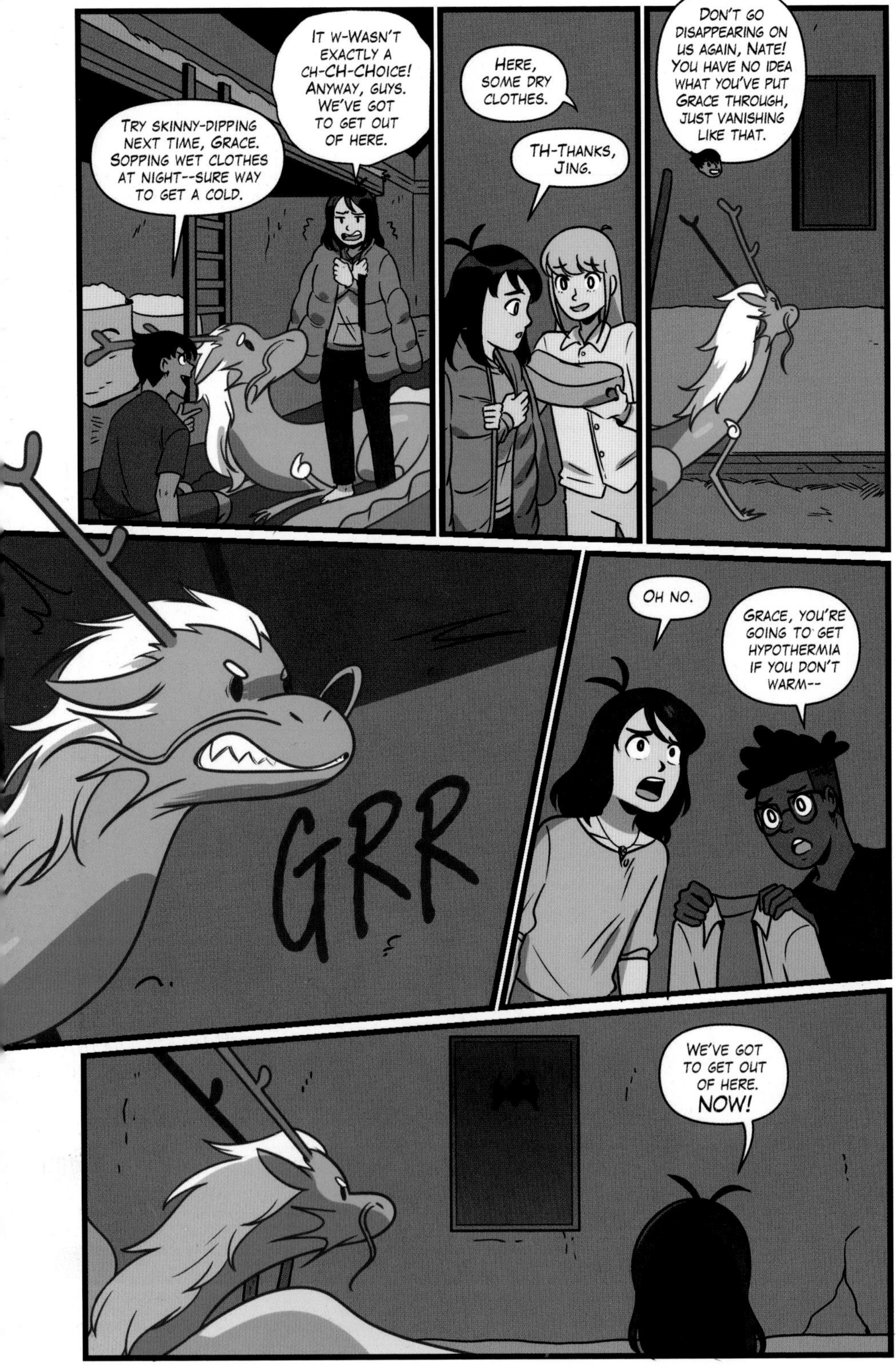
TRY SKINNY-DIPPING NEXT TIME, GRACE. SOPPING WET CLOTHES AT NIGHT--SURE WAY TO GET A COLD.
IT W-WASN'T EXACTLY A CH-CH-CHOICE! ANYWAY, GUYS. WE'VE GOT TO GET OUT OF HERE.
HERE, SOME DRY CLOTHES.
TH-THANKS, JING.
DON'T GO DISAPPEARING ON US AGAIN, NATE! YOU HAVE NO IDEA WHAT YOU'VE PUT GRACE THROUGH, JUST VANISHING LIKE THAT.
GRR
OH NO.
GRACE, YOU'RE GOING TO GET HYPOTHERMIA IF YOU DON'T WARM--
WE'VE GOT TO GET OUT OF HERE. NOW!

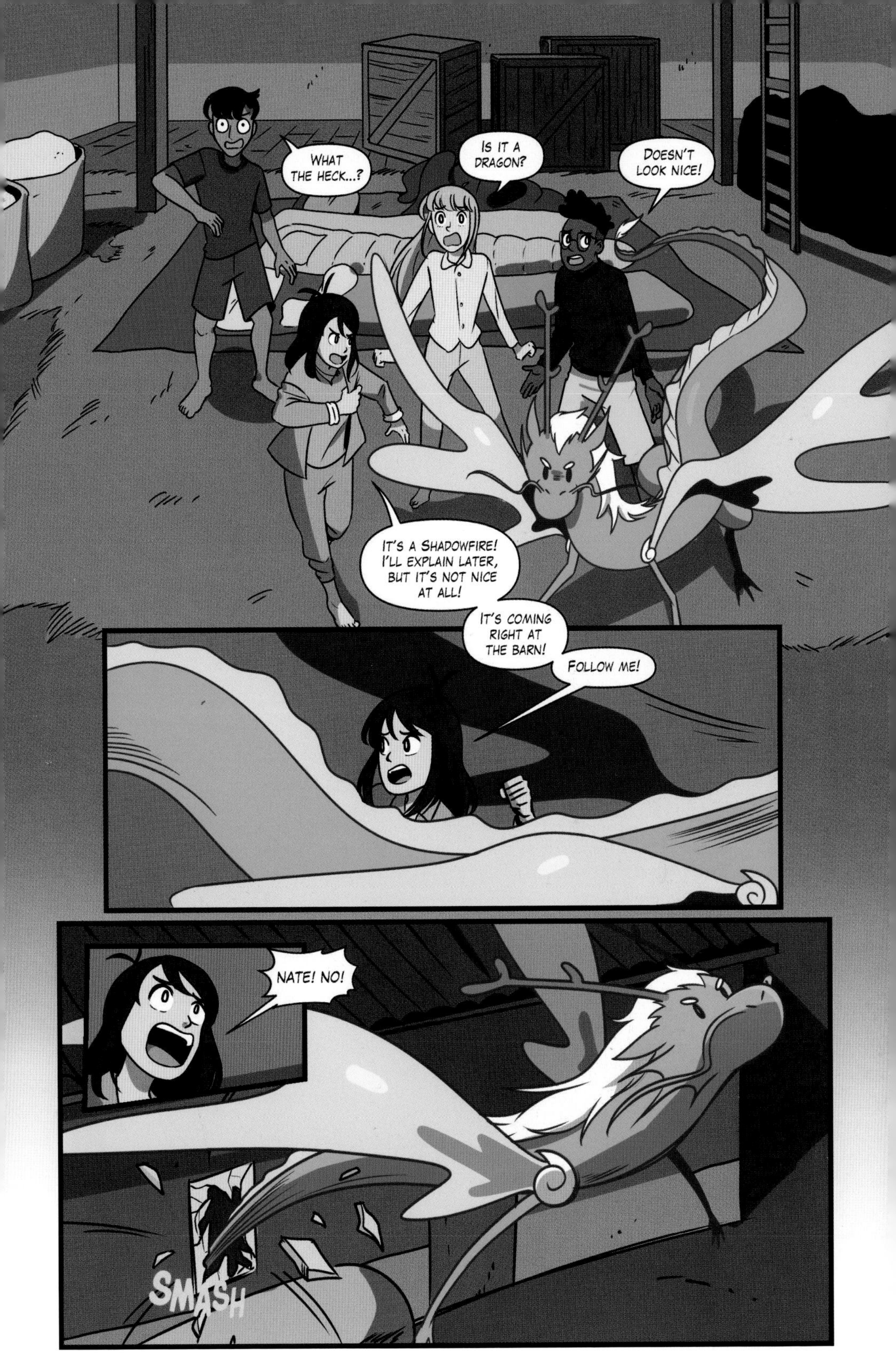
WHAT THE HECK...?
IS IT A DRAGON?
DOESN'T LOOK NICE!
IT'S A SHADOWFIRE! I'LL EXPLAIN LATER, BUT IT'S NOT NICE AT ALL!
IT'S COMING RIGHT AT THE BARN!
FOLLOW ME!
NATE! NO!
SMASH

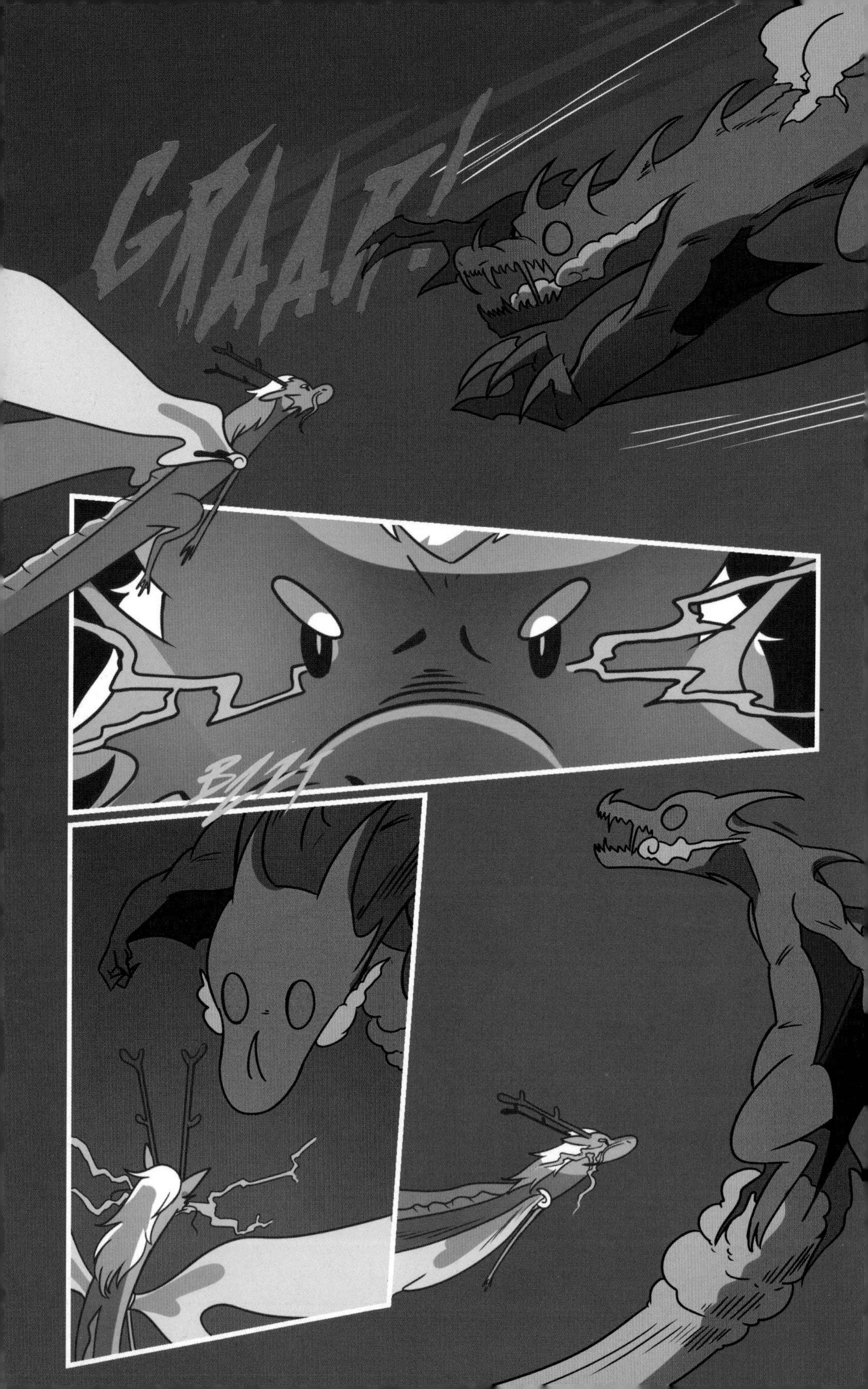
GRAAR!
BZZT

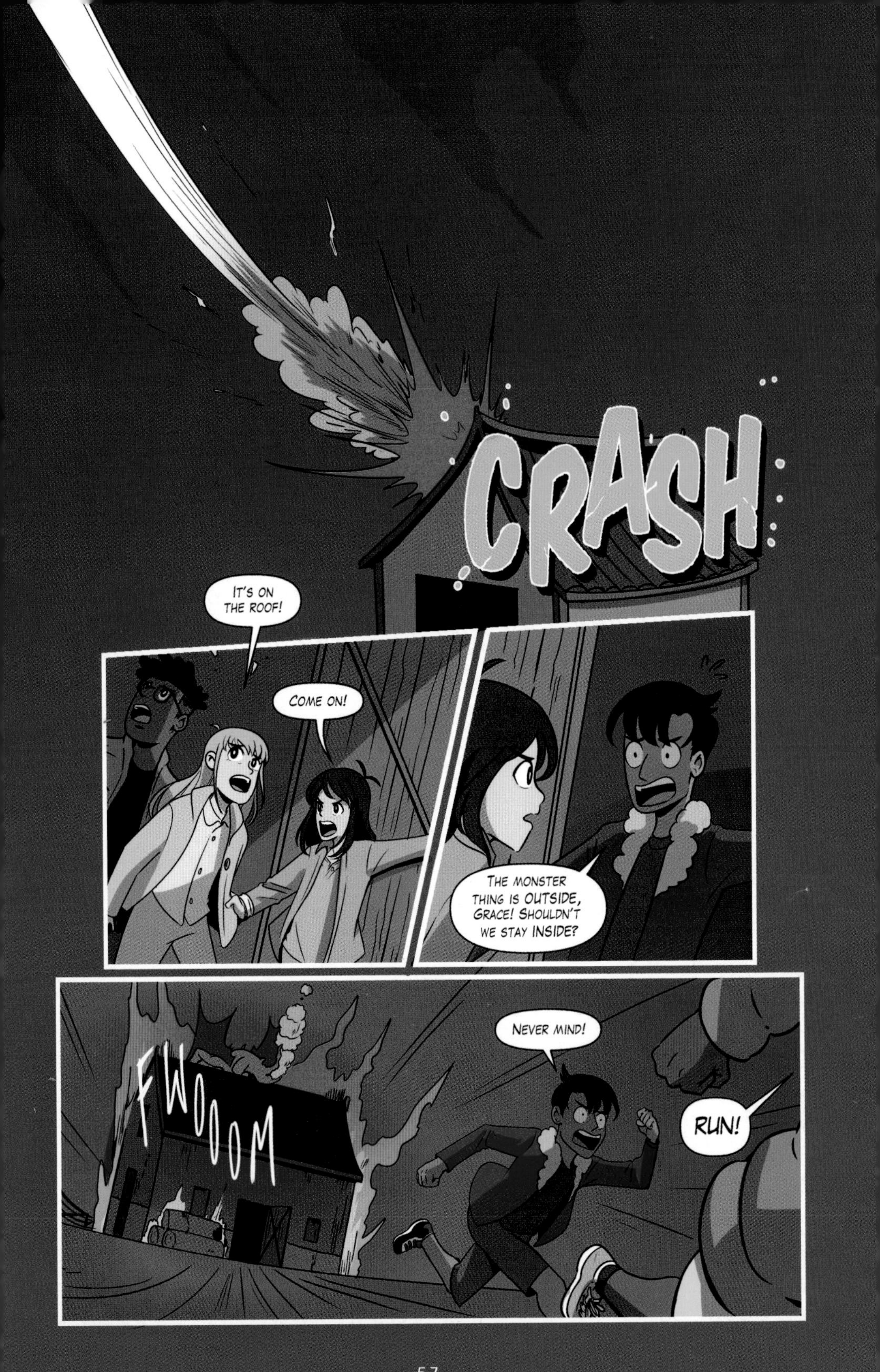
CRASH
IT'S ON THE ROOF!
COME ON!
THE MONSTER THING IS OUTSIDE, GRACE! SHOULDN'T WE STAY INSIDE?
FWOOOM
NEVER MIND!
RUN!

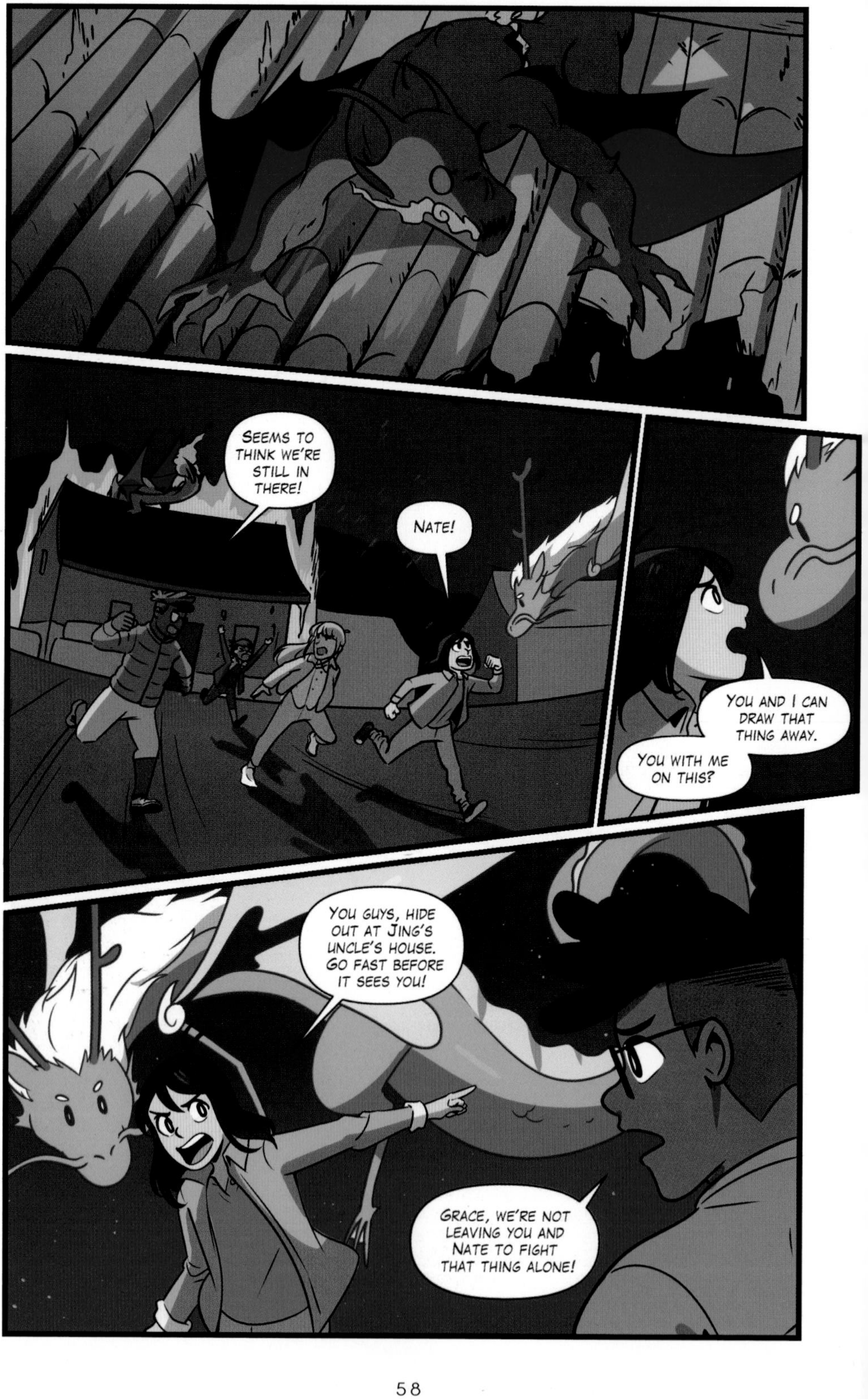
SEEMS TO THINK WE'RE STILL IN THERE!
NATE!
YOU AND I CAN DRAW THAT THING AWAY.
YOU WITH ME ON THIS?
YOU GUYS, HIDE OUT AT JING'S UNCLE'S HOUSE. GO FAST BEFORE IT SEES YOU!
GRACE, WE'RE NOT LEAVING YOU AND NATE TO FIGHT THAT THING ALONE!

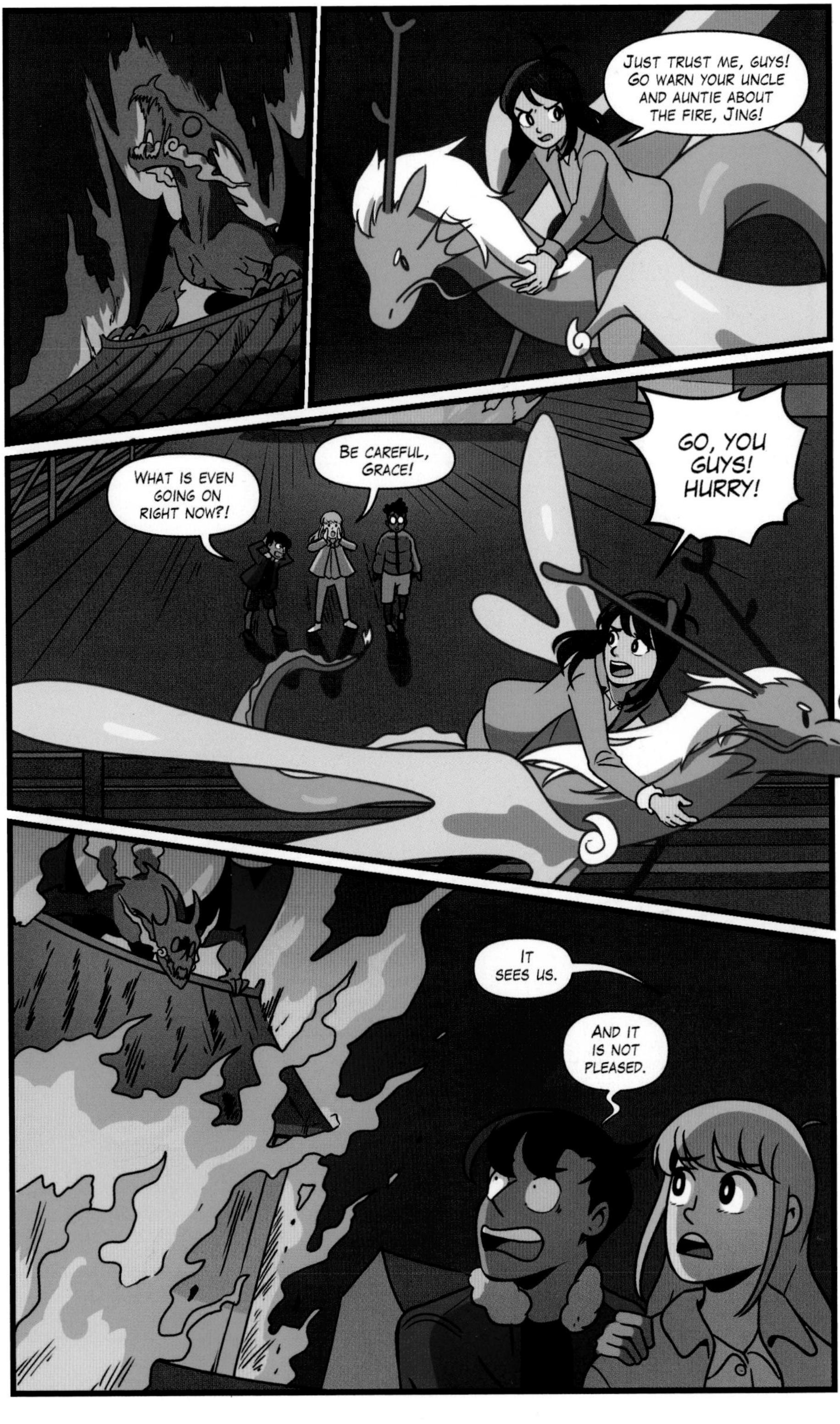
JUST TRUST ME, GUYS! GO WARN YOUR UNCLE AND AUNTIE ABOUT THE FIRE, JING!
WHAT IS EVEN GOING ON RIGHT NOW?!
BE CAREFUL, GRACE!
GO, YOU GUYS! HURRY!
IT SEES US.
AND IT IS NOT PLEASED.

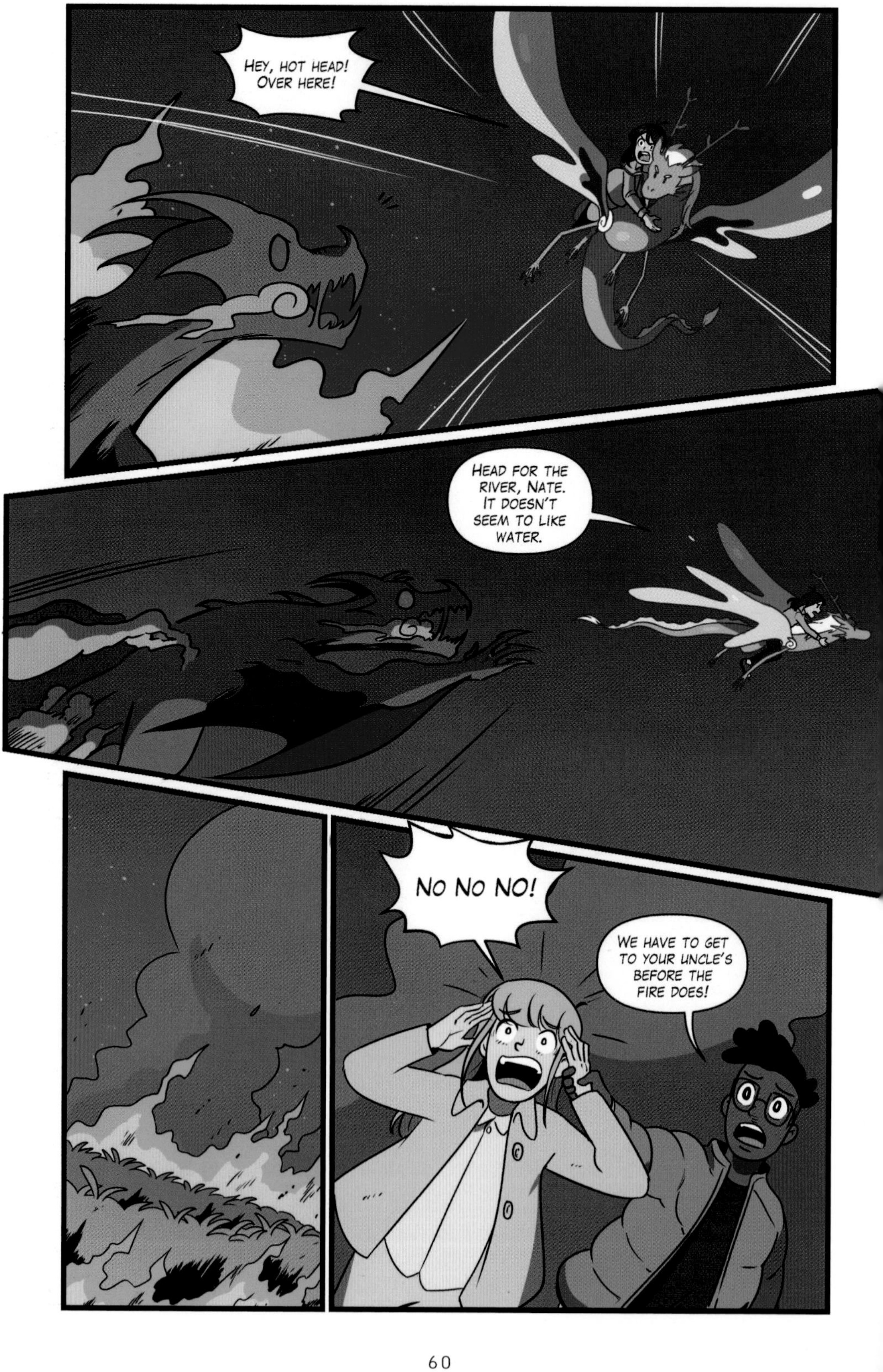
HEY, HOT HEAD! OVER HERE!
HEAD FOR THE RIVER, NATE. IT DOESN'T SEEM TO LIKE WATER.
NO NO NO!
WE HAVE TO GET TO YOUR UNCLE'S BEFORE THE FIRE DOES!

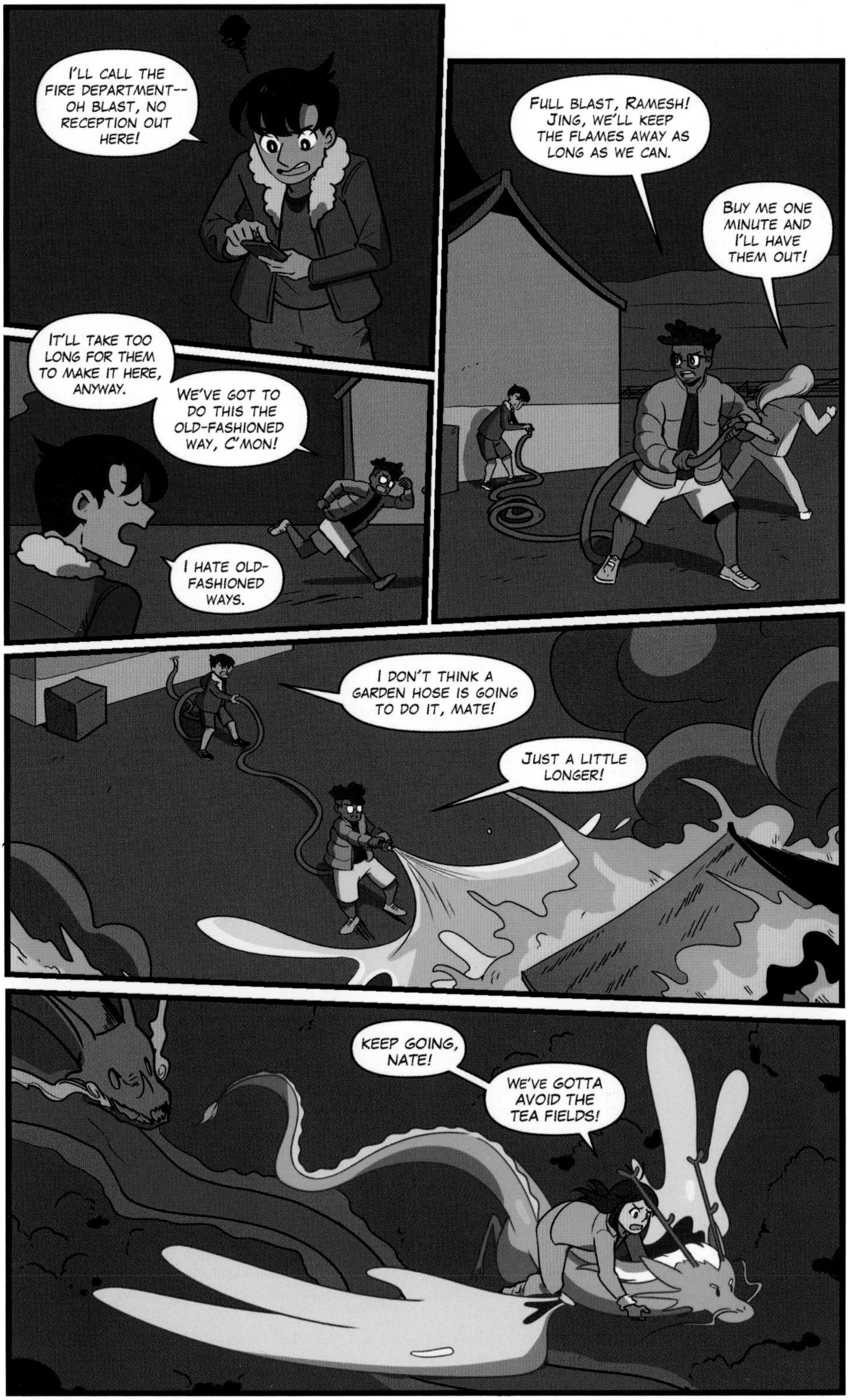
I'LL CALL THE FIRE DEPARTMENT-- OH BLAST, NO RECEPTION OUT HERE!
IT'LL TAKE TOO LONG FOR THEM TO MAKE IT HERE, ANYWAY.
WE'VE GOT TO DO THIS THE OLD-FASHIONED WAY, C'MON!
I HATE OLD-FASHIONED WAYS.
FULL BLAST, RAMESH! JING, WE'LL KEEP THE FLAMES AWAY AS LONG AS WE CAN.
BUY ME ONE MINUTE AND I'LL HAVE THEM OUT!
I DON'T THINK A GARDEN HOSE IS GOING TO DO IT, MATE!
JUST A LITTLE LONGER!
KEEP GOING, NATE!
WE'VE GOTTA AVOID THE TEA FIELDS!

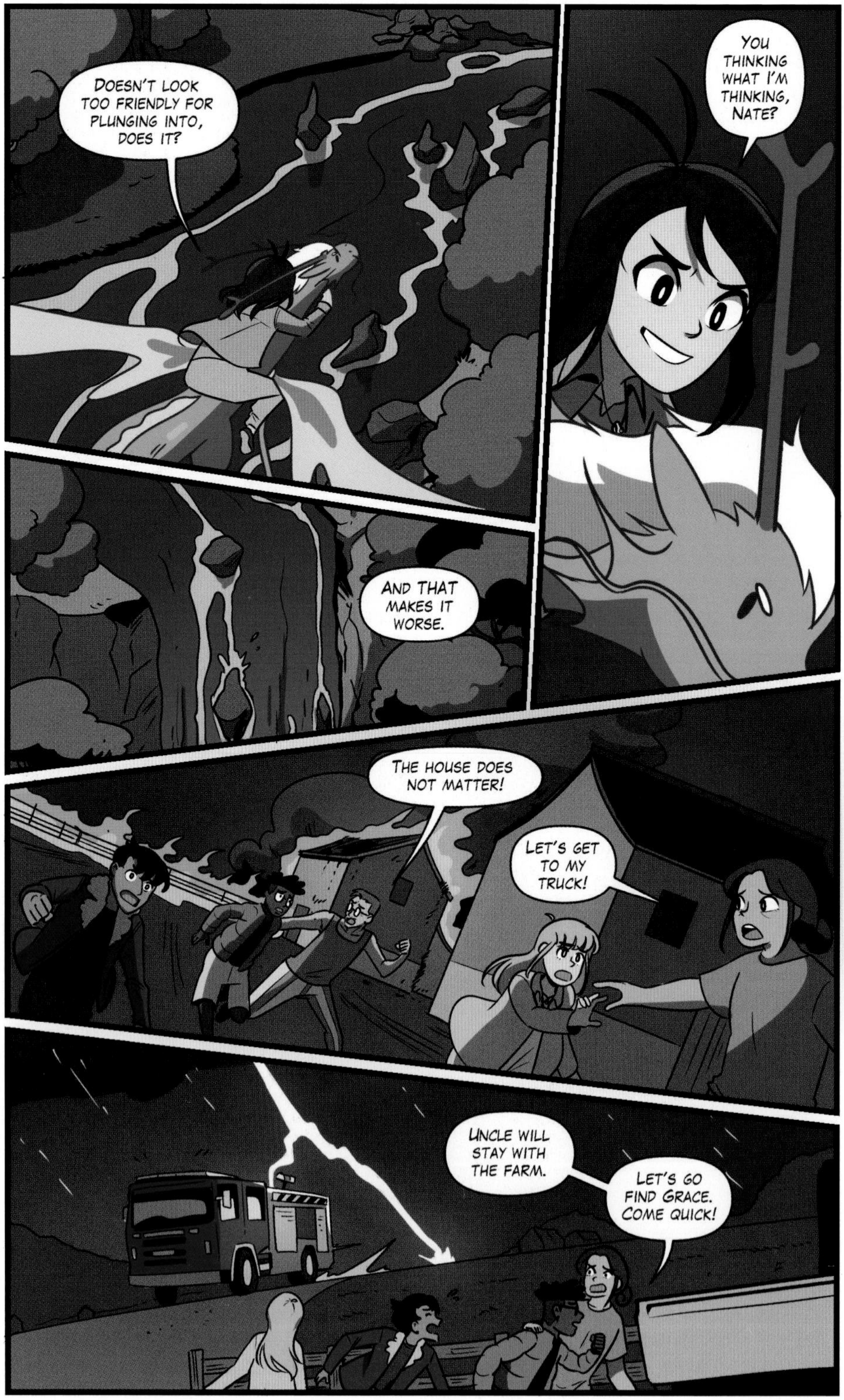
DOESN'T LOOK TOO FRIENDLY FOR PLUNGING INTO, DOES IT?
YOU THINKING WHAT I'M THINKING, NATE?
AND THAT MAKES IT WORSE.
THE HOUSE DOES NOT MATTER!
LET'S GET TO MY TRUCK!
UNCLE WILL STAY WITH THE FARM.
LET'S GO FIND GRACE. COME QUICK!

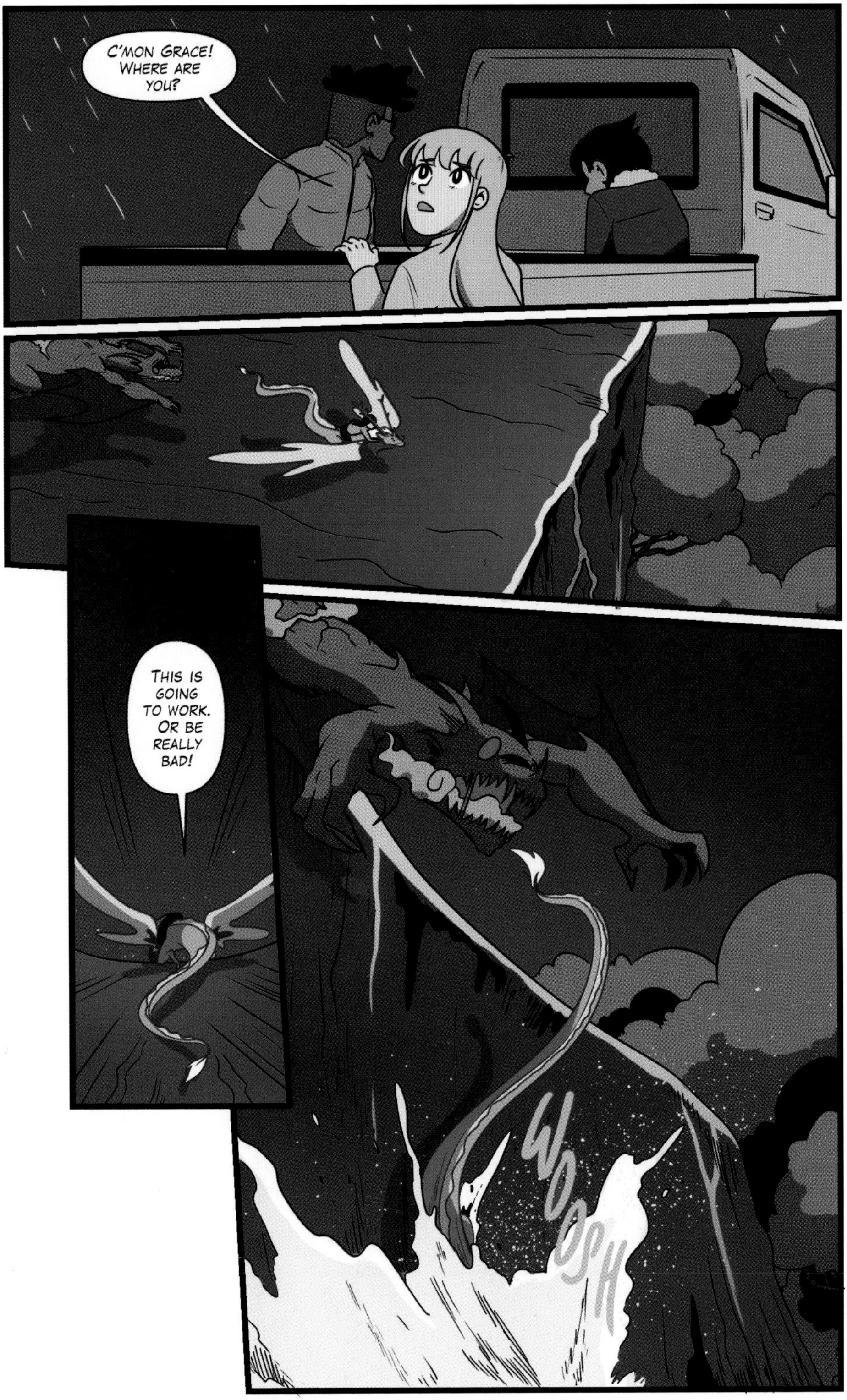
C'MON GRACE! WHERE ARE YOU?
THIS IS GOING TO WORK. OR BE REALLY BAD!
WOOSH

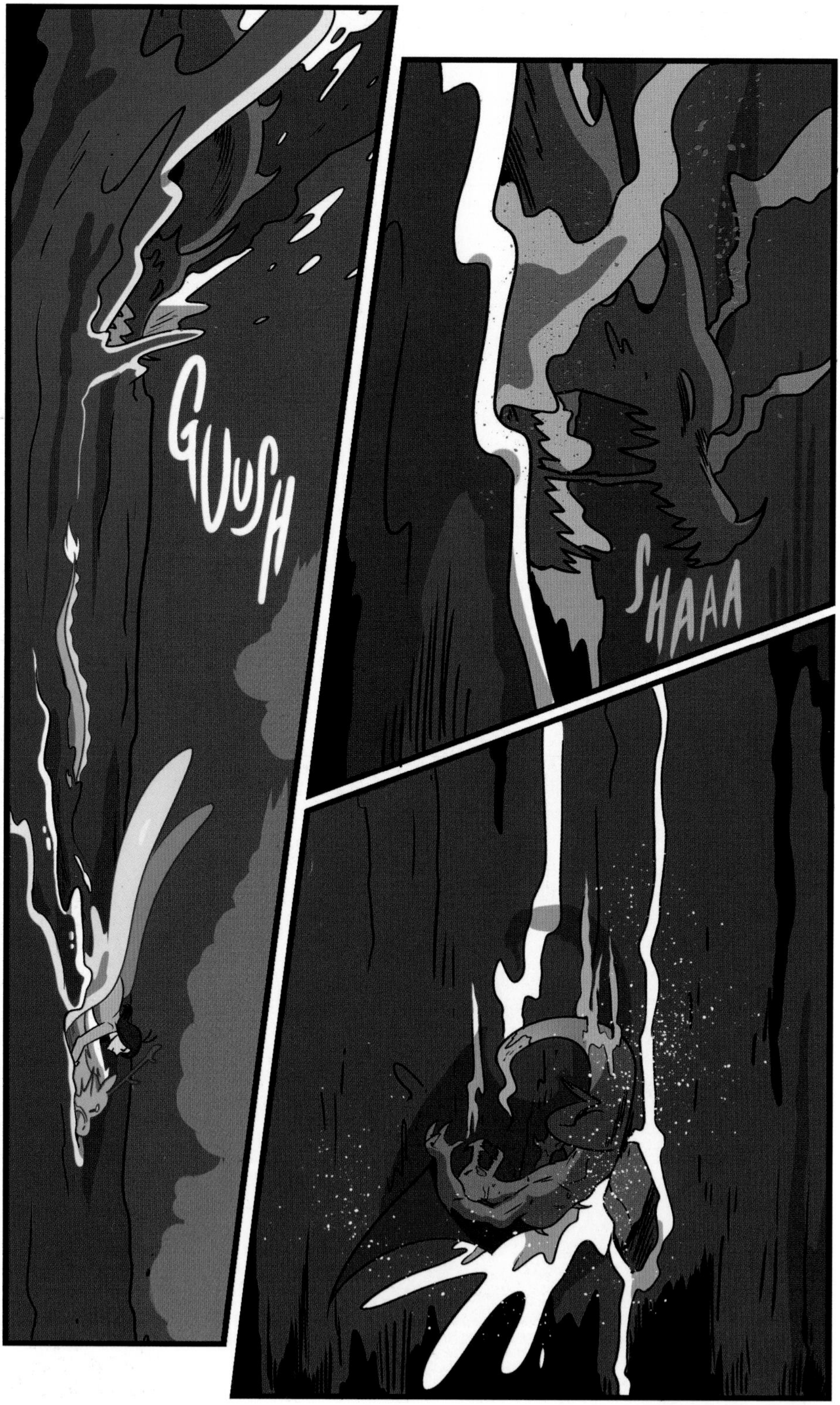
GUUSH
SHAAA

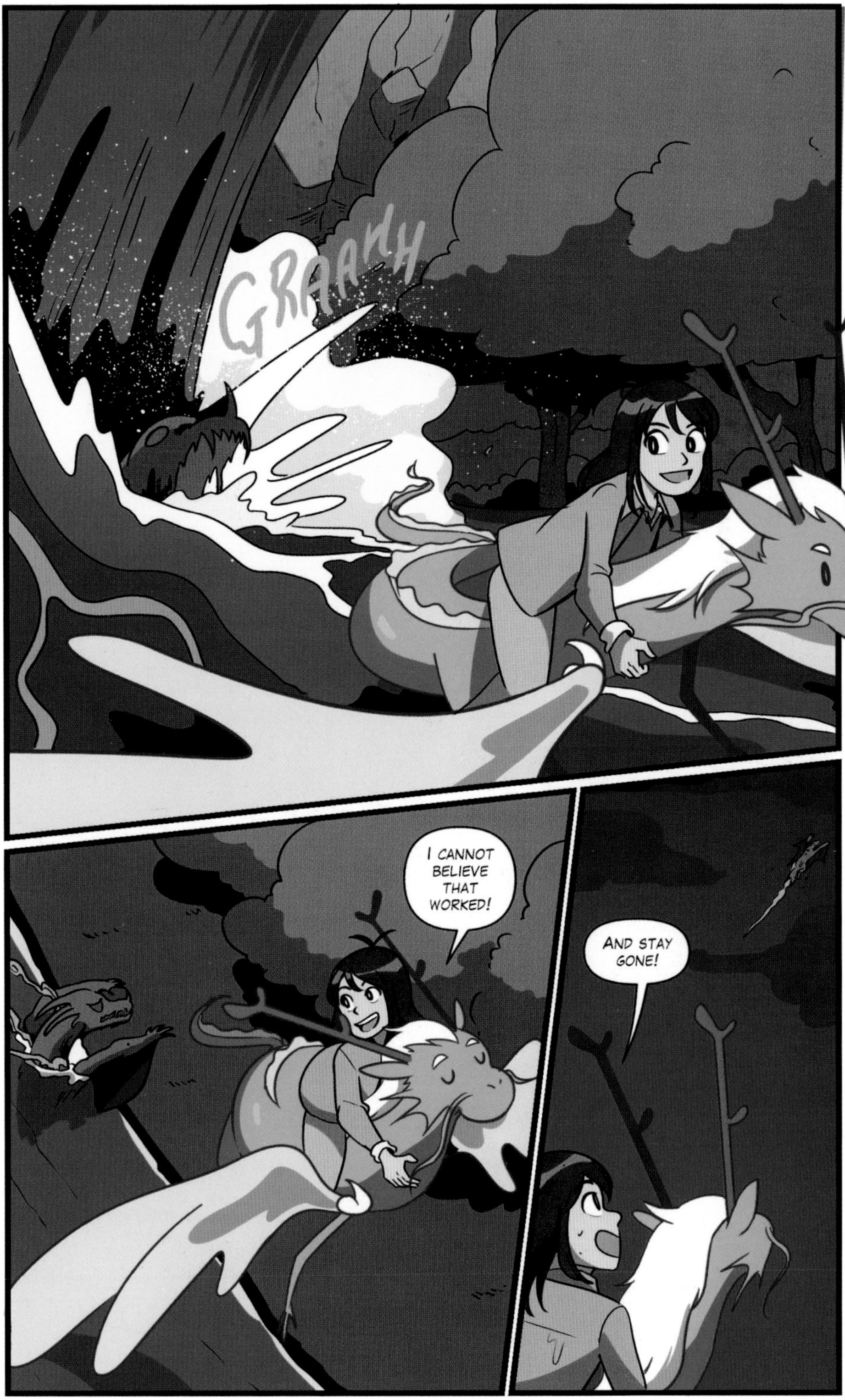
GRAAHH
I CANNOT BELIEVE THAT WORKED!
AND STAY GONE!

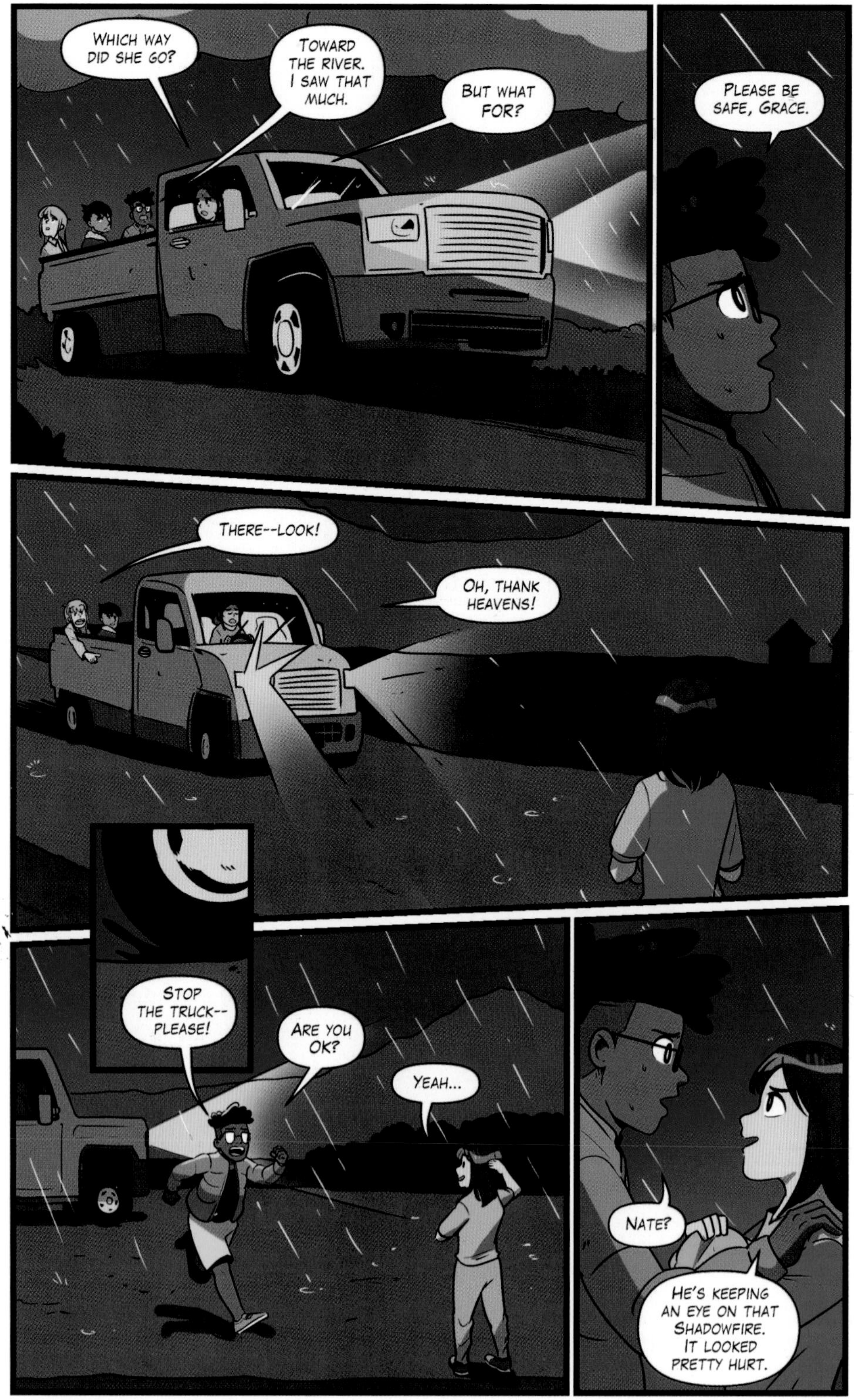

WHICH WAY DID SHE GO?
TOWARD THE RIVER. I SAW THAT MUCH.
BUT WHAT FOR?
PLEASE BE SAFE, GRACE.
THERE--LOOK!
OH, THANK HEAVENS!
STOP THE TRUCK-- PLEASE!
ARE YOU OK?
YEAH...
NATE?
HE'S KEEPING AN EYE ON THAT SHADOWFIRE. IT LOOKED PRETTY HURT.

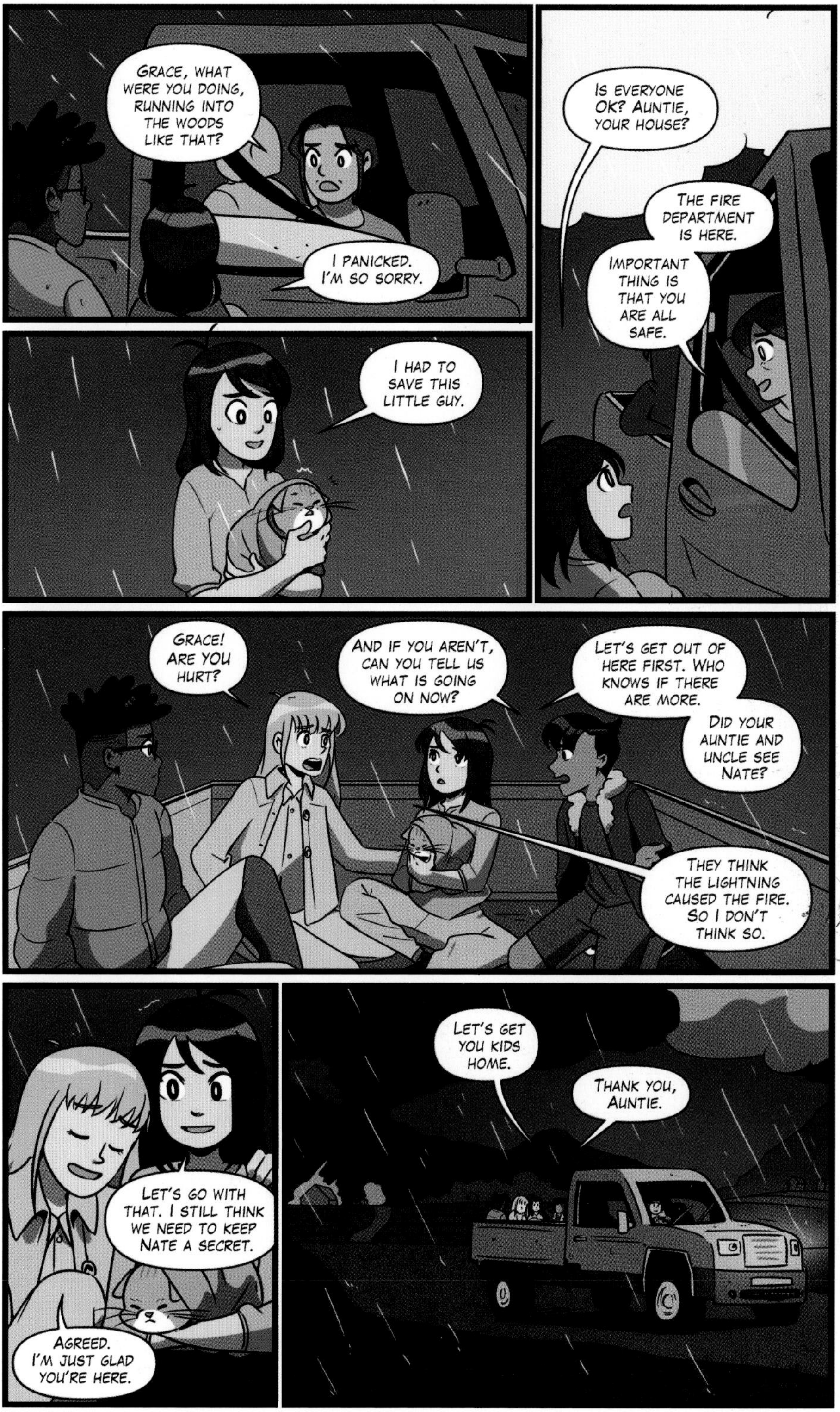
GRACE, WHAT WERE YOU DOING, RUNNING INTO THE WOODS LIKE THAT?
I PANICKED. I'M SO SORRY.
IS EVERYONE OK? AUNTIE, YOUR HOUSE?
THE FIRE DEPARTMENT IS HERE.
IMPORTANT THING IS THAT YOU ARE ALL SAFE.
I HAD TO SAVE THIS LITTLE GUY.
GRACE! ARE YOU HURT?
AND IF YOU AREN'T, CAN YOU TELL US WHAT IS GOING ON NOW?
LET'S GET OUT OF HERE FIRST. WHO KNOWS IF THERE ARE MORE.
DID YOUR AUNTIE AND UNCLE SEE NATE?
THEY THINK THE LIGHTNING CAUSED THE FIRE. SO I DON'T THINK SO.
LET'S GO WITH THAT. I STILL THINK WE NEED TO KEEP NATE A SECRET.
AGREED. I'M JUST GLAD YOU'RE HERE.
LET'S GET YOU KIDS HOME.
THANK YOU, AUNTIE.

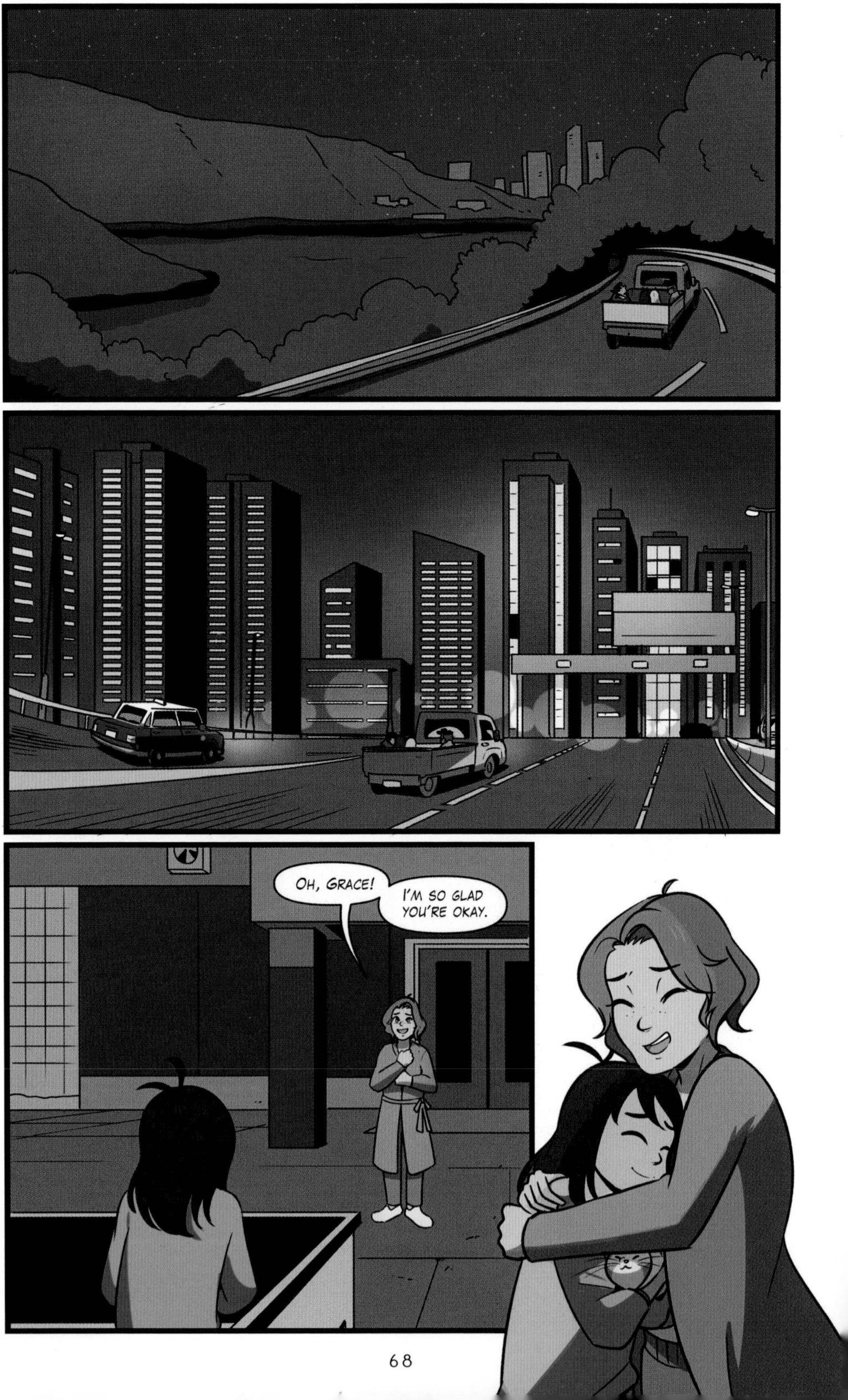
OH, GRACE!
I'M SO GLAD YOU'RE OKAY.

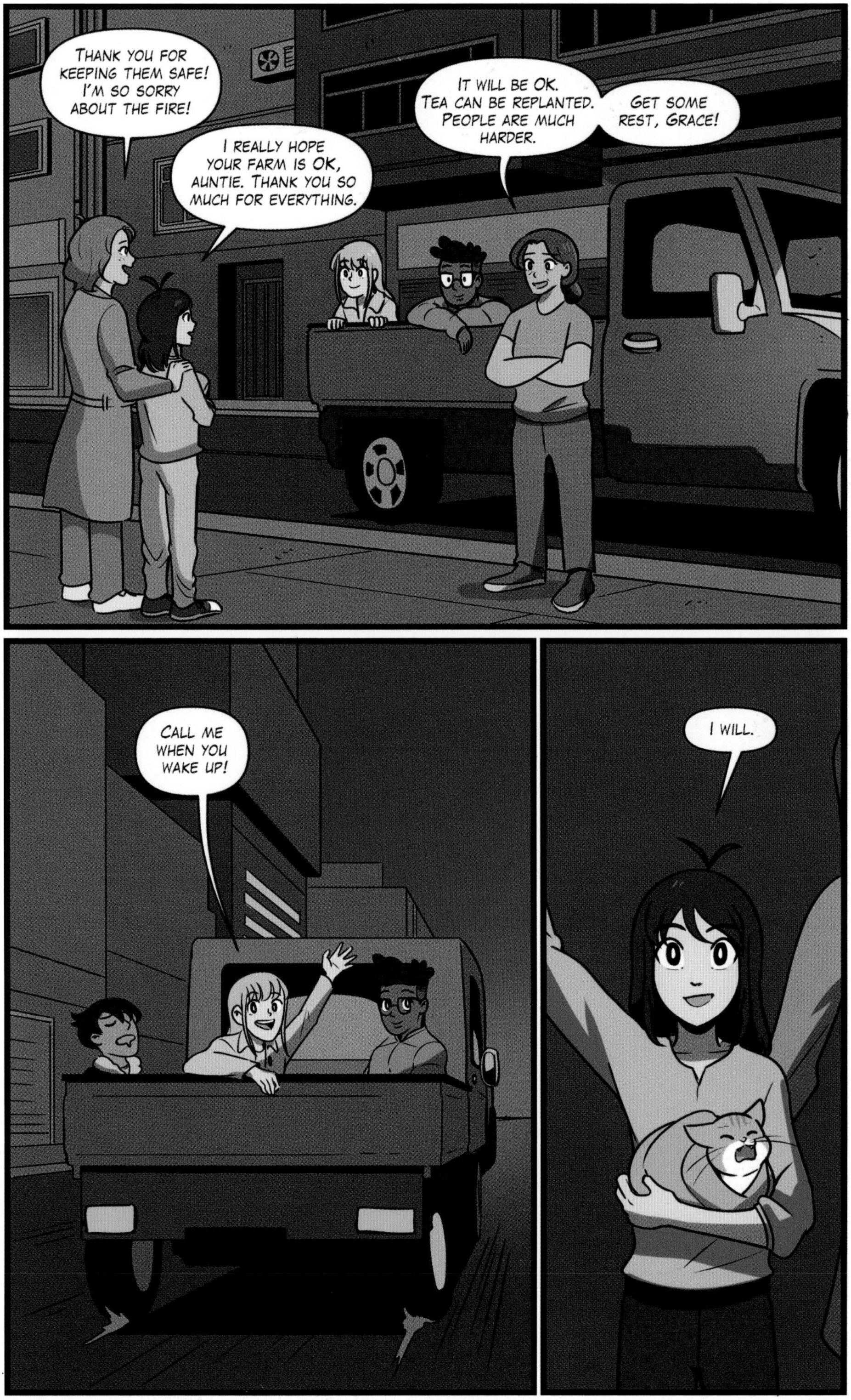
THANK YOU FOR KEEPING THEM SAFE! I'M SO SORRY ABOUT THE FIRE!
I REALLY HOPE YOUR FARM IS OK, AUNTIE. THANK YOU SO MUCH FOR EVERYTHING.
IT WILL BE OK. TEA CAN BE REPLANTED. PEOPLE ARE MUCH HARDER.
GET SOME REST, GRACE!
CALL ME WHEN YOU WAKE UP!
I WILL.

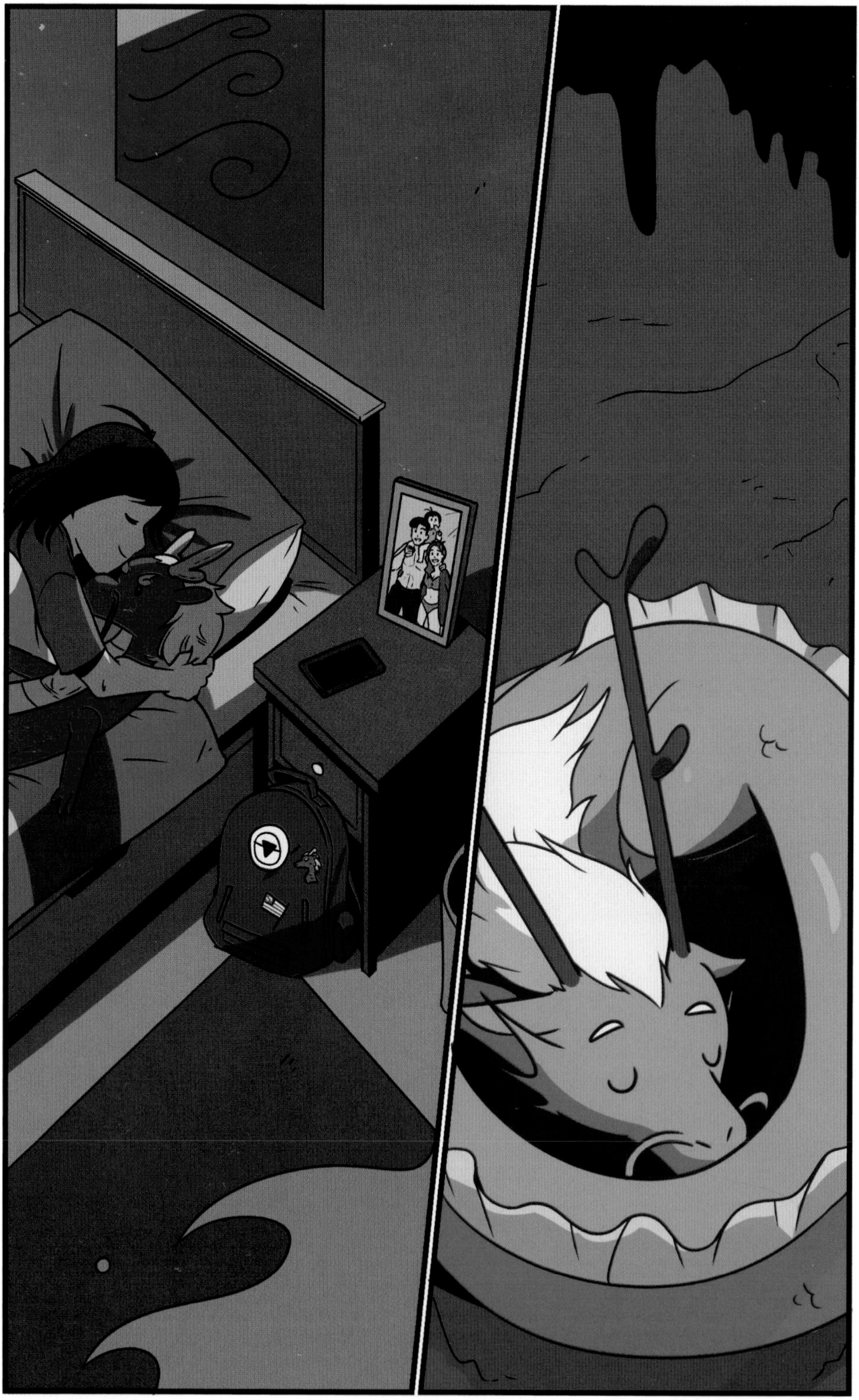

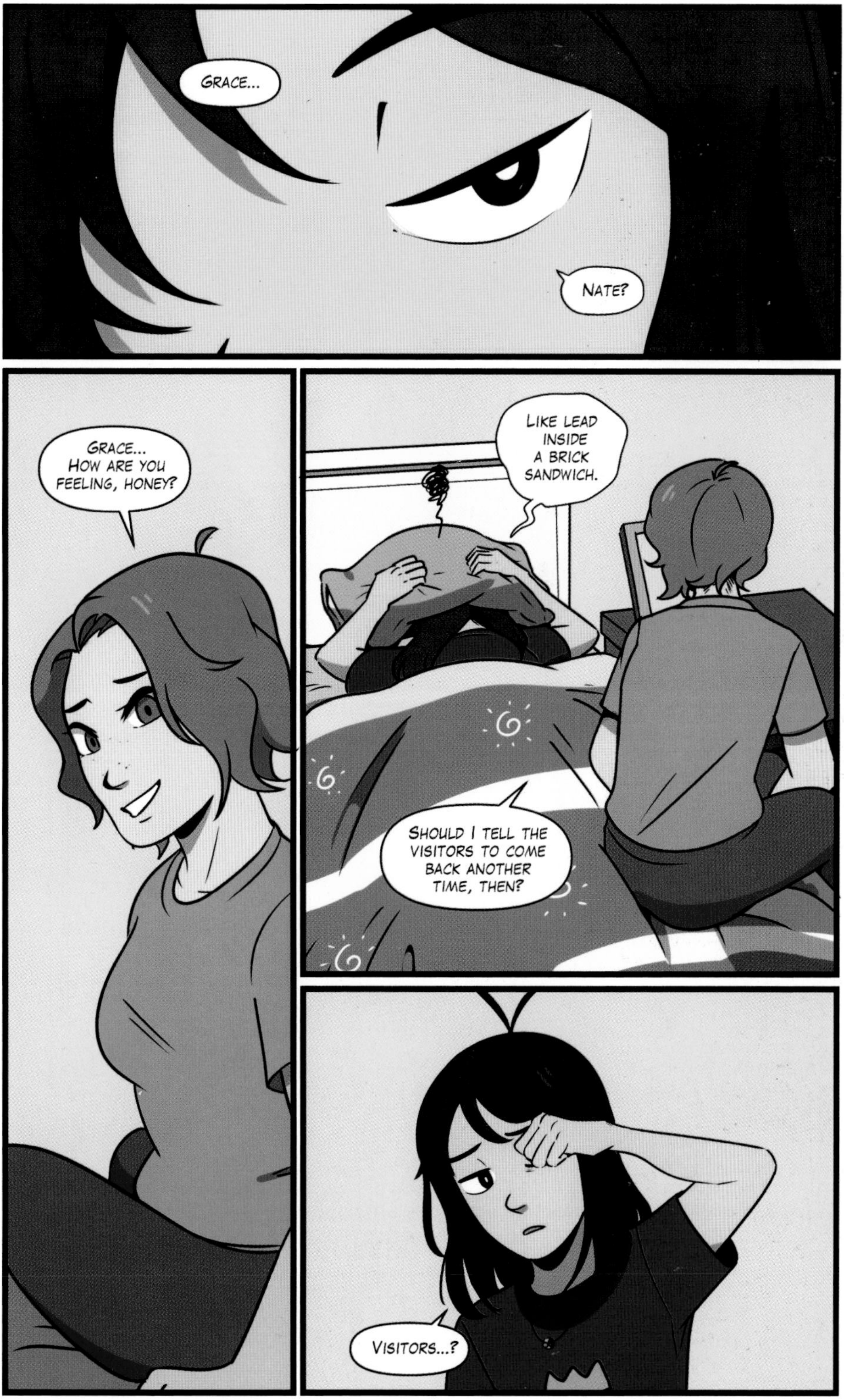
GRACE...
NATE?
GRACE... HOW ARE YOU FEELING, HONEY?
LIKE LEAD INSIDE A BRICK SANDWICH.
SHOULD I TELL THE VISITORS TO COME BACK ANOTHER TIME, THEN?
VISITORS...?

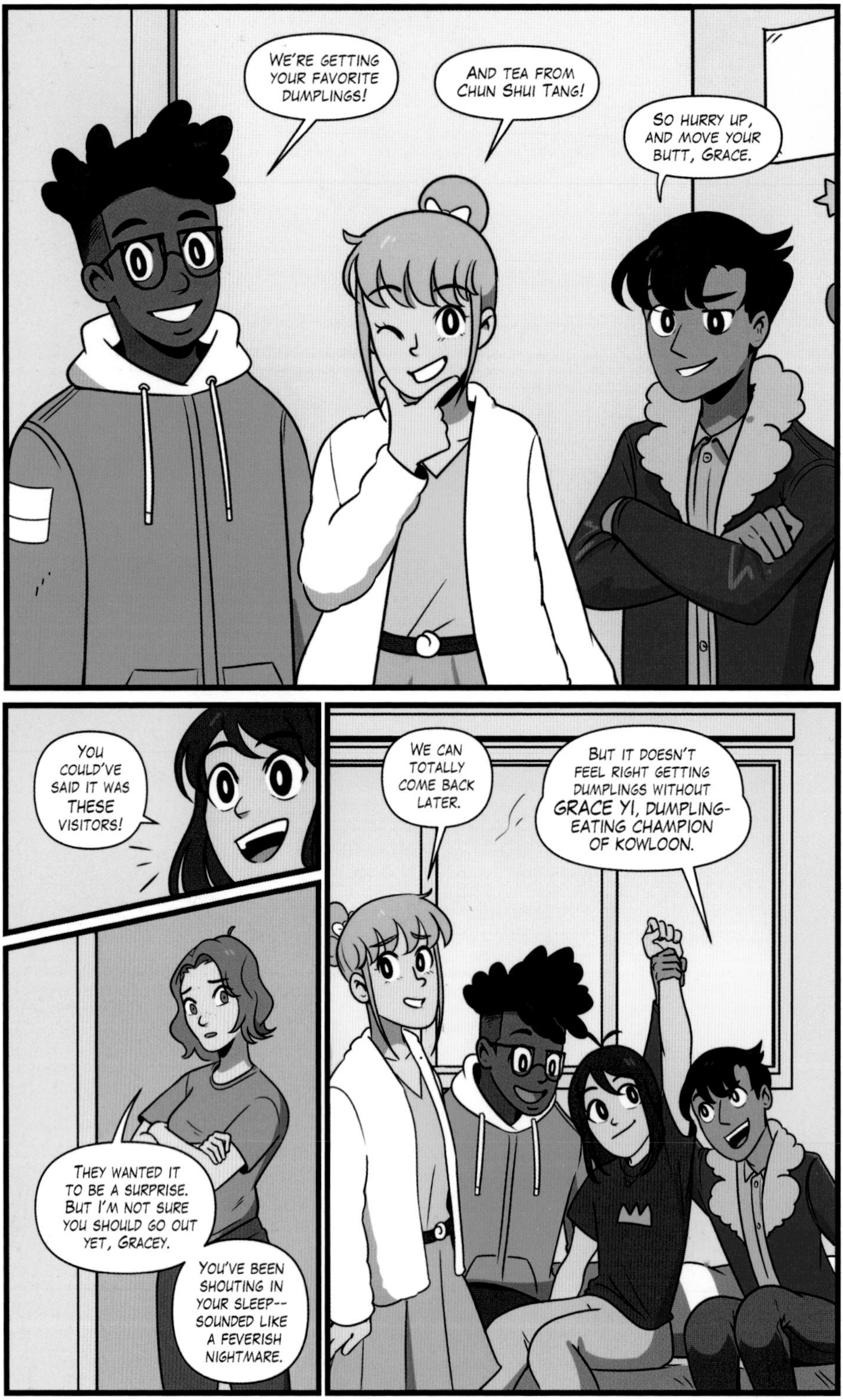
WE'RE GETTING YOUR FAVORITE DUMPLINGS!
AND TEA FROM CHUN SHUI TANG!
SO HURRY UP, AND MOVE YOUR BUTT, GRACE.
YOU COULD'VE SAID IT WAS THESE VISITORS!
THEY WANTED IT TO BE A SURPRISE. BUT I'M NOT SURE YOU SHOULD GO OUT YET, GRACEY.
YOU'VE BEEN SHOUTING IN YOUR SLEEP-- SOUNDED LIKE A FEVERISH NIGHTMARE.
WE CAN TOTALLY COME BACK LATER.
BUT IT DOESN'T FEEL RIGHT GETTING DUMPLINGS WITHOUT GRACE YI, DUMPLING-EATING CHAMPION OF KOWLOON.

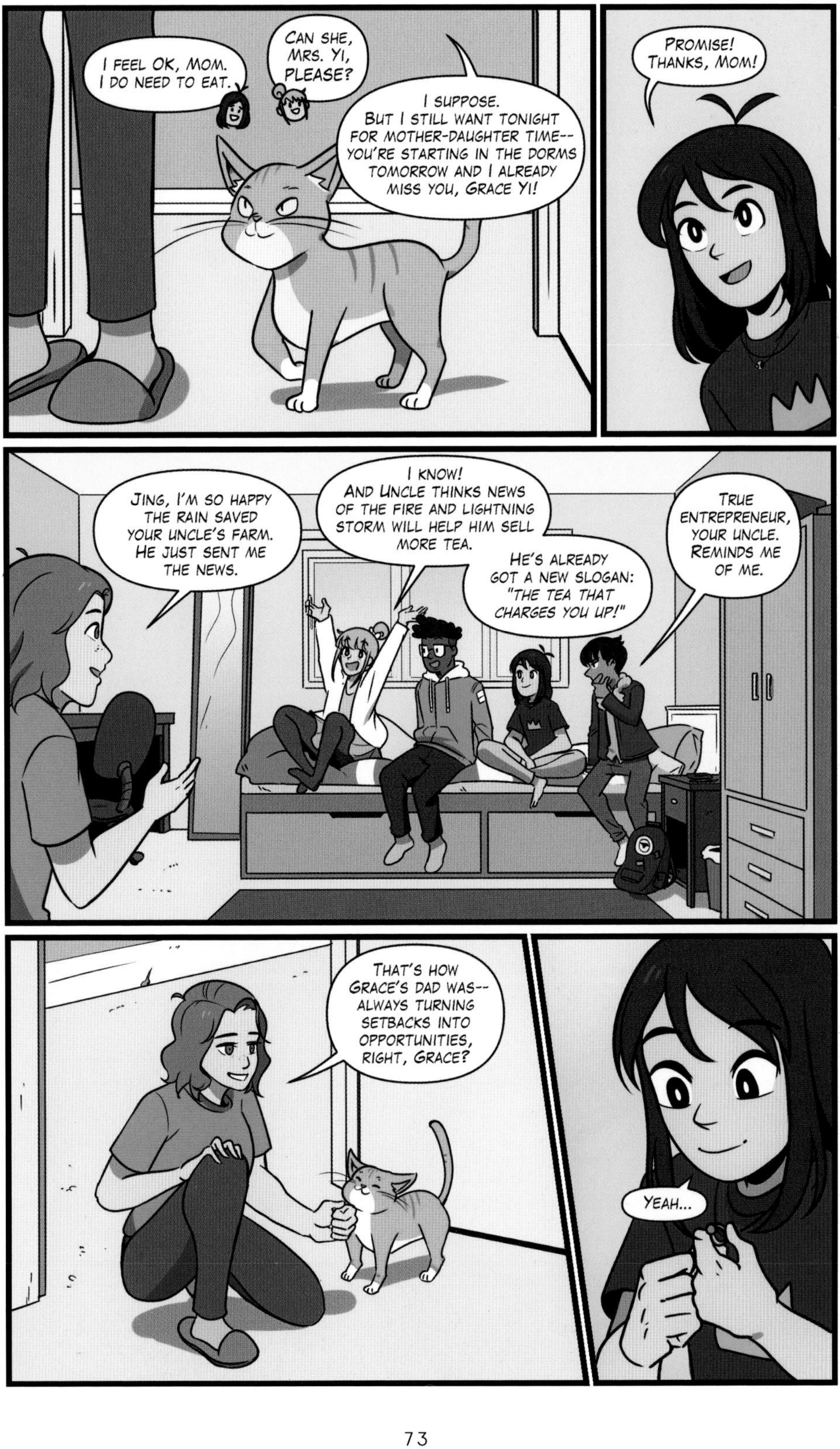
I FEEL OK, MOM. I DO NEED TO EAT.
CAN SHE, MRS. YI, PLEASE?
I SUPPOSE. BUT I STILL WANT TONIGHT FOR MOTHER-DAUGHTER TIME--YOU'RE STARTING IN THE DORMS TOMORROW AND I ALREADY MISS YOU, GRACE YI!
PROMISE! THANKS, MOM!
JING, I'M SO HAPPY THE RAIN SAVED YOUR UNCLE'S FARM. HE JUST SENT ME THE NEWS.
I KNOW! AND UNCLE THINKS NEWS OF THE FIRE AND LIGHTNING STORM WILL HELP HIM SELL MORE TEA.
HE'S ALREADY GOT A NEW SLOGAN: "THE TEA THAT CHARGES YOU UP!"
TRUE ENTREPRENEUR, YOUR UNCLE. REMINDS ME OF ME.
THAT'S HOW GRACE'S DAD WAS--ALWAYS TURNING SETBACKS INTO OPPORTUNITIES, RIGHT, GRACE?
YEAH...

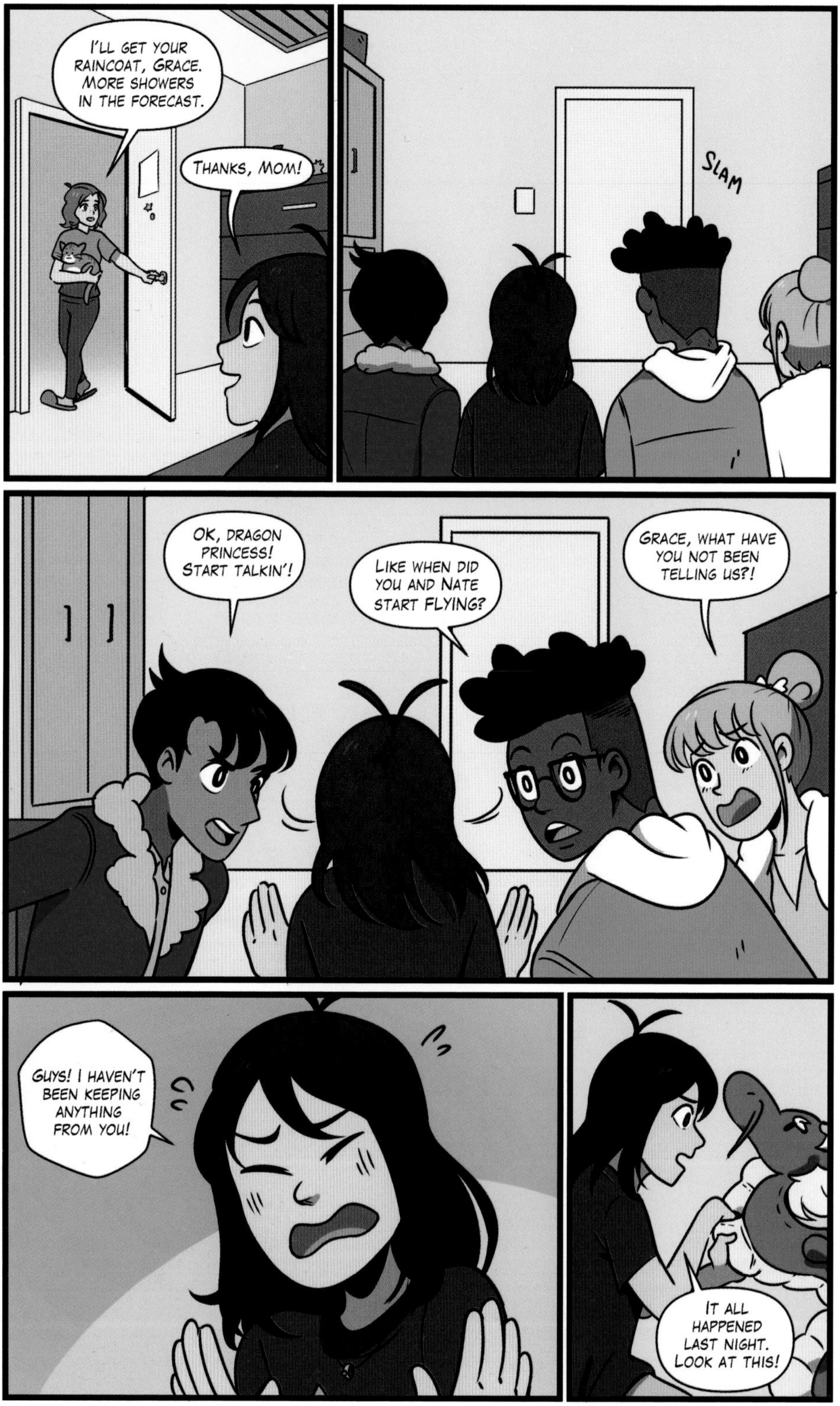
I'LL GET YOUR RAINCOAT, GRACE. MORE SHOWERS IN THE FORECAST.
THANKS, MOM!
SLAM
OK, DRAGON PRINCESS! START TALKIN'!
LIKE WHEN DID YOU AND NATE START FLYING?
GRACE, WHAT HAVE YOU NOT BEEN TELLING US?!
GUYS! I HAVEN'T BEEN KEEPING ANYTHING FROM YOU!
IT ALL HAPPENED LAST NIGHT. LOOK AT THIS!

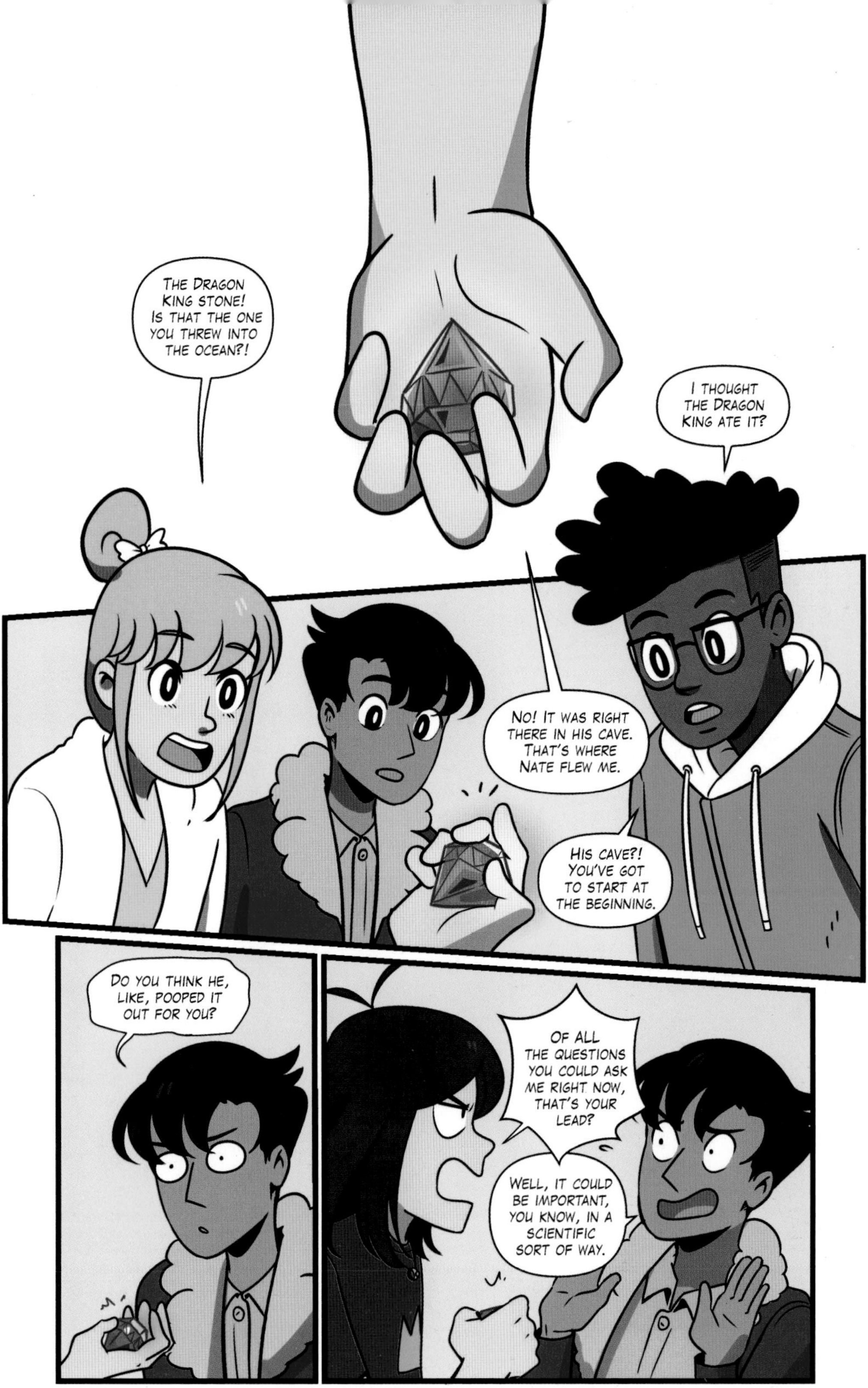
THE DRAGON KING STONE! IS THAT THE ONE YOU THREW INTO THE OCEAN?!
I THOUGHT THE DRAGON KING ATE IT?
NO! IT WAS RIGHT THERE IN HIS CAVE. THAT'S WHERE NATE FLEW ME.
HIS CAVE?! YOU'VE GOT TO START AT THE BEGINNING.
DO YOU THINK HE, LIKE, POOPED IT OUT FOR YOU?
OF ALL THE QUESTIONS YOU COULD ASK ME RIGHT NOW, THAT'S YOUR LEAD?
WELL, IT COULD BE IMPORTANT, YOU KNOW, IN A SCIENTIFIC SORT OF WAY.

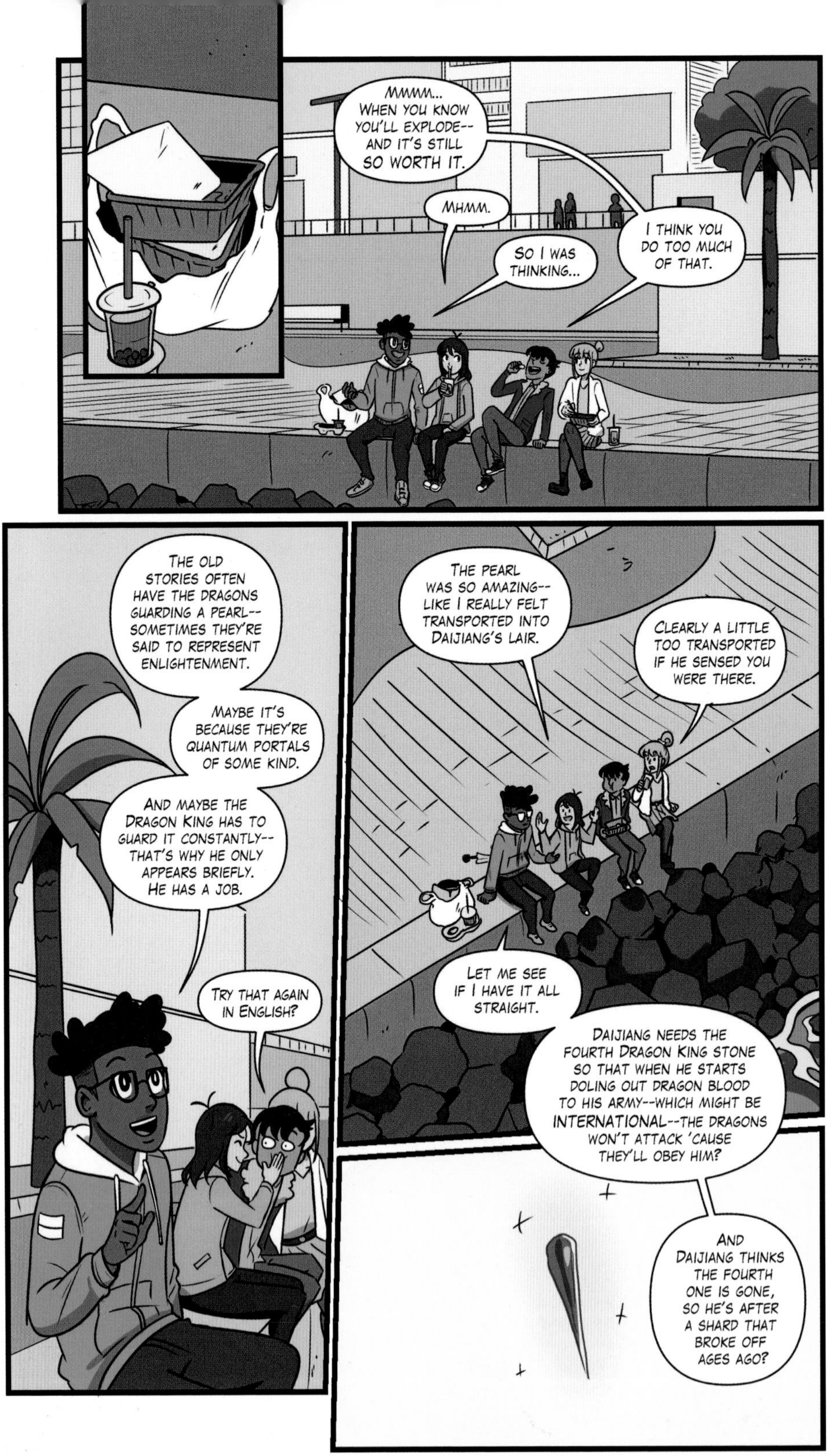

MMMM... WHEN YOU KNOW YOU'LL EXPLODE-- AND IT'S STILL SO WORTH IT.
MHMM.
SO I WAS THINKING...
I THINK YOU DO TOO MUCH OF THAT.
THE OLD STORIES OFTEN HAVE THE DRAGONS GUARDING A PEARL-- SOMETIMES THEY'RE SAID TO REPRESENT ENLIGHTENMENT.
MAYBE IT'S BECAUSE THEY'RE QUANTUM PORTALS OF SOME KIND.
AND MAYBE THE DRAGON KING HAS TO GUARD IT CONSTANTLY-- THAT'S WHY HE ONLY APPEARS BRIEFLY. HE HAS A JOB.
TRY THAT AGAIN IN ENGLISH?
THE PEARL WAS SO AMAZING-- LIKE I REALLY FELT TRANSPORTED INTO DAIJIANG'S LAIR.
CLEARLY A LITTLE TOO TRANSPORTED IF HE SENSED YOU WERE THERE.
LET ME SEE IF I HAVE IT ALL STRAIGHT.
DAIJIANG NEEDS THE FOURTH DRAGON KING STONE SO THAT WHEN HE STARTS DOLING OUT DRAGON BLOOD TO HIS ARMY--WHICH MIGHT BE INTERNATIONAL--THE DRAGONS WON'T ATTACK 'CAUSE THEY'LL OBEY HIM?
AND DAIJIANG THINKS THE FOURTH ONE IS GONE, SO HE'S AFTER A SHARD THAT BROKE OFF AGES AGO?

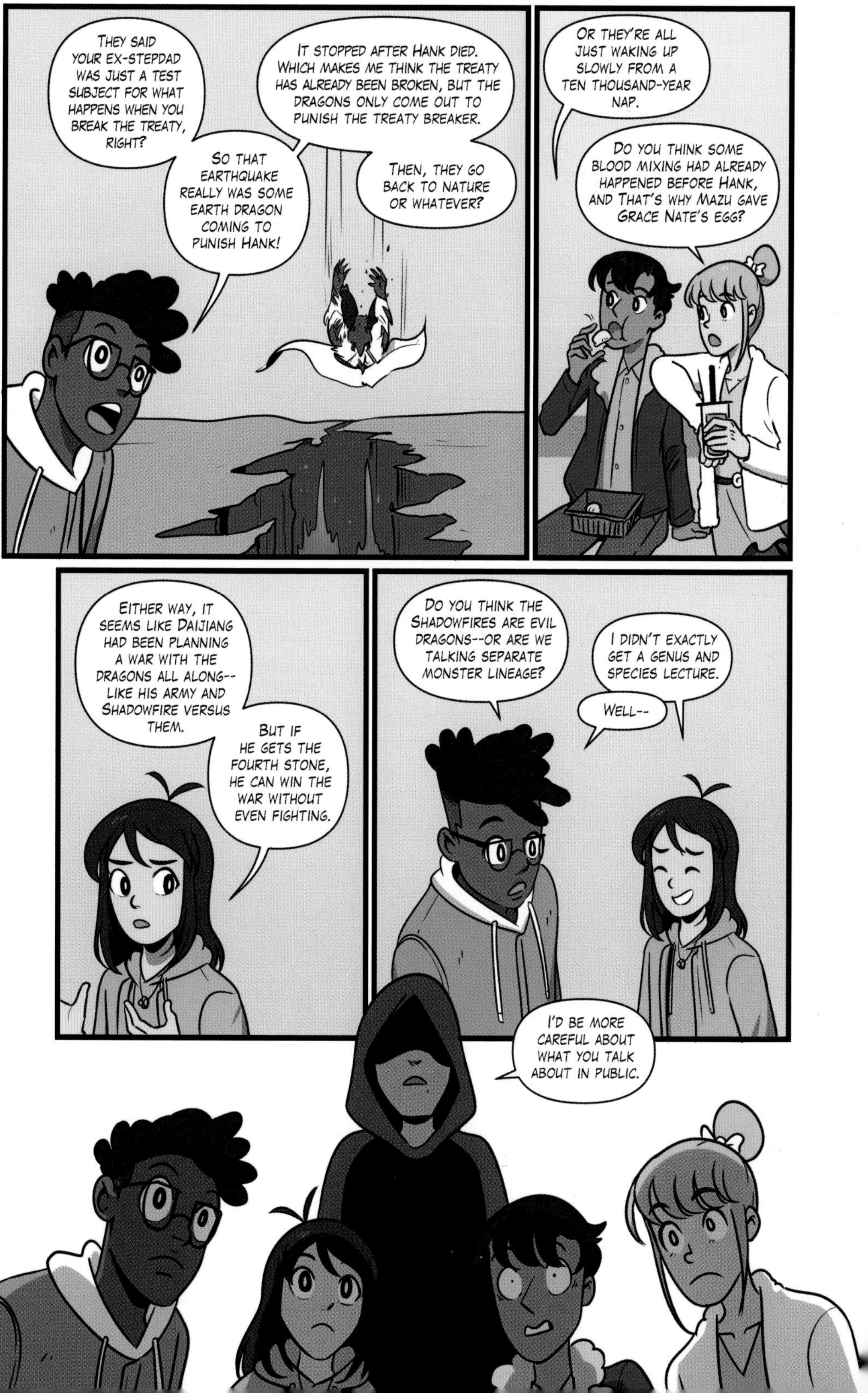
They said your ex-stepdad was just a test subject for what happens when you break the treaty, right?
So that earthquake really was some earth dragon coming to punish Hank!
It stopped after Hank died. Which makes me think the treaty has already been broken, but the dragons only come out to punish the treaty breaker.
Then, they go back to nature or whatever?
Or they're all just waking up slowly from a ten thousand-year nap.
Do you think some blood mixing had already happened before Hank, and that's why Mazu gave Grace Nate's egg?
Either way, it seems like Daijiang had been planning a war with the dragons all along--like his army and Shadowfire versus them.
But if he gets the fourth stone, he can win the war without even fighting.
Do you think the Shadowfires are evil dragons--or are we talking separate monster lineage?
I didn't exactly get a genus and species lecture.
Well--
I'd be more careful about what you talk about in public.

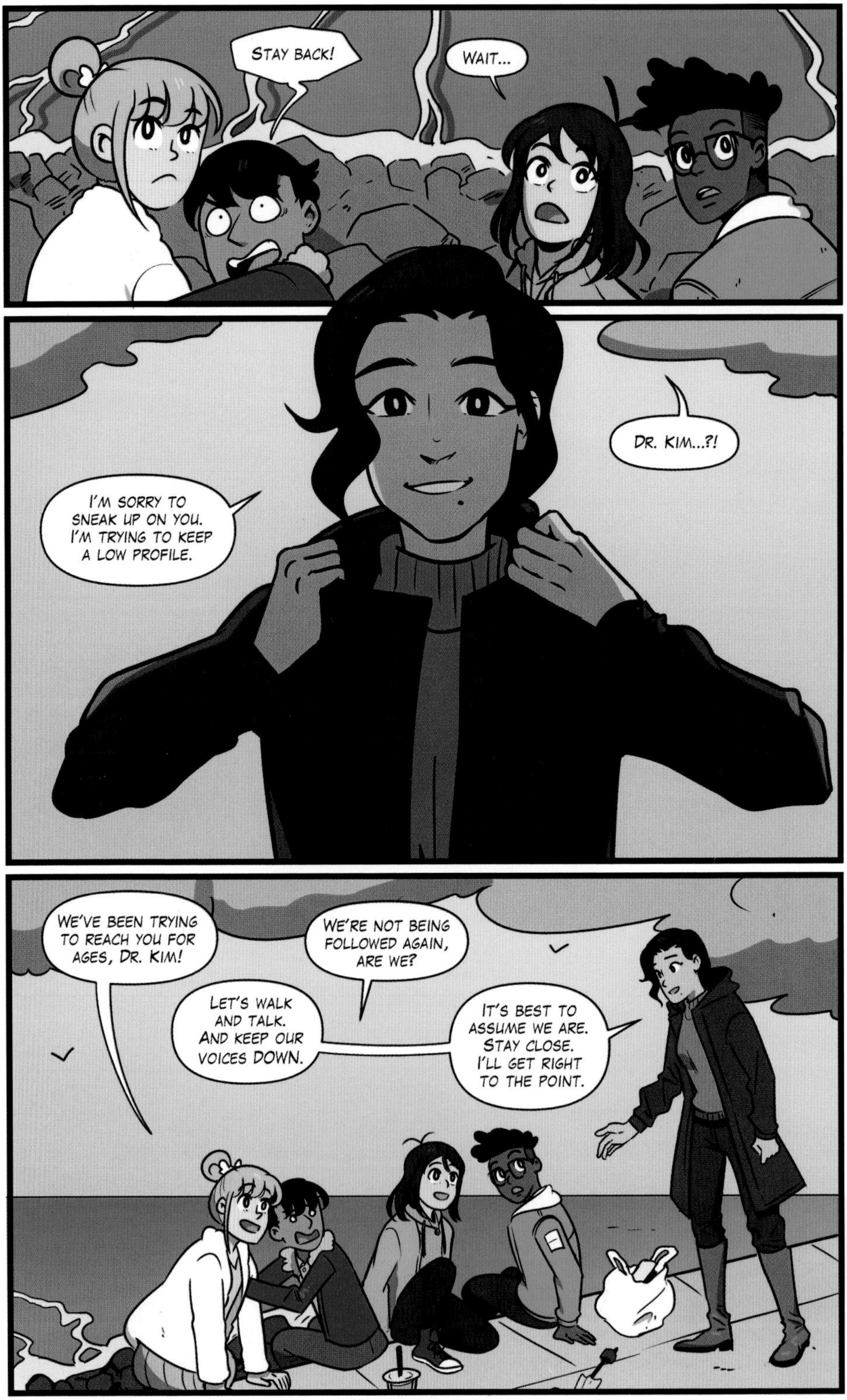
STAY BACK!
WAIT...
DR. KIM...?!
I'M SORRY TO SNEAK UP ON YOU. I'M TRYING TO KEEP A LOW PROFILE.
WE'VE BEEN TRYING TO REACH YOU FOR AGES, DR. KIM!
WE'RE NOT BEING FOLLOWED AGAIN, ARE WE?
LET'S WALK AND TALK. AND KEEP OUR VOICES DOWN.
IT'S BEST TO ASSUME WE ARE. STAY CLOSE. I'LL GET RIGHT TO THE POINT.

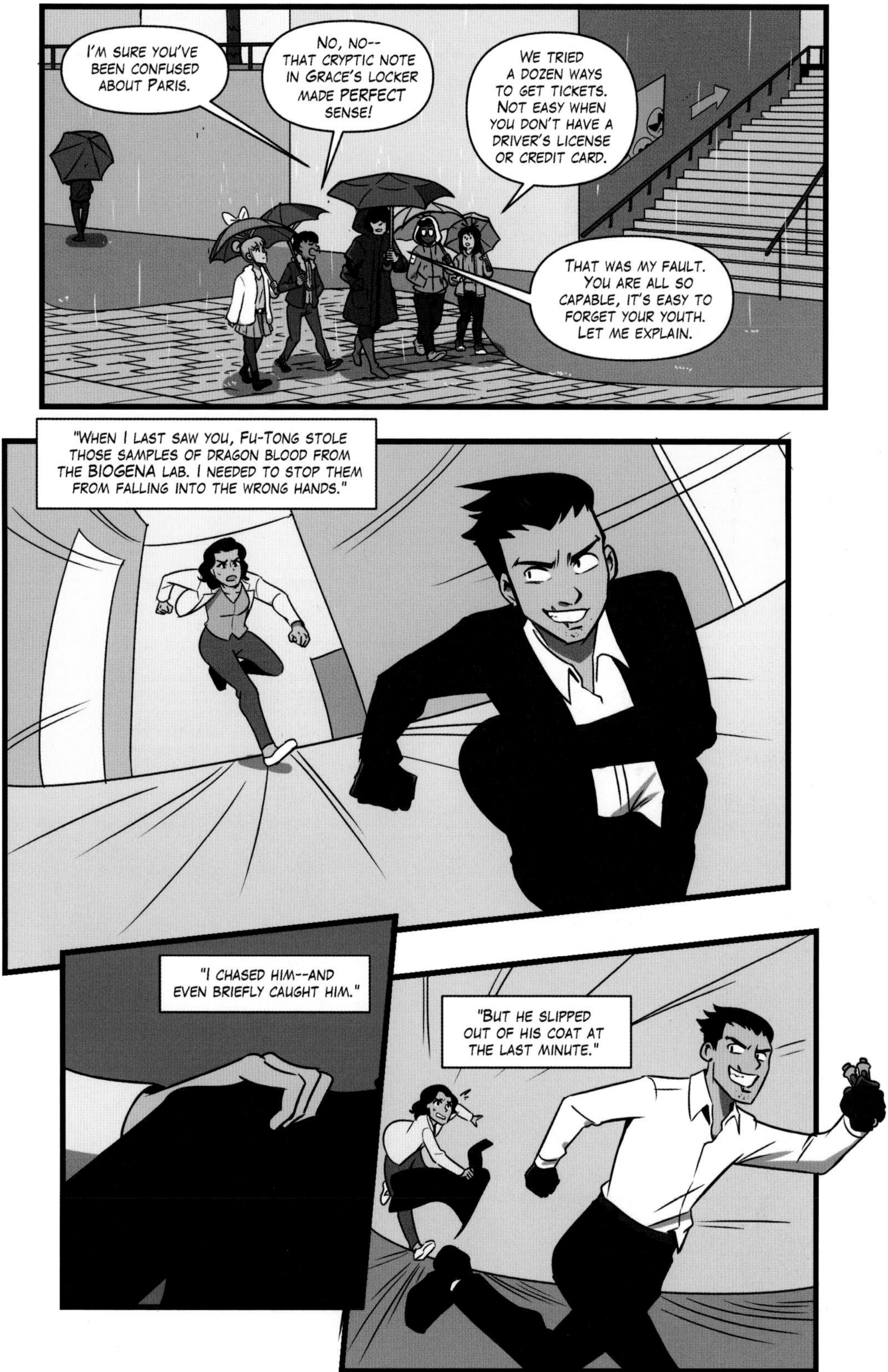
I'M SURE YOU'VE BEEN CONFUSED ABOUT PARIS.
NO, NO-- THAT CRYPTIC NOTE IN GRACE'S LOCKER MADE PERFECT SENSE!
WE TRIED A DOZEN WAYS TO GET TICKETS. NOT EASY WHEN YOU DON'T HAVE A DRIVER'S LICENSE OR CREDIT CARD.
THAT WAS MY FAULT. YOU ARE ALL SO CAPABLE, IT'S EASY TO FORGET YOUR YOUTH. LET ME EXPLAIN.
"WHEN I LAST SAW YOU, FU-TONG STOLE THOSE SAMPLES OF DRAGON BLOOD FROM THE BIOGENA LAB. I NEEDED TO STOP THEM FROM FALLING INTO THE WRONG HANDS."
"I CHASED HIM--AND EVEN BRIEFLY CAUGHT HIM."
"BUT HE SLIPPED OUT OF HIS COAT AT THE LAST MINUTE."

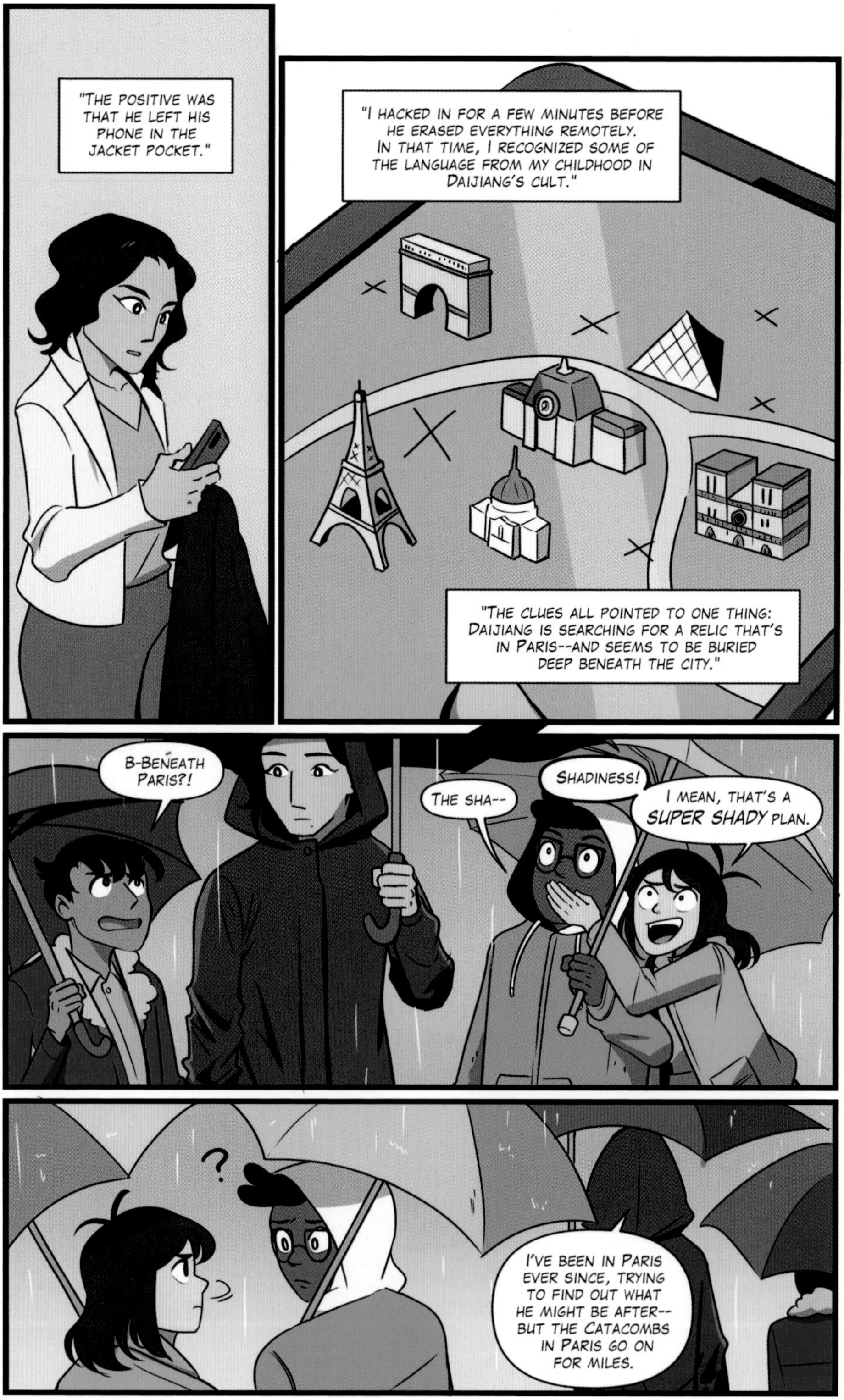
"THE POSITIVE WAS THAT HE LEFT HIS PHONE IN THE JACKET POCKET."
"I HACKED IN FOR A FEW MINUTES BEFORE HE ERASED EVERYTHING REMOTELY. IN THAT TIME, I RECOGNIZED SOME OF THE LANGUAGE FROM MY CHILDHOOD IN DAIJIANG'S CULT."
"THE CLUES ALL POINTED TO ONE THING: DAIJIANG IS SEARCHING FOR A RELIC THAT'S IN PARIS--AND SEEMS TO BE BURIED DEEP BENEATH THE CITY."
B-BENEATH PARIS?!
THE SHA--
SHADINESS!
I MEAN, THAT'S A SUPER SHADY PLAN.
?
I'VE BEEN IN PARIS EVER SINCE, TRYING TO FIND OUT WHAT HE MIGHT BE AFTER--BUT THE CATACOMBS IN PARIS GO ON FOR MILES.

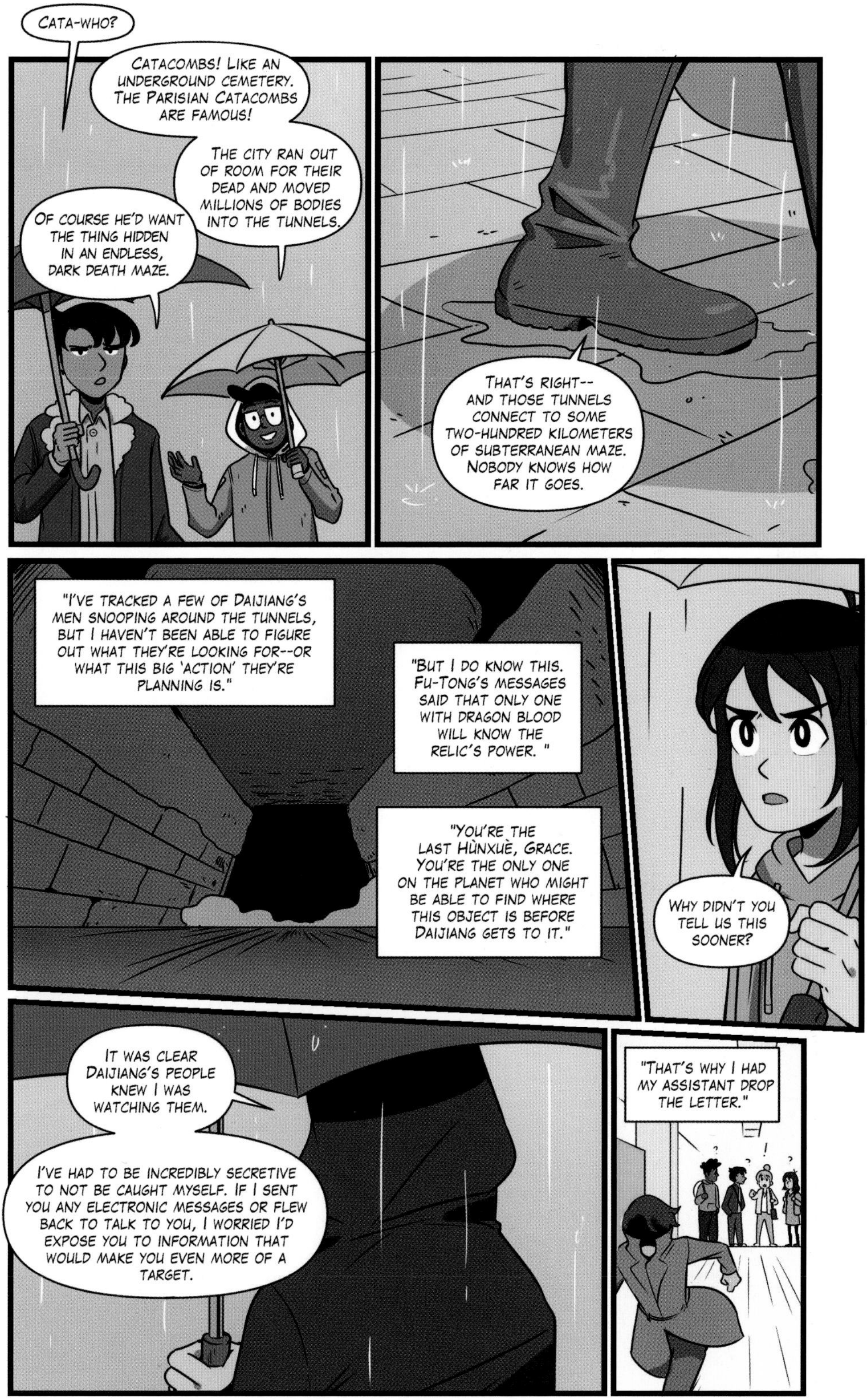

Cata-who?
Catacombs! Like an underground cemetery. The Parisian Catacombs are famous!
The city ran out of room for their dead and moved millions of bodies into the tunnels.
Of course he'd want the thing hidden in an endless, dark death maze.
That's right-- and those tunnels connect to some two-hundred kilometers of subterranean maze. Nobody knows how far it goes.
"I've tracked a few of Daijiang's men snooping around the tunnels, but I haven't been able to figure out what they're looking for--or what this big 'action' they're planning is."
"But I do know this. Fu-Tong's messages said that only one with dragon blood will know the relic's power. "
"You're the last Hùnxuè, Grace. You're the only one on the planet who might be able to find where this object is before Daijiang gets to it."
Why didn't you tell us this sooner?
It was clear Daijiang's people knew I was watching them.
I've had to be incredibly secretive to not be caught myself. If I sent you any electronic messages or flew back to talk to you, I worried I'd expose you to information that would make you even more of a target.
"That's why I had my assistant drop the letter."
? ? ! ?

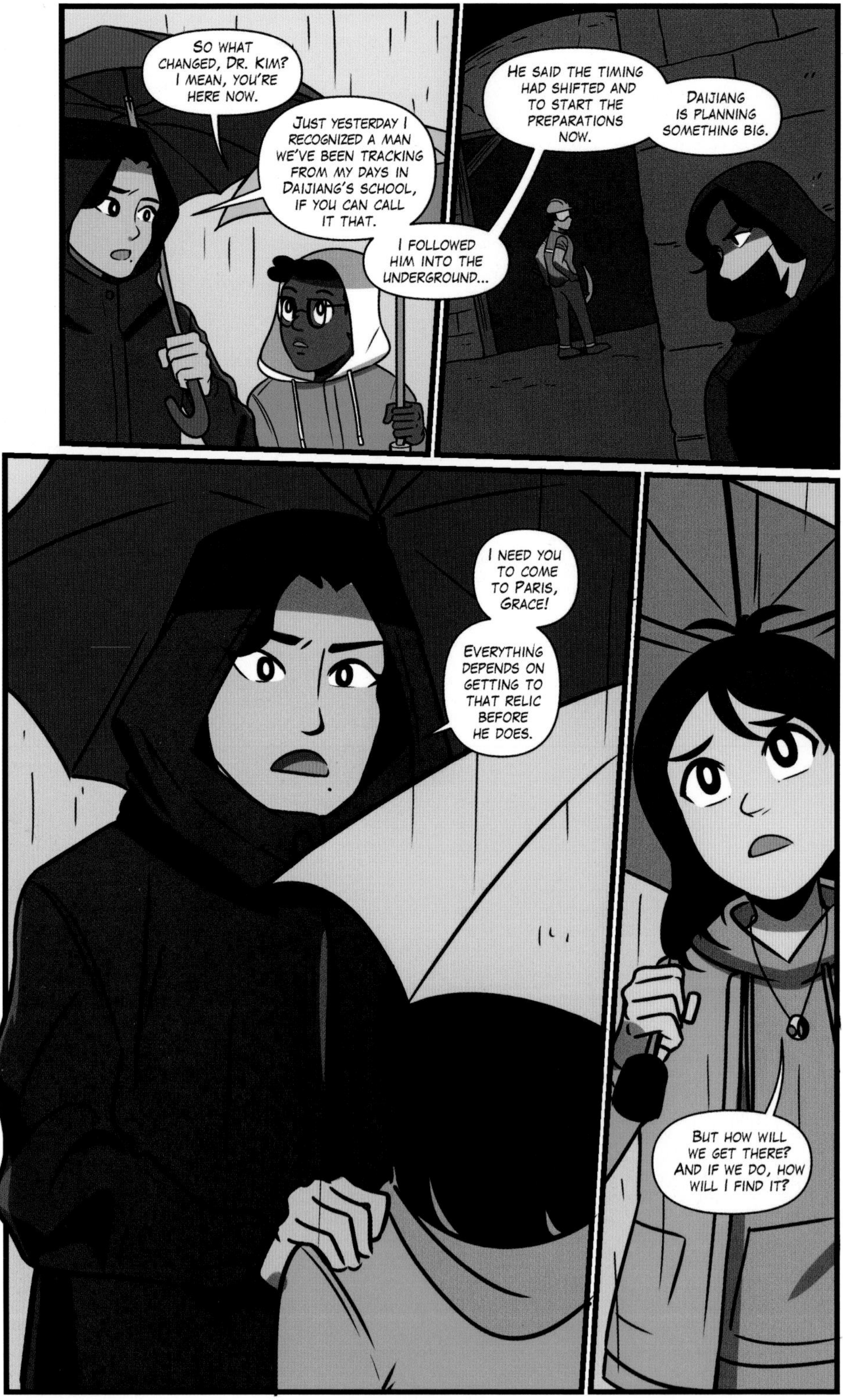
So what changed, Dr. Kim? I mean, you're here now.
Just yesterday I recognized a man we've been tracking from my days in Daijiang's school, if you can call it that.
I followed him into the underground...
He said the timing had shifted and to start the preparations now.
Daijiang is planning something big.
I need you to come to Paris, Grace!
Everything depends on getting to that relic before he does.
But how will we get there? And if we do, how will I find it?

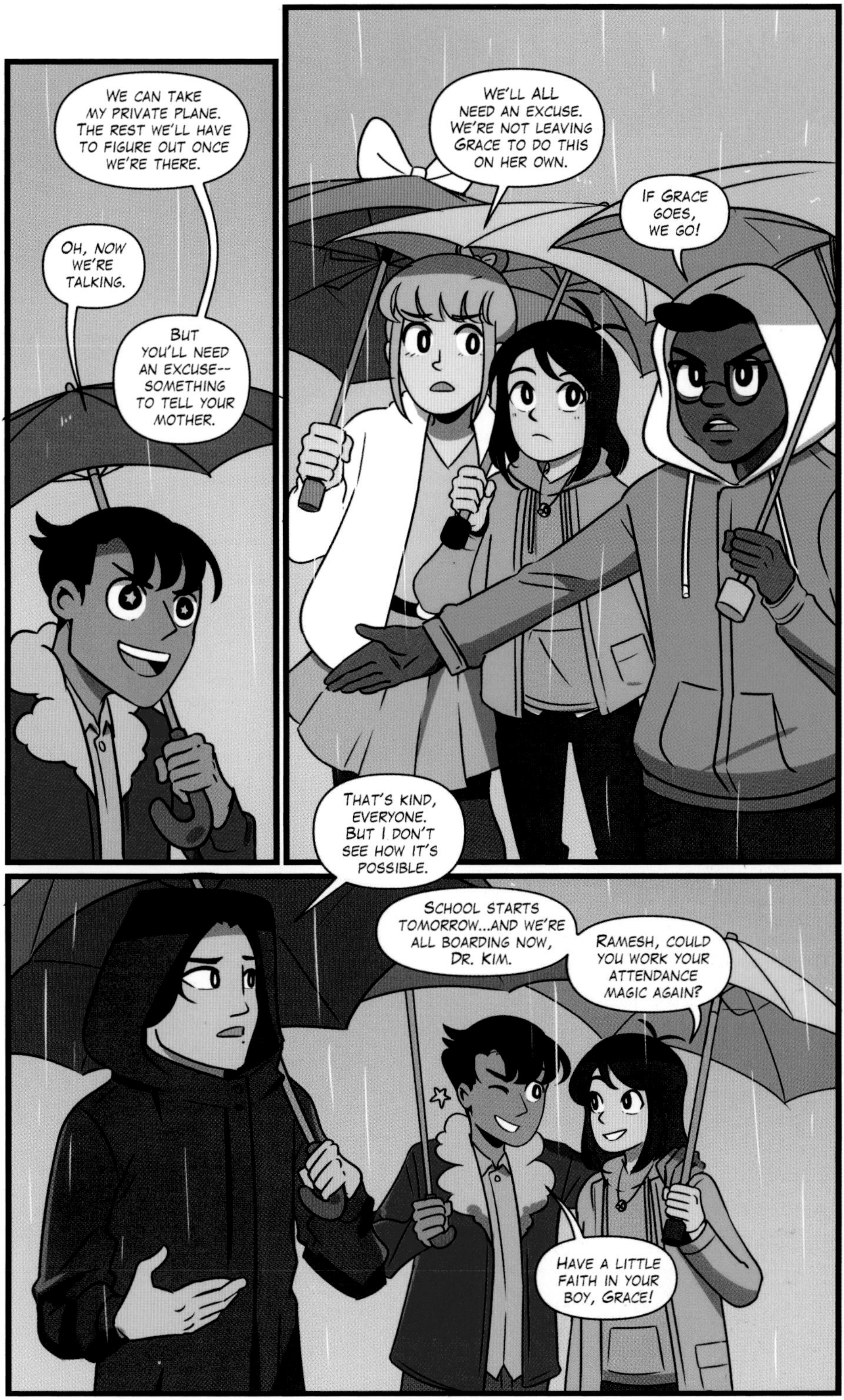
WE CAN TAKE MY PRIVATE PLANE. THE REST WE'LL HAVE TO FIGURE OUT ONCE WE'RE THERE.
OH, NOW WE'RE TALKING.
BUT YOU'LL NEED AN EXCUSE-- SOMETHING TO TELL YOUR MOTHER.
WE'LL ALL NEED AN EXCUSE. WE'RE NOT LEAVING GRACE TO DO THIS ON HER OWN.
IF GRACE GOES, WE GO!
THAT'S KIND, EVERYONE. BUT I DON'T SEE HOW IT'S POSSIBLE.
SCHOOL STARTS TOMORROW...AND WE'RE ALL BOARDING NOW, DR. KIM.
RAMESH, COULD YOU WORK YOUR ATTENDANCE MAGIC AGAIN?
HAVE A LITTLE FAITH IN YOUR BOY, GRACE!

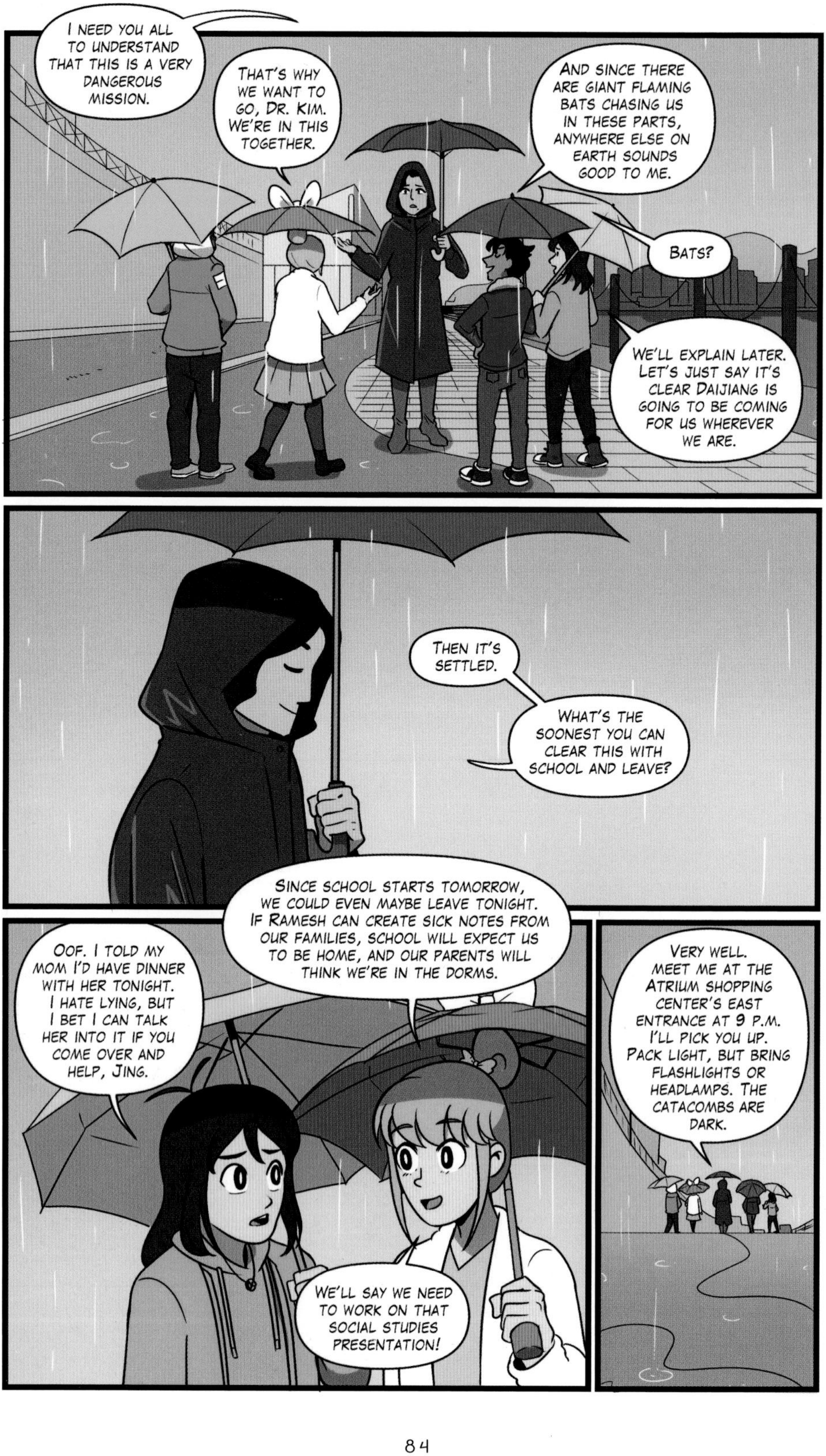
I NEED YOU ALL TO UNDERSTAND THAT THIS IS A VERY DANGEROUS MISSION.
THAT'S WHY WE WANT TO GO, DR. KIM. WE'RE IN THIS TOGETHER.
AND SINCE THERE ARE GIANT FLAMING BATS CHASING US IN THESE PARTS, ANYWHERE ELSE ON EARTH SOUNDS GOOD TO ME.
BATS?
WE'LL EXPLAIN LATER. LET'S JUST SAY IT'S CLEAR DAIJIANG IS GOING TO BE COMING FOR US WHEREVER WE ARE.
THEN IT'S SETTLED.
WHAT'S THE SOONEST YOU CAN CLEAR THIS WITH SCHOOL AND LEAVE?
SINCE SCHOOL STARTS TOMORROW, WE COULD EVEN MAYBE LEAVE TONIGHT. IF RAMESH CAN CREATE SICK NOTES FROM OUR FAMILIES, SCHOOL WILL EXPECT US TO BE HOME, AND OUR PARENTS WILL THINK WE'RE IN THE DORMS.
OOF. I TOLD MY MOM I'D HAVE DINNER WITH HER TONIGHT. I HATE LYING, BUT I BET I CAN TALK HER INTO IT IF YOU COME OVER AND HELP, JING.
WE'LL SAY WE NEED TO WORK ON THAT SOCIAL STUDIES PRESENTATION!
VERY WELL. MEET ME AT THE ATRIUM SHOPPING CENTER'S EAST ENTRANCE AT 9 P.M. I'LL PICK YOU UP. PACK LIGHT, BUT BRING FLASHLIGHTS OR HEADLAMPS. THE CATACOMBS ARE DARK.

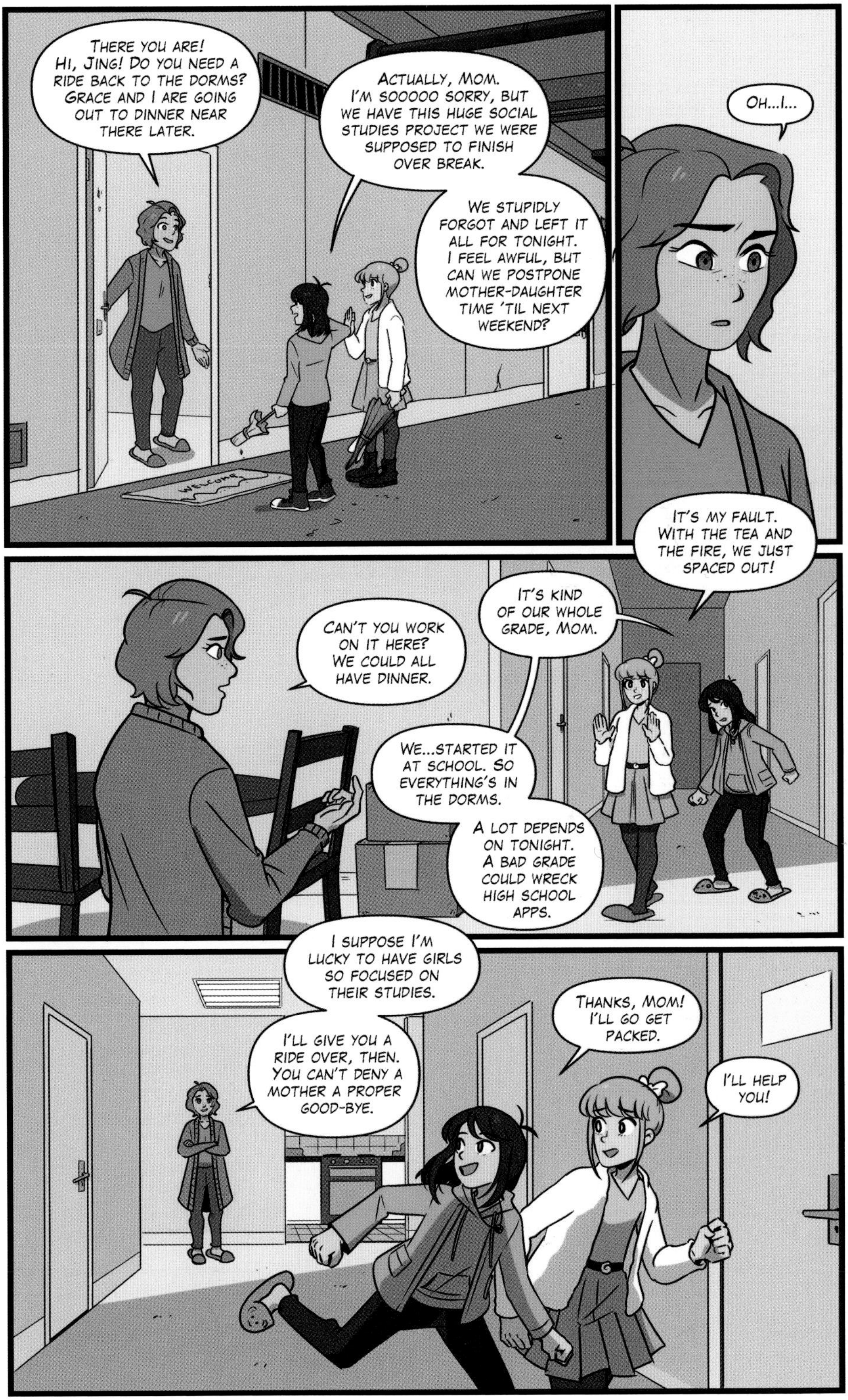

THERE YOU ARE! HI, JING! DO YOU NEED A RIDE BACK TO THE DORMS? GRACE AND I ARE GOING OUT TO DINNER NEAR THERE LATER.
ACTUALLY, MOM. I'M SOOOOO SORRY, BUT WE HAVE THIS HUGE SOCIAL STUDIES PROJECT WE WERE SUPPOSED TO FINISH OVER BREAK.
WE STUPIDLY FORGOT AND LEFT IT ALL FOR TONIGHT. I FEEL AWFUL, BUT CAN WE POSTPONE MOTHER-DAUGHTER TIME 'TIL NEXT WEEKEND?
WELCOME
OH...I...
IT'S MY FAULT. WITH THE TEA AND THE FIRE, WE JUST SPACED OUT!
CAN'T YOU WORK ON IT HERE? WE COULD ALL HAVE DINNER.
IT'S KIND OF OUR WHOLE GRADE, MOM.
WE...STARTED IT AT SCHOOL. SO EVERYTHING'S IN THE DORMS.
A LOT DEPENDS ON TONIGHT. A BAD GRADE COULD WRECK HIGH SCHOOL APPS.
I SUPPOSE I'M LUCKY TO HAVE GIRLS SO FOCUSED ON THEIR STUDIES.
I'LL GIVE YOU A RIDE OVER, THEN. YOU CAN'T DENY A MOTHER A PROPER GOOD-BYE.
THANKS, MOM! I'LL GO GET PACKED.
I'LL HELP YOU!

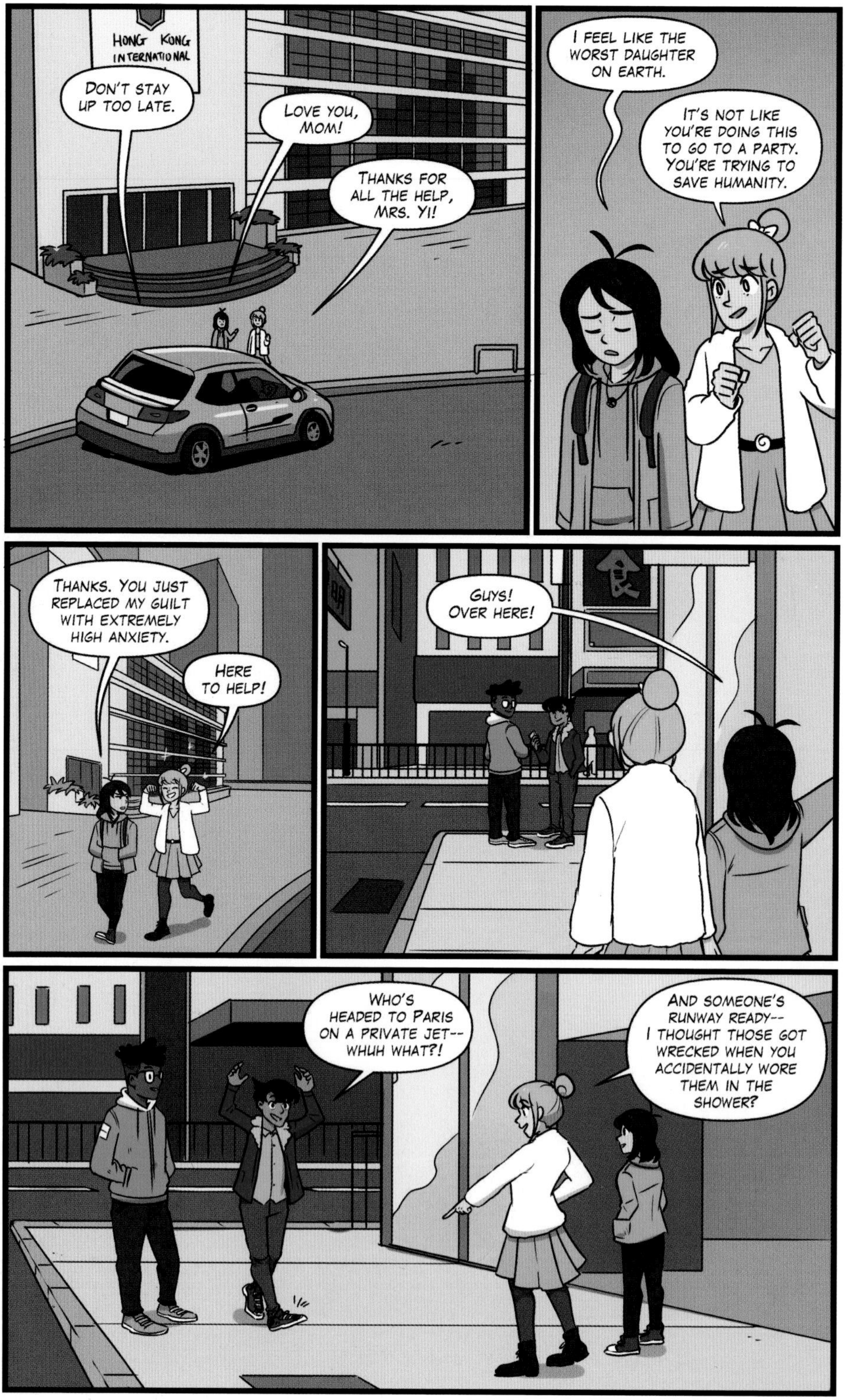
HONG KONG INTERNATIONAL
DON'T STAY UP TOO LATE.
LOVE YOU, MOM!
THANKS FOR ALL THE HELP, MRS. YI!
I FEEL LIKE THE WORST DAUGHTER ON EARTH.
IT'S NOT LIKE YOU'RE DOING THIS TO GO TO A PARTY. YOU'RE TRYING TO SAVE HUMANITY.
THANKS. YOU JUST REPLACED MY GUILT WITH EXTREMELY HIGH ANXIETY.
HERE TO HELP!
GUYS! OVER HERE!
WHO'S HEADED TO PARIS ON A PRIVATE JET-- WHUH WHAT?!
AND SOMEONE'S RUNWAY READY-- I THOUGHT THOSE GOT WRECKED WHEN YOU ACCIDENTALLY WORE THEM IN THE SHOWER?

OOOH, LOOK WHAT YOU MADE ME DO! LOOK WHAT YOU MADE ME--

NOOOOOOO!

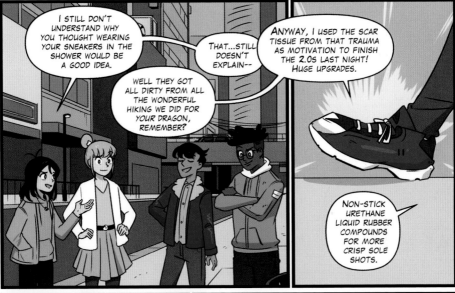

I STILL DON'T UNDERSTAND WHY YOU THOUGHT WEARING YOUR SNEAKERS IN THE SHOWER WOULD BE A GOOD IDEA.

THAT...STILL DOESN'T EXPLAIN--

WELL THEY GOT ALL DIRTY FROM ALL THE WONDERFUL HIKING WE DID FOR YOUR DRAGON, REMEMBER?

ANYWAY, I USED THE SCAR TISSUE FROM THAT TRAUMA AS MOTIVATION TO FINISH THE 2.0S LAST NIGHT! HUGE UPGRADES.

NON-STICK URETHANE LIQUID RUBBER COMPOUNDS FOR MORE CRISP SOLE SHOTS.

SAY STINKY FRENCH CHEESE!

RAMESH.

BUT HERE'S THE TRUE WIZARDRY... SMOKE SCREEN!

SMOKE SCREEN?

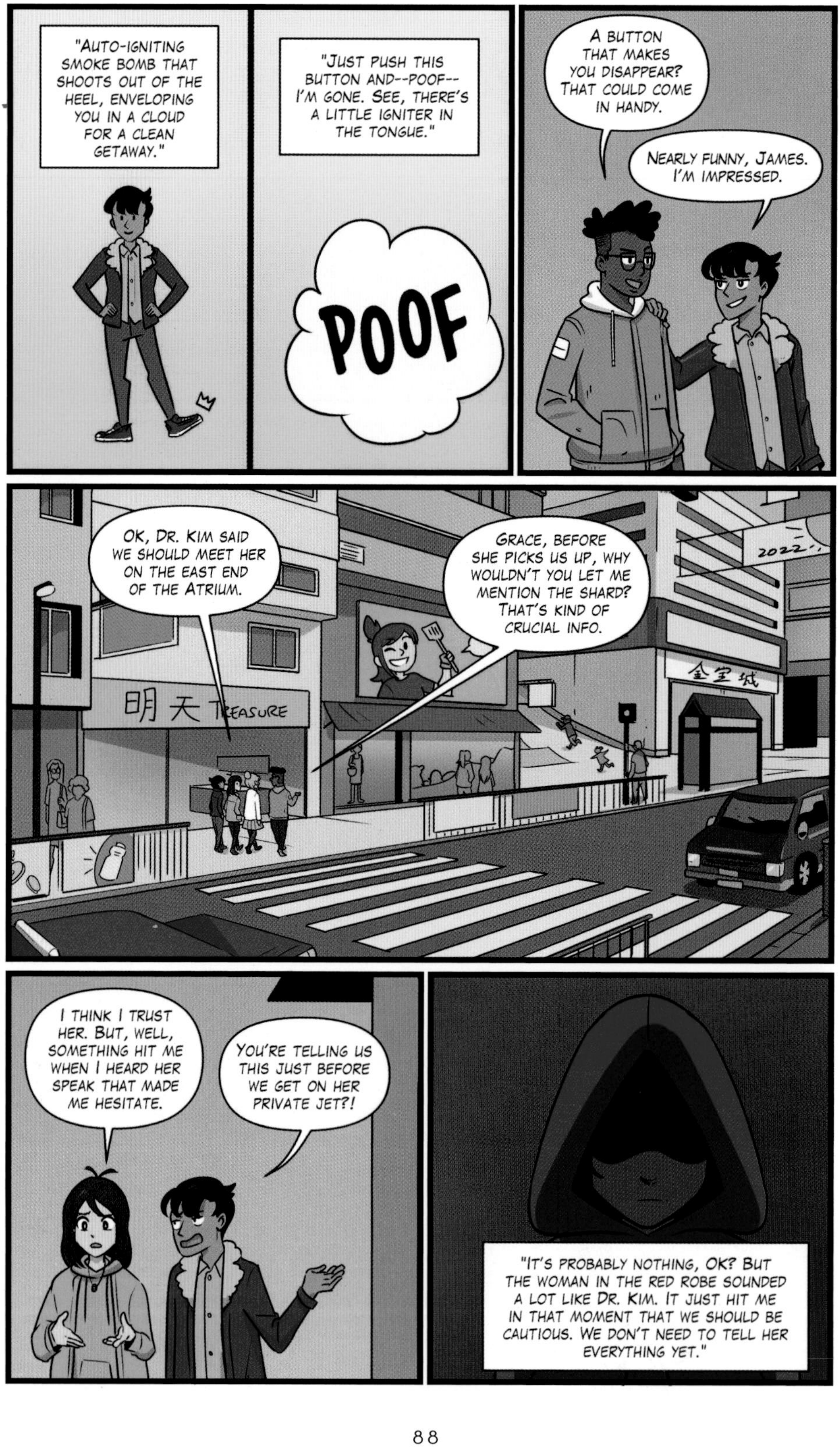
"AUTO-IGNITING SMOKE BOMB THAT SHOOTS OUT OF THE HEEL, ENVELOPING YOU IN A CLOUD FOR A CLEAN GETAWAY."
"JUST PUSH THIS BUTTON AND--POOF--I'M GONE. SEE, THERE'S A LITTLE IGNITER IN THE TONGUE."
POOF
A BUTTON THAT MAKES YOU DISAPPEAR? THAT COULD COME IN HANDY.
NEARLY FUNNY, JAMES. I'M IMPRESSED.
OK, DR. KIM SAID WE SHOULD MEET HER ON THE EAST END OF THE ATRIUM.
GRACE, BEFORE SHE PICKS US UP, WHY WOULDN'T YOU LET ME MENTION THE SHARD? THAT'S KIND OF CRUCIAL INFO.
明天 TREASURE
金宝城
2022
I THINK I TRUST HER. BUT, WELL, SOMETHING HIT ME WHEN I HEARD HER SPEAK THAT MADE ME HESITATE.
YOU'RE TELLING US THIS JUST BEFORE WE GET ON HER PRIVATE JET?!
"IT'S PROBABLY NOTHING, OK? BUT THE WOMAN IN THE RED ROBE SOUNDED A LOT LIKE DR. KIM. IT JUST HIT ME IN THAT MOMENT THAT WE SHOULD BE CAUTIOUS. WE DON'T NEED TO TELL HER EVERYTHING YET."

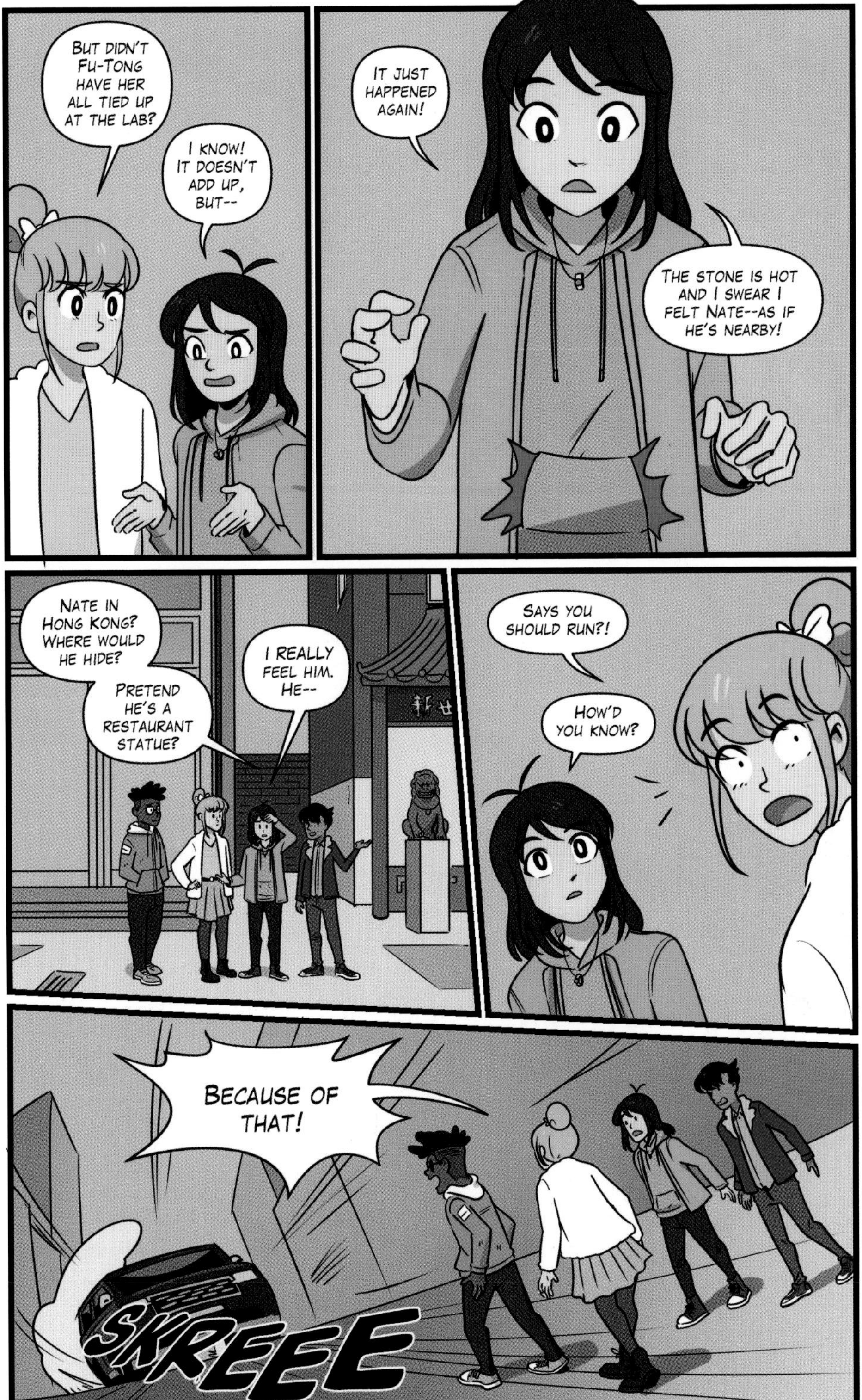
But didn't Fu-Tong have her all tied up at the lab?
I know! It doesn't add up, but--
It just happened again!
The stone is hot and I swear I felt Nate--as if he's nearby!
Nate in Hong Kong? Where would he hide?
Pretend he's a restaurant statue?
I really feel him. He--
Says you should run?!
How'd you know?
Because of that!
SKREEE

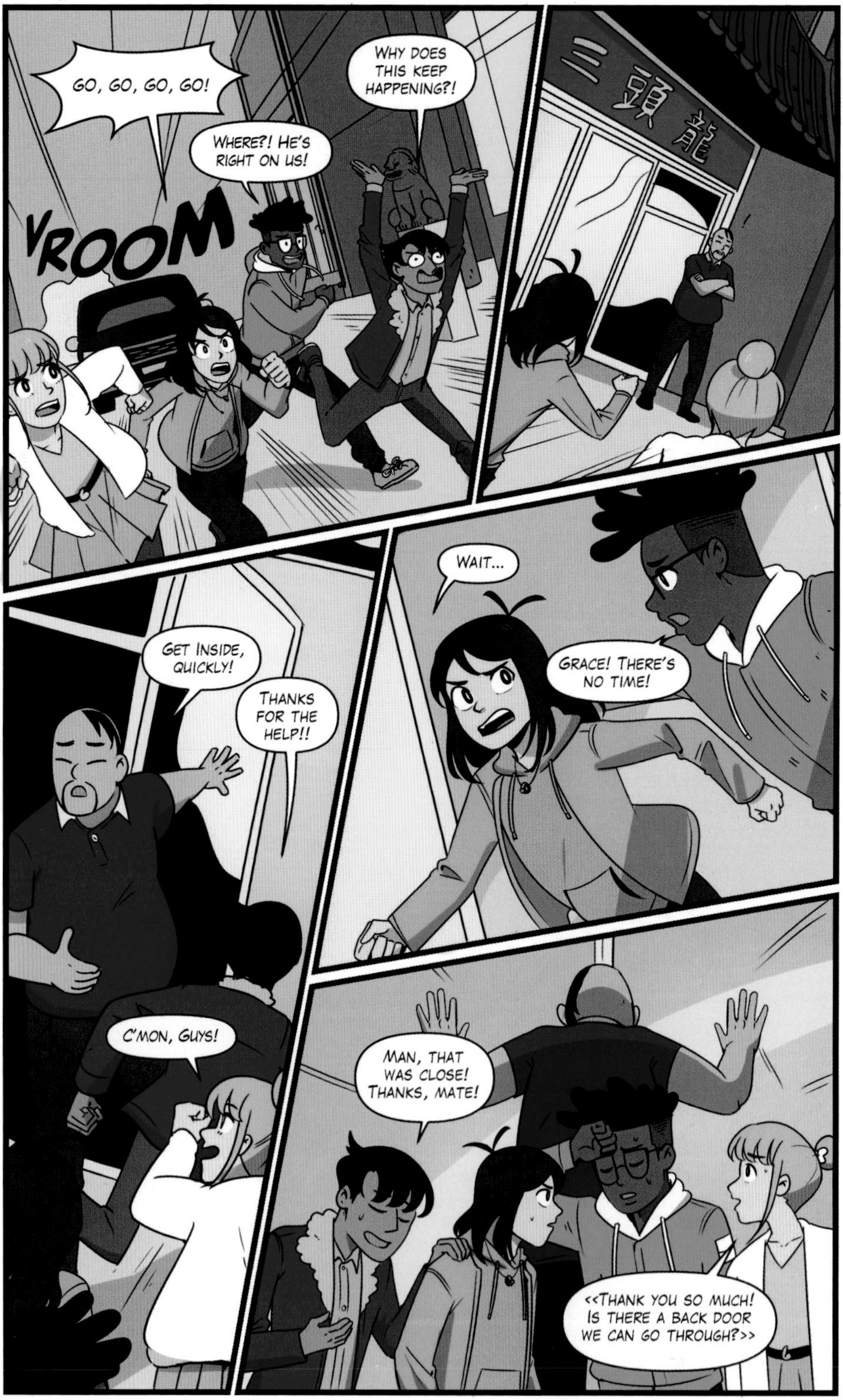
GO, GO, GO, GO!
WHERE?! HE'S RIGHT ON US!
WHY DOES THIS KEEP HAPPENING?!
VROOM
三頭龍
WAIT...
GRACE! THERE'S NO TIME!
GET INSIDE, QUICKLY!
THANKS FOR THE HELP!!
C'MON, GUYS!
MAN, THAT WAS CLOSE! THANKS, MATE!
<<THANK YOU SO MUCH! IS THERE A BACK DOOR WE CAN GO THROUGH?>>

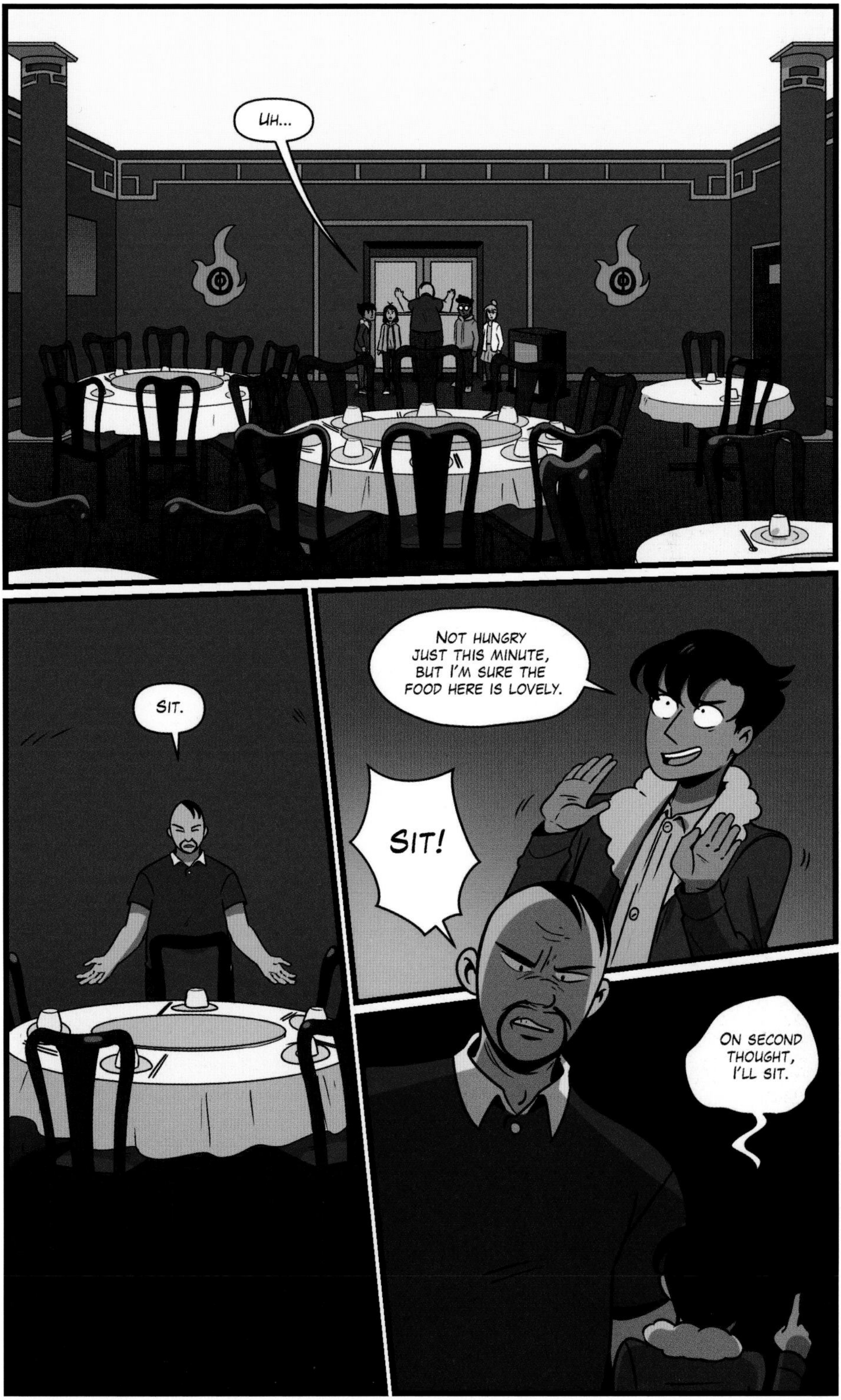
UH...
SIT.
NOT HUNGRY JUST THIS MINUTE, BUT I'M SURE THE FOOD HERE IS LOVELY.
SIT!
ON SECOND THOUGHT, I'LL SIT.

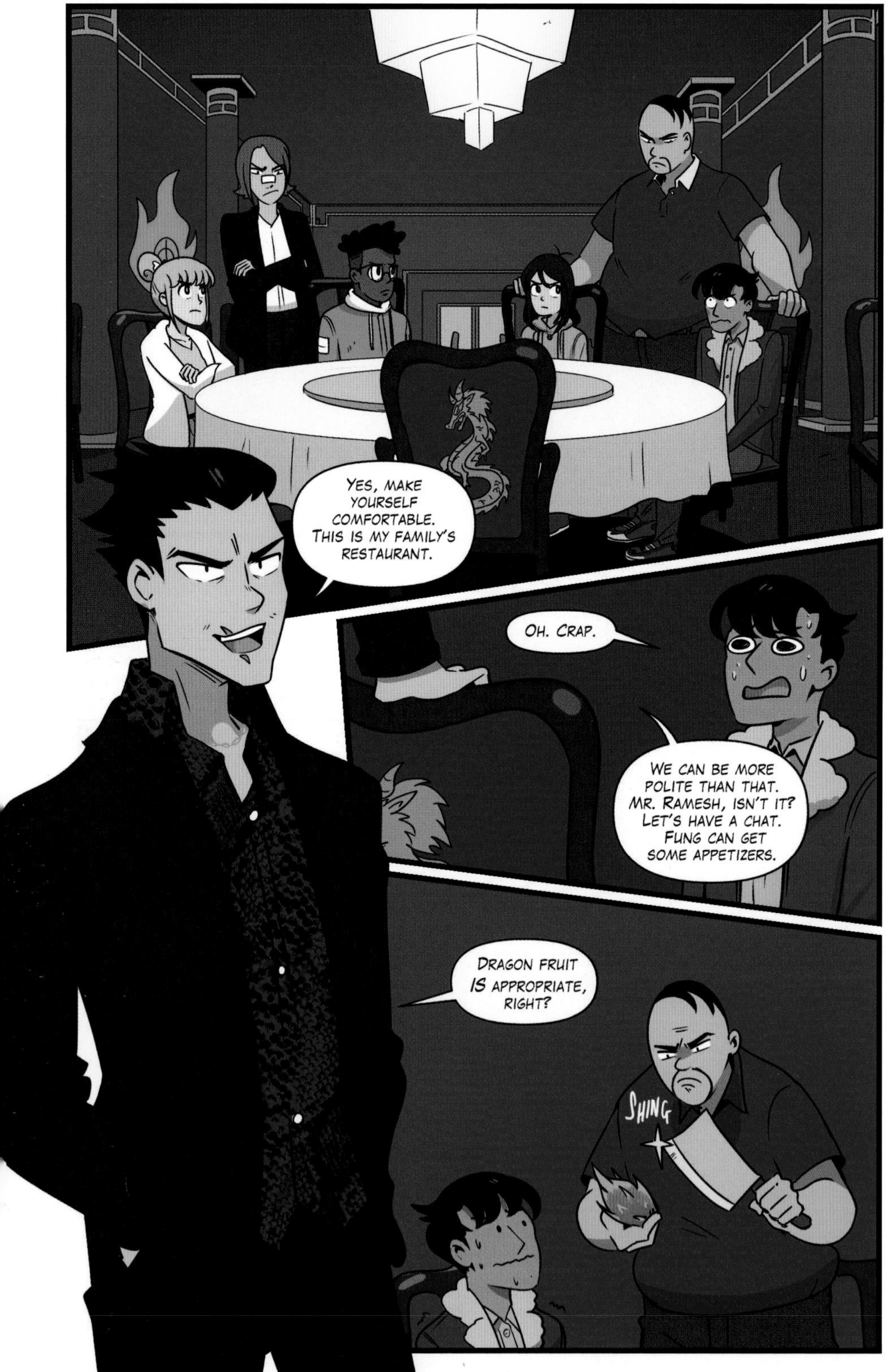
YES, MAKE YOURSELF COMFORTABLE. THIS IS MY FAMILY'S RESTAURANT.
OH. CRAP.
WE CAN BE MORE POLITE THAN THAT. MR. RAMESH, ISN'T IT? LET'S HAVE A CHAT. FUNG CAN GET SOME APPETIZERS.
DRAGON FRUIT IS APPROPRIATE, RIGHT?
SHING

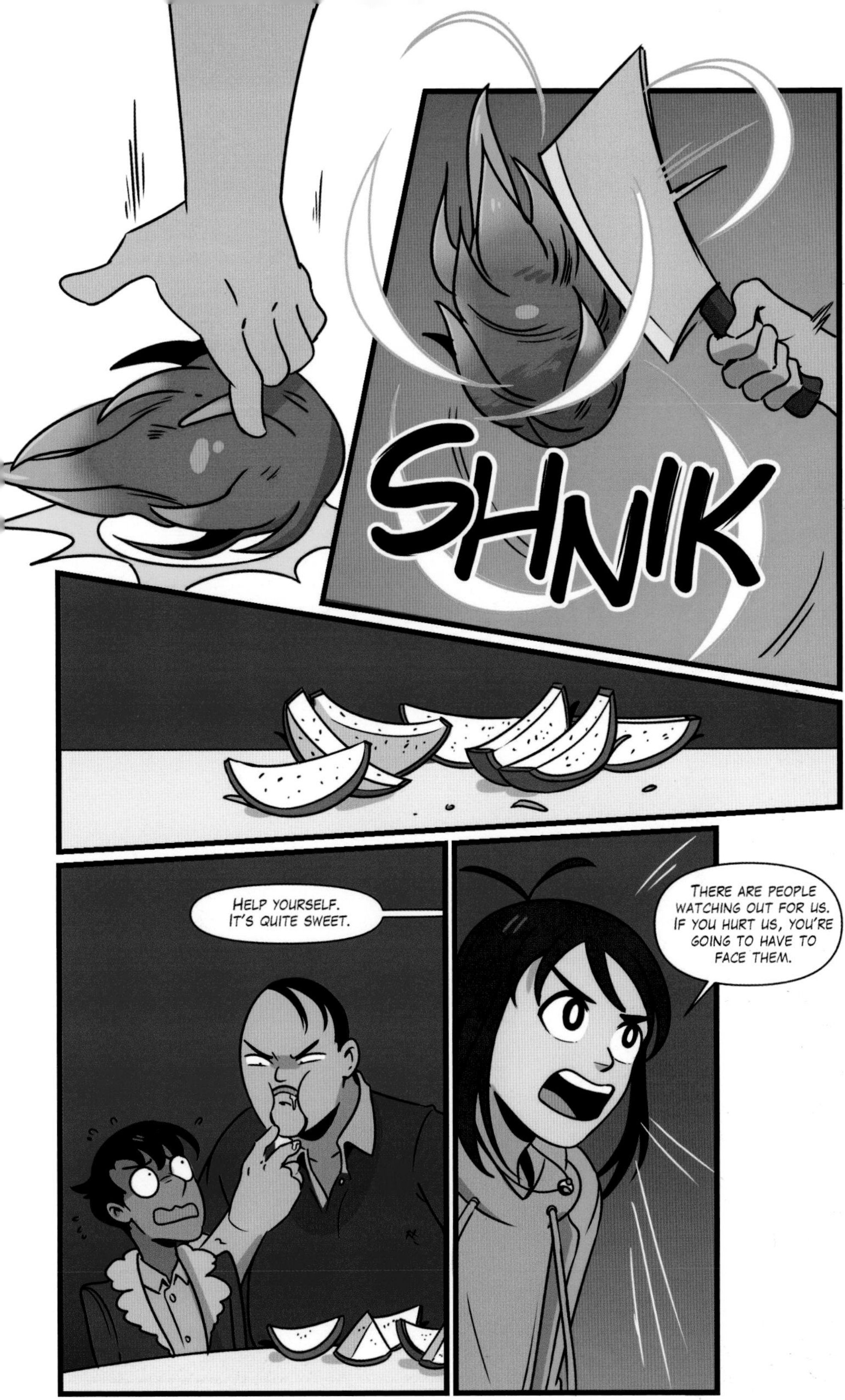
SHNIK
HELP YOURSELF. IT'S QUITE SWEET.
THERE ARE PEOPLE WATCHING OUT FOR US. IF YOU HURT US, YOU'RE GOING TO HAVE TO FACE THEM.

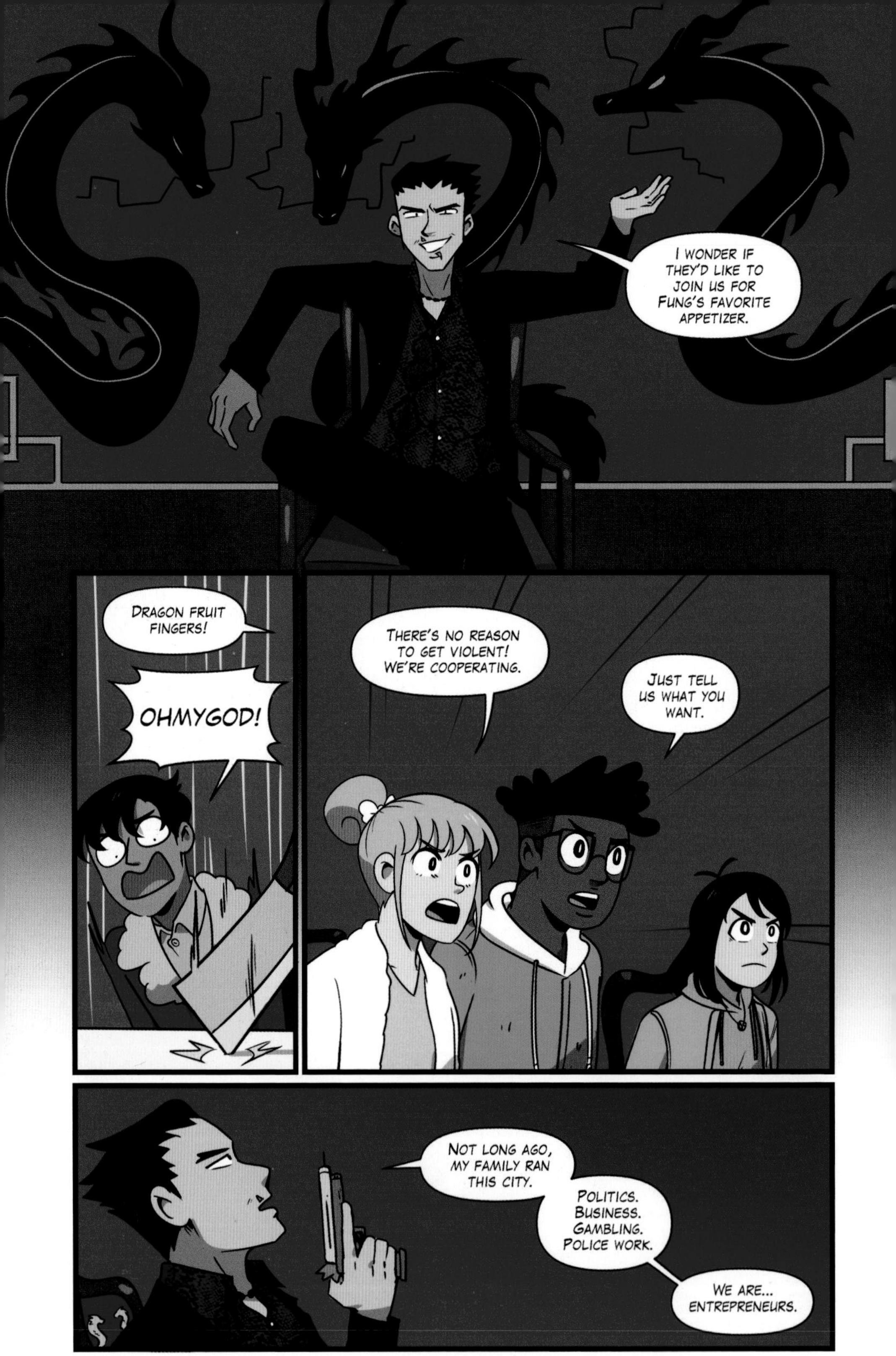
I WONDER IF THEY'D LIKE TO JOIN US FOR FUNG'S FAVORITE APPETIZER.
DRAGON FRUIT FINGERS!
OHMYGOD!
THERE'S NO REASON TO GET VIOLENT! WE'RE COOPERATING.
JUST TELL US WHAT YOU WANT.
NOT LONG AGO, MY FAMILY RAN THIS CITY.
POLITICS. BUSINESS. GAMBLING. POLICE WORK.
WE ARE... ENTREPRENEURS.

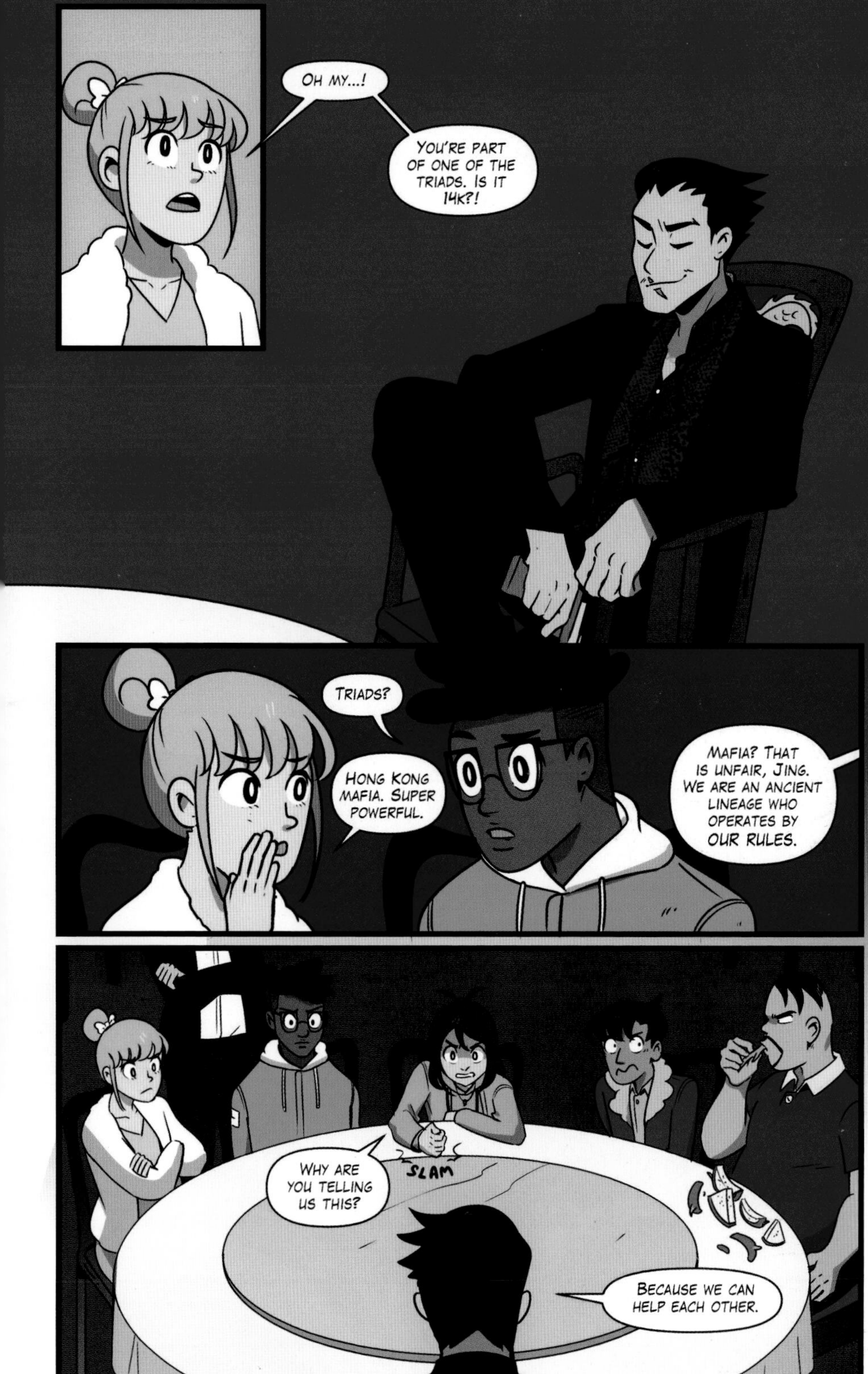
OH MY...!
YOU'RE PART OF ONE OF THE TRIADS. IS IT 14K?!
TRIADS?
HONG KONG MAFIA. SUPER POWERFUL.
MAFIA? THAT IS UNFAIR, JING. WE ARE AN ANCIENT LINEAGE WHO OPERATES BY OUR RULES.
SLAM
WHY ARE YOU TELLING US THIS?
BECAUSE WE CAN HELP EACH OTHER.

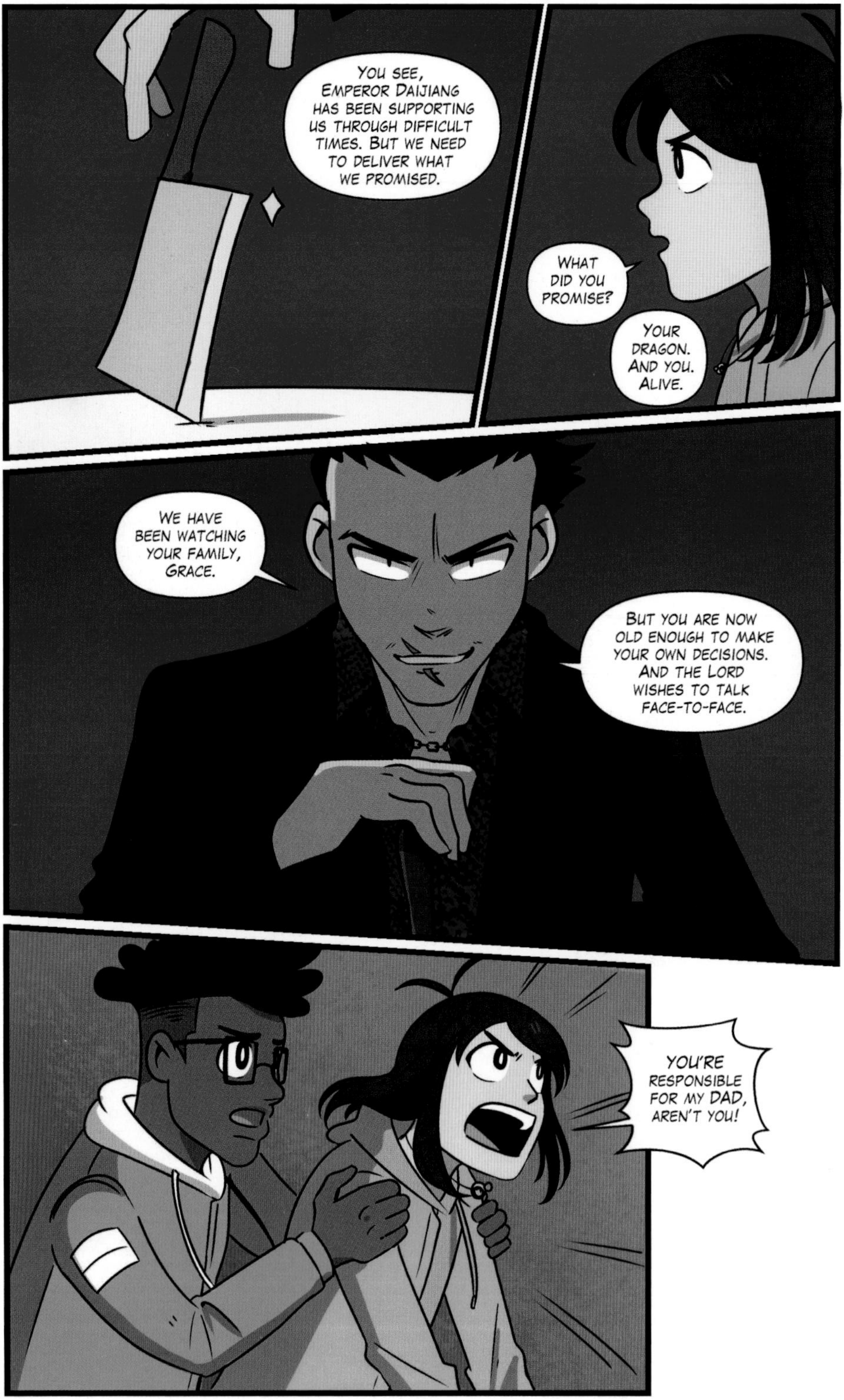
You see, Emperor Daijiang has been supporting us through difficult times. But we need to deliver what we promised.
What did you promise?
Your dragon. And you. Alive.
We have been watching your family, Grace.
But you are now old enough to make your own decisions. And the Lord wishes to talk face-to-face.
You're responsible for my DAD, aren't you!

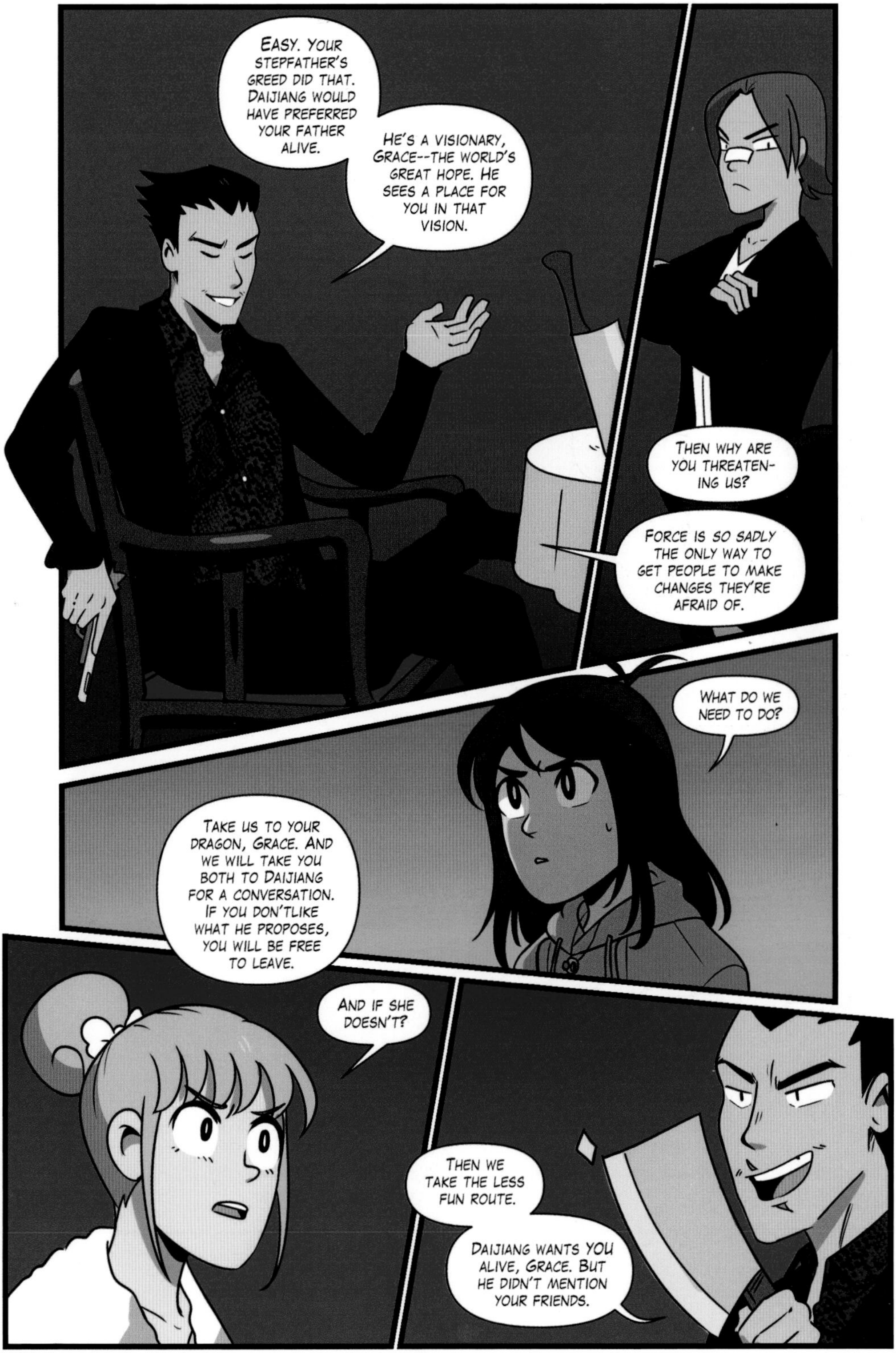
EASY. YOUR STEPFATHER'S GREED DID THAT. DAIJIANG WOULD HAVE PREFERRED YOUR FATHER ALIVE.
HE'S A VISIONARY, GRACE--THE WORLD'S GREAT HOPE. HE SEES A PLACE FOR YOU IN THAT VISION.
THEN WHY ARE YOU THREATEN-ING US?
FORCE IS SO SADLY THE ONLY WAY TO GET PEOPLE TO MAKE CHANGES THEY'RE AFRAID OF.
WHAT DO WE NEED TO DO?
TAKE US TO YOUR DRAGON, GRACE. AND WE WILL TAKE YOU BOTH TO DAIJIANG FOR A CONVERSATION. IF YOU DON'TLIKE WHAT HE PROPOSES, YOU WILL BE FREE TO LEAVE.
AND IF SHE DOESN'T?
THEN WE TAKE THE LESS FUN ROUTE.
DAIJIANG WANTS YOU ALIVE, GRACE. BUT HE DIDN'T MENTION YOUR FRIENDS.

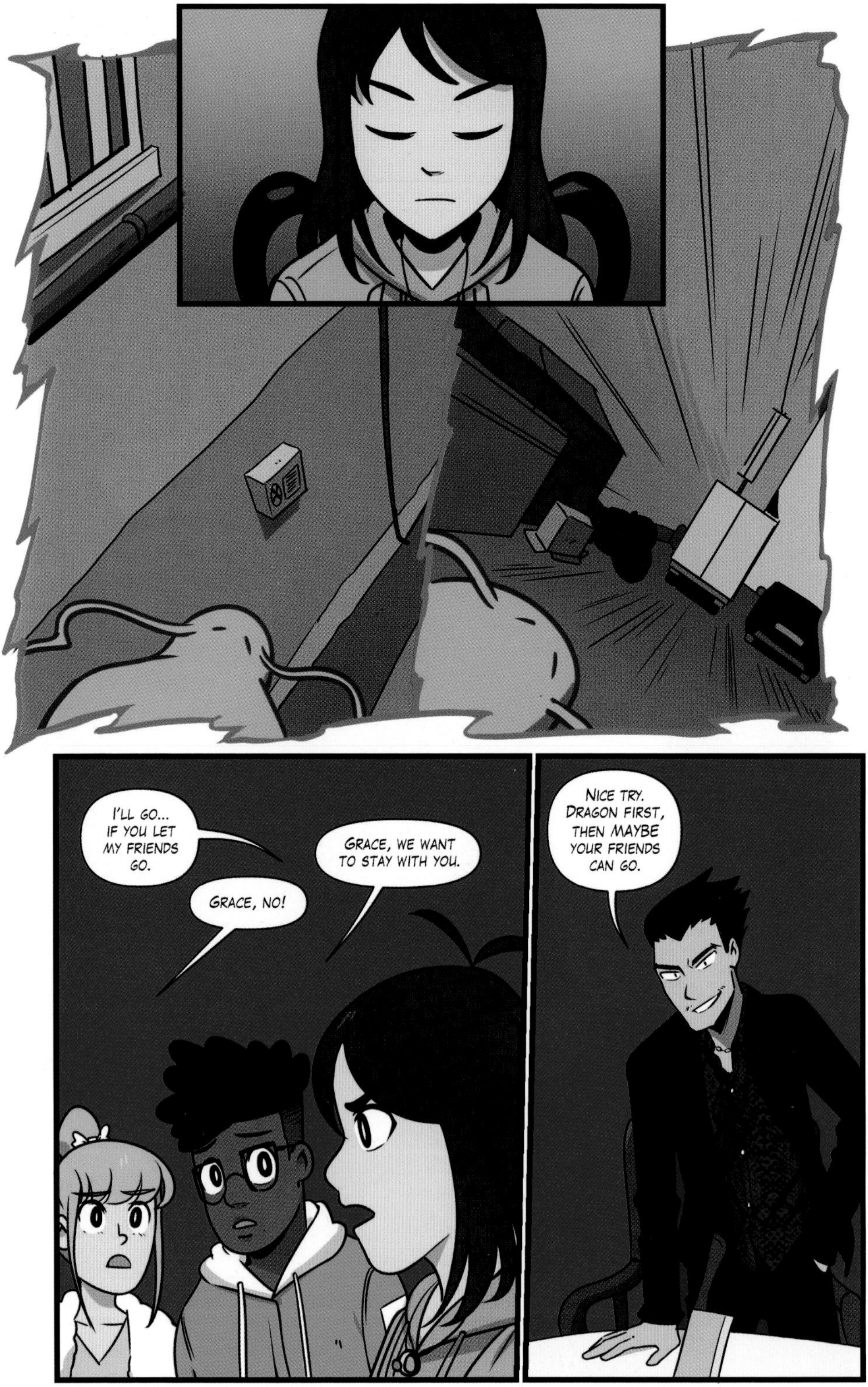

I'LL GO... IF YOU LET MY FRIENDS GO.
GRACE, NO!
GRACE, WE WANT TO STAY WITH YOU.
NICE TRY. DRAGON FIRST, THEN MAYBE YOUR FRIENDS CAN GO.

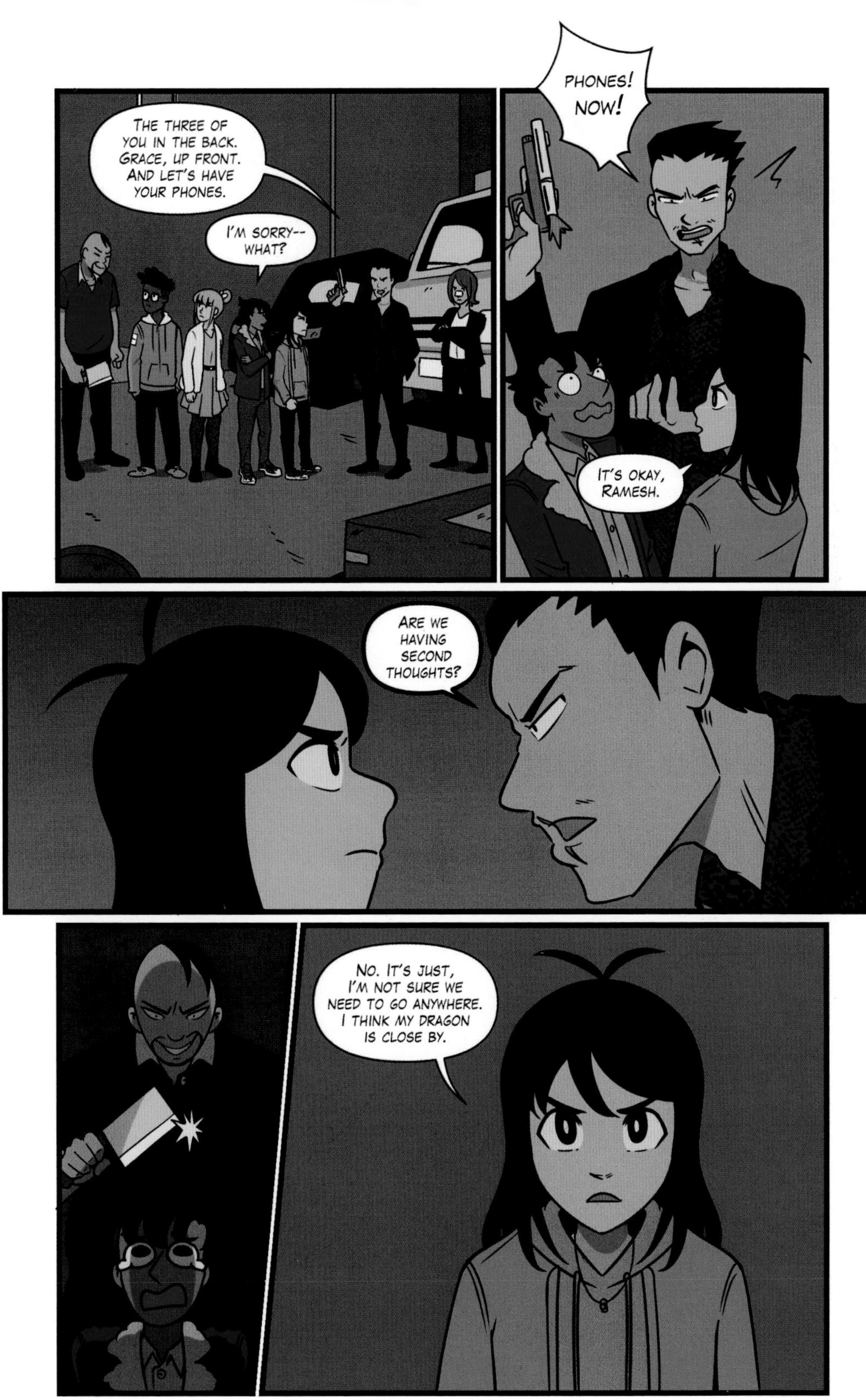
THE THREE OF YOU IN THE BACK. GRACE, UP FRONT. AND LET'S HAVE YOUR PHONES.
I'M SORRY-- WHAT?
PHONES! NOW!
IT'S OKAY, RAMESH.
ARE WE HAVING SECOND THOUGHTS?
NO. IT'S JUST, I'M NOT SURE WE NEED TO GO ANYWHERE. I THINK MY DRAGON IS CLOSE BY.

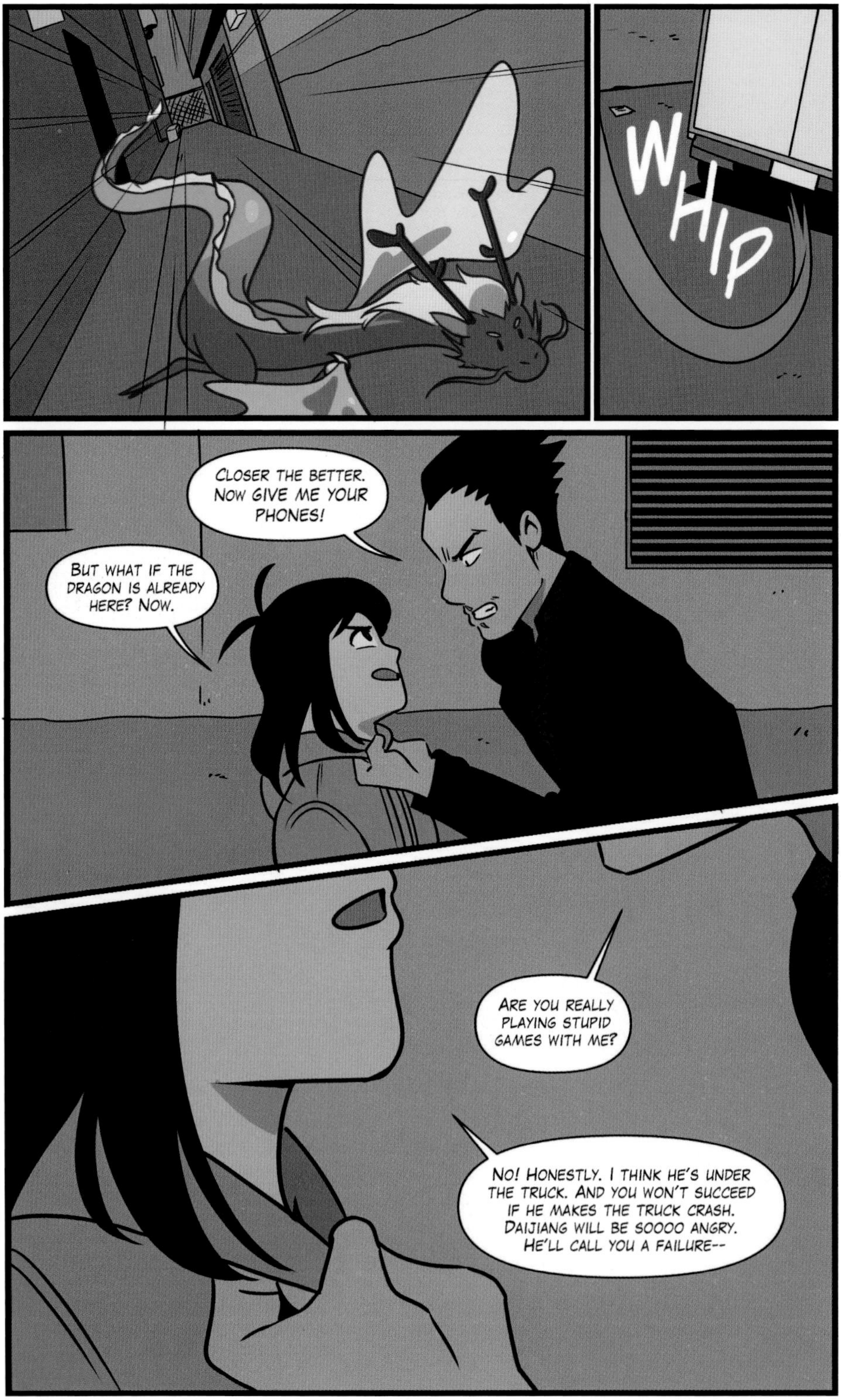
WHIP
CLOSER THE BETTER. NOW GIVE ME YOUR PHONES!
BUT WHAT IF THE DRAGON IS ALREADY HERE? NOW.
ARE YOU REALLY PLAYING STUPID GAMES WITH ME?
NO! HONESTLY. I THINK HE'S UNDER THE TRUCK. AND YOU WON'T SUCCEED IF HE MAKES THE TRUCK CRASH. DAIJIANG WILL BE SOOOO ANGRY. HE'LL CALL YOU A FAILURE--

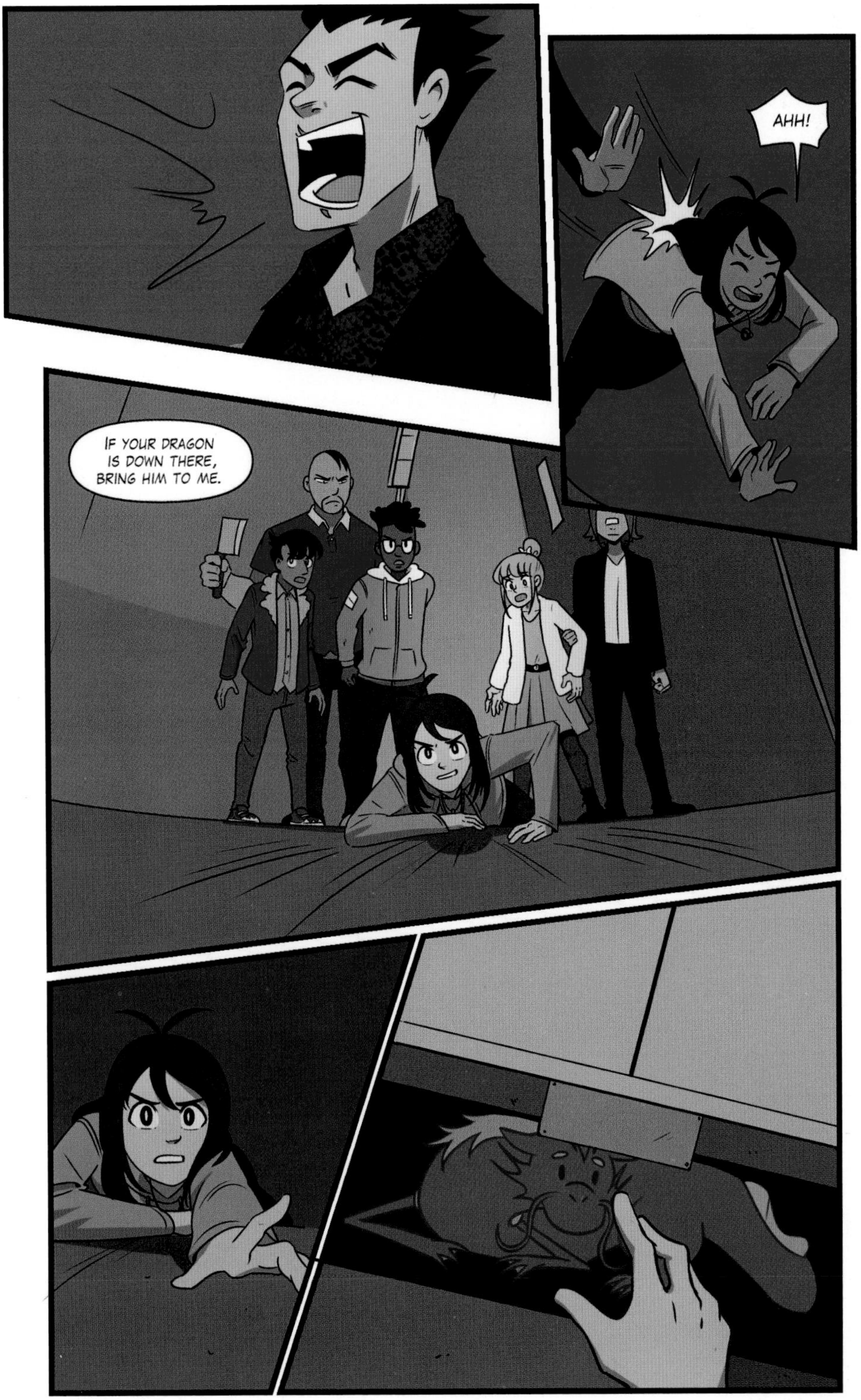
AHH!
IF YOUR DRAGON IS DOWN THERE, BRING HIM TO ME.

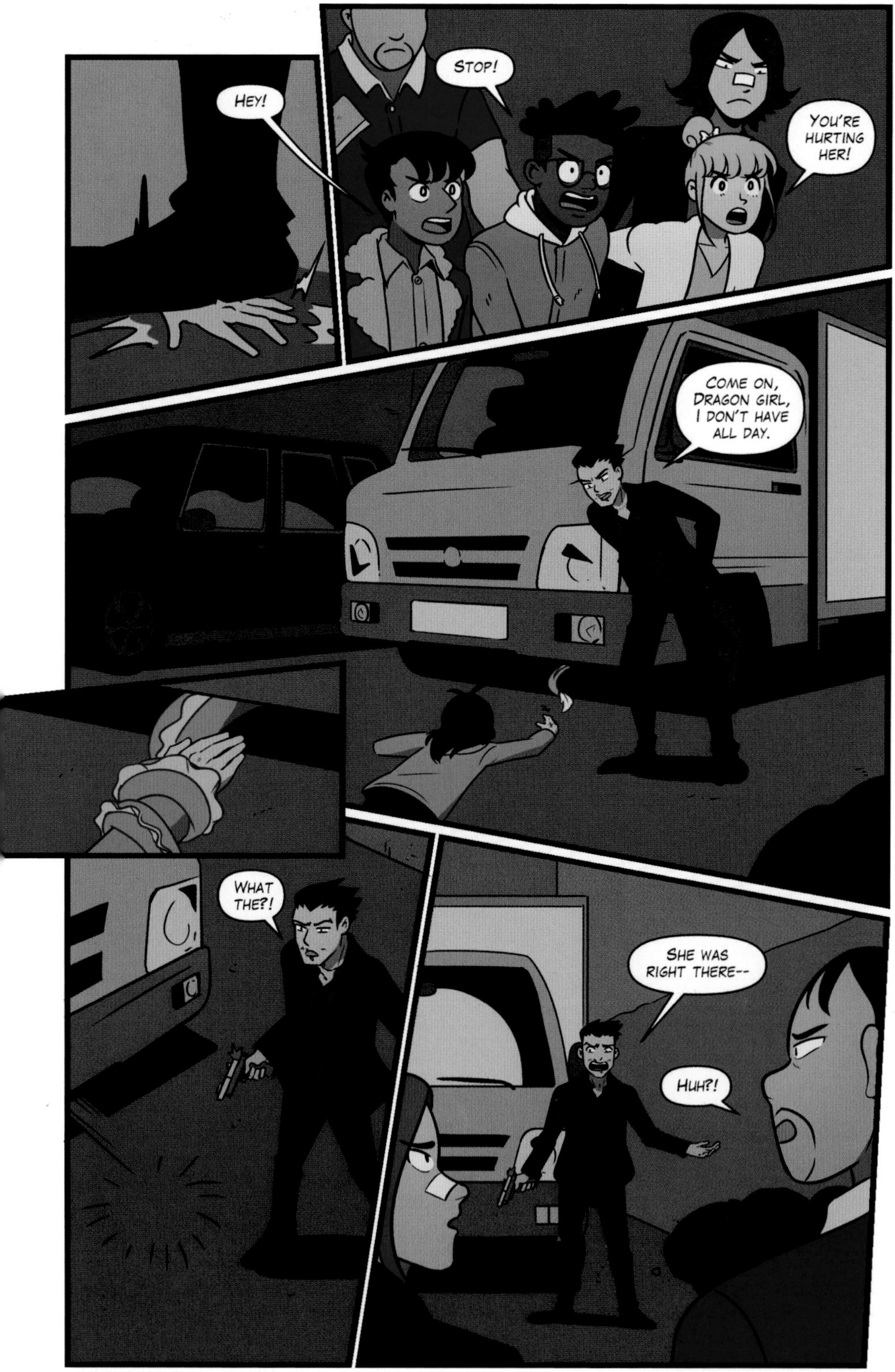
Hey!
Stop!
You're hurting her!
Come on, Dragon girl, I don't have all day.
What the?!
She was right there--
Huh?!

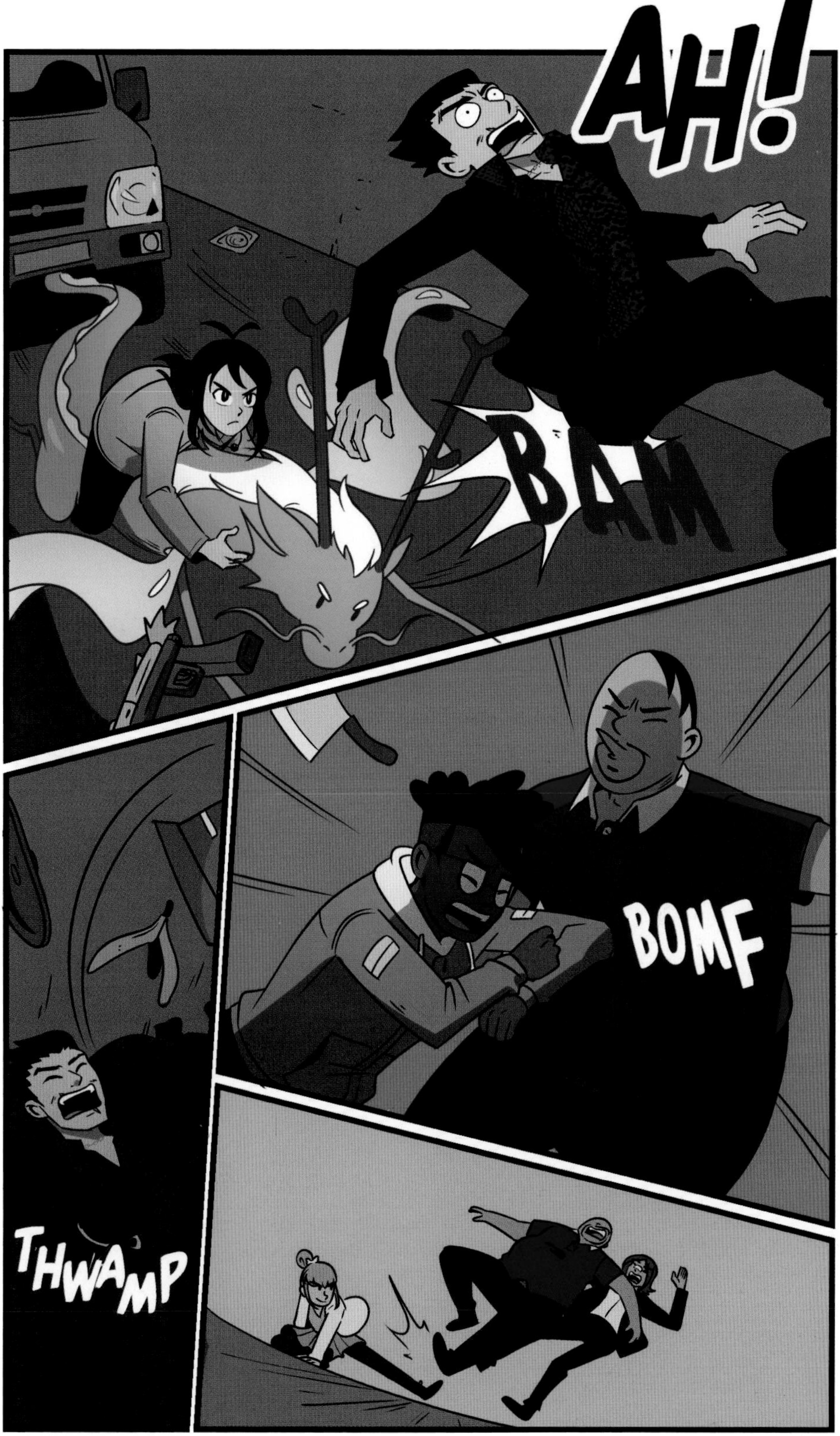
AH!
BAM
BOMF
THWAMP

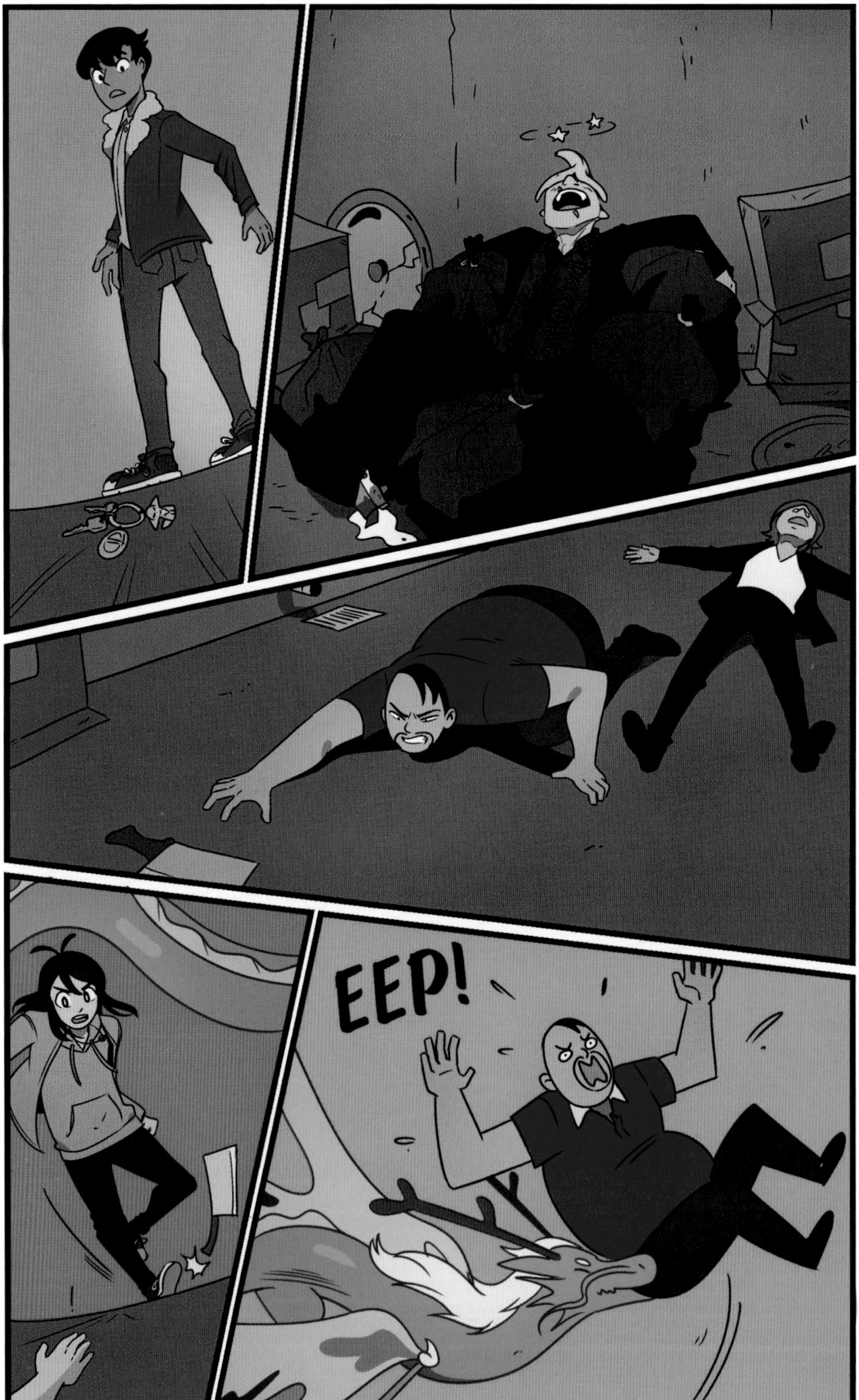
EEP!

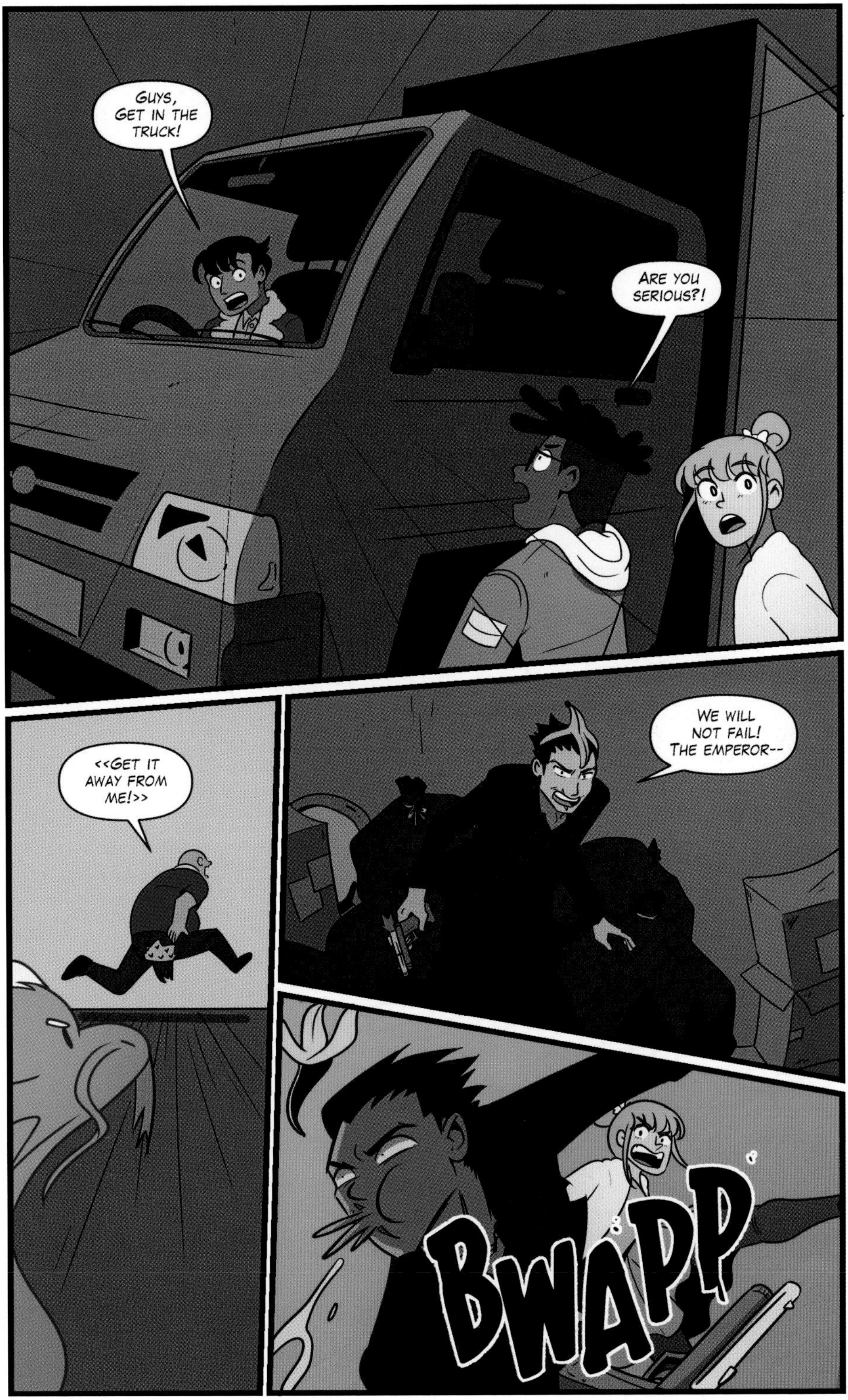
GUYS, GET IN THE TRUCK!
ARE YOU SERIOUS?!
<<GET IT AWAY FROM ME!>>
WE WILL NOT FAIL! THE EMPEROR--
BWAPP

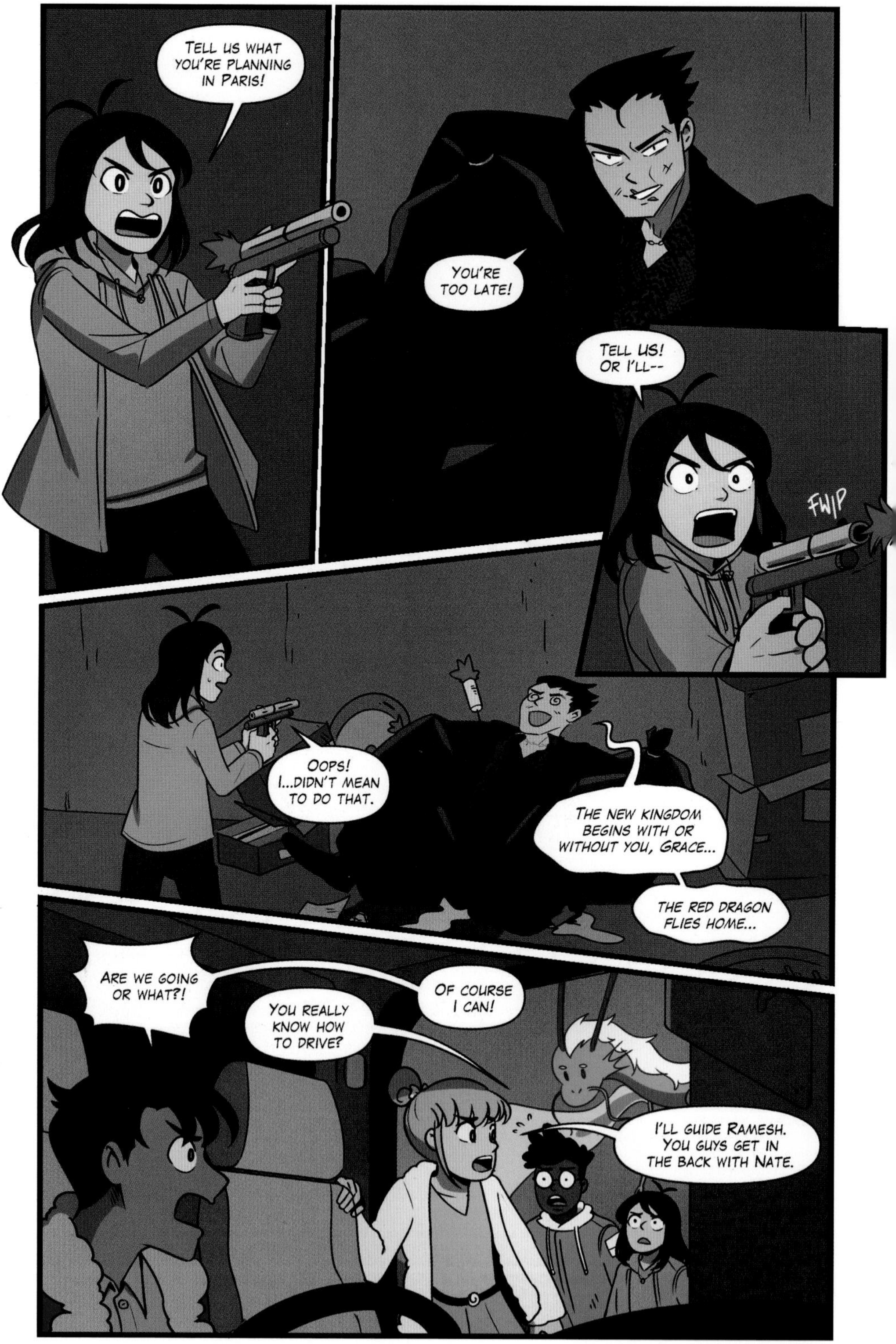
TELL US WHAT YOU'RE PLANNING IN PARIS!
YOU'RE TOO LATE!
TELL US! OR I'LL--
FWIP
OOPS! I...DIDN'T MEAN TO DO THAT.
THE NEW KINGDOM BEGINS WITH OR WITHOUT YOU, GRACE...
THE RED DRAGON FLIES HOME...
ARE WE GOING OR WHAT?!
YOU REALLY KNOW HOW TO DRIVE?
OF COURSE I CAN!
I'LL GUIDE RAMESH. YOU GUYS GET IN THE BACK WITH NATE.

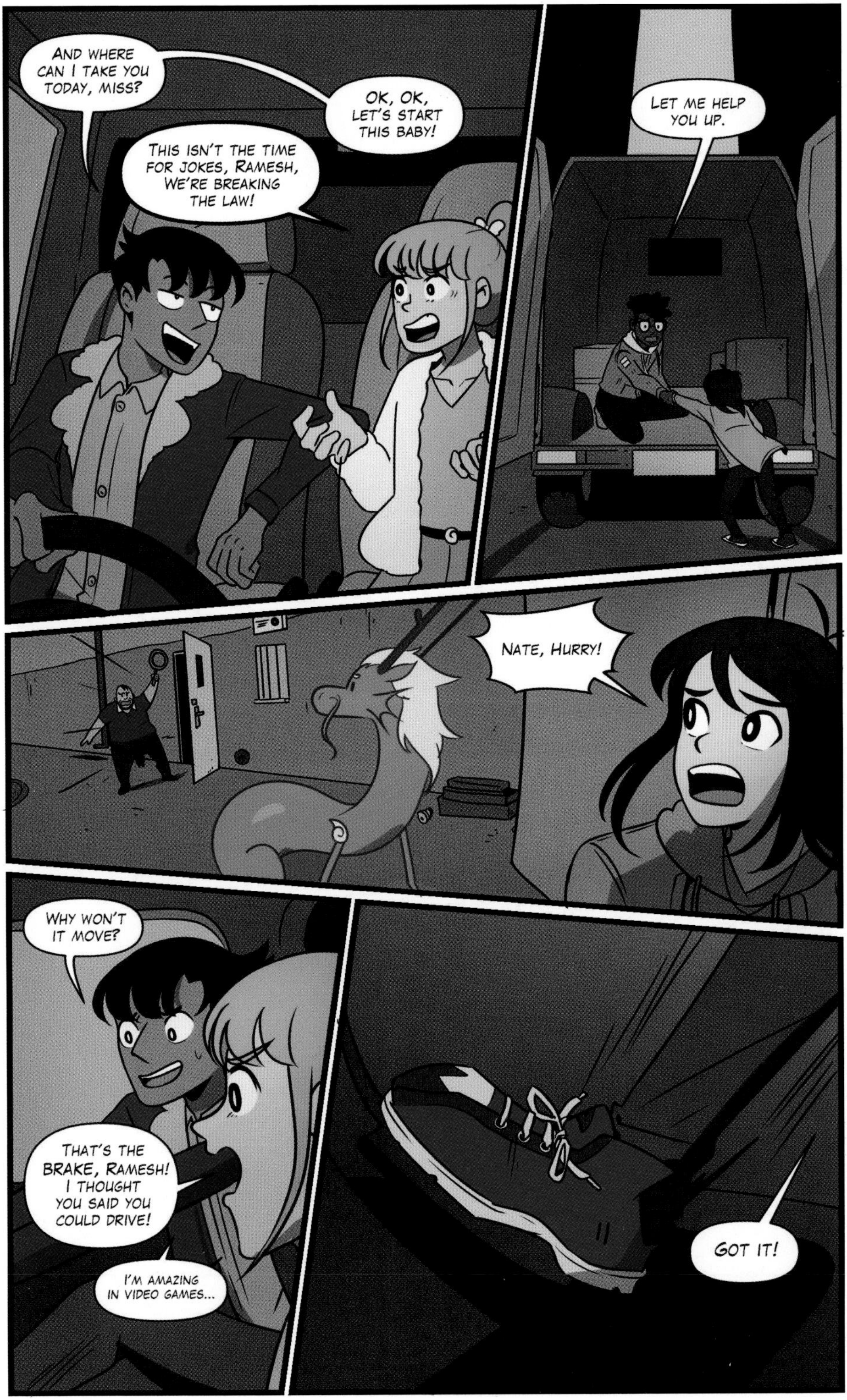
AND WHERE CAN I TAKE YOU TODAY, MISS?
THIS ISN'T THE TIME FOR JOKES, RAMESH, WE'RE BREAKING THE LAW!
OK, OK, LET'S START THIS BABY!
LET ME HELP YOU UP.
NATE, HURRY!
WHY WON'T IT MOVE?
THAT'S THE BRAKE, RAMESH! I THOUGHT YOU SAID YOU COULD DRIVE!
I'M AMAZING IN VIDEO GAMES...
GOT IT!

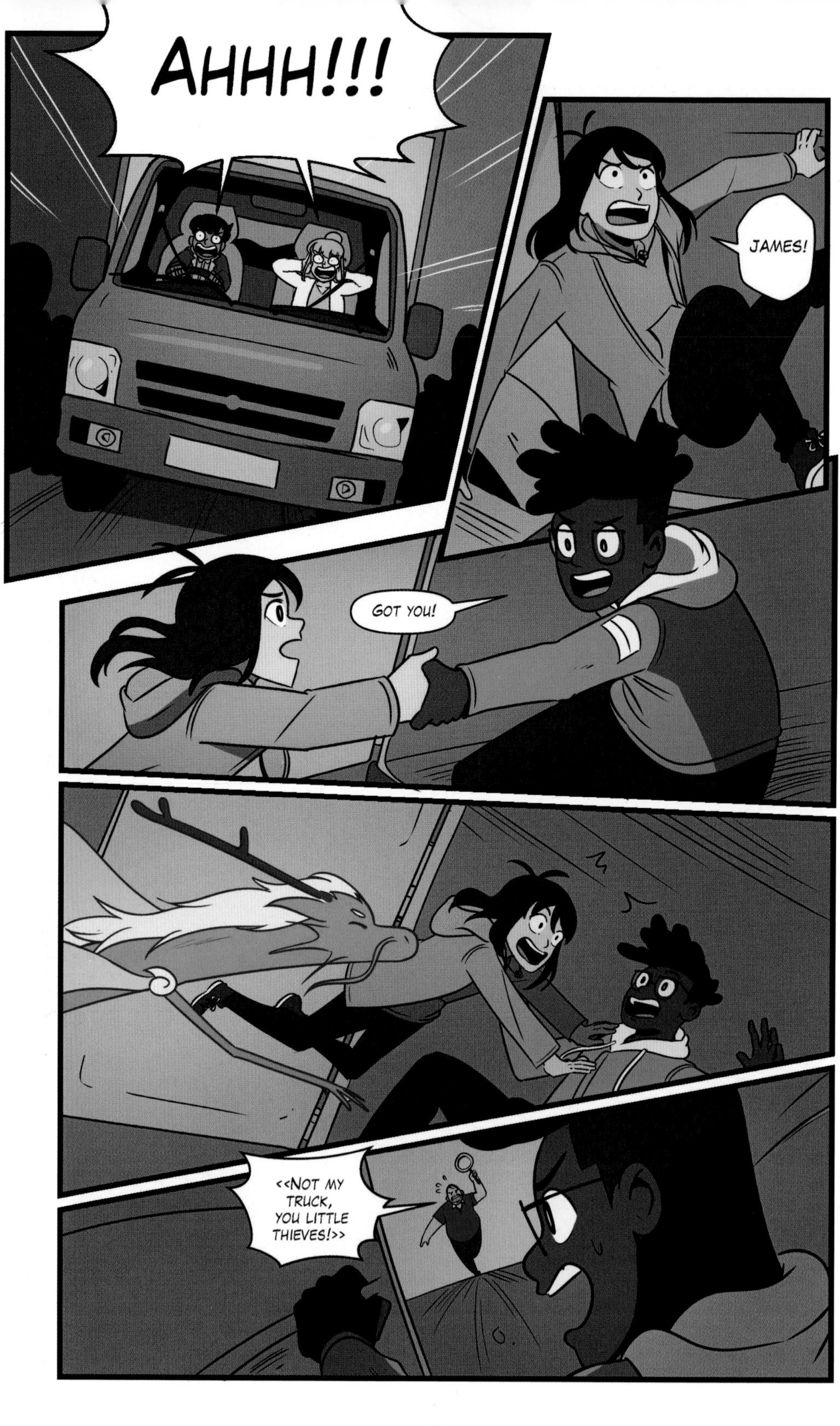
AHHH!!!
JAMES!
GOT YOU!
<<NOT MY TRUCK, YOU LITTLE THIEVES!>>

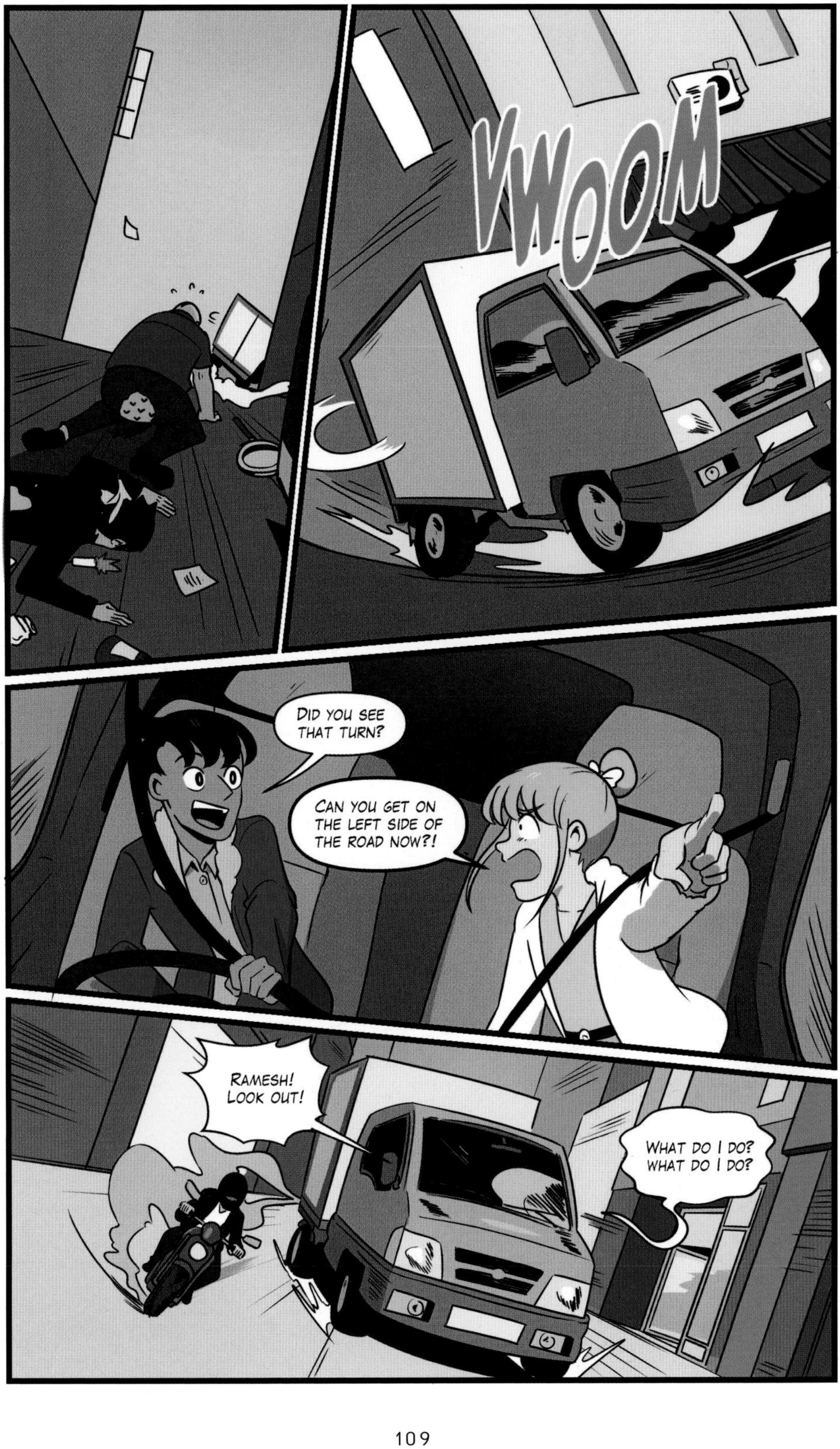
VWOOM
DID YOU SEE THAT TURN?
CAN YOU GET ON THE LEFT SIDE OF THE ROAD NOW?!
RAMESH! LOOK OUT!
WHAT DO I DO? WHAT DO I DO?

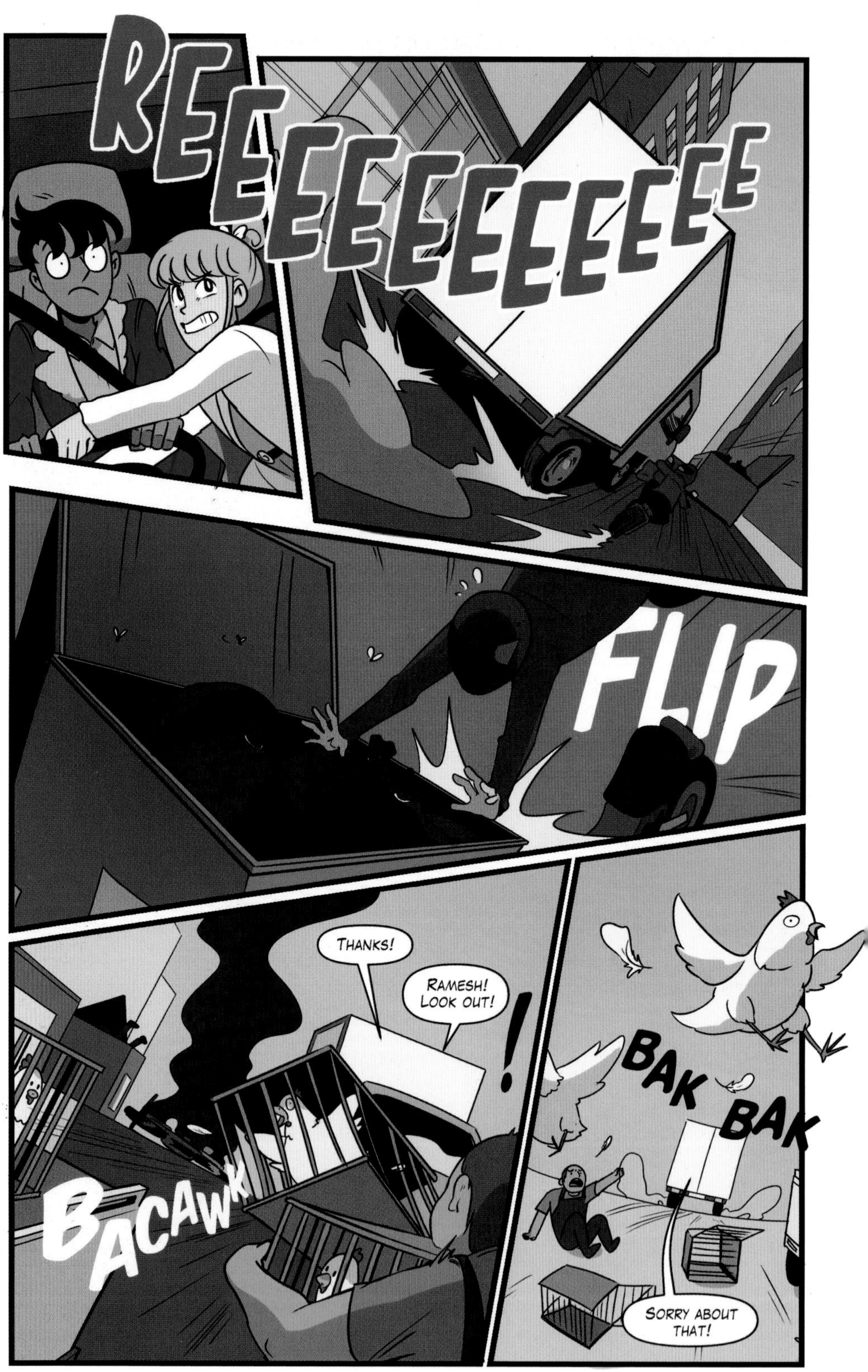
REEEEEEEEEEEEE
FLIP
THANKS!
RAMESH! LOOK OUT!
!
BACAWK
BAK BAK
SORRY ABOUT THAT!

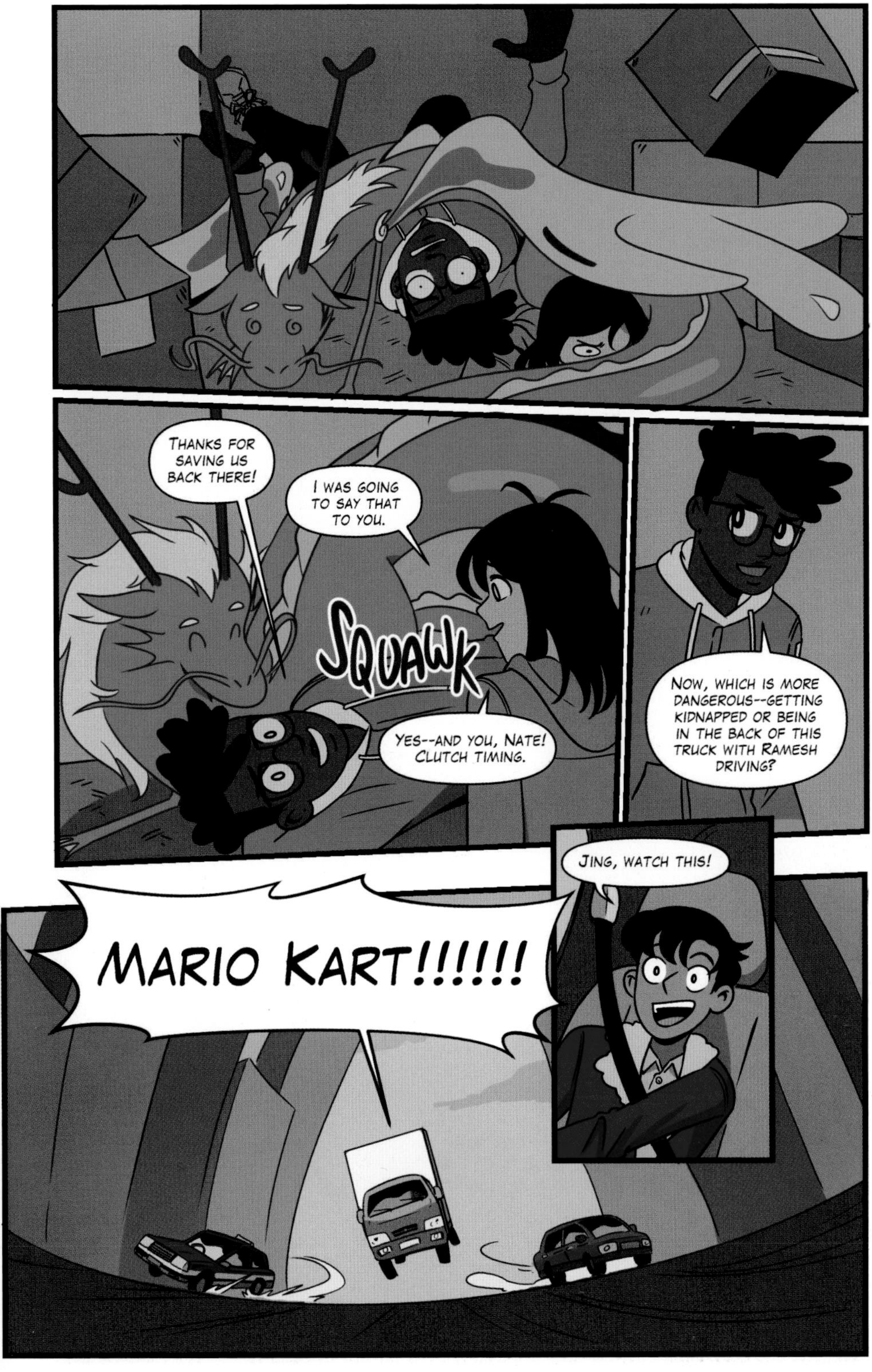
THANKS FOR SAVING US BACK THERE!
I WAS GOING TO SAY THAT TO YOU.
SQUAWK
YES--AND YOU, NATE! CLUTCH TIMING.
NOW, WHICH IS MORE DANGEROUS--GETTING KIDNAPPED OR BEING IN THE BACK OF THIS TRUCK WITH RAMESH DRIVING?
JING, WATCH THIS!
MARIO KART!!!!!!

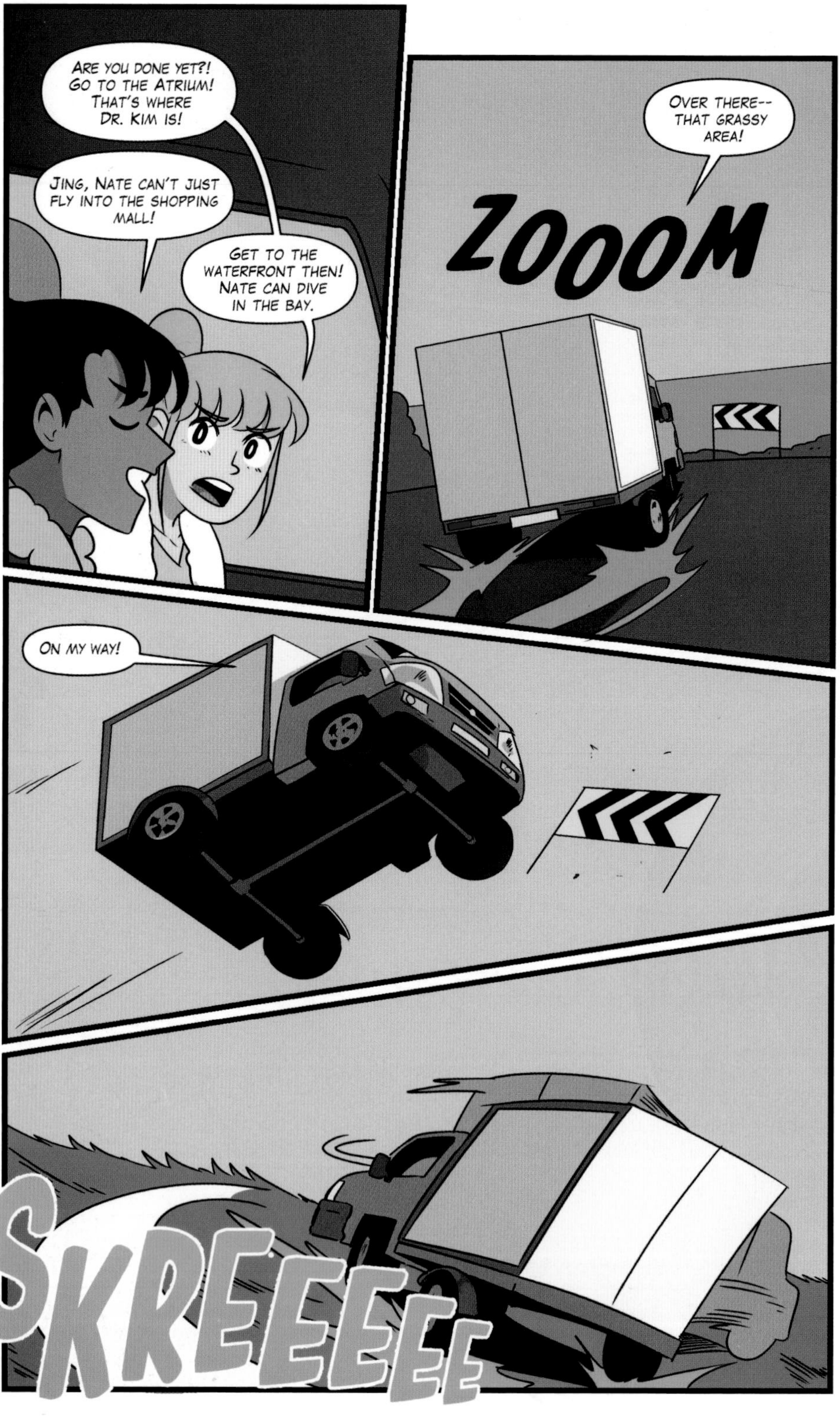
ARE YOU DONE YET?! GO TO THE ATRIUM! THAT'S WHERE DR. KIM IS!
JING, NATE CAN'T JUST FLY INTO THE SHOPPING MALL!
GET TO THE WATERFRONT THEN! NATE CAN DIVE IN THE BAY.
OVER THERE-- THAT GRASSY AREA!
ZOOOM
ON MY WAY!
SKREEEEEE

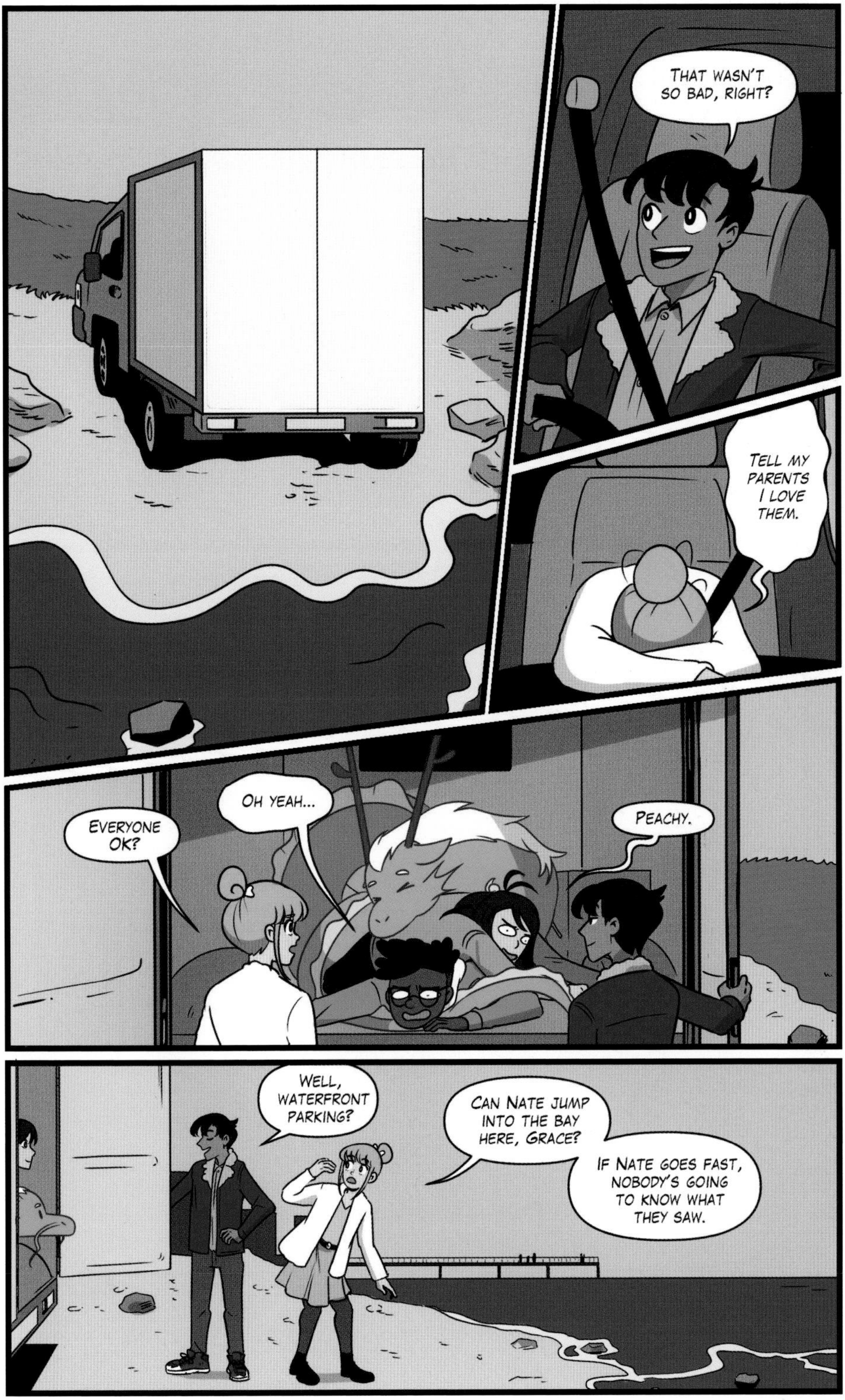
THAT WASN'T SO BAD, RIGHT?
TELL MY PARENTS I LOVE THEM.
EVERYONE OK?
OH YEAH...
PEACHY.
WELL, WATERFRONT PARKING?
CAN NATE JUMP INTO THE BAY HERE, GRACE?
IF NATE GOES FAST, NOBODY'S GOING TO KNOW WHAT THEY SAW.

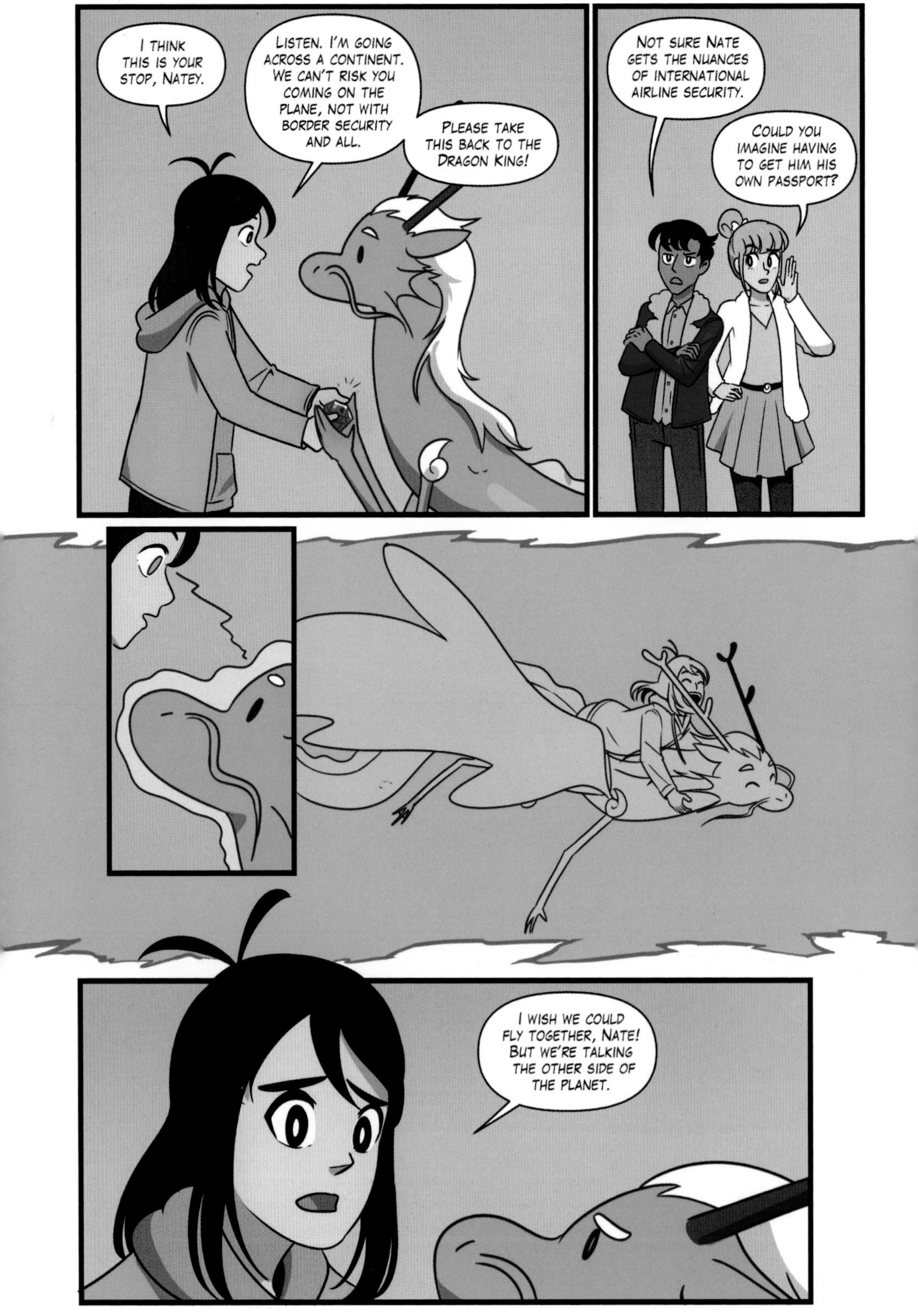
I THINK THIS IS YOUR STOP, NATEY.
LISTEN. I'M GOING ACROSS A CONTINENT. WE CAN'T RISK YOU COMING ON THE PLANE, NOT WITH BORDER SECURITY AND ALL.
PLEASE TAKE THIS BACK TO THE DRAGON KING!
NOT SURE NATE GETS THE NUANCES OF INTERNATIONAL AIRLINE SECURITY.
COULD YOU IMAGINE HAVING TO GET HIM HIS OWN PASSPORT?
I WISH WE COULD FLY TOGETHER, NATE! BUT WE'RE TALKING THE OTHER SIDE OF THE PLANET.

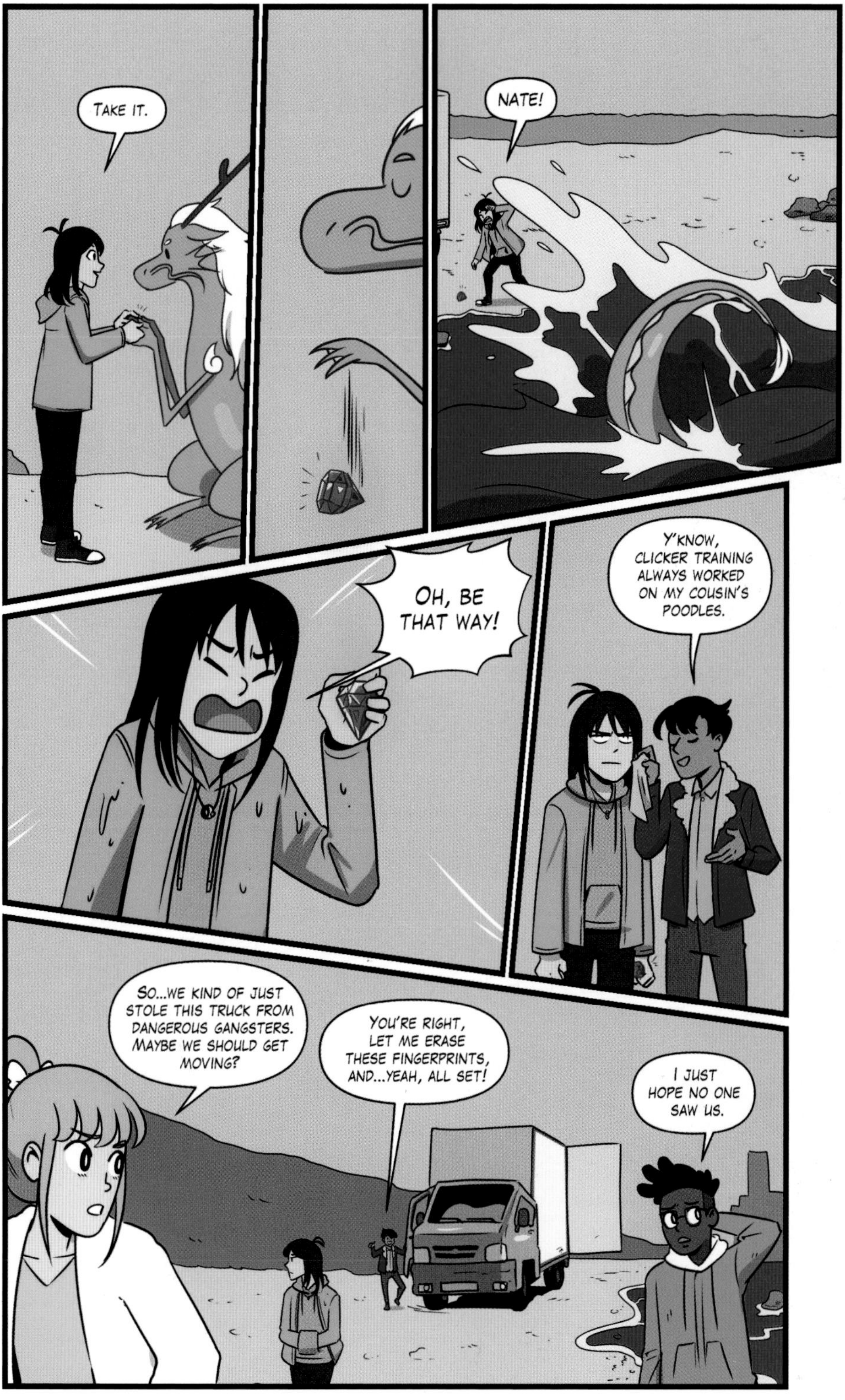
TAKE IT.
NATE!
OH, BE THAT WAY!
Y'KNOW, CLICKER TRAINING ALWAYS WORKED ON MY COUSIN'S POODLES.
SO...WE KIND OF JUST STOLE THIS TRUCK FROM DANGEROUS GANGSTERS. MAYBE WE SHOULD GET MOVING?
YOU'RE RIGHT, LET ME ERASE THESE FINGERPRINTS, AND...YEAH, ALL SET!
I JUST HOPE NO ONE SAW US.

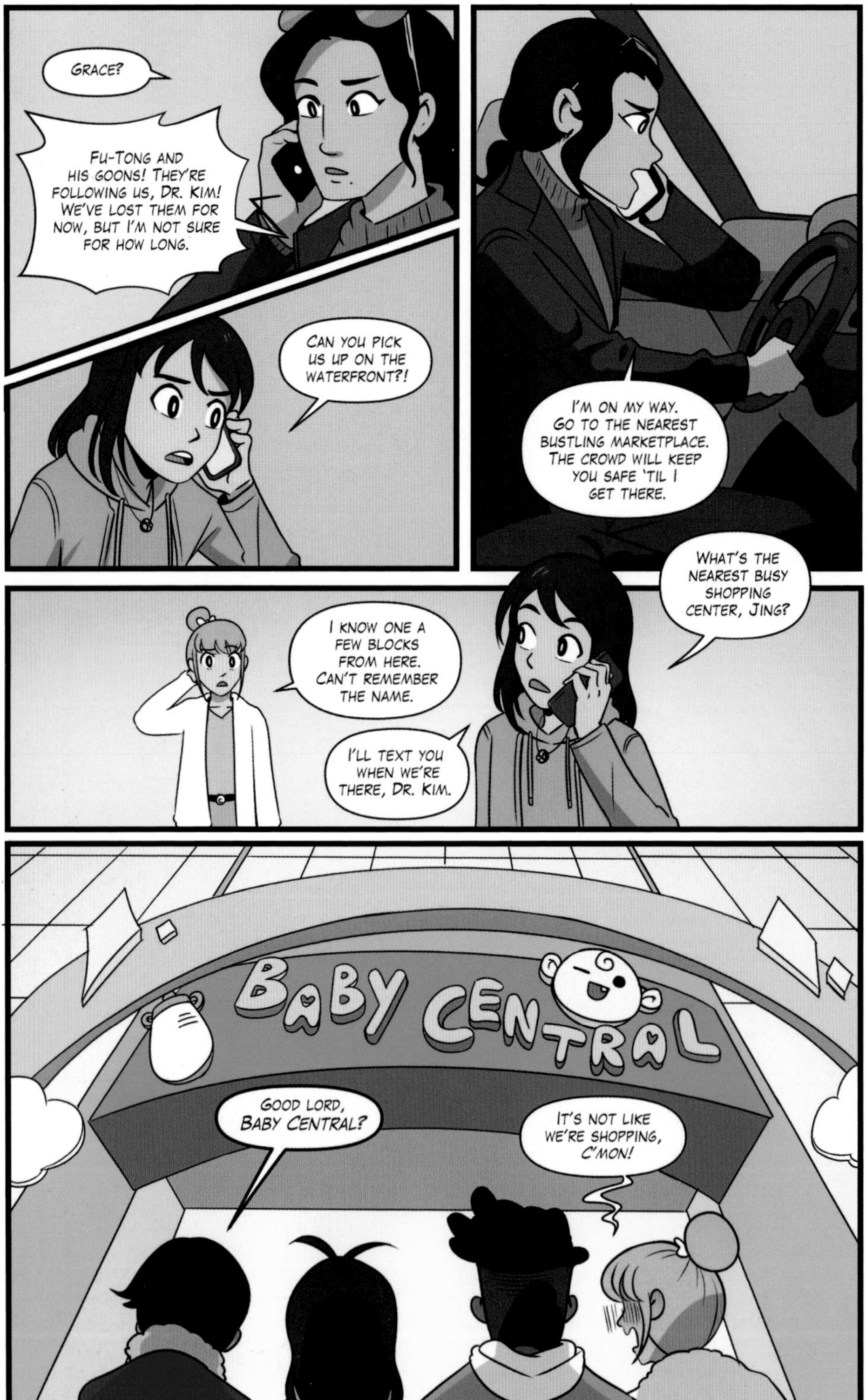
GRACE?
FU-TONG AND HIS GOONS! THEY'RE FOLLOWING US, DR. KIM! WE'VE LOST THEM FOR NOW, BUT I'M NOT SURE FOR HOW LONG.
CAN YOU PICK US UP ON THE WATERFRONT?!
I'M ON MY WAY. GO TO THE NEAREST BUSTLING MARKETPLACE. THE CROWD WILL KEEP YOU SAFE 'TIL I GET THERE.
WHAT'S THE NEAREST BUSY SHOPPING CENTER, JING?
I KNOW ONE A FEW BLOCKS FROM HERE. CAN'T REMEMBER THE NAME.
I'LL TEXT YOU WHEN WE'RE THERE, DR. KIM.
BABY CENTRAL
GOOD LORD, BABY CENTRAL?
IT'S NOT LIKE WE'RE SHOPPING, C'MON!

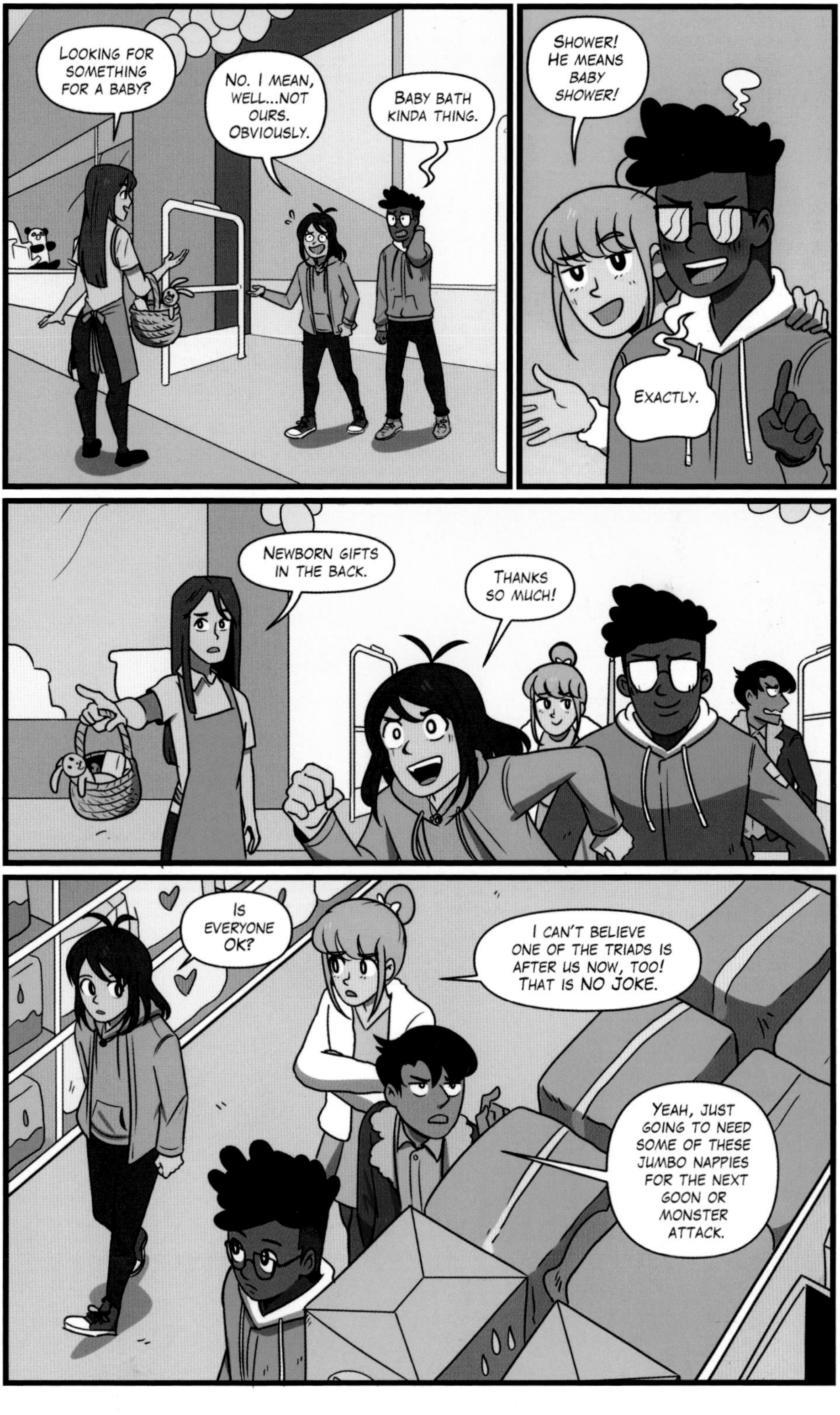

LOOKING FOR SOMETHING FOR A BABY?
NO. I MEAN, WELL...NOT OURS. OBVIOUSLY.
BABY BATH KINDA THING.
SHOWER! HE MEANS BABY SHOWER!
EXACTLY.
NEWBORN GIFTS IN THE BACK.
THANKS SO MUCH!
IS EVERYONE OK?
I CAN'T BELIEVE ONE OF THE TRIADS IS AFTER US NOW, TOO! THAT IS NO JOKE.
YEAH, JUST GOING TO NEED SOME OF THESE JUMBO NAPPIES FOR THE NEXT GOON OR MONSTER ATTACK.

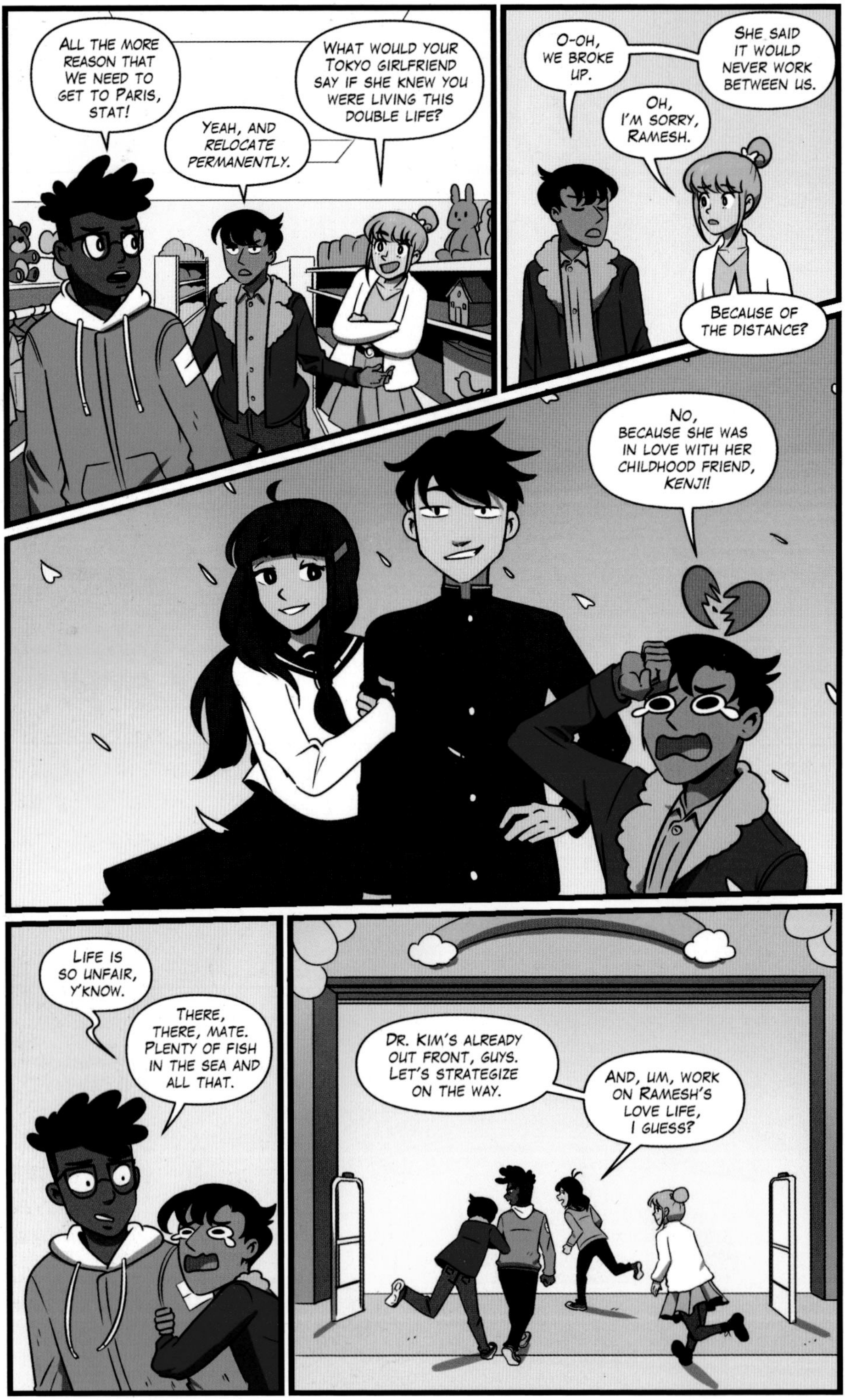
ALL THE MORE REASON THAT WE NEED TO GET TO PARIS, STAT!
YEAH, AND RELOCATE PERMANENTLY.
WHAT WOULD YOUR TOKYO GIRLFRIEND SAY IF SHE KNEW YOU WERE LIVING THIS DOUBLE LIFE?
O-OH, WE BROKE UP.
SHE SAID IT WOULD NEVER WORK BETWEEN US.
OH, I'M SORRY, RAMESH.
BECAUSE OF THE DISTANCE?
NO, BECAUSE SHE WAS IN LOVE WITH HER CHILDHOOD FRIEND, KENJI!
LIFE IS SO UNFAIR, Y'KNOW.
THERE, THERE, MATE. PLENTY OF FISH IN THE SEA AND ALL THAT.
DR. KIM'S ALREADY OUT FRONT, GUYS. LET'S STRATEGIZE ON THE WAY.
AND, UM, WORK ON RAMESH'S LOVE LIFE, I GUESS?

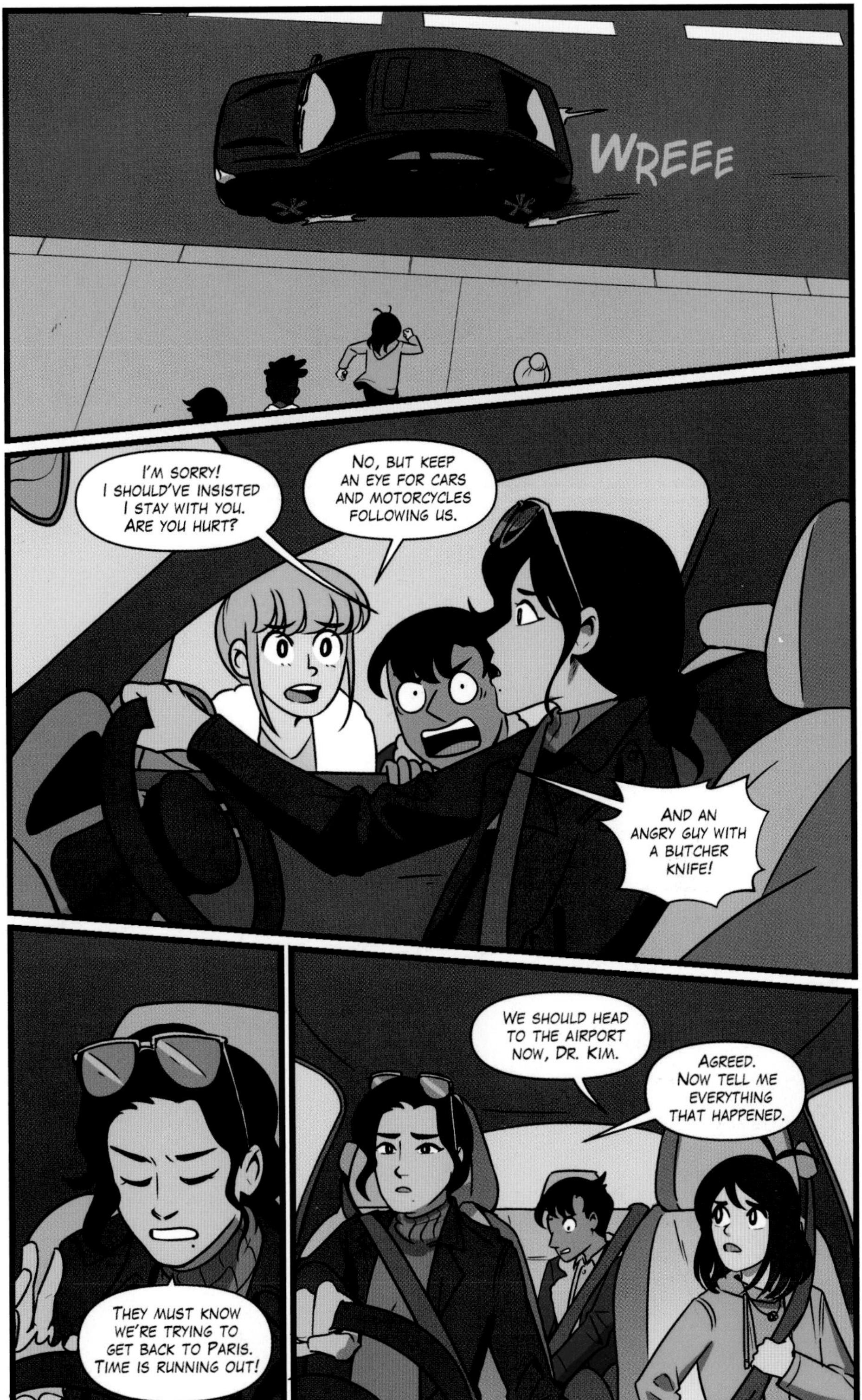
WREEE
I'M SORRY! I SHOULD'VE INSISTED I STAY WITH YOU. ARE YOU HURT?
NO, BUT KEEP AN EYE FOR CARS AND MOTORCYCLES FOLLOWING US.
AND AN ANGRY GUY WITH A BUTCHER KNIFE!
THEY MUST KNOW WE'RE TRYING TO GET BACK TO PARIS. TIME IS RUNNING OUT!
WE SHOULD HEAD TO THE AIRPORT NOW, DR. KIM.
AGREED. NOW TELL ME EVERYTHING THAT HAPPENED.

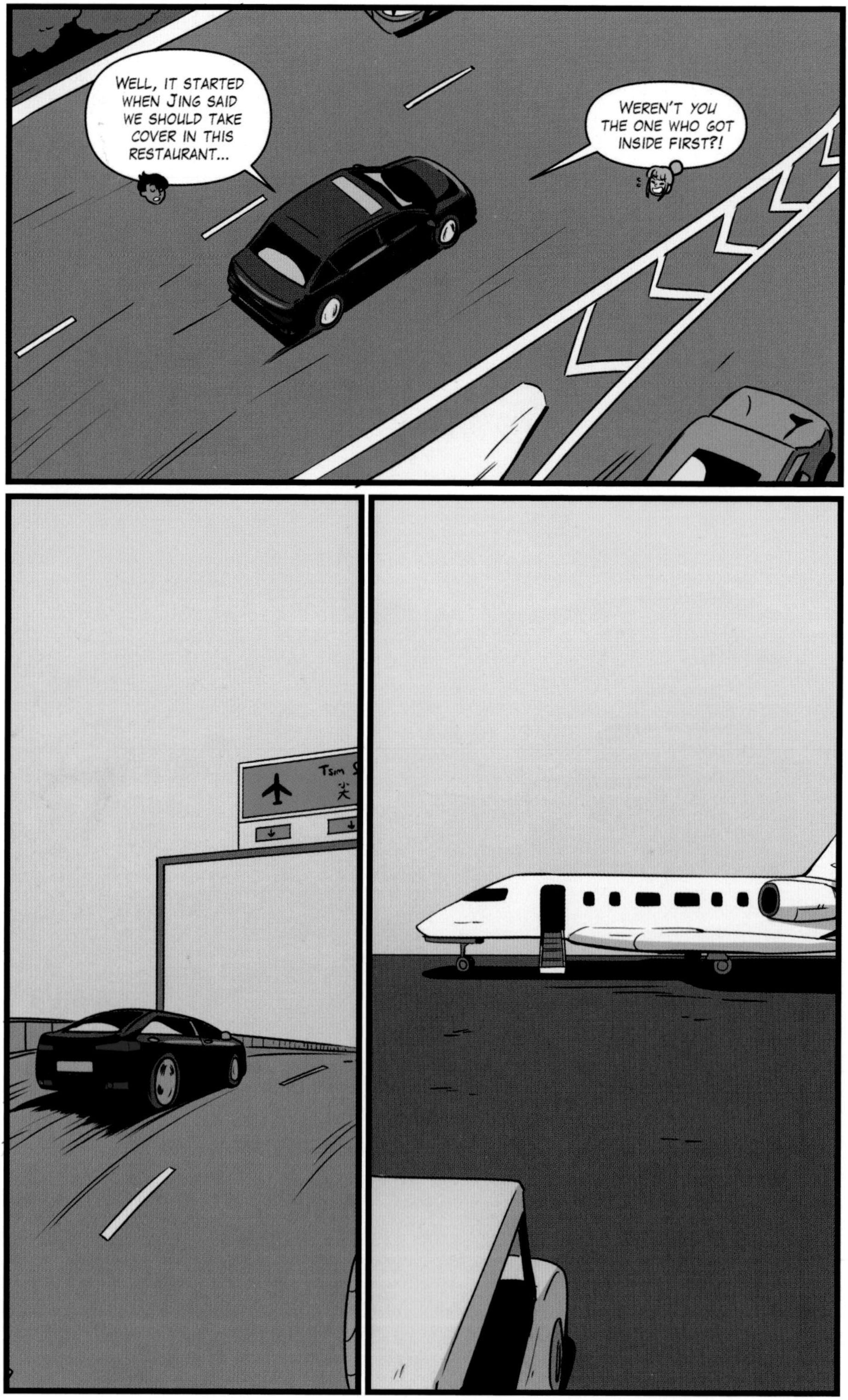
WELL, IT STARTED WHEN JING SAID WE SHOULD TAKE COVER IN THIS RESTAURANT...
WEREN'T YOU THE ONE WHO GOT INSIDE FIRST?!

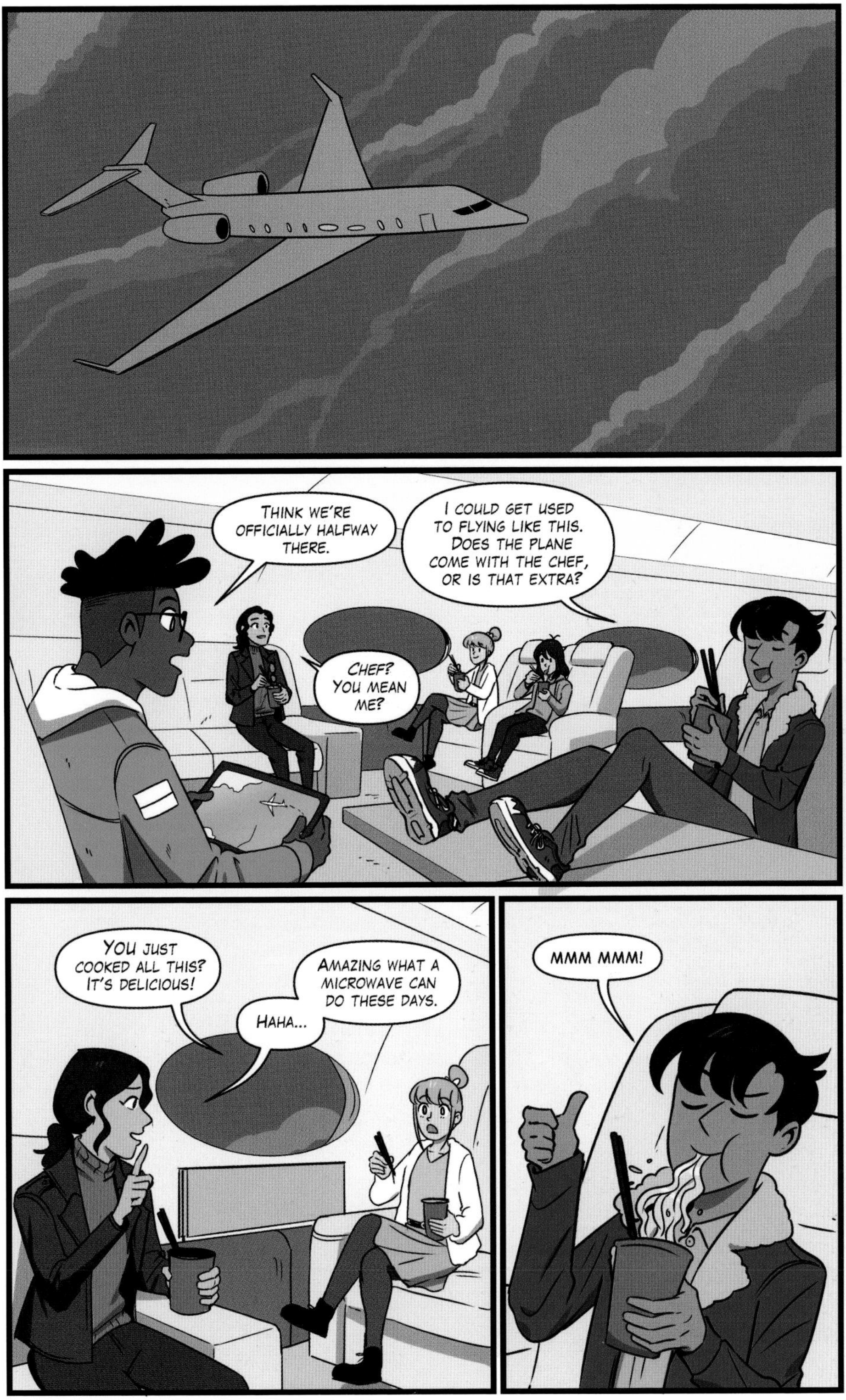
THINK WE'RE OFFICIALLY HALFWAY THERE.
I COULD GET USED TO FLYING LIKE THIS. DOES THE PLANE COME WITH THE CHEF, OR IS THAT EXTRA?
CHEF? YOU MEAN ME?
YOU JUST COOKED ALL THIS? IT'S DELICIOUS!
AMAZING WHAT A MICROWAVE CAN DO THESE DAYS.
HAHA...
MMM MMM!

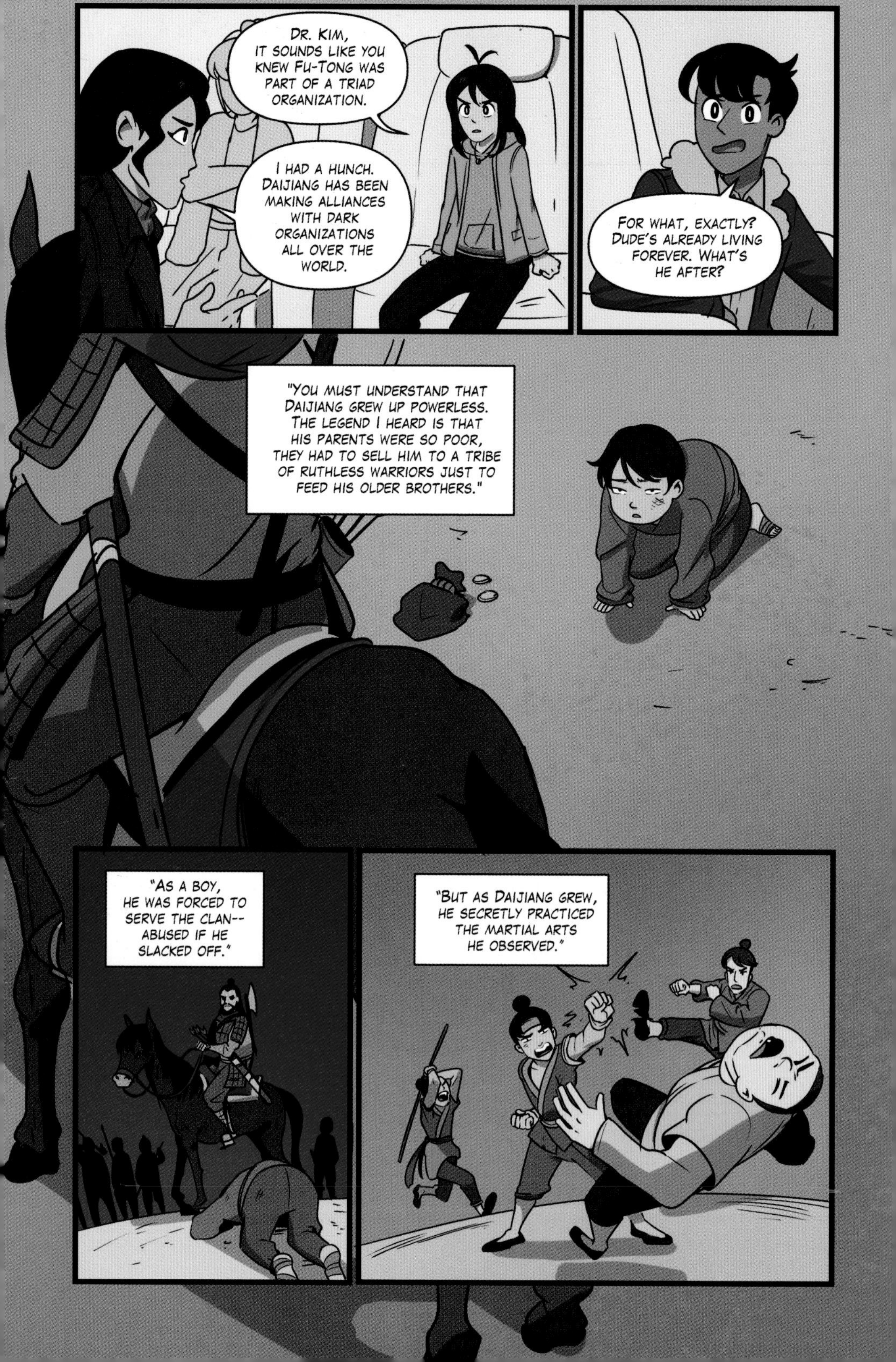
Dr. Kim, it sounds like you knew Fu-Tong was part of a triad organization.
I had a hunch. Daijiang has been making alliances with dark organizations all over the world.
For what, exactly? Dude's already living forever. What's he after?
"You must understand that Daijiang grew up powerless. The legend I heard is that his parents were so poor, they had to sell him to a tribe of ruthless warriors just to feed his older brothers."
"As a boy, he was forced to serve the clan-- abused if he slacked off."
"But as Daijiang grew, he secretly practiced the martial arts he observed."

"WHEN HE WAS JUST SIXTEEN, HE CHALLENGED THE LEADER TO A DUEL AND KILLED HIM."

"HE WENT ON TO LEAD THE CLAN TO BECOME ONE OF THE MOST POWERFUL FORCES OF THE REGION UNTIL THE YELLOW EMPEROR BROUGHT HIM INTO HIS ARMY.

"OF COURSE, YOU KNOW DAIJIANG TRIED TO OVERTAKE THAT ARMY AS WELL. FIGHTING FOR MORE POWER IS ALL HE HAS EVER KNOWN."

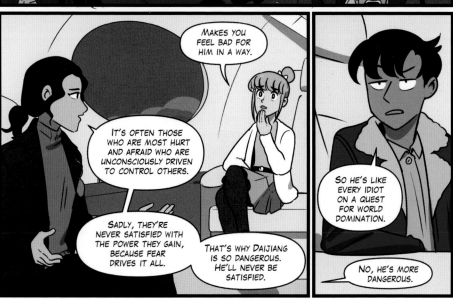

MAKES YOU FEEL BAD FOR HIM IN A WAY.

IT'S OFTEN THOSE WHO ARE MOST HURT AND AFRAID WHO ARE UNCONSCIOUSLY DRIVEN TO CONTROL OTHERS.

SADLY, THEY'RE NEVER SATISFIED WITH THE POWER THEY GAIN, BECAUSE FEAR DRIVES IT ALL.

THAT'S WHY DAIJIANG IS SO DANGEROUS. HE'LL NEVER BE SATISFIED.

SO HE'S LIKE EVERY IDIOT ON A QUEST FOR WORLD DOMINATION.

NO, HE'S MORE DANGEROUS.

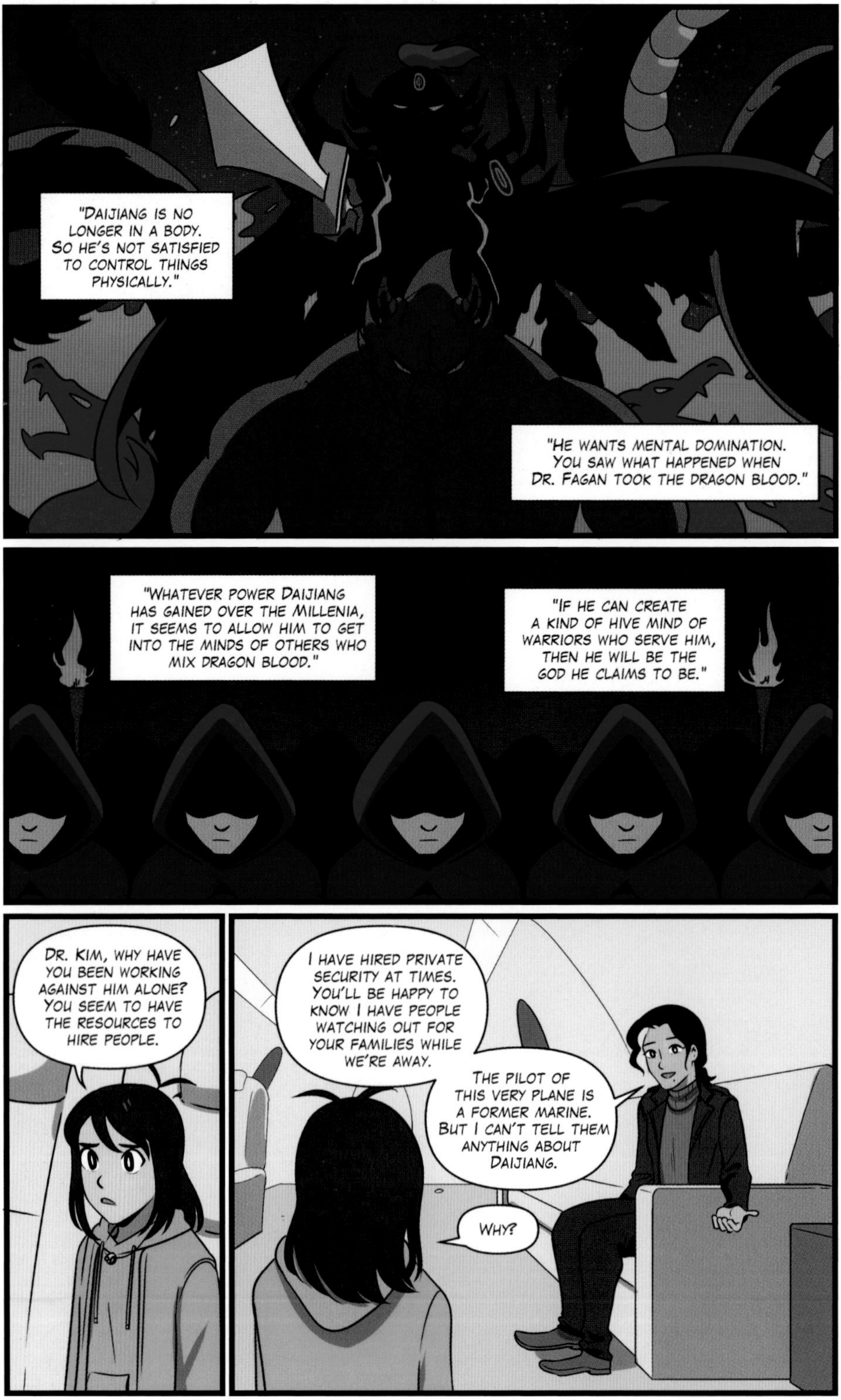
"Daijiang is no longer in a body. So he's not satisfied to control things physically."
"He wants mental domination. You saw what happened when Dr. Fagan took the dragon blood."
"Whatever power Daijiang has gained over the Millenia, it seems to allow him to get into the minds of others who mix dragon blood."
"If he can create a kind of hive mind of warriors who serve him, then he will be the god he claims to be."
Dr. Kim, why have you been working against him alone? You seem to have the resources to hire people.
I have hired private security at times. You'll be happy to know I have people watching out for your families while we're away.
The pilot of this very plane is a former marine. But I can't tell them anything about Daijiang.
Why?

"I DIDN'T GO HOME, BECAUSE I WAS WORRIED I'D DRAW DAIJIANG'S SOLDIERS TO MY FAMILY."

DO YOU REMEMBER I TOLD YOU I ESCAPED DAIJIANG'S CAMP?

"BUT DAIJIANG'S SOLDIERS WENT TO MY HOME ANYWAY."

I NEVER SAW MY PARENTS OR MY SISTER AGAIN.

THAT'S AWFUL!

YOU MEAN HE...?

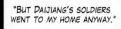

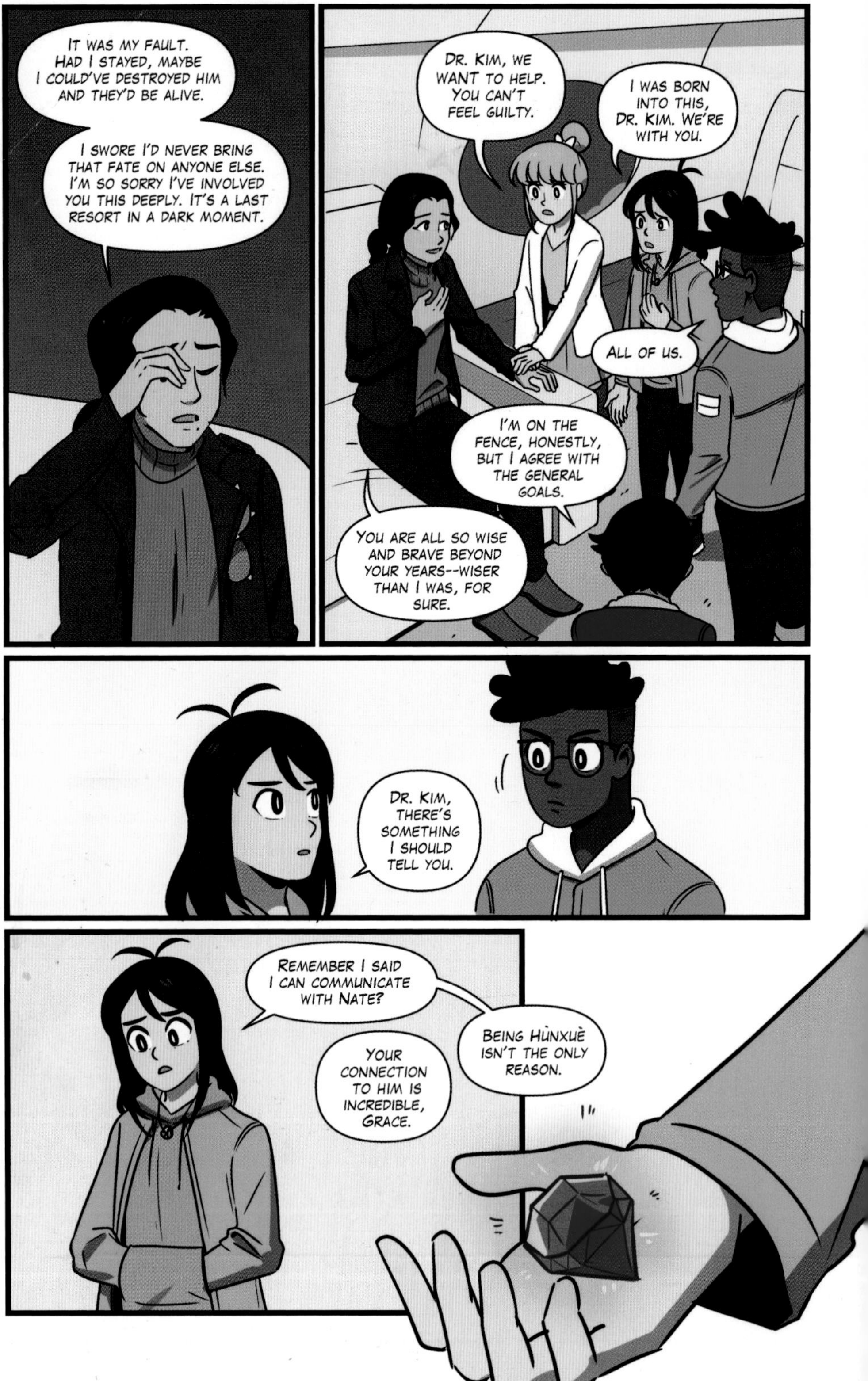
It was my fault. Had I stayed, maybe I could've destroyed him and they'd be alive.
I swore I'd never bring that fate on anyone else. I'm so sorry I've involved you this deeply. It's a last resort in a dark moment.
Dr. Kim, we want to help. You can't feel guilty.
I was born into this, Dr. Kim. We're with you.
All of us.
I'm on the fence, honestly, but I agree with the general goals.
You are all so wise and brave beyond your years--wiser than I was, for sure.
Dr. Kim, there's something I should tell you.
Remember I said I can communicate with Nate?
Your connection to him is incredible, Grace.
Being Hùnxuè isn't the only reason.

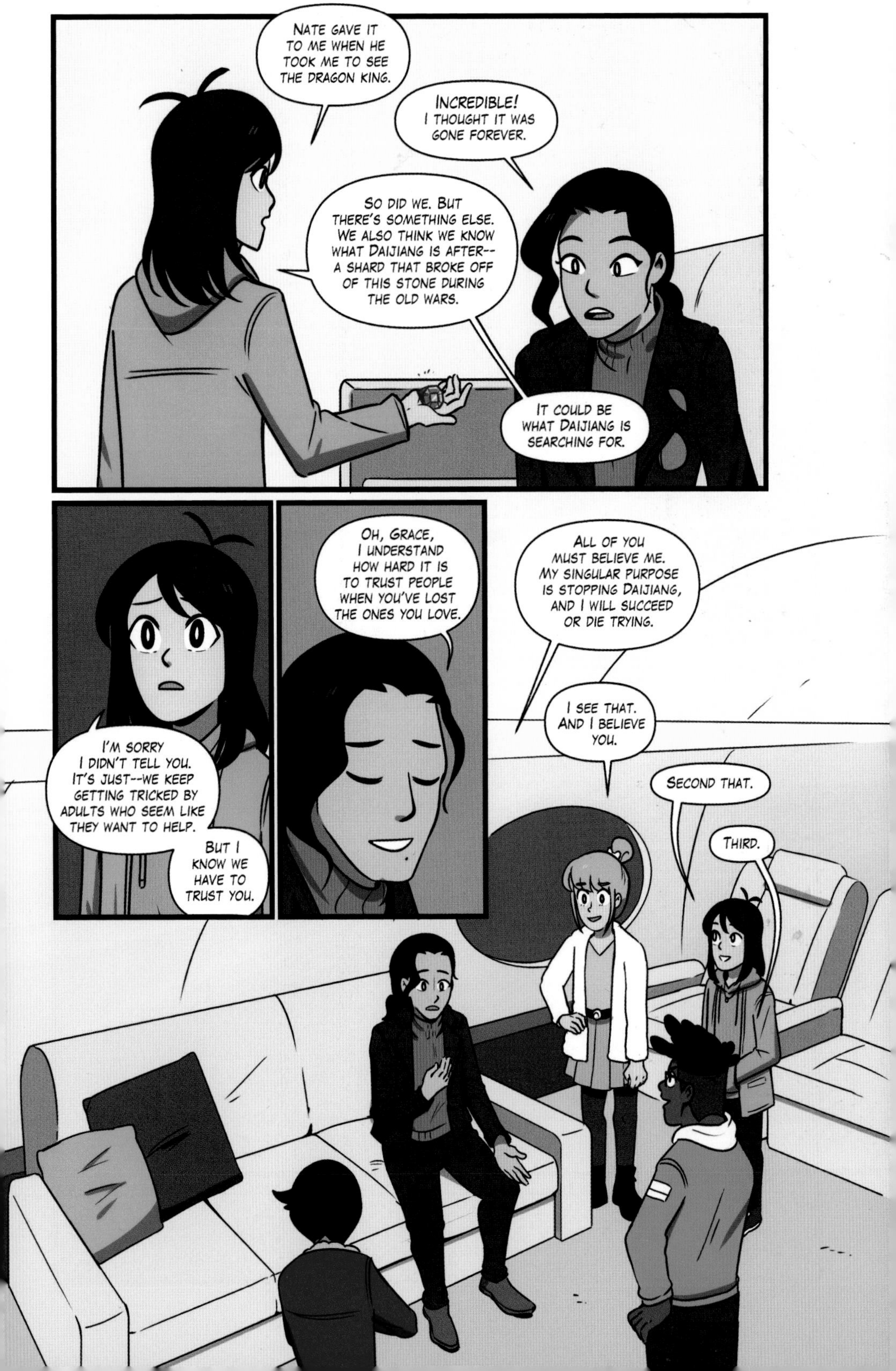
NATE GAVE IT TO ME WHEN HE TOOK ME TO SEE THE DRAGON KING.
INCREDIBLE! I THOUGHT IT WAS GONE FOREVER.
SO DID WE. BUT THERE'S SOMETHING ELSE. WE ALSO THINK WE KNOW WHAT DAIJIANG IS AFTER-- A SHARD THAT BROKE OFF OF THIS STONE DURING THE OLD WARS.
IT COULD BE WHAT DAIJIANG IS SEARCHING FOR.
I'M SORRY I DIDN'T TELL YOU. IT'S JUST--WE KEEP GETTING TRICKED BY ADULTS WHO SEEM LIKE THEY WANT TO HELP.
BUT I KNOW WE HAVE TO TRUST YOU.
OH, GRACE, I UNDERSTAND HOW HARD IT IS TO TRUST PEOPLE WHEN YOU'VE LOST THE ONES YOU LOVE.
ALL OF YOU MUST BELIEVE ME. MY SINGULAR PURPOSE IS STOPPING DAIJIANG, AND I WILL SUCCEED OR DIE TRYING.
I SEE THAT. AND I BELIEVE YOU.
SECOND THAT.
THIRD.

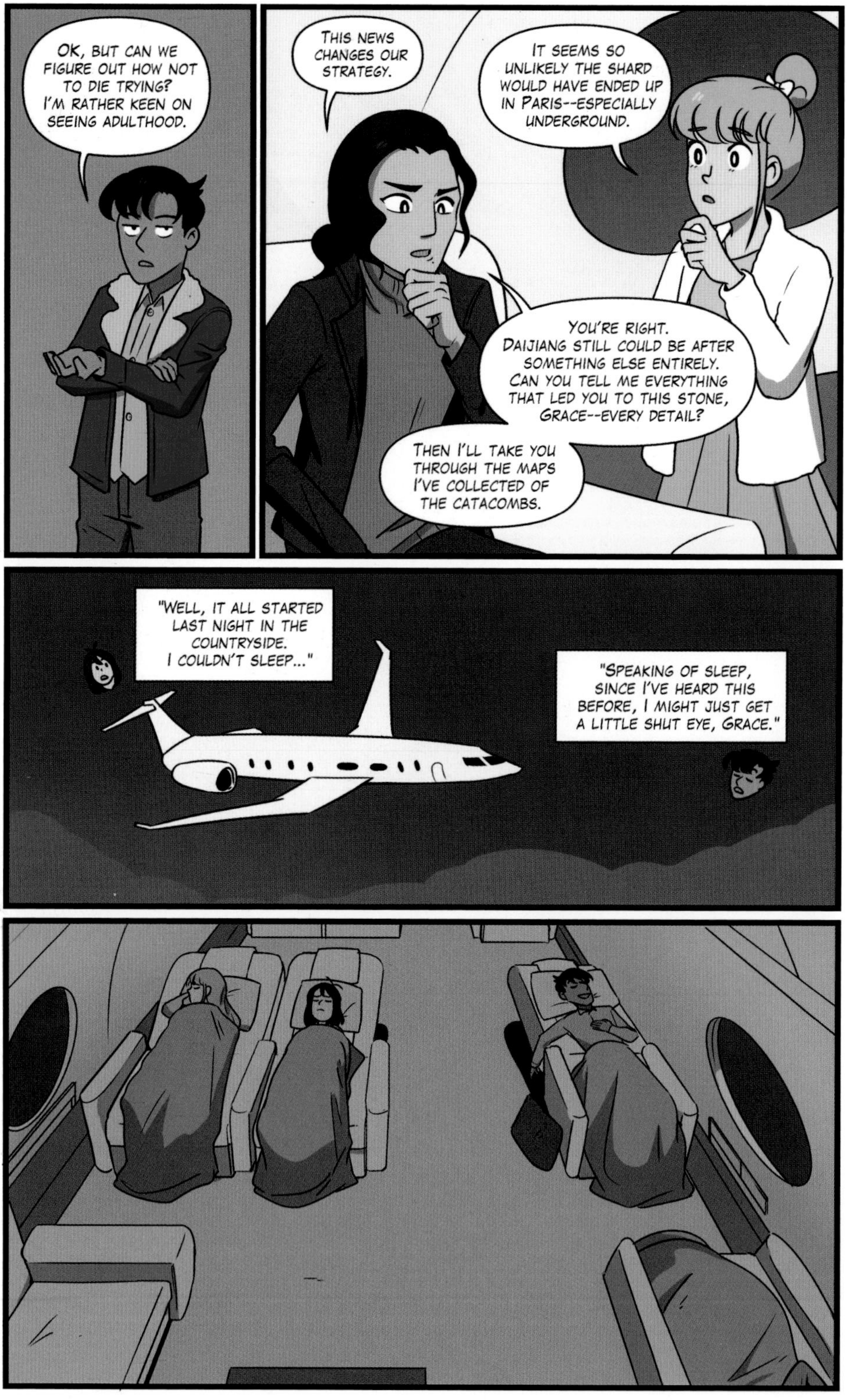
OK, BUT CAN WE FIGURE OUT HOW NOT TO DIE TRYING? I'M RATHER KEEN ON SEEING ADULTHOOD.
THIS NEWS CHANGES OUR STRATEGY.
IT SEEMS SO UNLIKELY THE SHARD WOULD HAVE ENDED UP IN PARIS--ESPECIALLY UNDERGROUND.
YOU'RE RIGHT. DAIJIANG STILL COULD BE AFTER SOMETHING ELSE ENTIRELY. CAN YOU TELL ME EVERYTHING THAT LED YOU TO THIS STONE, GRACE--EVERY DETAIL?
THEN I'LL TAKE YOU THROUGH THE MAPS I'VE COLLECTED OF THE CATACOMBS.
"WELL, IT ALL STARTED LAST NIGHT IN THE COUNTRYSIDE. I COULDN'T SLEEP..."
"SPEAKING OF SLEEP, SINCE I'VE HEARD THIS BEFORE, I MIGHT JUST GET A LITTLE SHUT EYE, GRACE."

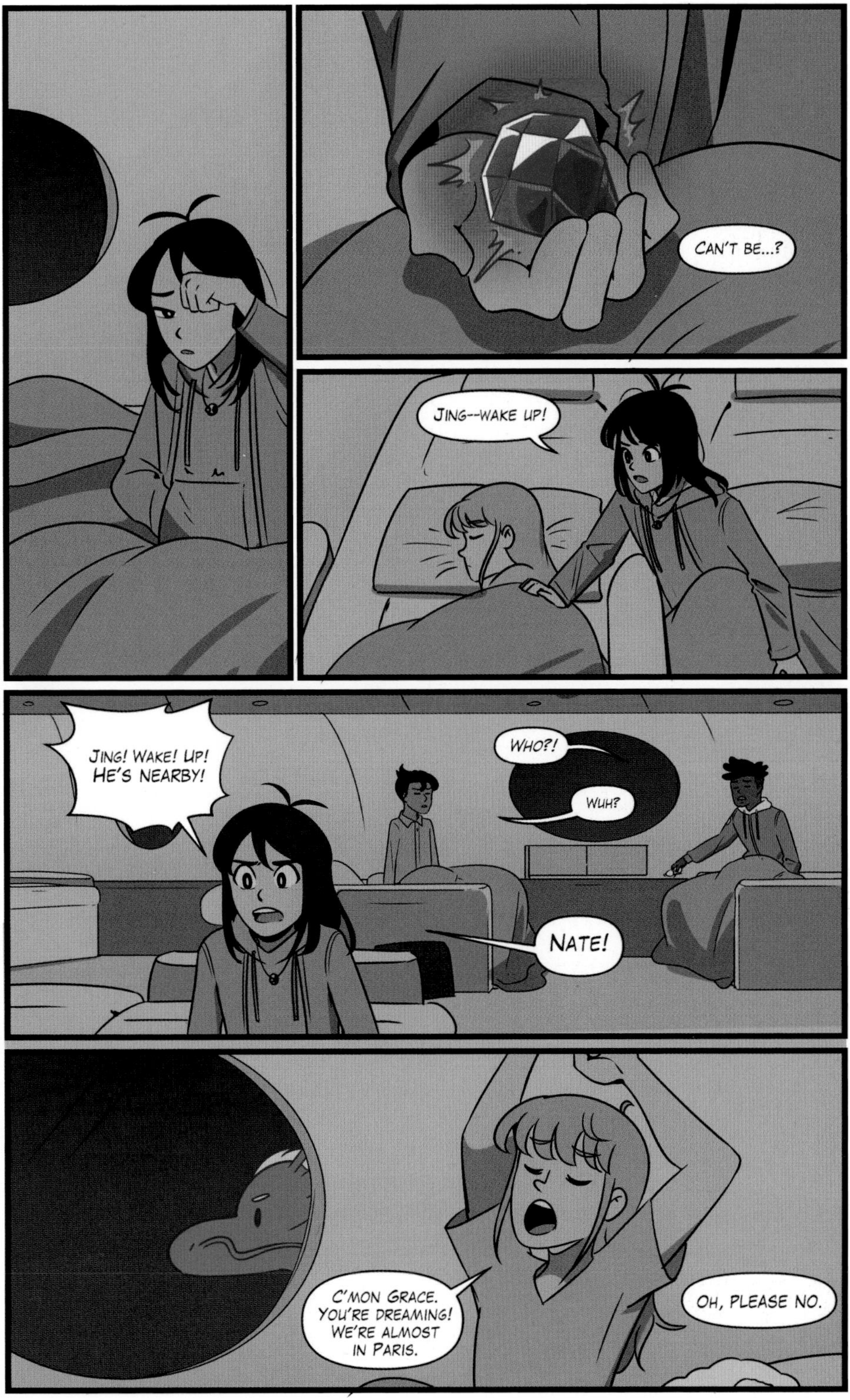
CAN'T BE...?
JING--WAKE UP!
JING! WAKE! UP! HE'S NEARBY!
WHO?!
WUH?
NATE!
C'MON GRACE. YOU'RE DREAMING! WE'RE ALMOST IN PARIS.
OH, PLEASE NO.

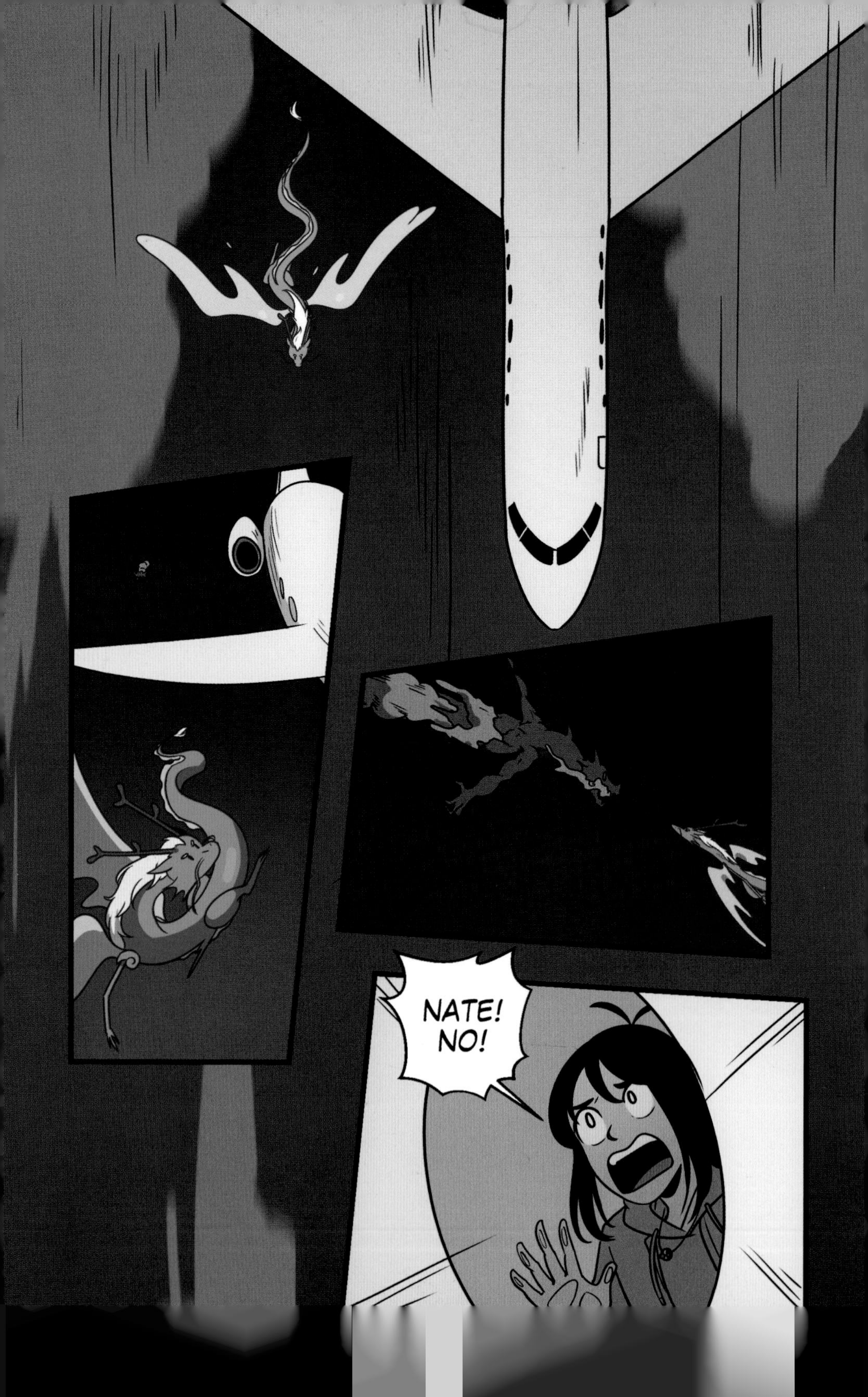
NATE! NO!

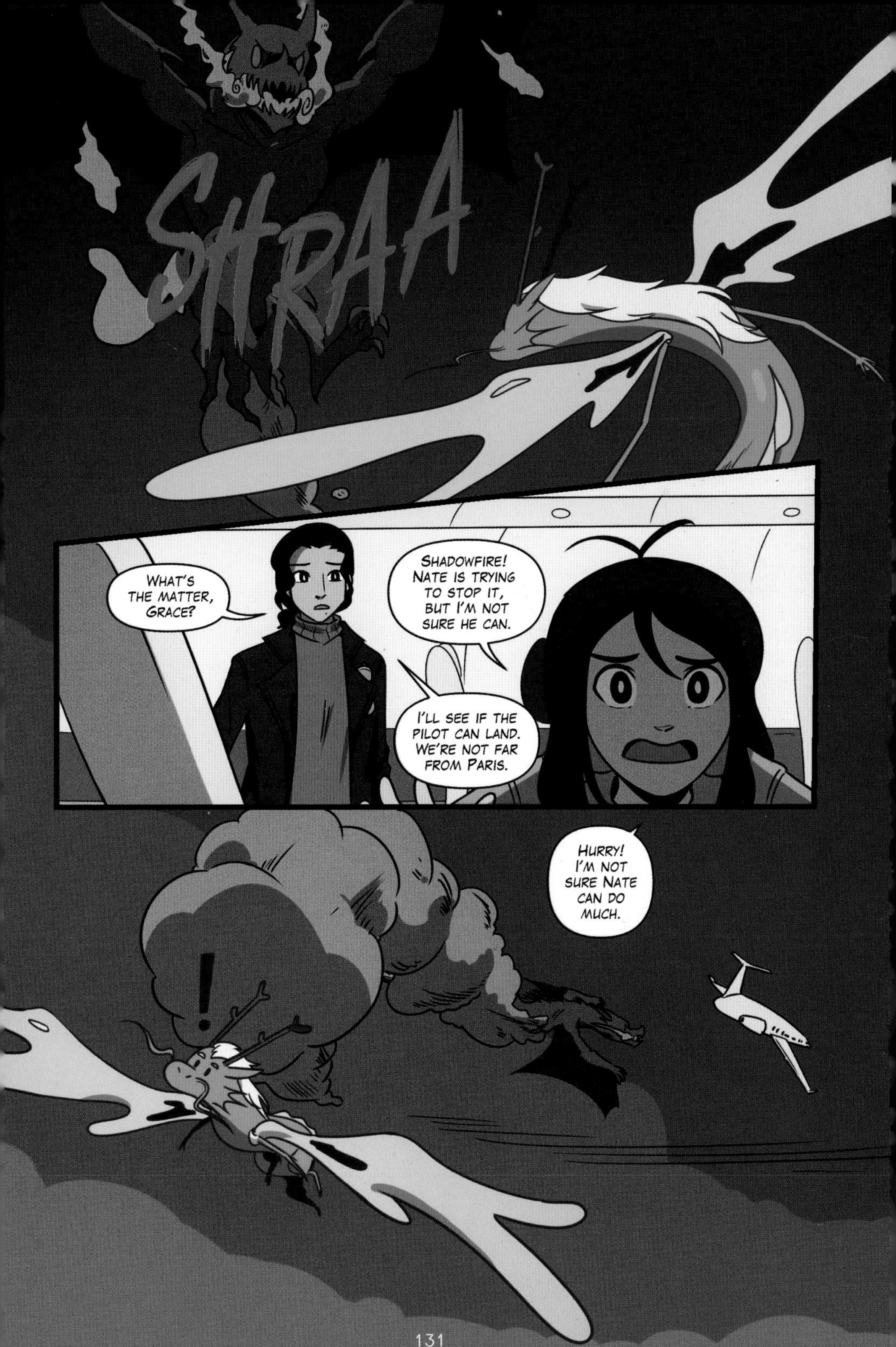
SHRAA
WHAT'S THE MATTER, GRACE?
SHADOWFIRE! NATE IS TRYING TO STOP IT, BUT I'M NOT SURE HE CAN.
I'LL SEE IF THE PILOT CAN LAND. WE'RE NOT FAR FROM PARIS.
HURRY! I'M NOT SURE NATE CAN DO MUCH.
!

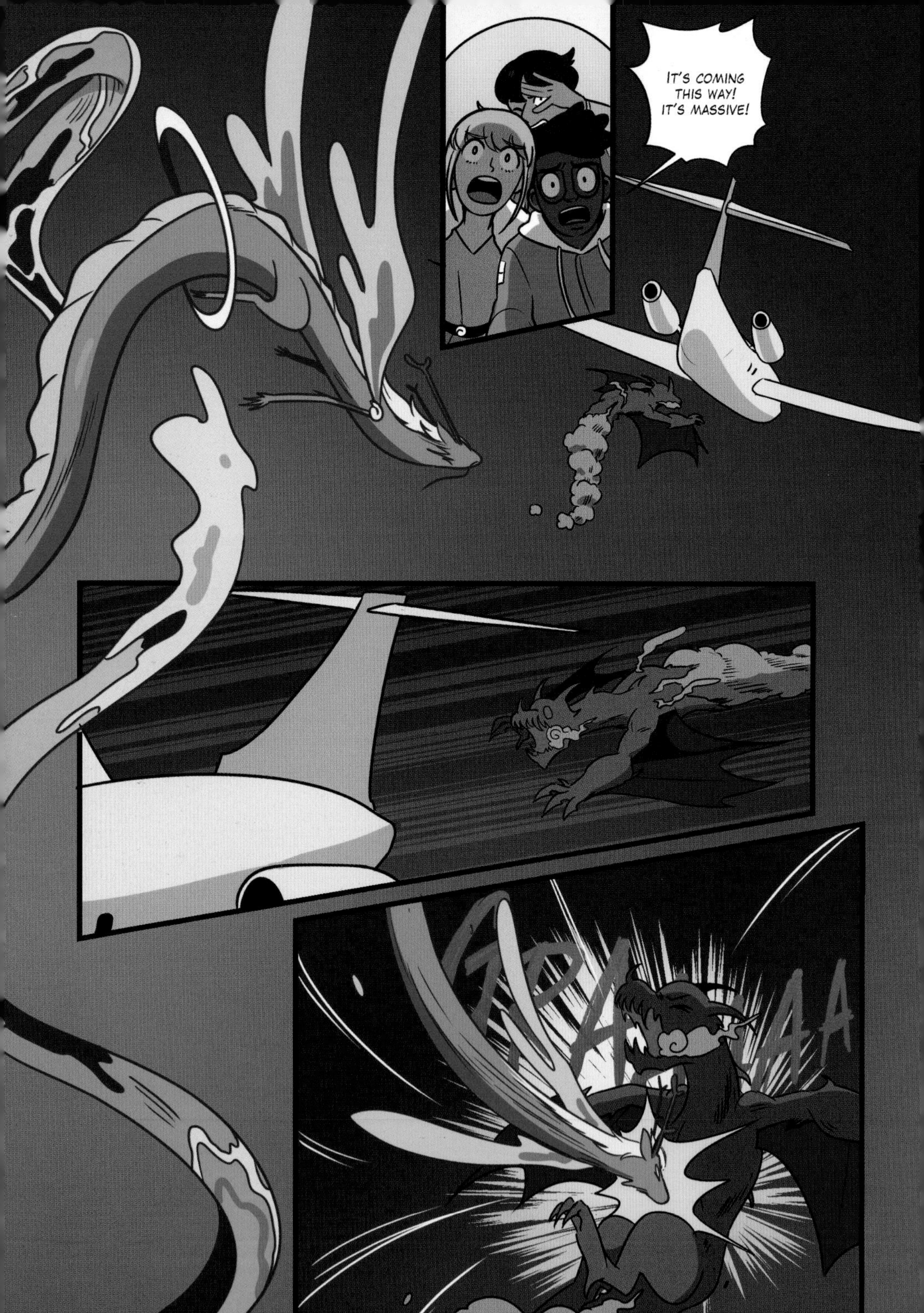
IT'S COMING THIS WAY! IT'S MASSIVE!

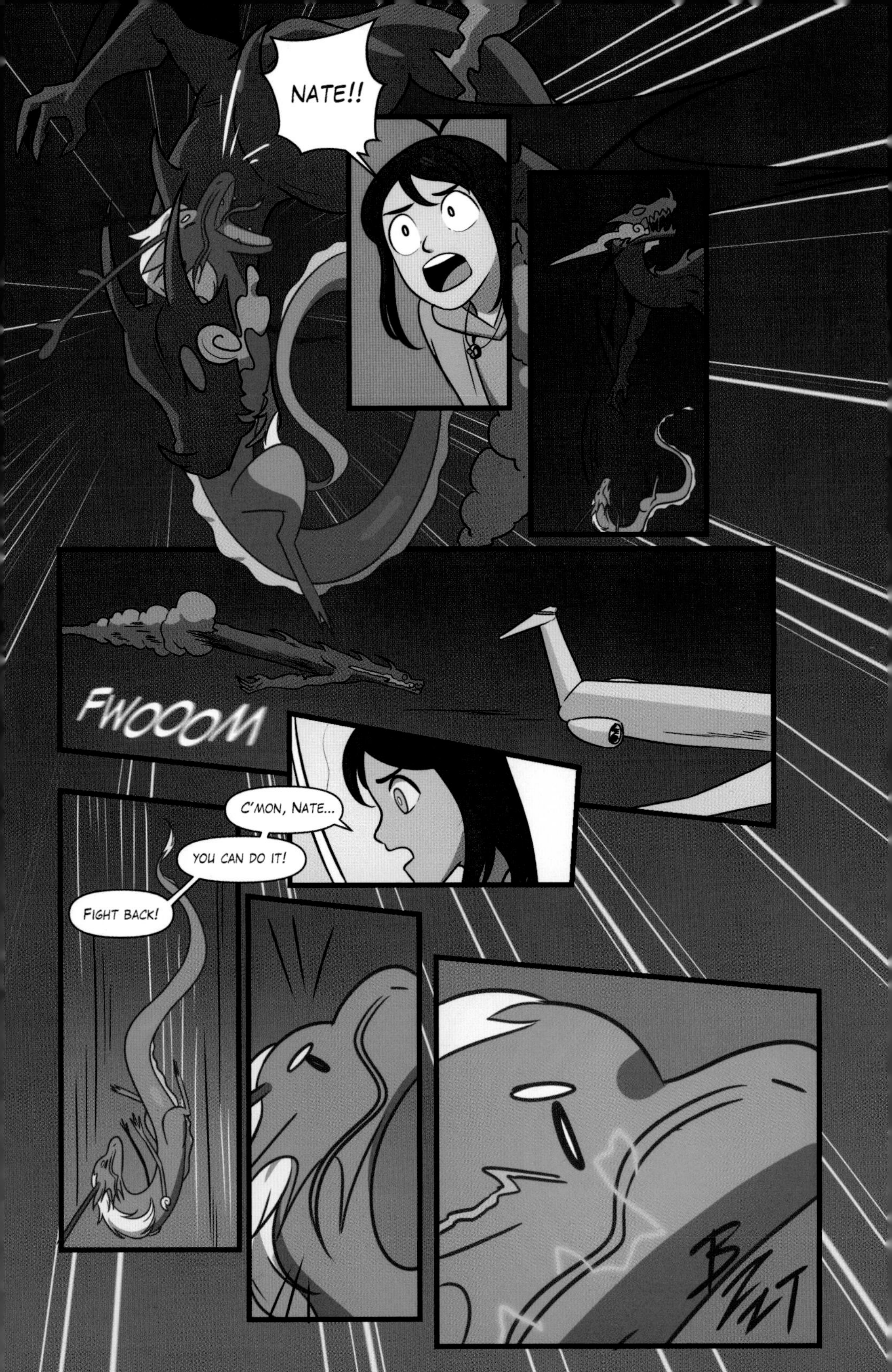
NATE!!
FWOOOM
C'MON, NATE...
YOU CAN DO IT!
FIGHT BACK!

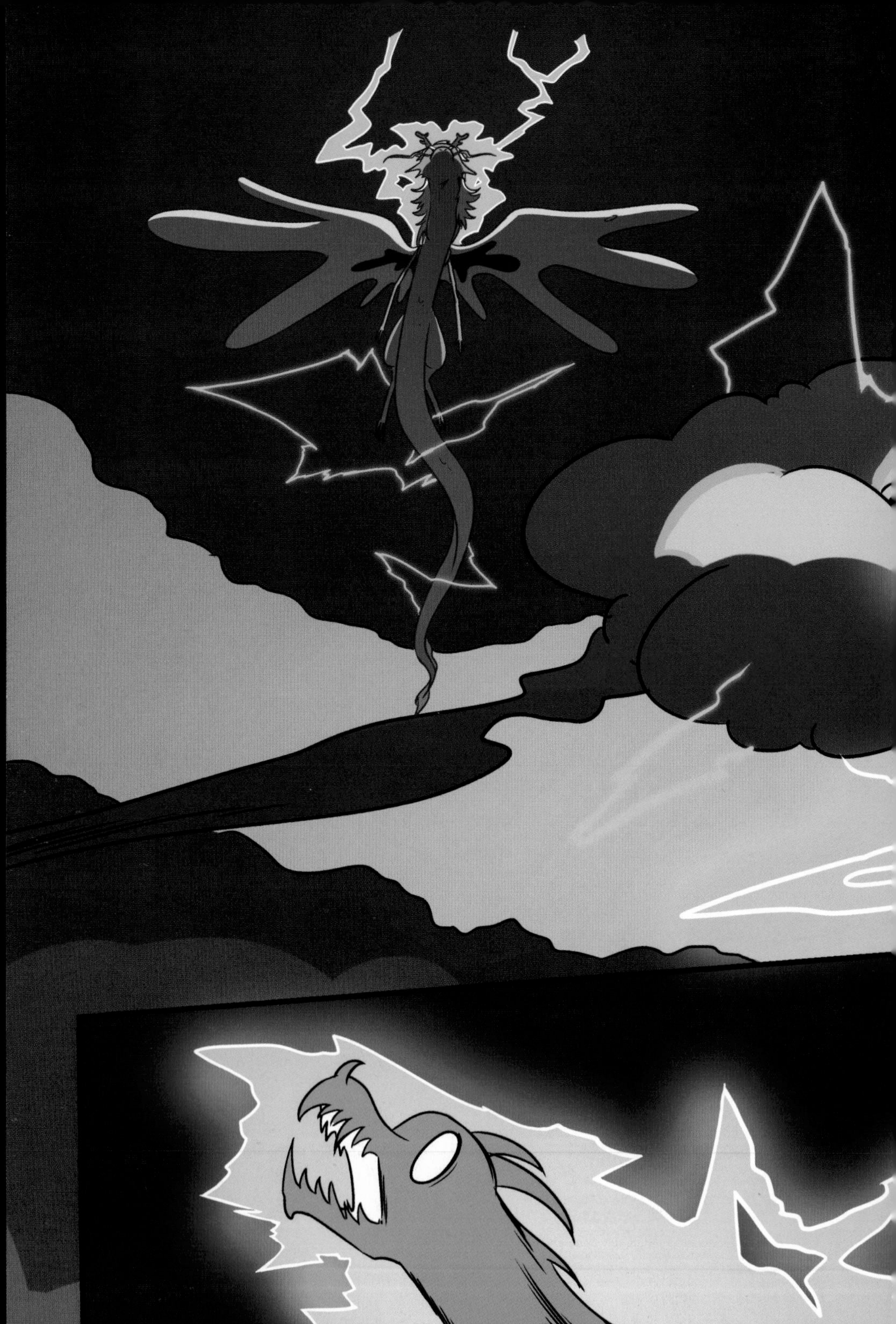

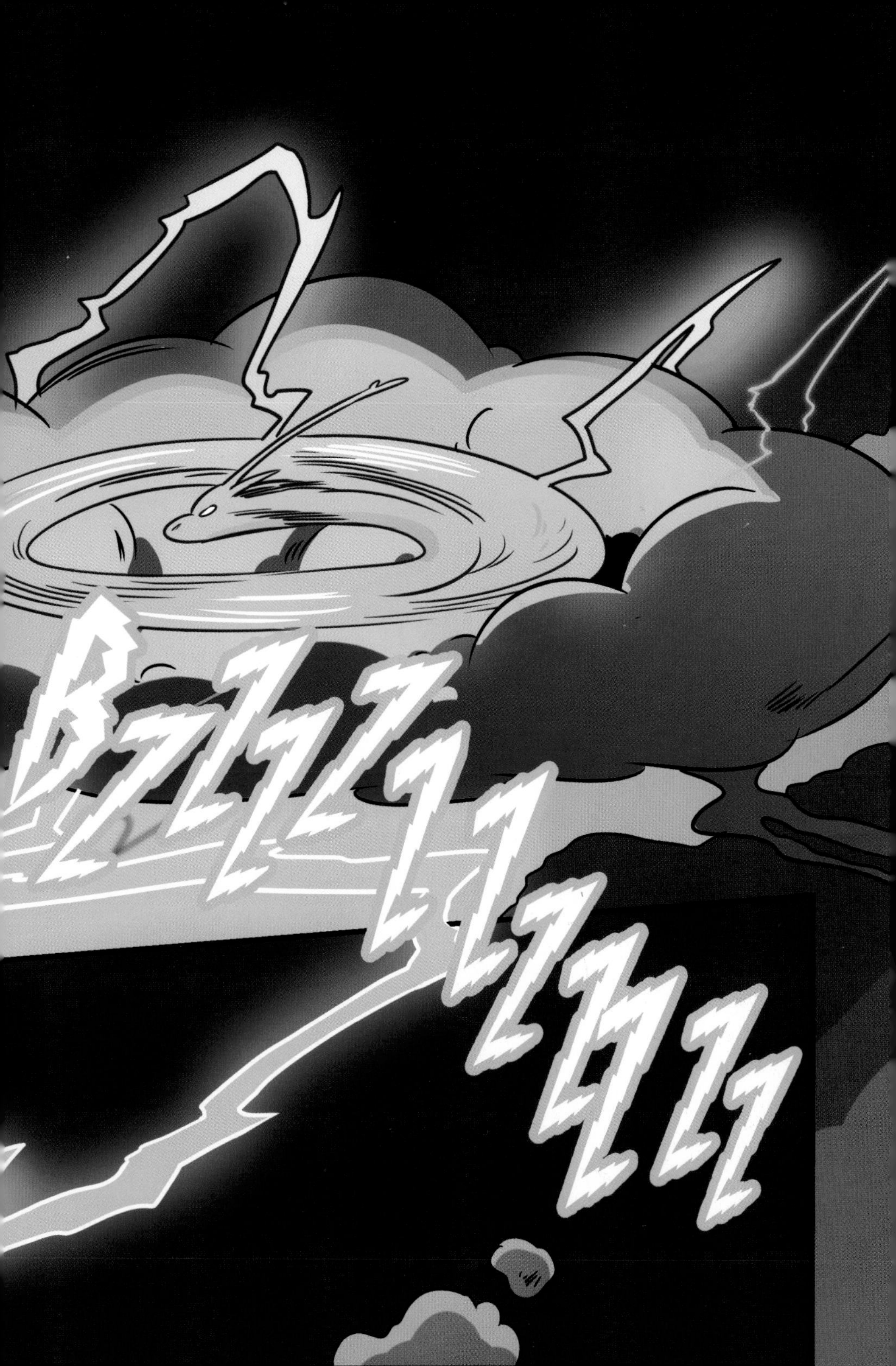
BZZZZZZZZZZZZ

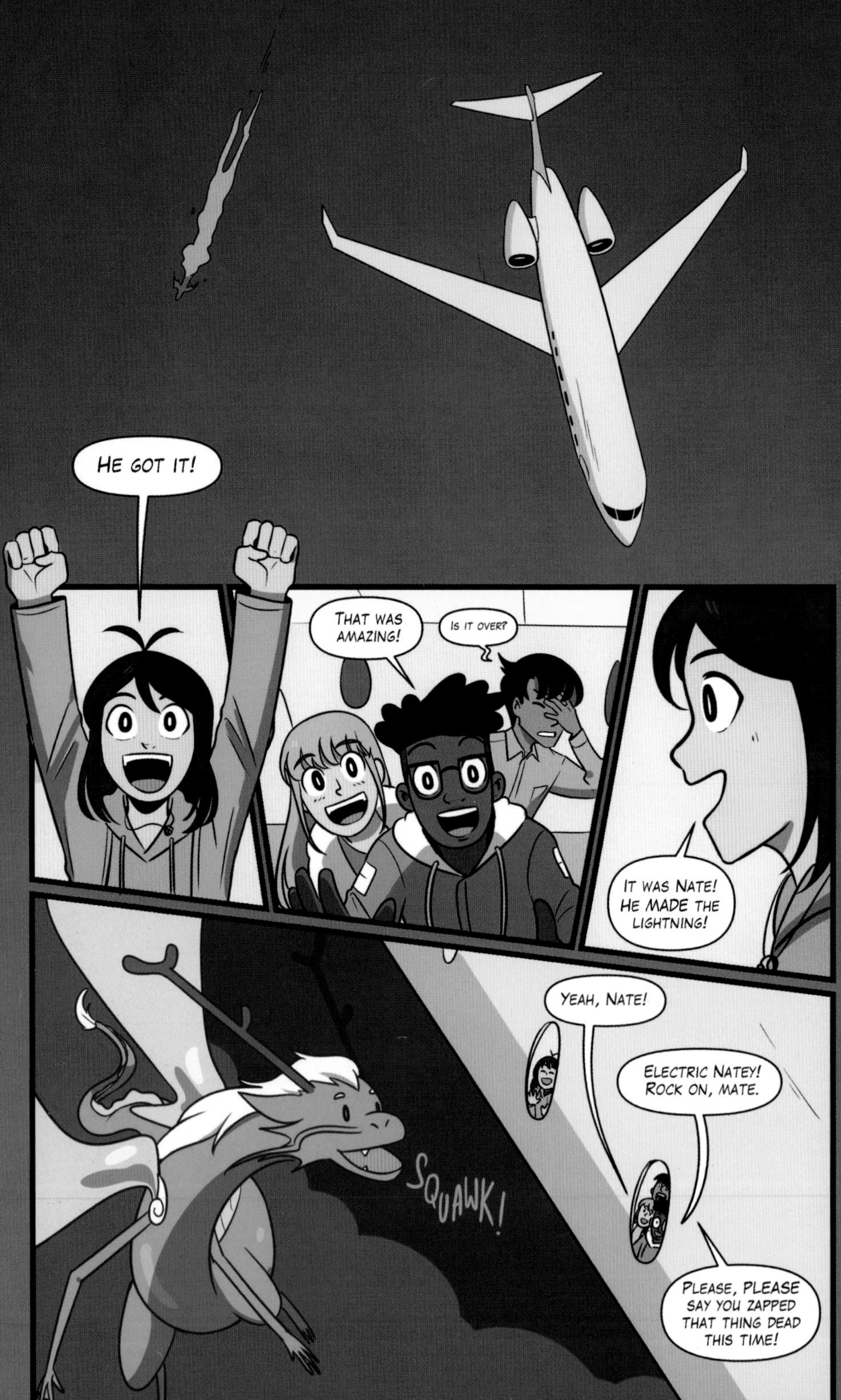

He got it!
That was amazing!
Is it over?
It was Nate! He MADE the lightning!
Yeah, Nate!
Electric Natey! Rock on, mate.
Please, PLEASE say you zapped that thing dead this time!
SQUAWK!

DR. KIM! NATE GOT IT!

THAT'S GREAT! HE SHOULD KEEP TRACKING US, GRACE. MY PILOT IS LANDING IN A SMALL AIRPORT OUTSIDE PARIS.

WE'LL BE ON THE GROUND SHORTLY.

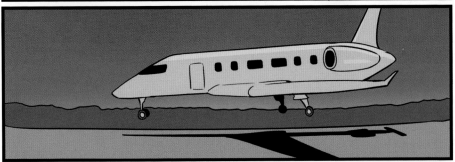

HERE HE COMES!

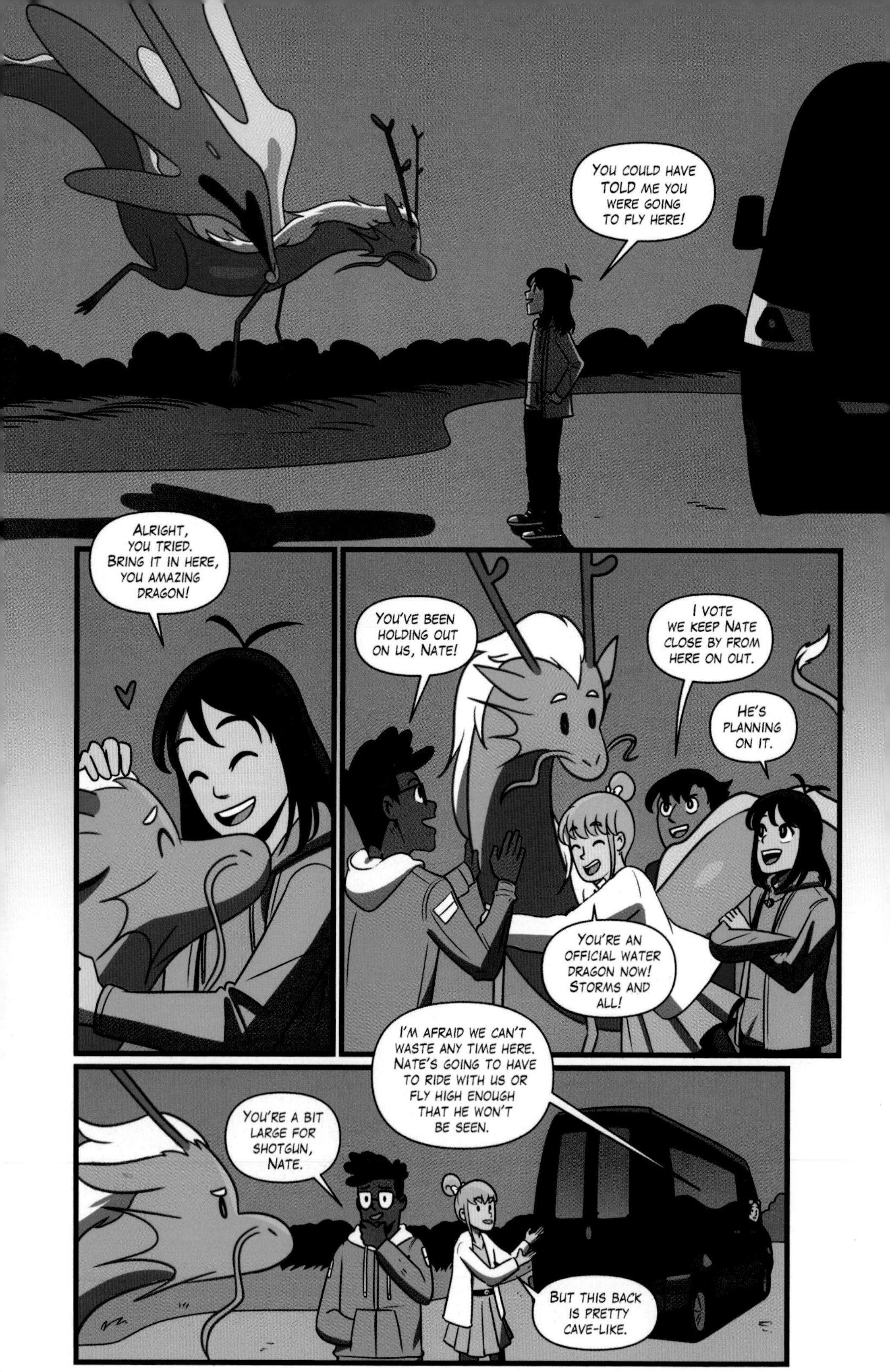

YOU COULD HAVE TOLD ME YOU WERE GOING TO FLY HERE!
ALRIGHT, YOU TRIED. BRING IT IN HERE, YOU AMAZING DRAGON!
YOU'VE BEEN HOLDING OUT ON US, NATE!
I VOTE WE KEEP NATE CLOSE BY FROM HERE ON OUT.
HE'S PLANNING ON IT.
YOU'RE AN OFFICIAL WATER DRAGON NOW! STORMS AND ALL!
I'M AFRAID WE CAN'T WASTE ANY TIME HERE. NATE'S GOING TO HAVE TO RIDE WITH US OR FLY HIGH ENOUGH THAT HE WON'T BE SEEN.
YOU'RE A BIT LARGE FOR SHOTGUN, NATE.
BUT THIS BACK IS PRETTY CAVE-LIKE.

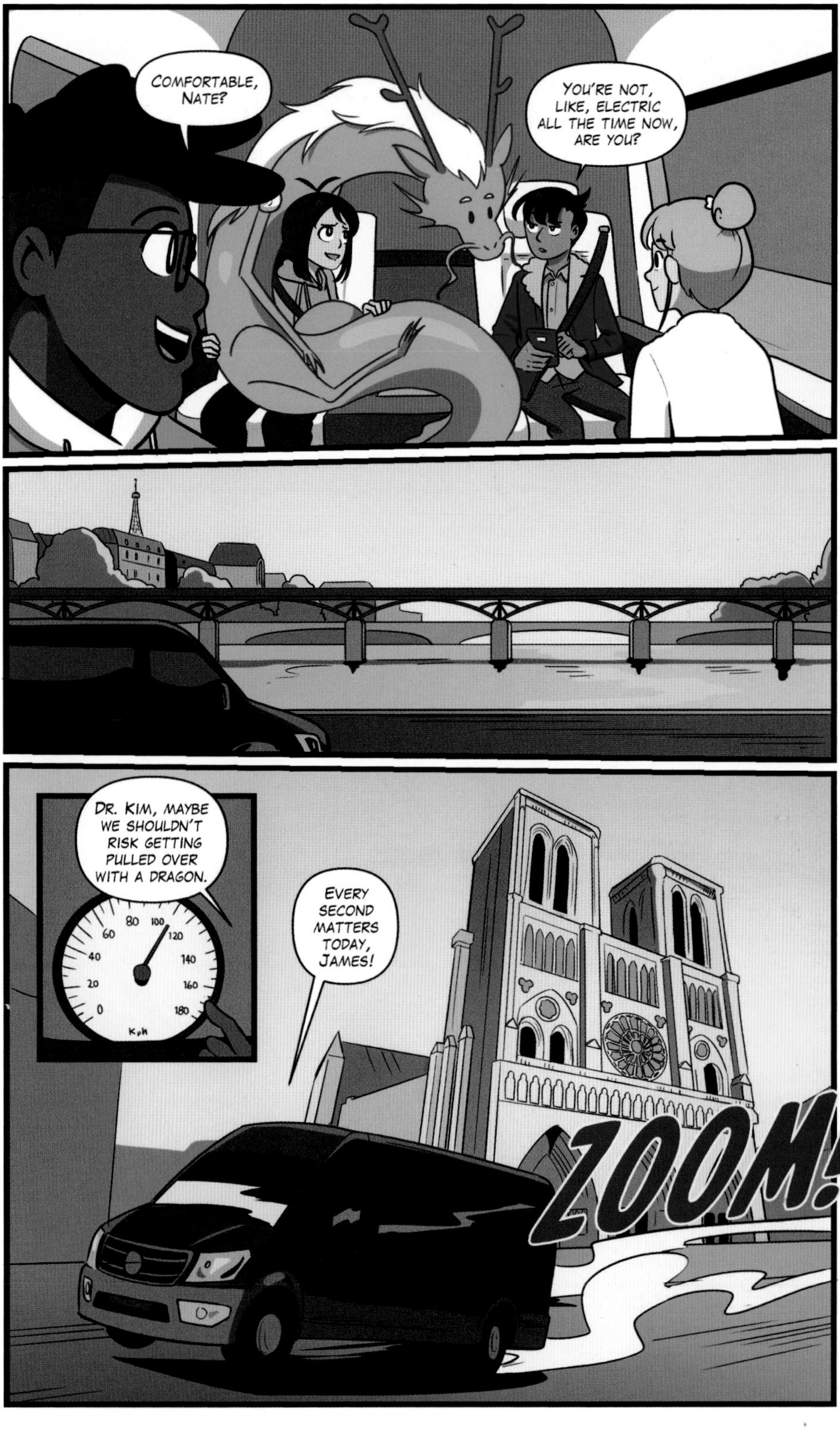
COMFORTABLE, NATE?
YOU'RE NOT, LIKE, ELECTRIC ALL THE TIME NOW, ARE YOU?
DR. KIM, MAYBE WE SHOULDN'T RISK GETTING PULLED OVER WITH A DRAGON.
EVERY SECOND MATTERS TODAY, JAMES!
ZOOM!

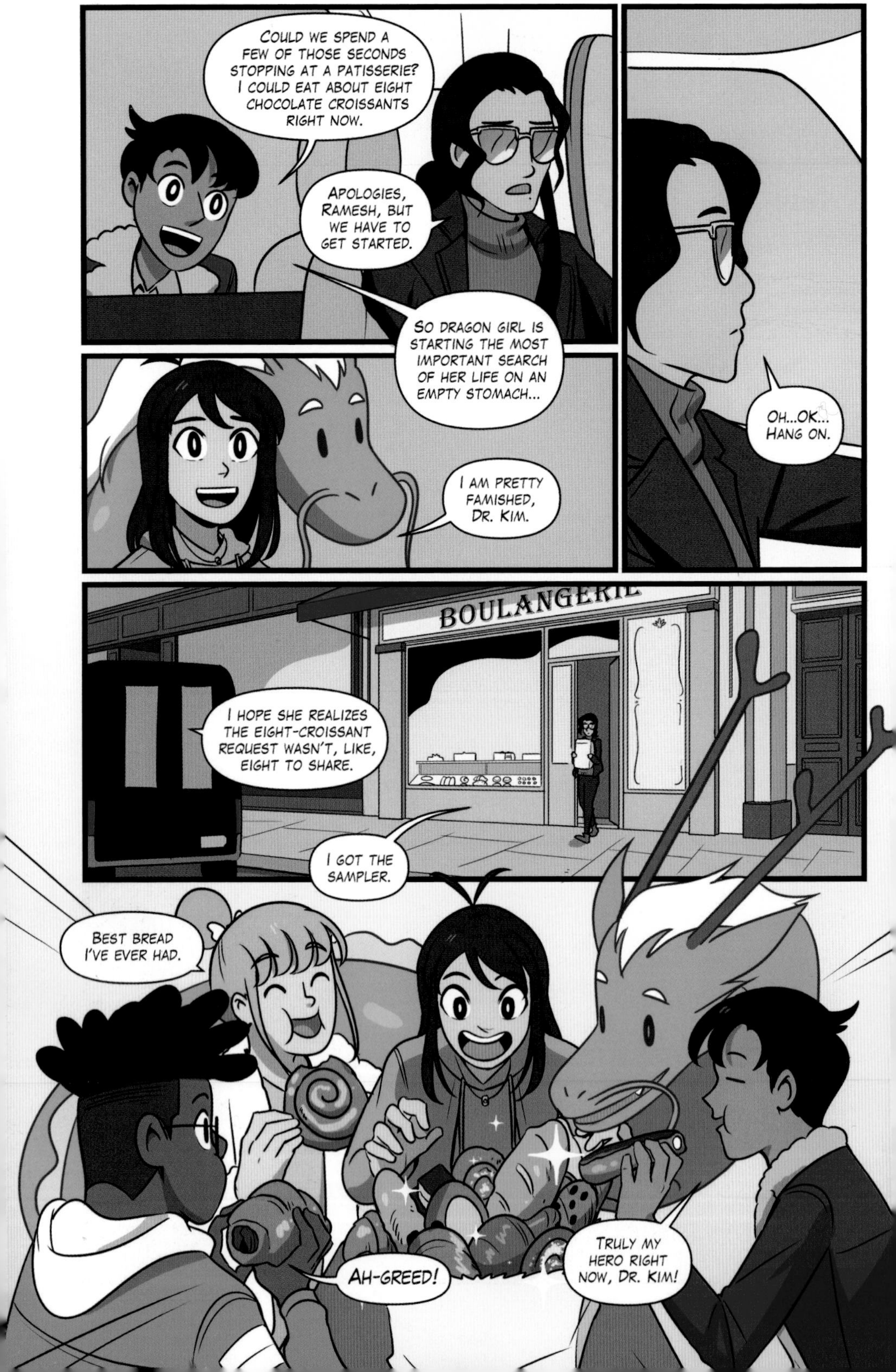
Could we spend a few of those seconds stopping at a patisserie? I could eat about eight chocolate croissants right now.
Apologies, Ramesh, but we have to get started.
So dragon girl is starting the most important search of her life on an empty stomach...
I am pretty famished, Dr. Kim.
Oh...OK... Hang on.
BOULANGERIE
I hope she realizes the eight-croissant request wasn't, like, eight to share.
I got the sampler.
Best bread I've ever had.
Ah-greed!
Truly my hero right now, Dr. Kim!

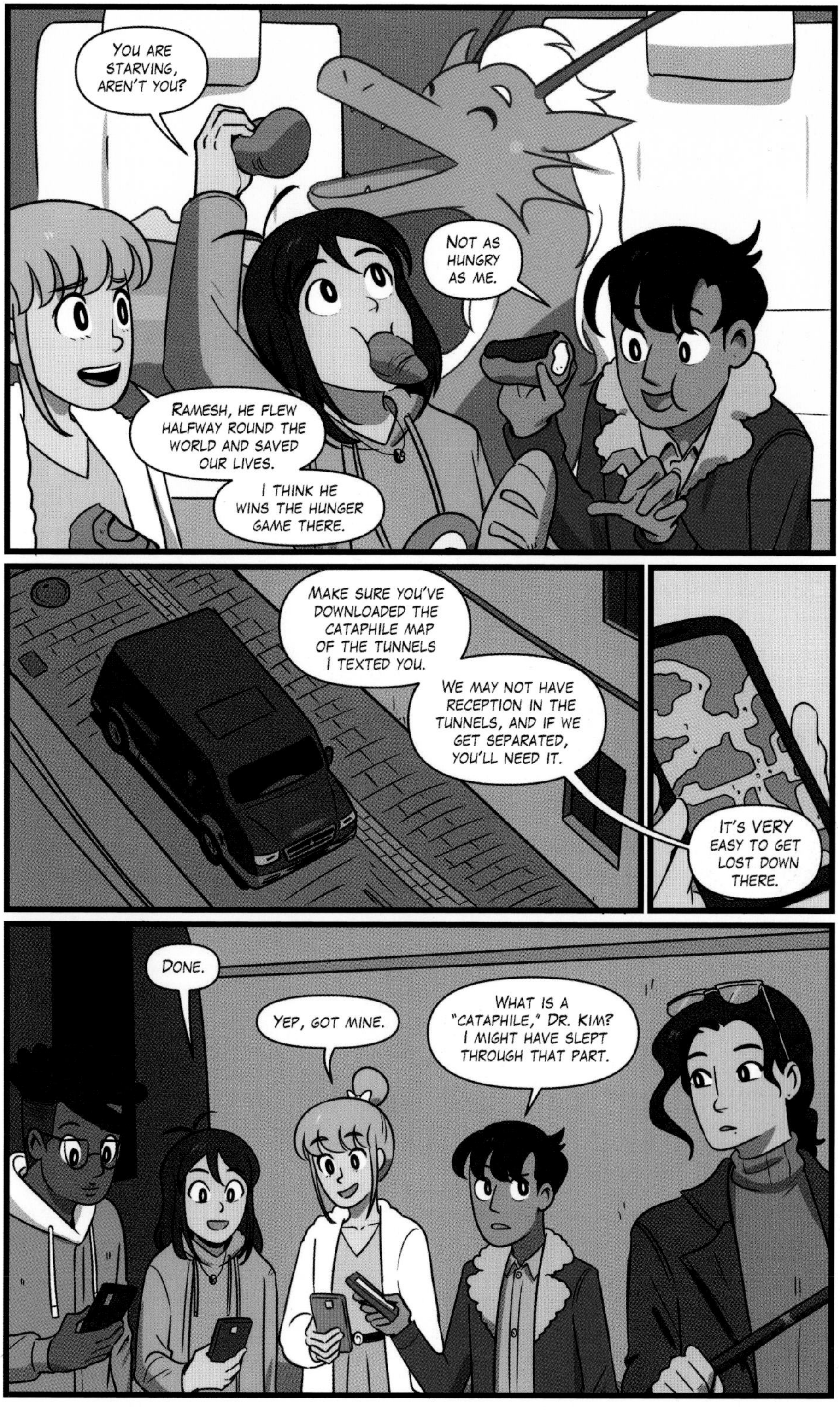
YOU ARE STARVING, AREN'T YOU?
NOT AS HUNGRY AS ME.
RAMESH, HE FLEW HALFWAY ROUND THE WORLD AND SAVED OUR LIVES.
I THINK HE WINS THE HUNGER GAME THERE.
MAKE SURE YOU'VE DOWNLOADED THE CATAPHILE MAP OF THE TUNNELS I TEXTED YOU.
WE MAY NOT HAVE RECEPTION IN THE TUNNELS, AND IF WE GET SEPARATED, YOU'LL NEED IT.
IT'S VERY EASY TO GET LOST DOWN THERE.
DONE.
YEP, GOT MINE.
WHAT IS A "CATAPHILE," DR. KIM? I MIGHT HAVE SLEPT THROUGH THAT PART.

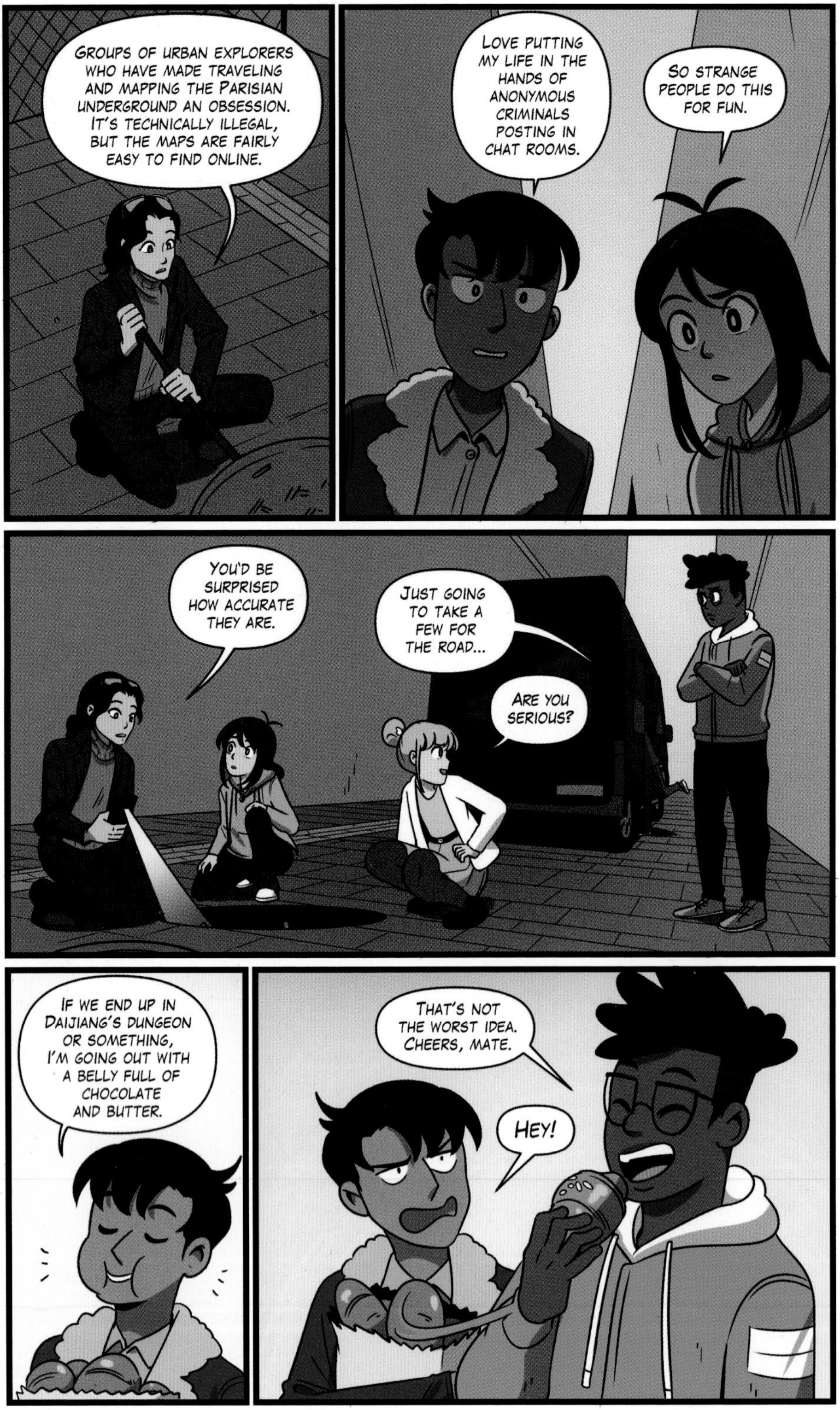
GROUPS OF URBAN EXPLORERS WHO HAVE MADE TRAVELING AND MAPPING THE PARISIAN UNDERGROUND AN OBSESSION. IT'S TECHNICALLY ILLEGAL, BUT THE MAPS ARE FAIRLY EASY TO FIND ONLINE.
LOVE PUTTING MY LIFE IN THE HANDS OF ANONYMOUS CRIMINALS POSTING IN CHAT ROOMS.
SO STRANGE PEOPLE DO THIS FOR FUN.
YOU'D BE SURPRISED HOW ACCURATE THEY ARE.
JUST GOING TO TAKE A FEW FOR THE ROAD...
ARE YOU SERIOUS?
IF WE END UP IN DAIJIANG'S DUNGEON OR SOMETHING, I'M GOING OUT WITH A BELLY FULL OF CHOCOLATE AND BUTTER.
THAT'S NOT THE WORST IDEA. CHEERS, MATE.
HEY!

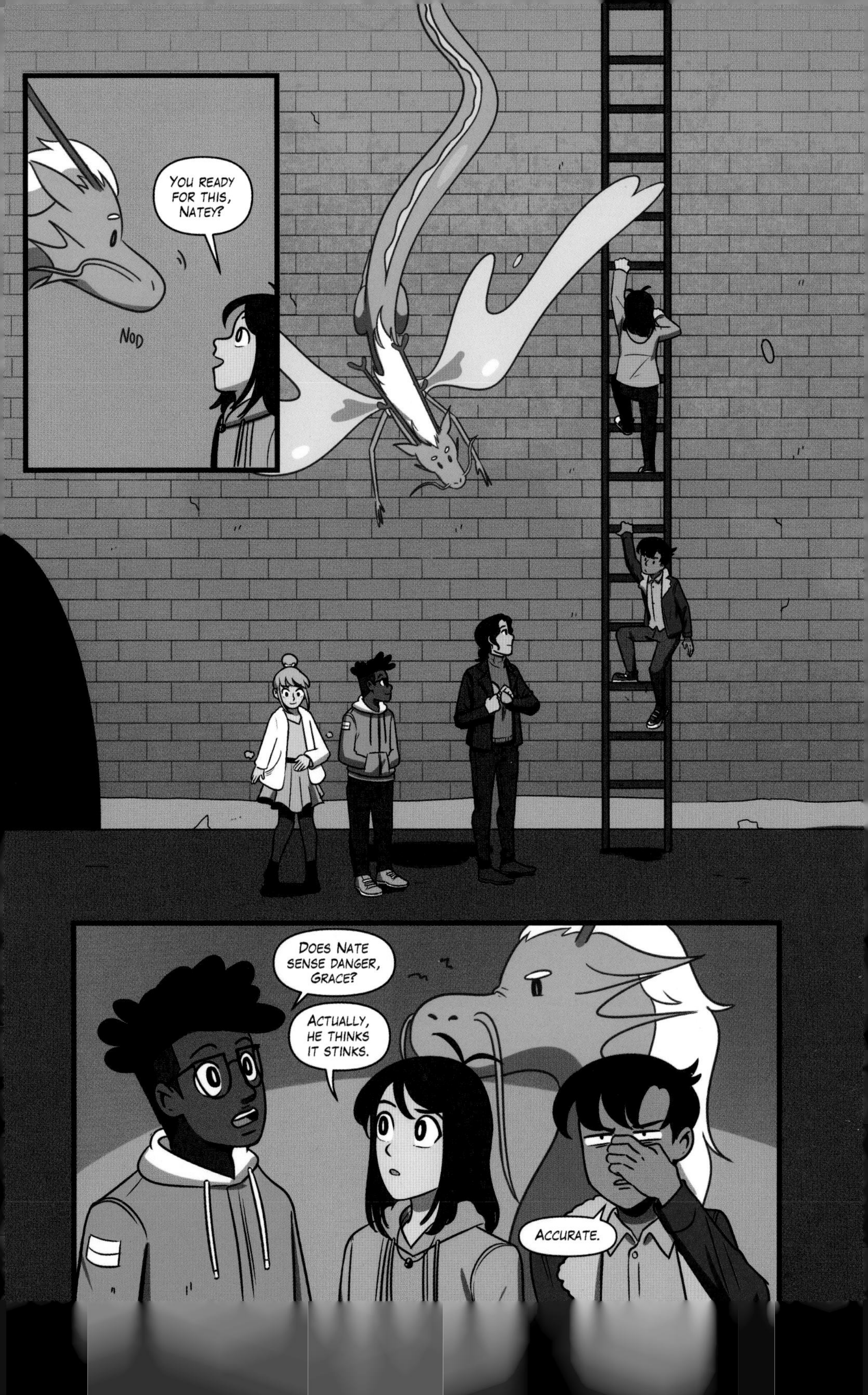
YOU READY FOR THIS, NATEY?
NOD
DOES NATE SENSE DANGER, GRACE?
ACTUALLY, HE THINKS IT STINKS.
ACCURATE.

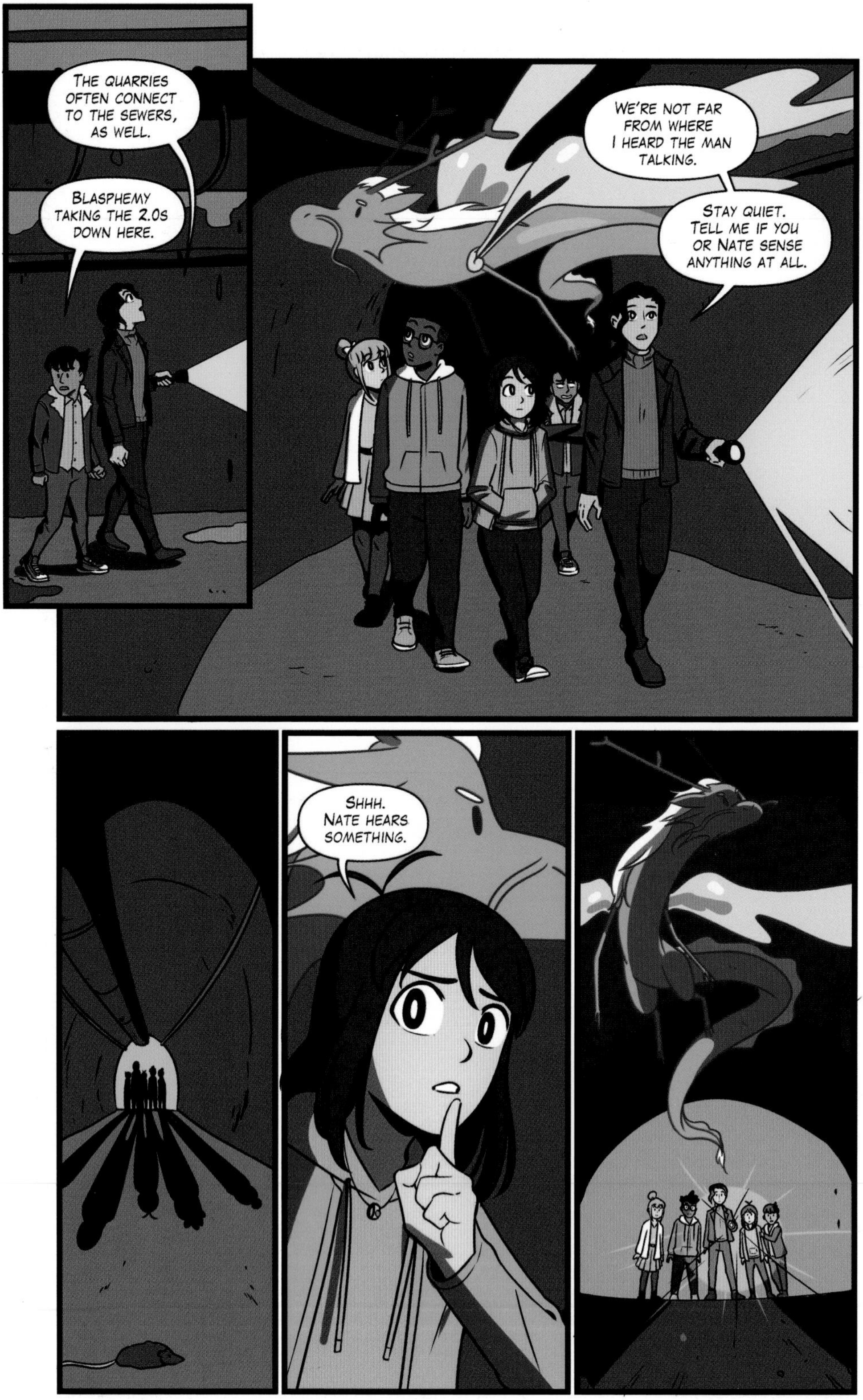
The quarries often connect to the sewers, as well.
Blasphemy taking the 2.0s down here.
We're not far from where I heard the man talking.
Stay quiet. Tell me if you or Nate sense anything at all.
Shhh. Nate hears something.

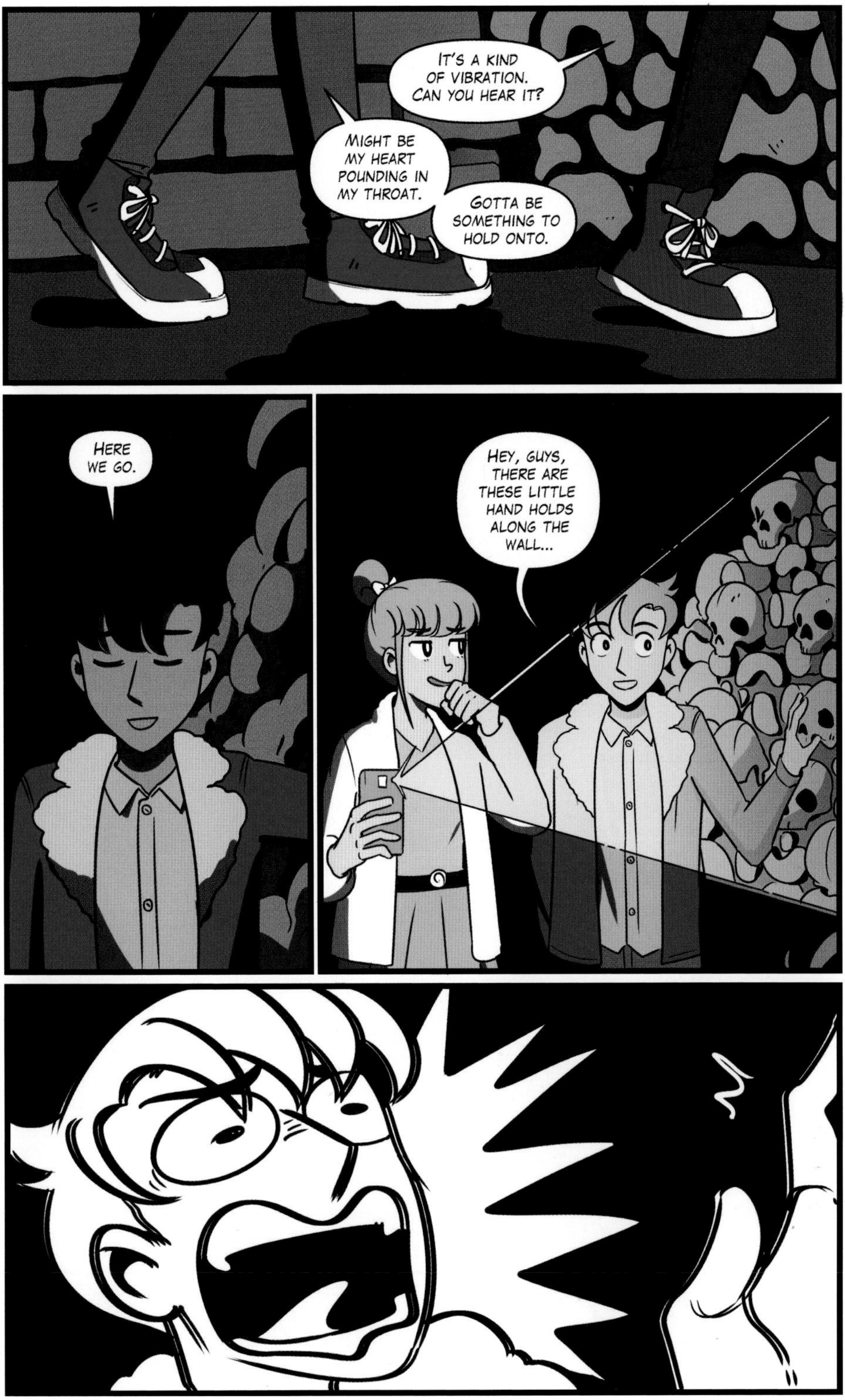
IT'S A KIND OF VIBRATION. CAN YOU HEAR IT?
MIGHT BE MY HEART POUNDING IN MY THROAT.
GOTTA BE SOMETHING TO HOLD ONTO.
HERE WE GO.
HEY, GUYS, THERE ARE THESE LITTLE HAND HOLDS ALONG THE WALL...

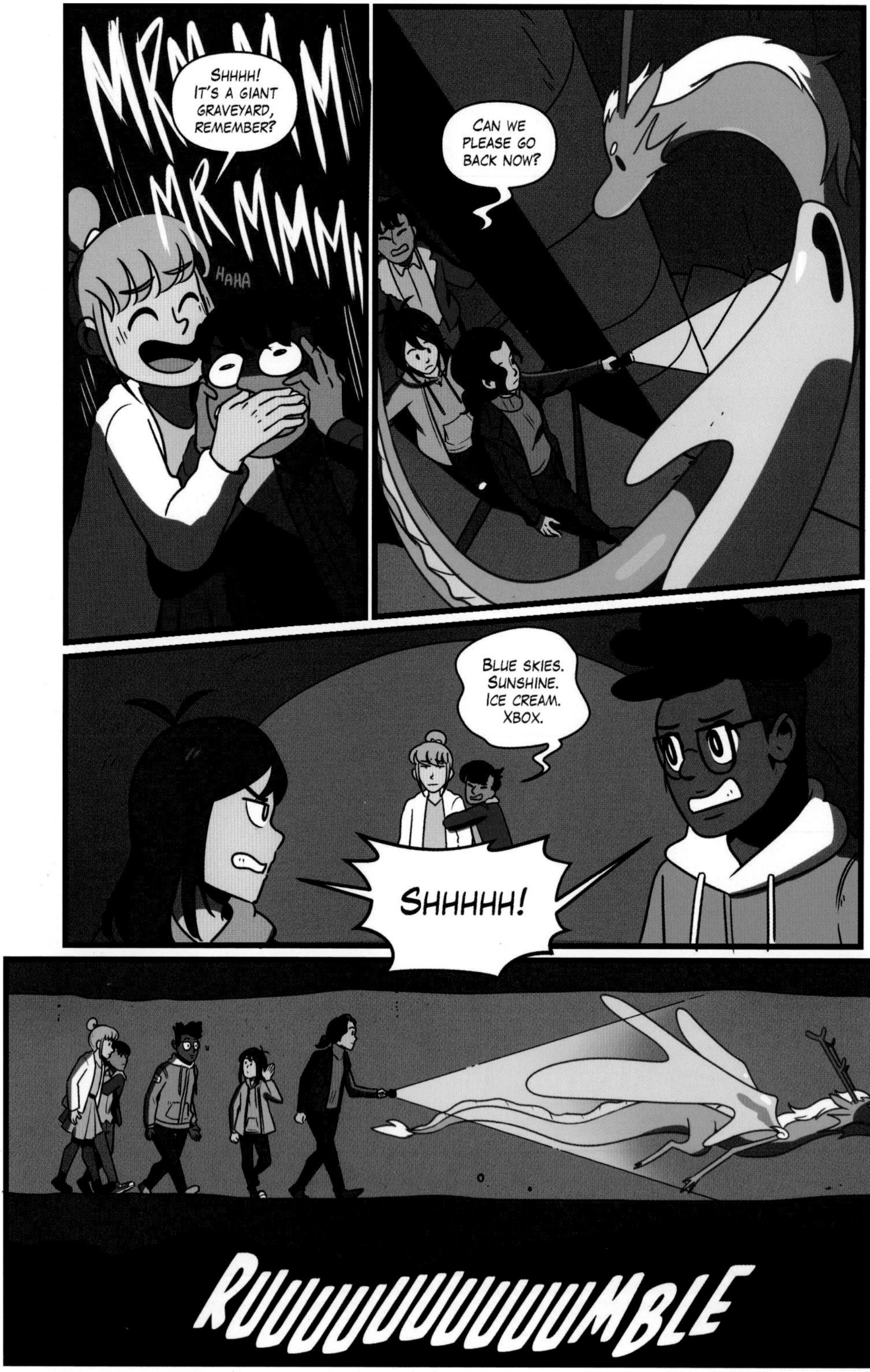
MRMMM MRMMM
SHHHH! IT'S A GIANT GRAVEYARD, REMEMBER?
HAHA
CAN WE PLEASE GO BACK NOW?
BLUE SKIES. SUNSHINE. ICE CREAM. XBOX.
SHHHHH!
RUUUUUUUUUUMBLE

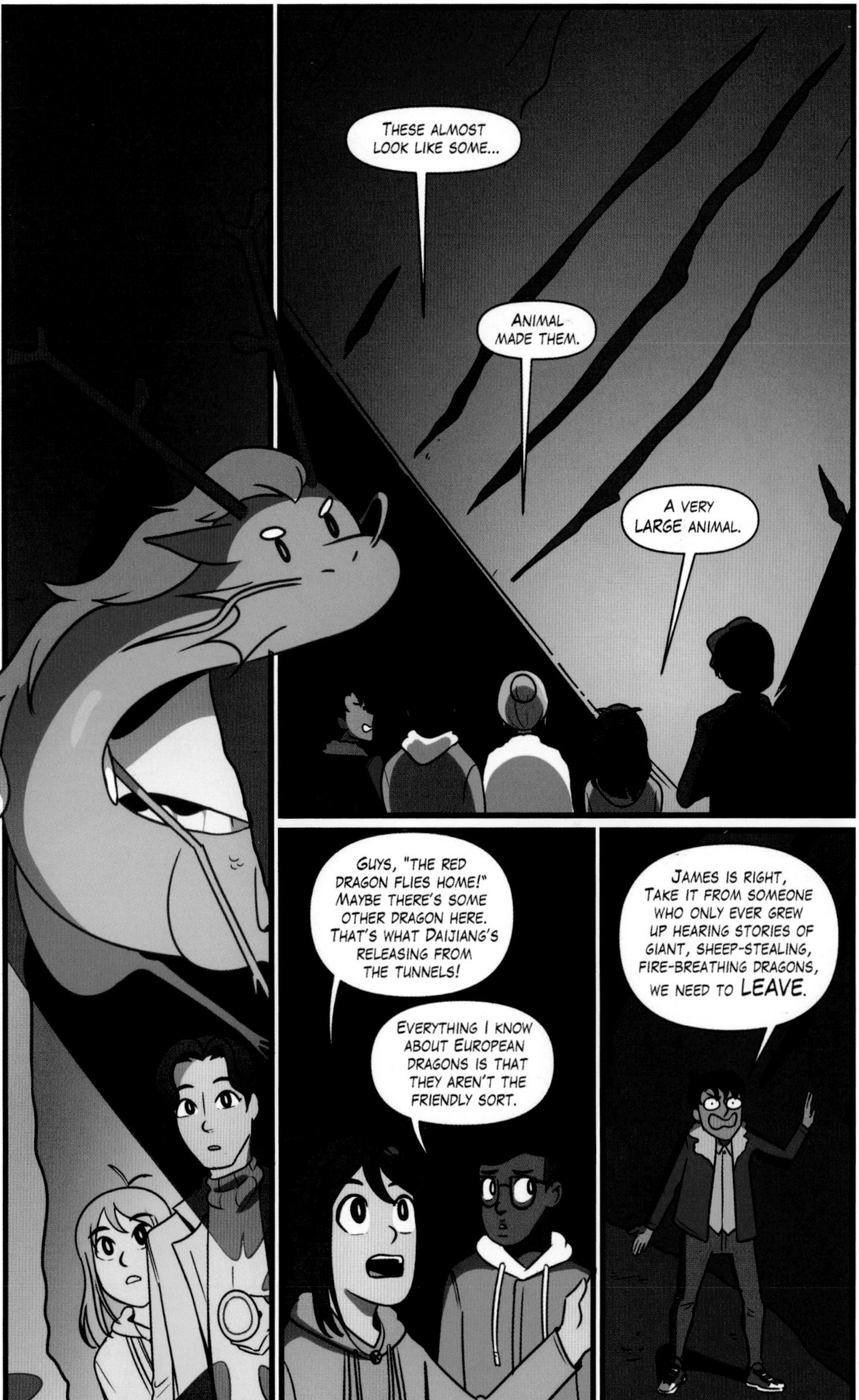
THESE ALMOST LOOK LIKE SOME...
ANIMAL MADE THEM.
A VERY LARGE ANIMAL.
GUYS, "THE RED DRAGON FLIES HOME!" MAYBE THERE'S SOME OTHER DRAGON HERE. THAT'S WHAT DAIJIANG'S RELEASING FROM THE TUNNELS!
EVERYTHING I KNOW ABOUT EUROPEAN DRAGONS IS THAT THEY AREN'T THE FRIENDLY SORT.
JAMES IS RIGHT, TAKE IT FROM SOMEONE WHO ONLY EVER GREW UP HEARING STORIES OF GIANT, SHEEP-STEALING, FIRE-BREATHING DRAGONS, WE NEED TO LEAVE.

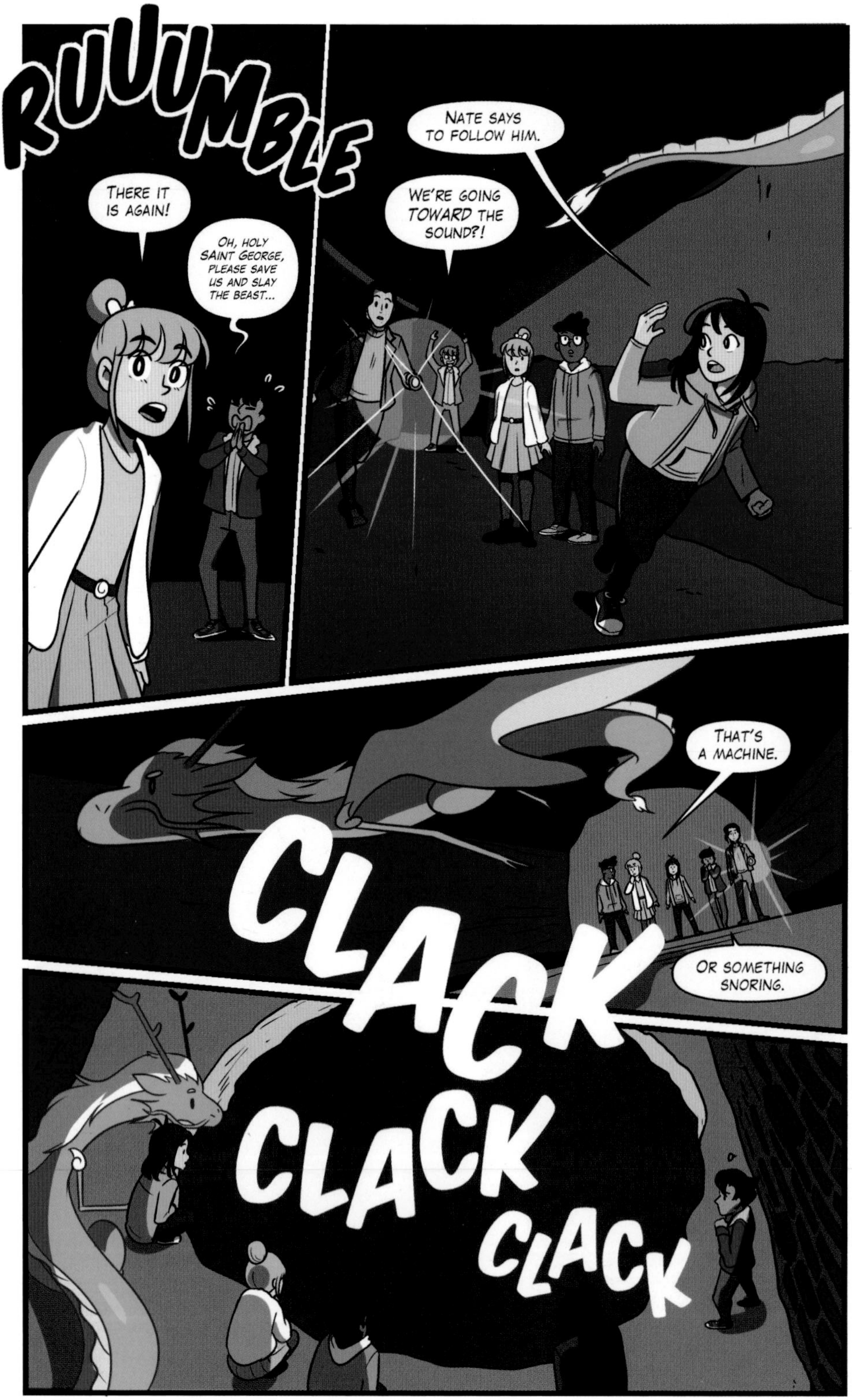
RUUUMBLE
THERE IT IS AGAIN!
OH, HOLY SAINT GEORGE, PLEASE SAVE US AND SLAY THE BEAST...
NATE SAYS TO FOLLOW HIM.
WE'RE GOING *TOWARD* THE SOUND?!
THAT'S A MACHINE.
OR SOMETHING SNORING.
CLACK
CLACK
CLACK

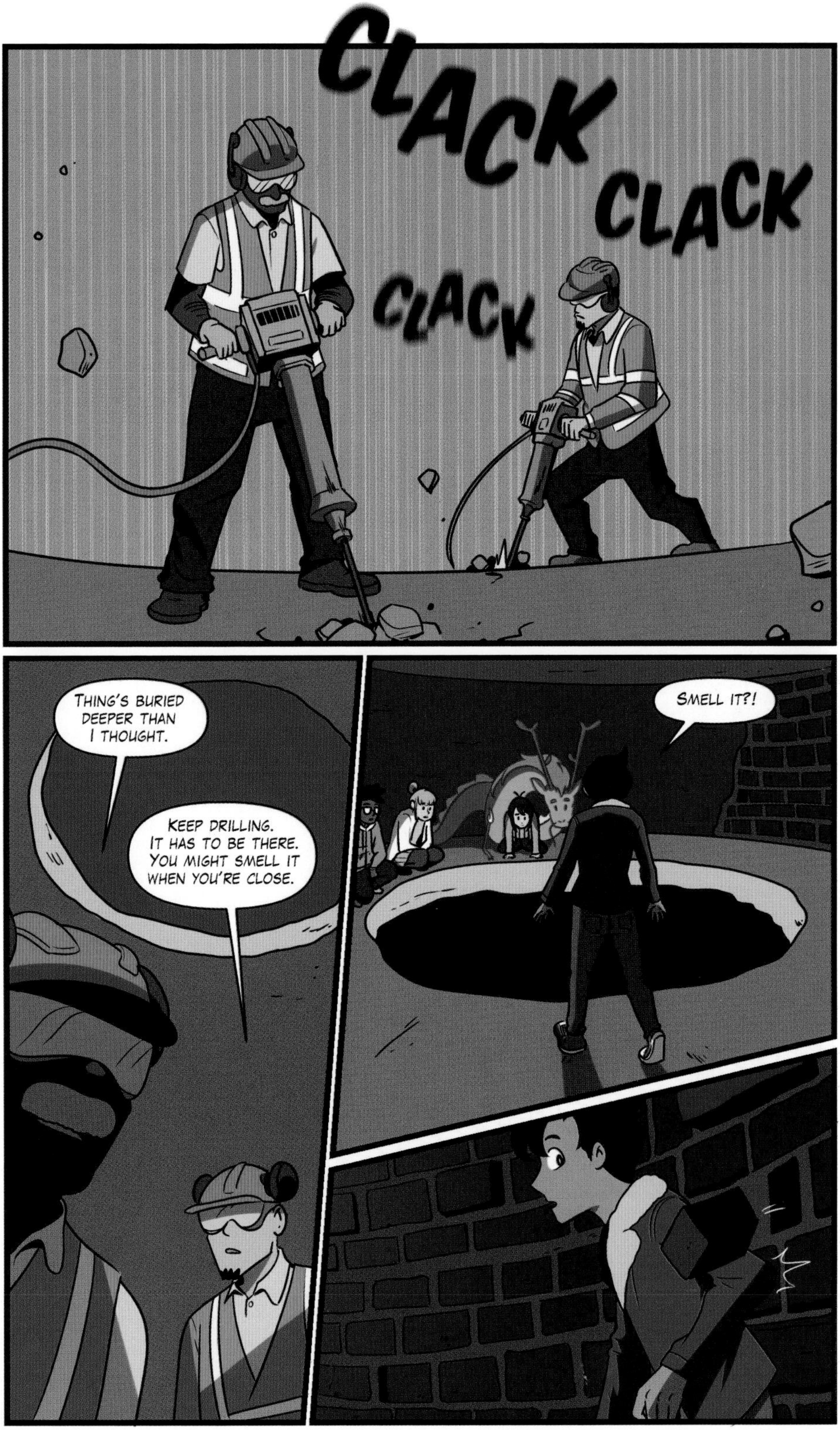
CLACK
CLACK
CLACK
THING'S BURIED DEEPER THAN I THOUGHT.
KEEP DRILLING. IT HAS TO BE THERE. YOU MIGHT SMELL IT WHEN YOU'RE CLOSE.
SMELL IT?!

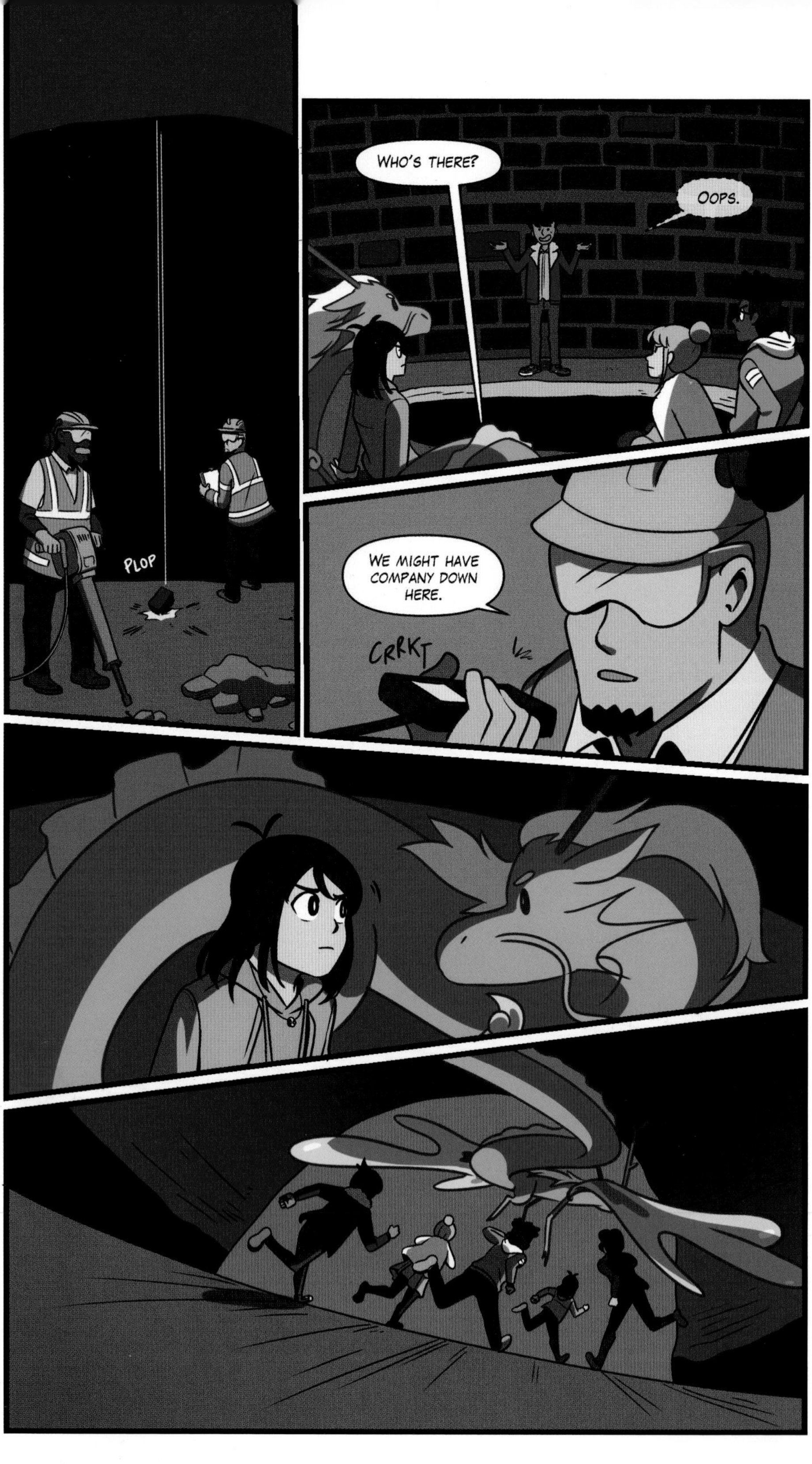
PLOP
WHO'S THERE?
OOPS.
WE MIGHT HAVE COMPANY DOWN HERE.
CRRKT

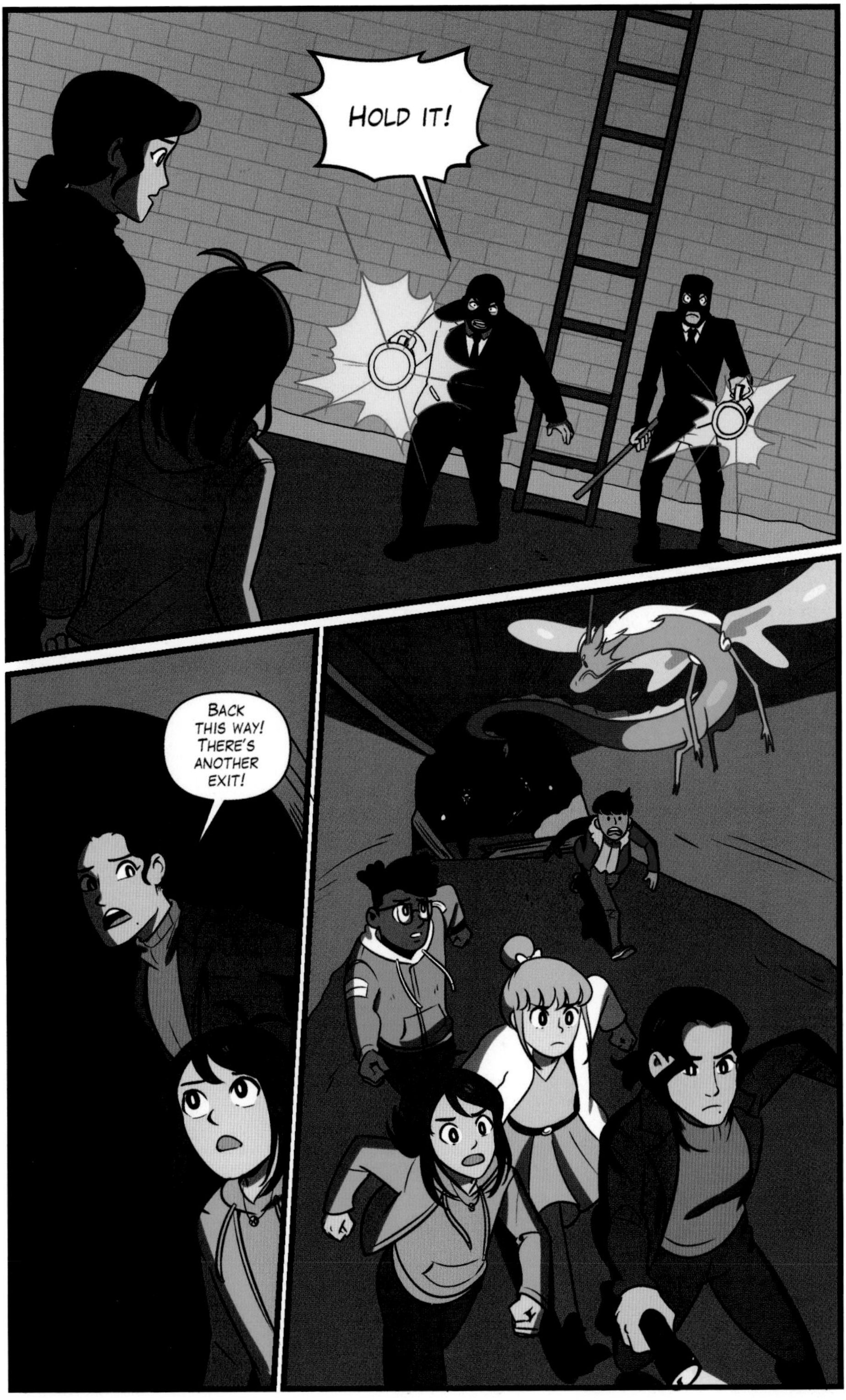
HOLD IT!
BACK THIS WAY! THERE'S ANOTHER EXIT!

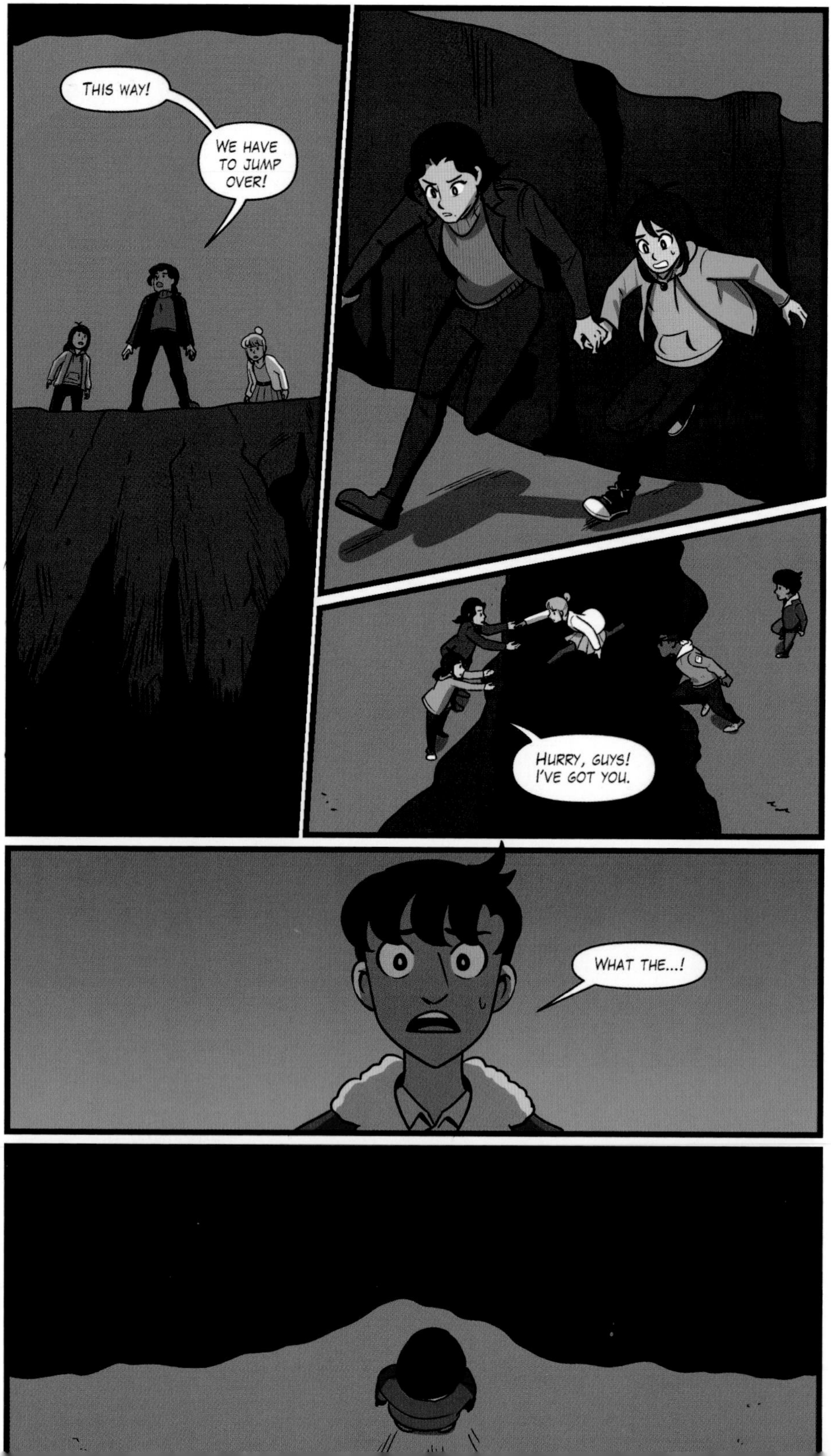
THIS WAY!
WE HAVE TO JUMP OVER!
HURRY, GUYS! I'VE GOT YOU.
WHAT THE...!

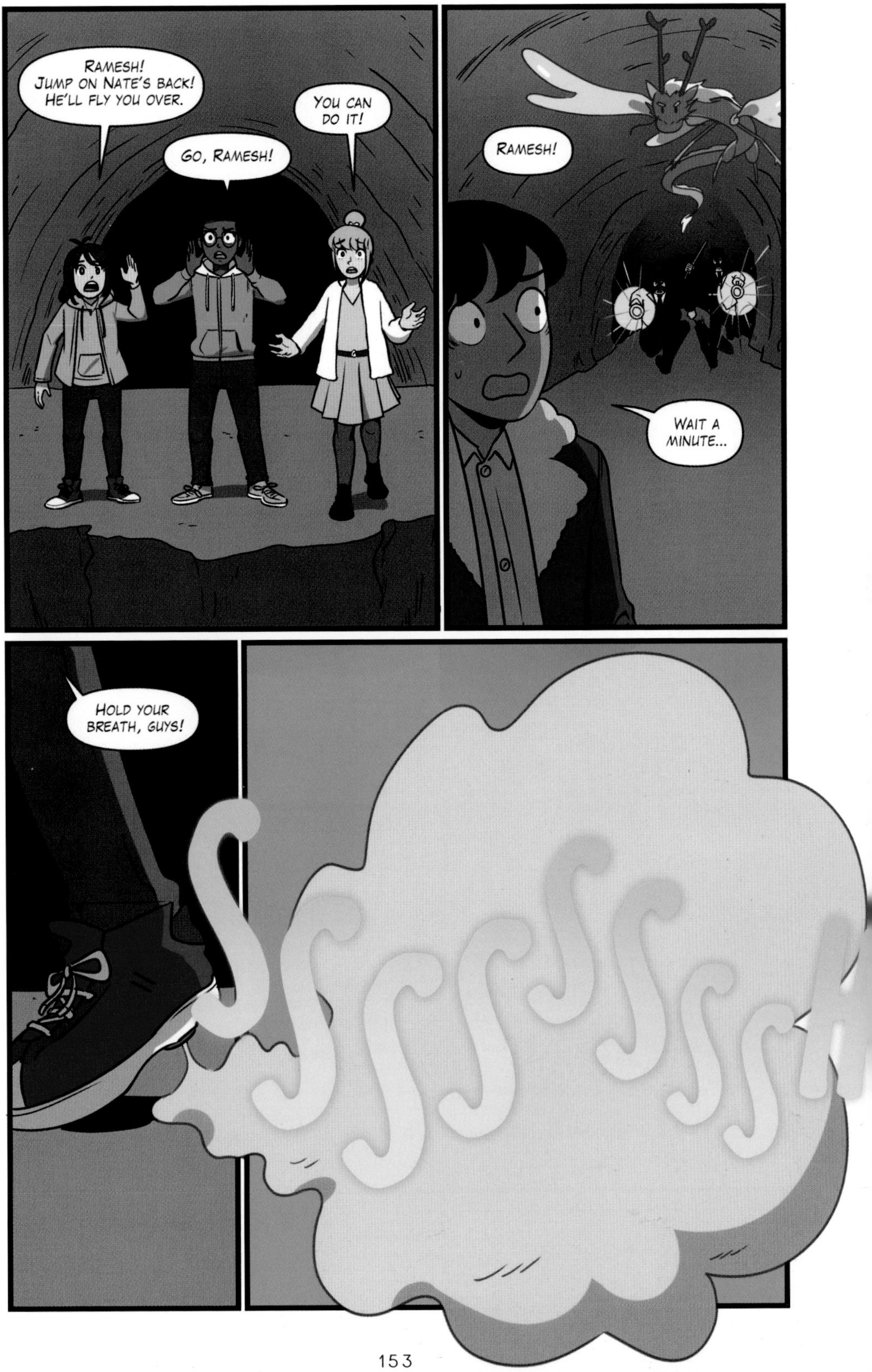
RAMESH! JUMP ON NATE'S BACK! HE'LL FLY YOU OVER.
GO, RAMESH!
YOU CAN DO IT!
RAMESH!
WAIT A MINUTE...
HOLD YOUR BREATH, GUYS!

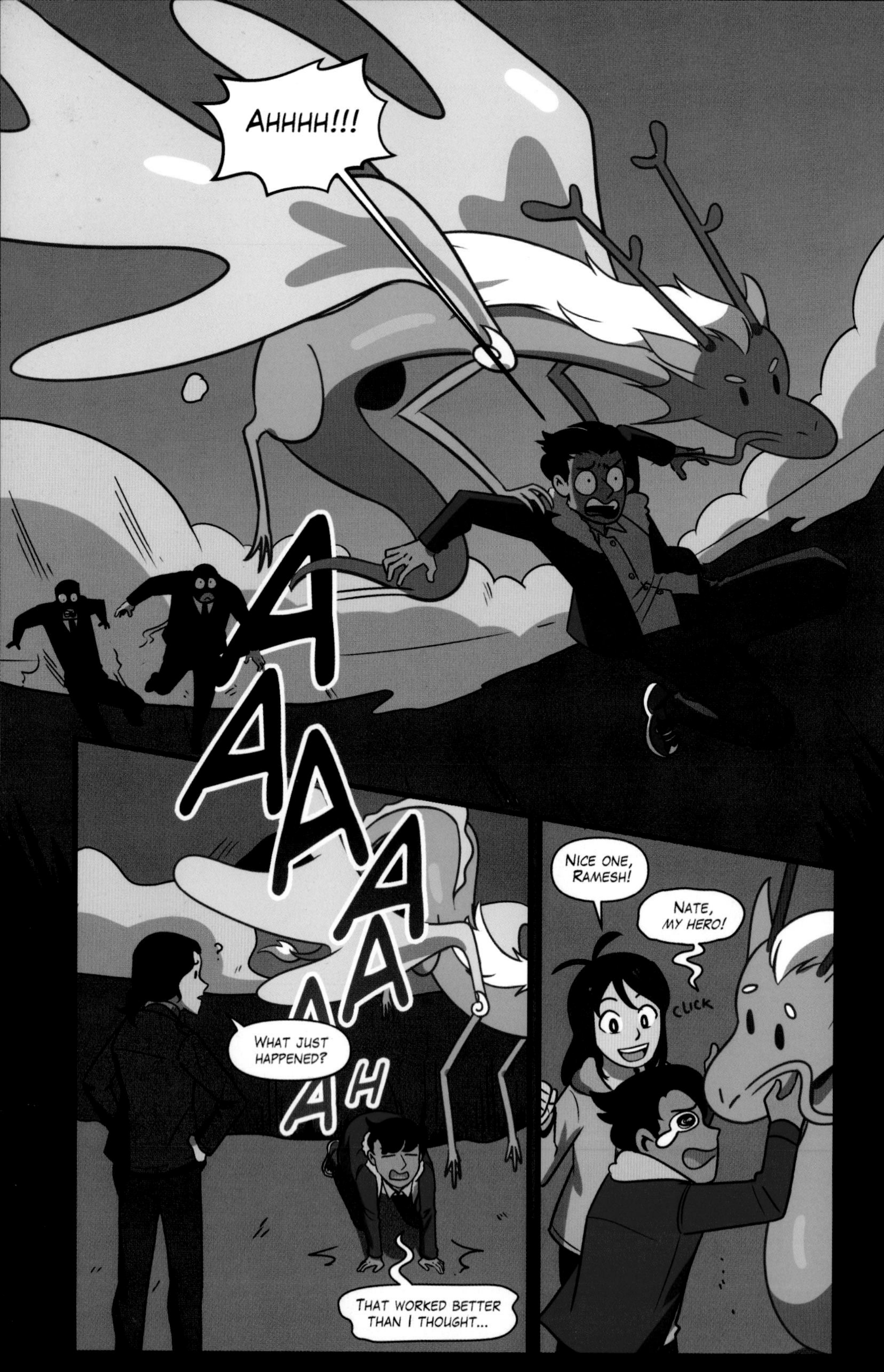
AHHHH!!!
AAAAAAAAH
WHAT JUST HAPPENED?
THAT WORKED BETTER THAN I THOUGHT...
NICE ONE, RAMESH!
NATE, MY HERO!
CLICK

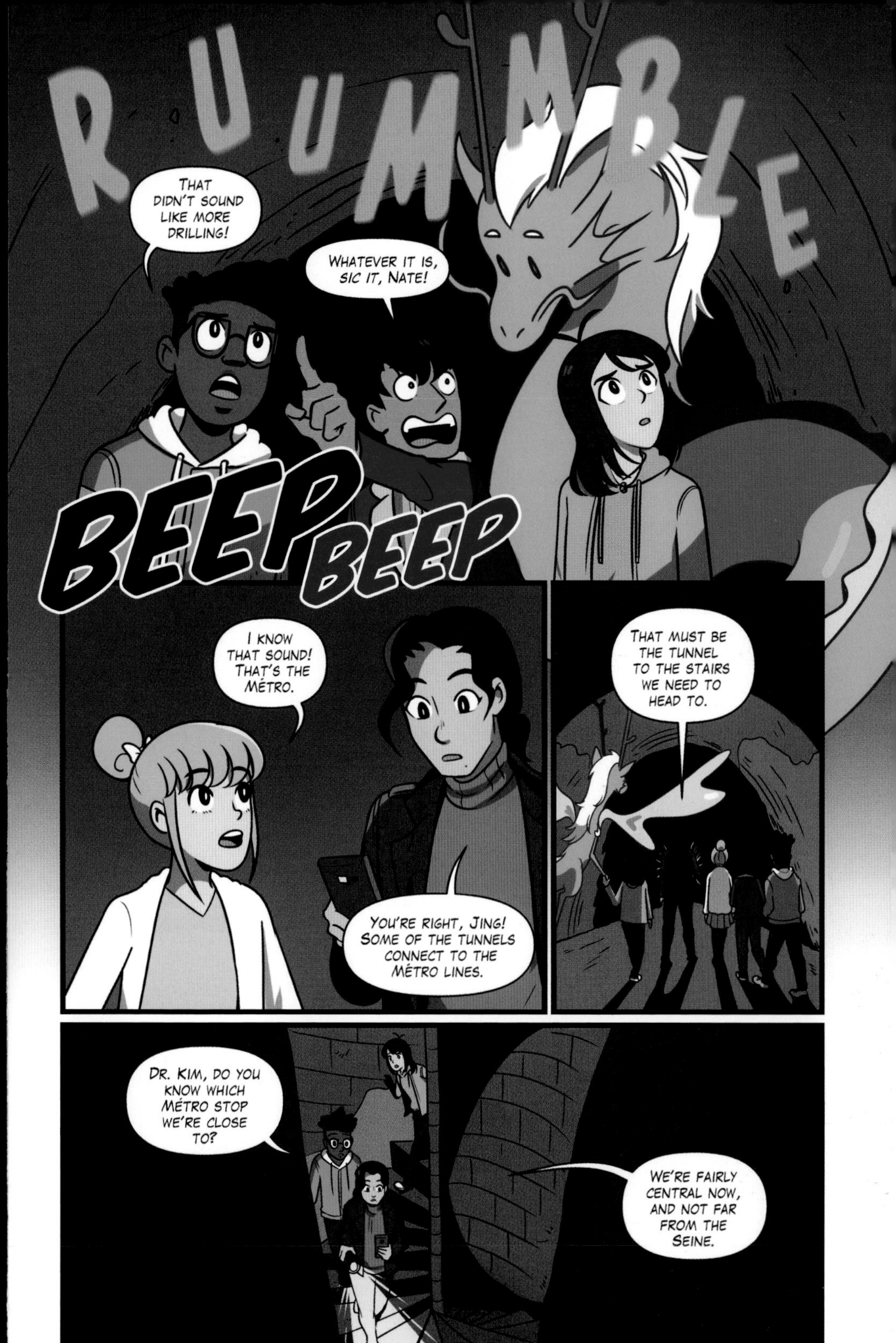
RUMMBLE
THAT DIDN'T SOUND LIKE MORE DRILLING!
WHATEVER IT IS, SIC IT, NATE!
BEEP BEEP
I KNOW THAT SOUND! THAT'S THE MÉTRO.
YOU'RE RIGHT, JING! SOME OF THE TUNNELS CONNECT TO THE MÉTRO LINES.
THAT MUST BE THE TUNNEL TO THE STAIRS WE NEED TO HEAD TO.
DR. KIM, DO YOU KNOW WHICH MÉTRO STOP WE'RE CLOSE TO?
WE'RE FAIRLY CENTRAL NOW, AND NOT FAR FROM THE SEINE.

I THOUGHT SO!

IT'S THE LOUVRE!

THE LOUVRE?

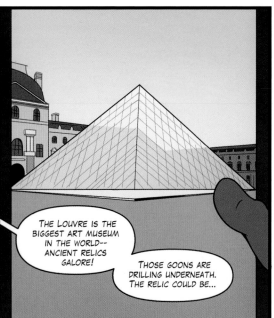

THE LOUVRE IS THE BIGGEST ART MUSEUM IN THE WORLD-- ANCIENT RELICS GALORE!

THOSE GOONS ARE DRILLING UNDERNEATH. THE RELIC COULD BE...

OF COURSE, IN THE MUSEUM!

YOU THINK THEY'RE TRYING TO TUNNEL IN?!

MAYBE. OR THEY'RE KNOCKING OUT THE ELECTRICITY-- SHUTTING DOWN THE SECURITY SYSTEM.

OR BUSTING THE SEWER LINE? REMEMBER HE SAID YOU CAN SMELL IT.

SOMETHING TELLS ME THE BIG ACTION PLAN ISN'T BACKING UP THE MUSEUM TOILETS.

MAYHEM BREAKS OUT WHEN PEOPLE CAN'T GO.

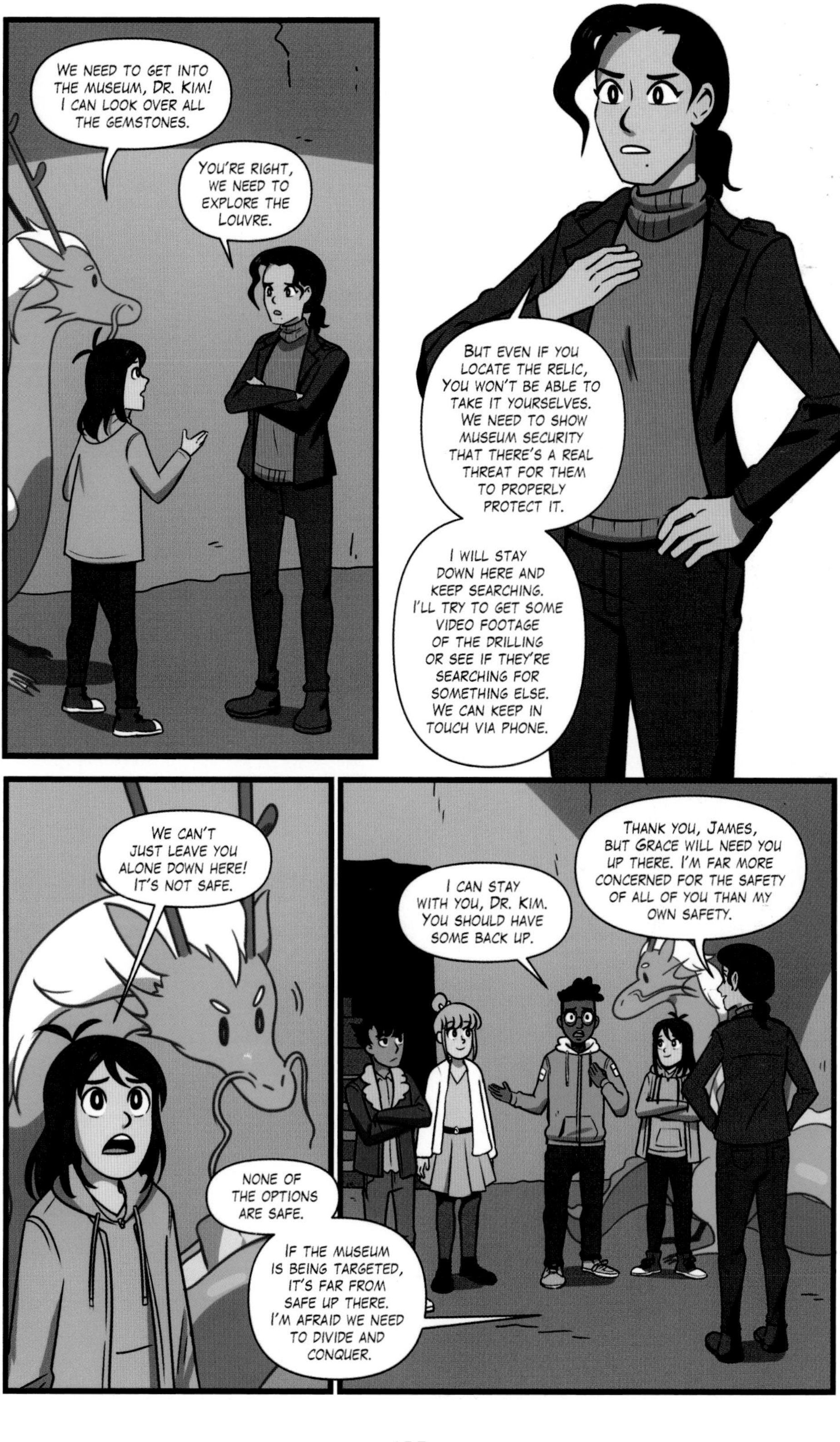
WE NEED TO GET INTO THE MUSEUM, DR. KIM! I CAN LOOK OVER ALL THE GEMSTONES.
YOU'RE RIGHT, WE NEED TO EXPLORE THE LOUVRE.
BUT EVEN IF YOU LOCATE THE RELIC, YOU WON'T BE ABLE TO TAKE IT YOURSELVES. WE NEED TO SHOW MUSEUM SECURITY THAT THERE'S A REAL THREAT FOR THEM TO PROPERLY PROTECT IT.
I WILL STAY DOWN HERE AND KEEP SEARCHING. I'LL TRY TO GET SOME VIDEO FOOTAGE OF THE DRILLING OR SEE IF THEY'RE SEARCHING FOR SOMETHING ELSE. WE CAN KEEP IN TOUCH VIA PHONE.
WE CAN'T JUST LEAVE YOU ALONE DOWN HERE! IT'S NOT SAFE.
NONE OF THE OPTIONS ARE SAFE.
IF THE MUSEUM IS BEING TARGETED, IT'S FAR FROM SAFE UP THERE. I'M AFRAID WE NEED TO DIVIDE AND CONQUER.
I CAN STAY WITH YOU, DR. KIM. YOU SHOULD HAVE SOME BACK UP.
THANK YOU, JAMES, BUT GRACE WILL NEED YOU UP THERE. I'M FAR MORE CONCERNED FOR THE SAFETY OF ALL OF YOU THAN MY OWN SAFETY.

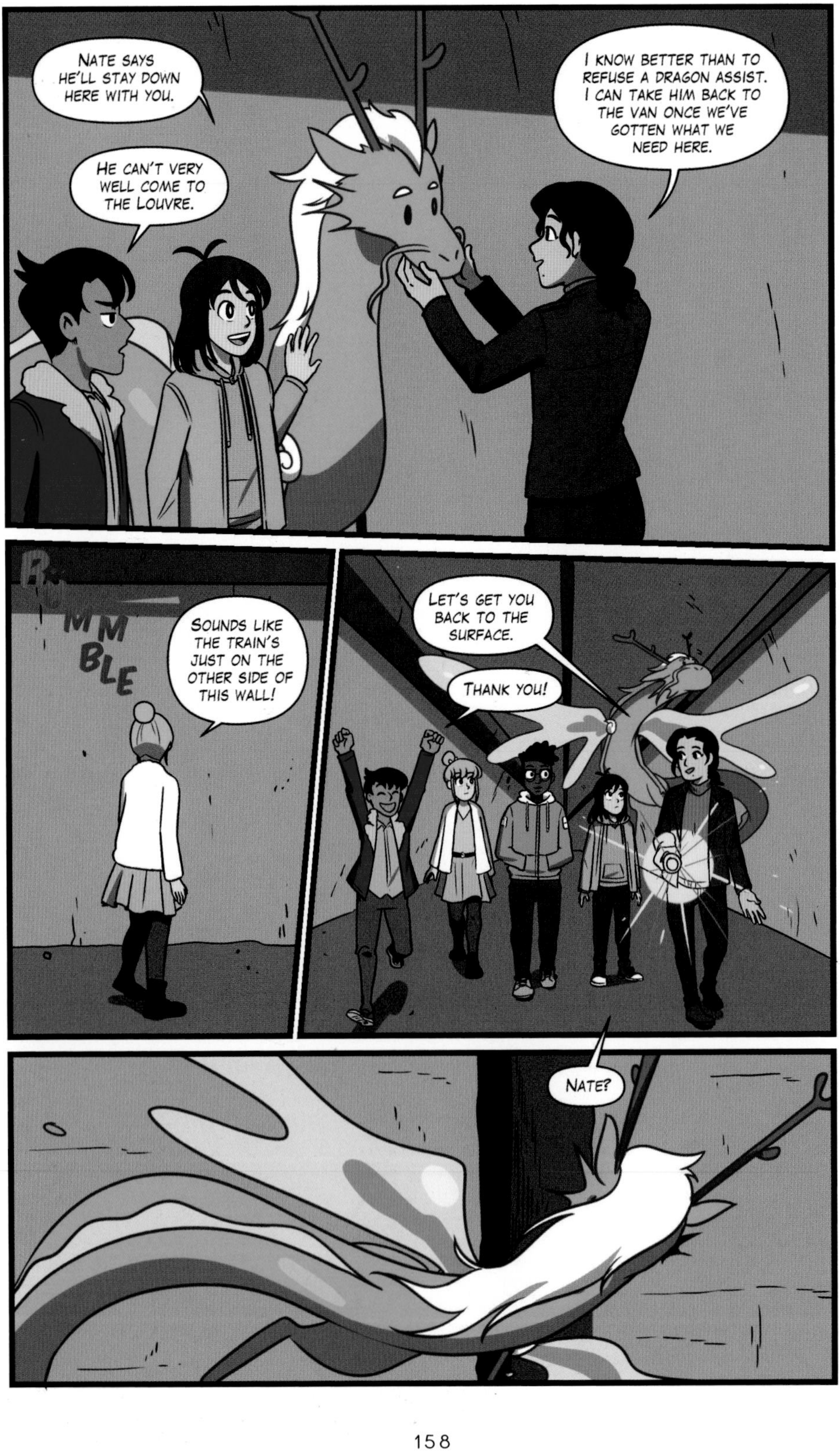
NATE SAYS HE'LL STAY DOWN HERE WITH YOU.
HE CAN'T VERY WELL COME TO THE LOUVRE.
I KNOW BETTER THAN TO REFUSE A DRAGON ASSIST. I CAN TAKE HIM BACK TO THE VAN ONCE WE'VE GOTTEN WHAT WE NEED HERE.
RUMMBLE
SOUNDS LIKE THE TRAIN'S JUST ON THE OTHER SIDE OF THIS WALL!
LET'S GET YOU BACK TO THE SURFACE.
THANK YOU!
NATE?

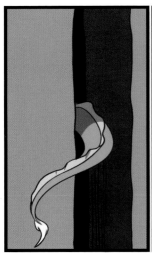

GUYS, OVER HERE! NATE FOUND THE TRACKS.

YES, I THINK THIS IS IT.

TAKE MY CREDIT CARD AND BUY THE PREMIUM TICKETS TO SKIP THE LONG LINE-- AND REMEMBER TO KEEP YOUR EYES PEELED FOR SUSPICIOUS ACTIVITY AND PEOPLE.

THE LOUVRE IS HUGE, RIGHT? ANY IDEA WHERE WE SHOULD START, DR. KIM?

THE BIGGEST STASH OF GEMS IS THE FRENCH CROWN JEWELS, BUT IT'S UNLIKELY THE SHARD WOULD HAVE ENDED UP THERE.

I'D STICK WITH THE EASTERN AND NEAR EASTERN ART EXHIBITS FIRST.

NOW, HURRY. THE MUSEUM IS OPENING SOON.

PLEASE BE SAFE, DR. KIM!

I AM THANKFUL TO ALL OF YOU. YOUR COURAGE AND COMPASSION ARE TRULY HEROIC.

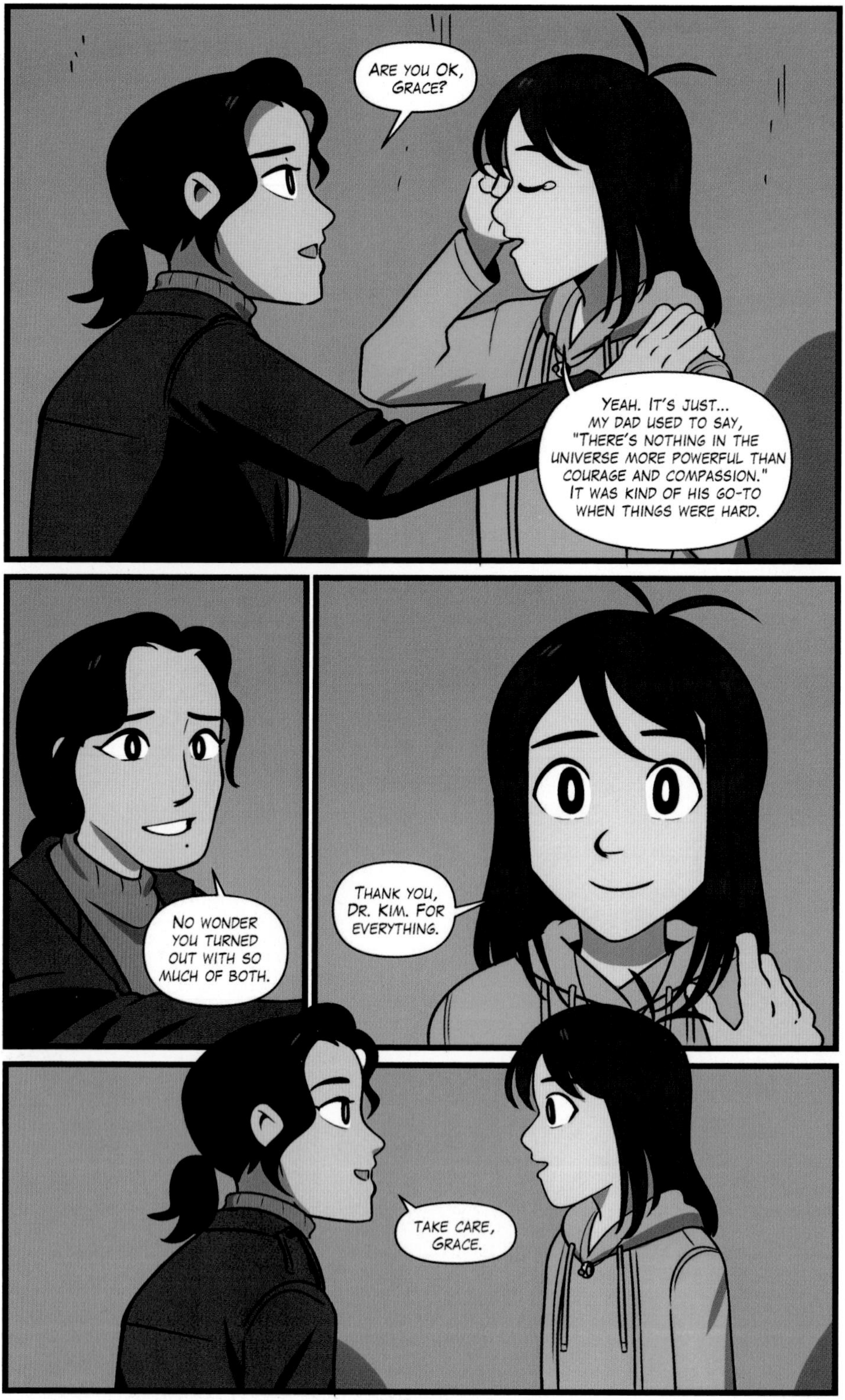
ARE YOU OK, GRACE?
YEAH. IT'S JUST... MY DAD USED TO SAY, "THERE'S NOTHING IN THE UNIVERSE MORE POWERFUL THAN COURAGE AND COMPASSION." IT WAS KIND OF HIS GO-TO WHEN THINGS WERE HARD.
NO WONDER YOU TURNED OUT WITH SO MUCH OF BOTH.
THANK YOU, DR. KIM. FOR EVERYTHING.
TAKE CARE, GRACE.

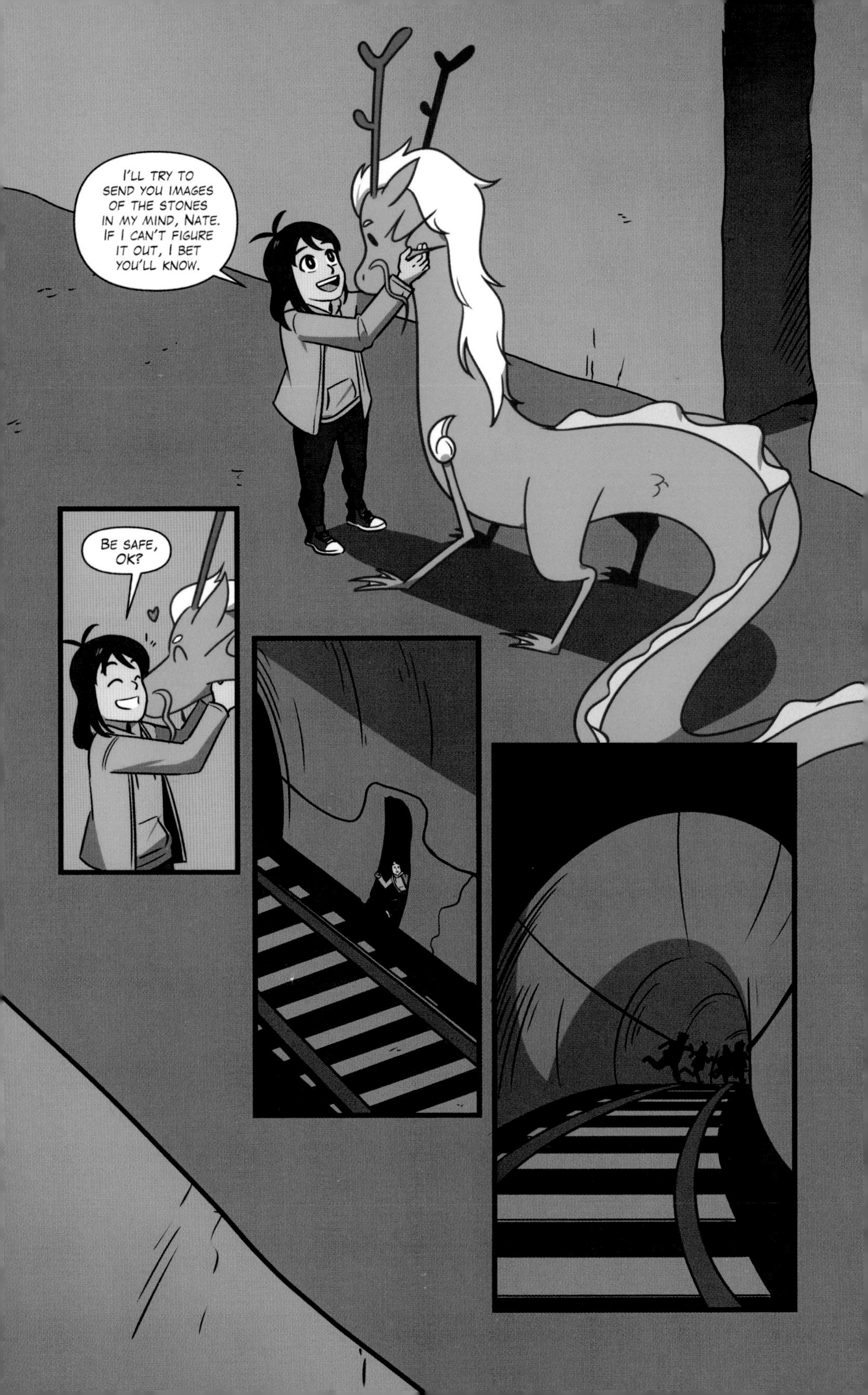
I'LL TRY TO SEND YOU IMAGES OF THE STONES IN MY MIND, NATE. IF I CAN'T FIGURE IT OUT, I BET YOU'LL KNOW.
BE SAFE, OK?

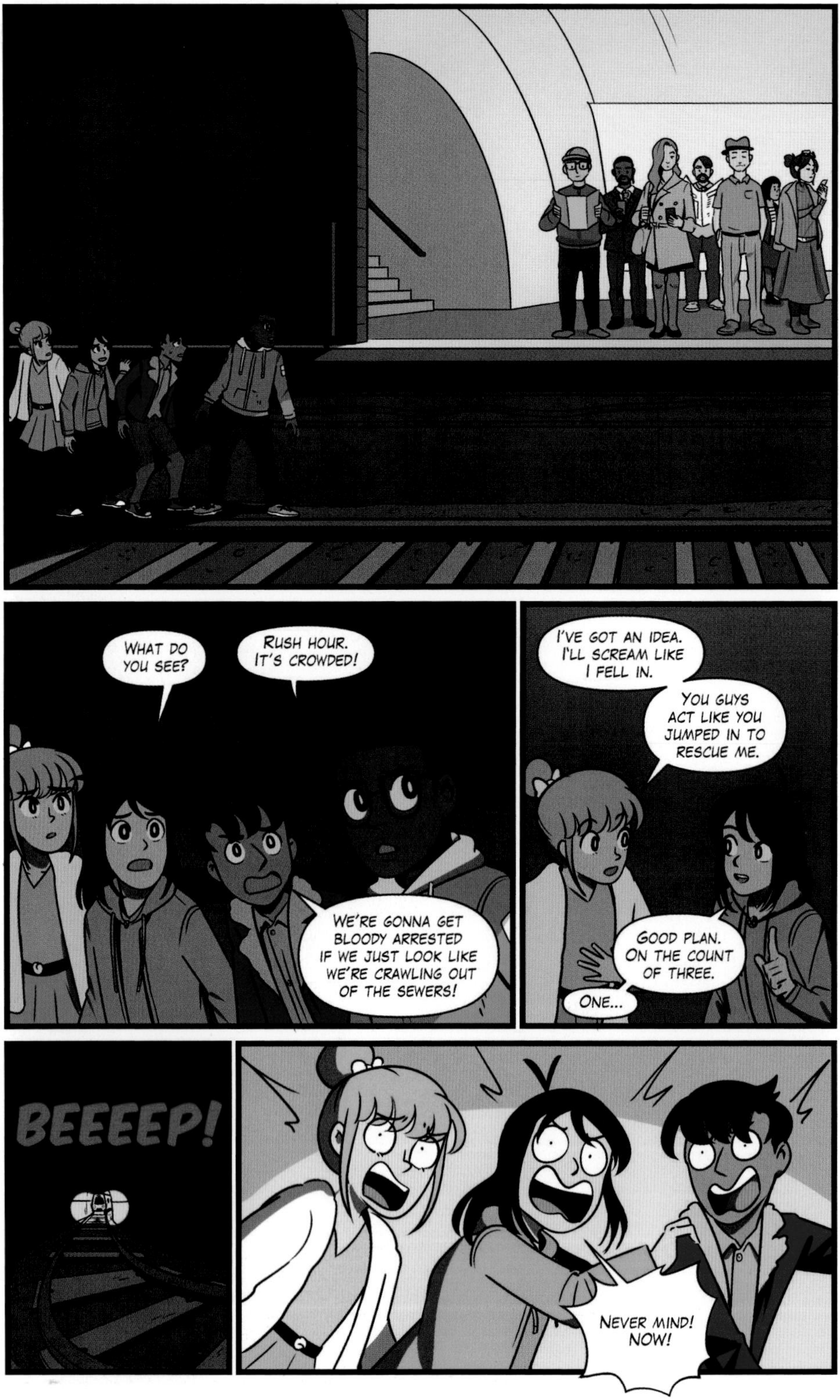
WHAT DO YOU SEE?
RUSH HOUR. IT'S CROWDED!
WE'RE GONNA GET BLOODY ARRESTED IF WE JUST LOOK LIKE WE'RE CRAWLING OUT OF THE SEWERS!
I'VE GOT AN IDEA. I'LL SCREAM LIKE I FELL IN.
YOU GUYS ACT LIKE YOU JUMPED IN TO RESCUE ME.
GOOD PLAN. ON THE COUNT OF THREE.
ONE...
BEEEEP!
NEVER MIND! NOW!

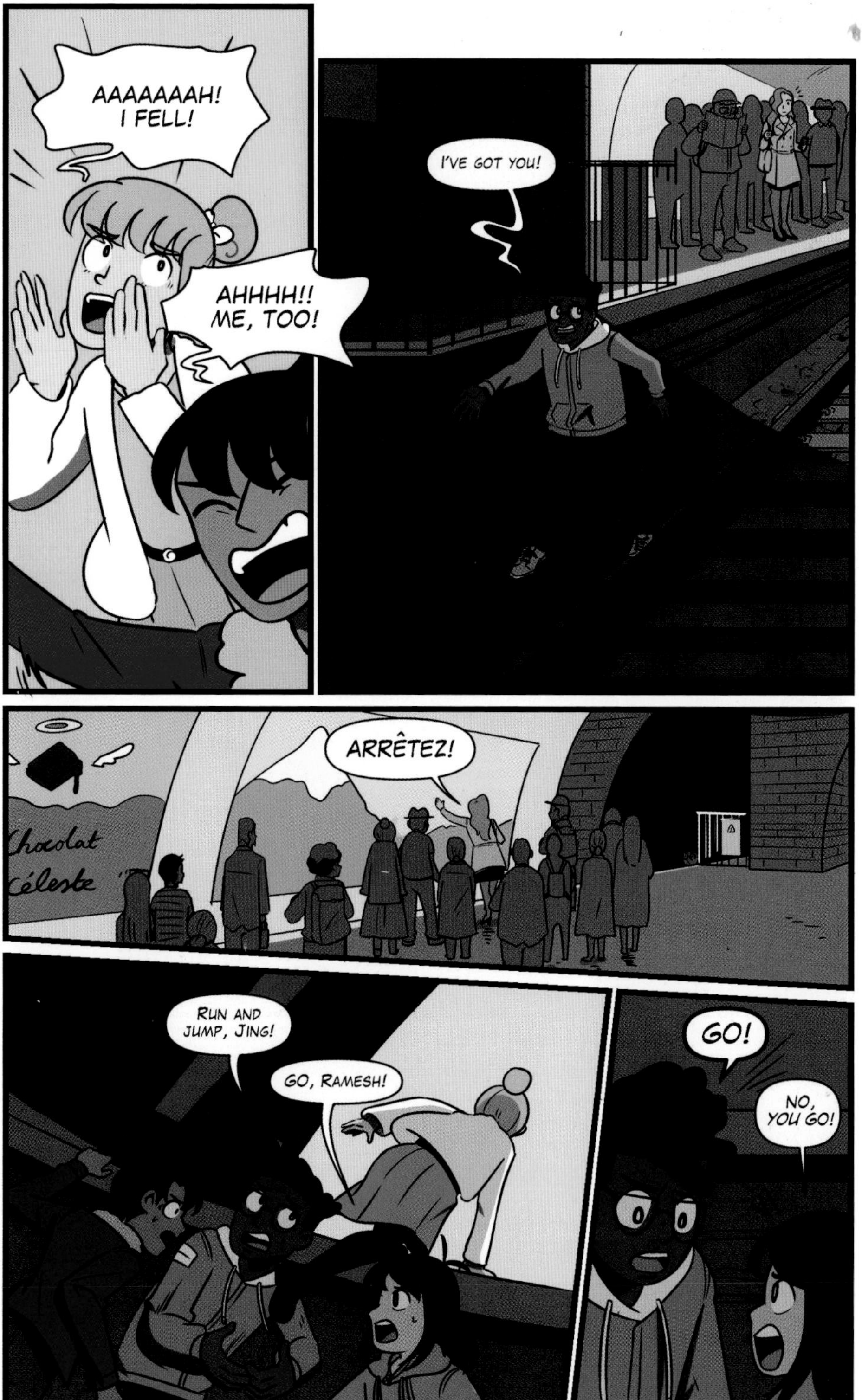
AAAAAAAH! I FELL!
AHHHH!! ME, TOO!
I'VE GOT YOU!
ARRÊTEZ!
Chocolat céleste
RUN AND JUMP, JING!
GO, RAMESH!
GO!
NO, YOU GO!

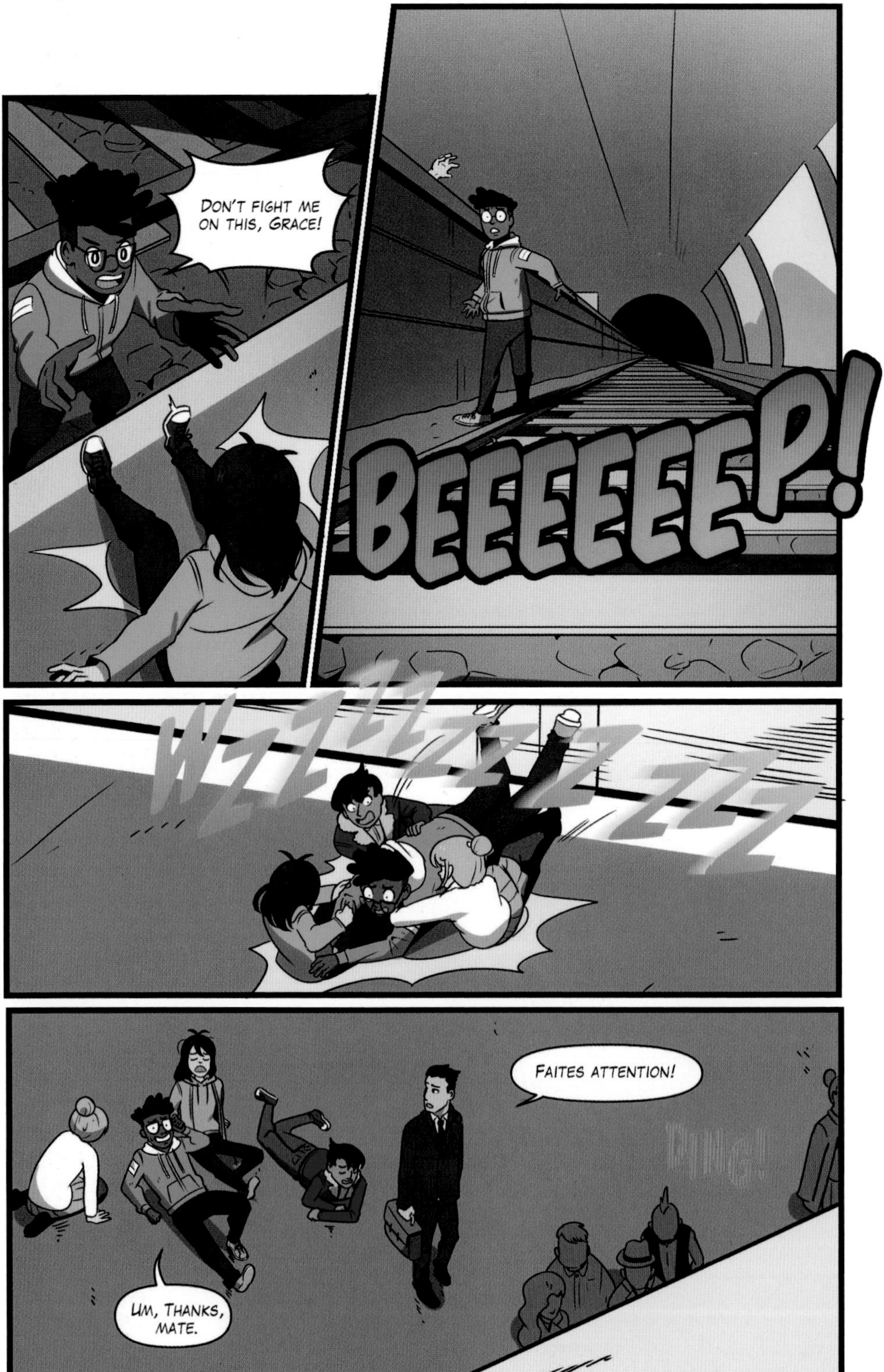
DON'T FIGHT ME ON THIS, GRACE!
BEEEEEEP!
FAITES ATTENTION!
DING!
UM, THANKS, MATE.

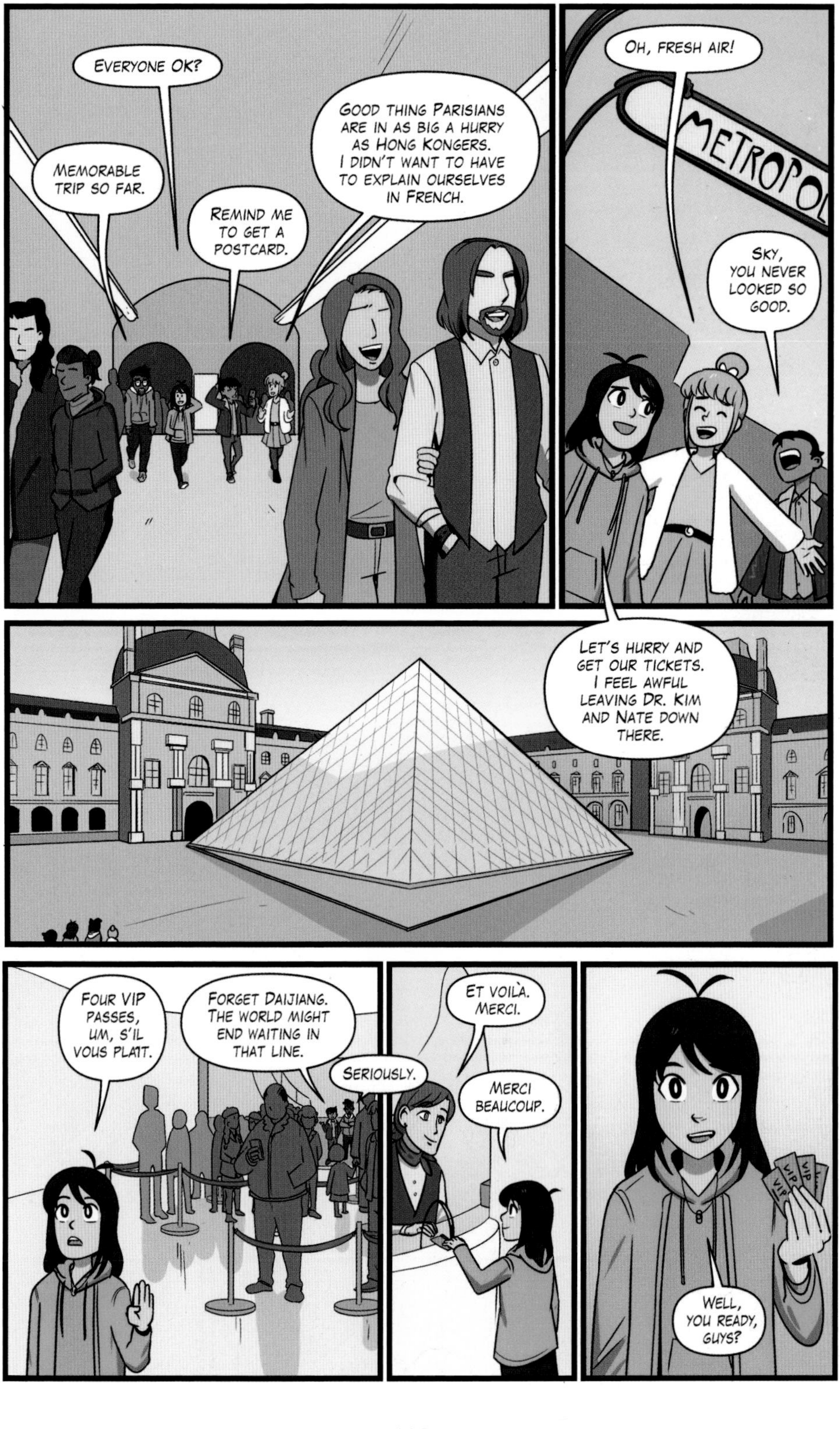
EVERYONE OK?
MEMORABLE TRIP SO FAR.
REMIND ME TO GET A POSTCARD.
GOOD THING PARISIANS ARE IN AS BIG A HURRY AS HONG KONGERS. I DIDN'T WANT TO HAVE TO EXPLAIN OURSELVES IN FRENCH.
OH, FRESH AIR!
METROPOL
SKY, YOU NEVER LOOKED SO GOOD.
LET'S HURRY AND GET OUR TICKETS. I FEEL AWFUL LEAVING DR. KIM AND NATE DOWN THERE.
FOUR VIP PASSES, UM, S'IL VOUS PLAIT.
FORGET DAIJIANG. THE WORLD MIGHT END WAITING IN THAT LINE.
SERIOUSLY.
ET VOILÀ. MERCI.
MERCI BEAUCOUP.
VIP
WELL, YOU READY, GUYS?

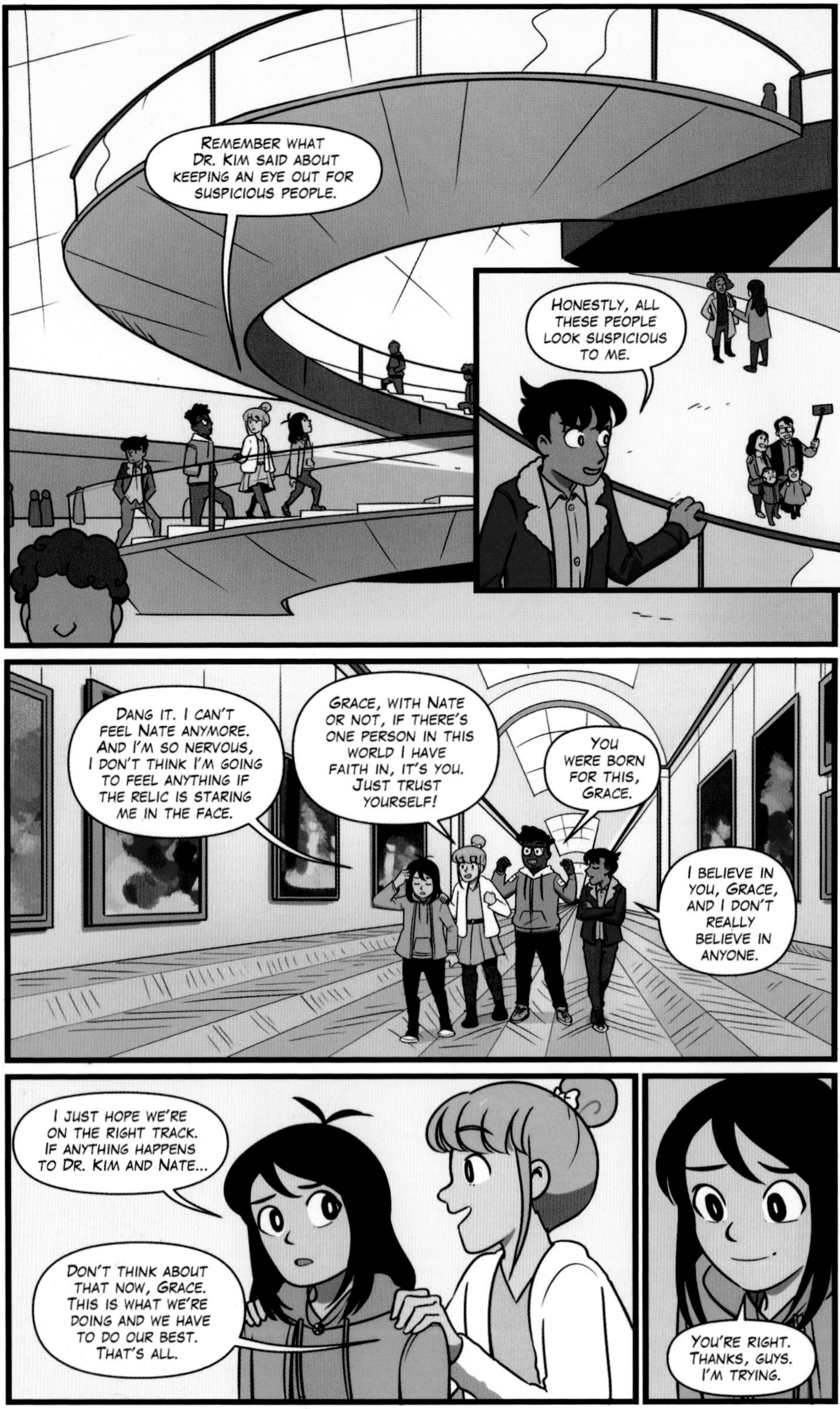

REMEMBER WHAT DR. KIM SAID ABOUT KEEPING AN EYE OUT FOR SUSPICIOUS PEOPLE.
HONESTLY, ALL THESE PEOPLE LOOK SUSPICIOUS TO ME.
DANG IT. I CAN'T FEEL NATE ANYMORE. AND I'M SO NERVOUS, I DON'T THINK I'M GOING TO FEEL ANYTHING IF THE RELIC IS STARING ME IN THE FACE.
GRACE, WITH NATE OR NOT, IF THERE'S ONE PERSON IN THIS WORLD I HAVE FAITH IN, IT'S YOU. JUST TRUST YOURSELF!
YOU WERE BORN FOR THIS, GRACE.
I BELIEVE IN YOU, GRACE, AND I DON'T REALLY BELIEVE IN ANYONE.
I JUST HOPE WE'RE ON THE RIGHT TRACK. IF ANYTHING HAPPENS TO DR. KIM AND NATE...
DON'T THINK ABOUT THAT NOW, GRACE. THIS IS WHAT WE'RE DOING AND WE HAVE TO DO OUR BEST. THAT'S ALL.
YOU'RE RIGHT. THANKS, GUYS. I'M TRYING.

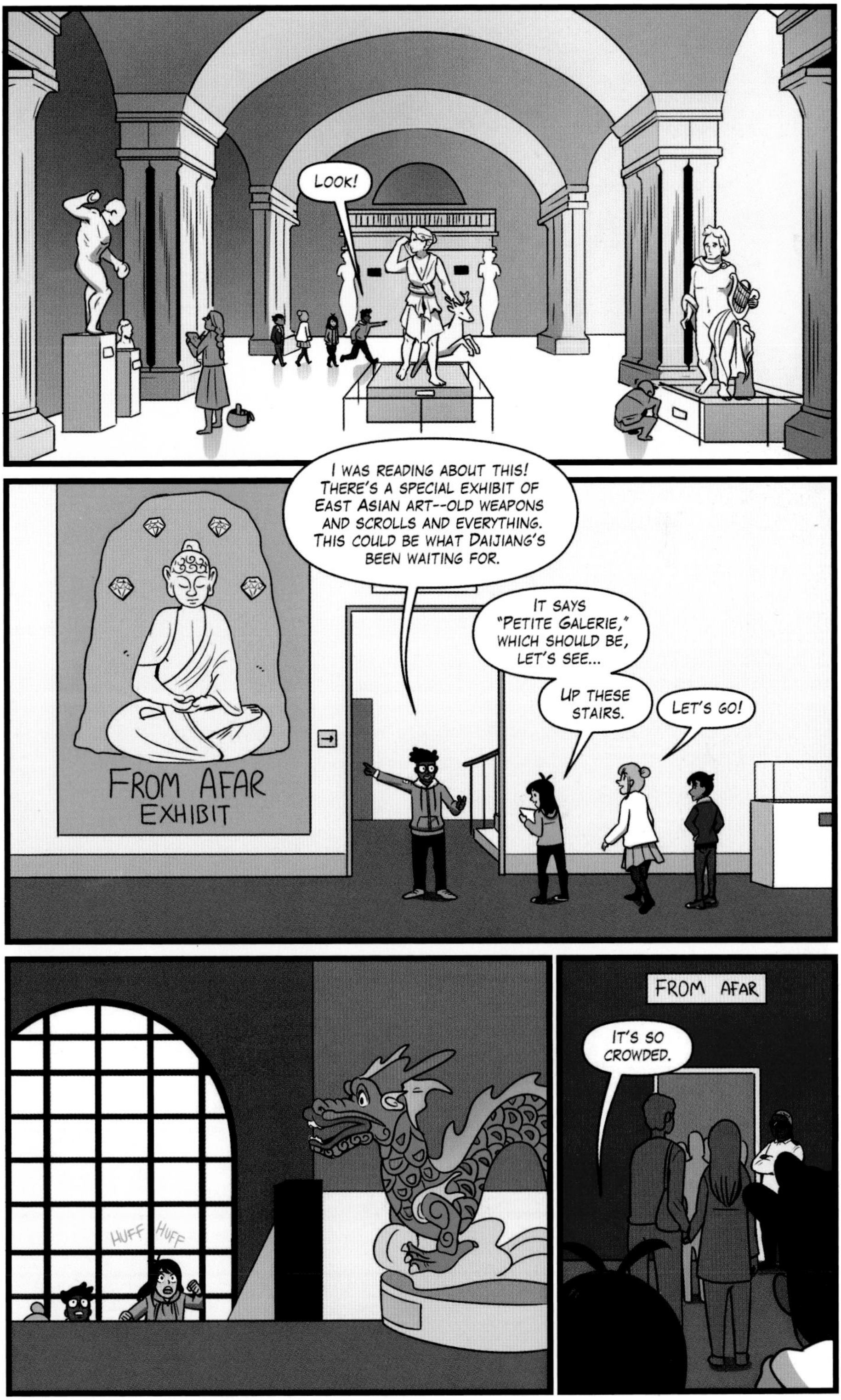
LOOK!
I WAS READING ABOUT THIS! THERE'S A SPECIAL EXHIBIT OF EAST ASIAN ART--OLD WEAPONS AND SCROLLS AND EVERYTHING. THIS COULD BE WHAT DAIJIANG'S BEEN WAITING FOR.
FROM AFAR EXHIBIT
IT SAYS "PETITE GALERIE," WHICH SHOULD BE, LET'S SEE...
UP THESE STAIRS.
LET'S GO!
HUFF HUFF
FROM AFAR
IT'S SO CROWDED.

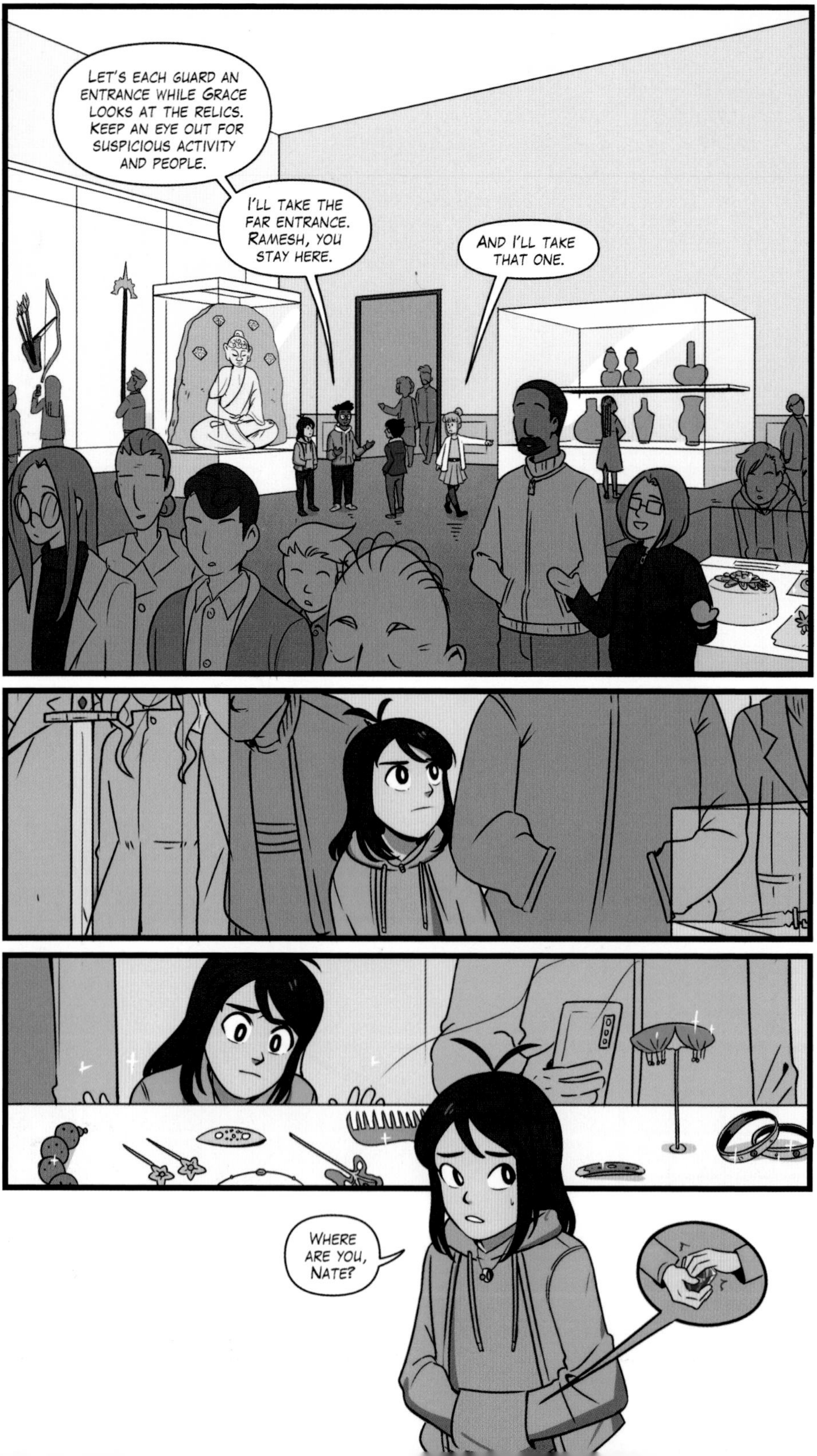
LET'S EACH GUARD AN ENTRANCE WHILE GRACE LOOKS AT THE RELICS. KEEP AN EYE OUT FOR SUSPICIOUS ACTIVITY AND PEOPLE.
I'LL TAKE THE FAR ENTRANCE. RAMESH, YOU STAY HERE.
AND I'LL TAKE THAT ONE.
WHERE ARE YOU, NATE?

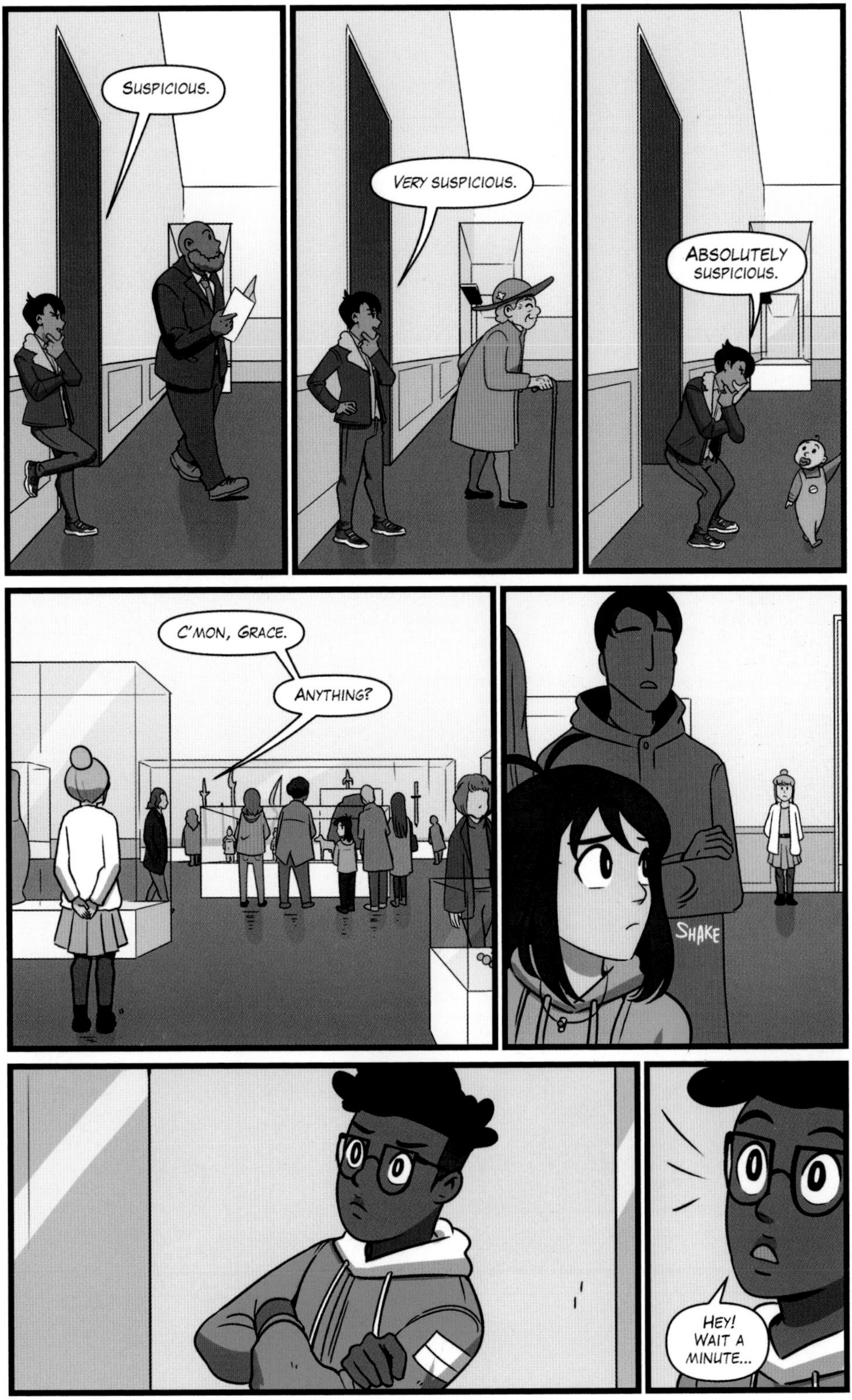
SUSPICIOUS.
VERY SUSPICIOUS.
ABSOLUTELY SUSPICIOUS.
C'MON, GRACE.
ANYTHING?
SHAKE
HEY! WAIT A MINUTE...

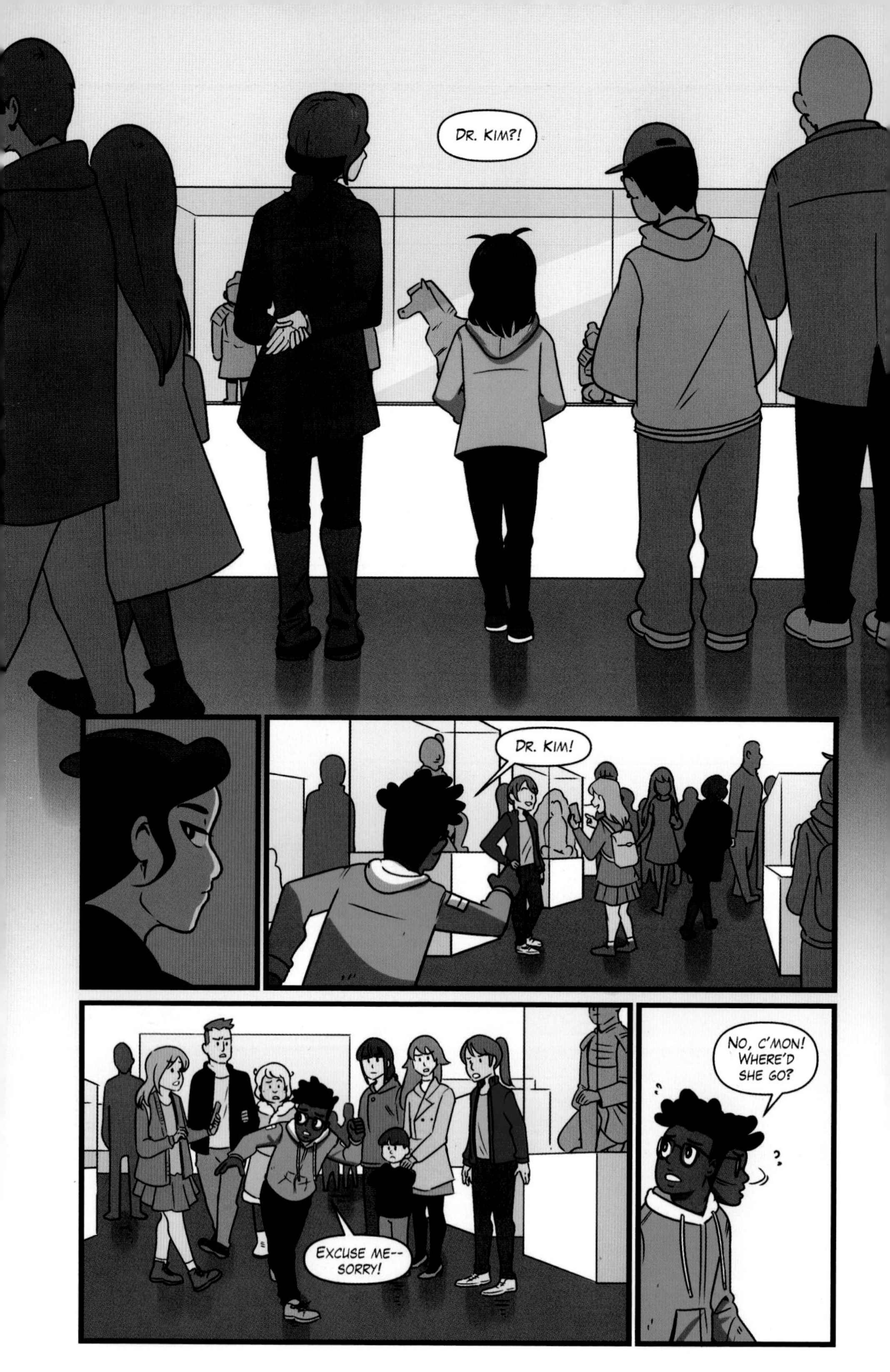
DR. KIM?!
DR. KIM!
EXCUSE ME--
SORRY!
NO, C'MON!
WHERE'D
SHE GO?

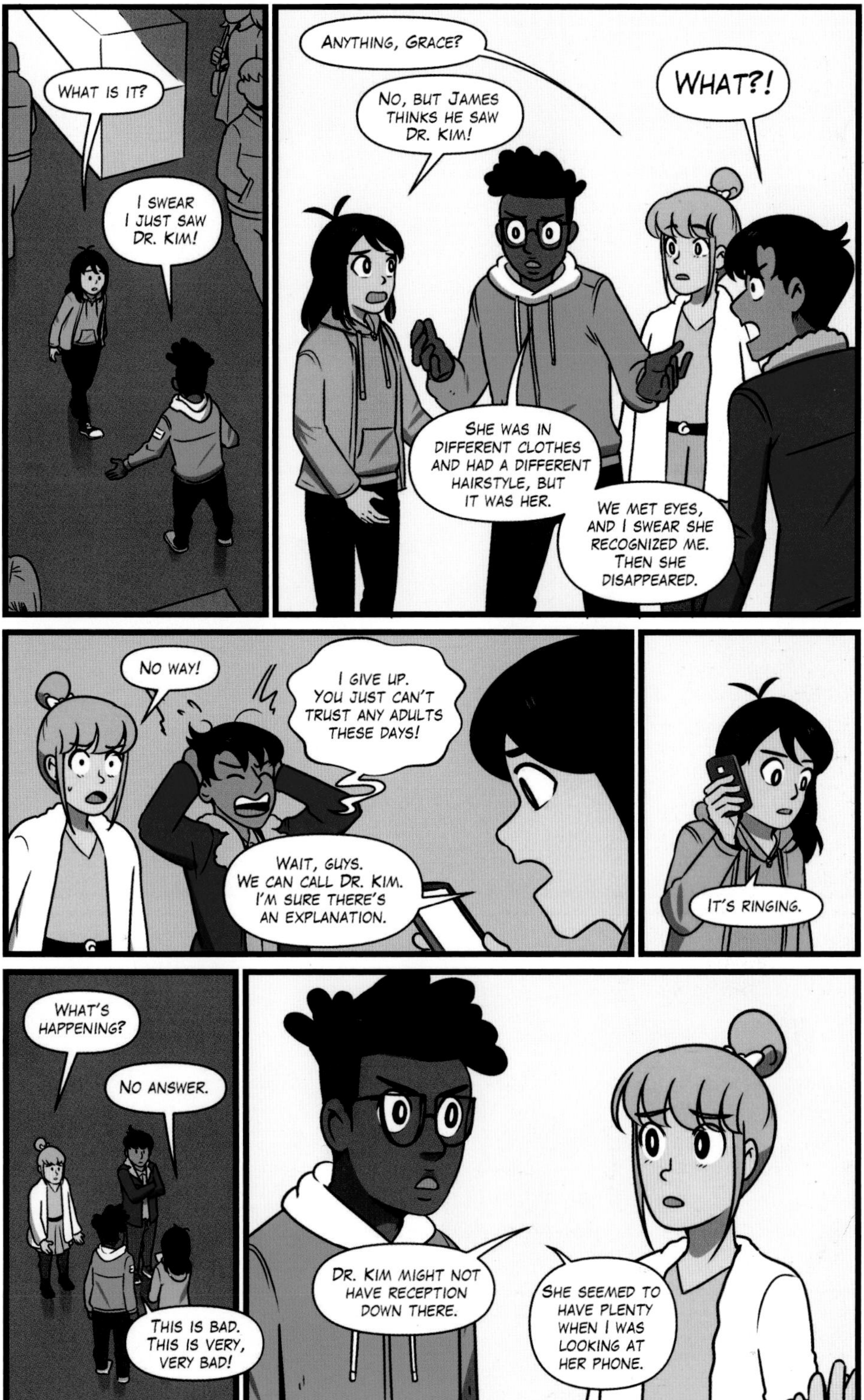
WHAT IS IT?
I SWEAR I JUST SAW DR. KIM!
ANYTHING, GRACE?
NO, BUT JAMES THINKS HE SAW DR. KIM!
WHAT?!
SHE WAS IN DIFFERENT CLOTHES AND HAD A DIFFERENT HAIRSTYLE, BUT IT WAS HER.
WE MET EYES, AND I SWEAR SHE RECOGNIZED ME. THEN SHE DISAPPEARED.
NO WAY!
I GIVE UP. YOU JUST CAN'T TRUST ANY ADULTS THESE DAYS!
WAIT, GUYS. WE CAN CALL DR. KIM. I'M SURE THERE'S AN EXPLANATION.
IT'S RINGING.
WHAT'S HAPPENING?
NO ANSWER.
THIS IS BAD. THIS IS VERY, VERY BAD!
DR. KIM MIGHT NOT HAVE RECEPTION DOWN THERE.
SHE SEEMED TO HAVE PLENTY WHEN I WAS LOOKING AT HER PHONE.

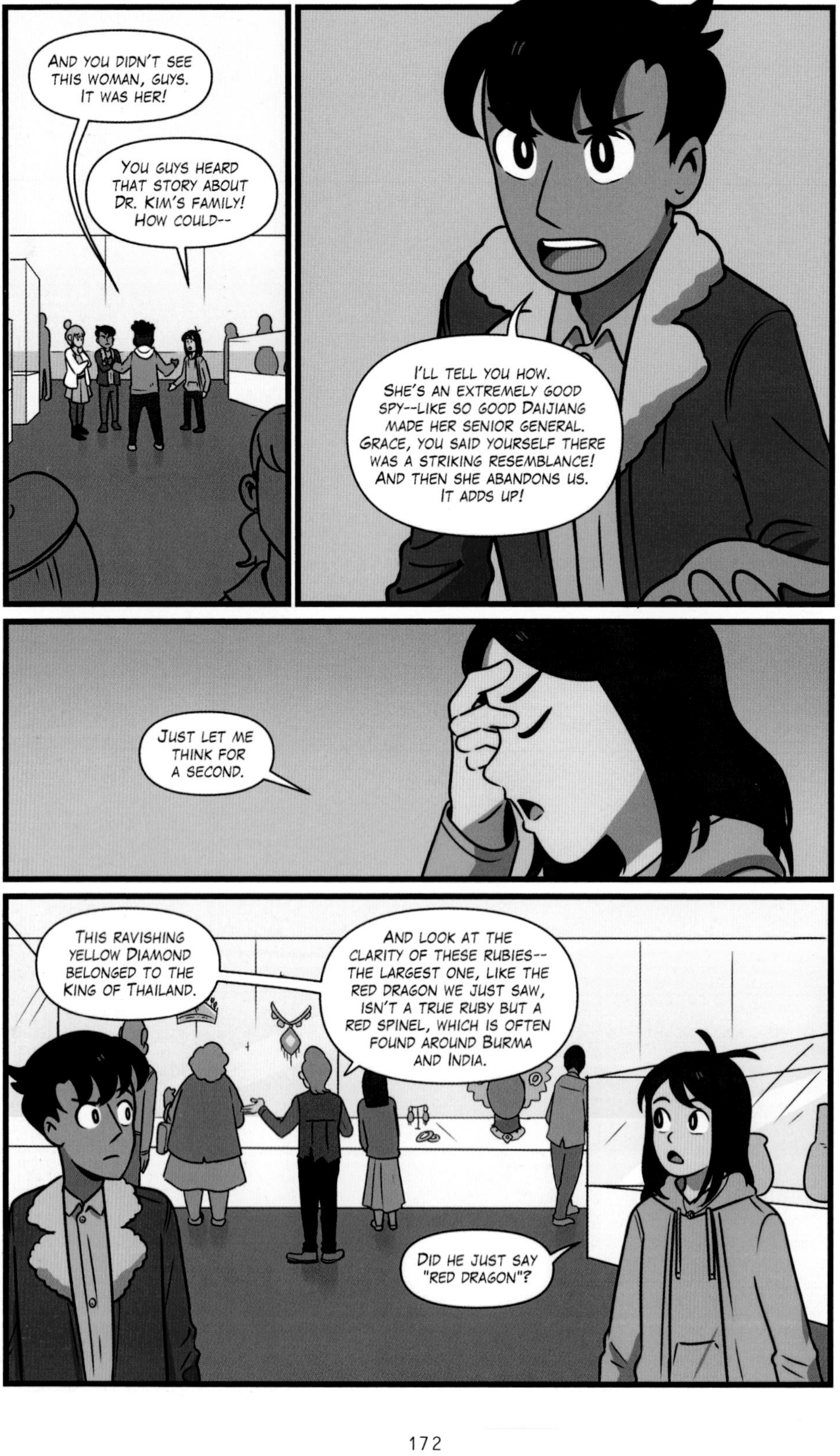

AND YOU DIDN'T SEE THIS WOMAN, GUYS. IT WAS HER!
YOU GUYS HEARD THAT STORY ABOUT DR. KIM'S FAMILY! HOW COULD--
I'LL TELL YOU HOW. SHE'S AN EXTREMELY GOOD SPY--LIKE SO GOOD DAIJIANG MADE HER SENIOR GENERAL. GRACE, YOU SAID YOURSELF THERE WAS A STRIKING RESEMBLANCE! AND THEN SHE ABANDONS US. IT ADDS UP!
JUST LET ME THINK FOR A SECOND.
THIS RAVISHING YELLOW DIAMOND BELONGED TO THE KING OF THAILAND.
AND LOOK AT THE CLARITY OF THESE RUBIES--THE LARGEST ONE, LIKE THE RED DRAGON WE JUST SAW, ISN'T A TRUE RUBY BUT A RED SPINEL, WHICH IS OFTEN FOUND AROUND BURMA AND INDIA.
DID HE JUST SAY "RED DRAGON"?

"THE RED DRAGON FLIES HOME!" LIKE FU-TONG SAID!

YEAH, AND I REMEMBER DR. KIM COMPLETELY BRUSHING IT ASIDE WHEN WE MENTIONED IT.

SO SORRY, BUT THAT RED DRAGON YOU MENTIONED, WHERE--

I'M IN THE MIDDLE OF A TOUR--

FRENCH CROWN JEWELS! DENON WING!

THANKS A MILLION!

FRENCH CROWN JEWELS! DENON WING!

AND DR. KIM TOLD US NOT TO PRIORITIZE THE FRENCH CROWN JEWELS! I SAY WE GET. OUT. OF. HERE. NOW!

I SAY WE GET TO THOSE CROWN JEWELS.

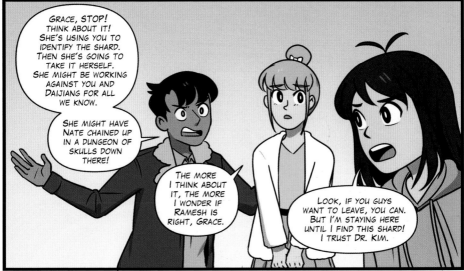

GRACE, STOP! THINK ABOUT IT! SHE'S USING YOU TO IDENTIFY THE SHARD. THEN SHE'S GOING TO TAKE IT HERSELF. SHE MIGHT BE WORKING AGAINST YOU AND DAIJIANG FOR ALL WE KNOW.

SHE MIGHT HAVE NATE CHAINED UP IN A DUNGEON OF SKULLS DOWN THERE!

THE MORE I THINK ABOUT IT, THE MORE I WONDER IF RAMESH IS RIGHT, GRACE.

LOOK, IF YOU GUYS WANT TO LEAVE, YOU CAN. BUT I'M STAYING HERE UNTIL I FIND THIS SHARD! I TRUST DR. KIM.

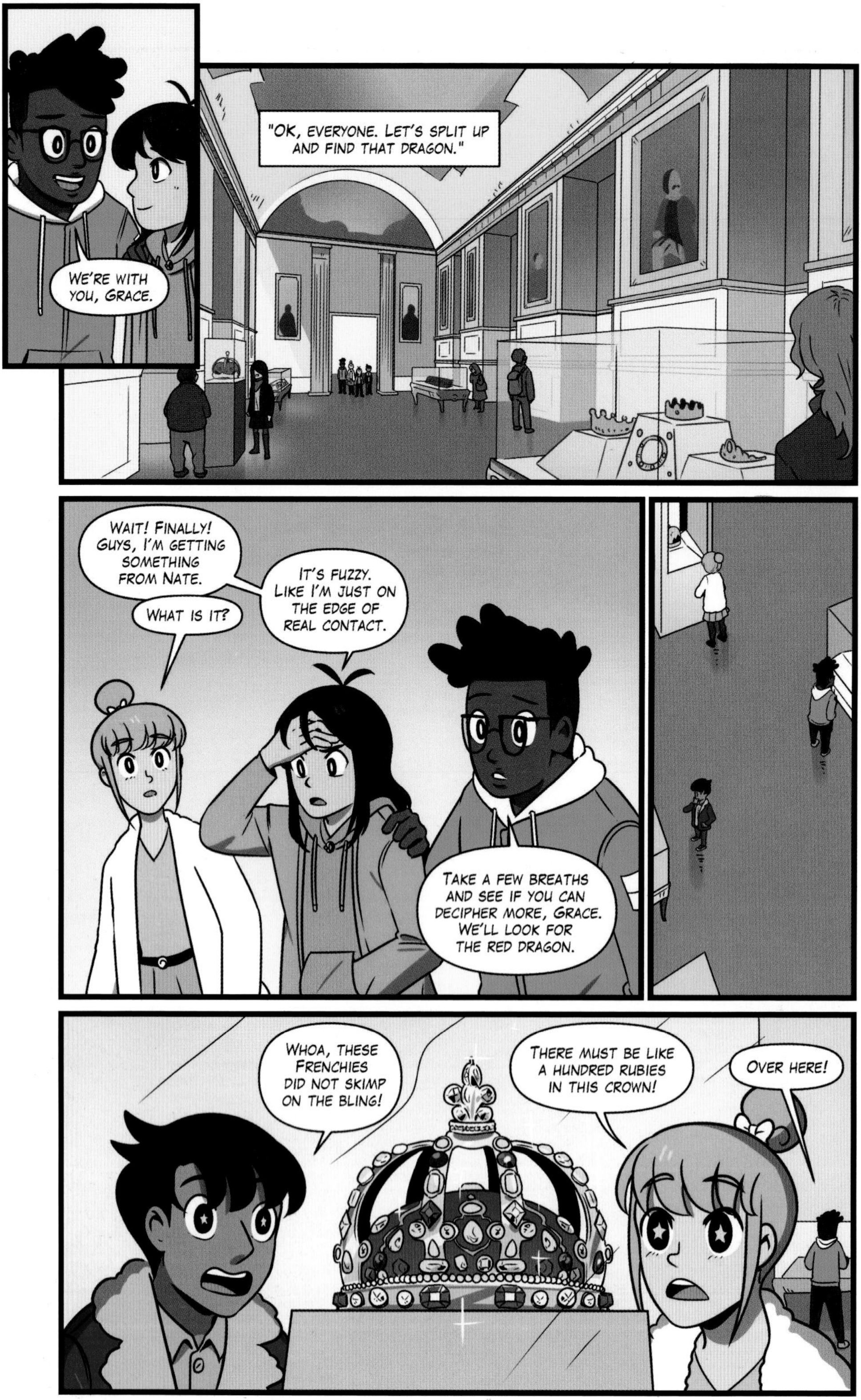
WE'RE WITH YOU, GRACE.
"OK, EVERYONE. LET'S SPLIT UP AND FIND THAT DRAGON."
WAIT! FINALLY! GUYS, I'M GETTING SOMETHING FROM NATE.
WHAT IS IT?
IT'S FUZZY. LIKE I'M JUST ON THE EDGE OF REAL CONTACT.
TAKE A FEW BREATHS AND SEE IF YOU CAN DECIPHER MORE, GRACE. WE'LL LOOK FOR THE RED DRAGON.
WHOA, THESE FRENCHIES DID NOT SKIMP ON THE BLING!
THERE MUST BE LIKE A HUNDRED RUBIES IN THIS CROWN!
OVER HERE!

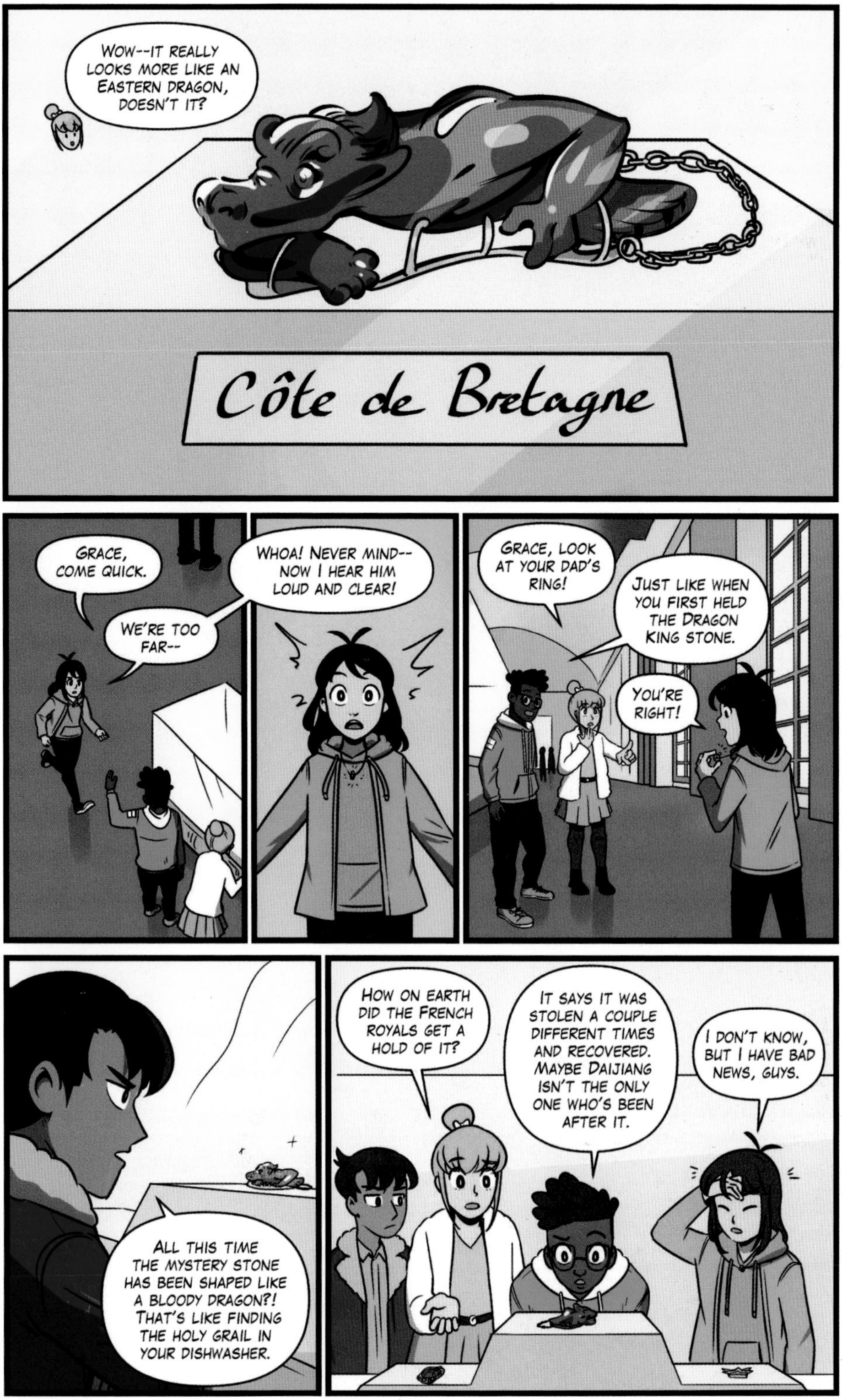
WOW--IT REALLY LOOKS MORE LIKE AN EASTERN DRAGON, DOESN'T IT?
Côte de Bretagne
GRACE, COME QUICK.
WE'RE TOO FAR--
WHOA! NEVER MIND-- NOW I HEAR HIM LOUD AND CLEAR!
GRACE, LOOK AT YOUR DAD'S RING!
JUST LIKE WHEN YOU FIRST HELD THE DRAGON KING STONE.
YOU'RE RIGHT!
ALL THIS TIME THE MYSTERY STONE HAS BEEN SHAPED LIKE A BLOODY DRAGON?! THAT'S LIKE FINDING THE HOLY GRAIL IN YOUR DISHWASHER.
HOW ON EARTH DID THE FRENCH ROYALS GET A HOLD OF IT?
IT SAYS IT WAS STOLEN A COUPLE DIFFERENT TIMES AND RECOVERED. MAYBE DAIJIANG ISN'T THE ONLY ONE WHO'S BEEN AFTER IT.
I DON'T KNOW, BUT I HAVE BAD NEWS, GUYS.

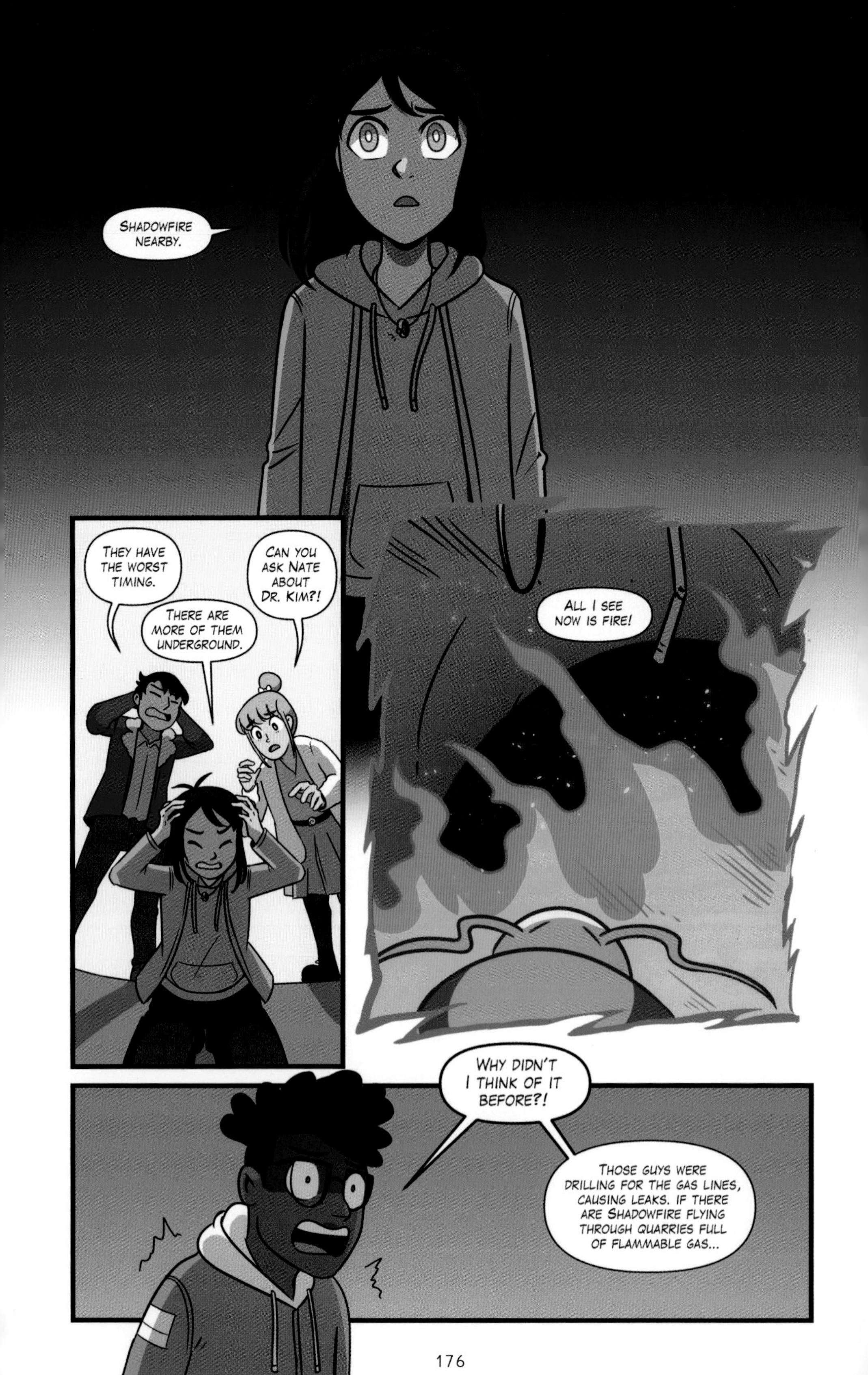

SHADOWFIRE NEARBY.
THEY HAVE THE WORST TIMING.
THERE ARE MORE OF THEM UNDERGROUND.
CAN YOU ASK NATE ABOUT DR. KIM?!
ALL I SEE NOW IS FIRE!
WHY DIDN'T I THINK OF IT BEFORE?!
THOSE GUYS WERE DRILLING FOR THE GAS LINES, CAUSING LEAKS. IF THERE ARE SHADOWFIRE FLYING THROUGH QUARRIES FULL OF FLAMMABLE GAS...

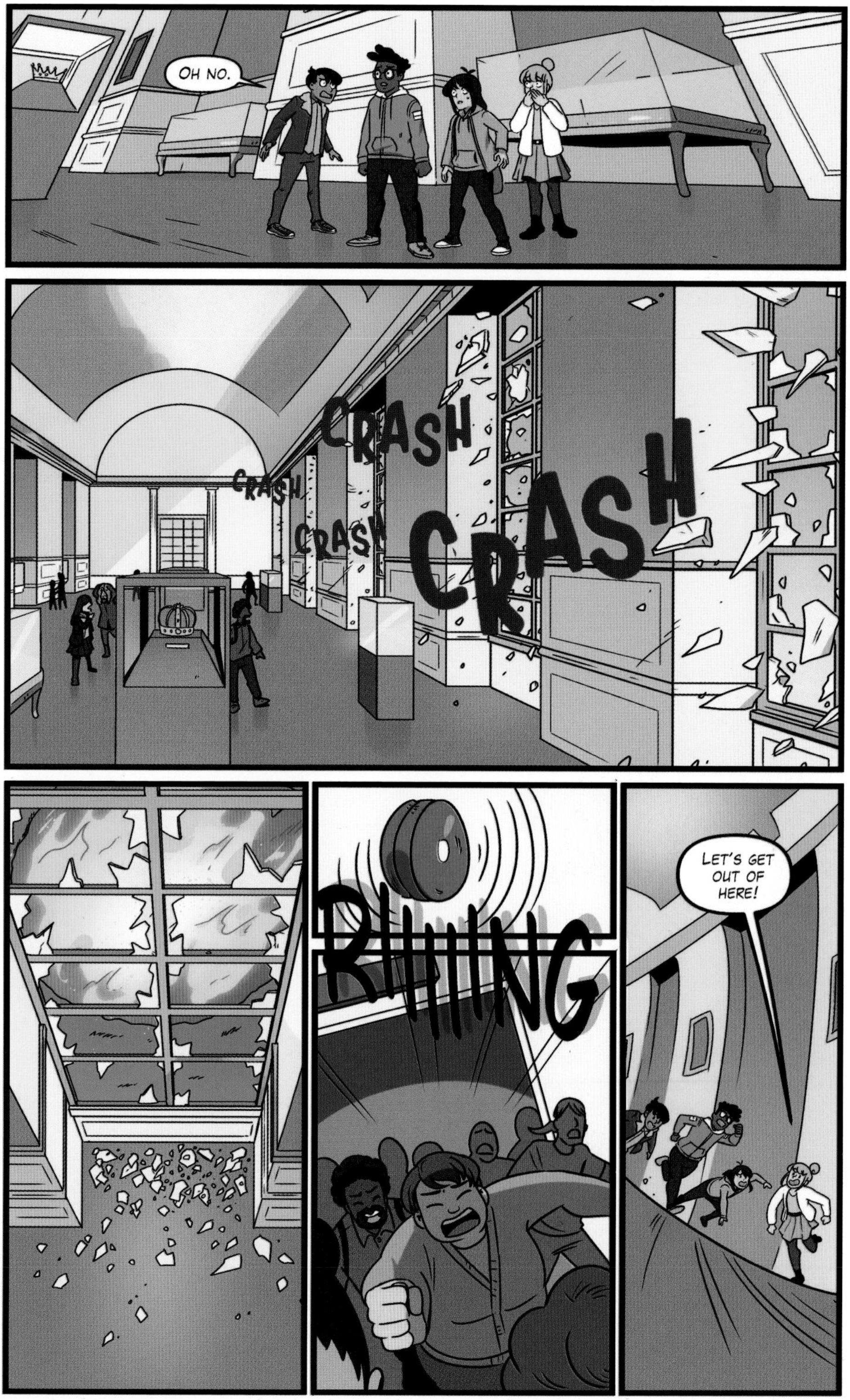
OH NO.
CRASH
CRASH
CRASH
CRASH
RIIIING
LET'S GET OUT OF HERE!

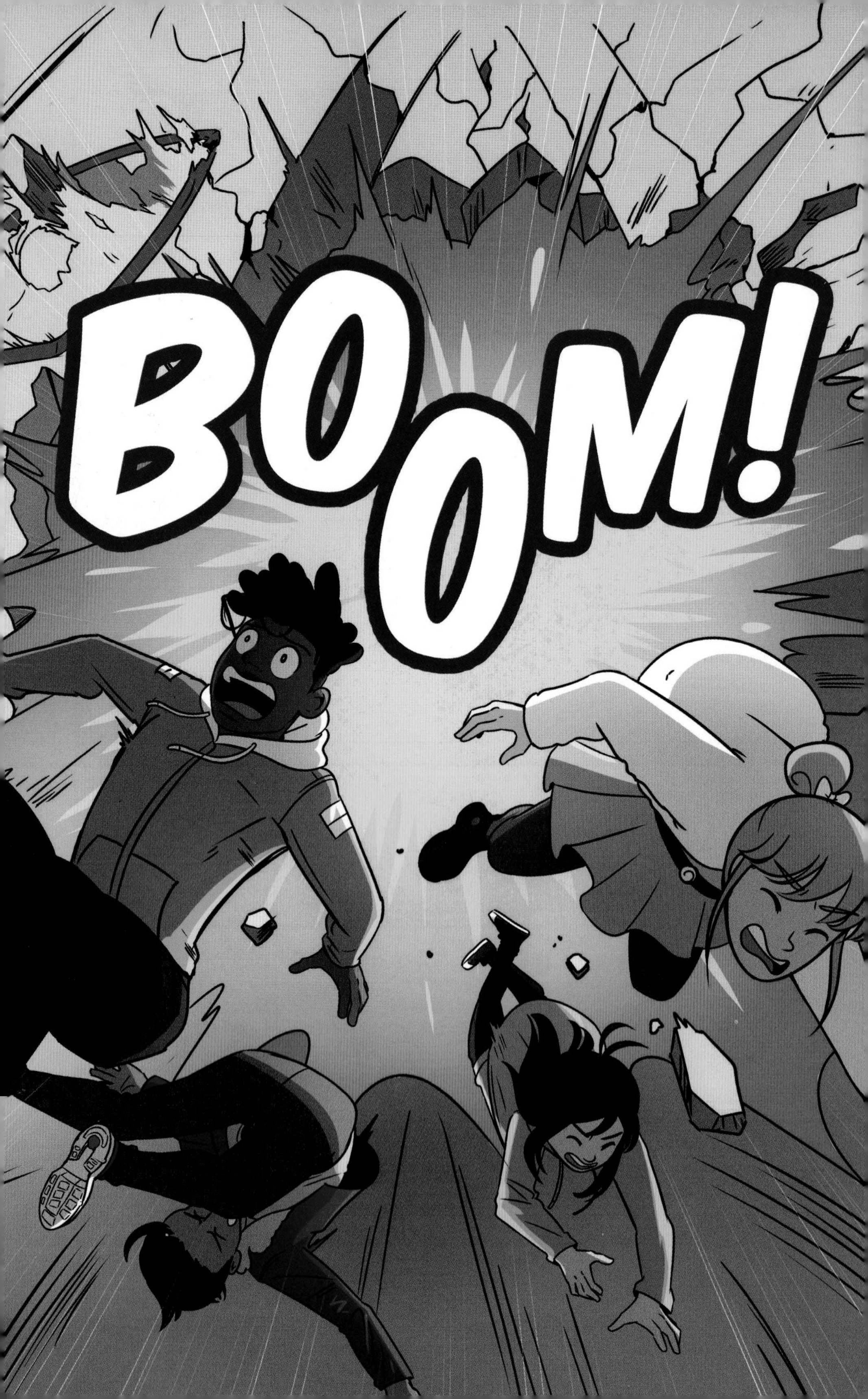
BOOM!

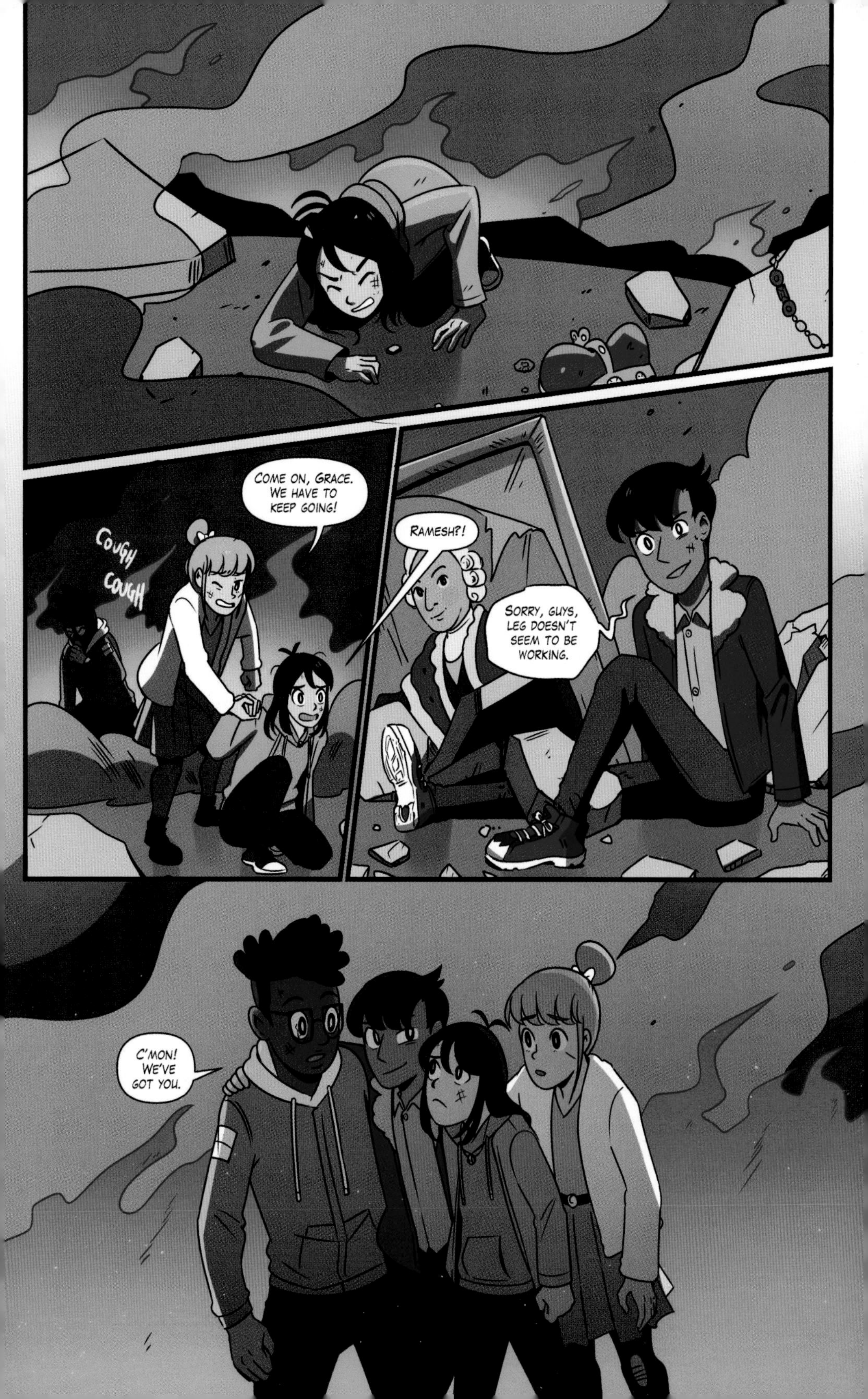

COUGH
COUGH
COME ON, GRACE. WE HAVE TO KEEP GOING!
RAMESH?!
SORRY, GUYS, LEG DOESN'T SEEM TO BE WORKING.
C'MON! WE'VE GOT YOU.

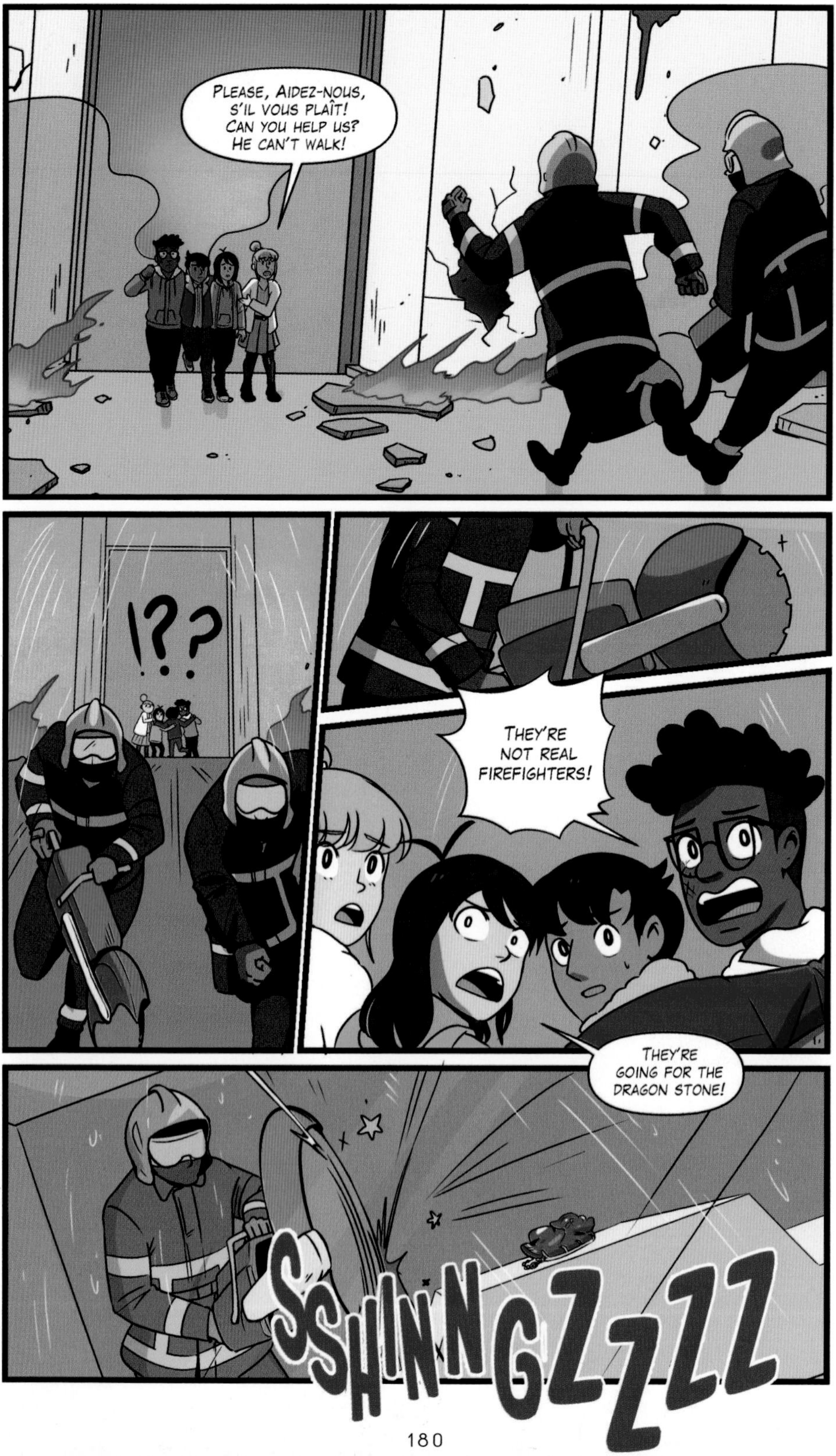
PLEASE, AIDEZ-NOUS, S'IL VOUS PLAÎT! CAN YOU HELP US? HE CAN'T WALK!
!??
THEY'RE NOT REAL FIREFIGHTERS!
THEY'RE GOING FOR THE DRAGON STONE!
SSHINNGZZZZ

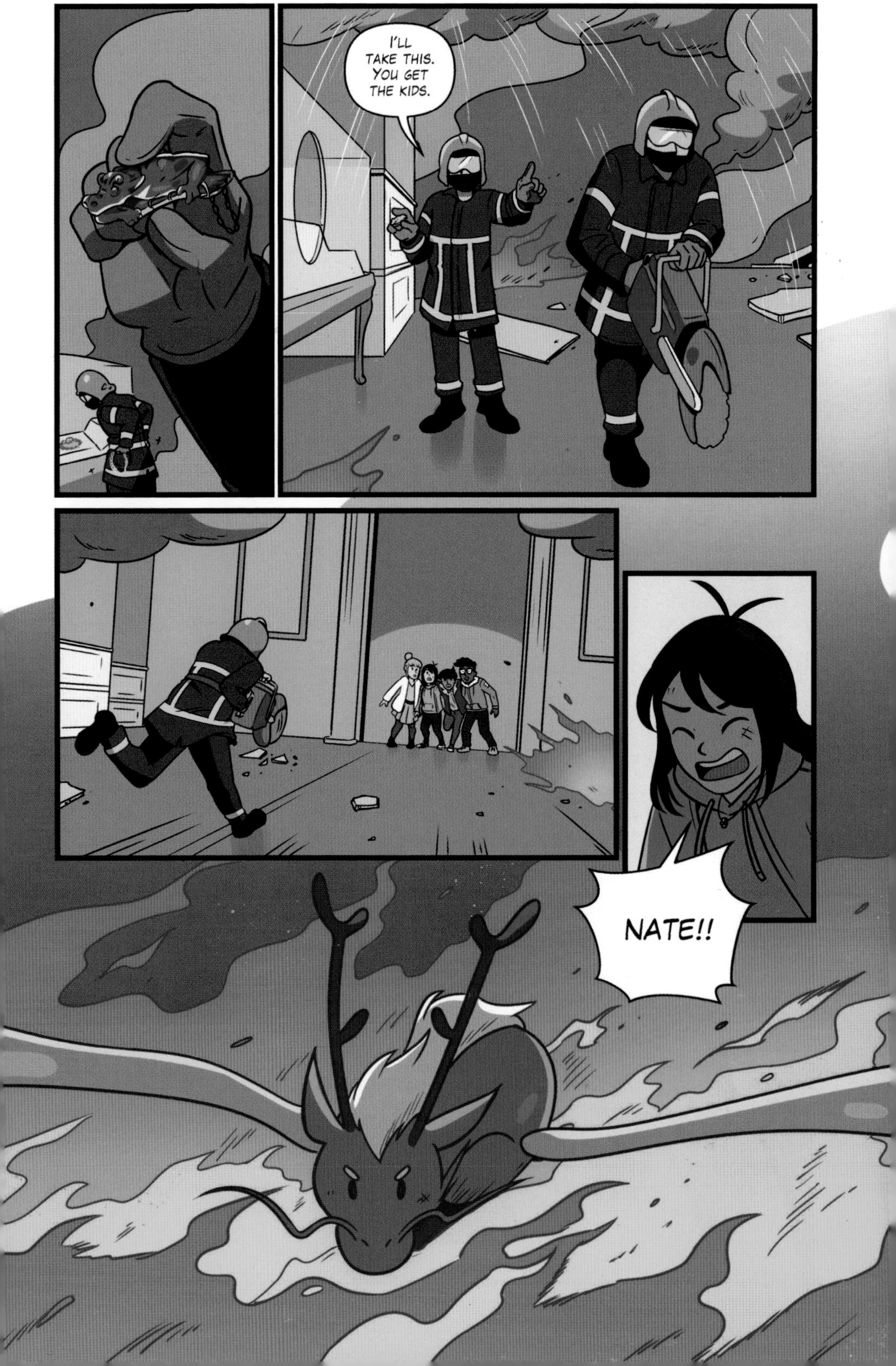
I'LL TAKE THIS. YOU GET THE KIDS.
NATE!!

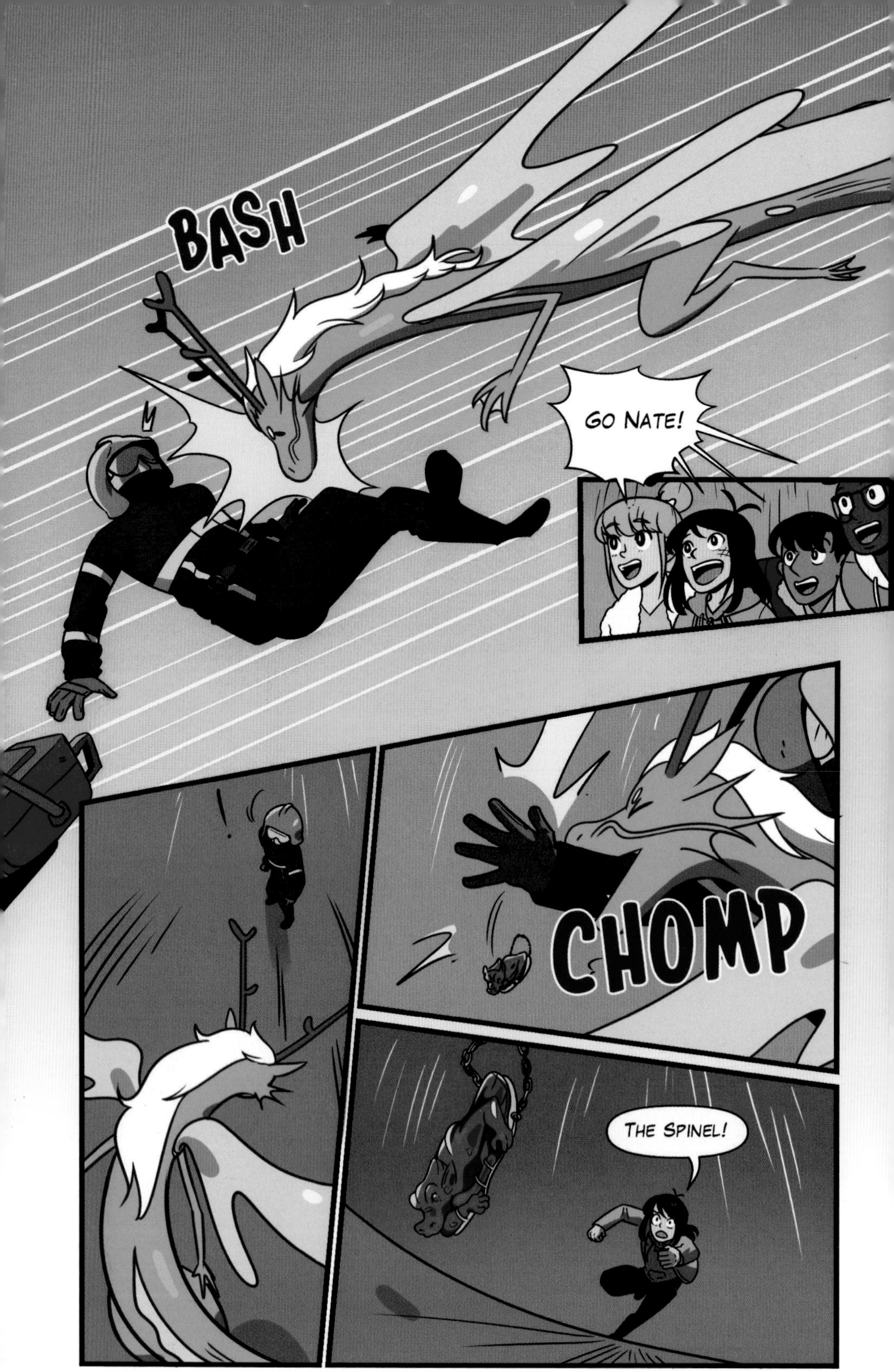
BASH
GO NATE!
CHOMP
THE SPINEL!

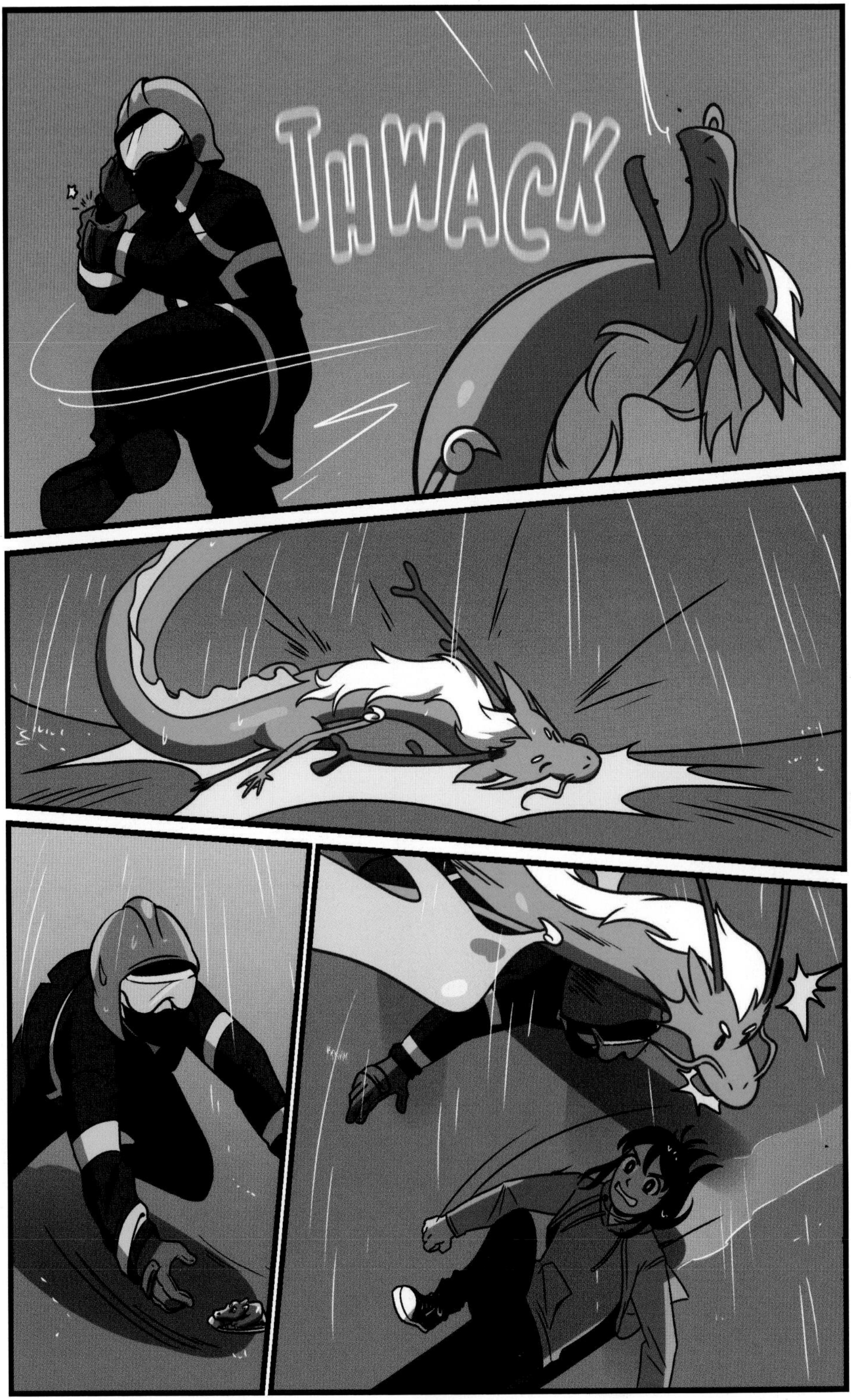
THWACK

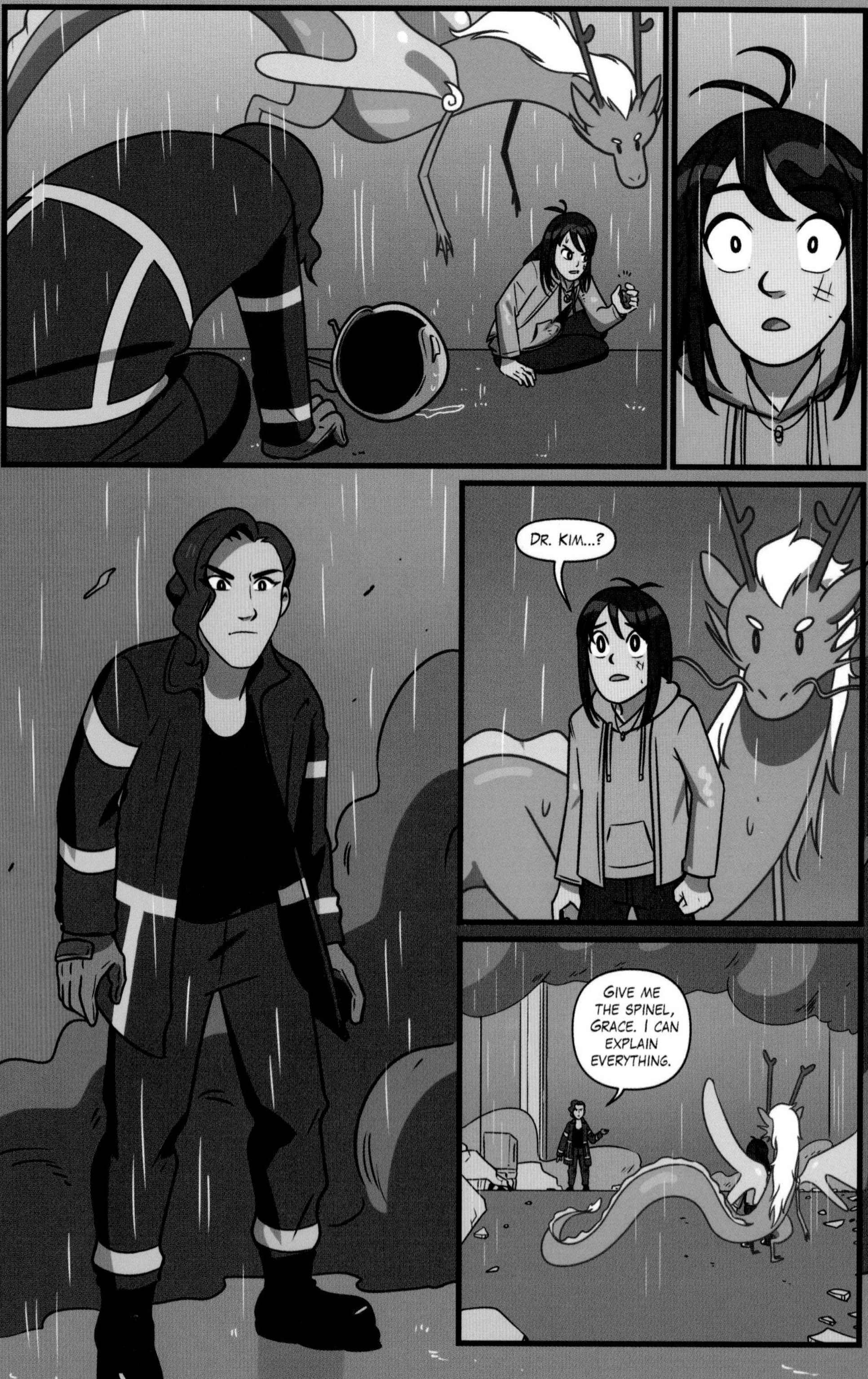
Dr. Kim...?
Give me the spinel, Grace. I can explain everything.

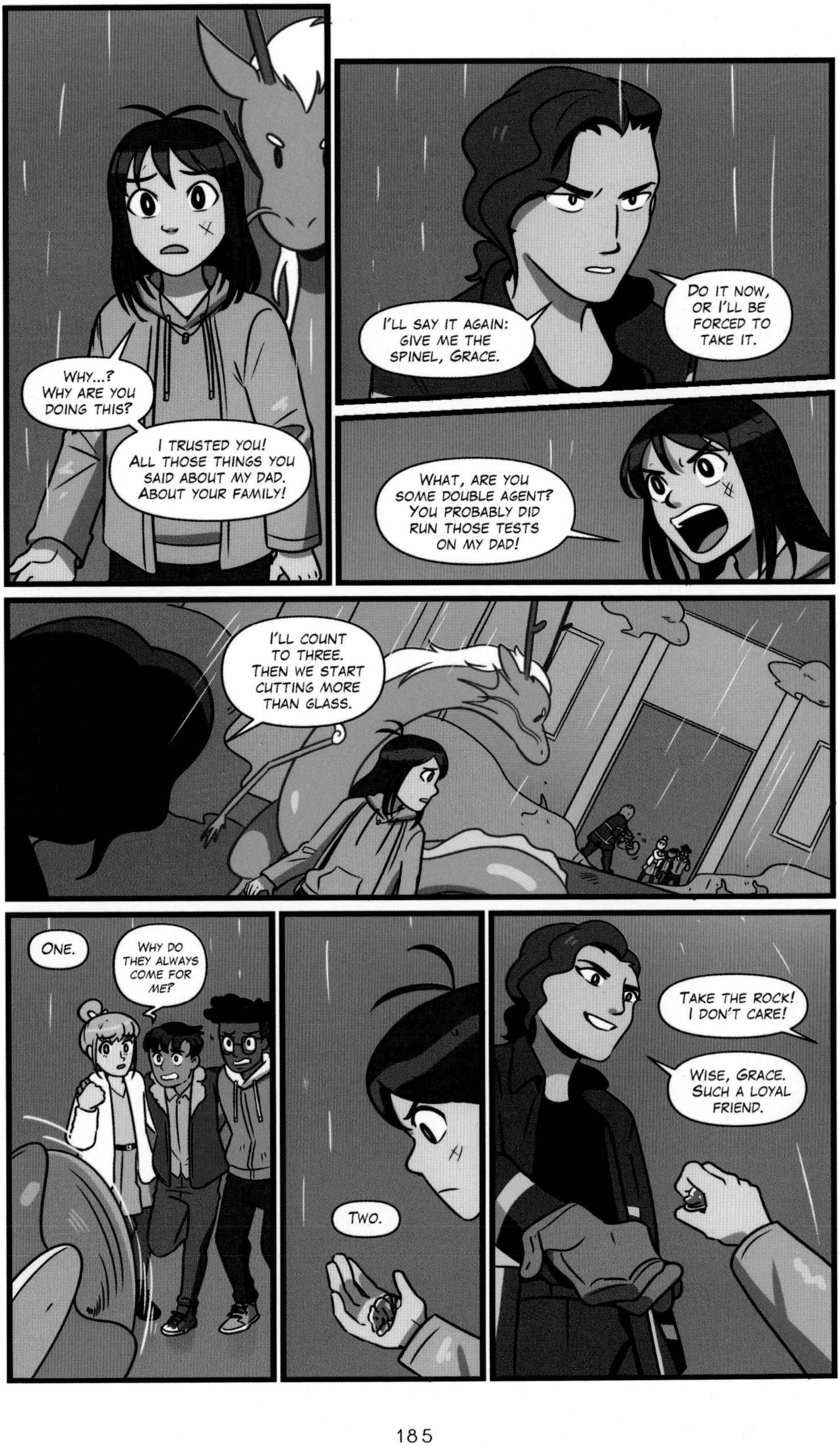
WHY...? WHY ARE YOU DOING THIS?
I TRUSTED YOU! ALL THOSE THINGS YOU SAID ABOUT MY DAD. ABOUT YOUR FAMILY!
I'LL SAY IT AGAIN: GIVE ME THE SPINEL, GRACE.
DO IT NOW, OR I'LL BE FORCED TO TAKE IT.
WHAT, ARE YOU SOME DOUBLE AGENT? YOU PROBABLY DID RUN THOSE TESTS ON MY DAD!
I'LL COUNT TO THREE. THEN WE START CUTTING MORE THAN GLASS.
ONE.
WHY DO THEY ALWAYS COME FOR ME?
TWO.
TAKE THE ROCK! I DON'T CARE!
WISE, GRACE. SUCH A LOYAL FRIEND.

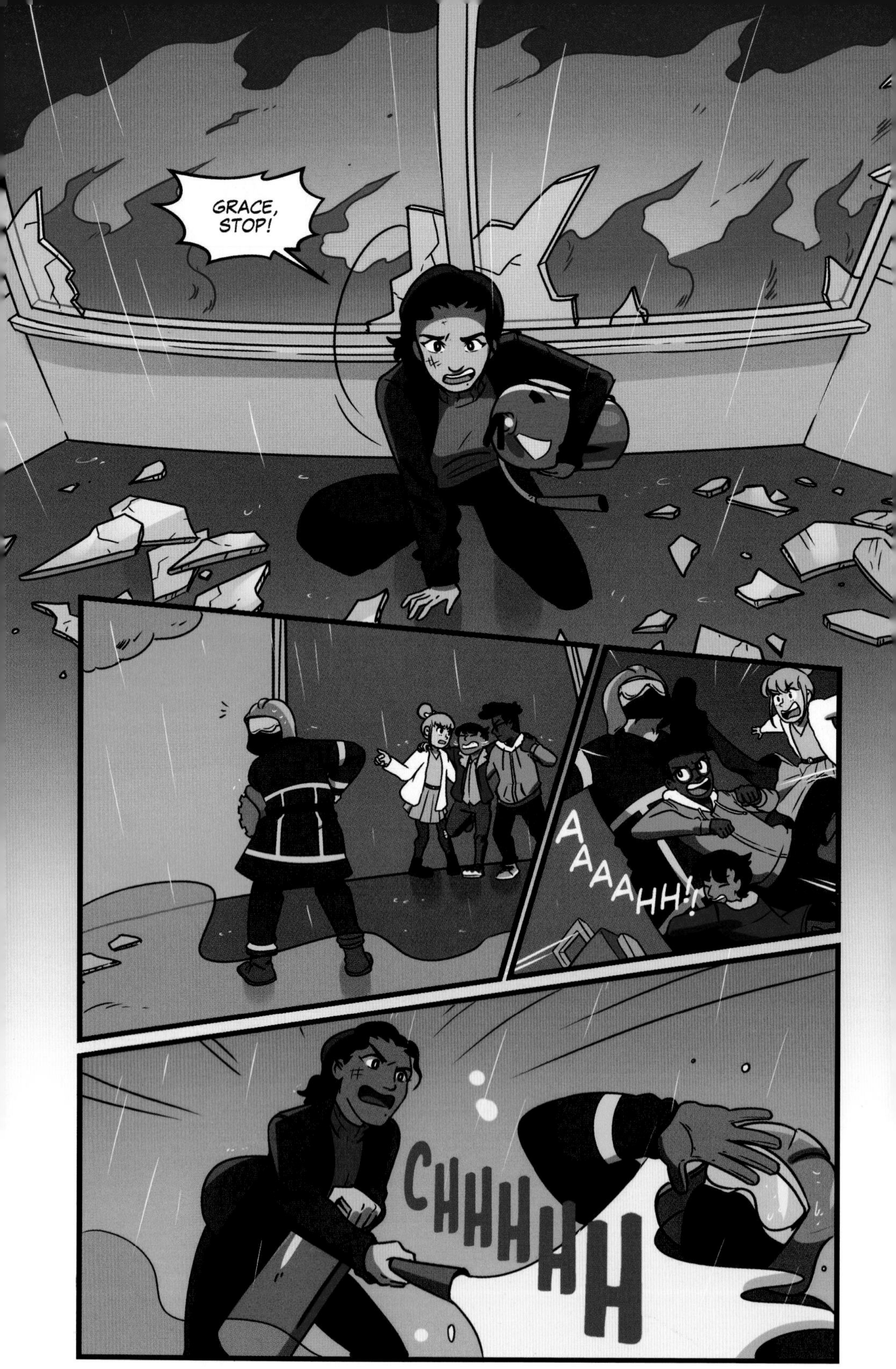
GRACE, STOP!
AAAAHH!!
CHHHHHH

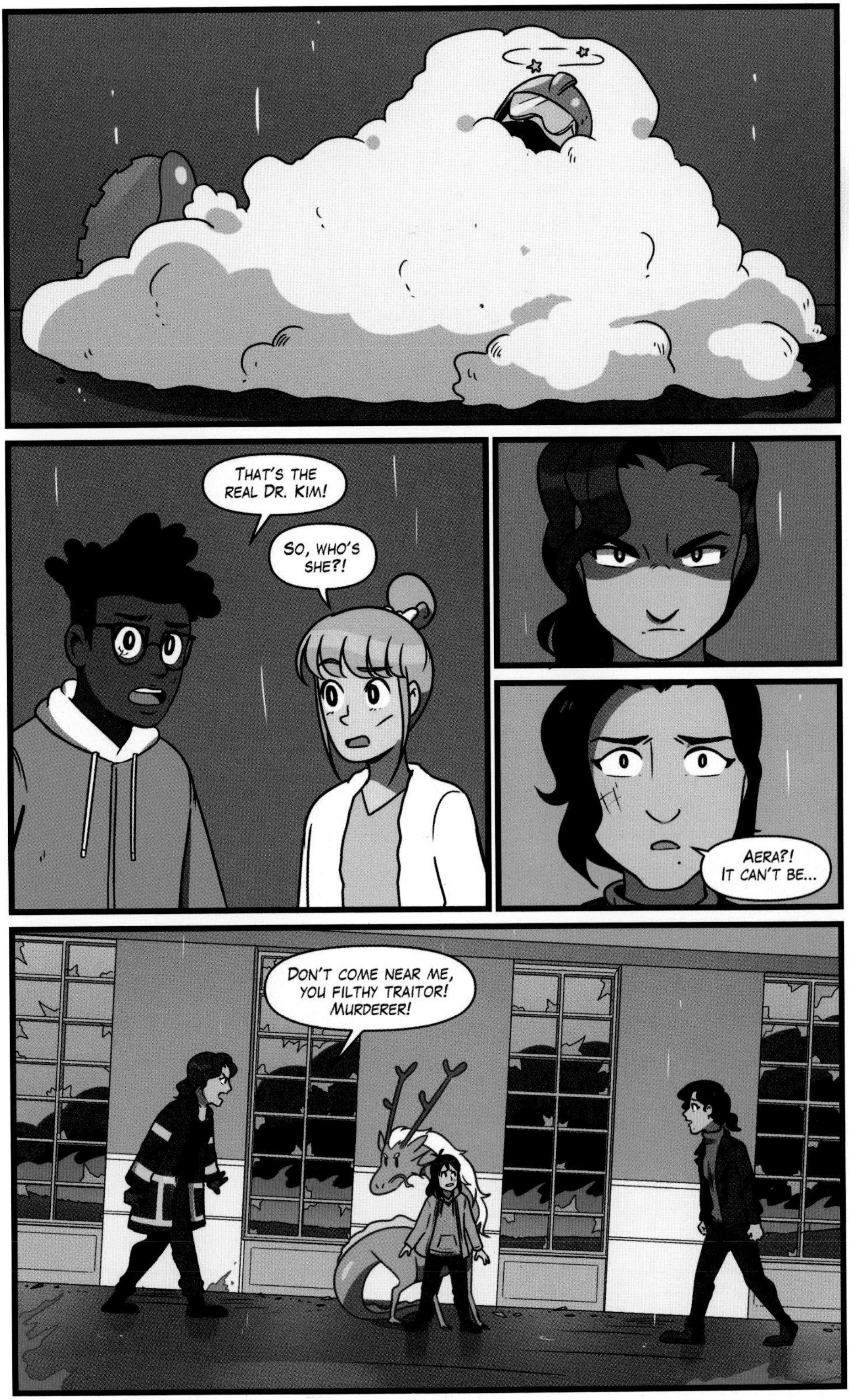
THAT'S THE REAL DR. KIM!
SO, WHO'S SHE?!
AERA?! IT CAN'T BE...
DON'T COME NEAR ME, YOU FILTHY TRAITOR! MURDERER!

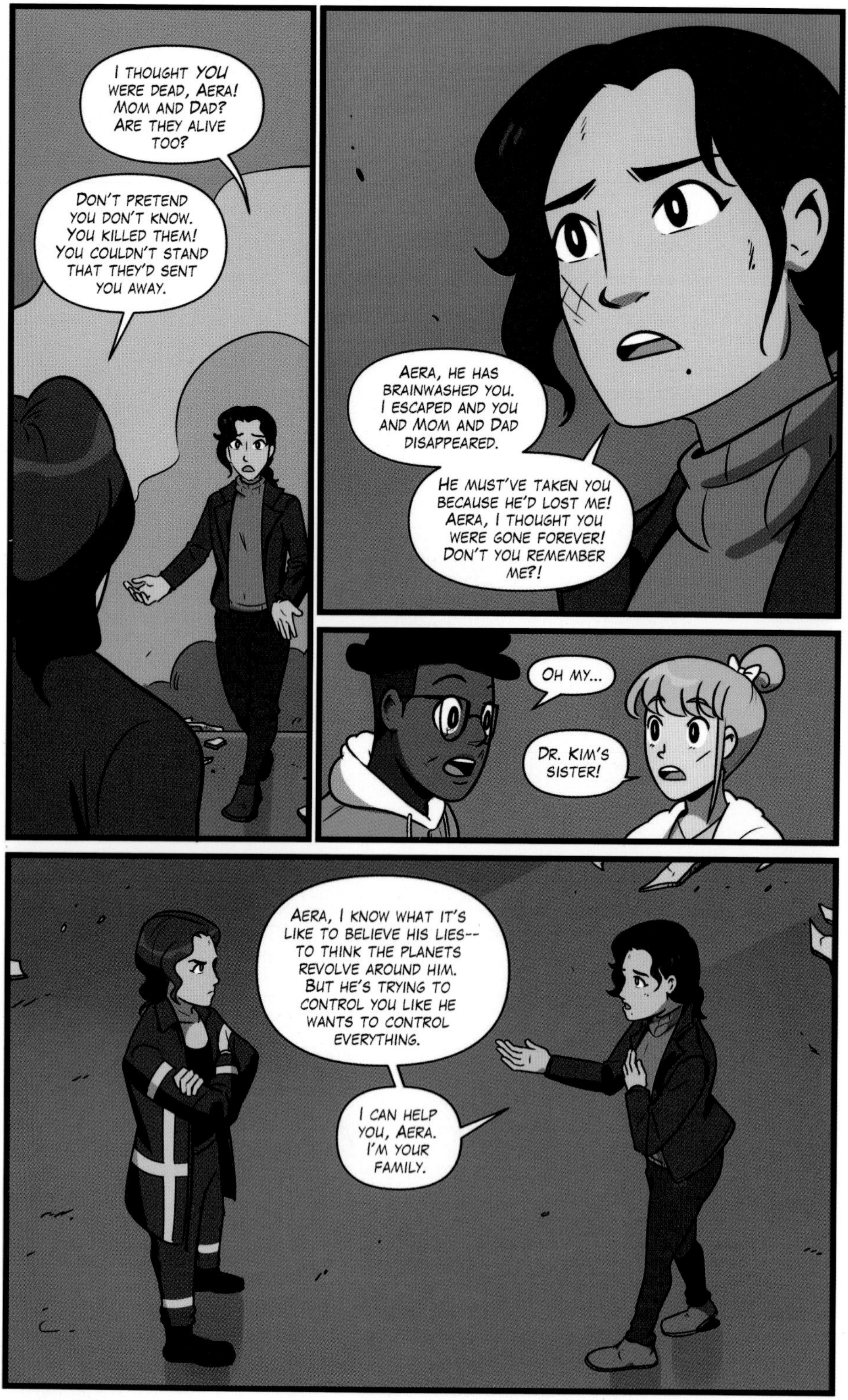
I THOUGHT YOU WERE DEAD, AERA! MOM AND DAD? ARE THEY ALIVE TOO?
DON'T PRETEND YOU DON'T KNOW. YOU KILLED THEM! YOU COULDN'T STAND THAT THEY'D SENT YOU AWAY.
AERA, HE HAS BRAINWASHED YOU. I ESCAPED AND YOU AND MOM AND DAD DISAPPEARED.
HE MUST'VE TAKEN YOU BECAUSE HE'D LOST ME! AERA, I THOUGHT YOU WERE GONE FOREVER! DON'T YOU REMEMBER ME?!
OH MY...
DR. KIM'S SISTER!
AERA, I KNOW WHAT IT'S LIKE TO BELIEVE HIS LIES-- TO THINK THE PLANETS REVOLVE AROUND HIM. BUT HE'S TRYING TO CONTROL YOU LIKE HE WANTS TO CONTROL EVERYTHING.
I CAN HELP YOU, AERA. I'M YOUR FAMILY.

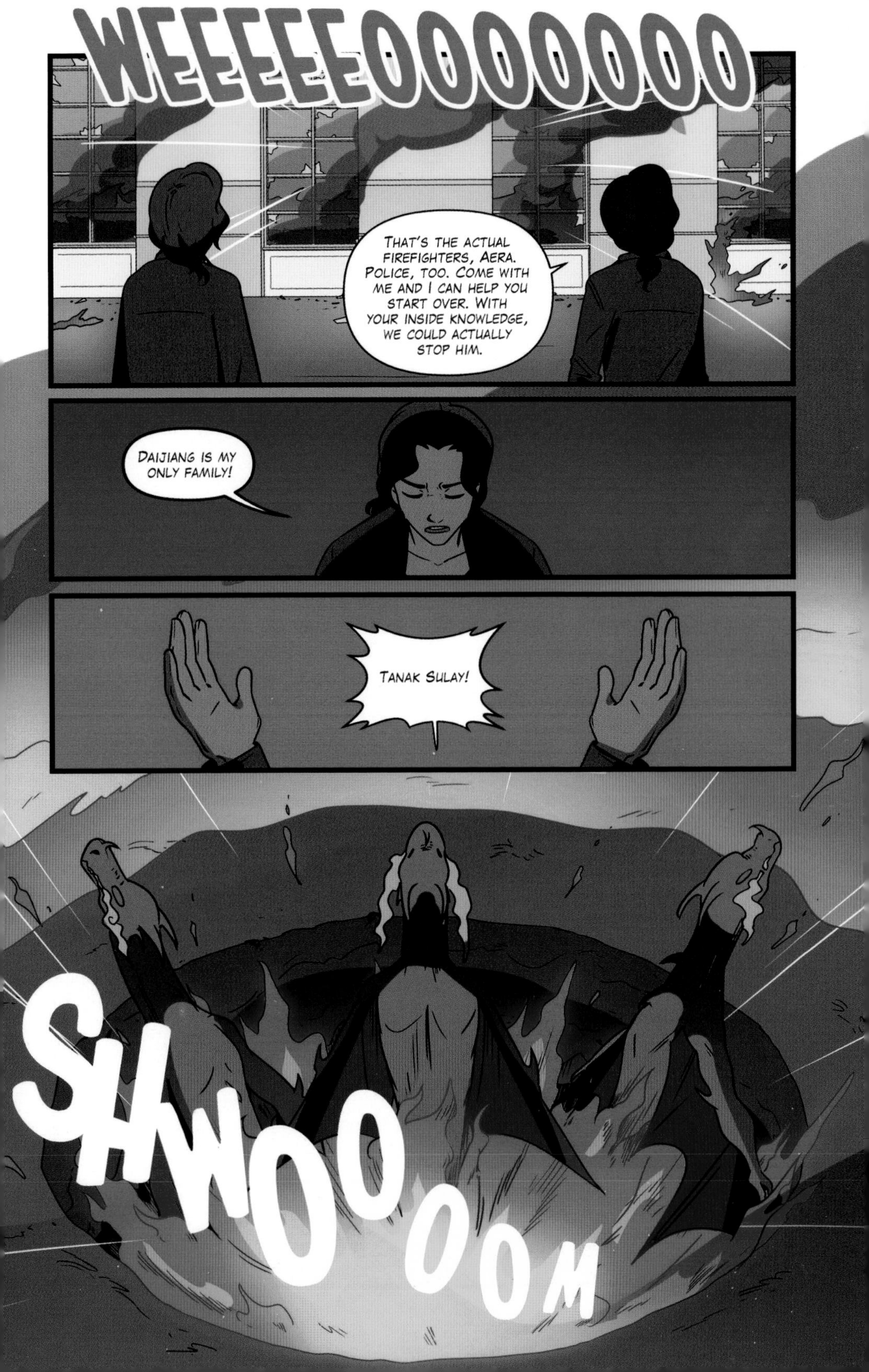
WEEEEEOOOOOOOO
THAT'S THE ACTUAL FIREFIGHTERS, AERA. POLICE, TOO. COME WITH ME AND I CAN HELP YOU START OVER. WITH YOUR INSIDE KNOWLEDGE, WE COULD ACTUALLY STOP HIM.
DAIJIANG IS MY ONLY FAMILY!
TANAK SULAY!
SHWOOOOM

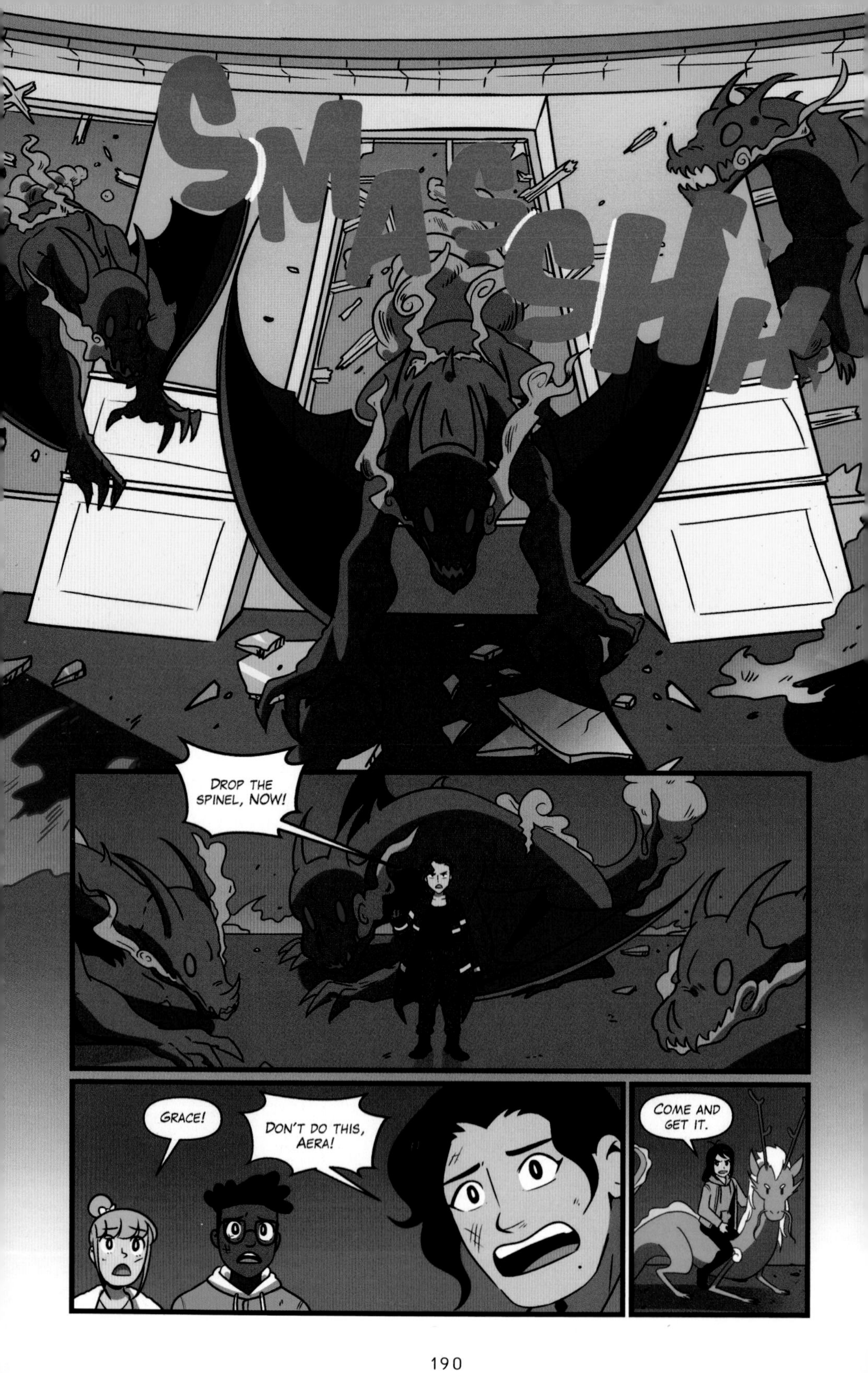
SMASSHH
DROP THE SPINEL, NOW!
GRACE!
DON'T DO THIS, AERA!
COME AND GET IT.

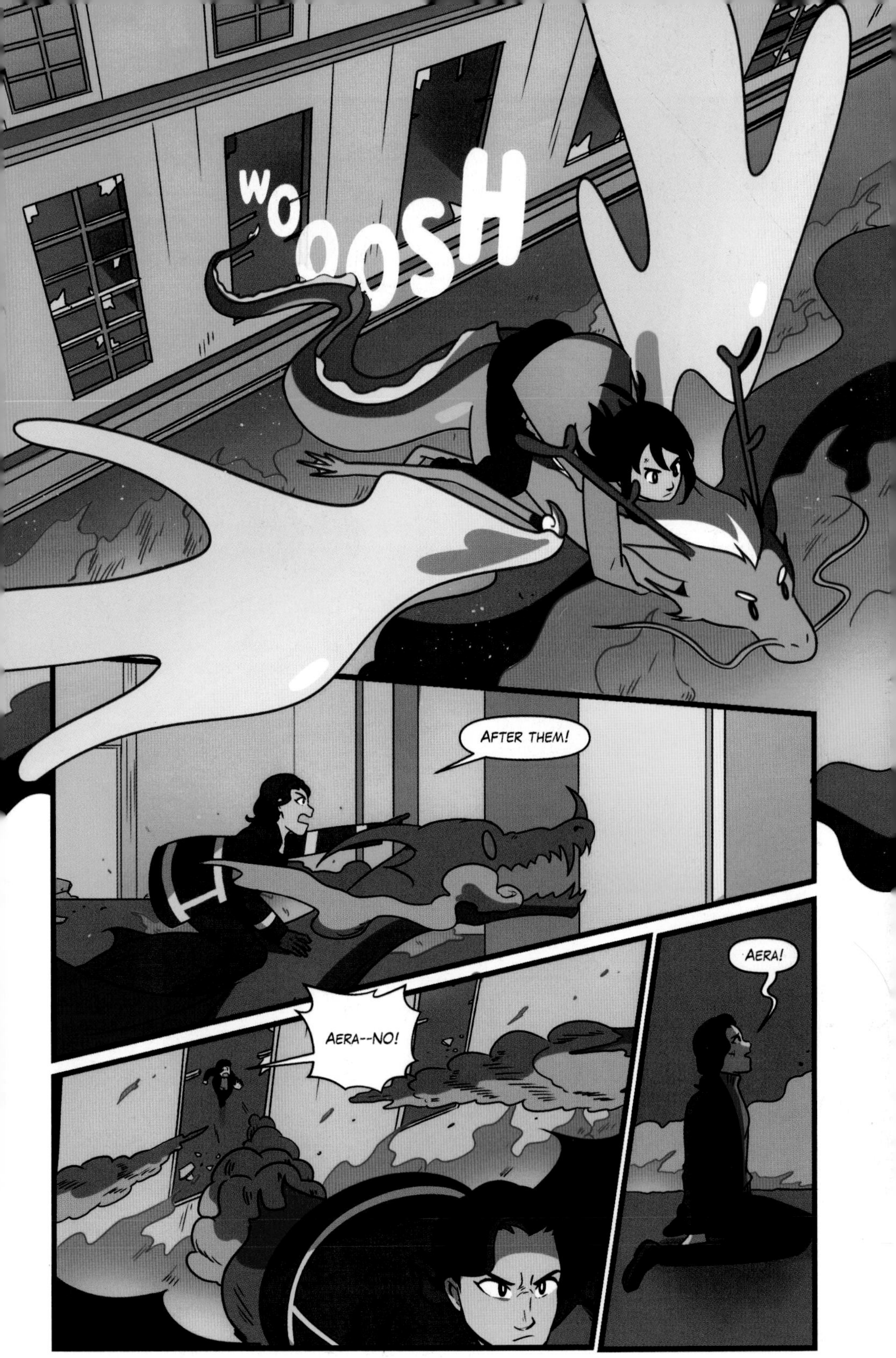
WOOOSH
AFTER THEM!
AERA!
AERA--NO!

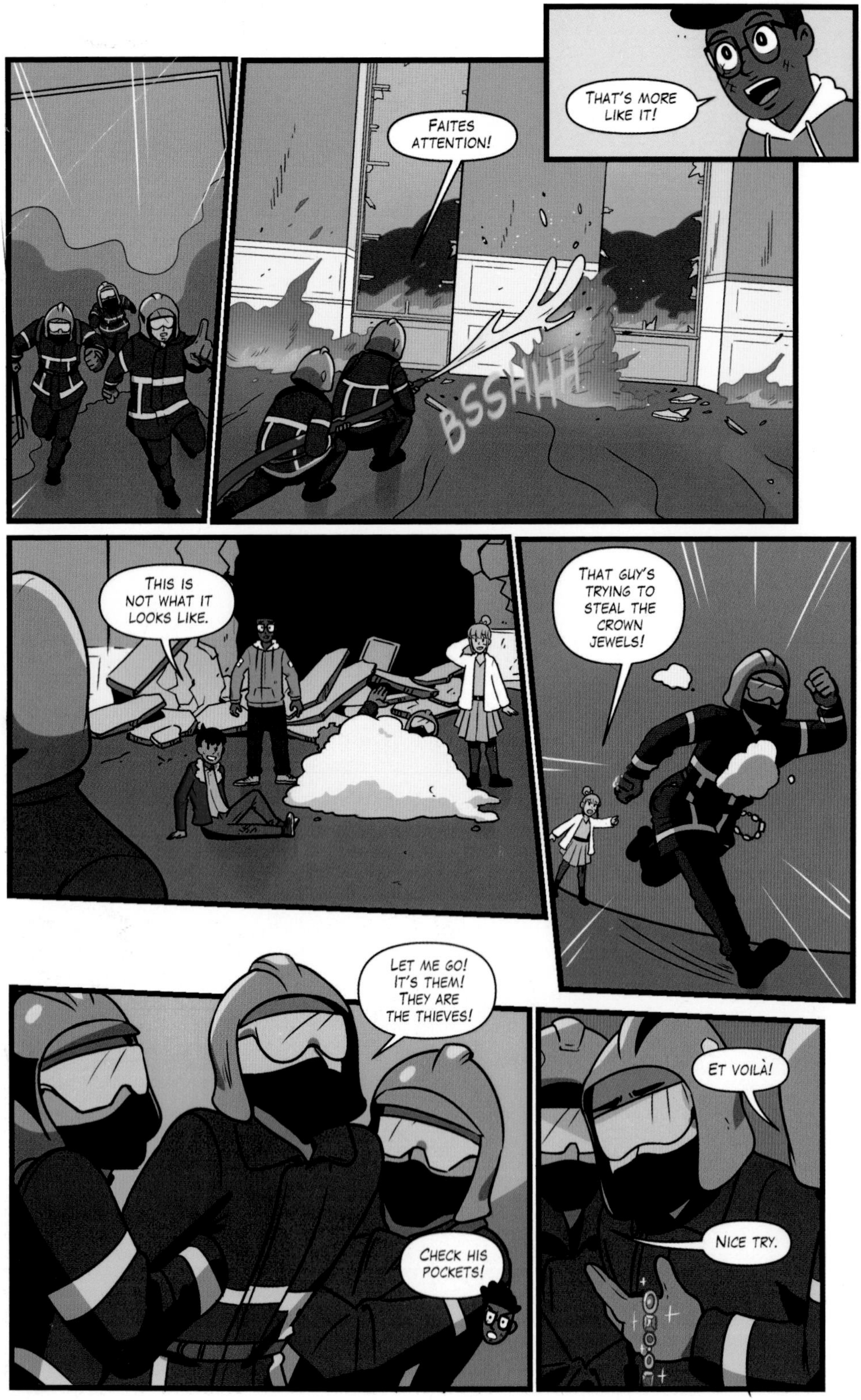
FAITES ATTENTION!
THAT'S MORE LIKE IT!
BSSHHH
THIS IS NOT WHAT IT LOOKS LIKE.
THAT GUY'S TRYING TO STEAL THE CROWN JEWELS!
LET ME GO! IT'S THEM! THEY ARE THE THIEVES!
CHECK HIS POCKETS!
ET VOILÀ!
NICE TRY.

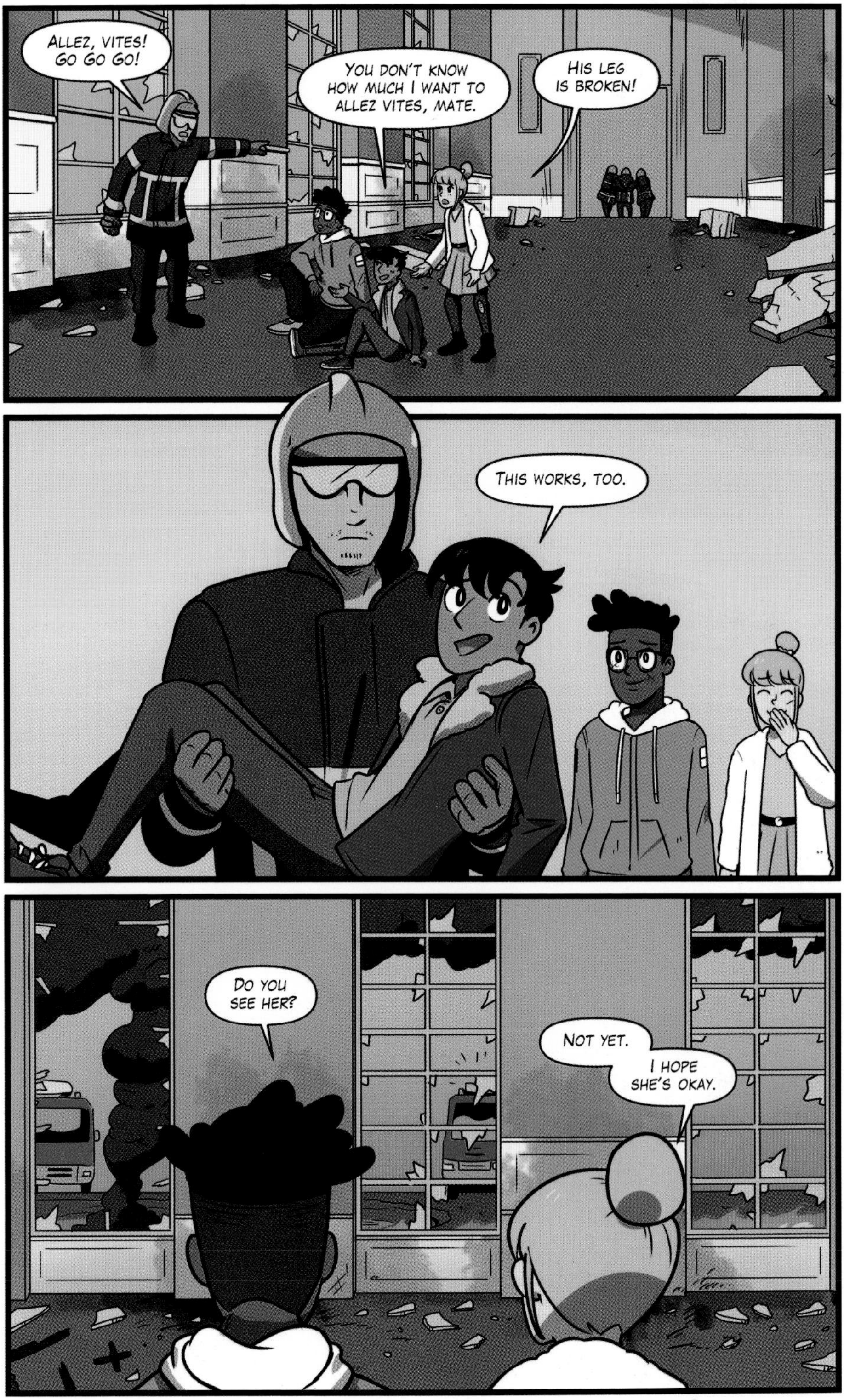
ALLEZ, VITES! GO GO GO!
YOU DON'T KNOW HOW MUCH I WANT TO ALLEZ VITES, MATE.
HIS LEG IS BROKEN!
THIS WORKS, TOO.
DO YOU SEE HER?
NOT YET.
I HOPE SHE'S OKAY.

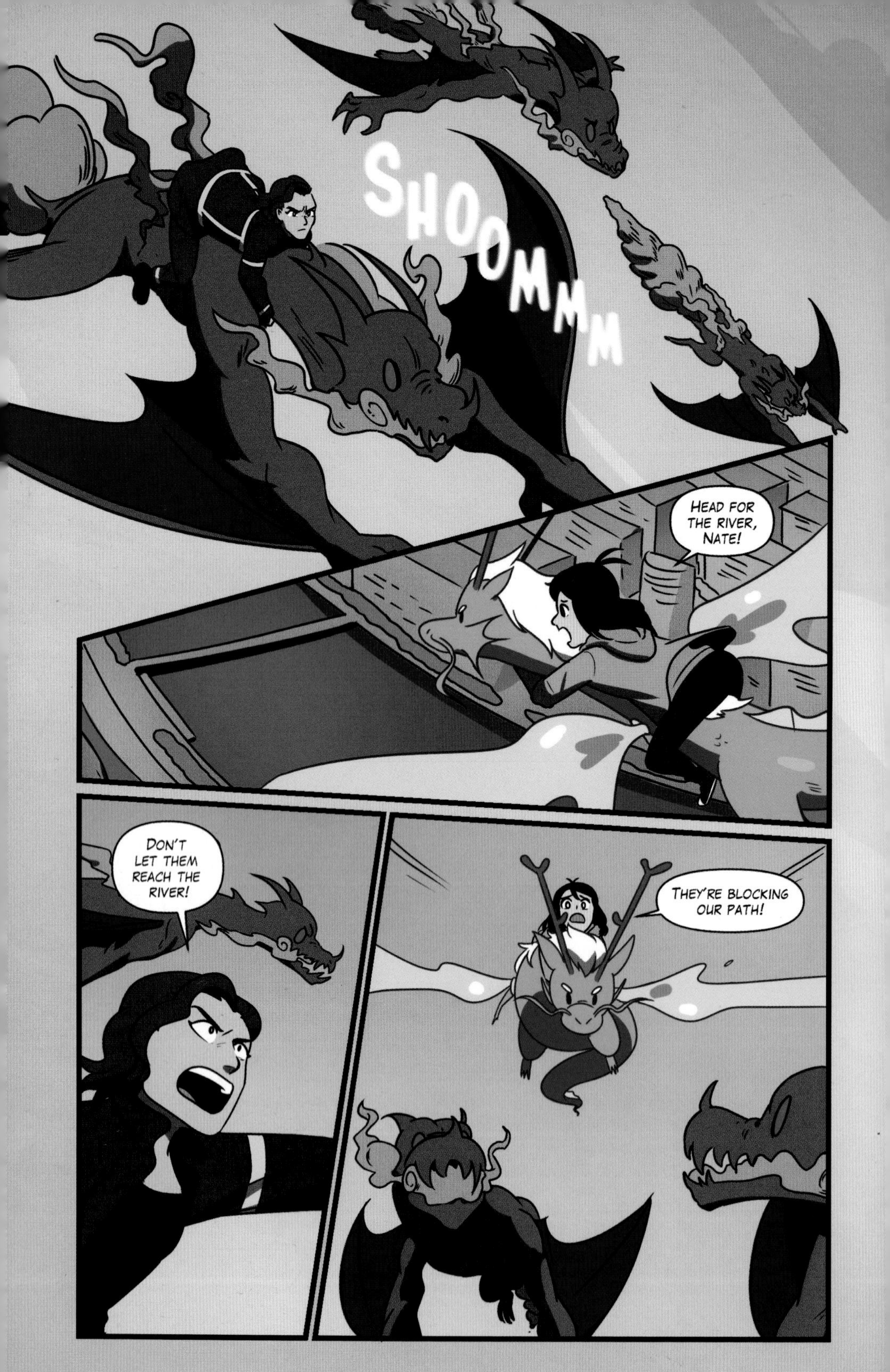
SHOOMMMM
HEAD FOR THE RIVER, NATE!
DON'T LET THEM REACH THE RIVER!
THEY'RE BLOCKING OUR PATH!

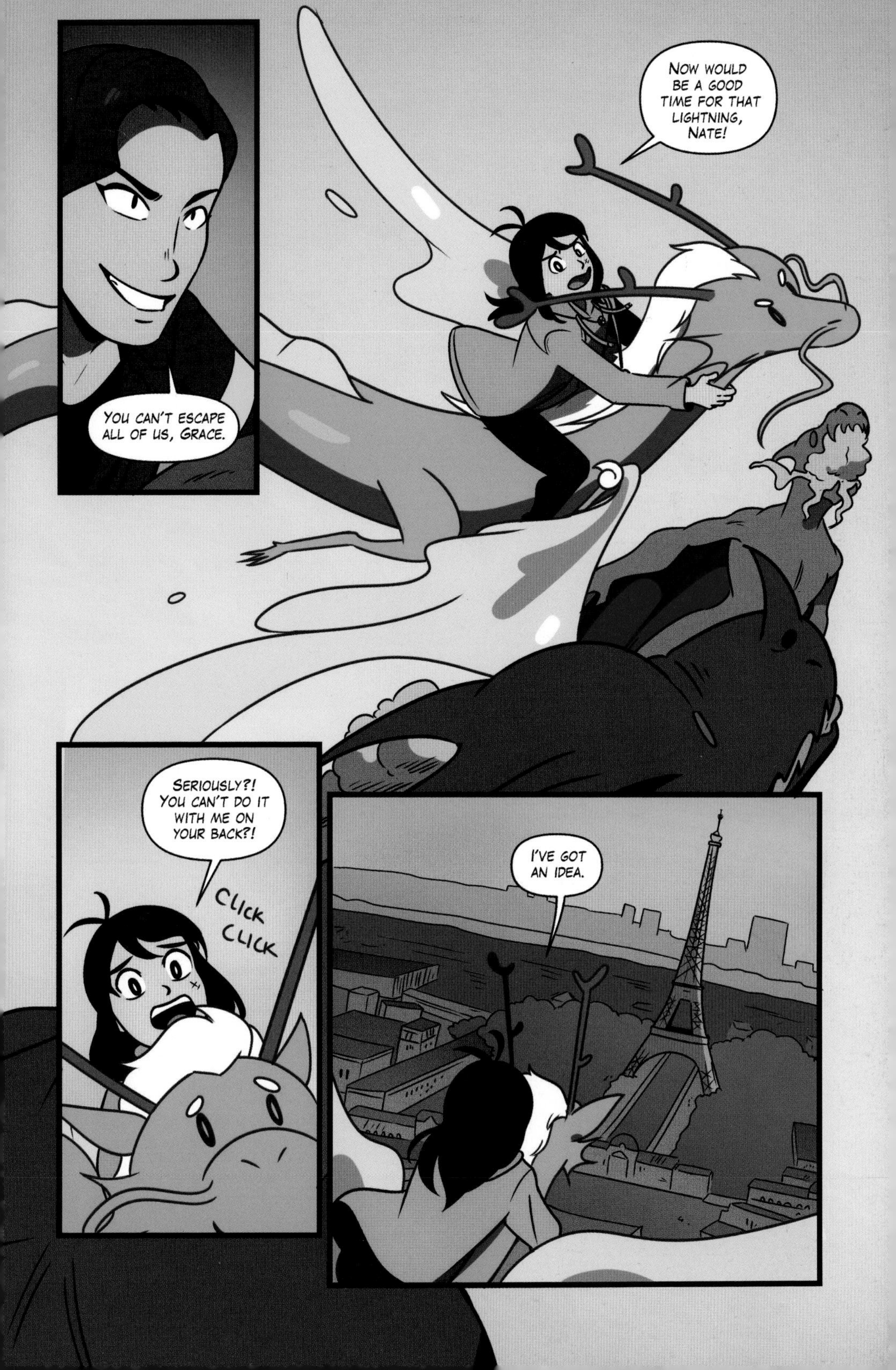
YOU CAN'T ESCAPE ALL OF US, GRACE.
NOW WOULD BE A GOOD TIME FOR THAT LIGHTNING, NATE!
SERIOUSLY?! YOU CAN'T DO IT WITH ME ON YOUR BACK?!
CLICK CLICK
I'VE GOT AN IDEA.

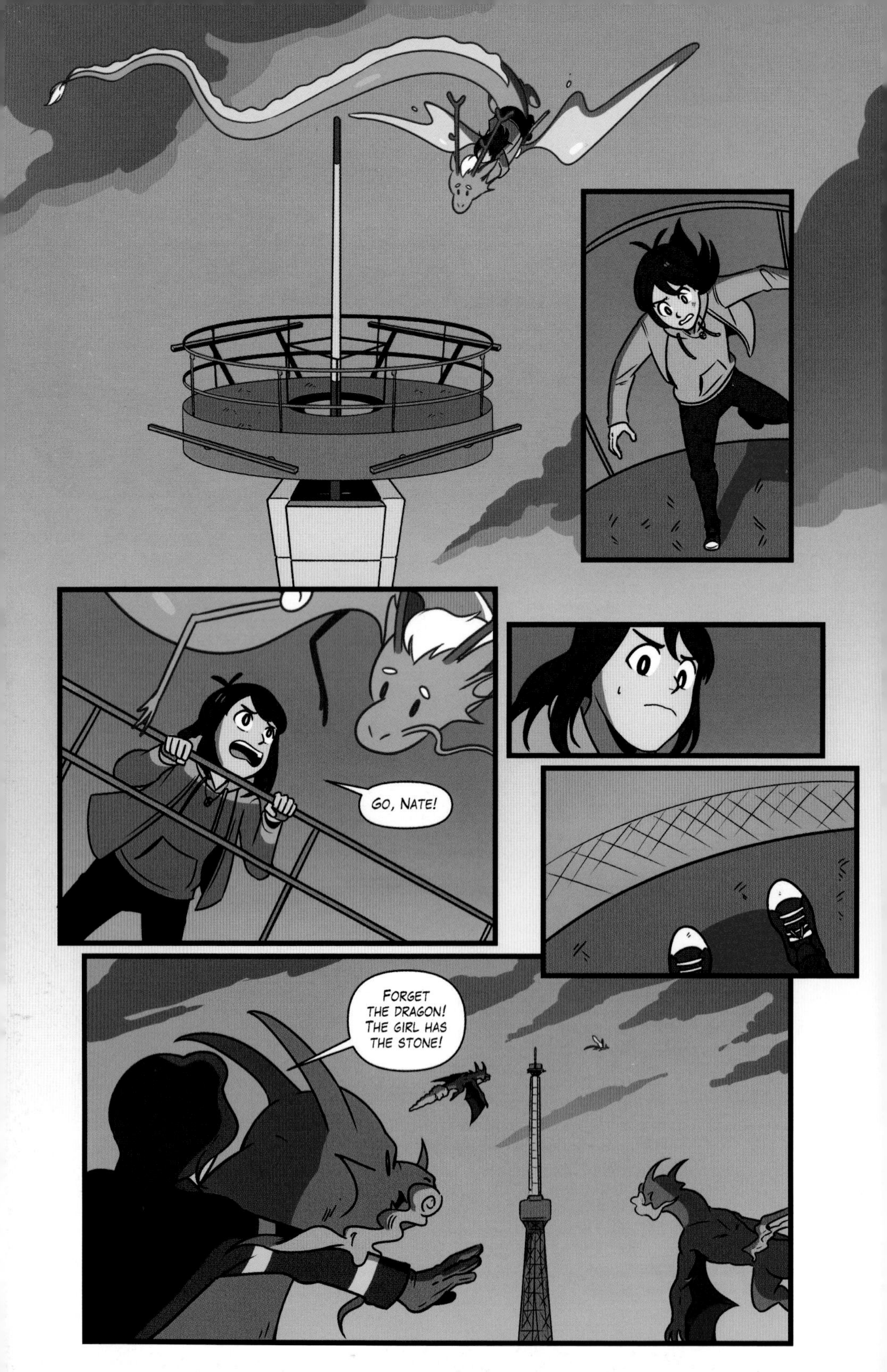
GO, NATE!
FORGET THE DRAGON! THE GIRL HAS THE STONE!

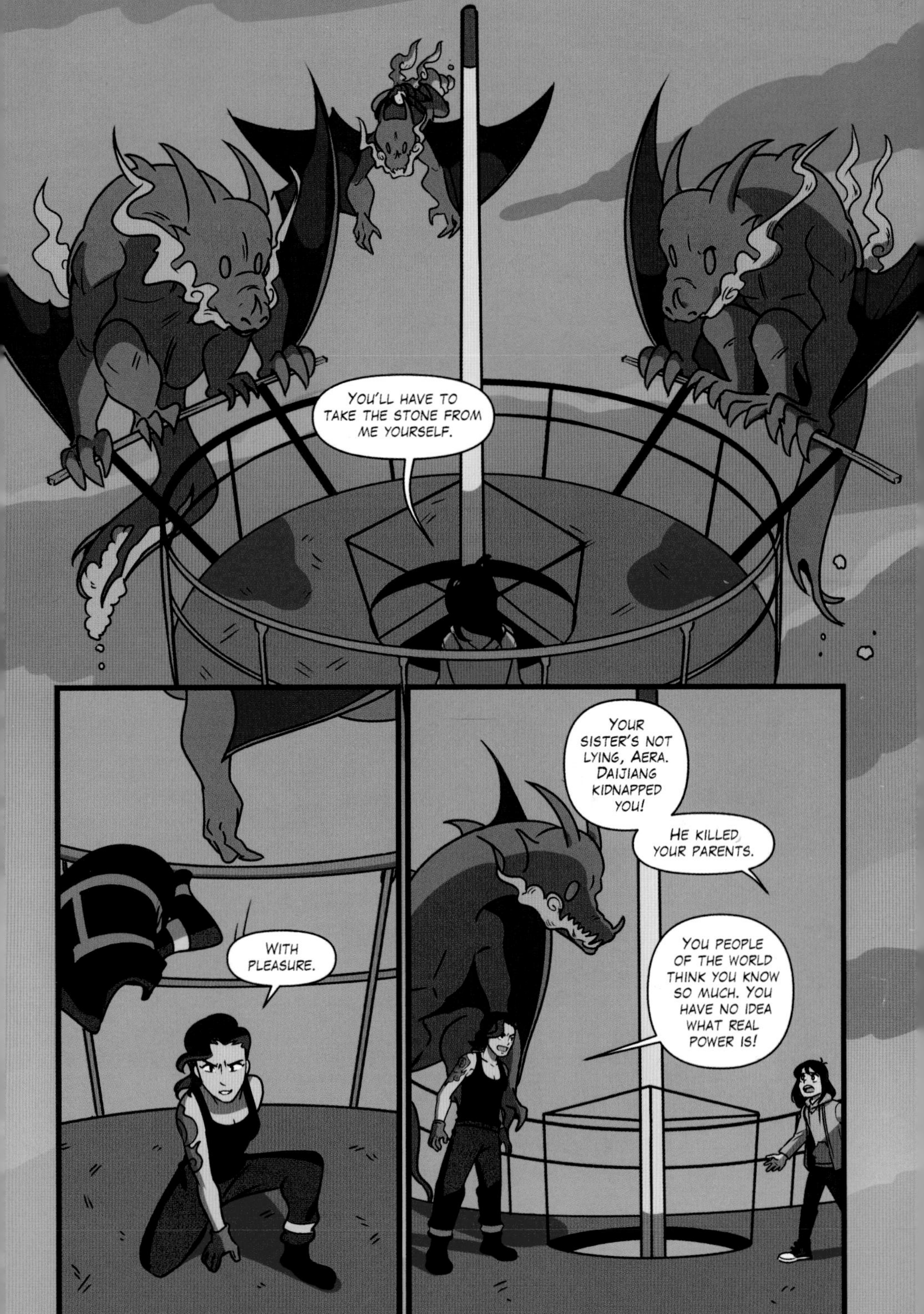

YOU'LL HAVE TO TAKE THE STONE FROM ME YOURSELF.
WITH PLEASURE.
YOUR SISTER'S NOT LYING, AERA. DAIJIANG KIDNAPPED YOU!
HE KILLED YOUR PARENTS.
YOU PEOPLE OF THE WORLD THINK YOU KNOW SO MUCH. YOU HAVE NO IDEA WHAT REAL POWER IS!

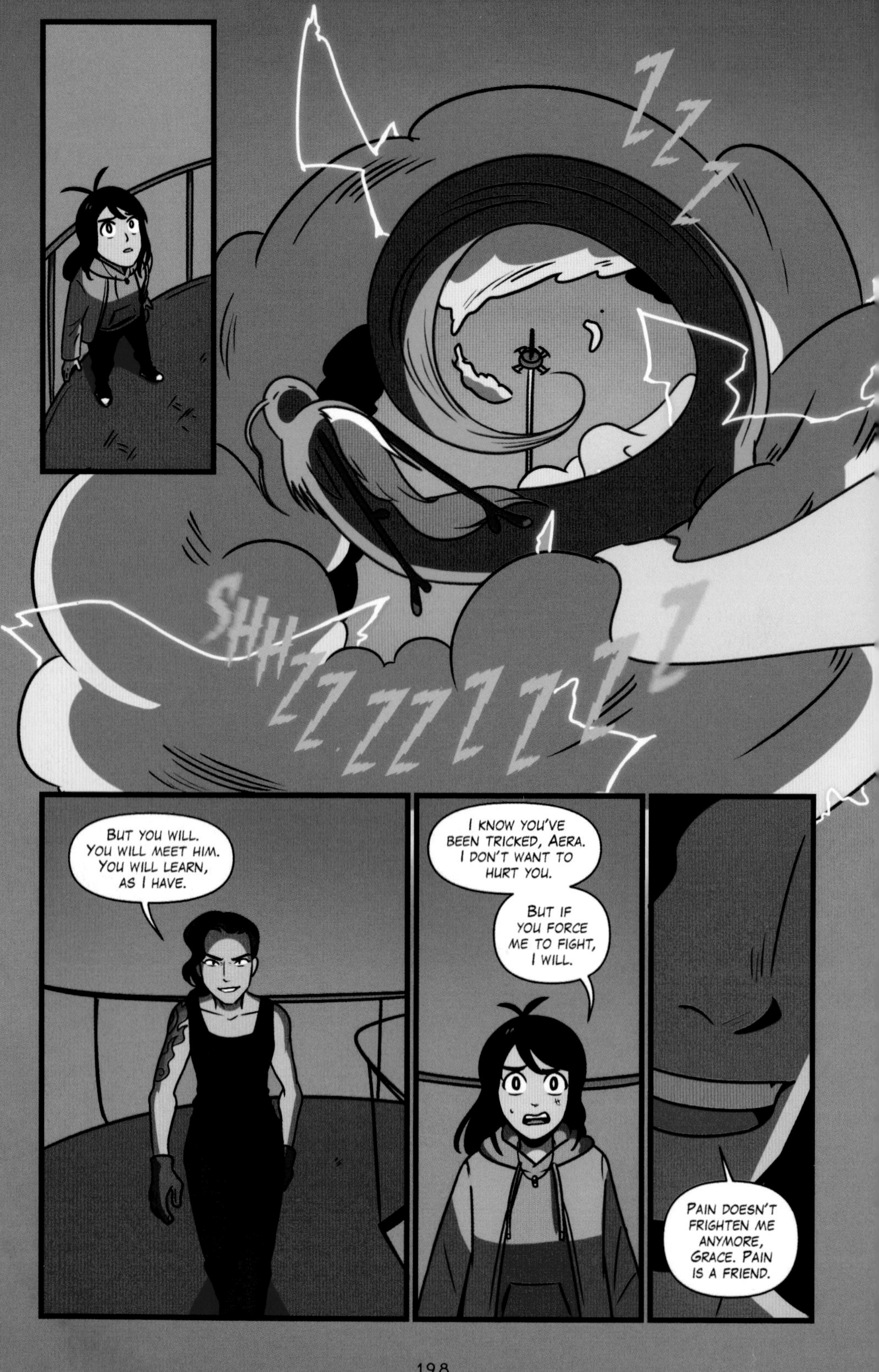
SHHZZZZZZZ
ZZZ
But you will. You will meet him. You will learn, as I have.
I know you've been tricked, Aera. I don't want to hurt you.
But if you force me to fight, I will.
Pain doesn't frighten me anymore, Grace. Pain is a friend.

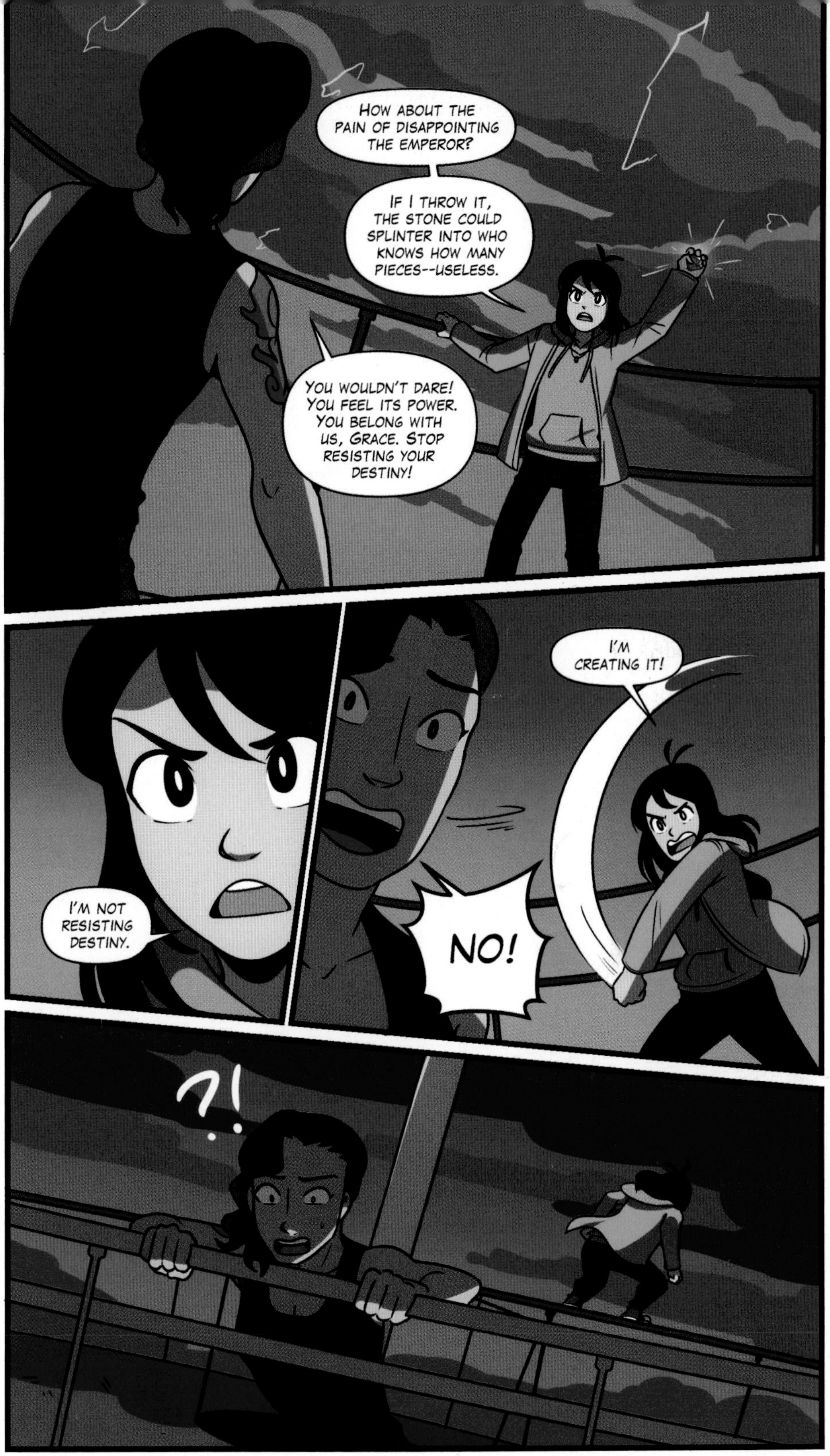
HOW ABOUT THE PAIN OF DISAPPOINTING THE EMPEROR?
IF I THROW IT, THE STONE COULD SPLINTER INTO WHO KNOWS HOW MANY PIECES--USELESS.
YOU WOULDN'T DARE! YOU FEEL ITS POWER. YOU BELONG WITH US, GRACE. STOP RESISTING YOUR DESTINY!
I'M NOT RESISTING DESTINY.
I'M CREATING IT!
NO!
?!

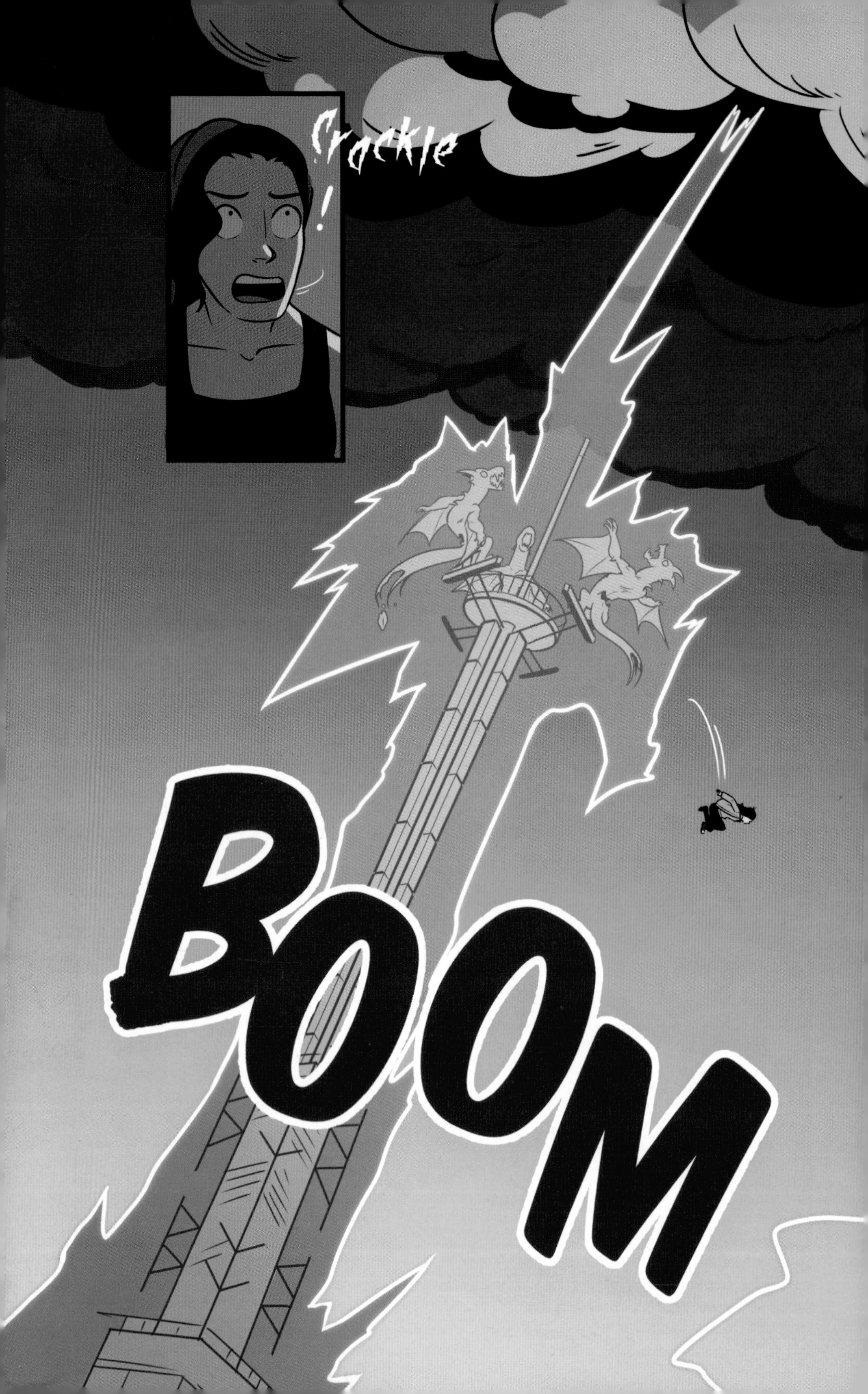
Crackle
!
BOOM

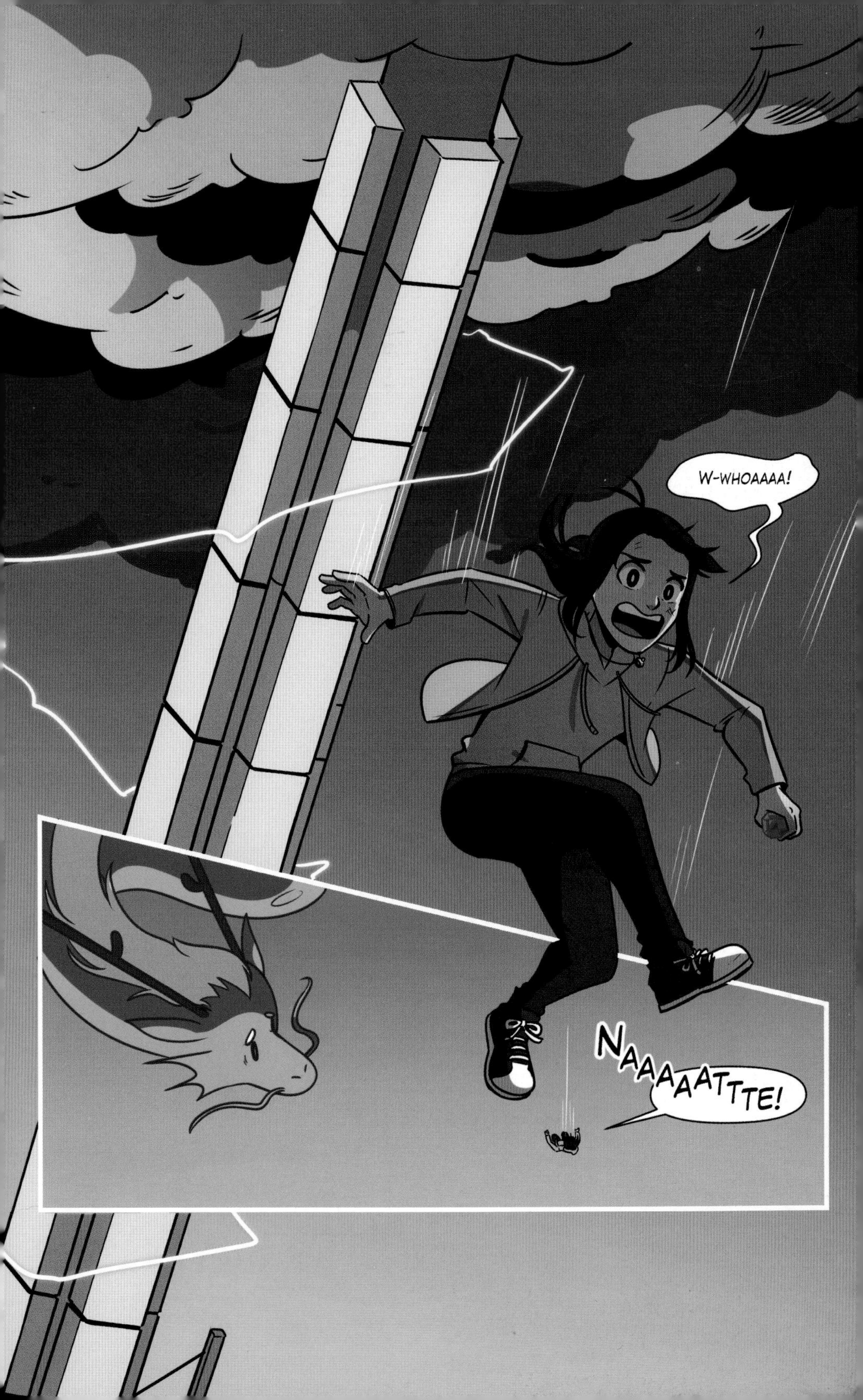
W-WHOAAAAA!
NAAAAATTTE!

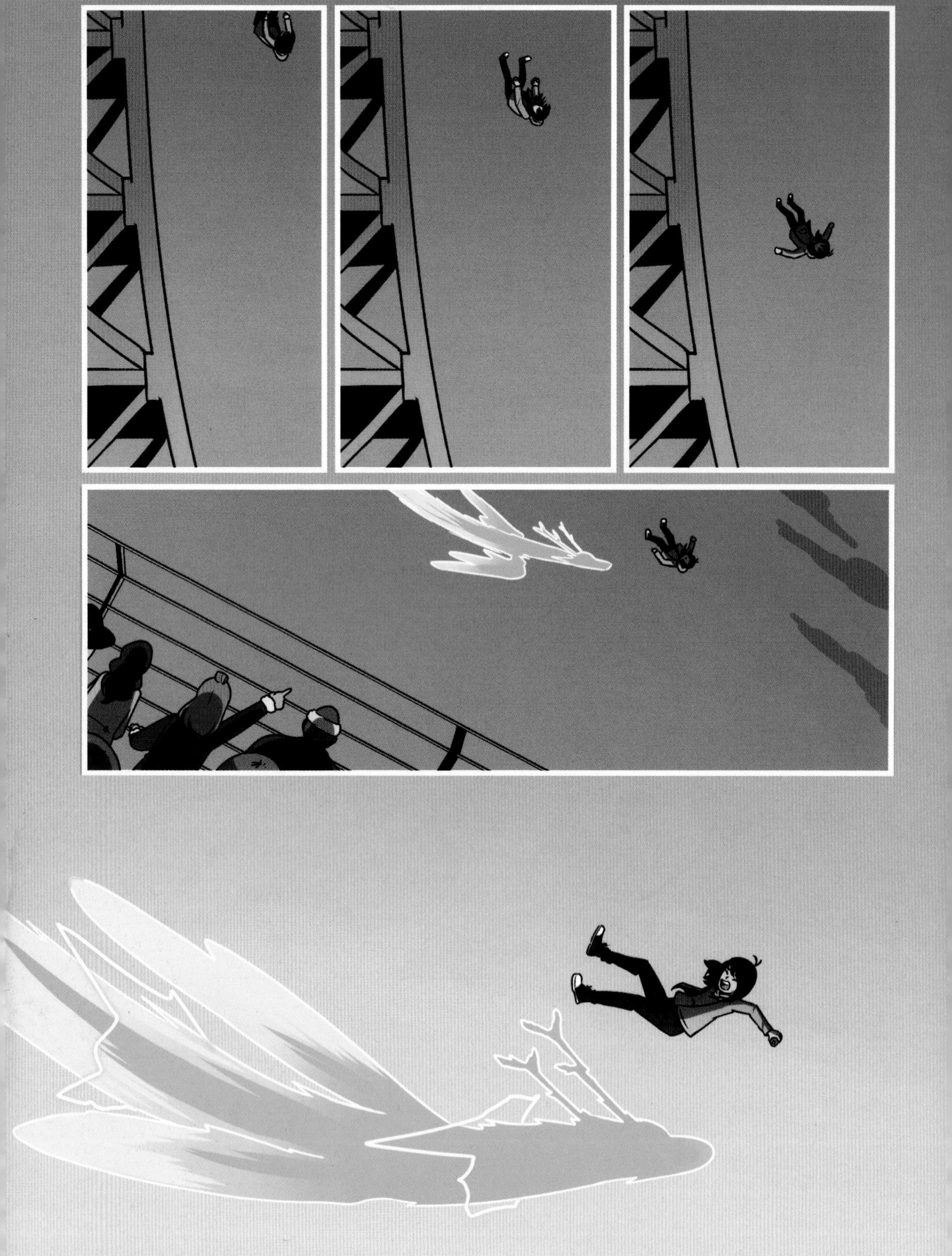

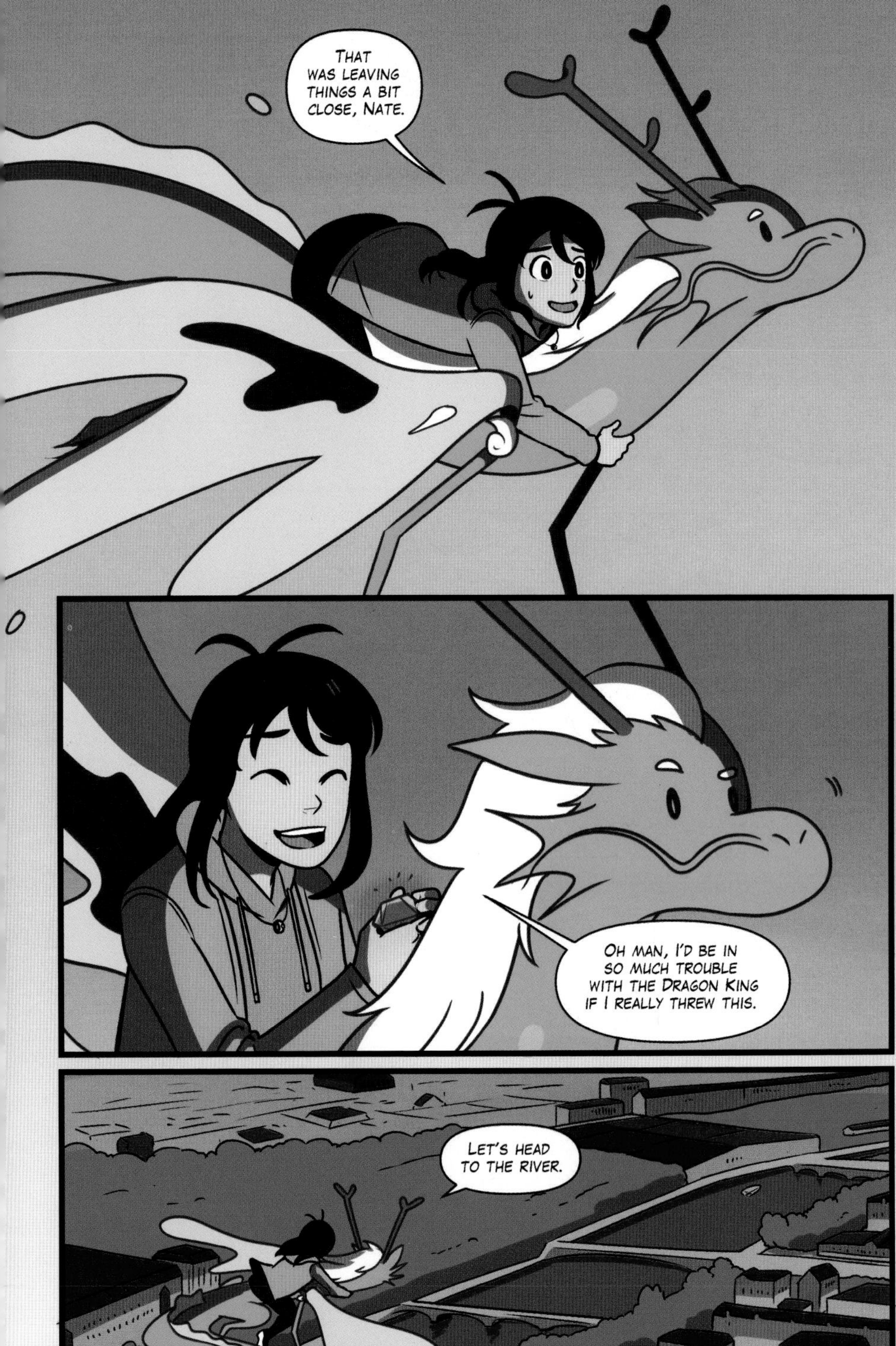
THAT WAS LEAVING THINGS A BIT CLOSE, NATE.
OH MAN, I'D BE IN SO MUCH TROUBLE WITH THE DRAGON KING IF I REALLY THREW THIS.
LET'S HEAD TO THE RIVER.

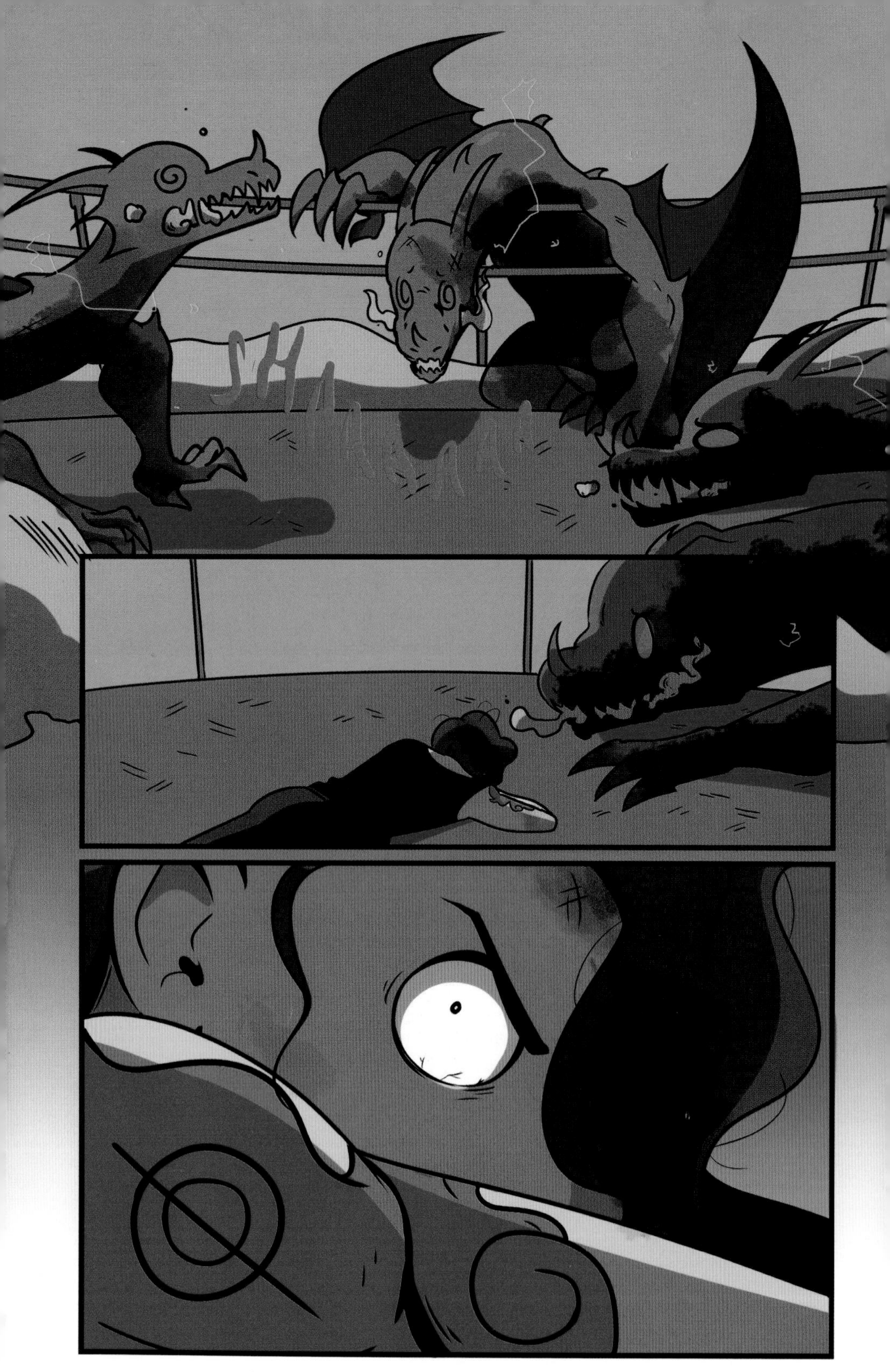
SHAAAAAA

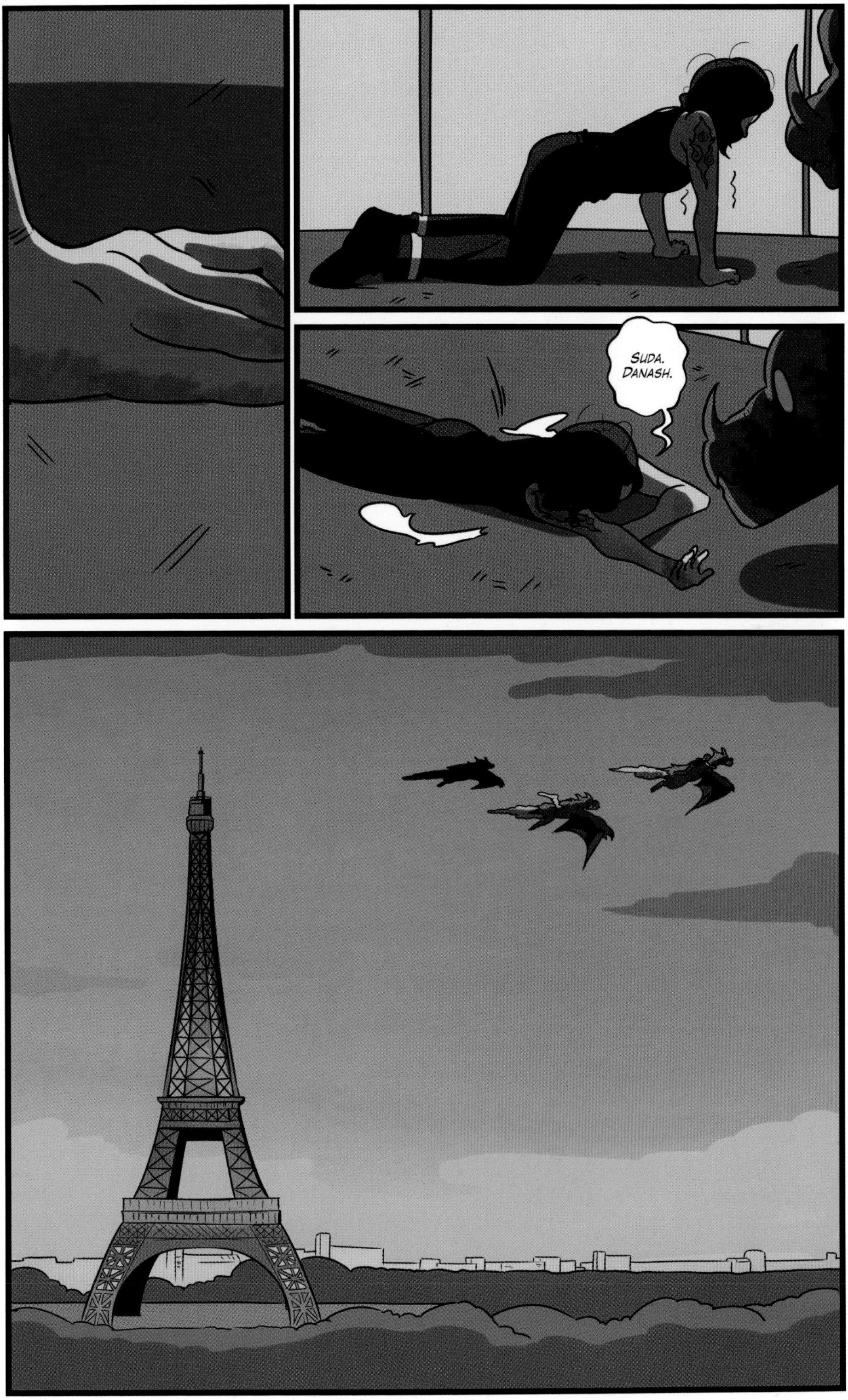
SUDA. DANASH.

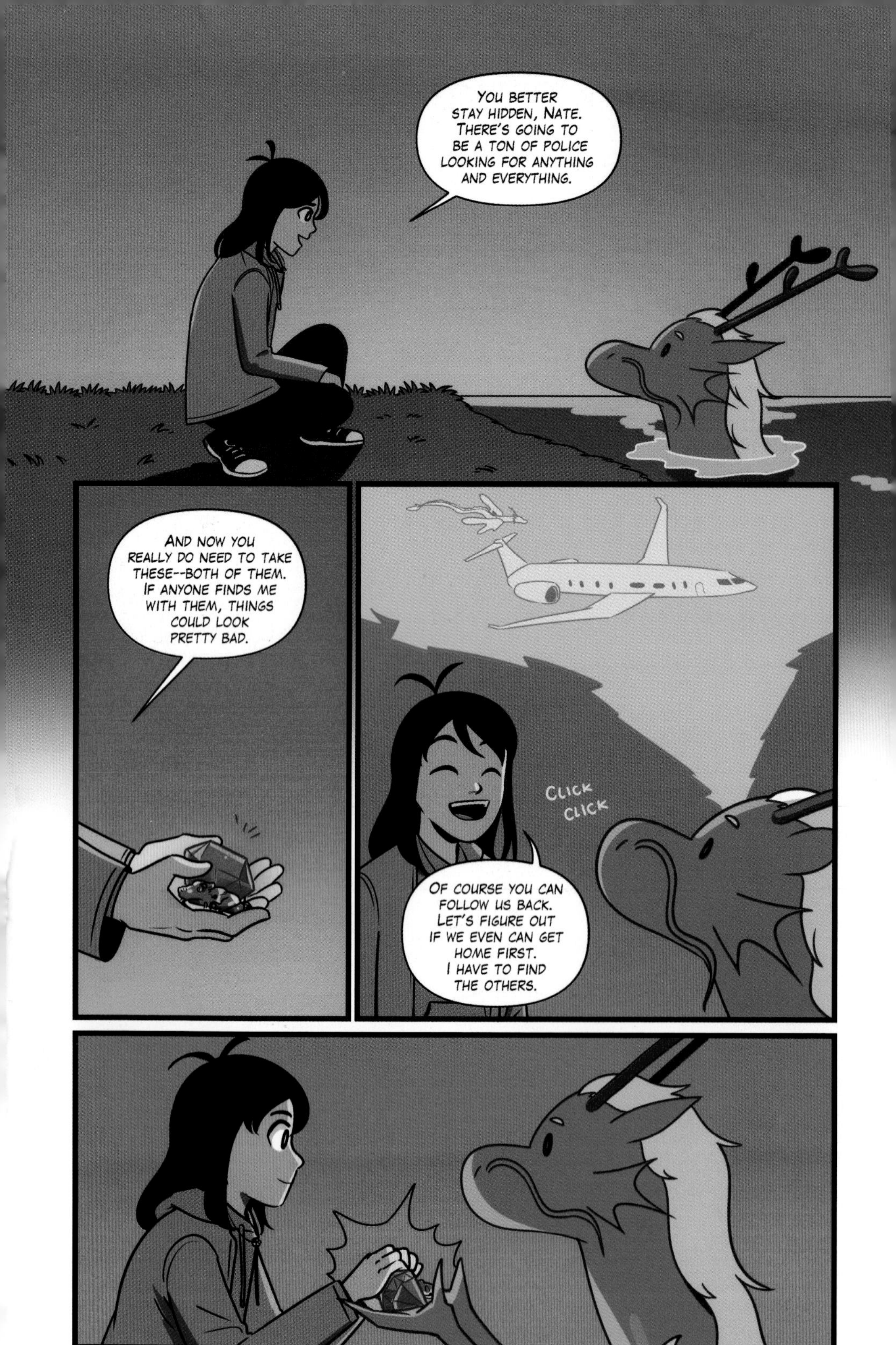
YOU BETTER STAY HIDDEN, NATE. THERE'S GOING TO BE A TON OF POLICE LOOKING FOR ANYTHING AND EVERYTHING.
AND NOW YOU REALLY DO NEED TO TAKE THESE--BOTH OF THEM. IF ANYONE FINDS ME WITH THEM, THINGS COULD LOOK PRETTY BAD.
CLICK CLICK
OF COURSE YOU CAN FOLLOW US BACK. LET'S FIGURE OUT IF WE EVEN CAN GET HOME FIRST. I HAVE TO FIND THE OTHERS.

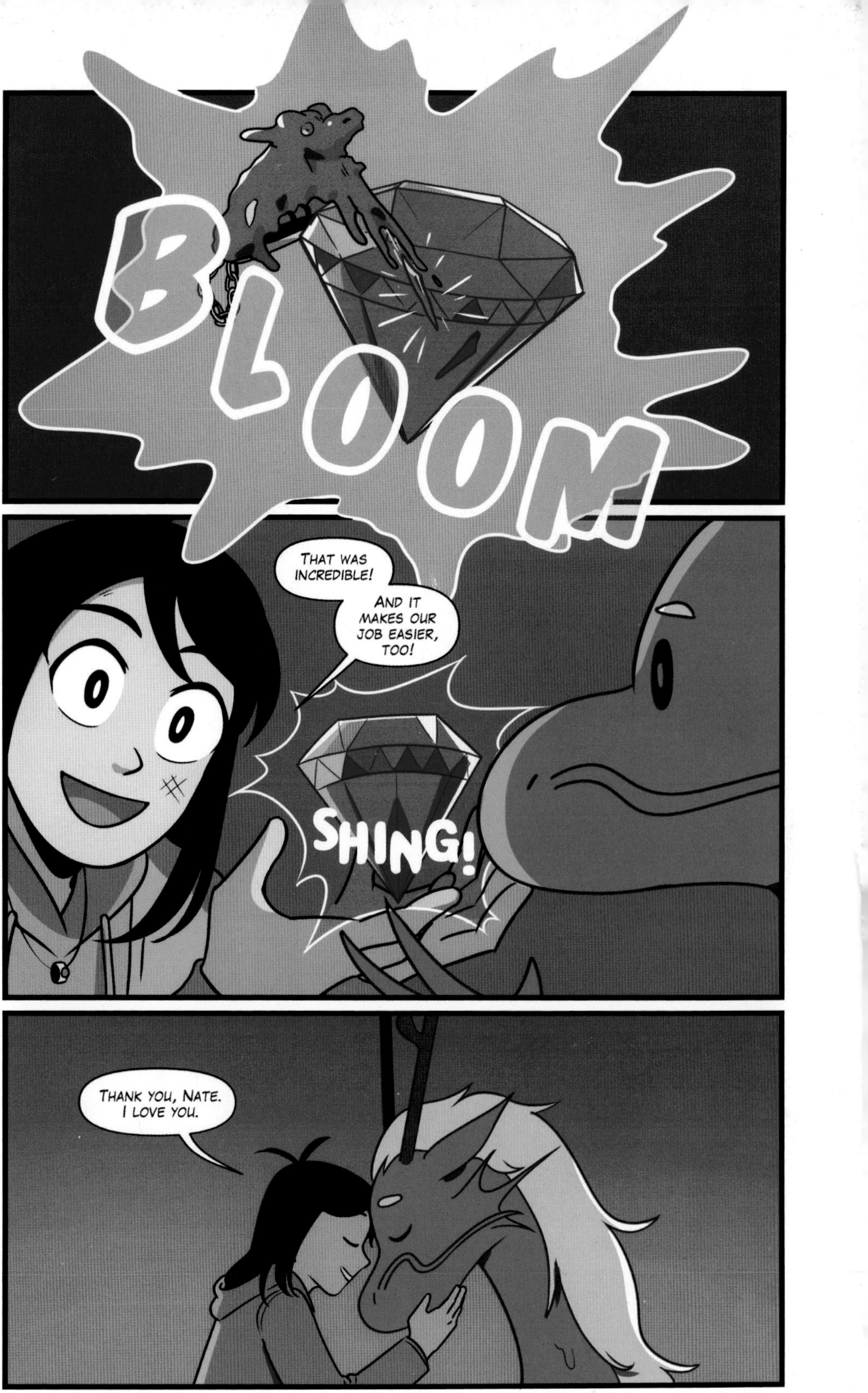
BLOOM
THAT WAS INCREDIBLE!
AND IT MAKES OUR JOB EASIER, TOO!
SHING!
THANK YOU, NATE. I LOVE YOU.

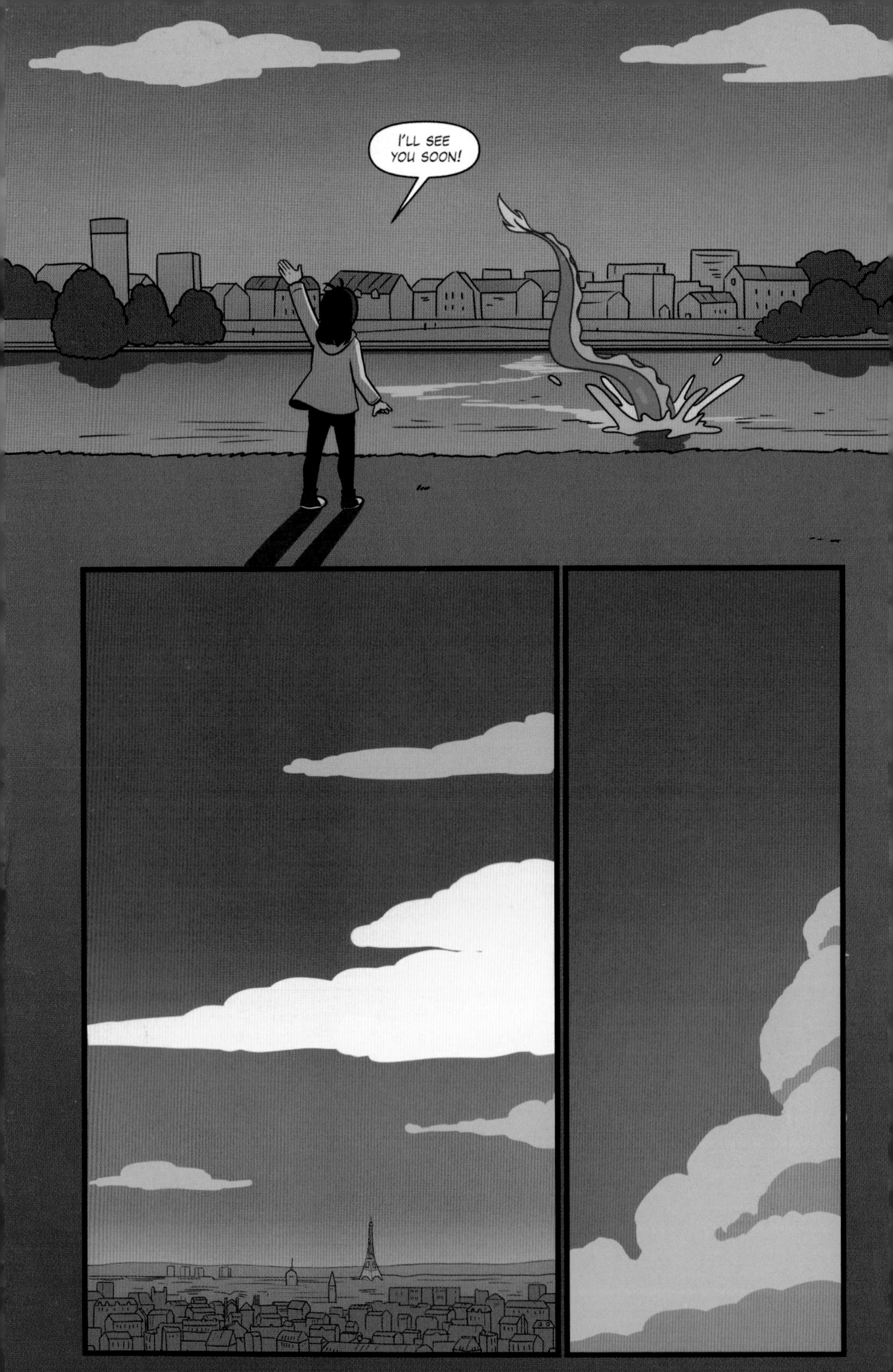
I'LL SEE YOU SOON!

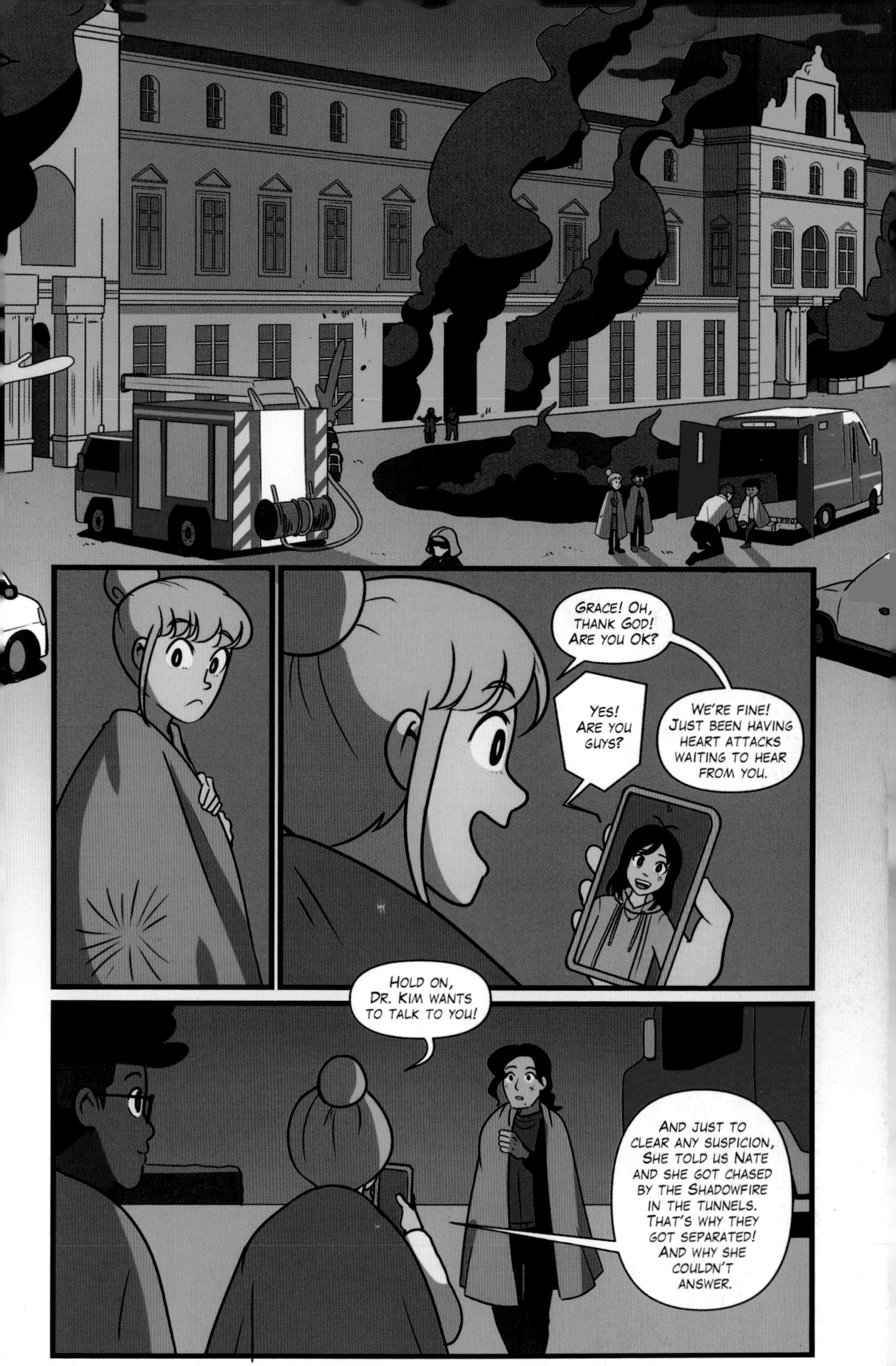
GRACE! OH, THANK GOD! ARE YOU OK?
YES! ARE YOU GUYS?
WE'RE FINE! JUST BEEN HAVING HEART ATTACKS WAITING TO HEAR FROM YOU.
HOLD ON, DR. KIM WANTS TO TALK TO YOU!
AND JUST TO CLEAR ANY SUSPICION, SHE TOLD US NATE AND SHE GOT CHASED BY THE SHADOWFIRE IN THE TUNNELS. THAT'S WHY THEY GOT SEPARATED! AND WHY SHE COULDN'T ANSWER.

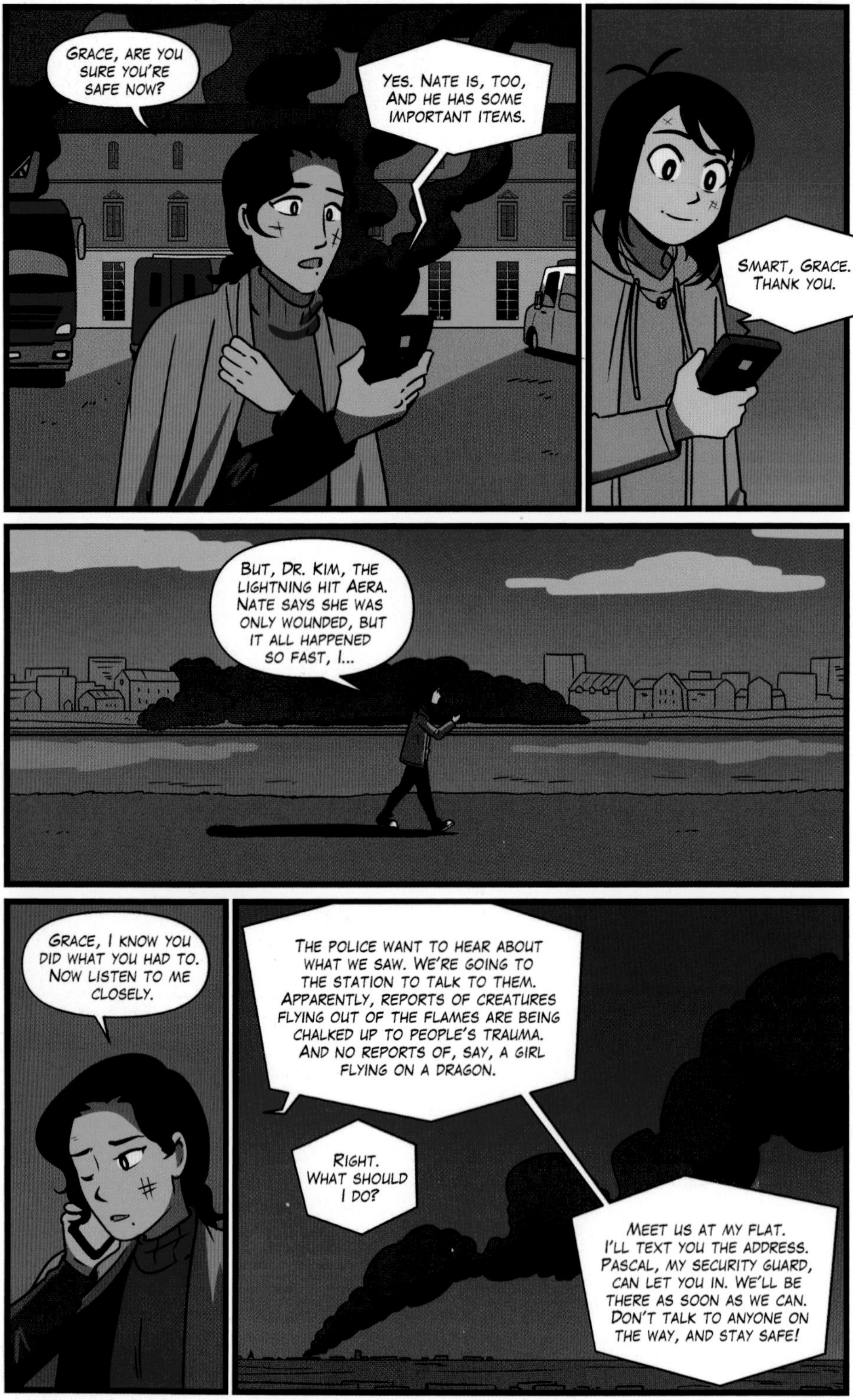
GRACE, ARE YOU SURE YOU'RE SAFE NOW?
YES. NATE IS, TOO, AND HE HAS SOME IMPORTANT ITEMS.
SMART, GRACE. THANK YOU.
BUT, DR. KIM, THE LIGHTNING HIT AERA. NATE SAYS SHE WAS ONLY WOUNDED, BUT IT ALL HAPPENED SO FAST, I...
GRACE, I KNOW YOU DID WHAT YOU HAD TO. NOW LISTEN TO ME CLOSELY.
THE POLICE WANT TO HEAR ABOUT WHAT WE SAW. WE'RE GOING TO THE STATION TO TALK TO THEM. APPARENTLY, REPORTS OF CREATURES FLYING OUT OF THE FLAMES ARE BEING CHALKED UP TO PEOPLE'S TRAUMA. AND NO REPORTS OF, SAY, A GIRL FLYING ON A DRAGON.
RIGHT. WHAT SHOULD I DO?
MEET US AT MY FLAT. I'LL TEXT YOU THE ADDRESS. PASCAL, MY SECURITY GUARD, CAN LET YOU IN. WE'LL BE THERE AS SOON AS WE CAN. DON'T TALK TO ANYONE ON THE WAY, AND STAY SAFE!

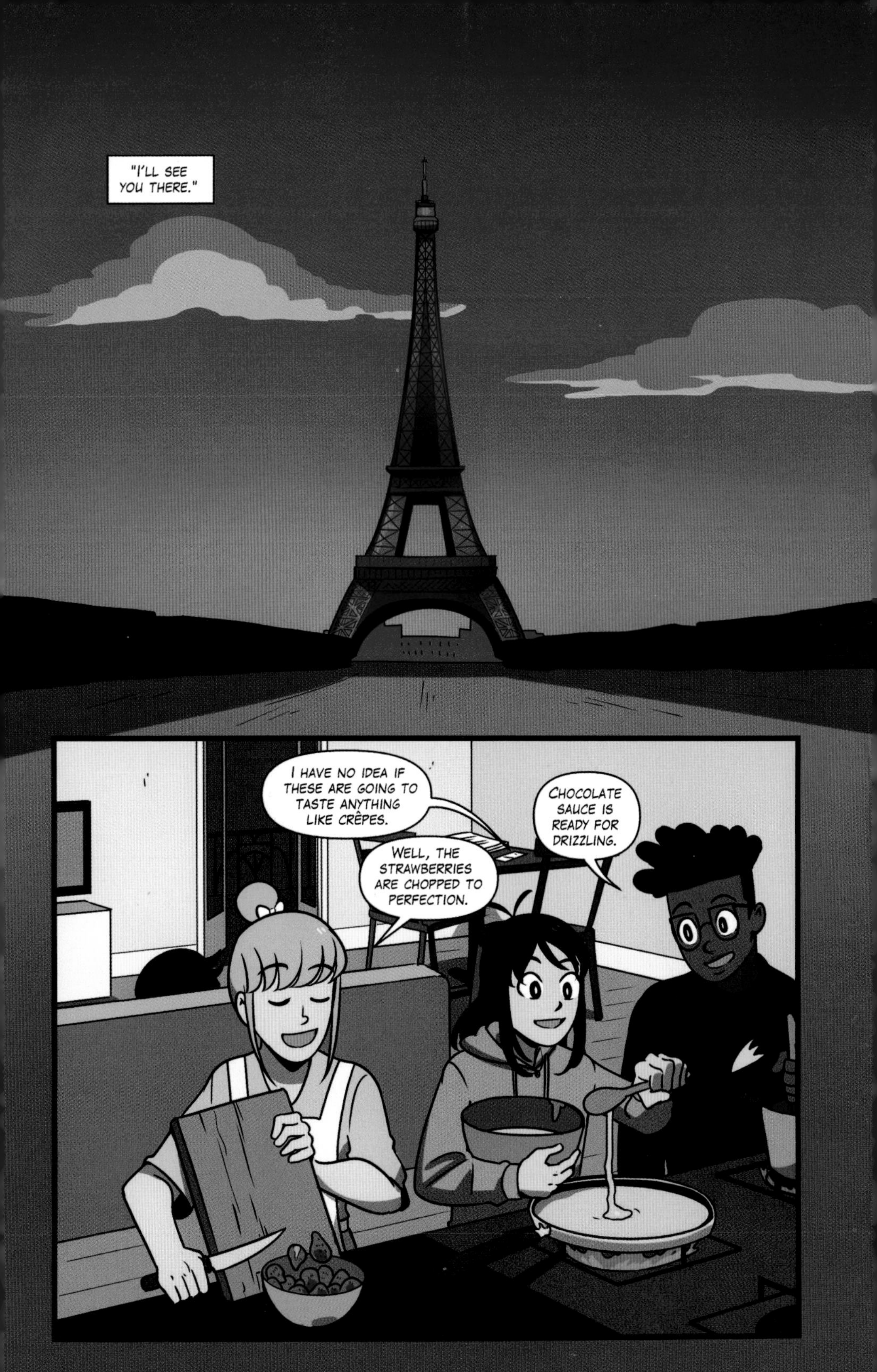
"I'LL SEE YOU THERE."
I HAVE NO IDEA IF THESE ARE GOING TO TASTE ANYTHING LIKE CRÊPES.
WELL, THE STRAWBERRIES ARE CHOPPED TO PERFECTION.
CHOCOLATE SAUCE IS READY FOR DRIZZLING.

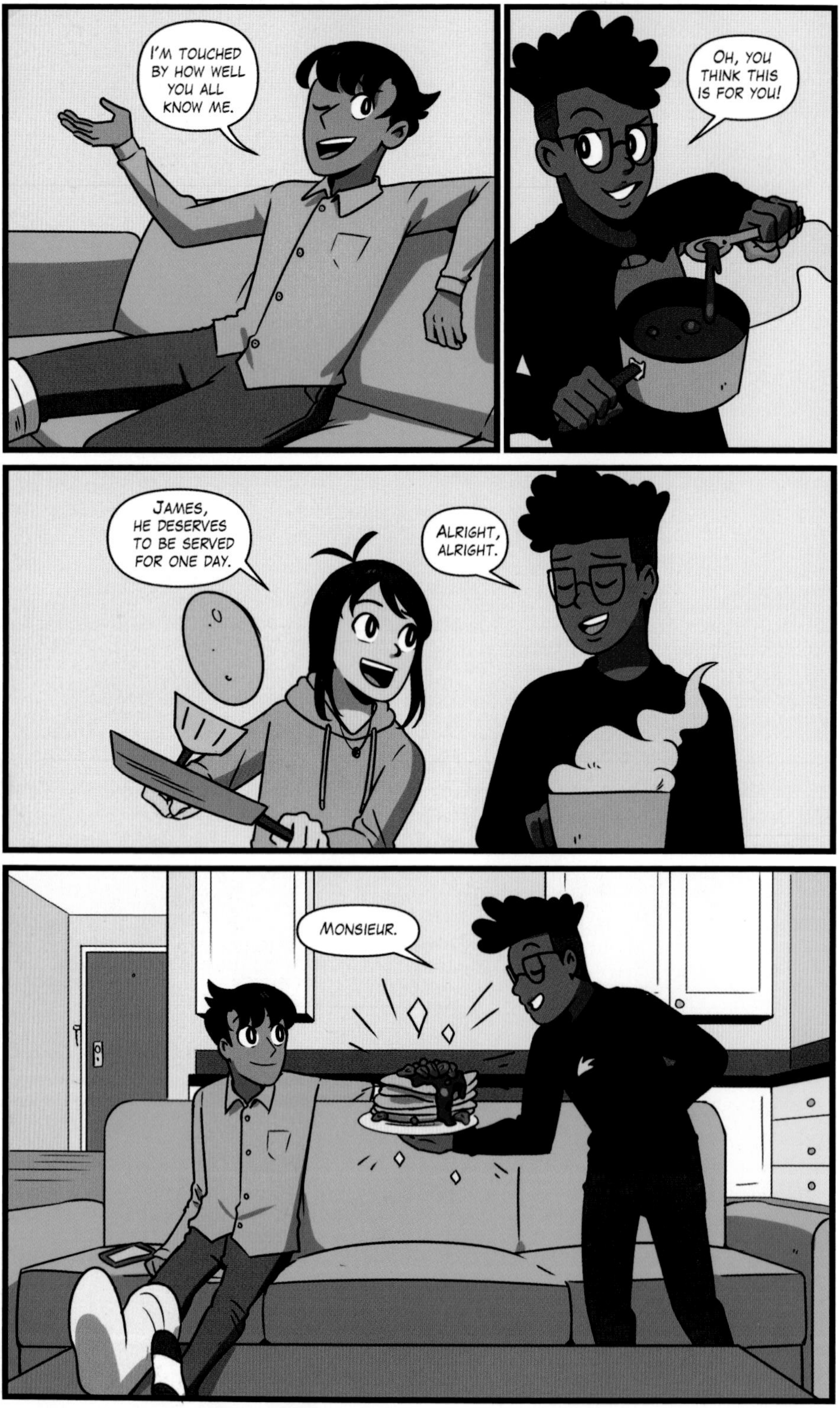
I'M TOUCHED BY HOW WELL YOU ALL KNOW ME.
OH, YOU THINK THIS IS FOR YOU!
JAMES, HE DESERVES TO BE SERVED FOR ONE DAY.
ALRIGHT, ALRIGHT.
MONSIEUR.

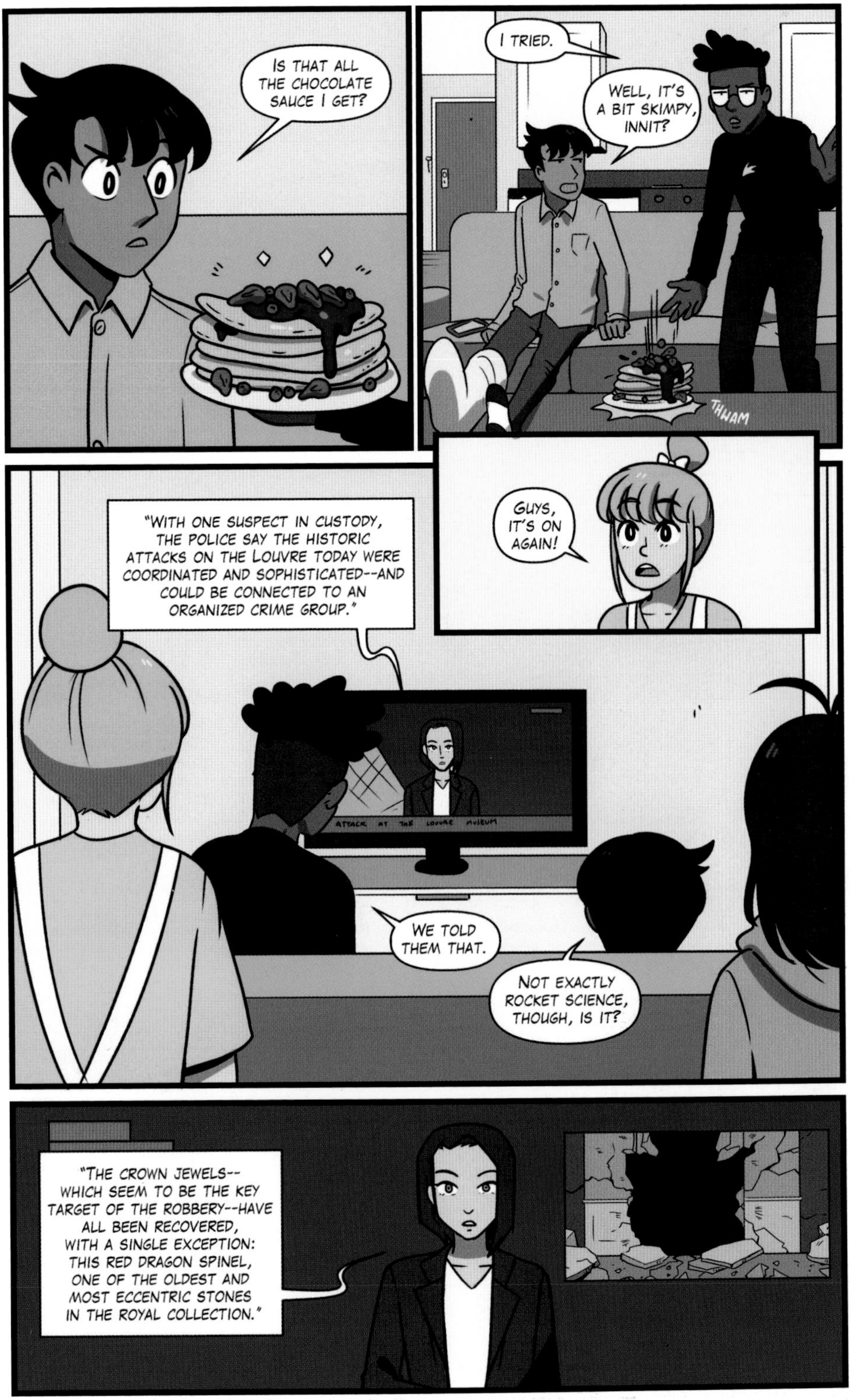
IS THAT ALL THE CHOCOLATE SAUCE I GET?
I TRIED.
WELL, IT'S A BIT SKIMPY, INNIT?
THWAM
GUYS, IT'S ON AGAIN!
"WITH ONE SUSPECT IN CUSTODY, THE POLICE SAY THE HISTORIC ATTACKS ON THE LOUVRE TODAY WERE COORDINATED AND SOPHISTICATED--AND COULD BE CONNECTED TO AN ORGANIZED CRIME GROUP."
ATTACK AT THE LOUVRE MUSEUM
WE TOLD THEM THAT.
NOT EXACTLY ROCKET SCIENCE, THOUGH, IS IT?
"THE CROWN JEWELS-- WHICH SEEM TO BE THE KEY TARGET OF THE ROBBERY--HAVE ALL BEEN RECOVERED, WITH A SINGLE EXCEPTION: THIS RED DRAGON SPINEL, ONE OF THE OLDEST AND MOST ECCENTRIC STONES IN THE ROYAL COLLECTION."

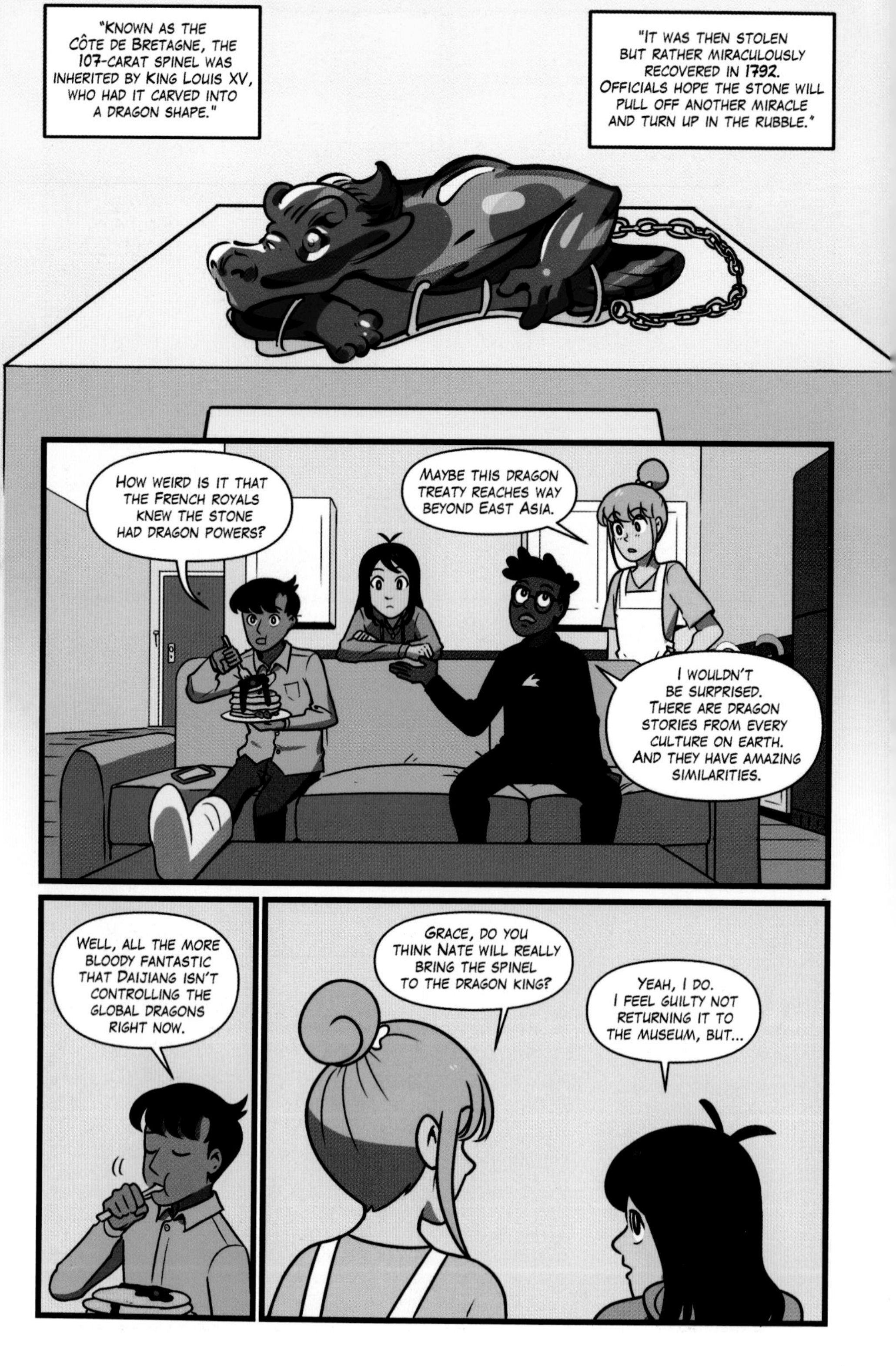
"Known as the Côte de Bretagne, the 107-carat spinel was inherited by King Louis XV, who had it carved into a dragon shape."
"It was then stolen but rather miraculously recovered in 1792. Officials hope the stone will pull off another miracle and turn up in the rubble."
How weird is it that the French royals knew the stone had dragon powers?
Maybe this dragon treaty reaches way beyond East Asia.
I wouldn't be surprised. There are dragon stories from every culture on Earth. And they have amazing similarities.
Well, all the more bloody fantastic that Daijiang isn't controlling the global dragons right now.
Grace, do you think Nate will really bring the spinel to the Dragon King?
Yeah, I do. I feel guilty not returning it to the museum, but...

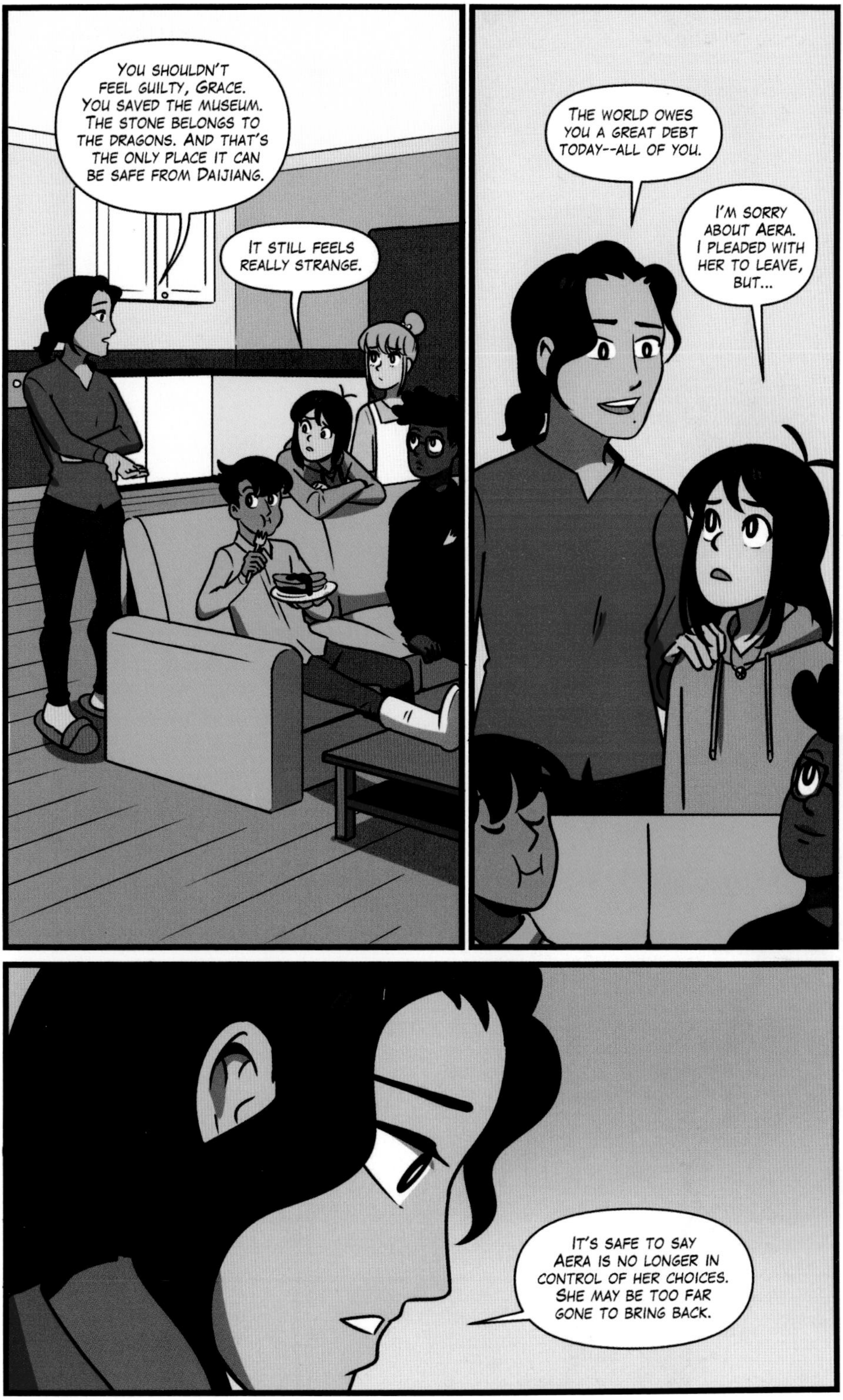
YOU SHOULDN'T FEEL GUILTY, GRACE. YOU SAVED THE MUSEUM. THE STONE BELONGS TO THE DRAGONS. AND THAT'S THE ONLY PLACE IT CAN BE SAFE FROM DAIJIANG.
IT STILL FEELS REALLY STRANGE.
THE WORLD OWES YOU A GREAT DEBT TODAY--ALL OF YOU.
I'M SORRY ABOUT AERA. I PLEADED WITH HER TO LEAVE, BUT...
IT'S SAFE TO SAY AERA IS NO LONGER IN CONTROL OF HER CHOICES. SHE MAY BE TOO FAR GONE TO BRING BACK.

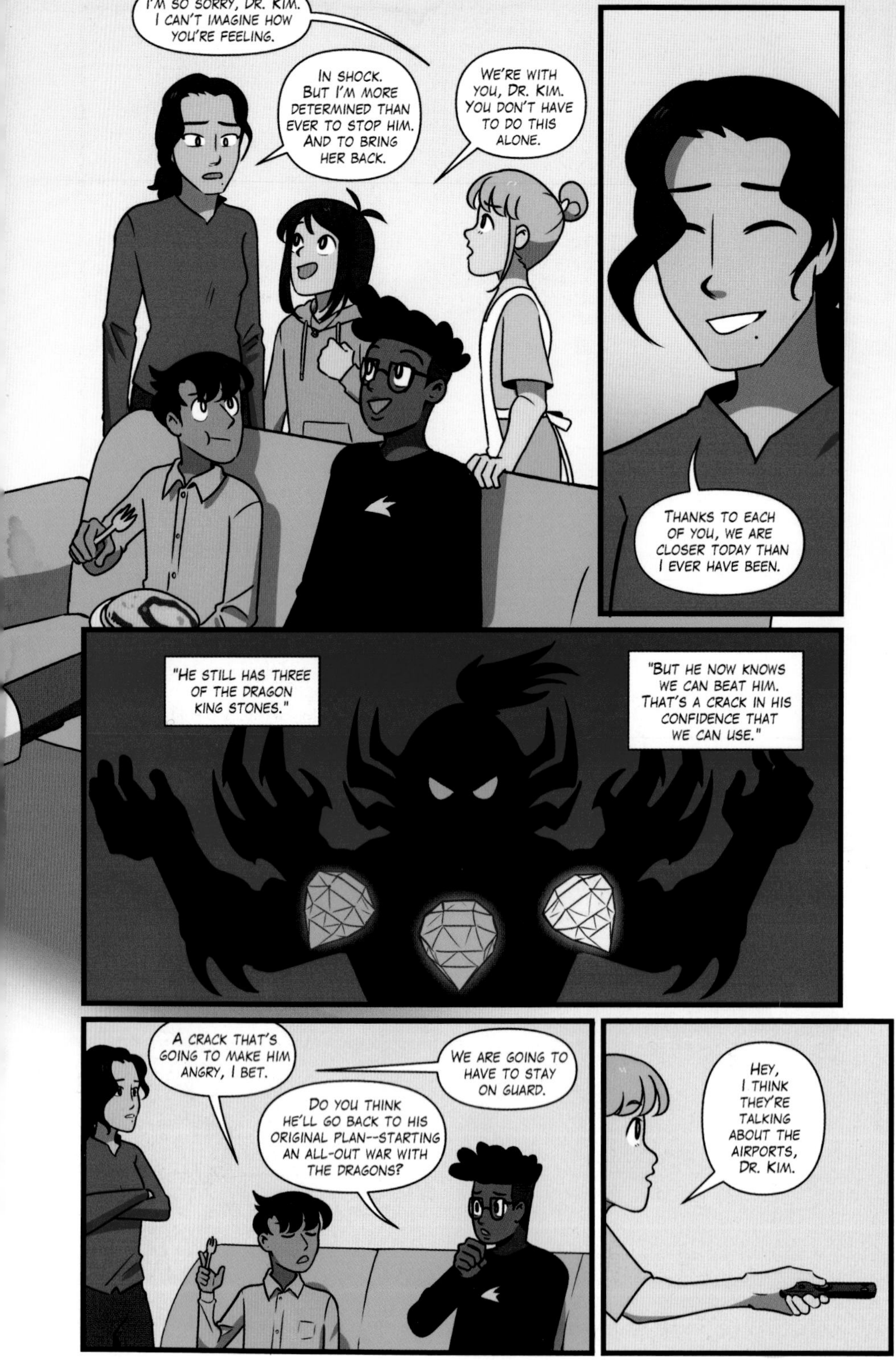
I'M SO SORRY, DR. KIM. I CAN'T IMAGINE HOW YOU'RE FEELING.
IN SHOCK. BUT I'M MORE DETERMINED THAN EVER TO STOP HIM. AND TO BRING HER BACK.
WE'RE WITH YOU, DR. KIM. YOU DON'T HAVE TO DO THIS ALONE.
THANKS TO EACH OF YOU, WE ARE CLOSER TODAY THAN I EVER HAVE BEEN.
"HE STILL HAS THREE OF THE DRAGON KING STONES."
"BUT HE NOW KNOWS WE CAN BEAT HIM. THAT'S A CRACK IN HIS CONFIDENCE THAT WE CAN USE."
A CRACK THAT'S GOING TO MAKE HIM ANGRY, I BET.
WE ARE GOING TO HAVE TO STAY ON GUARD.
DO YOU THINK HE'LL GO BACK TO HIS ORIGINAL PLAN--STARTING AN ALL-OUT WAR WITH THE DRAGONS?
HEY, I THINK THEY'RE TALKING ABOUT THE AIRPORTS, DR. KIM.

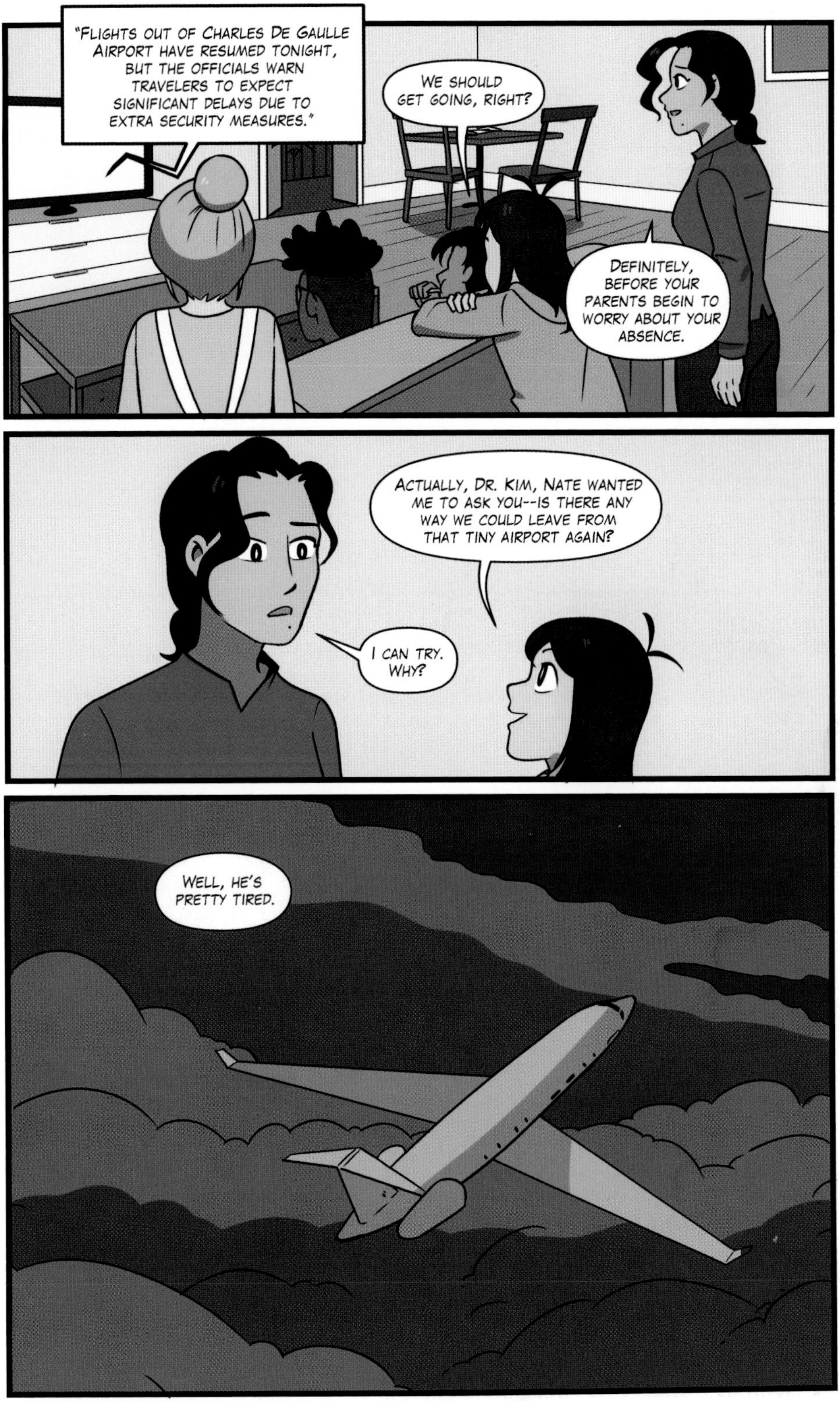
"FLIGHTS OUT OF CHARLES DE GAULLE AIRPORT HAVE RESUMED TONIGHT, BUT THE OFFICIALS WARN TRAVELERS TO EXPECT SIGNIFICANT DELAYS DUE TO EXTRA SECURITY MEASURES."
WE SHOULD GET GOING, RIGHT?
DEFINITELY, BEFORE YOUR PARENTS BEGIN TO WORRY ABOUT YOUR ABSENCE.
ACTUALLY, DR. KIM, NATE WANTED ME TO ASK YOU--IS THERE ANY WAY WE COULD LEAVE FROM THAT TINY AIRPORT AGAIN?
I CAN TRY. WHY?
WELL, HE'S PRETTY TIRED.

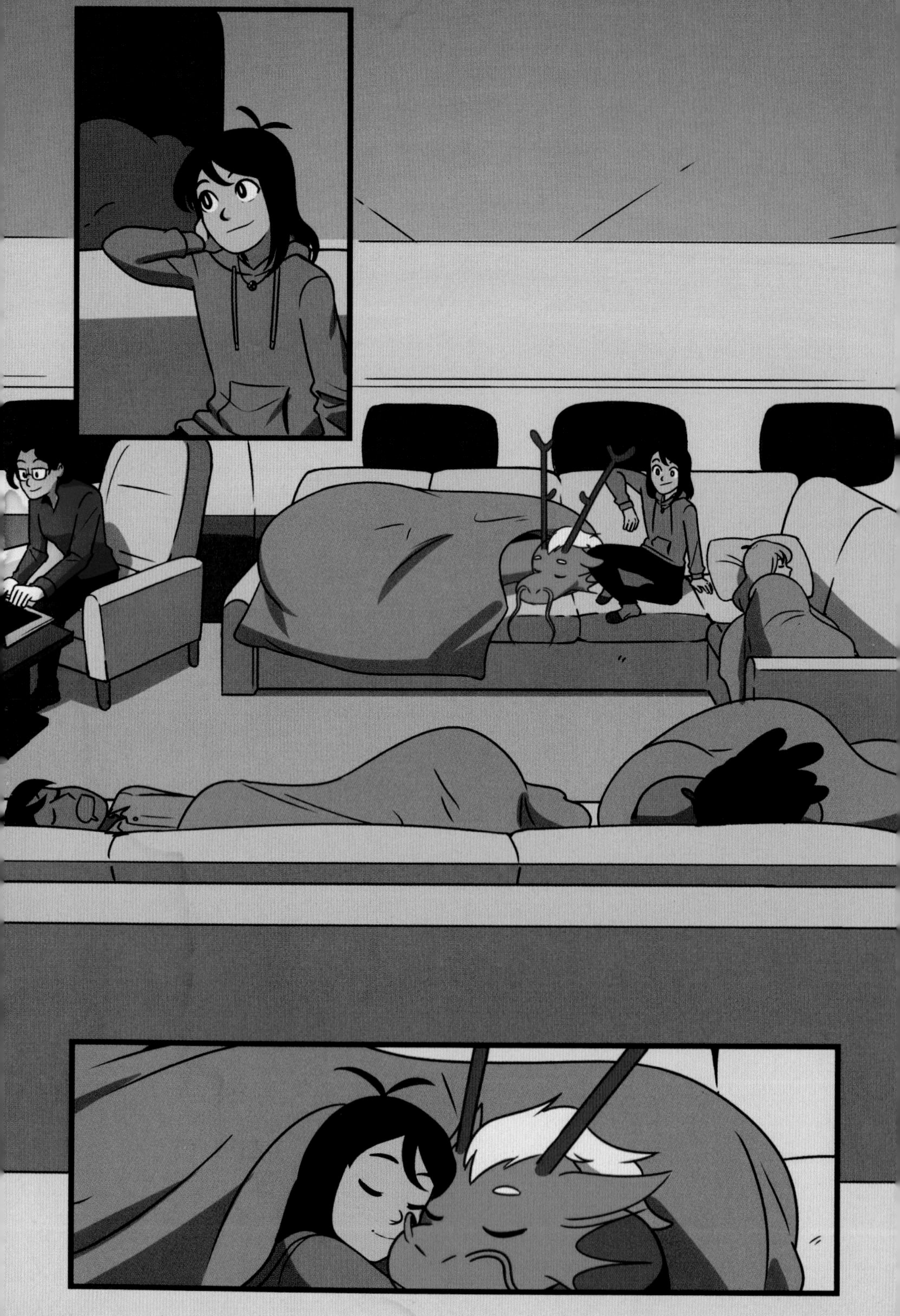

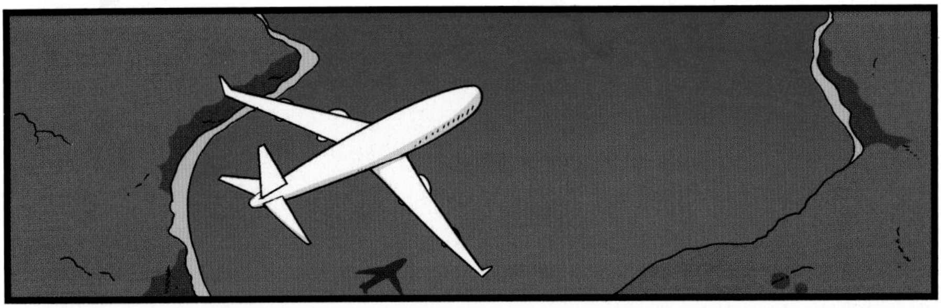

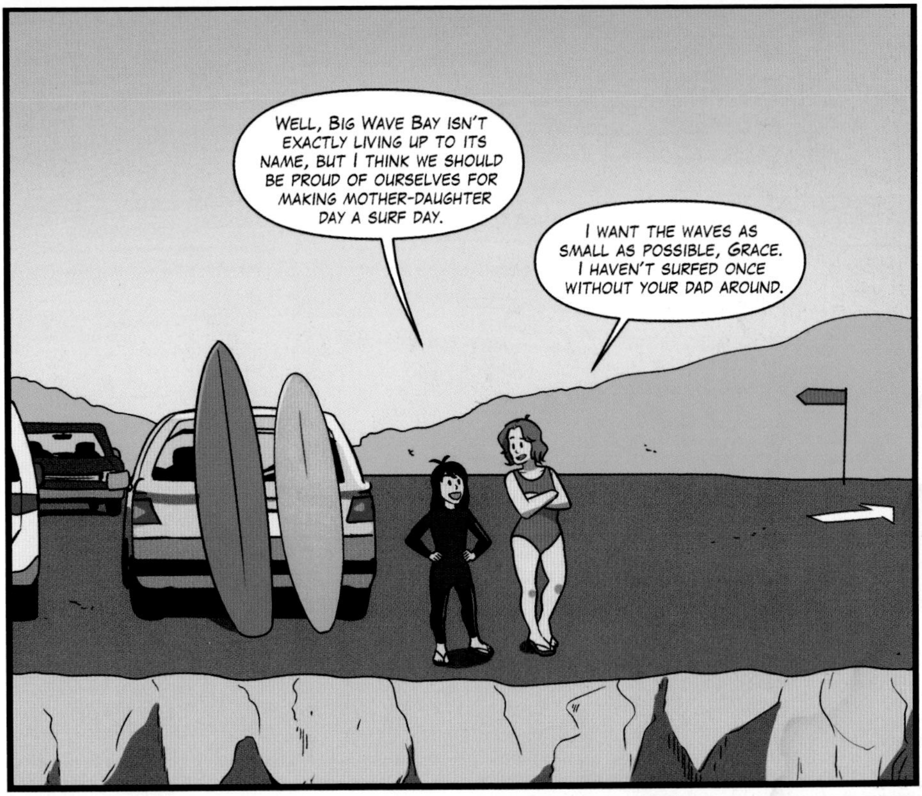
WELL, BIG WAVE BAY ISN'T EXACTLY LIVING UP TO ITS NAME, BUT I THINK WE SHOULD BE PROUD OF OURSELVES FOR MAKING MOTHER-DAUGHTER DAY A SURF DAY.
I WANT THE WAVES AS SMALL AS POSSIBLE, GRACE. I HAVEN'T SURFED ONCE WITHOUT YOUR DAD AROUND.

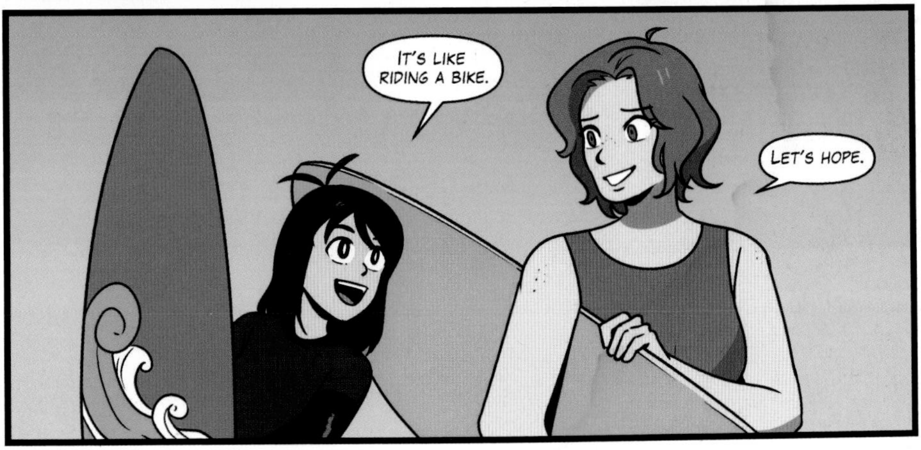
IT'S LIKE RIDING A BIKE.
LET'S HOPE.

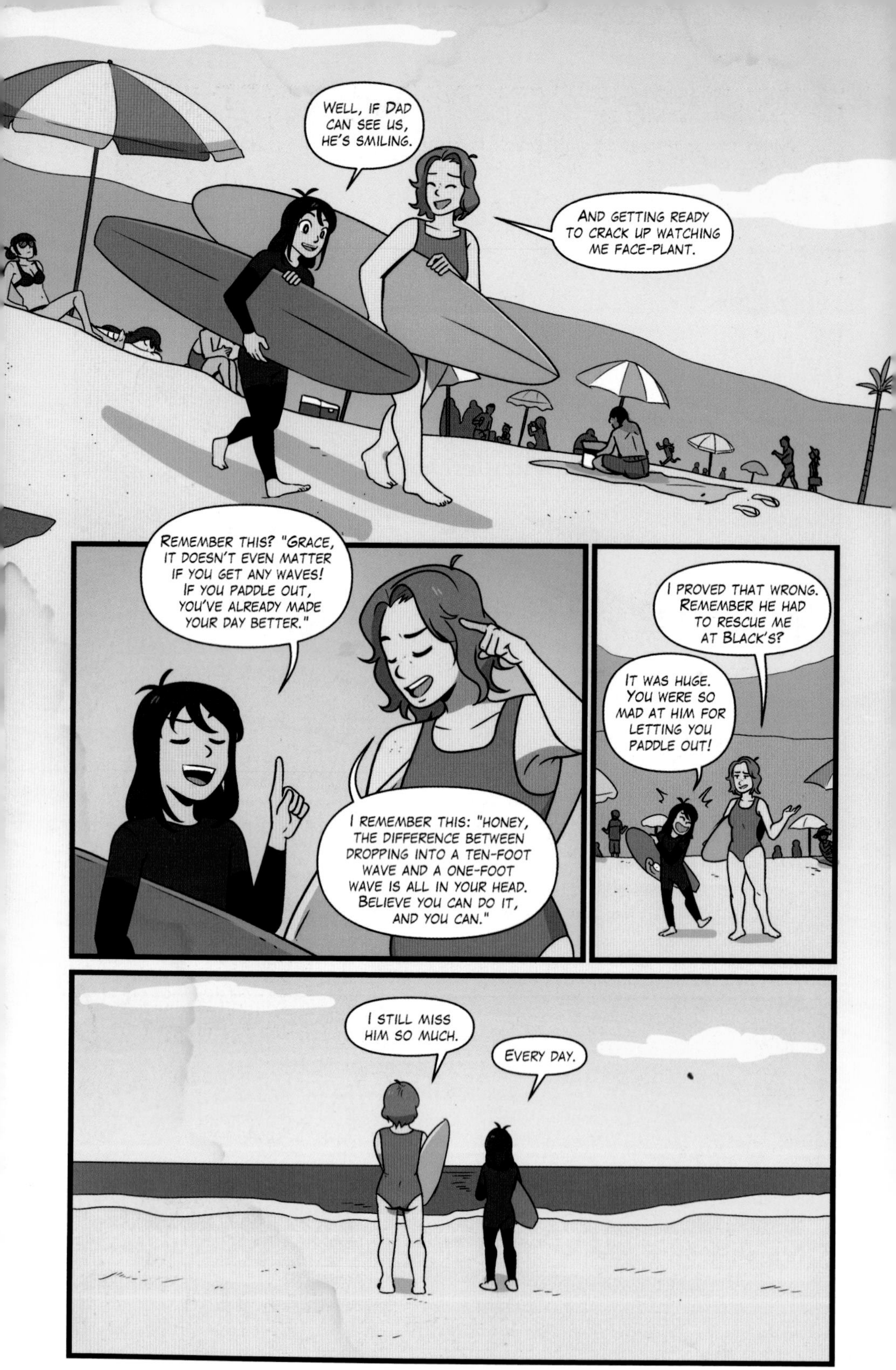
WELL, IF DAD CAN SEE US, HE'S SMILING.
AND GETTING READY TO CRACK UP WATCHING ME FACE-PLANT.
REMEMBER THIS? "GRACE, IT DOESN'T EVEN MATTER IF YOU GET ANY WAVES! IF YOU PADDLE OUT, YOU'VE ALREADY MADE YOUR DAY BETTER."
I REMEMBER THIS: "HONEY, THE DIFFERENCE BETWEEN DROPPING INTO A TEN-FOOT WAVE AND A ONE-FOOT WAVE IS ALL IN YOUR HEAD. BELIEVE YOU CAN DO IT, AND YOU CAN."
I PROVED THAT WRONG. REMEMBER HE HAD TO RESCUE ME AT BLACK'S?
IT WAS HUGE. YOU WERE SO MAD AT HIM FOR LETTING YOU PADDLE OUT!
I STILL MISS HIM SO MUCH.
EVERY DAY.

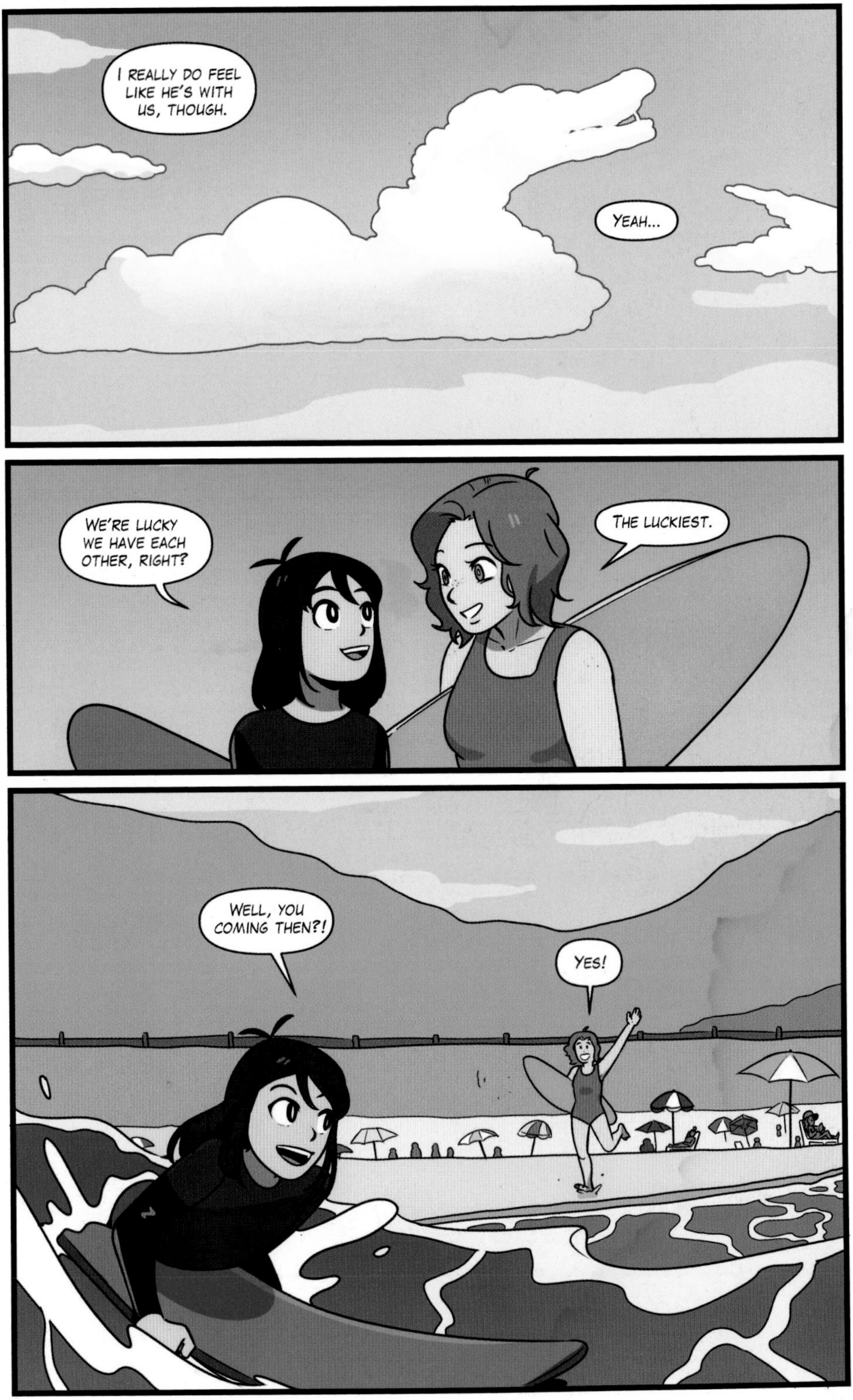
I REALLY DO FEEL LIKE HE'S WITH US, THOUGH.
YEAH...
WE'RE LUCKY WE HAVE EACH OTHER, RIGHT?
THE LUCKIEST.
WELL, YOU COMING THEN?!
YES!

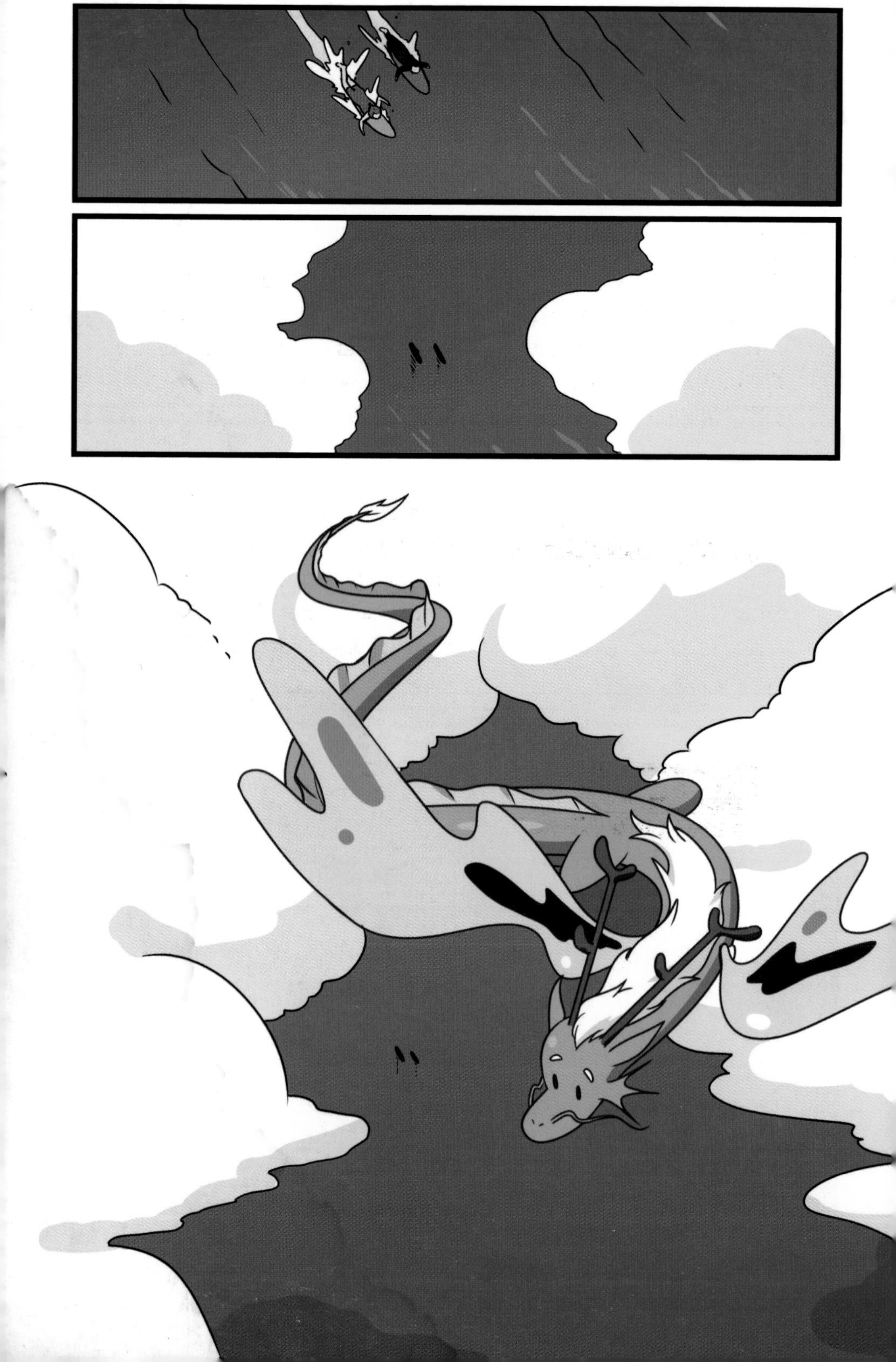